"That bruise is—terribly nasty," I said.

"It'll heal," Jeremy Bond answered shortly.

"You fought quite viciously, not at all like a gentleman."

"Who said I was a gentleman?"

"I've the feeling you've been in a great many fights."

"A great many," he admitted. "Won 'em all, too."

"And yet—yet you're not a violent man."

"Not unless I need to be, lass. Ordinarily I'm the sweetest, mildest chap you'd care to meet—cuddly, in fact." Bond moved a step nearer. "A woman needs to be cuddled now and then," he said in a low, melodious voice. "She needs to be held loosely and stroked and petted, needs to have a man blow gently into her ear and murmur sweet, silly words that make her glow all over and stretch like a well-fed cat. You need that, Marietta. I'd love to cuddle you."

"You're altogether too forward," I said stiffly.

"I want you, Marietta . . ."

Books by Jennifer Wilde

Dare to Love
Love's Tender Fury
Love Me, Marietta

Published by
WARNER BOOKS

Love Me, Marietta

by Jennifer Wilde

WARNER BOOKS

A Warner Communications Company

WARNER BOOKS EDITION

Cover art by Max Ginsburg

Warner Books, Inc., 75 Rockefeller Plaza, New York, N.Y. 10019

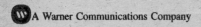 A Warner Communications Company

Printed in the United States of America

First Printing: October, 1981

10   9   8   7   6   5   4   3   2   1

*This one is for my friends Joanie and Nicholas Guild,
brilliant achievers, magnificent hosts,
beautiful people indeed.*

Love Me, Marietta

BOOK ONE
The Lover

One

As I stepped outside I saw him standing there at the end of the street again, his stance deliberately casual, his hands thrust into the pockets of his heavy navy blue coat. I paused on the steps, staring at him. He turned his back to me and sauntered around the corner. I felt a tremor of alarm. Who was he? Why was he watching the apartment? I had observed him at least half a dozen times during the past two weeks, a tall, heavyset man with coarse features and shaggy black hair, always wearing dark breeches and that heavy coat even though the weather was unseasonably warm.

Derek scoffed at my apprehension. When I had described the man to him and mentioned my alarm, he had curled his lips in that deprecatory smile I knew so well.

"My dear Marietta," he had replied, "it's perfectly natural for strange men to stare at you on the street. You're an unusually beautiful woman, and, I might add, your mode of dress invites such inspection."

That last remark had infuriated me. Derek loved me, I had no doubt about that, but ever since we had left Natchez and taken the apartment in New Orleans I had sensed a touch of disapproval in his manner toward me. He loved me and was going to marry me as soon as we returned to England, but I had the feeling he had never completely forgiven me for my past, for Jeff and Helmut and those tumultuous years of our separation. Derek knew all that had happened to me during that period, yet after he had won his court case in England and claimed the Hawke estates usurped by his uncle and cousins, he had come back to America to find me. Surely that was proof of his love. The niggling doubts I had had of late were clearly absurd.

Lifting my skirts to avoid a puddle, I moved down the street. It had rained quite furiously this morning, but now it was decidedly sultry, despite a heavy, overcast sky. The air was oppressive, laced with a tang of salt, and I could smell tar and exotic spices and that hint of mildew always present in New Orleans. Afternoon noises abounded, the cry of hawkers from the market, the rumble of wheels over rough cobblestones, the screech of a parrot perched on a swing beyond one of the ornate wrought-iron balconies. The city was alive with movement and color, yet a curious atmosphere of lethargy prevailed, perhaps because of the heat.

It was certainly too warm for anyone to be wearing a heavy navy blue coat. I paused briefly, turning to look behind me. The man was not in sight, yet I still had the feeling I was being observed. Perhaps it was my imagination, I told myself, but I could almost feel a pair of hostile eyes boring into my back. The sensation was so strong it was almost like physical contact. I frowned, turning the corner and making my way through the labyrinth of colorful stalls of the market. Chickens in flimsy wooden cages squawked. A plump woman in apron and blue bandana shrieked angrily as a small boy tried to steal an orange from her stall. The reek of fish was almost unbearable.

Why should the man be watching me? Despite Derek's remark about my beauty and mode of dress, I knew the man wasn't merely someone who liked to admire attractive women from a safe distance. I had sensed something hostile about him from the first, as though . . . as though he were planning something sinister. Pausing to inspect a barrow of mangoes and pomegranates, I picked up one of them and casually studied it, pretending to be totally absorbed. Out of the corners of my eyes I looked back the way I had come. The man was lounging near a bin of coffee beans, his eyes sullen as he stared at me. I put the mango down and, filled with a sudden resolve, headed straight toward him with a determined step.

I intended to confront him, to demand to know why he was following me. He seemed to read my intention and was clearly alarmed. Turning quickly, he hurried past several bins of shrimp and eel and disappeared. I stopped, both angry and frustrated. Confronting him was one thing, pursuing him through the market was quite another. I tried to tell myself he was merely a sneak thief who had been patiently waiting an opportunity to snatch my reticule, but that was a feeble explanation. Sneak thieves didn't skulk around for days on end, spying on potential victims, and if he had robbery in mind there were certainly far more prosperous-looking people idling about the city.

"I say, is something wrong?"

I turned to look at the man who had addressed me. He was very tall, with a lean, muscular physique admirably shown off by a modish pearl-gray suit cut to emphasize his broad shoulders and slender waist. His knee boots were gleaming black leather, his waistcoat black and white striped satin, and a neckcloth of vivid blue silk nestled beneath his chin. His eyes were blue, too, audaciously so, merry, mocking eyes full of life. His rich brown hair was excessively thick and wavy, one heavy wave tumbling jauntily over his forehead. His nose was slightly crooked and his full pink mouth was much too wide, but these flaws only served to heighten his inordinate good looks.

"I beg your pardon?" I said stiffly.

"I asked if something was wrong. You look extremely distressed."

"Nonsense."

"I was wondering if it had something to do with that brute hanging about a minute ago, the chap in the heavy coat. He was eyeing you quite intensely, not that I blame him, mind you. You're something worth eyeing."

"Excuse me," I retorted, moving past him.

He executed a quick, jaunty step and sauntered along beside me for all the world like a friendly, overgrown pup. I stopped and turned to give him an icy look impossible to misconstrue. He backed away a couple of steps in mock alarm and grinned at me. It was an intolerably engaging grin, the grin of a naughty little boy who wanted only to please.

"May I say something?" he inquired.

"I have a feeling you'll say it whether I grant permission or not."

"I just want to say you've got the most beautiful hair I've ever seen. It's like red gold, gorgeous."

"Thank you," I snapped.

"The rest of you is rather nice, too."

"I may as well be frank," I informed him, "I'm not interested. Not at all. You're quite handsome and you have considerable charm, but you've made a mistake."

"Did you think I had something in *mind?* I was merely trying to be gallant."

"Trying a mite too hard, I'd say."

"I saw you standing at the stall and I saw that brute eyeing you and then saw him run off when you approached him, and I thought he might be planning some kind of mischief. Dangerous-looking chap, if you ask me, definitely spooky. I wouldn't be at all surprised if he carried a *knife*."

"I thank you for your concern," I replied, "but it's really none of your affair."

"A gorgeous lass like you really shouldn't be traipsing about alone, you know," he said. "The city's full of villains. You need someone to look out for you. You need a protector."

"I'm quite capable of taking care of myself."

"I doubt that, lass," he informed me.

His tone was serious now. I studied him more closely. The jaunty manner and audacious good looks were undoubtedly deceiving. I sensed a toughness beneath the exterior, a subtle ruthlessness in those taut cheekbones and the curve of his mouth. I judged him to be in his early to mid thirties, and I felt he could be quite as dangerous as the man who had run away.

"I'm not a prostitute," I told him.

"I never assumed you were."

"If that's what you're looking for, you'll have no difficulty finding one. They're quite numerous."

"I'm aware of that."

"I imagine you are," I retorted.

He smiled a curious half-smile, one corner of his mouth curling up in a lopsided way that was both endearing and a little alarming. The indigo blue eyes were still mocking but there was a certain hardness in them now, and I couldn't help but feel a certain uneasiness. The stranger obviously had quite a temper, and he wasn't at all pleased by my smart retort. He stared at me for a moment or so as though debating whether or not to give me a good shaking, and then the hardness left his eyes and he relaxed, all charm again.

"I was merely trying to be helpful, lass."

"I appreciate that. Now, if you'll excuse me, I'll be on my way."

"I'll accompany you, if you don't mind."

"I do."

"I'm sorry about that, but I'm accompanying you anyway. I didn't like the look of that chap, nor did I like the way he looked at you. I have the feeling he might turn up again."

"Now just a minute—" I protested.

"Look, lass, I don't intend to argue with you. Why don't you just shut up. I'll walk along beside you until you reach your destination, and then I'll be on my way. If it's rape you're afraid of, forget it. I've yet to rape a red-haired beauty in broad daylight, in the middle of a market."

I ignored his remark and moved on briskly past the stalls. He strolled beside me with infuriating ease, moving with a long, bouncy stride, the tails of his jacket flapping.

"Actually, I've always preferred brunettes," he confided. "For rape, I mean. Skinny ones. A skinny brunette is always your best bet for a good, rousing rape."

"I don't find you at all amusing, sir."

"Jeremy Bond," he said, "at your service."

He managed to execute a mock bow, arm extended, without breaking stride. He was indeed audacious, altogether too cocky and sure of himself. Mr. Jeremy Bond was undoubtedly a rogue. I had seen all too many like him when I worked at Rawlins' Place, jaunty, handsome ne'er-do-wells who lived off their wit and charm. They had the morals of alley cats and no scruples whatsoever, invariably causing trouble sooner or later.

"Couldn't we move at a more leisurely pace?" he inquired. "I'm easily winded. Cigars. I have a passion for 'em. Never could resist a good cigar—or a skinny brunette."

I smiled in spite of myself. Jeremy Bond grinned.

"You're insufferable, Mr. Bond."

"And you, lass, take yourself much too seriously. You're

entirely too defensive. A bit of banter never hurt anyone. I've half a mind to move on and leave you to that lout who's been stalking you."

"I wish you would."

"You're too lovely, alas. I could never live with myself if I didn't see that you'd reached your destination safely."

Enough was enough. I stopped and stared at him with icy disdain. We had passed through the market and were on a particularly narrow street with rows of shops on either side. A knife sharpener and his cart blocked the sidewalk ahead, two stout matrons waiting patiently as he honed the blades of their scissors. The noise of steel on stone was unnerving. I grimaced. Jeremy Bond put his hands in his trouser pockets and stood watching me with his head tilted to one side, his shoulders slightly hunched. That wave of rich brown hair completely concealed one eyebrow. The other was arched expectantly.

"You've lovely eyes, too," he confided. "Deep, deep blue, like sapphires. I may as well confess, lass, I've fallen hopelessly in love. I knew it was bound to happen one of these days, but I never expected it to happen so suddenly."

"Mr. Bond, if you don't go away and stop bothering me this instance I intend to scream at the top of my voice."

"You do, lass, and I'll punch you on the jaw. I have a notorious right hook, can fell the stoutest Goliath with one blow."

"I have the feeling you *would!*"

"Sure I would," he said candidly. "Now that we understand each other, you might show a little appreciation for my gallantry. You might even tell me your name."

"I prefer not to."

I moved on, stepping into the street to get around the knife sharpener and his customers. Jeremy Bond strode along beside me, and, in truth, I was rather relieved. The man in the navy blue coat disturbed me far more than I cared to admit. He seemed to present a genuine threat, whereas I knew full well I could handle Mr. Bond.

"You won't tell me?" he asked.

"I certainly won't."

"Let me guess, then. I'll bet it's—uh—" He paused,

cocking his head again. "Clarinda," he said. "You look like a Clarinda, perhaps a Letitia. Am I right?"

"You're not even warm."

A large carriage came rumbling down the street. I was so preoccupied that I hardly even noticed it. Jeremy Bond gasped, seized me by the upper arms, and jerked me back onto the sidewalk. My skirts billowed up, slapping against the side of the carriage as it hurtled past.

"My God, lass! You really *don't* have any business being out alone! You would have let that bloody fool run you down!"

"If you hadn't been harrassing me I wouldn't have been preoccupied!" I retorted.

I was trembling visibly, dangerously near tears. Had he not swung me out of the way, I would have been crushed beneath the carriage wheels. My knees seemed to go weak. Jeremy Bond sensed my state and kept hold of my arms, holding them gently now. A frown creased his brow, and his lovely blue eyes were full of concern.

"Look, lass," he said, "I'm sorry."

"I—I am, too. You may let go of me now."

"Sure you're all right?"

I nodded, and although he released me, he looked ready to grab me again if I should show the least sign of faintness. His eyes were tender now, and they seemed to be looking into my soul. Audacious he might be, a ruthless scoundrel as well, but I knew instinctively that Jeremy Bond understood women better and cared for them more deeply than any man I had ever known. Derek loved me, yes, and Jeff Rawlins had loved me with all his soul, but neither of them had ever displayed the tender concern for my well-being this stranger displayed.

"Thank you," I said.

"My fault, I fear. I *was* harrassing you."

"Do you always approach strange women with such—such vigor?"

"Rarely," he replied. "Actually, I'm generally a model of deportment, the delight of maiden aunts."

"I rather doubt that, Mr. Bond."

"Your raving beauty made me lose all reason."

"There you go again."

"Shall we continue on our way? Incidentally, where are we going?"

"I'm on my way to Madame Lucille's."

"Ah, New Orleans' finest dressmaker, once the creator of Pompadour's most sumptuous gowns."

I was surprised. "You know Lucille?"

"I've paid a few bills that came from her establishment," he said, very nonchalantly.

He would have, I thought. A man like Jeremy Bond would undoubtedly have a mistress, a beautiful and extremely expensive creature with languorous eyes and creamy tan skin, one of the lush quadroons favored by the bucks of New Orleans, and Lucille's establishment was the favorite of those lovely and elegant ladies. Corinne had been gowned by Lucille. Corinne . . . I wondered what had become of that exquisite, tragic beauty who had loved Jeff almost as much as he had loved me. Jeff. New Orleans was filled with memories of him. I'd be glad when we finally left the city.

"Who is he?" Jeremy Bond inquired.

"I'm afraid I don't know what you're talking about."

"The man. The one you were thinking of just now."

I gazed at him, utterly dismayed. Jeremy Bond smiled.

"No, lass, I don't read minds, but I fancy I'm able to read faces. For a moment there your eyes were filled with love—and loss. When a beautiful woman has that look in her eyes, there's always a man."

I made no reply. His perception was disconcerting, and I had no intention of discussing Jeff Rawlins with him. Jeremy Bond made me extremely uncomfortable. He was a complete stranger, yet I felt he knew me as no man ever had, improbable as it might seem. We crossed a sun-filled square, leafy trees casting pale violet-blue shadows over dusty gray brick walls. A plump Negro woman in faded blue dress and white bandana fanned herself as she watched two little boys push a tiny sailboat across the water in the fountain.

"Lucille's is just around the corner," I said.

"I'll see you to the door, lass."

"If you insist."

We walked the rest of the way in silence, stopping in front of the shop. A gorgeously attired blonde opened the door and came down the steps, her pink silk skirts rustling seductively.

She paused a moment to adjust her elbow-length white gloves, casually eyeing Bond as she did so. He boldly assessed her, lids half-shrouding blue eyes dark with appreciation. I tapped my foot impatiently until the blonde moved on, looking over her shoulder to cast a final provocative glance at Bond.

"You'd better hurry," I said icily.

"Not my type," he replied. "Besides, you've already ruined me for other women."

"You never stop, do you?"

"I'm quite serious, lass."

He grinned. He really was extraordinarily good-looking with those broad, flat cheekbones and the deep cleft in his chin. The full mouth and slightly crooked nose added a rakish touch, keeping the face from being too handsome and making it far more interesting. Tall, virile, undeniably magnetic, he had that irresponsible air that most women found irresistible. He brushed the heavy brown wave from his brow. It promptly tumbled back down. A dangerous man, I thought, much too charming, much too perceptive. It was just as well I hadn't told him my name. Impulsive as he was, he might attempt to see me again, and Derek would hardly be pleased.

"Thank you for escorting me, Mr. Bond."

"My pleasure, lass. Shall I wait for you?"

"Certainly not!"

"This chap in the coat, I didn't like his looks, not at all. Looked to me like he had something nasty in mind. He might try to accost you on your way back home."

"I rather doubt it."

"When shall I see you again?" he asked.

"You shan't," I replied.

"You're wrong, lass."

"I happen to be living with another man, Mr. Bond. We're going to be married."

"I've always liked a bit of competition," he confided.

I had had quite enough of Mr. Jeremy Bond. I gave him a look that should have reduced him to ashes.

"You haven't a prayer," I told him.

"I'm going to have you, lass. Wait and see."

I saw no reason whatsoever to reply to this outrageous remark. Lifting my skirts demurely, I moved up the steps and entered the shop, closing the door behind me. A bell tinkled above my head, and Lucille peered out of the back room to see who had entered. Looking through the glass pane in the door, I could see Jeremy Bond standing at the foot of the steps, smiling a broad, devilish smile. After a moment he shook his head, thrust his hands back into his pockets, and started back down the street with that long, bouncy stride. If he hurried, he should be able to catch up with the blonde in no time at all.

Two

Lucille came bustling out of the workroom, gray hair piled precariously atop her head, cheeks heavily rouged, dangling garnet earrings swaying. She wore her habitual black taffeta dress, the full skirt crackling, the long sleeves covering her wrists. Sharp, shrewd, avaricious, Lucille was an artist, creating gorgeous gowns that were shockingly overpriced. She was also one of the city's great gossips, and little went on in New Orleans that she didn't know about.

"Ah," she said, peering over my shoulder, "I see you've met the notorious Mr. Bond. It was inevitable, my dear, a woman as lovely as you, a man as appreciative of beauty as he."

She clacked her tongue as he strode on down the street and out of sight. I drew myself up, pretending offense. Lucille smiled. Crafty old meddler that she was, she knew I was interested in the gossip she was ready to pass on, but I assumed an air of casual indifference.

"Is the gown ready?" I inquired.

"One final fitting, my dear. I want to be certain the bodice hugs you just so. Do you *know* him?"

"Mr. Bond accosted me on the street. He was extremely forward. I gave him a piece of my mind."

"Most women would *adore* being accosted by him," she informed me. "He has a *shocking* reputation with the ladies, my dear. They can't seem to get enough of him, and he treats them wretchedly—a fancy dinner, a shiny bauble, a quick tumble in the bedroom, and then he moves on to fresh territory. Janine Devereaux swallowed poison when he left her, it took them ever so long to revive her. The Devereaux family shipped the poor girl off to Paris. I hear she's entered a convent."

"Pity," I said. "Shall we move on to the fitting room? I'd like to wear the gown tonight. Derek is taking me out to dinner."

"Ah, the handsome Lord Hawke. And has he *married* you yet?"

"You know quite well he hasn't," I said stiffly. "I told you that we intend to marry in England. Derek wants the wedding to be held in the family chapel at Hawkehouse. It's traditional."

Lucille made a face. "Tradition," she snipped, "such foolishness. If he had any sense at all he'd have married you in Natchez, as soon as you recovered from that dreadful ordeal."

"He explained his reasons for waiting. I accepted them. I think a traditional wedding will be lovely."

"A wedding's a wedding, my dear," she replied, leading the way into the elegant fitting room. "If it were *me*, I'd want the knot to be tied as soon as possible. I'd be very *nervous* otherwise."

"It isn't you," I snapped.

Lucille clacked her tongue again. "And when are you *going* to England?"

"As soon as he can buy passage for us. It's extremely difficult, Lucille. This dreadful revolution raging in the East has made passage to England terribly expensive and hard to manage. Everyone wants to return to England, afraid the conflict will reach this part of the country, as well it might."

"Pooh, what happens up there doesn't affect us in the least. These Americans! So unruly, so ungrateful. Not that the English are any better, mind you. He's trying to buy passage?"

"He's been trying for the past few weeks. He had some business to take care of in New Orleans—property to sell, loose ends to tie up—but that's concluded now. As soon as we can get berth we'll be leaving New Orleans. I *told* you all that, Lucille."

"And you came to me for your trousseau. A good thing, too, my dear. You were practically *naked* when you arrived from Natchez. But then all your lovely clothes were destroyed in the fire."

"Yes," I said.

"Such a tragedy. Your husband killed, too, though from what I understand that was a *blessing.*"

"I don't care to discuss it, Lucille," I said, irritated and unwilling to discuss the past. Lucille knew everything, of course. She had made gowns for me back when I was living with Jeff and working at Rawlins' Place, and she was privy to all the details of my turbulent past. Still, despite her prying and her penchant for scandal, she was the finest dressmaker in the country. The new wardrobe she had made for me was stunningly beautiful, and this last gown was the *pièce de résistance.*

"I'll say one thing for your handsome Hawke, my dear, he pays his bills. I sent him a statement last Tuesday. He paid in full that afternoon. More than I can say for most of my customers. Your Mr. Rawlins was shameless when it came to bills. I had to dun and dun."

"Lucille—"

"Charming, though, so charming. I didn't *mind* being owed by a man like that one. Do you remember the gold gown, my dear?"

"I remember, Lucille."

"Quite the loveliest gown I ever created—until now. When your handsome lord sees you in the red—la!" she exclaimed, clicking her tongue. "I shall hate not being able to dress you in the future, my dear."

"I'll never find anyone in England as accomplished as

you," I told her. "I'm very eager to try on the new gown, Lucille."

"As well you should. It's my masterpiece. If you'll undress, my dear, I'll fetch the gown."

She scurried away, garnet earrings swaying, black taffeta crackling, and I took off my dress, handing it to an assistant who had come in to help. The girl disappeared, and I stood in front of the three-way mirror in my petticoat, examining myself as though the woman reflected were a stranger. The cheekbones were high and aristocratic, the nose finely chiseled, the mouth full and pink, but the sapphire blue eyes were sad and wise, the eyes of a woman who has seen too much and known great anguish. Nothing of the girl remained. There was a new maturity, an undeniable patina of sophistication.

I ran my fingers through the rich, coppery red waves that spilled thickly over my shoulders. Beautiful? Yes, men thought so. I was tall and slender with a superb figure, the white silk petticoat clinging to my full bosom, snugly encircling my narrow waist. The skirt belled out with row upon row of frothy white lace ruffles. Men found me desirable. They always had. I knew it was as much a curse as a blessing. Had Lord Robert Mallory not desired me, had he not taken me against my will six years ago, I would probably still be a governess, teaching other women's children to read and write and instructing them in the finer points of deportment.

I hadn't thought of Robert Mallory in a long time. When I refused to be the complaisant mistress he required, he and his wife had planted emeralds in my luggage and accused me of theft. I had been convicted, shipped to America as an indentured servant to be bought by the highest bidder. Derek Hawke had purchased me in order to "save" me from Jeff Rawlins, who had wanted to sell me to a brothel and turn a neat profit. Jeff . . . he had purchased me himself when Derek turned me out, but he had never intended to sell my letter of indenture. He had torn it into tiny shreds, flinging them into the air and giving me my freedom. He had loved me with a passionate intensity few women ever know, and it had ultimately cost him his life.

I wondered if I would ever be able to forgive myself for what had happened to Jeff. Unable to love him the way he loved me, I had continued to think of Derek Hawke, and when Derek had come back into my life I had made little effort to resist him. Jeff had discovered us together and had challenged Derek to a duel. How well I remembered the horror of that day, the fog, the oak trees, the terrible blasts of gunfire. I had held Jeff in my arms, hating myself as the life seeped out of him, smiling through my tears as he declared his love for a final time.

Derek had hated me, too. Incensed because I had caused him to take another man's life, he had turned against me, had deserted me, and, determined to survive, I had married Helmut Schnieder in Natchez, the gravest mistake of my life. Schnieder was a beast, a sadist who had married me only that I might provide a cover for his incestuous relationship with his own sister. When I had helped the poor girl flee from his clutches, he had gone insane with rage, had set in motion a terrible revenge I had been spared only by Derek's intervention.

He had come back for me. He had hated me, yes, or at least he had thought so at the time, but he had discovered that he couldn't live without me. I was in his blood, he claimed, and without the triumph of winning the Hawke estates back from his uncle and cousins meant nothing. He had returned to America to find me . . . and now, at long last, we were together. I loved him with all my heart and soul, as I had from the first, and I knew that he loved me as well. Cool, remote, moody, he might not show his love as openly as Jeff had, as other men might, but it was there nonetheless, binding us together irrevocably.

Of course he would marry me. I understood the delay. I was in agreement. A formal wedding at Hawke house would make our bond even more permanent. If I had ever entertained doubts about his intentions, that merely showed my own lack of understanding. I could see why he wanted to wait until our vows could be said in traditional fashion. I would be Lady Hawke soon enough, and in the meantime we were together, sharing our love. The future was ours. The gnawing doubts and fears that had plagued me since our reunion were sheer foolishness.

Besides, the delay had enabled me to assemble a suitable trousseau. When I became Lady Hawke I would be dressed in splendor befitting my new position. Lucille had seen to that. I sighed and brushed an errant copper-red lock from my temple. Everything was going to be fine. I had faced a great deal of adversity during the past six years, but that was all behind me. I had found my love at last, and nothing would come between us.

"These girls!" Lucille exclaimed, coming into the room. "They chat and giggle and never get their work done. I have to stay on them every minute. Here it is, my dear. Shall we slip it on. Gorgeous! Simply gorgeous, perhaps my finest achievement."

The gown was a rich, deep red brocade embroidered all over with floral patterns in an even deeper red silk. The full, gathered skirt belled out over half a dozen red lace underskirts, and the bodice with its off-the-shoulder puffed sleeves was cut provocatively low. Lucille helped me into the sumptuous creation, fastening it in back and then stepping off to survey her handiwork, nodding vigorously as she did so.

"Yes, yes, just right! The cloth, the cut, exquisite simplicity. Those red lace panels I wanted would have spoiled it. You were right to talk me out of them, my dear, but then you always did have the right instincts. Rich, rich red, deeper red embroidery, no frills, no bows, no panels. I thought no, my dear, I may as well admit it. Red, with your hair? The color is perfect, and *you* dominate the dress, my dear. So rich a garment would wash out most women, you know."

"You've done a superb job, Lucille."

"Pompadour would have loved it, but she could never have carried it off. I had to dress her in pale, pale green and pink, the softest of lilacs, the lightest of grays. She wasn't nearly as beautiful as you are, my dear. Pompadour was never a beauty, you understand, but she had *talent*. The king was utterly captivated, and there wasn't a man in France who wouldn't have sold his soul for one night with her."

Lucille loved to babble about her association with the Royal Favorite. I patiently endured a few minutes of scandalous revelations while she tugged at the skirt and smoothed down the waist, critically examining the fit. Satisfied at last, she stepped back and sighed.

"Perfection!" she declared. "I've run up a cloak to go with it," she informed me. "Dark red velvet lined with paler red silk. I know you didn't *order* it, my dear, but the gown cries out for a matching cloak, and Lord Hawke has already paid for it. You'll want to do your hair up, perhaps a few ringlets dangling in back but *no* feathers, no hair ornaments of any kind, mustn't distract from the gown.''

She began to unfasten it in back. ''*He* always pays his bills on time, too,'' she said.

''Who are you talking about?''

''Your Mr. Bond. He's done business with me on more than one occasion. There was a lovely creature named Therese, magnolia skin, full pink lips, eyes as black as ink and full of allure. He kept her in a plush apartment and was apparently quite fond of her. He certainly *dressed* her well.''

I made no comment, telling myself I wasn't at all interested in Mr. Jeremy Bond.

''She was a flighty creature, alas. Shockingly unfaithful. Your Mr. Bond discovered her in bed with a handsome young dandy, the lad couldn't have been more than nineteen. My dear, they were actually *performing* when he walked into the bedroom. He cocked an eyebrow and told them to go on about their business, and the young man was quite distressed, as you can imagine. He grabbed his clothes and scurried away quick as a flash. Few men care to tangle with Bond, you understand. He has a vicious right and is devilishly accomplished with pistol and sword, as I'm sure you know.''

''I know nothing whatsoever about him.''

''*Anyway,* Therese started shrieking and wailing. She leaped out of bed and tried to throw herself into his arms. My dear, he *socked* her! She had a black eye for days! *Then* he took a pair of scissors and cut all the gowns he had bought her to pieces. Calm as could be, he was, destroying all those lovely clothes while she wailed and protested.''

''Apparently Mr. Bond doesn't like to be crossed.''

''Few men do, dear. Bond ran into the young man a few nights later at one of the gambling halls. The youth was terrified, of course, afraid Bond would come after *him*, but Bond merely smiled that peculiar lopsided smile of his and bought the boy a drink, told him he had extremely good taste in women. You must admit the man has *style*.''

''He sounds like a thorough scoundrel.''

''Oh, he *is*, my dear. That's part of his charm. Every

woman loves a rogue, and he makes no pretense at being anything else. Half the women in New Orleans are in love with him. They say he comes from one of the best families in England. Disgraced them years ago, they say, got himself thrown out of the Army as well."

"What does he do for a living?"

"He gambles quite a lot, and I understand he's done a bit of smuggling, but his main source of income seems to come from mysterious jobs. I suppose you could call him a mercenary. It seems that when someone wants a bit of work done that involves danger, they call upon your Mr. Bond."

"He *isn't* my Mr. Bond, Lucille. I don't even know the man."

"Pity," she said.

"He doesn't even know my name," I added.

"He *will*," Lucille assured me. "When Jeremy Bond has his heart set on something, he goes *after* it. It seems he has his heart set on you, my dear. Your handsome Lord Hawke is going to have some competition."

I stepped out of the glorious crimson gown and handed it to her. "Jeremy Bond doesn't interest me in the least," I informed her.

"You're female, my dear. You're interested, all right. The woman hasn't been *born* who isn't interested in a man like that. He's handsome, charming, rakish, has a mysterious background —oh yes, you're interested enough."

"Nonsense."

"If I were twenty years younger—twenty-five, perhaps— I'd go after him myself. I'd be courting disaster, of course, men like that *always* spell disaster for a woman, but that's part of their appeal."

She sighed, remembering days gone by as she left the room with the gown draped over her arm. I began to dress, irritated by all this talk about Jeremy Bond. I *wasn't* interested in him, the man was preposterous, a jaunty, swaggering rogue, yet I couldn't help but be intrigued by what Lucille had said about him. I stepped into the showroom a few moments later, and Lucille soon joined me, shoving back the stack of gray hair that threatened to spill over her forehead.

"I'll have the gown and cloak delivered to you right away," she informed me.

"Thank you, Lucille."

"It's been a joy dressing you, my dear. I shall miss you."

"You mean you'll miss the business," I teased.

"That, too," she confessed. "A person has to make ends meet, but mostly I'll miss my association with you. You're a rare creature, Marietta. You've got that special quality few women have. It's more than beauty, more than feminine allure. You attract—adventure, tumultuous emotions. Life will never be calm and easygoing for you, my dear. It will always be lived at the highest pitch of emotion—as, indeed, it has been."

"That's over," I said calmly. "Now that Derek and I are together I intend to live—very quietly."

Lucille smiled, clearly not believing me, but she did not pursue the matter. She patted her hair again and adjusted one of the dangling garnet earrings.

"Did you get the trunk safely?" she asked.

"Trunk?"

"Last week. The one the man in the navy blue coat delivered."

I caught my breath, a tremor of alarm awakening inside. It took considerable effort to keep my voice level when I spoke.

"There was—no trunk," I told her.

Lucille looked puzzled. "The man came in bold as brass," she said, "he said he had to deliver a new brassbound trunk to Lord Derek Hawke and had lost the address. He'd seen you coming out of the shop—said you were with Lord Hawke when he bought the trunk—and asked me if I could give him the address. I—hope it was all right."

I forced myself to look unconcerned. "There must have been some kind of mix-up," I replied.

"Hope he didn't deliver it to the wrong address," Lucille said. "These stevedore types, you can never depend on them. There was a shipment of velvet, my dear, the *finest* velvet, several bolts of lace as well, directly from France, and do you know that it was delivered to Madame Renaldo! She actually tried to *claim* it."

"These things happen."

"I must say, I was rather startled when the man came in. Rough-looking type he was, low, heavy brows, mean brown eyes, thick lips curling up at the corner. Gave me quite a start. I thought he intended to *rob* the place, but he was as polite as could be. So was his assistant."

"There was—another one?"

"Lad not more than twenty-five or six, a blond giant in a leather jerkin, good-looking in a coarse sort of way. I gave them the address, and the man in the navy blue coat thanked me and nodded, and they left. You didn't get the trunk?"

"It—it may have come. I'd better be going now, Lucille."

"You'll have the gown and cloak in an hour or two. They will be delivered to the proper address, I assure you, or I'll have that boy's hide. Do come in and see me again before you leave for England, my dear."

"I will," I promised.

Lucille took my hands and squeezed them and then accompanied me to the door, her taffeta skirt crackling. The bell over the door tinkled merrily. I stepped outside, trying to still the alarm. I had first seen the man in the navy blue coat two weeks ago, but it was only during the past week that I had observed him loitering near the apartment. He must have followed me to Lucille's, then conned the address from her with his tale of a trunk. He knew where I lived. He . . . he had a companion. They were planning some kind of mischief. I could feel it in my bones. Derek might not be concerned, but I was near panic.

I moved quickly down the street, lost in thought. Who were they? What did they want? I turned the corner and started blindly down the narrow street that led to the market, eager to get back and inform Derek of what Lucille had told me. I didn't see the man until I was almost upon him. He was leaning against the wall, watching me, and as I drew near he straightened up and moved onto the sidewalk, blocking my way.

"Hello, my beauty," he said gruffly. "In a hurry?"

I stopped, and my blood seemed to run cold. He was tall and muscular and blond. He wore a leather jerkin.

Three

My every instinct told me I must remain calm, calm and cool and aloof. I knew I mustn't let him suspect the panic that swept over me, panic so strong I felt my knees must surely give way beneath me. Heart pounding, I somehow managed to draw myself up haughtily, gazing at him with what I hoped was a level gaze. He returned the gaze with dark, mocking eyes, the tip of his tongue slowly moving across his lower lip.

"As a matter of fact, I *am* in a hurry," I said.

There was only the faintest tremor in my voice. I willed my heart to stop pounding, willed the waves of panic to recede. It's broad, open daylight, I told myself. Nothing could happen to me right here on the street, not with dozens of people within shouting distance. Behind him, at the end of the street, I could see pedestrians moving along the intersecting street, women with shopping baskets chattering gaily, several men striding along purposefully. All I would have to do was scream and a crowd would convene.

"Step aside," I said curtly.

"Not very friendly, are you?" he retorted.

"Not at all," I snapped.

"Figured you'd be snobby. Figured you'd think yourself too high an' mighty to chat with the likes of Will Hart. That's me name, Will Hart. I know who you are, know all about you."

"Indeed."

"I've 'ad me eye on you. Me an' Bert 'as. Bert told me to keep away from you, but me, I 'ad to get a close look. Ain't disappointed, either. Ain't a bit disappointed. You're one fetchin' wench, all right."

"Who—who is Bert?"

"That needn't concern you."

"Does he—does he wear a navy blue coat?"

"I ain't sayin'."

Will Hart scowled, his wide, thin lips pressed tightly together and turned down at the corners. In his middle twenties, he was at least six feet tall, perhaps taller. His features, though coarse, were not unattractive, the cheekbones broad and flat, the large nose well shaped. Heavy lids half-shrouded his eyes, and his thick, dark brows were arched, flaring at the corners. His blond hair was the color of dark honey, one wave falling heavily across his brow.

I memorized all these details so I could describe him later. He wore high, dirty brown boots, snug plum-colored breeches, and, beneath the leather jerkin, a coarsely woven white shirt with full balloon sleeves. His hands were very large, I observed, enormous and tanned with strong fingers capable of all kinds of cruelty. There was an aura of cruelty about all of him, a suggestion of brutal force and violence barely contained beneath the surface.

"You're mighty cool," he informed me. His gruff voice was a kind of scratchy growl coming deep from his chest. "Most wenches don't mind chattin' with me. Most of 'em fancy a chance to chat with Will Hart."

"I'm sure they do," I said.

"Most of 'em 'ave a fancy for what I got."

"I would imagine so, Will."

I forced a lilting, flirtatious tone. Convinced now I was in no real danger, I intended to get all the information I could from him, and I had the feeling it wouldn't be difficult to do. The man was clearly a womanizer, a crude, uneducated lothario obsessed with female flesh. He was vain about his virility and good looks, too, that was obvious. I had no doubt countless barmaids and loose-living shopgirls had made much over those enormous hands, those broad shoulders, fanning his vanity like so many slave girls stroking the ego of a cruel and despotic pasha.

My tone surprised him. Still scowling, he studied me now with eyes that were suddenly suspicious, and I met his gaze boldly, displaying an interest I was far from feeling. I was careful not to overdo it. I must play on that arrogant male vanity, but I mustn't spook him. He mustn't suspect my true motive. Relaxing, I allowed the suggestion of a smile to flicker on my lips as I brushed a lock of copper-red hair from my temple.

"Reckon you might fancy what I got, too," he growled.

"Don't be absurd," I retorted, deliberately unconvincing.

"Yeah, you'd fancy it all right."

Will Hart nodded, grinning, convinced his male allure was having its customary effect. Men like Will Hart were shockingly easy to manipulate, I reflected. Any reasonably intelligent woman with a modicum of appeal could have them eating out of her hand in no time at all. There was an element of risk involved, of course, particularly if the woman didn't intend to follow through, but I was willing to take that risk.

"Reckon them thin-blooded, aristocratic men ain't male enough to satisfy a wench like you," he said.

"How—how dare you. Move aside immediately or—I'll scream."

"You ain't gonna scream, wench."

I stared at him with false defiance and then allowed my eyes to soften as I took in his powerful shoulders, his slender waist, and the prominent bulge in the breeches below. All I had to do now was pull him in, carefully, subtly. I felt absolutely no remorse in resorting to such shabby tactics. I was determined to find out why he and the mysterious Bert had been watching me.

"Reckon that bloody toff you're livin' with don't have the goods a wench like you needs."

"I suppose you think you do."

"Yeah," he replied, nodding. "I got everything you need."

"Sure of yourself, aren't you?"

"Sure of you, wench. Bert, he told me you wudn't nearly as high an' mighty as you pretend ta be, said you wudn't nothin' but a whore at heart. You worked in a gamblin' hall, he said. Reckon you had th' men placin' bets left an' right, with plenty on th' side."

"Your Bert is quite mistaken!"

"He ain't mistaken. He knows all about you, all about that toff who shares your bed."

"Oh?"

"Knows all about you both, Bert does."

"Why should he be interested in us? Does he plan to rob the apartment?"

Will Hart emitted a coarse, derisive laugh. "Bert'n me ain't thieves," he growled, "nothin' as small time as that. Naw, we ain't plannin' to break into your apartment, wench."

"I have it," I said flirtatiously, "you plan to kidnap me and hold me for ransom. That's it, isn't it. You think that Lord Hawke is extremely wealthy and would pay a fortune to get me back safely."

"I ain't sayin' nothin' more. Bert'd be mad as hell if he knowed I even spoke to you."

"You're afraid of him?"

"I ain't afraid of no one! Bert may be th' boss of this piece of business, but he knows better'n to try an' shove Will Hart around. I wanted to get a good look 'fore we went ahead, an' I got it."

"I've the feeling you like what you see."

"I like it, yeah."

"Perhaps we could—talk."

"Talkin' ain't what I 'ave in mind, wench."

"That—maybe that could be arranged, too."

He nodded, dark eyes aflame with desire, lips parted. I felt my confidence beginning to ebb. I was playing a dangerous game indeed. Could I go through with it? I knew I should hurry away as fast as my feet would carry me, but I had already learned quite a bit. If I handled him properly, I felt sure that I could get Will Hart to reveal even more. I would suggest we go to one of the bars near the waterfront, and I would get him to drink several stout ales. I would flirt and simulate desire for him, and after I found out what I wanted to know I would make a hasty retreat.

"I—I feel rather thirsty," I said.

"I got me a thirst, too, wench."

"Perhaps we could have a drink, Mr. Hart—Will."

"Bert wouldn't like that."

"I'm sure he wouldn't," I said.

"Know what? I don't care at all. We'll have a drink, wench, and then I reckon I'll give ya what you're cravin'."

"We couldn't use the apartment," I said quickly.

"Wudn't plannin' to. Place I'm thinkin' a takin' you 'as rooms upstairs. Ain't too fine, mind you, no satin counterpanes an' fancy curtains, but then I don't imagine you're gonna be spendin' too much time inspectin' th' furniture."

His voice was thick, his dark eyes almost completely hidden by heavy, drooping lids. The man was a fool, putty in my hands, but he was also an extremely dangerous animal. Dare I carry on with this? Dare I take the risk involved? I had a moment of terrible apprehension, and then I steeled myself. Tangible danger would be much easier to face than the nebulous, shadowy threat I had felt ever since I first grew aware of the man in the navy blue coat. There would be dozens of other people in the bar, people all around us, and he hadn't a prayer of getting me upstairs to one of the "rooms."

"I—I really don't think I should," I said.

"You ain't gettin' coy on me, wench."

"It's not that. I find you very attractive—very interesting, I've always had a weakness for strong, blond men, but what if Lord Hawke found out? He'd throw me out."

"He ain't gonna find out. Who's gonna tell him?"

"I'm terribly nervous."

"Don't worry about your toff, wench. Me 'n Bert plan to take care of him real soon."

"Well—"

I hesitated, extremely convincing in my dilemma. Hart could tell that I found him sexually irresistible, that I desperately wanted to run my palms over that broad back and savor the strength in those powerful arms, and he could also see that I was worried about Derek. Derek represented wealth, fine clothes, elegant appointments, and while I felt no compunction in being unfaithful to him, I certainly didn't want to risk losing my luxurious nest. I managed to convey all this quite easily. When dealing with men, every woman is a consummate actress. Hart believed I was an elegant harlot as obsessed with sex as he, and I would play the role to the hilt in order to achieve my purpose.

"Reckon you need a little persuadin'," he growled.

"Per—haps we could meet later. I really don't think this is a good idea, Will. We need to—plan things. You—you do have marvelous hands, so strong. I'd like to feel them—"

"You'd like to feel 'em squeezin' your teats," he growled.

"I—"

"I'm gonna pleasure you like you ain't never been pleasured before, wench. I'm gonna make you squirm 'n holler 'n beg for more. You ain't gonna want to go back to your bleedin' toff when I'm through with you. You're gonna beg me to keep you."

"I have very expensive tastes, Will."

"An' I got connections, wench. You think I can't put my hands on plenty a money. You want jewels hangin' around that pretty neck? I'll choke you with jewels."

"You make it sound—very tempting."

"The minute I set eyes on you, wench, I knew what I wanted, knew what I 'ad to have. Bert pointed you out to me, we was hidin' behind some bushes n' you and your toff came strollin' by 'n 'That's them,' Bert says, 'that's Lord 'awke and his woman,' 'n my tool stood straight up and started throbbin' 'n I started makin' plans."

"You—wanted me."

"You was wearin' a yellow dress that fit real tight around your waist and exposed half your teats. Th' skirt was blowin' in th' breeze like yellow sails 'n your hair was blowin', too, and you was clingin' to 'is arm, and I vowed you was gonna cling to my arm like that 'fore too long."

"I'm extremely—flattered."

"A wench like you, she needs a real man."

"You're right," I whispered huskily.

I laid my hand on his arm, melting with submission, completely overwhelmed by his virile appeal and eager to experience his prowess. My eyes glowed with admiration now, and I was ready to throw all caution to the winds. Hart smiled a smile of savage satisfaction and licked his lower lip again. The bulge in his breeches strained painfully against the plum-colored cloth. It was going to be extremely difficult to get him to sit still for drinks while all the while his mind would be on the room upstairs and the pleasures it promised. I sighed and stepped back, looking into his eyes, abject, ready to provide those pleasures. He took a deep breath, his chest swelling.

"Reckon you're as eager as I am," he growled.

"I'm still—nervous. I'll have to have—something to drink first."

"You'll have your drink, wench, but first I'm gonna give you a little sample a what Will Hart's gonna do to you."

He seized me, throwing one arm around my waist, the other around my shoulders, jerking me against him and holding me so tightly I feared I would break in two. He thrust his head down and slammed his mouth over mine, kissing me with brutal greed, and I shuddered inside, fighting the impulse to kick and claw. Somehow I managed to endure, to relax, to mold my body against his powerful chest and thighs and simulate submission if not response. I felt I was going to smother, felt I was going to swoon as he forced my lips apart and stabbed his tongue firmly into my mouth. My head seemed to ring. I heard a pounding, clattering noise that grew louder, louder, and then I heard a mighty yell.

"Unhand that woman!"

Will Hart released me abruptly and shoved me against the wall so violently that the breath was knocked out of me. Dazed, my senses reeling, I saw Jeremy Bond racing down the street toward us, the tail of his pearl-gray jacket flying behind him, his rich brown hair flying, too, tumbling all over his head in a mad whirl of waves. Startled, enraged, nostrils flaring, Will Hart curled his hands into brutal fists, his legs spread wide apart as he waited for the onslaught. Bond charged on, moving faster, drawing nearer, and then he leaped into the air and hurled himself at Hart, hitting him with such impact that they both fell crashing to the ground, Hart landing on his back with a bone-bruising thud, Bond on top of him.

"No!" I cried.

Neither man heard me. They wrestled in a dreadful tangle, legs kicking, arms flailing, bodies rolling, Hart on top now, now Bond, his hands caught up in Hart's hair as he crashed the man's head against the pavement again, again, each crash making a horrible thud. Hart roared and reared up, raising his body, throwing Bond to one side, climbing to his feet like an outraged bull. Bond wrapped his arms around Hart's legs and brought the man crashing down again and again as they wrestled in a tangle of flailing limbs, grunting, pounding, rolling this way and that.

I closed my eyes and caught my breath, black wings fluttering inside my head, threatening to eclipse consciousness. I reeled for a moment in a dizzy void, leaning against the wall for support. Then I opened my eyes, stood up straight, and brushed veils of copper-red hair from my face, still out of breath. My shoulders hurt terribly where they had slammed against the rough brick, and I felt as though someone had viciously poked my backbone with a solid steel rod. I panted for a moment, trying to focus, listening all the while to those thudding, thumping, crunching noises.

Both men were on their feet now, both weaving, panting, snarling. Blood poured from a gash over Hart's right eyebrow. There was a purple-gray bruise on Bond's left cheekbone. Hart roared, swinging an arm in the air, powerful fist flying toward Bond's head. Bond ducked, darted, whirled, leaping on Hart's back, slinging an arm around his throat, falling to his knees again and bringing Hart down with him. Hart gurgled, struggling furiously, his face turning a terrible pink as Bond strained and squeezed, determined to strangle the life out of his opponent. Hart caught hold of Bond's wrist, trying to pull the arm away, jabbing viciously into Bond's chest with the elbow of his left arm. The deadly hold momentarily loosened, Hart threw his left arm back and caught hold of Bond's hair, jerking forward with all his might.

Bond lost his hold and came tumbling over Hart like an acrobat, landing on the pavement nimbly on all fours, leaping to his feet and whirling to deliver a savage kick to the side of Hart's head as the stunned, still wheezing man tried to climb to his feet. Hart fell back, spread out on the pavement, and Bond leaped onto his stomach, a knee on either side of Hart's thighs, his hands circling Hart's throat, thumbs pressing murderously into the soft, vulnerable flesh beneath the Adam's apple. Hart's eyes seemed to be popping out of their sockets, and he no longer had the strength to throw Bond off.

"Let go of him!" I cried. "You're killing him!"

"Shut up!" Bond yelled.

"Jeremy Bond, you let *go* of him!"

Bond continued to squeeze for perhaps three seconds longer, his vivid blue eyes glittering intensely, his teeth bared, and then he let go. He stood up and stepped back, breathing heavily, his chest rising and falling. He looked down at the man stretched out on the pavement, his eyes still gleaming with murderous intent. Hart wheezed and coughed, awful gurgling noises bubbling up from the walls of his bruised, near-broken throat. After a few moments he managed to lift himself up on his elbow. His vivid pink face gradually began to pale and return to its natural color. His dark, dazed eyes began to focus.

"On your feet!" Bond ordered.

"You almost *killed* him!"

"Shut up, Marietta."

I wondered how he had learned my name, but I was far too concerned about Hart to give it much thought at the moment. Hart shook his head a few times to clear it, then slowly, painfully got to his feet. He was so weak he could hardly stand, his knees dipping dangerously. Blood still trickled from the cut over his eyebrow. His lip was cut, beginning to swell. His shirt was torn, one sleeve ripped wide open, and his breeches were torn at the left knee, bruised, bloody kneecap visible.

"Are you all right?" I whispered.

Hart ignored me. He stared at Bond with dark, threatening eyes. "I'm gonna remember this," he growled.

"Do that, laddie."

"You're gonna pay, Bond. Yeah, I know your name, heard her say it. You're gonna be sorry."

Bond extended one arm the better to display an audaciously trembling hand, mocking the man with theatrical fear. Hart turned his mouth down, desperately wanting to throw himself into the fray again, caution holding him back. After a moment he turned to look at me with venomous brown eyes.

"You're gonna be sorry, too, wench. You was just leadin' me on, never 'ad no intention a lettin' me ram it in ya. You was just tryin' to get me to talk, makin' a fool a me. No woman's gonna make a fool a Will Hart."

Head lowered, hair dipping over his brow, Jeremy Bond moved slowly toward Hart with fists balled, ready to swing again. Hart backed off, in no shape to take another beating.

"Move along, laddie," Bond said. His voice was low, laced with menace. "Be quick about it, too, if you don't want me to finish chokin' the life out of your worthless body."

Hart glared at both of us for a few moments, and then he turned and walked painfully down the street, limping visibly. Bond watched until Hart had turned the corner, disappearing from sight, and then he sighed heavily, brushed unruly brown locks out of his eyes and looked at me. His coat was torn, his fine boots deplorably scuffed, his breeches stained with dirt. His black and white striped satin waistcoat was ripped in two places, and the blue silk neckcloth was all askew. The bruise on his cheekbone looked nasty indeed, and I noticed that his knuckles were scraped.

"Well?" he said.

"You've ruined everything!" I snapped.

"What the *hell* are you talking about?"

"I had him eating out of my hand! I had him exactly where I wanted him! If you hadn't come along I'd have found out *everything!*"

"Jesus!"

"You had to come charging in like—like some demented knight on a white horse and spoil all my plans!"

"I don't *believe* this. I don't *believe* it. Talk about *gratitude!*"

"No one *asked* you to interfere!"

"I see a great brute mauling you like a crazed animal, and I'm supposed to saunter on by without a how-de-do. What exactly did you think you were *doing*, lass?"

"That's none of your bloody business!"

"Keep it up, just keep it up. In a minute I'm going to slap you so hard your ears will ring for a week."

"You lay a hand on me and I'll bite it off!"

"God, you're gorgeous!"

"You look like a—a bedraggled gypsy! Your hair is damp and falling all over your head. Your clothes are filthy and torn."

"That's supposed to be *my* fault?"

"Just leave me alone, Mr. Bond. Just leave me alone."

"I've no intention of leaving you alone. I intend to stick close by your side till I see you safely home. The rate you're going, you'll start a bloody *riot* before you get two blocks."

"You're not going *anywhere* with me. If you so much as—"

His vivid blue eyes flashed. He stepped over to me and

seized my arms and shook me for a good two minutes, shook me so hard my head bobbed, my hair whirling in every direction. When he let go of me I gasped, but I dared not lash out at him as I longed to do. I wanted to cry, and I wasn't at all certain I wouldn't start sobbing at any minute.

"You're no gentleman," I said lamely.

"Do something with your hair, for God's sake. You look like a witch."

"Go to hell."

"A gorgeous witch, though, I'll grant that. Are you all right?"

"I'm fine," I said, brushing hair back with my hands. "Now will you *please* leave me alone."

"What was that all about?"

"I told you, it's none of your business."

"Want me to shake you again?"

"Don't you dare, you—you cad."

Jeremy Bond smiled, delighted to be called a cad. It was an utterly dazzling smile. A strange exhilaration filled me, a wild, bewildering, totally uncalled for feeling that curiously resembled joy. I finished straightening my hair, brushed my skirt and adjusted the bodice, trying to pull myself together. Bond straightened his neckcloth and smoothed down his waistcoat and flicked dirt from the elbows of his jacket.

"My suit's ruined," he remarked.

"I'll see that you get a new one!" I snapped.

"I haven't let a woman buy my clothes since—oh, since I was twenty-five years old, maybe twenty-six. You let 'em buy your clothes, let 'em pay your rent, and they start thinking they own you. Now," he continued, "are you going to tell me what that was about or do I have to choke it out of you?"

"He was—he works with the man in the navy blue coat, the man you saw watching me at the market. They're planning something—something sinister, I'm sure. He found me very—appealing, and I decided to play on that and get him to tell me what they're up to."

Jeremy Bond shook his head, dumbfounded. "Jesus," he repeated.

"I knew *exactly* what I was doing, Mr. Bond, I assure you."

"You intended to *sleep* with the brute?"

"Of course not! I intended to take him to a bar and—"

"And ply him with liquor and get him to chatter his head off, and then you thought you'd just sashay out of the place and be on your merry way."

"That's precisely what I planned to do."

"Of all the stupid, harebrained, numbskulled, *idiotic* ideas! Couldn't you see the lout was an *animal*?"

"I can handle myself, Mr. Bond. I've had quite a lot of experience with men—all kinds of men."

"I don't doubt *that* in the least."

"I don't think I care for your implication, Mr. Bond."

"I don't give a bloody hoot. If I hadn't come along when I did, that hulking brute would have pulled you into the nearest alley."

"I had everything under control."

"Like hell you did. I don't intend to argue. Come along now, I'm taking you home, and if you so much as *look* like you're going to give me trouble, I'll bash your head in."

'You're so very gallant," I said acidly.

He seized my wrist and gave it a savage tug, moving briskly down the street and forcing me to totter along behind him. Every time I tried to pull free he jerked my arm viciously. I stumbled along, my heels tapping on the pavement with a crazy rat-tat-tat. When we reached the busy intersection he stopped, waiting for carriages to pass before crossing. Pedestrians gave us curious stares, but Bond couldn't have cared less.

"You can let go of me," I said.

"Going to behave yourself?"

I nodded, not nearly as angry as I should have been. There was something about him that made it impossible to be really angry with him. He was a rogue, undeniably so, but there was an endearing quality that made something dance inside of me. I wondered if he really had let women keep him when he was younger. He must have been a preposterously handsome youth, I thought, with that cleft in his chin, those broad cheekbones, those devilish blue eyes and quirkily arched eyebrows. Many women, particularly older ones, must have been more than willing to pay his bills.

"I *will* see that you get a new suit," I said.

"No you won't, lass. Thanks just the same though."

We crossed the street and, a few moments later, were passing through the market again, surrounded on all sides by color and bustle. Bond strolled along with that bouncy, relaxed stride, his fingers curled loosely around my elbow. I felt wonderfully safe and secure, not even bothering to look around for the man in the navy blue coat. In truth, I had almost forgotten about him. As we passed a bin of apples, Bond paused, inspecting them intently, finally selecting a very large, very red one and flipping a coin to the plump, flaxen-haired woman standing behind the bin.

"Thanks, luv," she said.

"You've got the best apples in town," he told her, treating her to one of his smiles.

" 'Ere, luv, let me dust it off for you."

She took the apple from him and wiped it on her faded blue apron until it gleamed a bright ruby red. When she gave it back to him, he grinned and tickled her under her chubby chin. The woman glowed visibly, ready to kill for him. There should be a law against such outrageous charm, I thought, a bit put out that he hadn't bought me an apple. He chomped on his treasure noisily as we moved on through the market, passing trays of shiny black eels and shelves laden with aromatic spices and carts piled high with multicolored flowers. Gossipy voices rose in a merry babble.

"We turn down here," I said.

"I know the way," he informed me.

"How could you possibly?"

Bond took another bite of his apple, guiding me around the corner with his hand loosely clasped about my elbow. "Lucille told me where you lived, lass. Told me your name, told me a bit of your history, told me everything I wanted to know."

"Damn her!"

"I went back to fetch you, you see. You'd already gone, and Lucille was in a chatty mood. After I'd learned all I needed to know, I started after you, and that's when I happened upon your little tryst."

"What did Lucille tell you?"

"Enough," he replied.

"I'll never buy another gown from her!"

"Mustn't blame Lucille. I have this way with women, you see. I can get 'em to tell me *anything*."

I let that one pass. We strolled by lovely, walled gardens, elaborate, romantic wrought-iron balconies festooning the brick houses beyond. I could smell mimosa and azalea and the bougainvillaea that spilled over the pale gray walls in a profusion of purple blossom. A haze of sultry heat hung over the city, a soft, clinging heat that seemed to gently stroke one's skin. Bond finished his apple and casually tossed the core over one of the walls. A few moments later we stopped in front of the large wrought-iron gates that led into the courtyard of the building where Derek and I were staying.

"Here we are," Bond said, "safe and sound."

"Yes," I said quietly.

"It's been most interesting, lass."

He smiled, a quiet, reflective smile this time, his blue eyes full of tenderness as they peered into mine. The tenderness was quite genuine, and I was startled. How could he possibly feel that way toward me, and how could I possibly be entertaining a desire to reach up and gently touch his cheekbone where it was bruised? He looked lazy now, lethargic, his eyelids drooping over those eyes that spoke of an emotion I had known precious little of in my lifetime. Men had rarely displayed tenderness toward me, never so openly as Bond did now. Perhaps they were afraid to be tender. Bond, I sensed, was utterly secure in his emotions, giving free rein to all of them.

"That bruise is—terribly nasty," I said.

"It'll heal."

"You fought quite viciously, not at all like a gentleman."

"Who said I was a gentleman?"

"I've the feeling you've been in a great many fights."

"A great many," he admitted. "Won 'em all, too."

"And yet—yet you're not a violent man."

"Not unless I need to be, lass. Ordinarily I'm the sweetest, mildest chap you'd care to meet—cuddly, in fact. I'm terrific on a cold winter night when a storm's raging outside and a fire burning within. Woman I used to know said I was the cuddliest man she'd ever known, and she'd known quite a few."

I made no reply. Bond moved a step nearer.

"A woman needs to be cuddled now and then," he said in a low, melodious voice. "She needs to be held loosely and stroked and petted, needs to have a man blow gently into her ear and murmur sweet, silly words that make her glow all over and stretch like a well-fed cat. You need that, too, Marietta."

"I—"

"You're very tense, uncertain, on edge."

"You're quite mistaken, Mr. Bond."

"I know women, lass. I'd love to cuddle you."

"You're altogether too forward," I said stiffly.

"I want you, Marietta."

"You—you don't even know me."

"I know enough. I know I want to hold you and protect you and ease that tension inside you. You're a beautiful woman, Marietta, maybe the most beautiful I've ever seen. I want to make you *feel* beautiful."

"Mr. Bond, if Lucille spoke so freely, she no doubt told you I was living with Lord Derek Hawke, that we intend to be married as soon as we get to England."

"Yeah," he said lazily, "she told me all that."

"I happen to love him with all my heart."

"He's not the man for you, lass."

"How could you possibly know?"

"Because you're not happy."

"You have no way of knowing whether I'm—"

"A woman in love—a woman loved properly in return—wears her happiness in her eyes, on her cheeks, on her lips, wears it like an invisible garment, a glorious garment that gives her an aura everyone can see."

"Nonsense."

"It's true, lass."

"I—this conversation has gone quite far enough. I—I suggest you look for someone else. I suggest you track down that blonde in pink silk who came out of Lucille's as we stood outside."

"Already have," he confessed. "Her name's Helena. She has a sumptuous apartment. Her protector is sixty years old and only visits her on Tuesdays and Thursdays."

"You certainly didn't waste any time!"

"I rarely do," he confided.

"*Goodbye*, Mr. Bond."

"We'll be seeing each other, lass."

"Don't count on it!"

I opened the gates and stepped into the courtyard, slamming them shut behind me. They made a loud, clanging noise that was extremely final. Jeremy Bond lingered on the pavement a moment, peering at me through the fancy iron curlicues, a smile on his lips, a rich brown wave splayed untidily over his brow. The garden was abloom with fragrant flowers. The fountain splashed softly, water spilling from one small white marble basin into the larger one below, a plump, mossy cupid perched on top. Bond looked at me, cocky, confident, determined, and then he nodded and strode away.

I stood in the garden for several minutes, bewildered, disturbed, filled with conflicting emotions. I would have to tell Derek what happened. I wondered what I was going to say—and just how much I would have to conceal.

Four

Derek was out when I finally stepped inside the apartment, and I was vastly relieved. My dress was stained, my hair was in shambles, and my face was probably dirty as well. He would certainly have questioned me had he seen me in this condition, and I intended to relate my story on my own terms without his prodding. He had gone out on business, I knew, and probably wouldn't be back until five. That would give me plenty of time to pull myself together, to get my thoughts—and emotions—in order.

I took a very long, very hot bath, washing my hair as well.

The water was extremely relaxing, and I luxuriated in it, savoring the warmth and the scent of soap. I was calm now, in complete control, no longer disturbed by those emotions Jeremy Bond had stirred inside. The man was extremely attractive, extremely charming. Any woman would respond to that, but I was sensible enough to realize it meant absolutely nothing. He was clearly irresponsible, with a checkered past, and I intended to waste no more time thinking about him.

Climbing out of the tub, I wrapped myself up in a large towel and began to dry off, the soft, nubby cotton caressing my skin. Will Hart and the man in the navy blue coat seemed figures out of a bad dream, distant, dimly remembered, not real at all now that I was back in the apartment, but I knew the danger they represented was real indeed. They weren't planning to rob, Hart had said, nor were they planning a kidnapping. Although he hadn't said so, I had had the impression that I wasn't a target at all, that their business had to do with Derek alone. "Don't worry about your toff, wench," Hart had said, "Me 'n Bert plan to take care of him real soon."

What had he meant? I cursed Jeremy Bond for bursting upon the scene when he did. If he hadn't come along, I would have been able to learn much more. It would have been risky, yes, but I was no stranger to risk, nor was I unfamiliar with men like Hart. I felt certain I could have handled him. He was vicious, a brutal animal, but I had guile and intelligence, weapons always more than a match for brute strength. Jeremy Bond might know a great deal about women, but I knew a great deal about men, all kinds of men. It was knowledge learned of necessity, and there had been times in my past when my very survival had depended on it.

As I dried my hair, I thought of Jack, the brawny, illiterate sailor whom I had turned to during my passage across the ocean to the colonies as an indentured servant. Had it not been for his protection, I might never have made it. Young, merry, uncomplicated, he had cherished me like some treasured pet, smuggling extra food to me, helping me endure the incredibly squalid and brutal conditions on board.

My hair dry, I slipped into a thin cotton petticoat with a low-cut neckline and a very full skirt festooned with ruffles, and then I sat down at the dressing table to brush the flowing mass of copper-red locks. I would never forget Jack Reed or his kindness. I would never forget Jeff either, or Helmut Schnieder, or Lord Robert Mallory. I would never forget young Bruce Trevelyan, so gentle, so sensitive, so in love with me, or the dreadful Brennan brothers who had kidnapped me on the Trace and staked me out like a goat, hoping to lure Jeff to his death.

So many men . . . but there was only one man who mattered, the man who had bought and paid for me and taken me to that rundown plantation in Carolina, the man who owned me still, body and soul. My love for him was as much a part of me as blood and flesh and bone. It coursed inside me, singing in my veins, so strong at times it was almost frightening.

Derek Hawke was not an easy man to love. Moody, remote, frequently cold, he dwelled inside himself, keeping all emotions under tight control and almost never displaying affection or humor. He was coolly detached, and it was difficult to reach the man behind that icy wall of reserve, yet he was capable of passionate rage, as I had reason to know, and sexual passion shattering in its intensity. When he made love to me, it was with splendid fury, almost as though he despised himself for the need of release, despised me for arousing those fires banked up inside him, and afterward, when he was spent, that wall of icy reserve went up again. There were no tender words, no soft caresses, no gentle smiles of repletion. It was as though I were in bed with a stranger totally untouched by that warm glow of aftermath.

My mind went back to that day in Natchez when I had strolled in the garden behind the inn. Finally having recovered from that night of insanity when Helmut had tried to kill me and, in so doing, brought about his own destruction, I had been in a very pensive mood, filled with a vague sadness as I moved slowly past the neatly arranged beds of flowers toward the edge of the cliff. It had been late afternoon, the sky pale and stained with yellow on the horizon as the sun began its gradual descent.

As I stood there near the edge of the cliff, the wind lifting my skirt and blowing soft strands of hair across my cheek, Derek had come for me. Lean, handsome, stern, he looked very much the English aristocrat in his perfectly tailored black trousers and frock coat, his white satin waistcoat patterned with maroon silk flowers, his neckcloth of matching maroon silk. His gray eyes had been solemn, filled with concern for me, solemn still as he told me that he had loved me from the first.

"It took me a long time to realize it," he said grimly, "and still I fought it. Even after I returned to England and won my case to obtain my inheritance, I felt little triumph. Without you it meant nothing. I came back for you because I had to. Life without you is life without meaning."

He had taken me into his arms then, kissing me with an urgent passion that was incredibly tender as well, and when he raised his head I had seen love glowing in his eyes. The icy wall had vanished. The Derek who held me was a softer, more loving Derek than I had ever known before.

"I'll never let you go," he had murmured. "The past is over, Marietta. The future is ours—together."

Those words had filled me with joy, and I had found great comfort in them. I was willing to forget the past, to bury forever those years of turmoil and torment and, with Derek, step into a bright and sun-filled future, but I knew he couldn't forget. He couldn't forget those days in Carolina when I had been his bond servant and had caused his financial ruin when I helped Adam and Cassie escape. He couldn't forget my years with Jeff Rawlins or my disastrous marriage to Helmut. The past was still there, an invisible barrier between us. He loved me. He had come back to America to claim me, but now that I was his he was strangely discontent.

Deep inside, I sensed the reason why. He loved me, yes, but he loved me in spite of himself. His love for me was a compulsion, beyond his control, as mine for him was, and I sensed that he would have been much happier if he had been able to forget me, if he had been able to select a cool, demure, virginal English girl to be his bride, a girl with breeding and background and blood as blue as his, a girl worthy of becoming Lady Hawke and serving as chatelaine in that ancestral hall he had finally claimed as his rightful heritage. I had a fine education, could be as cool and demure and aristocratic as any pink and blonde miss. I had blue blood, too, for my father had been the Duke of Stanton, but my mother had been a barmaid at the Red Lion Inn, and with the inbred snobbery he couldn't really help, Derek couldn't forget that, couldn't forget I was illegitimate and, worse, far from pure.

Sensibly, I faced that fact. Derek didn't want to love me, but he did, and I intended to prove that I was worthy of that love. Once we were married and living in Hawke house, he was going to be very, very proud of me. I was going to make him proud. I was going to make him forget the circumstances of my birth and the events of these past six years. The Marietta he knew, the indentured servant in her white cotton blouse and ragged brown skirt, and, later on, the hostess of a gambling hall in sumptuous golden gown, would be replaced by the elegant, gracious, serene lady of Hawkehouse, the wife who entertained his friends with ease, who ran the great house efficiently, whose primary concern would be his comfort and happiness—for I was going to make him happy.

It would take time, I realized that, but I was going to break down that icy wall and set free the troubled prisoner within. Behind that wall lived a man afraid to show tenderness and affection, afraid to let down his defenses and allow another to touch his heart. He had given his heart once, long ago, to a woman named Alice. He had married her, and her promiscuous unfaithfulness had soured him on all women and made him wary of those emotions he had once felt for her. The treachery of his uncle and cousins had embittered him even more, turning him into the cold, cynical, often cruel man I had first known in Carolina, yet even then I had sensed that wasn't the real Derek Hawke. The real Derek I had glimpsed only rarely, on those few occasions when he had let the wall down.

He was wary still, distrustful, holding himself in and unable to express the love I knew he felt for me. He could express it sexually, with a violent, plunging force that left us both shaken, but one day, I vowed, he would be able to express it in gentle words, in loving glances, in thoughtful, unconscious smiles. I would destroy that wall he had built around himself. With my love and devotion I would restore his faith in love, and I would banish all those fears that plagued him. He needed my love. He needed my understanding. He needed all that I was prepared to give freely, patiently, and without restraint. Derek wasn't an easy man to love, no, but he was the only man in the world who could cause this tender fury inside of me.

Sighing deeply, I put down the hairbrush. My hair fell in rich, gleaming waves now, a dark red-gold, deep, coppery highlights shining as I smoothed my hand over it, moving a thick wave from my temple. I gazed at my reflection for several moments, thinking of Derek, thinking of the past, and my sapphire-blue eyes were sad. Sad? Why should I be sad? I was in love with Derek, and Derek loved me. We were together at last, after so much conflict, and we were going to be married. Those eyes that looked back at me so pensively should be sparkling with happiness. Those high, aristocratic cheekbones should be flushed with joy.

"A woman in love—a woman loved properly in return—wears her happiness in her eyes, on her cheeks, on her lips," Jeremy Bond had said, "wears it like an invisible garment, a glorious garment that gives her an aura everyone can see."

What did *he* know about it? I got up abruptly and stepped to the wardrobe, taking out a thin white cotton dressing robe, the long, full sleeves with lacy ruffles at the wrists, the full skirt billowing with row upon row of ruffles gathered on thin yellow ribbon. Tying the wide yellow sash around my waist, I left the bedroom, moving into the spacious parlor. Rays of sunlight slanted through the louvered windows, making hazy yellow-gold patterns on the pale rose and blue carpet, intensifying the shadows already spreading over the soft ivory walls.

Compared to Derek, Jeremy Bond was a whimsical, will-o'-the-wisp figure, a foolish, frivolous dandy who happened to have been blessed with preposterous good looks and even more preposterous charm. He quite clearly lived off his wits, jaunting about from place to place with a head full of grandiose schemes that, if the truth were known, were probably far from honest. He was extremely tough, much tougher than he looked, and he was undoubtedly ruthless—I had sensed ruthlessness immediately—and he was altogether too forward, as dangerous in his way as ten Will Harts would be.

Ruefully, I reminded myself that I had resolved to waste no more time thinking about him, but it had, after all, been a most unusual encounter and Bond had a very strong presence. Presence? Yes, he had that. For all his whimsy, for all his blarney, he was an extremely commanding figure, undeniably virile and charged with potent sexual magnetism. I had felt that magnetism, of course, I was female, it was only natural, and loving Derek did not render me blind to any male allure but his. I had felt his magnetism, but I had not responded to it in the least. I had seen the man for exactly what he was, a charming rogue who would bring emotional disaster to any woman foolish enough to take him seriously.

Still, I had been rather hard on him. When he saw me in Will Hart's arms, he had jumped to the obvious conclusion and hadn't hesitated an instant, came charging to the rescue like a murderous savage, lips spread back, teeth bared, his eyes gleaming with murderous intent. He hadn't fought like a whimsical dandy. He had fought like a tough, hardened, experienced brawler who would kill if need be. Hart had been no match for him, although he was much heavier, far more muscular. I supposed I should have been at least a tiny bit grateful to him, but the man was so thoroughly infuriating I had lashed out at him like a shrew. It was just as well, I thought. If I had shown the least bit of gratitude, displayed the least bit of weakness, there was no telling what kind of advantage the rogue would have tried to take.

Sunlight touched the crystal pendants dangling from the chandelier and gleamed on the cut-glass bowl holding the roses I had gathered from the garden this morning. The apartment was lavishly appointed, furnished with opulent splendor, but Derek could easily afford to lease such a place. He was a very wealthy man now, his estate bringing in thousands and thousands of pounds each year. There were a number of tenant farms, a tin mine in Cornwall, a coal mine in Wales, several pieces of prime real estate in the city of London. No wonder his uncle and two cousins had tried their best to cheat him of his rightful inheritance. It had taken so many years for him to finally win what was his, and it had taken a great deal of money, too, money he had tried to raise in Carolina, working in the cotton fields alongside his slaves, money he had finally acquired after becoming a smuggler, risking God only knew what kind of danger.

He was in danger now, too. I hadn't been able to find out exactly what kind of nefarious deed Hart and his colleague in the navy blue coat were planning, but I had learned enough to know they meant Derek some kind of harm. I felt that familiar tremor of alarm. If anything happened to Derek . . . but nothing was going to happen to him. I intended to tell him what had happened, giving him a carefully expurgated version, and Derek would certainly take every precaution. Hart and the mysterious Bert might be dangerous ruffians, but Derek was perfectly capable of taking care of himself. He could, I knew, be as hard and lethal as a cold steel blade if he had to be.

Hearing footsteps outside, I stepped into the foyer with walls covered in pale yellow silk. The door opened. Derek stepped inside, bearing a large white and gold box with Lucille's signature printed elegantly on top. I moved toward him. He grimaced.

"Bankrupting me, I see," he remarked, indicating the box with a curt nod of the head. "I ran into the delivery boy outside the gates, relieved him of his burden. I've the feeling whatever this contains is terribly expensive."

"Terribly," I admitted.

Derek strode into the parlor, setting the box down on one of the low mahogany tables that flanked either end of the pale rose velvet sofa. He gave a heavy, exasperated sigh and brushed an errant lock of jet black hair from his brow. He wasn't really exasperated, I knew. If there was one thing Derek didn't quibble about, it was money. He encouraged me to spend as much as I liked.

"Another gown?" he inquired.

I nodded. "A matching cloak as well."

"It figures."

"You know very well I'm worth it, Derek."

"I suppose."

"You *know* I am," I said teasingly.

"All right, you're worth it."

"You said that very grudgingly."

"I've had an extremely busy, extremely frustrating afternoon, Marietta. I'm really not in any mood for playful chatter."

"Pardon *me*."

"I'm not in any mood for feminine pouting either. If you must look like a wounded doe, please get out of my sight. Go try on your new gown or something."

"You really *are* irritable," I remarked. "Still no passage?"

"Still no passage," he retorted. "Those goddamn rebels have fouled up everything. People are afraid the conflict's going to spread down here and there's a great deal of unrest. Passage to England is at a premium, very few ships are going there, and those that are have been booked solid."

"How much longer are we going to have to remain in New Orleans?"

"I'm not certain. There's a ship leaving in two and a half weeks, *The Blue Elephant*, preposterous name for a ship. It's huge, the sides covered with flaking blue paint, but it looks seaworthy enough. It'll be loaded to the gills with frightened loyalists from Natchez."

"You think you might be able to book passage on it?"

"I might. Chap who had already taken a cabin decided to stay on for a few more months, ordered the captain to sell the space to the highest bidder. The captain's being extremely canny about it, taking sealed bids, refusing to indicate what the top price might be. Insufferable bastard. I'd gladly have throttled him."

"You bid?" I inquired.

Derek nodded, stepping over to the mahogany sideboard to pour himself a brandy from the cut-glass decanter. He was tense, frustrated, in a very bad mood, his gray eyes grim, his mouth tight, a deep furrow between his arching black brows. He had always been an impatient man, impatient to get things accomplished, impatient with people less exacting than he. He splashed liquor into the glass and took a deep swallow, staring out the window with grim preoccupation.

"Did you make a high bid?" I asked.

He turned around to glare at me. "Of course I did," he snapped. "I'm quite as eager to get out of this city as you are, Marietta. I have a great many responsibilities back in England."

"Perhaps we'll be able to leave on *The Blue Elephant*. I find the name rather charming—a great blue elephant ponderously riding the waves. Don't scowl like that, Derek. I hate to see you scowl."

Derek took another swallow of brandy, ignoring my remark. He was wearing elegant knee boots of polished black leather and snug navy blue breeches, the cloth molded against his long, powerful legs. His light blue satin waistcoat was stitched with navy blue leaves, his navy blue frock coat cut superbly to emphasize his broad shoulders and slender waist. A severe black silk neckcloth nestled under his chin. The fine, London-made clothes somehow only stressed that buccaneer air he had, and he looked like nothing so much as a handsome, aristocratic pirate, cool and capable of merciless plunder.

"The dress is really splendid," I said brightly. "Lucille outdid herself. It's red brocade, a rich, rich red—I know you don't like me to wear red, Derek, heaven knows *why*—but when you see me in this you're going to be very pleased. I intend to wear it tonight."

"I'm not interested in your clothes, Marietta."

"Damn you, Derek! Sometimes you're—absolutely insufferable!"

"You knew what kind of man I was when you cast your lot with mine." His voice was cool, totally unperturbed.

"Sometimes I think you take pride in being difficult."

Derek put down his empty glass and removed his frock coat, tossing it onto one of the pale blue velvet chairs. "No, Marietta," he said patiently, "I don't take pride in it. I don't particularly relish being the way I am, but I have no intention of becoming the chatty, fawning Romeo you seem to desire."

"I'd hate it if you fawned over me!"

"Indeed?"

"I wouldn't want you to chatter either."

"No?"

"I wouldn't mind if you were a bit more like Romeo."

He frowned, pulling off the black silk neckcloth. "Sweet words under the balcony are not my style," he said. "I've never been a romantic man, Marietta. I've never been overly demonstrative. I don't know why women demand constant reassurance. You know perfectly well how I feel about you. Would I be here with you if I didn't feel that way?"

"That's not the point."

He gave me an exasperated look and took off his waistcoat, tossing it on top of the coat and neckcloth. The shirt he wore beneath was of very fine, very thin white lawn, the sleeves full and billowing, the tail tucked loosely into the waistband of his breeches. I gazed at him, loving him so, wanting to hold him close and smooth away that furrow over the bridge of his nose. I was so very lucky, I told myself, the luckiest woman alive. He might be difficult, but there were very few women who wouldn't gladly have changed places with me.

"I'm sorry," I said quietly. "I know you've had a difficult afternoon. I know how hard it's been selling all that property you owned here, tying up all the loose ends so we can leave."

"I'd rather have been here with you," he replied.

That surprised me. "Really?" I said.

"Making love to you is far more pleasant than haggling over property with potential buyers who expect to make a killing. I enjoy making love to you. As a matter of fact I'd like to do it right here, right now, right over there on that sofa."

"I—"

"The prospect doesn't appeal to you?"

"I'd adore it, Derek, but—there's something I need to tell you."

"It can't wait?"

"I'd like to tell you now. It's terribly important. Something happened, you see, and—I'm worried, Derek."

He frowned again and poured himself another brandy and stood leaning with buttocks and thighs against the sideboard, looking at me with cool gray eyes, a curl at one corner of his mouth. I took a deep breath in order to brace myself, and then I related my tale. I told him about the man in the heavy navy blue coat following me to the market, told him of my encounter with Will Hart after I left Lucille's. I had already decided it wouldn't be wise to mention Jeremy Bond.

"I was walking down the street, quite preoccupied, and he just stepped out in front of me. He said his name was Will Hart. He knew who I was. He knew a lot about me, about you, too. He—I was terrified, naturally, but I managed to stay calm. I asked him what he wanted, and he said he and his friend Bert—the man in the coat—had been watching us for a long time. He said—he indicated they were planning to do you some kind of harm."

"He just volunteered this information?"

"I know it seems surprising, but he wasn't overly bright. He was trying to intimidate me, he may have planned to do something to me. I deliberately tried to coax information from him, and I would have learned more if two men hadn't come along. They were well dressed, highly respectable-looking men," I lied, "and when Hart saw them approaching he hurried away."

Derek's expression hadn't changed an iota. He had listened with a cool, imperturbable look in his eyes, seemingly as disinterested as he would have been had I been relating a bit of gossip I'd overheard at the dress shop. I had expected a less stony reaction.

"I don't suppose I was ever in any real danger," I said, "not there on the street in broad daylight, but it was highly upsetting, Derek."

"I imagine it was. I was a fool to ever allow you to go out alone."

"The pair of them are planning to *do* something."

"Perhaps."

"It doesn't *worry* you?"

"Not particularly."

"I'm frightened, Derek."

"You needn't be. I can take care of myself, Marietta. I can take care of you, too, although it seems I've been negligent of late. You won't go out again by yourself. You won't leave this apartment unless I'm with you. The man's name was Hart, you say?"

"Will Hart. The other man's name was Bert. He told me. Do you *know* them?"

He shook his head. "The names mean nothing to me."

"I wonder who they are."

"A couple of disgruntled chaps out to settle an old score perhaps. I met dozens of the sort when I was smuggling, and I'm afraid I wasn't always too patient with them. I was a stern taskmaster, and the men who worked under me were expected to toe the line. Hart and the other might well be former employees who hold a grudge against me—I never paid attention to names when I was in that business."

"I want you to carry a pistol, Derek."

Derek finished his second brandy and set the glass aside, folding his arms across his chest and peering at me with an inscrutable expression. He wasn't a bit disturbed by what I had told him. That chilly calm infuriated me. I wanted to rail

56

at him, but I knew it would be futile. With that jet black hair and those chiseled features, now as immobile as a statue's, he looked formidable indeed. I told myself any ruffian would think twice before trying to accost him, but it was very little comfort. I'd feel much better if he would agree to carry a pistol. I knew it would be a mistake to press the matter.

"I love you," I said quietly. "If anything happened to you I—"

"Nothing's going to happen to me," he interrupted. "Don't give it another thought, Marietta." He lifted his eyes to glance at the exquisite gilt ormolu clock on the mantle. "It's after six," he said, "too late for our tryst on the sofa, I suppose. I want to bathe, and if I know you, my dear, it'll take you at least two hours to properly adorn yourself."

He strolled casually out of the room, the long, soft white sleeves billowing. I felt empty, depleted by all the varied emotions I had so recently experienced. I should have known he would react that way—rather, that he would not react at all. The beautiful clock ticked steadily, softly, filling the silence with gentle metallic clicks. I needed him. I needed to cling to him and feel the strength of his arms, the warmth of his body. I needed comfort and reassurance, and he should have known that. He shouldn't have walked out. I gazed at the long, plushly upholstered rose velvet sofa, thinking of what might have been. I fervently wished I had waited to tell him about Will Hart.

Five

Derek had ordered the carriage for eight o'clock, and now, at seven-thirty, he stepped into the doorway of the bedroom with an impatient look in his eyes, a look that blazed into exasperation when he saw that I was still wearing my dressing robe. He was, of course, completely dressed, in fine black knee boots, superbly cut black breeches and frock coat, shiny black silk neckcloth and a waistcoat of heavy steel-gray silk with narrow black stripes. He looked severe, formal and devastatingly handsome, scowl notwithstanding.

"I *detest* waiting," he snapped.

"We have half an hour," I said airily. "There's no need to work yourself up, Derek. I'll be ready in plenty of time. I've already done my makeup and hair, as you can see. All I have to do now is dress."

"If you're not ready in twenty-five minutes, I'm leaving without you. I happen to be starving."

"If you're that hungry I could step into the kitchen and fix something to tide you over. You know how slow the service is at Damon's. People don't really go there to eat, though the food's magnificent. They go there to be seen and savor the luxury."

"Stop babbling and put on your dress," he grumbled.

I smiled to myself as he moved angrily back into the parlor and lighted a cigar. I could smell the fragrant aroma of smoke and fine tobacco. He began to pace back and forth like a caged panther as, still smiling, I removed the robe. I couldn't refrain from teasing him now and then, prodding that restless impatience, gently fanning that so easily fired irritation. Derek didn't know how to relax, but I planned to teach him in days to come.

Putting the dressing robe aside, I slipped into the petticoat Lucille had created to go with the gown, the frail red silk bodice snugly caressing my breasts and clinging to my waist, the full, rustling red skirts belling out in splendor. The undergarment alone made me feel like a queen, the skirts lifting and floating with a soft silken music as, unable to resist, I made a graceful whirl in front of the full-length mirror.

Almost reluctantly, I slipped the gown on over it, fastening it in back and smoothing the waist down, spreading the rich, rich deep-red brocade skirt over the underskirts. If I had felt like a queen before, I felt even more like one now. No, not like a queen, a queen had to be grand and formal, constantly aware of her dignity. I felt like a *grande amoureuse,* a bewitchingly beautiful *amoureuse* who captivated kings and made queens despair. With its off-the-shoulder puffed sleeves, seductively low neckline and form-fitting bodice, its lush, luscious skirt spreading out in sumptuous folds, the gown would make any woman feel this way.

The red brocade was embroidered all over with tiny flowers in an even deeper red silk, and the very simplicity of the cut was its greatest glory. The gown needed no frills, no bows, no panels. Lucille had surpassed herself, and I had followed her advice. I had done my hair up in a carefully arranged, seemingly careless arrangement of waves, three long ringlets dangling down in back. I had brushed my lids with the faintest suggestion of blue-gray shadow, tinted my cheeks with a pale, barely discernible blush of pink. My lips were pink, too, naturally so, and my blue eyes did indeed seem to sparkle like sapphires.

How long had it been since I had felt this way in a garment? Much, much too long. Perhaps the last time had been when I was wearing the golden ball gown Lucille had created for the dance at Rawlins' Place. That seemed such a long time ago, and now the man who had caused me such anguish, such indecision that night was waiting for me in the next room, still pacing back and forth as he smoked his cigar. I had wanted him that night when he came so brazenly into the ballroom, ruthlessly determined to have me even though he knew I had committed myself to Jeff. Loving Jeff in a very special way, fiercely loyal to him, I had tried so hard to resist Derek Hawke, had tried to hate him for so brutally casting me aside in Carolina, but I had been unable to deny the feelings he stirred anew. I had been much too weak to resist his demands. I hadn't wanted to hurt Jeff . . . and in the end I had caused his death.

I closed my eyes for a moment, willing away the past. The future was all that mattered now, my future with Derek. I stepped over to the bed to remove the cloak from its nest of tissue paper, and it was then that I discovered the gloves Lucille had slipped into the box as an afterthought, long red velvet gloves the identical dark red of the embroidered flowers. I moved back over to the mirror, pulling them on, smoothing them over my elbows, and then I took one final look at myself in the glass.

The dress was cut daringly low, my breasts swelling against the cloth and rising round and full, half-exposed, the sleeves dropping down and leaving my shoulders quite bare. The bold, beautiful red of the gown made my hair seem an even richer copper-red, darker, providing a dramatic contrast with the sapphire blue of my eyes. I had never, I knew, looked more striking, more desirable, and it was with supreme confidence that I stepped into the parlor, pausing just inside in order to better observe Derek's reaction.

He was leaning against the fireplace, one elbow propped on the mantle beside the clock. His cigar was clamped between his teeth, a surly expression on his face. He looked up. He took the cigar out of his mouth and stared at me with gray eyes that gradually darkened with desire. He tossed the cigar into the fireplace, his eyes still on me. I could see him struggling with himself, trying to control those fierce emotions smoldering inside.

"You like what you see?" I asked lightly.

"I've never seen anything lovelier in my life."

His voice was deep. His gray eyes grew even darker, but the desire was gone now, replaced by stern disapproval.

"Lu—Lucille did a splendid job," I said.

"She did indeed."

" 'Pompadour would have loved it,' she said. She used to dress Pompadour, you know. This gown makes me feel—so gloriously female."

"Wear it with pleasure tonight," he said. "You'll never wear it again."

"I certainly shall. It cost a fortune."

"It's a whore's gown. It's calculated to make every man who sees you in it want to bed you immediately. That's what I wanted to do a moment ago. However elegant, however expensive, it's the gown of a whore."

My cheeks flushed with anger. "I'll take the dress off immediately!"

Derek glanced at the clock. "There isn't time," he remarked. "I'd never be able to take you to a respectable restaurant attired like that, but then Damon's is hardly respectable. Fetch your cloak."

"I'm not going," I said icily.

"I don't intend to argue, Marietta."

"That's what you think of me, isn't it? You think I'm a whore! Perhaps I am. Perhaps I've *had* to be!"

"We're not going to have a scene, Marietta."

"Damon's isn't respectable, no, but then neither is this apartment, this neighborhood. You could have rented a place in the right part of town, where the gentry live, but instead we're staying in this—this exclusive red-light district where rich men keep their mistresses."

"Fetch your cloak," he repeated, cool in the face of my anger.

"You've never taken me to a respectable restaurant, Derek. It's always been Damon's. Are you ashamed of me? Is that it?"

"You're being quite irrational," he said calmly.

"I think not. I think I'm making perfect sense. That's why we haven't married yet. You don't really want to marry me."

Derek sighed wearily, stepped into the bedroom, and returned with the long red velvet cloak. He started to place it over my shoulders. I pulled away. He scowled fiercely, seized my arms, and pulled me back. I stood in stony silence as he placed the soft, luxurious folds over my shoulders and reached around in front to fasten it at my throat. The clock struck eight. I could hear the carriage pulling up in front.

"I'm not going, Derek."

"You're going," he said sternly.

"I don't *want* to go now."

He fetched his own cloak, swirled it around his shoulders and gave me a look that clearly brooked no argument. The anger inside me was cold now, icy cold. I would go, all right. If I didn't go willingly, he was quite capable of dragging me out of the apartment by force, and I preferred to preserve what dignity I could. He adjusted the hang of his heavy black cloak, a magnificent cloak lined with steel gray silk. His face was expressionless, his manner remote. He strode into the foyer and opened the front door, waiting.

I hesitated a moment longer and then followed him. He

locked the door behind us and, pocketing the key, moved toward the gates. The courtyard was bathed in moonlight, the air scented heavily with the perfume of flowers. The fountain splashed quietly. Derek held the gates open for me, closed them with a firm clank and helped me into the carriage. I sat, stiffly as he climbed in beside me and pulled the door shut. He rapped on the roof with his knuckles, and the carriage began to move, wheels skimming over the cobbles, the horses' hooves clattering noisily.

"There's no point in pouting," he remarked.

"Sometimes I actually detest you, Derek."

"I'm sorry about that, my dear."

Neither of us spoke again as the carriage moved through the labyrinth of narrow streets that grew more and more congested as we neared the restaurant. Derek sat with his hands on his knees, and in the moonlight that streamed in through the window I studied those long, beautifully shaped hands I knew so well, hands that could grip with brutal strength, hands that could caress lightly, fingertips touching flesh as though savoring the texture of satin. Moonlight gleamed on the signet ring he wore on his left hand, the ring he had worn ever since he returned from England, the ring he had fought so hard to acquire. It was silver, very, very old, the metal dark, the top a small silver circle with a black onyx hawk embedded skillfully.

The ring had been passed down from generation to generation, and it was a symbol of his position, his place in the world, of all that the name Hawke stood for in that elite world of English aristocracy. He wore it with pride, a constant reminder of who he was. Derek was very much a part of that world, had spent years fighting for his right to belong, to wear the ring, and in my heart I knew that I could never belong, not truly. I could adapt, yes, and I could win token acceptance, even admiration, but I would always be an outsider, never really a part. Derek knew that, too. In my anger, I had hit upon a truth neither of us could honestly deny: Derek didn't want to marry me. I now faced that truth squarely.

He loved me, and he would honor the commitment he had made, but he did not *want* to marry me. Love me though he might, he would always secretly resent the fact that my blood was not as blue as his, my background shady and open to criticism. I might make him happy—I *would* make him happy—but the resentment would remain no matter how hard he tried to suppress it. I knew he would always disapprove of me, no matter how much he loved me, no matter how much I tried to win his complete approval. Earlier this afternoon, while I was waiting for him, I had told myself otherwise, had painted a glowing picture of our future, but now, as the carriage stopped in front of the brightly lighted entrance, I no longer tried to fool myself.

Derek climbed out and reached in to help me down, taking my hand firmly, pulling me toward him. My crimson skirts rustled as I stepped down, and a gentle breeze caused my cloak to billow. Derek spoke tersely to the driver, giving him instructions, and then he escorted me into the elegant silver-gray and blue foyer of the most expensive, the most famous restaurant in New Orleans, a restaurant no "respectable" woman would dream of entering. He removed my cloak, removed his own and checked them both. His face was immobile as he led me toward the wide, curving archway that opened into the main room.

Damon's was the epitome of subdued elegance. There was no glitter, no gilt, no opulent plush. The walls were covered with a pale gray silk. The draperies that covered the windows were of deep blue velvet over cloth of silver, similar draperies framing those smaller archways leading to "private" rooms where a gentleman could dine undisturbed with his companion of the evening. Graceful white columns supported the pale, sky-blue ceiling traced with silver designs, and the chandeliers dripped with crystal pendants that reflected soft candlelight with silvery-violet glints. This main room was extremely large, circular in shape, patrons dining at tables covered with snowy cloths, sitting in fine rosewood chairs upholstered in pale violet or sky-blue brocade. Music played quietly, a soothing, unobtrusive background to the tinkle of china and crystal, the hum of low voices.

An atmosphere of extremely refined, extremely discreet sin prevailed, as subtle as expensive perfume. Although men frequently came in alone or arrived in groups, no women were allowed without a male escort. The women who dined here were the most beautiful in New Orleans, sumptuously gowned, exquisitely coifed, candlelight enhancing magnolia-smooth complexions and gleaming in dark worldly eyes. These women lived in opulent apartments similar to the one I shared with Derek, welcoming lovers who kept them in luxury, showered them with jewels, paid dearly for the privilege of showing them off at Damon's. In these circles, a man's mistress was a prized possession as important to his image as the house he owned, the carriage he drove, the thoroughbred stables he maintained, and the men who dined at Damon's could afford the best New Orleans had to offer.

As the maitre d' led us to our table, I could feel the women watching me with carefully veiled hostility, the men staring with open admiration. Derek helped me into my chair, his face still expressionless. I felt naked and exposed, extremely vulnerable in the gown that, so short a time ago, had given from such a joyous feeling. I realized that I was no different than the other women who sipped champagne and toyed with their pheasant. Without a wedding ring on my finger, I was exactly like them, living off a man, totally dependent on his generosity. Until now it had never bothered me. Until now I had never given it a thought. I resented it now. I resented Derek bringing me here night after night, exposing me to the stares of worldly men and envious women.

"Champagne?" he inquired.

"I think not."

"Are you going to sulk?"

"I'm not sulking, Derek. I'm very angry."

"Over the dress?"

"Over what you implied."

"I didn't call you a whore. I said it was a whore's gown."

"You make me feel like a whore."

"That's absurd," he said coldly, studying the menu. "Oysters, I think, and pheasant. Asparagus with sauce. Lemon ice afterward. And champagne." He closed the menu and looked at me. "You're going to be my wife, Marietta, and Lady Hawke must dress in gowns suitable to her position."

"I'm not Lady Hawke yet."

"That's quite true. You know the reason why."

"I know the reason you *told* me. You said you wanted to be married at Hawkehouse, in the chapel. If—if you really loved me, that wouldn't matter. You'd have married me before we left Natchez."

"You doubt my intentions?"

"I didn't—not before."

"And now, after a silly argument, you think I don't want to marry you at all. You think I want to keep you as my whore. Is that it? It's not terribly rational, Marietta. You know what I feel for you."

"Do I?"

"You damn well should know," he said crisply. "If you expect me to vow eternal devotion every hour on the hour, you're due a disappointment. I love you, goddamnit. Now drink your champagne."

He thrust a glass toward me, his gray eyes smoldering. He was genuinely angry now, tense with anger, and I fell silent, knowing it would be unwise to pursue the matter further. Eyes lowered, I toyed with the champagne glass, watching the tiny golden bubbles fizzle to the surface with soft explosions. Derek drank several glasses, and when our food came he ate heartily. I hardly touched the food, occasionally pushing it from side to side, unable to eat. The waiter removed our plates and brought the lemon ice in small silver dishes.

"I didn't mean to hurt you, Marietta," he said wearily.

"I know you didn't. You never do."

"You're much too sensitive."

"If I'm sensitive, it's because my position is so vulnerable. I'm not your wife. At the moment I'm no different from any of these women here. I feel very insecure. I can't help it."

"That will all be changed soon enough, Marietta."

"I know. I don't mean to be unreasonable, Derek, but we were apart for such a long time—so many things happened— I'm afraid something else will happen. I lost you twice. I don't think I could stand losing you again."

"You're not going to lose me."

His anger was gone, and although his manner could hardly be called tender, it was at least conciliatory. His voice was low, and his eyes met mine with a steady gaze. The candlelight seemed to polish his lean, handsome face, burnishing his cheekbones, creating faint shadows beneath them. His jet hair gleamed darkly with blue-black highlights.

"I wanted to please you," I said.

"I know that, Marietta."

"I wanted to be beautiful for you."

Another man would have told me that I *was* beautiful, that I didn't need a new gown to enhance the beauty that was ever-present, that would glow incandescently even were I wearing rags. Another man would have taken my hand and stroked it gently, apologizing for his harshness and soothing the tension with quiet, reassuring words. Derek merely frowned and told me to eat my lemon ice before it melted, but that was his way, and I didn't want another man.

"I do hope we get passage on *The Blue Elephant*," I remarked.

"We'll know soon enough."

"It's going to seem strange, returning to England. I left it under—under such adverse circumstances. I left it in chains, a convicted thief, sentenced to fourteen years of servitude. I'll be returning as your bride-to-be. Life is full of ironies."

Derek finished his dessert. A waiter came to our table with a silver pot of coffee, pouring the steaming, aromatic liquid into elegant, paper-thin china cups. My lemon ice had indeed melted. I nodded to the waiter, indicating that he could remove the dish.

"I don't really feel a part of England," I continued quietly. "I don't feel I belong there. For some reason I feel I belong here—in America. I've grown to love this country."

Derek elevated an eyebrow. "I suppose next you'll be wanting to go north and take up arms with the rebels."

"They do have just grievances, Derek."

"Perhaps so, but violence and bloodshed is no way to solve them. They'll be put down soon enough, order restored."

"England—English law—can be very harsh. I have reason to know that."

"I thought you were eager to return."

"I am, but only because of you. I'm eager to become your wife, eager to start our new life together, but if it weren't for that—" I hesitated. "If you were to tell me we were going to settle permanently here in America, I'd have no desire to see England again."

"England is my home."

"And your home is my home," I told him.

Derek didn't seem to hear me. He stiffened, staring across the room with gray eyes that were suddenly hostile. Startled, I turned to see what had caused such a sudden change in him. I caught my breath, and I could feel a flush tinting my cheeks. Jeremy Bond had just entered Damon's with a gorgeous blonde, the same blonde who had come out of Lucille's this afternoon. He had spotted us at our table. He said something to the blonde and started toward us with that long, bouncy stride. The blonde frowned and followed the maitre d' to a table on the other side of the room.

I tried to control my breathing, tried to still the panic inside. I hadn't told Derek about Bond. If Derek found out that I'd already met him, he'd know I had been withholding information. He'd wonder why. Desperately striving to appear casual, I lifted the coffee cup to my lips, set it down. The cup clattered noisily in the saucer, but Derek didn't notice. His eyes never once left Bond, who drew nearer and nearer, finally reaching our table with a mocking smile on his lips.

"Hawke," he said. "It's been a long time."

Derek nodded curtly. "Bond," he said.

"I saw you sitting over here, thought I'd pop over to say hello." He gave me a friendly glance and returned his attention to Derek. "I must say, you seem to be doing very well for yourself, Hawke. Last time I saw you you were carting a keg of illegal rum through a swamp, yelling at the others to keep up."

Derek made no reply. His eyes were dark with hostility.

"Glad to see you've come up in the world," Bond continued jauntily. "I say, aren't you going to introduce me to your lovely companion?"

Derek merely glared. Bond grinned.

"No? Hardly sporting of you, old cháp, but then if *I* were dining with such a breathtaking beauty, I wouldn't care to introduce her to another man either."

He looked at me again, his vivid blue eyes full of mischief. He wore impeccably cut black breeches and frock coat and a white satin waistcoat embroidered with black silk flowers, an elegant white silk neckcloth nestling under his chin. That rich brown wave fell cockily over his brow. The audacious grin danced on his lips. I silently pleaded with him not to give me away. Bond was fully aware of my discomfort and sensed the reason why. His blue eyes teased me. He seemed to be full of laughter and devilment.

"Well," he said, "guess I'd better dash off now. Nice seeing you, Hawke. Nice seeing you, too," he added, giving me a jaunty nod.

He left to rejoin the blonde he had so cavalierly abandoned a few minutes before. Derek had been gripping the edge of the table as though ready to spring to his feet and start swinging. He relaxed his grip now, watching Bond's retreating figure with eyes that hadn't lost a bit of their hostility. I sipped my coffee, relieved but still shaken by the close call. It was not until Bond sat down that Derek turned back to me, and by that time I was completely composed.

"You know him?" I inquired casually.

"I've known him most of my life—since both of us were boys. His family's estate bordered ours. We hated each other then, and we hate each other now. Jeremy Bond is thoroughly disreputable, always has been."

"He seemed—quite charming."

"A lot of people have found him charming. They invariably regretted it."

I took another sip of coffee. "I take it he was involved in smuggling, too," I said.

"There's very little he hasn't been involved in," Derek retorted. "He was thrown out of Oxford, drummed out of the army, squandered a fortune on gambling and women. He left England in disgrace, disowned by his family, and for the past ten years he's made a precarious living as a gambler, as a smuggler, as a mercenary."

"A mercenary? He fights for money?"

"For a while there he had his own band of cutthroats. They fought Indians, fought pirates off the coast, fought anyone whose enemies could afford to pay the going price."

"It sounds terribly bloodthirsty."

"Bond's that, all right. That dapper, devil-may-care manner fools a lot of people. He's as hard as steel, utterly ruthless, utterly fearless. I admire his valor—I'll have to admit that most of his fighting was for a good cause—but he's completely irreverent and totally irresponsible. He abides by no rules but his own, refuses to take orders."

I finished my coffee, careful not to show too much interest.

"I suppose the two of you clashed when you were smuggling," I remarked.

"We were having some trouble with the pirates," Derek said. "They were hiding out in the swamps, lying in wait for us, stealing our goods. A lot of lives were lost. Bond and his men were hired to accompany us."

"And?"

"We had no more trouble with the pirates," he said tersely.

"I should think you'd be grateful to him."

"Bond and his men were as bad as the pirates. No discipline at all, as rowdy a band of ruffians as I've ever encountered. As soon as the pirates had been routed, he set up his own smuggling operation in direct competition with ours, stole some of our key men, damn near wrecked our business."

I thought that highly enterprising of him, but I knew it would be unwise to say so. I could see how Derek—so stern, so responsible, so conscious of background and duty and appearances—would clash with an irreverent rogue like Bond. Derek took himself very seriously, and I doubted that Bond had a serious bone in his body. He was unquestionably a scamp, but, however ruthless he might be, I couldn't believe he was a true villain. Even Derek had spoken highly of his valor.

"Are you finished?" Derek asked.

I nodded, pushing the coffee cup aside.

"We'd better go then. If I stay here much longer I might just march over there and punch his face in."

"You *do* hate him, don't you?"

Derek didn't answer. He paid the bill and led me toward the foyer, his gray eyes expressionless. Men and women stared again as I passed in the luxuriant red gown, but I paid no attention to the stares this time. In fact, I rather hoped Jeremy Bond *was* staring. Derek might not appreciate the gown, but I knew full well Bond would. Resisting an impulse to glance toward his table, I held Derek's arm, feeling much better than I had earlier.

As we stepped into the foyer, the front door opened, and a heavyset man with thick blond hair entered. He was of medium height, in formal attire, his complexion ruddy, his blue eyes friendly. He removed his cloak and checked it, smiling at the attendant, and then he turned and saw us. His lips parted in surprise.

"Hawke!" he exclaimed.

He smiled again, eyes full of pleasure, and hurried over to take Derek's hand in a firm grip. Derek seemed genuinely pleased to see him. They shook hands, and then Derek introduced me. The man's name was Stephen Howard. He was in his early forties, his attractive face pleasantly lined.

"I didn't know you were in New Orleans," Derek remarked.

"Nor I you," Howard replied. "You disappeared after the trial. No one knew *what* had happened to you."

"I had business here."

"As do I. Politics. Intrigue. A diplomat's life is never easy. We hope to secure the loyalty and support of the territory, but I fear there's a shocking amount of sympathy with the rebels. How long have you been here?"

"Ever since the trial."

"Just arrived a couple of weeks ago myself. I say, if you've been in America all this time you probably haven't heard about your uncle."

Derek was suddenly guarded. "What about him?"

"You don't know then. He died. His heart. It happened only a few days after he lost the case. Your cousin Roger blames you. The chap's extremely bitter, made all kinds of noise around London, vowed he was going to—" Howard cut himself short, realizing he was being indiscreet. "I—uh—perhaps we could discuss it later," he said.

"I'd like to hear about it now," Derek told him. "In privacy. We'll take one of the rooms and you can tell me while you dine."

"Your, uh, lovely bride-to-be might find it rather upsetting."

"I'm sending her home. Marietta, the doorman will summon our carriage. The driver will see you to the door. You'll be all right."

"But—"

Derek fetched my cloak and put it over my shoulders. "I don't know how long I'll be," he said brusquely. "Don't wait up for me."

Howard seemed slightly embarrassed by Derek's abruptness. He gave me an apologetic smile. The two men moved toward the archway, leaving me standing alone, disturbed, feeling abandoned. What had his cousin Roger said? What had he vowed? I felt a terrible alarm, and I resented Derek's abandoning me

70

like this, like . . . like I was a piece of excess baggage. He could have made an appointment to see Howard later. He could at least have seen me safely home and then returned to the restaurant.

Two couples came inside, the men in their fifties, silver-haired and richly attired, the women lush, lovely creoles with dark, creamy complexions and shining brown eyes. One wore ivory velvet, the other pale gold silk, and their perfume scented the air, musky and exotic. All four of them gave me curious looks, no doubt wondering what I was doing standing here alone, obviously upset about something. They went on into the restaurant, the heady perfume lingering in the air. From behind the recessed booth the check-out attendant gave me a curious look, too. Unaccompanied women did not linger in the foyer of Damon's, her eyes seemed to say. It wasn't done.

Frowning, I stepped outside and spoke to the doorman. He hurried away to see to the carriage. I was angry, upset, filled with a variety of conflicting emotions. I had told Derek all about Will Hart and the man in the bulky navy blue coat, and he had said I was not to go out alone again. Yet he sent me away without hesitation, at nighttime, too, without giving a moment's thought to any possible danger. What if Hart and his colleague had followed us to Damon's? What if they were standing in the shadows right now, watching me, waiting? It was taking the doorman an inordinately long time to return. I was beginning to feel genuine alarm when the door opened behind me, and someone stepped outside.

"Ah, here you are," Jeremy Bond said. "I was afraid I might have missed you. Are you ready to go?"

Six

He was wearing a long, beautifully cut black cloak lined with heavy white silk, the garment falling from his shoulders in rich folds that swept the ground. He smiled an engaging smile, as though this had all been arranged, and I couldn't help but feel a rush of relief. I wasn't about to let him suspect it, however. I looked at him with cool composure I was far from feeling.

"Just where do you think we're going?" I inquired.

"I'm taking you home, of course. Can't have you gadding about New Orleans alone, particularly at night. All sorts of villains abroad after the sun goes down."

"The doorman is fetching our carriage. I'll be quite all right, Mr. Bond. Lord Hawke would be *very* upset if he—"

"Damned ungallant of him, leaving you like that. I saw him coming back in with a heavyset blond chap, saw 'em go into one of the private rooms. Naturally, I thought he'd come back out in a minute or so. When he didn't, I realized he must have left you to get home by yourself."

"He and Mr. Howard had some important business to discuss."

"Important business be damned. Man's a bloody fool to leave you like this, particularly after what happened this afternoon. You told him about it, didn't you?"

"I told him—most of it."

"Didn't tell him about me, though. You were scared to death I was going to mention it when I came over to the table. I could see the panic in your lovely blue eyes."

"The carriage should be here in—"

"Let's walk," he suggested. "It's a grand night."

"There are all sorts of villains abroad," I reminded him.

"You're safe with me, lass," he assured me. "It's not too long a walk, only a few blocks. The exercise'll do you good."

"Mr. Bond, can you give me one good reason why I should let you walk me home?"

"Oh, I can do better than that. I can give you several. First of all, I'm an amiable chap, delightful company. Second, you're upset and need a shoulder to cry on. Mine are quite broad. Third, now that you know Hawke and I grew up together you can use those feminine wiles to get information out of *me*."

"What about Helena?" I inquired.

"You remembered her name, I see."

"I remembered," I said dryly.

"Helena can take care of herself. You, my dear, can't."

"You just walked out and left her at the table?"

Jeremy Bond nodded, a grin on his lips. "Upset her quite a bit," he admitted. "It wasn't the act of a gentleman, but then she knew I wasn't a gentleman when she agreed to go out with me. If I know Helena, she'll find someone to pay for her meal."

"You're quite dreadful."

He nodded again, thrusting his hands in his pockets, looking preposterously handsome and cocky. The doorman returned. The carriage pulled up. I told the driver I wouldn't be needing him. Jeremy Bond took my arm, and we started down the street. It was a balmy night, warm but not unpleasantly so. The sky was a deep, misty purple, glittering with stars barely visible behind the mist. Bond adapted that long, bouncy stride to match my own. I could feel the warmth of his body, the strength in the arm locked firmly around my own.

"Do you always treat women so wretchedly?" I asked.

"Like I treated Helena? Usually. They invariably come 'round for more. I suppose it's this devilish charm. Gets 'em every time."

"I don't think I've ever known a man quite so arrogant and conceited," I said, not at all unkindly.

"High time you did, lass. You don't want a grim, broody chap like Hawke. You want someone who can make you smile, make you laugh, make you feel like a million pounds when you wake up in the morning."

"I'm quite happy with Derek."

"I doubt that, lass. I doubt it mightily."

"I happen to love him."

"Really? A dour, severe fellow like that?"

"I love him very much."

Jeremy Bond shook his head, amazed. "Remarkable," he said.

"Was he—always so serious?"

"Always. Even as a boy. Stiff, formal, always scowling. He took himself very seriously, never knew how to relax and have a good time. He was a Hawke, you see, had to live up to the responsibility of the name. He was always the proper son, manners you wouldn't believe, stiff, formal, never indulged in any pranks, never got in trouble."

"And you, I imagine, were *always* in trouble."

"Always. The Bonds were aristocratic, too, frightfully aristocratic, our blood as blue as anyone's. You're never supposed to forget that. You're never supposed to forget your superiority to common folk. The family expected me to revere the family name, live up to it. They pointed to young Master Hawke as a model of deportment. *He* never got into fights with the farmers' brats. *He* never left muddy boot tracks in the hall or put frogs in the tutor's bed. He certainly never poured water out the second-floor window onto the heads of unsuspecting guests. I was, I fear, incorrigible."

"I don't doubt it."

"I found the life of English aristocracy insufferably dreary, far too stuffy and self-satisfied to suit a lad like me. The family gave up on me a long time ago. Booted me out, in fact."

"You didn't mind?"

"Hurt my pride a bit, I suppose, but I didn't really mind. I never knew my mother, you see. She died when I was born. My father was cold, my stepmother a horror, my older brother a dreadful prig, always reproving me, always criticizing. He was the fair-haired boy, of course, due to inherit everything. Bloody welcome to it."

There was just the faintest trace of bitterness in his voice, and I sensed that his family's disowning him had hurt him far more than he cared to acknowledge, even to himself. We turned down another street, moving at a leisurely pace. Lampposts made soft yellow pools at regular intervals, light spilling over the pavement and spreading over the walls. We could hear low voices and laughter coming from the balconies. Someone played a guitar, strumming quietly. The air was heavily perfumed, a languorous atmosphere prevailing over the district. Several prostitutes lingered in doorways, watching us pass, fanning themselves with palmetto fans, graceful, indolent creatures who were very much a part of the district's charm.

"You were booted out of the army, too," I said.

"Hawke told you quite a lot about me, I see. Yes, I was booted out. The military life was much too strict, had far too many rules and regulations. I like to make my own rules."

"I can see that."

"He told you I was a rotter, didn't he?"

"More or less," I replied.

"Suppose I am," Bond said quietly. "Everyone always *said* I was. After a while I started believing them. I do, however, have a good heart."

"Oh?"

"All I need is the right woman to reform me."

"I don't envy her the task."

"Oh, it would be a most delightful task," he assured me, "extremely rewarding."

We walked two more blocks and turned another corner, moving down a brightly lighted, bustling street lined with cafés and bars. Carriages of every description rumbled over the cobbles, and the pavements were crowded with pedestrians, lively young clerks in chap frock coats, pretending to be dandies and eyeing the pretty girls in second-hand finery who spent their days working behind counters, brawny stevedores who worked on the docks, sailors from all over the world. Music played loudly, almost drowned out by the roar of rowdy voices celebrating freedom from care. One could smell beer and sweat and face powder, fish and salt and sauerkraut. One could feel a merry, highly charged energy in the air.

"Want to stop for a beer?" Bond asked.

"I—I think not."

"I could use one myself, but I guess we're not really dressed for it."

"I've never been on this street before. Is it safe?"

"Safe as houses. An occasional brawl, nothing serious. Folks come here to have a merry time. Your real vice occurs down nearer the waterfront, knifings, shootings, hefty lads shanghaied by brutal press gangs, unsuspecting females whisked away to work in South American brothels."

"That actually happens?"

"White slavery, you mean? Sure it does. When they're not busy raiding and sinking trade ships or attacking coastal villages or waylaying smugglers in the swamps, Red Nick and his men do a thriving business in women. Kidnap 'em, sell 'em to brothels in Caracas, Rio de Janeiro, places like that."

"How horrible."

"A lot of the women are Mexican, taken from the villages, but quite a few come from New Orleans. Red Nick has regular contact with ruffians who supply him with women. Most of 'em he sells. The choicest of the lot he keeps for his men, holding them on an island stronghold off the coast of Texas."

"He's a pirate?"

"Most notorious pirate on the coast. The very name Red Nick strikes terror in the hearts of the authorities. They know about the island, have a pretty good idea where it's located, but it'd take an armada to capture it. Mostly they just try to stay out of his way."

"Have you ever met him?"

Bond shook his head. "Ran into some of his men a while back, crew of cutthroats hiding in the swamps, harassing the smugglers, not more than twenty or thirty. I, uh, helped get rid of 'em, but they represented only a handful of Red Nick's force. He must have three hundred men under his command."

"You seem to know quite a lot about him."

"I made it my business to find out all I could. He comes from Scotland originally, grew up in Edinburgh, had a fine education I understand. His name's Nicholas Lyon—they call him Red Nick because of his hair. He killed a man in Scotland when he was sixteen years old, was scheduled to hang. He escaped, killing a couple of guards in the process, took to the sea. By the time he was in his early twenties, he already had his own ship, eventually got his own fleet and began to concentrate on the coast."

Three drunken sailors came reeling out of a bar directly ahead of us, reeling pleasantly, all three grinning. Jeremy Bond moved me aside as they stumbled toward us. A pretty blonde girl in a faded pink dress and tattered, darker pink feather boa called one of the sailors by name and hurried toward him with a wide, laughing smile on her lips, her long jet earrings dangling. "You're a sight, you are!" she cried, linking her arm in his. He gave her a mighty hug. It touched me to see two young people so merry, so free of care. Bond was watching me. He seemed to read my mind.

"There hasn't been much of that in your life, has there?"

"What are you talking about?"

"High spirits. Merriment."

"I've not had much time for that sort of thing," I said quietly. "Life hasn't been easy, Mr. Bond."

"I know, lass."

"Lucille *did* tell you a lot, didn't she?"

He nodded. "There won't be much merriment in the future, either, not if you stay with Derek Hawke. You're not cut out for the kind of life he intends to live in England, lass."

"How would you know?" I asked.

"I know Hawke. And I know you."

"You don't know me at all," I retorted. "I never should have agreed to let you walk me home," I continued. "I should have taken the carriage. You really are terribly presumptuous!"

"And you're awfully touchy. It's true, you know, what I said. In your heart you know it's true."

"I know no such thing!"

My voice was cool and haughty. I pulled my arm from his, wishing I had the courage to abandon him entirely. I kept my eye on the carriages passing by, hoping to spot an empty one I might be able to hire. Bond grinned, striding along beside me, his elegant cloak swelling and fluttering behind him like dark, silk-lined wings. The heavy brown wave bounced on his forehead, dipping lower and lower until it almost covered one mischievous blue eye. I pretended to ignore him. When we reached the end of the street he took hold of my wrist, holding it tightly when I tried to pull free.

"This way," he said. "We'll cut through the market. It's shorter."

"Let go of my wrist!"

"Promise to behave?"

I refused to answer. He gave my wrist a brutal twist, still grinning. I gasped, startled.

"Promise?" he repeated.

"You're hurting me!"

"Not really. If I wanted to I could twist it a bit more, have you hollering in pain."

"Don't you dare!"

Bond chuckled, releasing my wrist. I rubbed it vigorously, giving him a vicious look.

"You'd like to slap me, wouldn't you?" he said.

"I'd dearly love to!"

"Don't quite dare though, do you?"

I saw no reason to answer him. I did indeed want to slap him. I wanted to slap him soundly, and at the same time I wanted to laugh. That surprised me. The man made it impossible to be really angry with him, at least for more than a few minutes. The little boy who had enjoyed naughty pranks was still very much in evidence, however virile and ruthless the man might be. His charm was almost overwhelming, quite, quite dangerous.

"Are we going to be friends?" he asked.

"Definitely not," I retorted. "However, as I was foolhardy enough to get myself into this situation, I may as well see it through. You may escort me the rest of the way."

He cocked a brow. "May I? Really?"

"I might just slap your face after all!"

He grinned, leading me across the street and into the poorly lighted labyrinth of the market. Only a few of the stalls were still open. The ground was littered with soiled cabbage leaves and limp carrots, shredded flowers, bits of paper. Torches burned here and there, but much of the area was in shadow, empty stalls closed up for the night. I could smell nuts roasting. A Negro woman moved wearily from stall to stall, bending down to pick up any piece of fruit or vegetable that might still be edible, dropping it into her basket. Jeremy Bond frowned darkly. Taking a wad of money from his pocket, he thrust it into the woman's hands. She looked up at him with tired brown eyes full of amazement, and Bond hooked his arm in mine, hurrying me along before the woman could thank him.

"I hate that!" he exclaimed. "If these bloody slaveholders are going to set their slaves free, they might at least provide them with some means of livelihood! Sometimes I detest my fellow man."

His voice rang with genuine indignation, the frown digging

a deep furrow over the bridge of his nose. We walked for a while in silence, Bond seething, eventually calming down. We passed bins of coffee beans, the beans glowing a rich red brown in the flickering torch light. Nearby, a husky blond man in a begrimed white apron was packing fish in a barrel of ice, grabbing the silvery fish by their tails, slapping them down onto the ice with resounding smacks. A plump woman with a magnolia blossom behind her ear examined a tray of oranges, idly inspecting them for flaws. We left the lighted area, strolling past rows of empty stalls half in shadow, a misty moonlight alleviating some of the darkness.

"That was a lovely thing you did back there," I said quietly. "You feel very strongly about it, don't you?"

"I feel strongly about a lot of things," he replied. "Does that surprise you?"

"Not at all."

"I can't abide injustice. I've spent a good part of my adult life fighting it in one way or another."

"Derek told me—he said you were a mercenary."

"I'm sure he did. It's true. I've hired my services as a fighter, as a killer if you choose, but I've never gone after any man or any group of men who weren't in the wrong, who didn't deserve to be squelched."

"You don't have to justify yourself to me, Mr. Bond."

"I just wanted to set the facts straight. Wouldn't want you to think I was really the cold-blooded killer Hawke undoubtedly made me out to be."

"He never implied that. He said he admired your valor. He said most of your fighting had been done for a good cause."

"Indeed? Thought the chap hated me."

"He does," I replied, "but he's always fair."

We passed under an archway, leaving the market, moving down a long, narrow passageway thick with blue-black shadows, our footsteps ringing on the cobbles. It never entered my head to be frightened, not with Jeremy Bond beside me. I felt perfectly safe and hadn't given Hart and his friend a single thought since we left Damon's. We left the passageway and started down the street beyond, lampposts glowing at every corner, an occasional carriage passing slowly.

"Have you killed many men?" I asked.

"Dozens and dozens," he said teasingly. "The army trained

me well, gave me all sorts of skills before they drummed me out. Only training I ever had, actually. Didn't learn a bloody thing at Oxford except how to cheat at cards. That stood me in good stead, too.''

"You're not half as bad as you pretend to be."

"Oh, I'm bad, lass. Never doubt it. Mothers warn their daughters about me every day. Of course that only makes the daughters more interested, makes me much more intriguing. Nothing enhances a man's appeal like a reputation for wickedness."

"Lucille told me about your reputation with women."

"I must remember to thank her," he said. "Gives me a definite advantage where you're concerned."

"Mr. Bond—"

"If you call me Mr. Bond one more time I fully intend to twist your arm quite savagely. Try 'Jeremy.' ''

"I don't know you well enough to call you by your first name."

"And stop being so goddamn coy."

"Really, Mr.—"

He gave me a warning look, his blue eyes dark with intent.

"I wasn't being coy," I said smoothly. "I can't abide coy women."

"You've been coy as hell," he informed me. "Why don't you just admit you find me attractive? You may be all wrapped up in Derek Hawke, you may even believe you love him, but you've wanted to go to bed with me ever since you first saw me this afternoon."

"You—you're quite wrong about that!"

"Why can't you admit it? There's no disgrace involved."

"I happen to love Derek."

"And you want to sleep with me."

"I don't intend to argue."

"No point in arguing. We both know it's true."

He had released my arm earlier, and now he thrust his hands into his pockets, hunching his shoulders forward, sauntering along at a leisurely pace. The handsome cloak billowed, fluttering gently. He was indeed wrong, I told myself. I did find him attractive, yes, I couldn't deny that, but the thought of sleeping with him had never entered my mind. His conceit knew no bounds. Because a great many women had made a fuss over him, had spoiled him deplorably, he arrogantly assumed every woman he met found him irresistible. Well, here was one who didn't. I had no desire to sleep with anyone but Derek.

"Angry?" he inquired.

"Not in the least," I said coldly.

"You are. I can tell."

"Your nonsense isn't worth getting angry about."

"It's not nonsense, Marietta. It's the truth. I'm a very honest man. I hoped you'd be honest, too."

"You hoped I'd be easy prey. You hoped—you thought you could offer your protection and I'd be so grateful I'd tumble into your arms the minute you gave the signal."

"You're right."

"I told you this afternoon—you're wasting your time."

Jeremy Bond grinned, hands in pockets, shoulders hunched, wave flopping on his forehead as he strolled beside me in that bouncy stride. He wasn't at all perturbed by the cool, aloof manner I assumed. I was extremely irritated, extremely disturbed, and I felt wonderfully, gloriously alive, as though I had downed a dozen glasses of champagne instead of one. Something seemed to sing inside of me, making joyous music that was felt, not heard. I told myself it was the lovely night, the perfumed air, the smooth caress of red silk against my skin.

Bond made no attempt to resume our conversation. He seemed to be preoccupied, lost in thought, the grin still curling on that wide, generous mouth. We walked down the street toward the apartment, passing the gray walls dripping with bougainvillaea. The balconies beyond were brushed with shadow, moonlight gilding the wrought iron. Lamps glowed behind curtained windows, making hazy yellow-gold squares in the night. New Orleans was at its most bewitching in the evening, sultry and romantic and imbued with an indolent charm that cast a spell over the senses. I was going to miss this city. I had known much sadness here, but I had known happiness, too, a kind of happiness I had never experienced before.

I was in a pensive mood by the time we reached the gates. The anger and irritation had vanished, and that joyous music had been replaced by a languor that seemed to steal over my entire body. Bond was silent, studying my face as we stood there in front of the gates. I felt no animosity toward him. I felt strangely passive, as though I no longer had a will of my own, as though I had been drugged by the fragrant perfume of roses, lulled by the soft night noises that rustled in the gardens. It had been a long walk, an eventful day, and I was weary, so weary I didn't protest when he touched my cheek, stroking it gently with his fingertips.

"You're lovely," he said. "You're the loveliest woman I've ever seen. I mean that, Marietta."

His voice was very low, and there was a husky catch in it, as though the words came from deep inside. I tilted my chin, looking up at him. His face was clearly visible in the moonlight, the eyes half-shrouded, dark blue now, full of meaning, sending a message it was impossible not to read. I noticed anew the generous, beautifully shaped mouth, the slightly crooked nose, the broad, flat cheekbones with skin stretched taut. He was a stranger, a man I barely knew, yet somehow I felt I knew him better than I had ever known any man. I felt he knew me, too, knew me as no man had.

"Thank you, Jeremy," I said quietly.

"There, you've said it. I didn't have to twist your arm after all."

"It's a beautiful name."

"On your lips it is. On your lips it's like music."

"I—I must go in."

He nodded slowly, opening the gates, leading me into the courtyard. The mossy white marble fountain spilled and splattered, filling the garden with a quiet, soothing sound. My skirts rustled as we moved across the patio, pausing near the fountain. A few fireflies drifted through the honeysuckle growing on trellises near the wall, their flickering, pale gold lights accentuating the darkness there. The center of the courtyard, where we were standing, was bathed in hazy moonlight that touched everything with silver. Although the night was warm, I shivered inside. I seemed to have lost control of myself, seemed to be in the middle of a beautiful dream that was disturbing as well, extremely disturbing.

"I love you," he said.

"No. You mustn't say that."

"I love you, Marietta."

"You couldn't. You want to sleep with me. I can understand that. I can understand—physical attraction, but love—love has nothing to do with it."

"Love has everything to do with it."

"You mustn't talk like this," I whispered.

"Are you afraid?"

"I love Derek. He loves me."

"He cast you aside once. He sold you to another man. Yes, I heard about that, too. A man who could do that couldn't love you, not the way you deserve to be loved."

"Please don't say anything more."

Jeremy Bond looked at me, his head tilted slightly to one side, his wavy brown hair very dark in the moonlight, his lips parted. I shivered again as he moved nearer and unfastened my cloak. It fell to the ground with a silken rustle. He took hold of my naked shoulders and pulled me against him. I closed my eyes as his lips lightly brushed the curve of my throat, my cheeks, my eyelids, finally settling over my own, covering them, pressing so gently, so sweetly. He curled one arm around my shoulders, drawing me nearer, and I seemed to melt against him as his other arm moved around my waist, fastening me to him as those warm, firm lips continued to plunder my own, insistent now, impatient for response I tried desperately to withhold. He made a low, moaning noise in his throat, kissing me until I seemed to spin into an oblivion of softly exploding sensation.

He withdrew his mouth, drawing back, still holding me, looking down into my eyes. I shook my head, pleading with him to release me, pleading silently, unable to speak. He unwound his arm from my waist and took hold of my arms, holding me away from him, studying me as he might study a precious, priceless work of art.

"Deny it now," he ordered gently. "Deny you want me as much as I want you."

"Don't," I begged.

"I don't know how it happened. I knew it would one day. I knew I would fall in love. I want you."

"No."

"I want you now. I want you tomorrow. I want you forever."

"You—those words—you don't mean—"

"I mean every one of them. I've never said them before,

not to any woman. You think I'm trying to seduce you—I am, yes, I admit it—because I need you, Marietta, because I love you."

That low, melodious voice seemed to come from far away, for I was still in the middle of a dream. This man, this moment, this magic inside me were all a part of the dream, and I knew none of it could be real. He couldn't be saying those words. I couldn't be feeling this glow that grew inside, a sweet, tingling ache that spread throughout me, demanding fulfillment, demanding release. I felt weak, so weak, and I would have crumpled to the ground had those strong hands not been holding me so firmly, the fingers gripping tightly, digging into my flesh. I still seemed to be spinning, and I wondered if I was going to swoon. I looked up into those eyes dark with desire yet filled with tenderness and awe.

"It's happened," he said. "We can't deny it."

"No."

"Love me."

"I—I can't."

He drew me to him and kissed me again, his lips caressing mine for a long, lovely moment that seemed to last forever yet ended too soon, leaving me with a painful ache, a need for completion. He turned me around, standing close behind me, curling one arm around my waist, wrapping the other around my throat, leaning forward to rest his chin on my shoulder. His cheek touched mine. I tried to pull away, but he held me fast, his forearm against the hollow of my throat. He rubbed his cheek against mine, murmuring a litany of love. I could hardly breathe. The sensations inside threatened to annihilate me completely. I prayed for the dream to end, prayed for sanity to return as he held me, gentled me, murmuring that litany that had no words, only feeling.

"No," I whispered. "No, Jeremy."

"Love me, Marietta."

"I love Derek."

"Love me."

I closed my eyes and steeled myself, and somehow I managed to drive back the sensations that swelled within me. I denied them, closed them away, standing rigidly in his arms now, cold, immobile, all warmth seeping out of me, replaced by resolution won against almost impossible odds. He sensed the change immediately. He straightened up, unwinding his arm from my throat, releasing my waist. I turned around, facing him with a level gaze it took incredible willpower to maintain. I wanted to touch that twisted nose and stroke that deep cleft in his chin. I wanted those arms around me again, wanted that warmth and strength and loving protection.

"You must go," I said.

"You want me, Marietta."

"I want only Derek."

"You felt—"

"I'm human," I said coldly. "I felt something, yes. Physical response. Nothing more. My love for Derek doesn't— hasn't made me immune to lips and arms and warmth. I responded to the touch, not to the man."

"I don't believe you," he said.

"Believe what you will, Mr. Bond."

He stood there a few feet away, his arms folded loosely across his chest, his legs wide apart, the cloak spilling from his broad shoulders and spreading out in rich, dark folds. The cocky, irreverent scamp might never have existed. The man who faced me was grave, very grave, his handsome face wearing an expression so serious it was alarming. The eyes that were usually full of laughter were grim. The lips designed for grinning were set in a hard line, turned down at the corners. He might never have smiled. He might never have made a teasing remark. He was another Jeremy Bond, a stranger indeed.

"I meant what I said, Marietta. I've fallen in love with you."

"I belong to another man."

"He doesn't deserve you. He shan't have you, not if I can help it."

"Please go, Mr. Bond."

"I have to leave New Orleans in the morning on business. I don't know how long I'll be gone—only a few days, I hope. When I return I fully intend to see you. I intend to take you away from him. You're not going to marry Derek Hawke. You're going to marry me."

His voice was cool, matter-of-fact. He meant what he said, I could tell that. He looked at me, wanting to say more, deciding against it. After a moment he frowned darkly and moved over to pick up my red velvet cloak where it had fallen. He placed it carefully, impersonally around my shoulders and then strode purposefully toward the gates. He opened them, stepped outside, closed them behind him. I could hear his footsteps loud and angry on the pavement as he walked on down the street, and I felt something that must have been relief. It had to be relief. It couldn't be disappointment. I wasn't certain what I felt, and I didn't dare examine it too closely. He was gone. That was the important thing. He was gone, and the dream was over at last. I knew it was going to haunt me for a long time to come.

Seven

Stephen Howard was surprised when he discovered that I was the one who had sent the message to his hotel, not Derek, and when he discovered that I was alone, he was clearly embarrassed and not a little uneasy. I couldn't help smiling to myself as I led him into the parlor. Big, genial, pleasantly attractive with his dark blond hair, mellow features, and friendly blue eyes, he was quite obviously ill at ease with women, particularly attractive women. Did he think I had lured him here in order to seduce him?

He followed me into the parlor as though it were a silken trap. He wore a beautifully tailored light brown frock coat with breeches to match, a dark brown neckcloth, and a rather dashing waistcoat patterned with gold, brown, and bronze leaves. The elegant attire merely emphasized that warm, comfortable feeling he seemed to exude. I liked him very much already, but I could see that it was going to be quite a task to put him at ease.

"Won't you sit down, Mr. Howard?" I invited.

"Well—uh—I don't know, Mrs.—uh—I don't know what to call you," he said miserably.

"You may call me Marietta."

"I'd rather not," he admitted.

"Miss Danver, then," I suggested. Until I became Lady Hawke I was still legally Mrs. Schnieder, but that was a name I would never use.

"Miss Danver, I—uh—I don't quite understand. The boy brought a note to my hotel. It asked me to come round immediately. It was signed by Hawke."

"I forged his signature," I said.

"You *did?*"

Stephen Howard was horrified. He glanced uneasily about the room as though checking for means of escape. I found his sunny disposition and lack of worldliness extremely refreshing. A woman who would forge a man's signature was capable of anything, his look seemed to say, and I smiled again, amused. He undoubtedly considered me a glamorous, wicked creature with ulterior motives, although today I wore a simple, demurely low-cut frock of topaz-colored silk.

"Derek spoke so highly of you when he came home the other evening," I said smoothly. "I—well, I must admit that I *did* have an ulterior motive in getting you here this way, Mr. Howard."

"Yes?" His apprehension grew.

"I may as well be frank with you, Mr. Howard. As you know, Derek and I are going to be married as soon as we get to England. I love him very much, and I—I do so want to be a good wife to him."

Howard found that quite admirable. He began to relax.

"I've met so few of his friends, Mr. Howard, and I sensed immediately that you'd be sympathetic. Derek said you were one of the kindest men he knew, one of the most honorable as well."

I was lying outrageously. Derek had said no such thing. When I had asked him about Howard and their talk in the private room at Damon's, he had cut me short, telling me it was none of my concern. He had been grim and uncommunicative ever since. I knew the talk had disturbed him far more than he cared to admit, and, as I could get no information from Derek, I had decided to try my luck with Howard. Knowing Derek would be out all afternoon, I had paid a boy to deliver the note to Howard's hotel, and I faced him now with a modest smile that begged him to be understanding.

"You want me to help you in some way?" he inquired.

I nodded. "Derek would be furious with me if he knew about this," I said, quite truthfully this time, "but I thought you and I could have a cozy little chat. *Do* sit down, Mr. Howard. I thought you might be able to tell me something about—oh, about his other friends, for instance, perhaps something about his family. I know so little about his life in England."

"I see," he said, visibly relieved.

"I feel terrible about deceiving you this way, even worse about forging Derek's signature, but I felt you'd understand. You håve a very understanding face. I noticed that the other night at Damon's."

"That's—uh—quite an interesting establishment," he said. "I don't ordinarily frequent such places, but a chap I know said I must dine there at least once."

"Derek and I go there often. It has a rather unsavory reputation, true, but their menu is the finest in the city. You *will* help me, won't you, Mr. Howard?"

"Of course, my dear."

Stephen Howard might have little experience with women, but he was gallant by nature and found this opportunity to be of assistance quite pleasant. He smiled a very warm smile and sat down in the chair I indicated. I poured a brandy for him, and he accepted it gratefully, completely at ease now, actually daring to look at me with open admiration. I settled on the sofa and spread my shimmering topaz skirt out, devoting the next few minutes to polite, flattering questions about his work.

"But you lead such an interesting life," I said.

"Not at all," he protested. "When I'm not involved in some diplomatic mission, like I am now, I spend most of my time puttering around Howard Hall. It's terribly large and draughty, but we have a very fine library, a fine cellar, too. I live there with my sister, admirable woman, Bella, but she's always knitting the most depressing garments for me. It's always a relief when I'm called upon to be of service to the Crown."

"Howard Hall sounds charming," I said. "Is it anywhere near Hawkehouse?"

"Not too far, actually. In the same district."

"I suppose you knew Derek when he was a boy."

"I knew him only slightly back then. I was ten years older, you understand. When I visited Hawkehouse as a young man he was still in his early teens, a rather stiff, formal youth who was extremely polite but not particularly interesting to a youth training for the diplomatic service. Actually, we didn't become friends until he returned to England. We ran into each other in London right before the trial began. I followed it with a great deal of interest."

"It was a terrible ordeal for him," I said, pretending to know much more than I did.

"Dreadful business," Howard agreed, "but justice was done, I'm pleased to say. His uncle was a bounder, no question about it, and his two sons aren't much better. There's still hope for young Robert. He's just turned thirty and I understand he's with the East India Company now, amassing a fortune in Bombay. Roger, of course, is a different story."

Stephen Howard ran a hand through his thick blond hair and frowned a deep frown that made furrows in his brow, his blue eyes severely disapproving as he thought about Roger Hawke. I held my breath, on edge, my pulse leaping. I had been leading the conversation up to this point all along, carefully manipulating him without his being aware of it, and I had to be even more careful now. Howard was indeed an honorable man, and if he even suspected that Derek hadn't discussed the matter with me, he would change the subject immediately.

"More brandy, Mr. Howard?" I asked.

"Don't mind if I do," he replied. "Fine brandy, fine as any we have in the cellar."

I smiled and took his glass, very, very casual. My hand shook slightly as I filled it. The decanter clattered against the rim of the glass and a few drops of liquor splattered. Fortunately, Howard didn't notice. I handed him the brimming glass and then strolled over to the window to peer out at the courtyard. It was drenched with sunlight.

"Derek was—quite disturbed when he came in the other night," I said, my back to him.

"And well he should be. His cousin Roger vowed he was going to have revenge, vowed he was going to return to Hawkehouse and wear the ancestral ring if it was the last thing he did, and he made no secret of his intentions. I heard him talking about it myself one night at Almack's, not three days after his father's death. I don't think I've ever seen such cold fury in my life. The man's dangerous."

"Derek doesn't seem to think so. He was disturbed, yes, but he said it was all just talk."

"Talk like that can't be ignored. There's no question that Hawke's the legal heir, that was settled once and for all in the courts, but if anything were to happen to him, his cousin Roger would be next in line. Roger said he was going to see Hawke in his grave. He blames Derek for his father's death, you see, claims forcing him to leave Hawkehouse was what brought it on."

I felt a cold chill steal over me. I folded my arms about my waist, still gazing out at the courtyard, not seeing it now, seeing only horror. A terrible premonition seized me, and for a moment I thought I might actually faint, black shadows encroaching, threatening to engulf me. The moment passed, and I forced myself to turn around, forced myself to move across the room and rearrange some flowers in a cut-glass vase.

"Derek says there's no cause for alarm," I said, surprised at how calm my voice sounded. "He doesn't believe his cousin Roger could actually be contemplating anything."

"I wouldn't count on that. Roger Hawke is probably the most unscrupulous man I've ever met, cold as ice, hard as steel. Not the sort of man I'd care to have as an enemy, I assure you."

"What does he look like?" I asked casually.

"Very tall, a bit taller than Hawke, I'd say, and very lean. He has the Hawke features, but they're harder, colder, lean cheeks, thin lips, gray eyes that seem to stare right through you. He wears a peruke most of the time, powdered in the French style. He dresses in the French style, too, knee breeches, embroidered brocade frock coats, lace at his wrists and throat. For some reason the frills and fripperies make him seem all the more ominous.''

"Is he married?"

"He was. His wife died. Some say he poisoned her, but then there are always rumors about a man like Roger Hawke. He spends quite a lot of time in Paris, has friends at the French court. I imagine that's where he is now. Shortly after he made all those noises at Almack's he dropped out of sight."

"He left London?"

"Apparently. Few people missed him, I assure you."

Howard shook his head and took another sip of brandy. I was in control of myself now, calm, but in the mirror across the room I could see that my cheeks were pale, my blue eyes very dark. Stephen Howard finished his brandy, setting his glass down just as the ormolu clock struck five. He looked up in surprise, and then he got quickly to his feet.

"I say, I had no idea it was so late. I have a very important meeting at seven o'clock. I really must be getting back to the hotel. I have a carriage waiting on the street."

"I appreciate your coming, Mr. Howard."

"Hope I was of some help."

"You've no idea how helpful you were," I said.

"You must call on Bella when you get to England," he said as I led him into the foyer. "She'll try to put you to work for her charitable causes, and she may *knit* something for you, but I'm sure you'll like her. I feel sure Bella will like you, too."

I opened the door for him. "I'll look forward to meeting her."

Howard hesitated in the doorway a moment, looking at me with friendly blue eyes, a warm smile on his lips, and then he took my hand in both of his.

"I must tell you something, my dear," he said. "I do hope you won't mind. When I saw you the other night in that—uh—quite remarkable red gown I had my reservations about you."

"Oh?"

"I thought you were quite lovely, quite charming, but I thought Hawke must be out of his mind to be thinking of marrying you and taking you back to England. I—well, I thought he was just dallying with you, telling you a lot of marlarky in order to keep you happy.''

"And now?" I asked.

"Now I think he's a lucky man indeed. I envy him."

He squeezed my hand and smiled again. If the rest of Derek's friends were as kind and compassionate as Stephen Howard, I'd have no difficulty at all when I became Lady Hawke, I thought, but I knew Howard was a rare man indeed. I put my free hand on his cheek for just a moment, thanking him silently. He let go of my hand and smoothed the lapels of his frock coat, slightly embarrassed.

"Goodbye, Miss Danver."

"I hope to see you again," I told him.

He nodded and started toward the gates. I closed the door and went back into the parlor, watching through the window as he opened the gates and climbed into the waiting carriage, and then I turned away, gazing at the elegantly appointed room without seeing anything but the chilling picture that was beginning to take shape in my mind, the pieces slowly fitting together. I thought of the man in the navy blue coat, the man named Bert who had been watching the apartment for over two weeks, following me when I went out, and I thought of Will Hart and the information I had obtained from him before Jeremy Bond burst upon the scene. I thought of Roger Hawke, seeing him clearly in my mind, tall and lean and lethal, elegantly attired in rich brocade and lace frills, coldly planning to take his revenge. All the pieces were in place now, and all of them fit perfectly. I saw the picture clearly. I knew the plan. I understood the motives behind it.

I tried not to panic. Panic would accomplish nothing. Alarm leaped inside of me, vibrant, so intense I had to grab hold of the drapery for support, my knees weak, threatening to buckle beneath me. I gripped the soft velvet so tightly I could feel it give, heard it ripping from its fastenings at the top. I let go. No, I told myself, no, you mustn't. You must be calm. You can't afford to give way. A kind of calm returned, and I clung to it as a drowning man might cling to a spar. I tried to think rationally, and after a while I succeeded. It was five-thirty now. Had so much time passed? Five-thirty already, and he hadn't returned. . . . What if something had happened? I forced the thought from my mind, desperately clinging to the spar of calm as the waves of panic splashed anew.

If I had figured it out, Derek had figured it out, too, had fit the pieces together just as I had done, and he would take the necessary precautions to ensure his safety. There was no cause for alarm. I told myself that over and over again until, at last, I believed it. Derek could take care of himself as well as any man, better than most. He was late, yes, but there was a perfectly good reason. They wouldn't try anything in broad daylight. No, no, they would lurk in the shadows, crouch in the darkness, waiting for just the right opportunity to do their foul deed in secrecy and silence. He would be home soon, and I would hold him tightly and then I could tremble, then I could give way and he would comfort me and drive away the alarm.

He knew. He probably knew far more than I did, and he hadn't discussed it with me because he had wanted to spare me this same alarm. He wanted to protect me, shelter me, spare me unnecessary worry, and I loved him for it. He had probably suspected something like this for a long time, perhaps ever since we came to New Orleans, and the talk with Stephen Howard had merely confirmed it. That would explain so much. That would explain his cool manner, his remoteness, the tension I sensed just beneath the surface. He had been irritable, harsh, unyielding, and I had felt shut out. I had been hurt. I understood now, and I blamed myself for resenting his manner when all the while he had merely been trying to protect me from needless alarm. When I had told him about the man in the navy blue coat, about my encounter with Hart, he had listened with cool indifference, doing his best to stem my worry by pretending to feel none himself. I had been angry and frustrated. I had wanted to rail at him. Now I wanted only to hold him.

Leaving the parlor, I deliberately found tasks to occupy myself. I took Derek's shirts out and refolded them. I dusted off his boots. I straightened my own clothes. An hour passed and the sun began to go down and the courtyard began to fill with dark orange-gold light and shadows began to spread over the walls. Shadows began to spread inside as well, and I lighted candles in every room. I ran out of tasks. The apartment began to seem like an opulent prison. The walls seemed to close in on me. I couldn't stand much more of this. If he didn't return soon, the waves would wash over me and I would drown in panic. I took down the first volume of Samuel Richardson's *Clarissa* and tried to read, but the words blurred together and it was impossible to concentrate.

Putting the book aside, I went out into the courtyard, trying to hold the panic at bay. The tiles were bathed in dark gold that slowly faded. The shadows were thickening. The fountain splashed quietly. Derek would be home any minute now, I told myself. Any minute now the carriage would pull up in front, and he would climb out and step into the courtyard and I would throw myself into his arms and everything would be all right. I must stay calm. I must think of something else. I mustn't let the panic sweep over me. I watched the shadows grow darker, from gray to blue-gray to black, watched the last dark golden rays fade until the tiles were a gleaming gray-white. The air seemed to take on a soft violet tint, and the first fireflies began to flicker in the shrubs, pale gold against the dark.

There had been fireflies four nights ago when I had been standing here in the moonlight with Jeremy Bond. I allowed myself to think about that evening, examining the scene in retrospect with cool objectivity. It still seemed a dream, unreal, hazy, without substance or texture. I couldn't deny the feelings he had aroused, but in the cold light of reality I could justify them to myself. I had been deeply disturbed when I stepped out of Damon's. I had been angry, frustrated, frightened as well, and I had felt rejected, too. Derek had been curt and abrupt, almost shoving me out the door, and Bond had appeared when I most needed comfort and companionship. He had sensed my vulnerability, had taken advantage of it, employing all his considerable charm in the hope of an easy conquest.

He had been smooth and skillful, an accomplished seducer who wooed with great finesse and far too much experience. He knew all the right words, all the right phrases, speaking them in a low, melodious voice that, at the time, had seemed all too sincere. He had said he loved me. I had almost believed him. He had said he intended to marry me, and that was absurd, a final ploy calculated to gain him the victory he had almost won. Yes, there had been a few dangerous moments when I had been on the verge of succumbing to the need and emotions inside, but loyalty to Derek and my love for him had prevented me from taking that disastrous plunge. I could never have forgiven myself if I had allowed Jeremy Bond to chalk up one more conquest. He had failed, and I would never see him again. He had said he was leaving New Orleans on business, and by the time he returned he would undoubtedly have put me out of his mind. He would undoubtedly find easier prey. Men like Jeremy Bond didn't like to be reminded of their failures.

I had felt physical desire, yes, I had indeed wanted to go to bed with him, I could admit that, but it had been a momentary aberration on my part, a matter of flesh responding to flesh, and it had nothing to do with true feeling, nothing to do with love. I loved Derek with every fiber of my being, and no matter how glibly he might use it, I doubted that Jeremy Bond knew the meaning of the word. I forgave myself for responding to him as I had, knowing it would never happen again. Strangely enough, the encounter with Bond seemed to strengthen my feeling for Derek.

The courtyard was almost dark now. The gleaming white tiles were barely visible beneath the layers of shadow, and the fountain was a blurry white shape not clearly defined. The dark gray sky was taking on a purple hue, pale stars not yet sparkling. A carriage came rumbling down the street. It stopped, and I felt a wave of relief, relief so great I was almost dizzy. I heard the iron gates opening, heard the carriage moving on down the street. Derek closed the gates and looked at me, clearly surprised.

"Thank God," I whispered.

"Marietta? Are you all right? Has anything happened?"

I shook my head, still dizzy with relief, and I hurried over to him and threw my arms around him, clinging to him, and he was surprised anew but not at all displeased. He wrapped his arms around me, gathering me to him, holding me very tightly.

"What's this?" he inquired.

"I—I'm just so relieved."

"You were worried about something?"

"I was worried about you."

"Well, now I'm back. Safe and sound. Feel better?"

I nodded, resting my head on his shoulder. His arms were so strong, holding me so securely. He was so tall, so firm, so solid, and I never intended to let him out of my sight again, never. He sighed, indulging me as an adult might indulge a child, not at all remote now, the wall momentarily vanished. Gently, he loosened his hold and curled one arm around my shoulders, leading me past the fountain, into the foyer.

"Quite a welcome," he remarked, closing the door.

"You were gone so long."

"That couldn't be helped."

"I'm so glad you're back."

"You're pale, Marietta. You're trembling."

"I can't help it."

"You were that worried?"

I nodded once more, and Derek studied my face. We were in the parlor now. His hands rested lightly on my shoulders, and his gray eyes were full of concern. That handsome face, usually so stern, was tender now. How long had it been since he had looked at me this way? How long? Weeks and weeks. He hadn't looked at me this way since that late afternoon in Natchez when we were in the gardens behind the inn, standing at the edge of the cliff. He moved one hand until it touched my throat, the fingers gently wrapping around it. He tilted my head back and leaned down and kissed me lightly on the lips, so lightly. I was trembling again.

"There," he said. "There. It's all right."

"I thought—"

"I know what you thought."

"I—I know about your cousin, Derek."

"Oh?"

He moved back. He took off his cloak and draped it across a chair. He was wearing a handsome navy blue suit, a white brocade waistcoat with tiny navy blue and black polka dots, a black silk neckcloth. His fine black leather boots were polished to a high sheen. He didn't seem at all disturbed. He seemed to be in a remarkably mellow mood. I had rarely seen him so relaxed.

"Stephen Howard came by this afternoon," I told him.

"Did he?"

"I—I sent for him, Derek."

"I see."

"I had to know what was going on, Derek. I had to."

"So you sent for Stephen Howard and tricked him into telling you about our conversation at Damon's."

"I know it was deceitful, but you wouldn't tell me and—"

"I didn't want you to worry, Marietta."

"I understand that now. I understand—everything."

"I was trying to protect you from unnecessary alarm. There was no need for you to worry, no need for you to be apprehensive. I suspected something was going on when you first told me about the man in the coat, and after you described your encounter with Will Hart, I was certain."

"You think your cousin—"

"I'm sure they're his hirelings."

"Derek—"

"There's nothing to worry about, Marietta."

He lifted the skirt of his frock coat, revealing the butt of a long and lethal-looking pistol. He pulled it out, examined it with expressionless eyes and set it aside. I shivered. Derek sighed, still relaxed, looking rather lazy, not at all angry.

"You carried it," I said.

"I've been carrying it for weeks."

"You never told me."

"I love you, Marietta. When you love someone, you shelter them. You protect them. You shivered just now when I took the gun out. Had you known I was carrying it you would have been ill with worry. I've been extremely preoccupied of late. I've been cold. No doubt I've been harsh."

"I—I was—"

"You thought I was having second thoughts about marrying you. You thought I was beginning to regret coming back to America for you. It isn't easy for me to love, Marietta. I'm not a demonstrative man. I do love you."

"I never really doubted it."

He elevated an eyebrow. "No?" he asked. His voice was almost teasing.

"Perhaps, just a little. You were so—so wretched to me when I came in wearing the red dress."

"I wanted to throw you on the floor and make brutal love to you. I had to restrain myself. I knew every man who saw you in the dress would feel the same savage quickening inside. That angered me. The thought of another man touching you filled me with cold fury.''

"You treated me so coldly. You almost shoved me out the door of Damon's.''

"I know. I felt badly about that. I shouldn't have sent you off alone, but I had to hear what Howard had to say. I wasn't thinking of anything else, and I felt you'd be safe with the driver.''

"I was hurt.''

"I realize that. I've hurt you many times. Never intentionally. No doubt I'll hurt you again. I'm frequently unfeeling. You've known that from the very beginning.''

"I loved you in spite of it.''

Derek smiled wryly and glanced at the clock. "I suppose we should be thinking of dinner,'' he said. "We'll go out. Not to Damon's. We'll go to one of those 'respectable' restaurants you mentioned the other night. If the respectable matrons and their respectable husbands are outraged to see a hussy like you in their midst, that'll just be too bad. If one of the men looks like he wants to rape you, I'll break his jaw.''

"I love you like this.''

"Oh? How am I?''

"Teasing. Tender. Accessible.''

"At the moment I feel extremely accessible,'' he said, looking at me with smoky gray eyes half-veiled by drooping lids. "That frock you're wearing may not be scarlet, may not leave you half-naked, but it's quite provocative nevertheless, and your hair's all shiny, like copper fire. Pity we have to go out to dinner.''

"We don't have to. There's cheese and bread, sausage I could slice. We have white wine, fruit.''

"You had your heart set on a respectable restaurant.''

"I don't feel—terribly respectable tonight.''

"No?''

I shook my head. The corners of his mouth lifted in another wry smile as he looked at me. I felt a warm, honey-sweet anticipation begin to build inside me, a lovely ache that grew slowly. I moved over to him and touched his cheek and then moved my hand up to smooth back locks of jet black hair. His gray eyes continued to hold mine, lids heavier still, drooping low, the smile curling still on his lips. This was the Derek I dreamed of, the Derek I could love openly and without restraint. The remote stranger was gone.

"We'll have a picnic," I murmured. "Here, in the parlor."

"That sounds tempting," he said.

"I love you, Derek."

"I know. I'm glad. I'm a very lucky man."

"You are indeed."

He curled his arms loosely around my waist and kissed my throat, my shoulder. I leaned back against his arms, running my palms over his broad back as his lips moved lower, lightly brushing the curve of my bosom.

"I'd better go get the food," I said.

"I suppose you must. I'm mightily hungry."

"I intend to take very good care of you."

"You always did," he said, pulling me nearer. "You polished my boots. You washed my shirts. You baked peach pies. Remember the pies?"

"I remember."

"You were a temptress, casting your spell over me, and how I fought it. I wanted a good excuse to whip you. I wanted to despise you. I couldn't, no matter how I tried."

"I know."

He drew me even nearer, arms like bands of steel crushing me to him, holding me fast, a willing captive. I stroked his back, running my palms over the smooth broadcloth, tilting my head back so that I could look up into those amorous gray eyes.

"I never wanted to love you," he continued. "I couldn't help myself. I hated women after Alice, despised them, and then you came along—a temptress with flaming copper-red hair and bold blue eyes and far too much spirit for an indentured servant. There were times when I wished I'd never bought you off that auction block, times when I cursed myself for the folly, but the moment I saw you standing there I knew I had to have you."

"You said you were merely saving me from Jeff."

"There was that," he admitted, "but that wasn't the main reason."

"You waited—so long to take me."

"I wanted to that first night, after the auction. You were

under the wagon, terrified of Indians, shivering, and I spread a blanket over you. You finally went to sleep, and I looked at you for a long, long time, wanting you and fighting it desperately. You were my property, bought and paid for, a convicted thief who gave herself such airs, who spoke in a disturbingly refined voice. It took great strength to keep from crawling under the wagon that night."

"I never suspected."

"You knew I wanted you, witch. You kept provoking me, luring me on, casting your spell until, finally, I couldn't help myself. You won."

"So did you," I told him. "I—I'd better see about the food now. I've a feeling we'll—continue this later."

"You can count on it," he promised.

I moved out of his arms and touched his face again and smiled, and then I went back to the tiny kitchen and took out cheese and hard sausage and bread. I sliced the sausage, sliced the cheese and bread, took out delicious-looking jade green grapes and washed them. The ache was still inside, a lovely, tormenting ache that grew lovelier the longer it was denied. He was in a rare mood, and I intended to cherish every moment of it, make every moment memorable. Arranging the food carefully, attractively on a tray, I took out the bottle of white wine, wishing there had been time to chill it, and then I returned to the parlor.

"You certainly took your time," he scolded.

"I wanted everything to be just right."

"So did I," he said.

He had put out most of the candles. The room was hazy with shadow, and a fire burned low behind the screen. He had spread blankets in front of the hearth, a soft pile of blankets covered with a pale satin counterpane. I was surprised, delighted, too. He smiled a lazy smile, padding toward me on bare feet, wearing only a heavy navy blue satin dressing robe, the sash tied loosely below his waist. I set the tray down, took the bottle over to the bar, and set it down while I looked for glasses. He came up behind me, placed his hands on my shoulders.

"The wine's warm," I said. "We'll have to drink it that way."

"No matter," he murmured.

He lifted my hair, kissed the back of my neck. I moved my shoulders in protest.

"I'll drop the glasses," I said.

"Forget the glasses."

"You're hungry."

"It can wait," he told me.

He turned me around and kissed me lazily, slowly, savoring my lips as a connoisseur might savor the finest, rarest wine, firm, warm lips parting my own. I knocked one of the glasses over. I clung to him, the heavy satin slippery beneath my fingers. He kissed me again, again, again, and the ache grew, spreading slowly throughout me, becoming almost unendurable. He led me away from the bar, his robe rustling with a soft, silken rustle, his bare feet making gentle thuds on the carpet. I felt weak, powerless, without will, and he led me toward the center of the room as he might lead an invalid. He paused, holding my arms, looking at me with sleepy, sensuous eyes.

"Your cheeks are flushed," he observed.

"It's terribly warm. The fire—"

"You're wearing too many clothes," he informed me.

He smiled and stepped behind me and began to unfasten the invisible hooks in back of my dress. I felt the bodice loosen, the beige silk gradually slipping from my breasts, falling forward, my breasts straining against the fragile white silk bodice of the petticoat beneath. He caught hold of the beige silk sleeves, slowly pulling them down my arms, so slowly, bending down to push the frock all the way to the floor. I stepped out of the circle of silk, shivering, and he stood in front of me now and, smiling lazily, hooked his thumbs in the thin straps of my petticoat, tugging at them. I felt the silk sliding over my breasts, cool and tormenting against my swollen nipples, and then my breasts were free and he bent down to kiss them.

I caught hold of his hair, tugging at it, unable to endure the torment now, unable to prolong it any longer. He kissed the swollen pink nipples and pushed the petticoat down, half a dozen skirts billowing, fluttering like frail petals. My eyes were closed, my head thrown back, my hair spilling behind me in a cascade of copper-red waves. He finished undressing me, kissing me here, there, kissing me again, finally lifting me up into his arms and carrying me over to the pallet in front of the hearth, lowering me onto the satin counterpane. The satin was cool and smooth and slippery beneath me, and I could feel the warmth of the fire on my skin. He stood over me with legs spread wide, looking down at me with his hands resting on his thighs.

"Beautiful," he said huskily.

"For you."

"It should always be like this."

"Always," I whispered.

I was adrift on a sea of sensations, the satin cool beneath my buttocks, the warmth of the flames on my skin, the warmth inside growing, tingling, my bones aching as though I were bound with velvet cords and being stretched on a velvet rack, the pain of physical need merging with the pleasure of anticipation. I could hear the soft crackle of the fire, a symphony of snapping pops as wood and bark were devoured, and I could hear the rustle of satin as I shifted my position, sliding on the slippery cloth. I could smell wood burning, and I could smell skin. I could smell desire, too, my own, his.

I looked up at him, seeing his calves, the skirt of his robe, his chest, all at a peculiar angle, the small roll of flesh beneath his jaw, the tip of his nose, his brow, covered now with unruly jet locks, his eyes like dark gray smoke, filled with desire. He rubbed his thighs, fingers sliding over the navy blue satin, and he smiled and caught hold of the two ends of the sash, slowly untying the loose knot. He parted the heavy folds and shrugged his shoulders and the robe fell to the floor behind him with a soft swoosh. In the firelight his body was bronze, tall, lean, superbly muscled.

"Now," he said.

Planting a knee on either side of my thighs, he bent his head down, his eyes darker now, gleaming with desire, his lips parted, wide, pink, drawing nearer my own, covering them. I closed my eyes and flung my arms around him, and he gradually lowered himself, my body a cushion for his, his weight crushing me, pinioning me to the pallet, welcome, so welcome, hard muscle covered with smooth, warm skin, his mouth holding my own captive, smothering the scream that swelled in my throat as he entered and we became one and the age-old dance began.

The music of our lovemaking was loud and lovely, and both of us were caught up in the rhythm, moving together, flesh parting to welcome flesh, flesh stroking, caressing, filling, and beautiful new sensations began to blossom, tight buds opening in soft explosions of pleasure that grew steadily more intense, emotion and feeling heightening each sensation, giving it shape and meaning. We danced together in perfect union, movement matching movement, and tenderness turned to fury by degrees, and by degrees the dance turned into combat, fierce combat. Fury possessed him, possessed me, and together we trembled on the brink of an abyss, struggling, straining, tottering, falling finally and hurtling into a void of shattering oblivion.

I held him close, savoring the splendor, and later, much later, he got up to put another piece of wood on the fire, poking at it until the flames began to lick the wood. I sat up, wrapping the satin counterpane around me, and he sighed heavily and pulled on his dressing robe, lazy, lethargic, his face seeming to sag just a little, faint mauve shadows under his eyes. He fetched the tray of food, bringing it back over to the pallet, sitting heavily beside me. He ate bread and sausage and cheese and I took a few grapes, not really hungry, replete. I lay back, gathering the counterpane over my breasts, watching him eat.

"Full?" I asked when he set the tray aside.

He nodded, still lazy, still lethargic. I lifted one arm and smoothed damp locks from his brow. The fire was popping anew, flames devouring the wood. The candles had almost burned down, light weak now, flickering, the room almost dark. One candle spluttered out, then another. Walls that had been washed in hazy gold light were spread with blue-gray shadow. Soon there was no light but the light of the fire. Derek was silent, lost in thought.

"This is lovely," I said. "I feel—so warm, so safe."

"You are safe, Marietta."

"Those dreadful men. Your cousin—"

"My cousin hired them, I feel sure. I feel sure he hired them to do away with me so that he could inherit. No doubt he felt that if something happened to me in America, there would be no inquiry. He wouldn't dare attempt anything in England, and we're leaving for England tomorrow night."

I was startled, so startled I could hardly speak. "What—what do you mean?" I finally asked.

"Departure date for *The Blue Elephant* has been moved up," he told me. "It leaves tomorrow night, at midnight. The bids were opened today and mine was highest. Everything is settled."

"I can hardly believe it."

"I can hardly believe it myself," he replied. "It's been extremely aggravating, extremely frustrating. I've been under a great deal of strain during these past weeks. I've taken it out on you."

"I understood—most of the time."

He stared at the fire, lost in thought again. His handsome face was half in shadow, chin, mouth and nose barely visible, broad cheekbones polished with firelight, eyes very dark, very grave, eyebrows straight and serious. His jet black hair was still slightly damp, beginning to dry in feathery puffs. I put my hand on his shoulder, stroked the back of his neck. He didn't seem to notice, staring at the flames without seeing them.

"Don't leave me," I said quietly.

He turned to look at me, surprised. "Leave you?"

"Don't—don't shut me out. Don't put that wall up around you again."

"What wall?"

"You're not even aware of it, are you?"

"Apparently not," he replied.

"You shut me out, Derek. There are times when I feel I'm absolutely alone, even though you're beside me. You retreat into yourself. You leave me and I can't reach you."

"I'm sorry, Marietta. I wish I could be the man you seem to want."

"You are the man I want. I'm just so glad we're actually leaving. I'm glad we're finally going to England. I'll feel so much better after we're married."

"That's been bothering you, hasn't it?"

"It has. I admit it. I haven't had much security in my life, Derek. A wedding ring will make all the difference."

"A ring matters so much?"

When I didn't answer, he sighed and pulled me roughly into his arms, cradling me against his chest, looking down into my eyes, and then he shook his head in exasperation that was only pretense. He smiled and pulled his signet ring off and, taking my hand, slipped it onto my finger. It was much too large, of course, much too loose, but I folded my finger back over it, deeply touched, so touched I found it difficult to hold back the tears.

"Feel better?" he asked.

"You didn't have to do that."

"You wanted a ring, you've got one. It'll have to do until you get a gold one. You'll have to tie some string around it to make it stay on properly. If you lose it, I fully intend to choke you to death."

"I won't lose it."

"I'm not going to leave you," he said. "In fact, I have something quite different in mind."

"Oh?"

"I think a celebration is in order."

"We'll drink the wine."

He lowered me back onto the pallet, shifting position so that he was leaning over me, his lips inches from my own.

"Later," he murmured.

I didn't argue.

Eight

The trunks had all been packed and sent on ahead to the ship, and the apartment looked strangely barren with all our personal effects removed. Derek had settled everything with the stout, stern-faced woman who had leased it to us, and she had come by earlier to inspect for damage, her dark black hair worn in a severe bun, her crisp blue skirts crackling as she examined each room with shrewd black eyes. Declaring herself satisfied, she reminded us to put out the candles when we left and then bustled away, counting the money Derek had given her.

The ormolu clock on the mantle struck the half hour. It was ten-thirty now, and the carriage would be arriving out front at any minute now. I was nervous, eager to be off, but Derek was utterly calm, almost chilly. His face was expressionless, his manner remote. Those wonderful hours of intimacy we had shared last night might never have been, and had the ring not been on my finger I might almost believe I had imagined them. I had wound a piece of twine around it on the underside, and it fit snugly now. I looked at it, remembering, and I told myself that last night had been merely a foretaste of what was to come once we were in England, settled in Hawke-house, all strain removed.

"Don't fret so," he told me. "We've plenty of time. It only takes a few minutes to drive down to the docks."

"I'm not fretting. I'm just nervous. I can't help it."

I had been nervous all day long, plagued by a vague apprehension I couldn't clearly define. Derek had assured me there was no more danger, but I wouldn't feel completely secure until the boat had pulled away from the dock and we were actually on our way. Packing had been an ordeal, and I had done most of it by myself. Derek had had to attend to some last minute business, leaving me alone for several hours during the middle of the afternoon. I had insisted he take the pistol with him. Grimacing irritably, he had lifted the skirt of his frock coat to reveal the butt. After he returned and after the trunks had been sent on to the ship, we had dined with Stephen Howard at his hotel. I had found it difficult to be civil, impossible to eat, had been so nervous I had had to suppress an urge to run screaming out of the dining room, and that hadn't improved Derek's mood at all.

"I do wish the carriage would get here," I said.

"It'll be here. I ordered it for ten-thirty."

"It's past that. What if we're late?"

"We're not going to be late, Marietta."

I found his calm infuriating. He stood beside the mantle with arms across his chest, his gray eyes betraying not the least sign of emotion. He was wearing polished black boots, fine black breeches with frock coat to match, and his waistcoat was a rich, dark maroon. He was so handsome, so remote, so insufferably cool. I realized in all fairness that today had been as much a strain for him as for me. Once we were on board he would relax.

I stepped over to the mirror to make a final examination. I had brushed my hair until it shone with deep copper highlights, and it fell to my shoulders in rich, heavy waves. My gown was a sumptuous turquoise brocade with narrow royal blue stripes. The puffed sleeves fell off the shoulder, the neckline was modestly low, and the skirt belled out from the snug waist to spread over half a dozen royal blue underskirts. It was one of Lucille's loveliest creations, not too formal for traveling, the kind of gown a lady would wear for casual entertaining in her stateroom.

"Do I look all right?" I inquired.

"You look fine, Marietta."

"Perhaps I should have worn the magenta satin."

"When we get to our stateroom you can change. You can change several times if you like. You can put on and take off every bloody gown you own."

"You needn't be so hateful," I snapped.

"I don't intend to fight with you," he said dryly.

"I don't want to fight. I just want the carriage to get here so we can be on our way. All day long I've felt like I was going to jump out of my skin."

"So I've noticed."

"You *could* have given me a little comfort instead of being so distant and cold."

"I suppose I could have. I've had other things on my mind."

—"Derek—"

"There's the carriage. Put on your cloak. I'll see to the candles."

I picked up the long royal blue cloak lined with turquoise and placed it over my shoulders, fastening it at my throat while Derek blew out the candles we had left burning. When he blew out the last one, darkness descended, pitch black darkness, and I was momentarily disoriented. Then I felt his hand close over mine. He led me into the foyer and out into the courtyard. It was misty with fog. When had the fog come in? Derek locked the door, placed the key on top of the door frame and led me past the fountain.

As he opened the gates I suddenly thought of Jeremy Bond. When he returned to New Orleans, I would be on my way to England. I wondered if he would come to the apartment to try and see me. How would he react when he discovered that I was already gone? Had he really meant any of those wild, foolish words he had said that night after he walked me home? Of course not. It had all been preposterous, and he was an utterly preposterous man. He would never know that I had left the city. He would never make an attempt to see me again. He probably didn't even remember my name.

Derek helped me into the carriage and climbed in beside me. He closed the door and rapped on the roof, and a moment later we were on our way. The fog was thick, a blurry, grayish-white veil that swirled and lifted occasionally to reveal a street lamp, part of a wall, an archway leading into a courtyard. The whirr of the wheels and the clop of the horses' hooves seemed strange and eerie, echoing against the thick, moving walls of fog, and the carriage seemed to rock and bounce like a small boat in a choppy sea. I took Derek's hand, holding it tightly. He squeezed my fingers and pulled my hand into his lap.

"Feel better?" he asked.

"A little. I don't know why I'm so nervous."

"We've both been under strain, Marietta."

"Derek, I know you said your cousin wouldn't dare try to do you harm once we're in England, but—do you really think the danger is over?"

"He couldn't risk attempting anything in England, not after all the talking he did, the threats he made. His one hope was to dispose of me while I was still over here, and he hired the wrong man to do the job."

"There were two of them."

"I would imagine he made a deal with the older one, the man in the heavy coat, in London, promising him so much money if he returned to England with proof of my death, and once he arrived in New Orleans the chap hired Hart to assist him. They're bumbling fools, both of them. They lurked around, waiting for the right opportunity to present itself, and now it's too late.''

"Your cousin must really hate you."

"He always has,'' Derek replied, ''and now that I've won my rightful inheritance he has even more reason to hate me. I imagine we'll have a confrontation one of these days,'' he continued, ''it's inevitable, but when it happens it'll be face to face, in broad daylight.''

He let go of my hand, withdrawing into himself again, and I leaned against the cushion and peered out at the fog. It seemed to be thinner here, lifting and parting, tearing open to show a flight of wooden steps, a string of lights, the corner of a warehouse. I realized we were nearing the docks, and the wind coming over the water was ripping the fog. The carriage rocked violently. I was pitched forward. Derek caught my shoulders, pulled me back, holding me as the carriage continued to jostle over the rough cobbles. After a few minutes the driver began to slow down, finally drawing to a full stop. Derek released me. Through the window I could see thick patches of fog that swirled and lifted, revealing huge stacks of boxes, coils of rope, the flaking hull of a ship, all dimly illuminated by three or four lanterns that swayed in the wind.

"I intend to speak to that fellow!'' Derek snapped. ''He had no business driving so recklessly.''

Scowling, he climbed out and helped me down. The wind caught my cloak immediately and sent it swooping back from my shoulders like madly fluttering blue and turquoise wings. Derek slammed the door of the carriage and started to step around to speak the driver. He had taken only three or four steps when the driver clicked the reins savagely, yelling at the horses. The carriage moved off at a frightening speed. My cloak came unfastened, lifted in the air, disappeared into the fog. I barely noticed. A cold hand seemed to clutch my heart.

"Derek!'' I whispered hoarsely.

"Keep calm!'' he ordered.

"It's a trap. That driver—he—he must have been in on it. The ship isn't leaving. There are no people. They set it up. They bribed the captain to tell you the ship was—''

"Shut up!"

Several moments passed. I was numb with terror. The fog lifted, parted, swirled like ghostly veils. I could hear water slapping against wood and wood groaning, and these noises somehow intensified the eerie silence that hung over the docks at this hour. The lanterns swayed, pouring dim yellow light over the crates, over the coils of rope. The gigantic old ship with its flaking blue hull rocked gently on the water, knocking against the dock, and it did indeed resemble a tired blue elephant. Through the fog I could discern several other ships moored nearby, cloaked in darkness like *The Blue Elephant*, tall masts a skeletal forest in the fog.

There was a loud clatter, a tinkling crash. One of the lanterns went out. Someone had thrown a rock at it. Pistol in hand, Derek motioned me to move behind him. Several more moments passed, the heavy silence broken only by sounds of water slapping, wood creaking. They were out there, lurking behind the boxes or crouching behind the bales of cotton, watching us, waiting. Another rock was thrown. Another lantern went out. There were just two wavering pools of light remaining, shadows intensified, the fog drifting, breaking, moving in a ghostly dance around us.

"What are we going to do?" I whispered.

"We're leaving," Derek said. His voice was frighteningly calm. "Stay behind me, Marietta."

He started moving away from *The Blue Elephant*, keeping close to the edge of the pier, near the water, skirting the stacks of wooden crates, the bales of cotton, and I followed, my heart pounding, my knees so weak I thought I would stumble and fall at any moment. Ten yards, twenty, and we passed under one of the remaining lanterns, dim yellow-orange light pouring down. Thirty yards, and *The Blue Elephant* was behind us, and it was dark, so dark, nests of shadows on every side, water slapping, sloshing, fog swirling, the smell of salt and tar and damp wood assailing our nostrils. There was another pool of light up ahead, at least fifty yards away, and we moved slowly toward it.

Both of us heard the footsteps, scuffling footsteps that echoed and seemed to come from all around. Were they ahead of us? Behind us? Following us on our left, darting from cover to cover? It was impossible to tell. Derek held up his arm, motioning me to stop, and we stood very still in the darkness, listening. They stopped, too. Where were they? From a distance came the sound of raucous laughter and music, muted, barely audible. The waterfront bars were not too far away. If we could reach them, there would be lights, hundreds of people, safety, and I knew that was what Derek had in mind. My terror was so intense it had gone beyond feeling, and a curious numbness had come over me now, a numbness almost like calm.

A brisk wind blew over the water, tearing at the fog, lifting it, driving it away, and suddenly strong rays of moonlight streamed down, illuminating the area with a clear silver light that sharpened details and darkened shadows. I saw the ships on our right, enormous black monsters crouching low on the water, and I saw the boxes, the bales, piled in awkward pyramids on our left, deep, blue-black shadows around them. I saw Derek's face, skin taut, mouth tight, his eyes alert. I saw the pistol in his hand, long, black, lethal. He knew how to use it. He was an expert. They didn't have a gun, I told myself. If they'd had a gun they would have fired earlier, when we were standing in the light just after the carriage drove away. Perhaps there was hope. Perhaps there was still hope.

I shivered, folding my arms in front of my waist, the wind tearing my hair, lifting my skirts. There were tears in my eyes. I hadn't been aware of them until Derek reached over to brush them away with his finger. Holding the pistol in his right hand, he wrapped his left arm around me, pulled me to him and kissed me on the lips, tenderly, so tenderly, telling me without words that everything was going to be all right, that he loved me. The kiss was all too brief. I clung to him for a moment, and then he gently withdrew, stepping back, turning around to watch the shadows. The moonlight wavered, washing the pier with silver, wisps of fog still floating, and Derek nodded, indicating that we should move on.

We proceeded slowly, cautiously, Derek keeping a sharp watch, gripping the pistol firmly, ready to fire. The music and laughter seemed nearer now, and in the distance I could see clusters of light. The moonlight began to fade, growing dimmer, dimmer, disappearing as a cloud passed over the moon. The darkness was total, a solid black shroud cloaking everything. I watched the shadows and saw one of them move, a dark, bulky shadow disengaging itself from the others, moving stealthily toward us. I screamed. Derek whirled around and saw the shadow and shoved me roughly aside, so roughly that I reeled, tottering backward, finally falling.

Derek raised the pistol to shoot, but before he could get a shot off the shadow lunged, falling on him, knocking the pistol out of his hand. I could see the two of them grappling, hugging each other, it seemed, locked in a deadly embrace, and I got to my knees, out of breath, my heart pounding again, hair spilling over my face. The cloud that had hidden the moon drifted past. Moonlight streamed down again, and I could see them clearly, the heavyset man in the bulky navy blue coat gripping Derek savagely around the waist, trapping his arms, Derek kicking his shin, breaking free, swinging his fist back to pound it into the man's stomach, cracking him across the jaw as the man bent over double in pain. The second blow sent him sprawling, landing on the wooden planks with a heavy thud, and Derek leaped upon him, seizing his throat. The man thrashed, kicked, struggled, toppling Derek over, rolling on top of him.

I saw the pistol. It had skidded across the pier. It was only a few feet away from where I knelt. Bruised, still out of breath, I doubted I could get to my feet, but I knew I had to get the pistol. I began to crawl toward it, and then someone shoved me viciously and I fell flat, lifting my head in time to see Will Hart reach down and pick up the pistol. He was dressed exactly as he had been before, in brown boots and plum-colored breeches and coarsely woven white shirt, the full gathered sleeves billowing, the leather jerkin shiny in the moonlight. He stood with his legs apart, watching the fierce combat, a smile playing on his lips.

I groaned, getting to my hands and knees. Hart turned and looked at me, the smile spreading into a leer. He stepped over to me, seized my hair, and jerked savagely, pulling me up. I couldn't restrain a scream of pain. He slung an arm around my throat, hard muscles tightening, cutting off the scream. Swooping black wings closed over my brain. I almost blacked out.

"I've been waitin' for this," he whispered, his lips at my ear. "I've been waitin' a long time."

I tried to speak. I couldn't. Hart tightened his grip, his arm curling, squeezing, and the blood rushed to my head. I closed my eyes and knew I was going to die, knew my throat was going to be crushed any second now. The pain was unbelievable. Orange and red lights seemed to whirl on my eyelids and I was in a black void, struggling to breathe, struggling to live. Hart loosened his hold, chuckling, and I gulped air, gasping, coughing. He continued to chuckle, delighted to have me in his power, savoring my pain.

"Be a good wench, now," he said in a crooning voice. "You be good and I'll let ya watch Bert cut your toff's 'eart out. 'E 'as a knife, Bert does, bloody fool 'adn't pulled it out yet, shoulda 'ad it in 'is 'and before 'e leaped on your toff."

Derek and the man in the navy blue coat were both on their knees now some ten yards from where we stood. Both were dazed, struggling to their feet, and Bert fumbled with the tail of his coat and pulled a knife out of a scabbard at his thigh. It glittered in the moonlight, long, sharp, hideous. He lunged at Derek, and Derek moved aside just in time to avoid the deadly blade that passed not a fraction of an inch from his side. He whirled, caught Bert's wrist, and twisted violently. Bert yelled and dropped the knife. Hart made an exasperated noise.

"Bloody fool," he said, "bloody bumblin' fool. Looks like I'll 'ave to settle your toff's stew myself. Nice he was carryin' this pistol."

Derek had Bert's arm wrenched up between his shoulder blades, and Bert was yelling, trying to break free. He reared forward, throwing an arm back, catching Derek's head in an awkward grip. They fell crashing to the planks, both of them losing their holds. Bert tried to get up. Derek caught his legs, jerking him back down. Bert's head banged loudly. Derek stood up, stunned, weaving and shaking his head to clear it. Bert groaned, reaching for the knife that was almost within his grasp. Derek kicked the knife and sent it skidding into the water.

Hart chuckled again and curled his arm tightly around my throat again and lifted his free arm. I saw the pistol in his hand and saw him pull the trigger. I heard the explosion and saw a violent orange flash and a puff of smoke and saw Derek clutching himself and reeling backward, stumbling, tripping on the edge of the pier, falling. I heard a loud splash, and I screamed again, the sound welling up in my bruised throat and splitting the air. The world seemed to spin, revolving faster and faster, and I fell into a merciful void of blackness.

"Th' ring, goddammit! Th' bloody ring. He ain't gonna give us tuppence if we don't give 'im th' bloody ring!"

The words seemed to come from a long way off. They were muffled, indistinct, part of a terrible dream. I opened my eyes and everything was blurred, black and silver and blue. It was several moments before I could focus, before I realized where I was. I was in a sitting position, leaning against a bale of cotton, and Hart and his colleague were standing a few feet away. Bert's face was bruised, contorted now with anger, and Hart wore a smug, mocking expression.

"You almost mucked it up, mate," he said. "If I 'adn't got 'is pistol 'e'd a kicked your feeble brains out."

"*You* mucked it up!" Bert growled. "You shot 'im, yeah, and he fell into th' water and 'e's got th' bloody *ring* on 'is finger. Now one of us is gonna have ta dive down there and find 'im and cut th' ring off 'is finger if 'e ain't already floated out to sea!"

"Don't get yourself in such an uproar, mate. I got it right 'ere. The wench 'ad it on 'er finger. I pulled it off. No one's gonna 'ave ta get wet tonight."

"Give it to me!" Bert ordered.

"I got it in my pocket. It's safe where it is."

"We're gonna 'ave ta kill th' wench, too," Bert said.

Hart shook his head. "I got plans for 'er," he said. "Big plans."

"We gotta kill 'er," Bert insisted. "She can identify botha us."

"She ain't gonna 'ave a chance ta identify us," Hart told him.

"You plan on keepin' 'er for yourself?"

"I plan on 'avin' a bit of sport, yeah, and when I get through with 'er I'm gonna turn a nice profit. Red Nick'll pay a fortune for a wench like 'er, pay double 'is usual price."

I heard the words clearly, but they didn't really register. They weren't real. None of this was real. I wasn't alive. I couldn't be alive. I knew I was dead, and I was glad, for there was no reason to live. I was dead. I had to be dead. I couldn't live. My throat hurt terribly and my shoulders ached, but I didn't feel the pain. I was incapable of feeling anything. I stared at the two men and listened to their voices, but none of it was real. I wondered if I was in hell.

" 'Ey," Bert said, "I didn't thinka that."

"No, mate, you didn't."

" 'E'll pay top price! We're gonna 'ave us a bloody fortune!"

"Not us, Bert," Hart said quietly.

"Hunh? Whatda you mean?"

Hart smiled and licked his lips and leveled the pistol at Bert's chest. "I got the ring, Bert. I got the wench. Why should I share with you?"

"Will! You ain't gonna do this! You ain't gonna double-cross me! Not me, not your mate!"

" 'Fraid I am, Bert."

"I'm th' one set this 'ole thing up! I made th' deal with 'im in London! I'm th' one who arranged everything, paid th' captain a bloomin' fortune to tell 'awke 'e 'ad passage and tell 'im th' ship was leavin' at midnight. I brought you in! I brought you in 'cause we was mates and I needed 'elp and I wanted my mate to 'ave a share!"

"Yeah," Hart agreed. "Looks like you made a mistake, Bert."

He pulled the trigger. Bert yelled, a look of amazement in his eyes as he grabbed his chest and blood spurted through his fingers. He fell to his knees, shaking his head, unable to believe what had happened. He continued to shake his head for several moments, moaning, blood spurting, and then his eyes glazed over and he fell face forward, his arms flailing out in front of him. Hart moved back, blew on the barrel of the pistol, and chuckled again.

I was in hell, yes, and the man in the leather jerkin was Satan, but where was his pitchfork, where were the flames? I caught hold of the bale of cotton and pulled myself up. I was standing, but my legs were numb. My whole body was numb. I couldn't feel anything. That was perfectly natural, I told myself. I was dead and in hell and I couldn't feel anything. The man in the leather jerkin looked at me, leering. He wedged the pistol into his waistband and started toward me, and I watched him quite calmly, not at all afraid. Why should I be afraid if I was already dead? He stopped in front of me and grinned, his dark eyes gleaming.

"You an' me are gonna 'ave a real good time," he said.

I looked at him with cool, level eyes, and I saw his wide, thin lips and his large, well-shaped nose. I saw the broad, flat cheekbones and gleaming eyes and the dark, arching brows that flared at the corners. His hair was blond and shaggy. Who would have thought that Satan had blond hair? I lifted my hand up as though to touch that heavy blond hair and watched quite objectively as my nails racked across his cheek, drawing blood. Satan yelled and jumped back and curled one huge hand into a fist. I saw the fist flying through the air toward me, and I felt something almost like pain, but I couldn't feel pain, of course, and I welcomed the blackness that swallowed me up, claiming me at last.

It was dark, so very dark, layers of thick black darkness covering me, and I was swimming through the blackness, swimming slowly, layers falling away. I was swimming, but I couldn't move my arms, and that was strange indeed. Something was holding me back, something coarse and scratchy that bit tightly into my wrists and made swimming much more difficult, but I continued nevertheless, swimming upward, parting layers of blackness, and it tasted awful. It tasted like cotton, cotton crammed against the roof of my mouth and holding my tongue down. I tried to get rid of the awful cotton taste, but I couldn't. I tried to move my arms in graceful strokes, but I couldn't do that either, and if I didn't surface soon I was going to drown.

I swam frantically now, plunging upward, black layers parting rapidly, growing lighter, grayish black now, now dark gray, no longer black, now misty gray stained with gold, yellow-gold flickering, growing brighter, hurting my eyelids. I opened my eyes and saw the candle flame across the room. I blinked and tried to sit up and couldn't. I was stretched out on a narrow bed. There was a gag in my mouth, and my wrists were tied to the bedposts. The room was small with a low, slanting roof, the tan walls stained with brownish circles caused by moisture. A hideous green carpet covered the floor, ragged with age, worn through in spots. Besides the bed, there was a crude wooden chair and a single table. The pewter candlestick stood on the table, a chipped porcelain chamber pot beside it.

I struggled for only a moment, trying to pull my wrists free. The coarse hemp bit into my flesh, tightening savagely as I pulled. There was no hope of freeing myself, I realized that immediately. A wad of cotton cloth had been crammed into my mouth, a handkerchief tied tightly across my lips to hold it in place. The shock and numbness had worn off, but I didn't panic. I knew what had happened. I could still feel the pain in my jaw. There was probably a bruise. Will Hart had knocked me out and brought me to this room and tied me securely, my left wrist bound to one bedpost, my right wrist to the other. He had gagged me so that I wouldn't scream and bring inquisitive neighbors up here. This was obviously an attic room, small, sordid, smelling of mildew and sweat and dirt.

I didn't care what happened to me now. There was no reason to go on living. Hart would use me, and if he didn't kill me I intended to kill myself at the first opportunity. I couldn't go on living with this anguish inside of me, this terrible anguish that made every moment an unendurable agony. I wished fervently that they had killed me when they killed Derek. I fervently prayed that Hart would kill me when he returned, when he had finished using me to assuage his lust. I wondered where he was. I wondered how long I had been here. An hour? Two? Longer?

It didn't matter. Nothing mattered. The candlelight flickered, burning low, washing the filthy walls with patterns of light and shadow. I could hear the wind blowing fiercely around the eaves, and from somewhere below came the sounds of raucous music, gruff, heavy voices, and shrill, feminine laughter, all muted, muffled, barely audible. Doors slammed, and there was a high-pitched yell and the sound of something breaking. I was in an attic room over one of the waterfront bars, or one of the brothels. It didn't matter where I was. It didn't matter at all.

Time passed. Half an hour? An hour? Time had no meaning. The anguish was so intense that each moment seemed an eternity. The muted sounds continued, and the candle burned lower, guttering, the flame leaping in a frenzied dance, finally going out. I lay in darkness for a long time, bound, gagged, consumed with anguish that was constant torture. Eventually, I heard footsteps, two sets of footsteps moving up a flight of wooden stairs that seemed nearby. The sound grew louder, and then the door opened and a dim shaft of light spilled into the room. I saw two men enter.

" 'Old on a minute," Hart said gruffly. "I'll light another candle, 'ave some right 'ere in the table drawer."

I could hear him fumbling about noisily. He muttered a curse and struck a match, dropped it, cursed again and struck another, holding it to the wick of the candle he had jammed into the pewter candlestick. A circle of golden light began to spread in softly diffused rays. Hart shook the match out and dropped it on the floor, turning to the man who had come in with him.

"Don't mind 'er," he said, nodding his head in my direction without looking at me. "Anything she 'ears she ain't gonna 'ave a chance to repeat, least not to anyone 'o'd care."

The tall, thin, coldly handsome man in the powdered white peruke turned to glance at me for perhaps half a second, his icy gray eyes betraying not the least sign of interest. He wore black pumps with low heels and silver buckles, white silk stockings molding his calves. His knee breeches and full-skirted frock coat were of pale blue satin, the coat elaborately embroidered with black and silver flowers. Lace spilled from his wrists, spilled from his throat in a frilly cascade. The soft white hair made his features seem even harsher. They were familiar features, all too familiar, but much harder than his cousin's had been.

So Roger Hawke hadn't gone to Paris after all. He had come to New Orleans to make sure the deed was done properly. He sniffed disdainfully, lifting a lace handkerchief to his nostrils.

"Hurry it up, man," he said sharply. "It's bad enough I had to meet you here at this ungodly hour. I don't want to expire from the stench."

"I 'ave the ring right 'ere. 'Ere it is."

Hawke took the ring, examined it without expression, and then dropped it into his pocket.

"You're certain he's dead?"

" 'E's dead, all right. Feedin' th' fish this very minute."

"Where's the man I hired to kill him?"

"Bert? 'E—uh—'e 'ad a bit of trouble, couldn't make it. 'E told me to collect for 'im."

"I see," Hawke replied.

He took out a roll of bills and calmly began to count them. The candlelight washed those cold, steely, handsome features, polishing the hard cheekbones, sketching shadows beneath them.

"What are you going to do with the woman?" he inquired.

"I 'ave plans for 'er."

"Kill her," Hawke said. "Kill her now."

His voice was totally devoid of emotion. He might have been telling Hart to step on a bug or swat a gnat. After that first, brief glance, he hadn't looked at me again. I might have been part of the furniture. He handed the money to Hart and lifted the lace handkerchief to his nostrils again, crinkling his nostrils.

"Do it now, man," Hawke ordered. "I don't like loose ends."

"Ain't gonna be no loose ends. She ain't gonna talk, I told ya. Soon as I finish pleasurin' her, I aim to turn a profit. Red Nick'll pay good money for 'er. 'E buys wenches, ships 'em to foreign parts to work on their backs in fancy 'ore 'ouses."

Roger Hawke was clearly displeased. His gray eyes were the color of steel and just as hard. His mouth was a thin, tight line. Hart scowled, stubbornly maintaining his position. Brutal, vicious, powerfully built, he looked like a puppy compared to Hawke. I had the feeling the taller man could have snapped him in two without so much as creasing his elegant frock coat. They stared at each other for a long moment, and then Hawke grimaced.

"Very well," he said dryly.

"Red Nick's men are in th' city right now, collectin' wenches. They'll be takin' 'em through the swamps less 'n a week from now, takin' 'em to a pickup point. A month from now she'll be in a 'ouse in Caracas. Ain't no one there gonna be interested in anything but 'er tail."

"If anything happens, Hart, if she gets away—"

"She ain't gettin' away. She's stayin' right 'ere in this room 'til Red Nick's men are ready to 'ead for th' swamps."

"If there are any slip-ups, you can expect several inches of steel through your gullet."

" 'Ey, are you threatenin' me?"

"Not at all," Hawke replied. "I'm stating fact."

His voice was dry, his face devoid of any kind of expression. Hart turned slightly pale. Roger Hawke lifted the lace to his nostrils one more time, the scent of perfume wafting across the room, and then he nodded curtly and left the room, his gorgeous frock coat rustling crisply. Hart stood with his hands curled into tight fists, his cheeks still pale as he listened to the footsteps descending the stairs. He scowled again as the sound faded away and crammed the money into his pocket, turning to look at me for the first time since he had entered the room. He forgot about Roger Hawke then. I could see him forgetting. He had only one thing on his mind now. He licked his lower lip, his brown eyes turning even darker as they filled with brutal desire.

As I watched him, a curious calm came over me. The anguish receded, and I shut it away, shut it deep inside me. There was no room for anguish now. Now there was room for nothing but strength. A few minutes ago there had been no reason to go on living. A few minutes ago I had wanted to die. I had a reason for living now, and I intended to survive. Someway, somehow, I was going to survive, and one day I was going to take my revenge on the man in the powdered wig and elegant French attire. As Will Hart began to unbuckle his belt, I made that vow. I was determined to keep it.

BOOK TWO
The Pirate

Nine

Most of the women were in a stupor as we trudged through the swamp, listless, dazed, a few of them sobbing, but the girl who tripped along beside me might have been on her way to a picnic. Petite, perky, she had long chestnut-brown hair and hazel eyes more green than brown. Her small pink mouth was undeniably saucy, and her cheekbones were dusted with a light, charming scattering of golden-tan freckles. She couldn't have been more than eighteen, I thought, but those greenish-brown eyes were filled with worldly wisdom far beyond her years.

"It's not the bloody *pirates* I'm afraid of," she confided in a chatty voice. "It's the alligators. These swamps are full of 'em. Snakes, too. I wish I hadn't remembered the snakes!"

She shivered quite dramatically, clutching her arms about her waist and peering around her with mock-nervous eyes. The minx was actually enjoying herself. I found that astounding under the circumstances. The pink cotton dress she wore might have been a party dress, torn and soiled though it was. It had puffed sleeves, an extremely low-cut bodice and a very snug waist, the swirling skirt fluttering up at the hem to reveal the ruffled white underskirts beneath.

"My name's Emmeline, luv," she said, "Emmeline *Jones*, quite a combination, I admit. My mother was French, my father English. Emmeline's much too prissy—that was my mother's contribution. You can call me Em, luv, all my friends do, and I figure we might as well be friends."

"I'm Marietta Danver."

"I knew you'd have a name like that, knew it the minute I saw you. Those elegant, aristocratic features, and that *dress!* Turquoise and royal blue brocade, royal blue *petticoats*—it must have cost a bleedin' fortune. I recognized the quality at once. Looks like something Lucille might of run up."

"You know Lucille?"

"I know *of* her, luv. A lass like me wouldn't have much occasion to go to a shop like hers, not unless she had a rich protector. I never had *any* protector, rich or poor. I've had to take what I could get ever since I was thirteen, and I was usually grateful for pennies."

"You've been on your own since you were thirteen?"

Emmeline Jones nodded, her long chestnut curls bouncing. "My father died when I was twelve. My mother remarried. Her husband was forty-two years old and had a taste for tender young flesh. I was terribly tender, terribly young. He had two sons, one eighteen, one twenty-three. They liked young things, too. Don't know how many times I was raped, luv. I figured if I was going to spread my legs three times a night I might as well get something out of it besides a collection of bruises. James, he was the eldest son, he liked to beat me up a bit afterwards, slap me around."

"How dreadful."

"My mother knew what was going on, of course. She didn't care. She always hated me, I never knew why. Anyway, one night James half-killed me, and I took a butcher knife and stabbed him in the shoulder—didn't kill him, wish I had—and while he was still bleedin' like a stuck pig I grabbed a few clothes and ran off, headin' straight for New Orleans. We were livin' in Baton Rouge when I took off."

"It must have been terrible for you," I said.

"It wasn't much *fun,* luv, I tell you for sure, but I did all right. I was independent, you see, never had a pimp, never worked in any of the houses. Me, I don't like to answer to anyone. I figured Red Nick's men would nab me one of these days. It was inevitable."

"You don't seem too upset," I observed.

"I try to look at the bright side, luv. I figure it can't be much worse than what I've been going through. New Orleans is a scary place for a lass on her own. There are too many elegant houses of joy, too many gorgeous Creoles workin' out of plush apartments. A lass like me, with this turned-up nose and these bloody freckles, she has to take her chances on the waterfront, and that isn't a picnic, I assure you.''

"I still don't see how you can be so cheerful.''

"I have plans, luv. I'm not workin' in any house in South America, I promise you. Red Nick keeps the best of the lot to serve his men on the island, two or three out of every batch rounded up, and I intend to be one of 'em. I intend to pick me out a high-rankin' pirate, one of his aides, maybe, and I'm going to fascinate him. I'm going to be so sweet and cuddly he'll cover me with jewels, and when I have enough jewels, I'm going to escape from the island and come back to the mainland a wealthy woman.''

"You sound quite confident.''

"A girl has to be confident nowadays, luv,'' Em replied. "Oh, I could weep and moan and carry on like that stuck-up blonde, that Nadine up there, the tall, skinny one who keeps sobbin' she's from one of the best families, but what good would it do? I intend to make the best of things, luv.''

"I admire your attitude.''

"I just wish there weren't so many alligators. See that *log* over there? It looks awfully suspicious to *me*. It might be a log, but then again it might be an alligator.''

"It's covered with bark,'' I said. "There are twigs broken off.''

"You never can tell, luv. They're terribly sneaky.''

I almost smiled. The girl was refreshingly cheerful, and there had been little cheer this past week. Hart had kept me in his room for five days before turning me over to the pirates, and we had been traveling for two days, leaving the city in five closed carriages, abandoning the carriages yesterday morning to begin our trek through the swamps. There were seventeen women in our group, only six men guarding us. They were a brutal-looking lot, heavily armed with knives and pistols and cutlasses, herding us along like cattle. The pirate who seemed to be in charge carried a long whip and used it mercilessly when one of the women stumbled or failed to keep up.

"At least they don't have us shackled,'' Em remarked. "I guess they figure there's no *need* for shackles. A girl'd be a fool to try and escape through this swamp with alligators and snakes underfoot, and any one of these ruffians would put a bullet through the heart of any girl who *did* try. Glad I'm walking beside you today, luv. They had me beside Nadine yesterday, and her weepin' and whinin' almost drove me out of my mind.''

"You there!" one of the pirates yelled. "Keep your mouth shut!"

"Go play with yourself!" she retorted.

The pirate scowled menacingly, placing one hand on the butt of his gun. He was a tall, husky lout with shaggy black hair and fierce blue eyes, a scar down one side of his face. He wore high black boots with flaring tops and snug black breeches and a loose, full-sleeved purple shirt tucked carelessly into his waistband. A cutlass hung at his thigh. A knife was thrust into his belt alongside the pistol. Em stuck her tongue out at him. He glared a moment longer and then grinned lasciviously. She blew him a kiss.

"Won't have any trouble with *that* one," she promised. "He likes me, took me last night. Took me three times, in fact. Wasn't too bad if you don't mind it rough and rugged. I kept him occupied, all right, got a few swallows of rum for thanks. Reckon he'll want to saddle me again when we camp tonight."

Each of the pirates had selected a woman the night before, using her when it wasn't his turn to stand guard. I had been fortunate. None of them had fancied me. The skinny blond named Nadine had shrieked in terror when one of the men had pulled her over to his blankets. She had fought viciously, shrieking all the while, and he had finally had to administer a savage beating and cram a gag in her mouth. The other pirates had laughed uproariously as their colleagues tamed the shrew.

"*Anyway*," Em continued, "I figured two heads are better than one, figured *two* of us might have a better chance of surviving if we became friends and stuck together. The minute I saw you with those marvelous high cheekbones and that gorgeous copper-red hair, I knew *you* weren't going to South America either. I wouldn't be surprised if Red Nick decided to keep you for himself."

"Do you think there's a chance?" I asked.

"I'd say it's a certainty, luv. Me, I'm all right to look at.

126

I've got nice eyes, nice hair, plenty of curves in the right places, and I've got spirit, too. The men like spirit. I'm better lookin' than most of these dogs they rounded up, but you—" Em shook her head, chestnut curls bouncing. "You're a bloody queen, luv. You're so beautiful I should hate your guts."

"I'm glad you don't, Em."

"You're so calm, so cool about everything. Haven't sobbed once. Haven't complained. Haven't shown the least sign of fear. I like that. I noticed it at once. *She's* going to survive, too, I said to myself. She's got brains as well as beauty, and if you're smart you'll make friends with her, I told myself, so I made a point of gettin' next to you when we started off this morning."

"And now we're friends," I said, squeezing her hand.

We continued to trudge over the damp, spongy ground, avoiding the strands of eerie gray moss that hung from the cypress trees, avoiding the thick roots and vines, frequently moving around pools of stagnant green water. Birds cried out, fluttering away in panic as we drew near, and once a thick, greenish-gray log reared up and thrashed its tail and opened its jaws to reveal rows of razor sharp teeth. Em clutched my hand tightly, almost crushing my fingers. The alligator made a peculiar noise that was half-hiss, half-growl and slithered away into the long brown grass. We heard a splash a few moments later as the creature dove into the water.

There was water all around us, horrible, fetid water covered with a thick coat of mossy green scum, fingers of solid ground reaching through it, dangerous patches of quicksand on either side. Only someone who knew the swamps well could have made his way through the treacherous labyrinth, and I understood why smugglers and pirates used the swamps for their nefarious trade. In places the cypresses and other trees were so thick, so festooned with moss and vines, that we could hardly pass through, and often we had to wade through several inches of muddy brown water. The six pirates forced us on with curses and shoves, and when any woman lagged she felt the lash across her shoulders.

We finally stumbled into a small clearing covered with dry brown grass and fallen logs. Cypress trees surrounded it, their gnarled, twisted branches covered with Spanish moss. Vines with small, peculiar shaped purple and blue flowers twisted around the tree trunks. The pirate with the whip ordered us to stop, and the women sank gratefully to the ground and onto logs. Em was highly suspicious of the logs, kicking one cautiously before deigning to sit on it. I sat down beside her, shoving a tangle of hair from my cheek. The pirates began to distribute food and water.

"It's about time!" Em snapped as one of them stopped in front of us with a canteen and a sack full of parched corn and dried beef.

"Shut up, slut!" he snarled.

"Oh, he's a charmer," she said, "but he *does* have nice shoulders."

The pirate looked at her with new interest. He was a hulking brute, his brown eyes sullen, his dark blond hair falling across his brow in short, ragged locks. He wore a red and black striped jersey and filthy black breeches. His black leather knee boots were scuffed and worn, and his belt sagged under the weight of his knives and gun. Em smiled at him pertly and batted her eyelashes at him.

"Come on, luv," she coaxed, "give us a little more corn, another piece of beef. You don't want us to starve, do you?"

"What's your name, slut?"

"Emmeline, luv, but you can call me Em."

"Why 'adn't I noticed you before?"

"You were too busy noticing that skinny Nadine. I saw you with her last night. *I* wouldn't shriek, I promise. Truth to tell, I'd probably enjoy it—I've always had a weakness for broad shoulders."

While she talked he had been steadily pouring corn into her lap, and now he tossed her an extra piece of dried-beef. Em smiled prettily, flirting outrageously. The pirate in the purple shirt who had taken her the night before came stalking over, his blue eyes hostile, the scar on his cheek a vivid pink slash.

"Back off, Dobbs!" he ordered. "This 'un's mine."

"Yeah?" Dobbs taunted. "Shove it, Ginty, or I'll put a knife through your craw."

Ginty gave Dobbs a mighty push, snarling viciously, and Dobbs stumbled and dropped the bag of food. The two men began to fight like tigers, gouging and grappling with murderous intent until three of the other pirates pulled them apart.

Dobbs' red and black striped jersey was torn. Ginty's jaw was badly scraped. Em perched on the log with an angelic expression, gathering up extra corn and tying it in a handkerchief, surreptitiously placing it in a hidden pocket of her skirt. She was going to survive, all right, and I was extremely pleased to have become her friend.

"See what I mean?" she said as the pirates moved away. "I have something special they all like. That Ginty, he was ready to kill, and Dobbs was eating out of my hand. These are small fry, luv, go-betweens. They don't even live on the island. The important chaps will be on the ship that picks us up, and I intend to pick out one of Red Nick's chief lieutenants and fascinate him out of his breeches."

"I've no doubt you will."

"You now, luv, you're a bit too high class for these louts, too regal and high-toned to appeal to 'em. Your kind of beauty leaves 'em cold, which is just as well—none of them bothered you last night, I noticed, doubt they'll bother you tonight. It'll be a different story when Red Nick sees you. He's an educated man, they say. They say he appreciates fine clothes, fine wine, fine women."

"Oh?"

"He's frightfully good-looking, too, I hear. Very tall and lean and hair the color of copper, eyes like blue ice. He's a cold, merciless killer who'd as soon run you through as look at you, but he has a definite weakness when it comes to beautiful women."

"Where did you hear all these things?"

"You hear a lot about Red Nick on the waterfront, luv. Here, take some of this beef and hide it. Is there a pocket on your skirt? No? Hide it in your bodice then—here, I'll wrap it up in a bit of my petticoat. A few hours from now you'll be glad we have these extra provisions."

Em tore off part of a petticoat ruffle, wrapped the beef in it and handed it to me. I thrust it between my breasts. Dobbs came stalking back to retrieve the bag he had dropped, but not before Em had scooped out several more handfuls of parched corn. She smiled sweetly and looked at him with admiring, angelic eyes. He scowled, handed her a canteen of water, and moved on to distribute food to some of the other women, cuffing Nadine viciously when she asked for more.

"That one's not going to last a breakfast spell," Em remarked, indicating Nadine. "She has the brains of a peacock. I may not have much book learning—my schooling stopped when I was ten—but I learned how to take care of myself in tricky situations. A girl has to."

"I know, Em. I've been in a few tricky situations myself."

"I suspected as much, luv. You may look like a duchess, may speak with a high-toned accent, but you've had your share of rough times, too. I sensed that immediately. I could see it in your eyes. I don't know how you happened to end up in a mess like this—I don't pry, luv, I mind my own business—but I have a feelin' a man was involved."

"You're right, Em," I said quietly.

Em reached over and took my hand, squeezing it encouragingly. "Don't you worry, luv," she told me. "We're in for some more rough times, I don't deny it—it's going to be scary—but you and me, luv, we're going to stick together and we're going to survive."

I nodded, giving her hand a return squeeze. This feisty little street sparrow in her ragged pink dress reminded me a great deal of Angie, the girl who had come to America on the convict ship with me. Angie had been feisty, too, with a face like an angel's and a vocabulary that would have made a stevedore blush. I had learned a great deal from her, and those lessons had stood me in good stead during the years that followed. Em had already displayed her ability to make the best of things, and having her at my side was going to make all this much easier to endure.

"The first thing we've got to do, luv, is make sure we end up on the island instead of in one of them houses. I don't see it as bein' a huge problem," she added.

"Neither do I," I told her.

"Now you're *talkin'*, luv! If we don't get eaten up by alligators, we're in business."

"On your feet, sluts!"

The pirate in charge cracked his whip. He was a blond giant with a patch over one eye and a filthy blue bandana tied around his head. He wore an olive-green frock coat with silver buttons, the once-elegant garment frayed now, torn on one side. His name was Quince, and he wielded the whip with vicious authority, a sadistic smile on his lips as he lashed one of the women across the shoulders.

"That one," Em said, shuddering. "He makes my blood run cold. You want to watch out for him, luv."

"I fully intend to."

"Hurry it up!" Quince yelled. "Get movin'!"

Dobbs and Ginty collected the canteens and lined us up again. A chubby, brown-eyed brunette in a blue dress saw a snake slithering toward her through the grass. She screamed and stumbled over a log, falling heavily on her stomach. Quince kicked her savagely and, seizing her by the hair, yanked her to her feet. The girl was in a state of shock, trembling uncontrollably. Quince slapped her across the face and shoved her into line, and we started through the thick grove of cypress trees, moving slowly of necessity, frequently tripping over the tangled roots.

The eerie, gray Spanish moss dangled down, brushing our cheeks, and swarms of insects filled the air, mosquitoes lighting on us with a soft, feathery touch that quickly turned into a painful sting. The cypress trees thinned out, and we moved alongside a stagnant green lake, greenish-gray logs resting in the muddy bank, frequently stirring to slide into the water. Em gripped my hand tightly, eyeing the alligators with considerable alarm. Turning away from the lake, we moved through another dense forest of trees, vines hanging down in treacherous loops, the ground damp and spongy. The mosquitoes were still with us, but one soon learned to ignore them, just as one learned to ignore the horrible, fetid smells.

We had been moving along for perhaps three hours when Quince yelled for us to halt. The forest had given out, and we were on the edge of another body of water, neither lake nor river but a sprawling green mass dotted with small islands covered with more trees. The pirates dragged three large, flat wooden boats out from under the shrubbery and ordered us to climb into them, Quince cracking his whip in the air, lashing it across the shoulders of any woman he felt moved too slowly.

"I'm not going to like this part," Em confided. "Never have trusted boats, luv, and these look mighty leaky."

"Step lively!" Quince roared.

Em and I climbed into one of the boats, sitting down on the wooden planks in the center. The skinny blonde named Nadine climbed in after us, as did the plump brunette in blue and two more women, one a terrified Negro girl who couldn't have been over fourteen, the other a lass with pale brown hair and sky-blue eyes that looked curiously empty. She was still in a state of shock. Dobbs clambered into the front of the boat, wielding a long, narrow pole. A pirate named Tremayne stood up in the rear, pushing us off with a similar pole.

"Careful there, luv," Em told him, "you don't want to tip us over. These waters are *full* of alligators."

Tremayne merely scowled at her. He was considerably younger than the other men, surely not more than twenty-five, a tall, muscular lad with dark brown eyes and sun-streaked brown hair. He wore high black boots, clinging gray cord breeches, and a blue and gray striped jersey that accentuated his powerful shoulders. A dark blue scarf was tied around his neck. He stood with legs wide apart, perfectly steady as the boat swayed in the water. Dobbs stood in front, using his pole with skill.

"How *deep* is this water?" Em asked.

"Not more 'n six feet," Tremayne growled. "Relax, wench, you're not gonna get wet."

"If I fall in, will you rescue me? I don't swim, you see."

Tremayne pretended to ignore her, but I could see him stealing looks at her as he and Dobbs poled us past one of the islands. The boat rocked alarmingly in the stagnant, greenish-brown water, the prow cutting through layers of scum. Nadine brushed pale blonde locks from her cheeks and rearranged her sky-blue brocade skirt, revealing the elegant lace underskirts beneath. Although the clothes were filthy now and deplorably tattered, I could see that they had come from Paris. The girl had a sharp, thin face and light green eyes, her pink mouth full and pouting. She spoke with a French accent.

"Where are they *taking* us?" she exclaimed.

"Far, far away," Em informed her. "Don't get so riled up, Nadine. You might tip us over."

"But I don't *belong* here! My father is an aristocrat. He'll pay a fortune to get me back! I'm not like the rest of you! I'm not a whore!"

132

"No?" Em said. "You could have fooled me. If you're so bloody high and mighty, what were you doing on the waterfront?"

"I was visiting a friend. He—he happened to be staying in one of those dreadful inns down there. I *begged* him to find better lodgings. I told him I couldn't keep going · down there."

"I'll wager Daddy didn't know about your little visits, luv. If there's anything I can't stand, it's a bloody hypocrite. At least I'm an *honest* whore, luv. I'll bet you didn't even *charge.*"

Nadine gave her a sullen look and glanced around apprehensively, gnawing her lower lip. The plump brunette was still trembling. I took her hand, gently squeezing it. The girl's hands were rough and red. I guessed that she had been a scullery maid, a sturdy, uneducated girl who clearly came from peasant stock. Her name, I knew, was Bessie, and I was almost certain she had been a virgin when she was abducted. I held her hand and smoothed hair from her temple. After a while her trembling ceased, but her large brown eyes continued to stare straight ahead seeing nothing but remembered horror.

Dobbs and Tremayne poled us past another of the islands and then guided the boat through a narrow opening among the trees and down a finger of water not more than twenty feet wide, muddy banks close on either side, tree limbs forming a moss-draped canopy overhead. The light was dim here, only a few pale rays of sunlight able to sift through the limbs. Strange birds cried out, and the moss floated in the air like thick smoke. We continued down the watery tunnel for at least an hour before turning down another, one boat ahead of us, the other following close behind.

A peculiar calm possessed me. I no longer heard the explosion and saw the puff of smoke and the violent orange streak, no longer saw the man I loved staggering backward, falling off the pier into the water, and I no longer felt the anguish that made life itself unendurable. That was locked up tightly inside of me, and there it would remain for the rest of my life, an integral part of me. One day, perhaps, I would allow myself to remember and feel the anguish again. One day, perhaps, I might even allow myself to cry, but that luxury would have to wait. Now there was room for nothing but this steely resolution to survive and take my revenge on Roger Hawke.

The horror I had experienced since that night had had no effect whatsoever. I had endured Will Hart's brutal embraces without a murmur, without a struggle. I had deliberately removed myself from the stark reality, had been cool and passive even as he thrust inside me repeatedly, exhausting himself in a frenzy of lust only to begin anew a short while later. I had told myself it was happening to someone else, and I seemed to observe things from a great distance, aloof and untouched, removed. That feeling of calm detachment had remained when he turned me over to the pirates, haggling with Quince over the price and finally accepting far less than he had anticipated.

All the while the resolution had grown inside me, and I could feel strength building steadily. I had survived horror before, and I would survive this, too. I had already found a strong ally in Em. My first objective, as was hers, was to avoid being shipped to South America with the rest of the women. Life on the island would be rugged indeed, but it would be better than its alternative, and escape would be a much greater possibility, particularly if we succeeded in making our captors believe we were resigned to our fates and intent only on making the best of things. I had no doubt Em would be able to fascinate the man she selected as her protector, but would I be able to fascinate the notorious Red Nick? I certainly hadn't fetched the price Hart had been expecting, and none of these men had shown the least interest in me, preferring the plump Bessie, the thin and haughty Nadine. Em said my beauty was too refined to appeal to this particular group of men. Would it appeal to Red Nick? If it didn't, I was in a great deal of trouble.

"Don't even consider it," Em said.

"Consider what?"

"Failure, luv. You've been sittin' there so silent, thinking, and I saw doubt in your eyes just now. You think he might not fancy you. There's not a chance of that, luv. The minute he sees you he's going to be hooked good and proper."

"What are you two talking about?" Nadine asked sharply.

"Nothing that concerns you, luv."

"You're planning, something, I can tell. You think you're so smart, both of you. You think you're going to escape. You haven't a prayer, but when that Red Nick person finds out who I *am* he'll turn me loose immediately. Daddy will reward him handsomely."

"Dream on, luv. You'll soon be spreading those skinny legs of yours for a flock of foreign-speakin' gents who couldn't care less who your daddy is. If they have any sense, they'll put a sack over your head first."

"You bitch!"

Em ignored the insult. Nadine sulked petulantly, her mouth pursed most unattractively, her light green eyes full of hostility. The men poled the boats out of the watery tunnel and across a sea of wavy gray-brown grass, the water not more than two or three feet deep here. Directly ahead of us, perhaps a quarter of a mile away, a strip of solid land stretched as far as the eye could see. It was heavily wooded, tall palm trees towering over the others. We reached it a short while later, and Dobbs and Tremayne leaped out, dragging the boat out of the water and ordering us to get out. Soon we were trudging through the trees. The horrible fetid smell was gone now, and the air was laced with a salty tang. The ground beneath our feet was solid, no longer damp and spongy. The swamps were behind us, the coast somewhere up ahead.

We took another short break. Dobbs and Ginty passed canteens around, allowing us only a brief swallow each. I took the opportunity to give Bessie one of the pieces of dried beef I had hidden. She accepted it silently, eyes staring blankly. Although I had tried to do it surreptitiously, Nadine saw me give the food to the girl and rushed over to report it to Quince, hoping to ingratiate herself. She received a fierce slap across the mouth for her efforts, and I waited for Quince to come over with his whip. He didn't even turn around to glance in our direction, clearly he had other things on his mind.

"That was a close one," Em said, standing beside me. "Nadine is a real prize, isn't she? If there's one thing I hate more than a hypocrite, it's a bloody squealer. She's going to get hers, all right. It's inevitable."

"You're gonna get yours, too," Tremayne told her.

Neither of us had noticed the muscular young pirate standing nearby, and I paled as I realized he, too, must have seen me give the food to Bessie. He stood in front of us now, hands on hips, but he didn't pay the least attention to me. He had eyes only for Em, and they were filled with appreciation of her raffish charms.

"Oh?" she said.

"Tonight," he retorted.

"You'll have to fight Dobbs and Ginty, luv. Both of them have staked a claim."

"Neither of 'em are gonna tangle with me, wench. I'm Red Nick's second-in-command."

"You *are*?"

"I'm over all these louts. Quince, he wields the whip, but me, I got the authority. I don't like anything, all I gotta do is say the word to Red Nick. He hasn't been happy with these roundups, the men were losing too many women. He sent me along this time to keep an eye on things, make a special report."

"Then you must live on the island?"

"Have my own place right across the courtyard from Red Nick's."

"How *fascinating*," Em remarked.

"You can forget about Dobbs and Ginty, wench. Tonight you're gonna share a blanket with *me*."

"I can hardly wait, luv."

Tremayne strolled away, his broad shoulders rolling under the snug blue and gray striped jersey. A blissful smile played on Em's small pink mouth, and her hazel eyes were positively aglow with delight.

"There you *are*," she said, "and he's not bad-looking either, nice features, wicked brown eyes, a *magnificent* physique. I couldn't be happier about it. After tonight he's not *about* to let me be shipped to Rio."

Quince cracked his whip and ordered us to get back in line, and we continued our march. The light was gradually fading, taking on a faint pinkish tint. The smell of salt was stronger now, a distinct tang that was marvelously refreshing. Palm fronds rattled overhead, and we were able to move much faster now that the ground was solid and there were no roots and vines to obstruct us. We marched for perhaps half an hour before the light turned dark orange, streaming through the trees in rapidly fading rays. The light was almost gone when I heard the roar of waves slapping over sand. Darkness had fallen entirely when we stumbled through the last line of trees and onto the broad beach.

"Thank God that's over," Em said. "No more alligators. Now all we have to worry about is sharks. I hear these waters are *alive* with 'em. I wonder if they ever sneak up on the beach?"

"I doubt it, Em."

"Never can tell. They're awfully sly and crafty."

Most of the women sank onto the sand in exhaustion. The pirates gathered up driftwood and lighted three fires that soon were blazing in crackling red-orange fury. Water and food were distributed, a paltry amount of the latter. Em and I were grateful for the extra we had been able to hide earlier on, although it didn't go far as we shared it with Bessie and the young Negro girl who huddled beside us. Her name was Corrie, and she had a frail, delicate beauty. The fires had begun to burn down when the pirates selected their partners for the night. Tremayne tapped Em on the shoulder and gave her a curt nod, indicating a spot beneath one of the palm trees. Nadine ran shrieking back toward the trees as Dobbs approached her. He lunged after her, slinging an arm around her throat and dragging her back.

Bessie, Corrie, and I were unmolested. We shivered miserably under the heavy blankets the pirates had tossed us, for the night was cold, the wind blowing over the water icy and unrelenting. Bessie sobbed in her sleep. Corrie continued to shiver. I finally managed to fall asleep despite the crash of the waves and the lurid sounds of coupling punctuated by screams. A faint golden streak was visible on the horizon when I woke. Em was shaking my shoulders. I sat up and rubbed my eyes. Everyone else was asleep, several of the pirates snoring.

"I found out all about him," she whispered. "He *has* a woman, her name is Maria, but here's the important part, luv—he's *tired* of her. She gives herself airs, has gotten much too big for her breeches. That's what Michael says."

"Michael?"

"Michael Tremayne, luv. Who did you *think* I meant? He

says Red Nick has his eye out for a replacement. Oh, luv, look! There's the ship! There on the horizon. Can you see it?''

She pointed. As the golden streak spread, spangling the water with flecks of dancing light, we could see the ship approaching. We watched in silence, and soon we could see the flag waving high on the tallest mast. It was solid black, and as it snapped in the wind we could see the skull and crossbones quite clearly. The ship stopped, riding the waves as anchor was dropped. Boats were lowered. Red Nick had come to pick up his goods.

Ten

Tremayne awakened and, seeing the ship and the approaching boats, roused the other pirates, suddenly taking on the authority he hadn't bothered to display earlier. He barked orders curtly, and even Quince hurried to obey. As early morning sunlight gleamed bright and drove away the pale pink of dawn, the youth with the stern brown eyes and broad shoulders took complete charge. The rest of the women were awakened. We were assembled in a ragged line. Bessie stared in front of her with empty eyes. Corrie trembled beside me, and I took her hand. Nadine fussed with her hair, primping for the new arrivals. The three boats bobbed on the water, drawing nearer.

"It's going to be all right, Corrie," I said.

"I'se afraid, Miz Marietta." Tears spilled down her cheeks.

"We're all afraid."

"My mistress, Miz Henrietta, she wudn't pleased with me. She didn't like the way I done her hair. She tole Mista Buck to sell me an' he sold me to the bad men. One uv 'em took my cherry. I bled somethin' awful. They'se goin' to put me in a bad place so's other men can stick their things in me.''

"Maybe not, Corrie. You—you must be brave.''

"I'll try, Miz Marietta, but I'se so scared.''

When the boats were a few yards from shore, the men leaped out, took hold of long ropes attached to the bows, and waded on to shore, pulling the boats behind them. There were six men, all dressed in motley pirate attire, bandanas around their heads, cutlasses at their sides, knives and pistols thrust into their belts. One of them, a sullen giant with coal black hair and a beak-like nose, approached Tremayne with a disgusted look in his fierce gray eyes.

"Not a very promisin' lot, Mike,'' he grumbled.

"A couple of 'em aren't so bad,'' Tremayne replied.

"The wench in pink, the one with the teats half hangin' out, she oughta fetch a good sum.''

"She's not for sale.''

"Keepin' her for yourself?''

Tremayne nodded. The pirate with the beak-like nose strolled slowly down the line of women, examining each one of us with a disgruntled expression. He wore tall black boots, black trousers, and a loose-fitting green shirt with full sleeves. His bandana was green, too, and a gold hoop dangled from his left earlobe. He paused in front of Nadine, clutching her chin in his hand, jerking her head from left to right.

"They like 'em skinny in Rio,'' he declared. "Once she's washed up and put in a new dress, this one'll do. She oughta bring a hundred pounds. How much you pay for her, Quince?''

"Didn't pay nuthin','' Quince retorted. "Nabbed her when she was comin' outta her lover's room. Clamped a hand over her mouth, dragged her down the back stairs.''

"How 'bout the rest of 'em?''

"Paid fifty pounds for the little nigger. Paid two hundred and fifty for that tall redhead. Hart wanted five hundred. Paid a hundred for that one in yellow, one of our agents nabbed her. The rest of 'em were snatched by our own men.''

"Total outlay three hundred pounds. Too bloody much. We won't get more'n a coupla thousand for the whole lot, less'n that if Mike means to keep the one with the teats.''

"We did the best we could,'' Quince protested.

"Your best ain't good enough, Quince. You come up with another lot like this, you and your men are gonna find yourselves manning the oars again. Red Nick's gonna be bloody unhappy when he sees these dogs."

"It ain't as easy as it used to be, Draper. Hart and the rest of 'em ain't supplyin' like they was, and me 'n the boys, we have to be careful, have to keep outta sight. Nabbin' a wench ain't all that simple."

Draper turned to Tremayne. "What do you think, Mike?"

"Quince and his boys know the swamps like the backs of their hands. That ain't to be sneezed at, Draper. Quince uses his whip a mite too much, and his boys are a mite rough on the wenches, but they hadn't lost any this time. Red Nick ain't been happy, but I don't reckon he could do much better. We put new men on the job, they're likely to spend the rest of their lives wanderin' these swamps tryin' to find a way out."

"That what you gonna tell Red Nick?"

Tremayne nodded. Draper wasn't happy, but he didn't care to argue with Red Nick's second-in-command. Instead, he kicked the sand with the toe of his boot and moved back down the line for a closer look at us. When he stopped in front of me, I met his fierce gaze with cool composure.

"Two hundred and fifty pounds for this one!" he snarled. "Quince musta been outta his mind! She looks like a bleedin' aristocrat, cold as ice. They ain't gonna line up for the likes of her."

"She's got something," Tremayne said flatly.

"Nothin' I can see," Draper retorted. "Let's get 'em on the boats and out to the ship. He don't want to tarry too long in these waters."

We were herded onto the boats. Corrie sat on one side of me, Em on the other, Bessie and two other women facing us. A husky pirate climbed in after he had pulled the boat into the water. He took up the oars, and we were on our way to the ship. Corrie sobbed. I slipped my arm around her, and she rested her head on my shoulder, trembling. The boat tipped precariously, riding the waves, the pirate rowing vigorously, muscles rolling beneath his jersey. Bessie stared at the water and gathered bunches of her blue skirt between her fingers, tugging at it, pulling, unaware of what she was doing.

"Are you all right, luv?" Em asked me.

"I'm fine, Em. It's the others I'm worried about. I wish we could do something for them."

"I know the feeling, luv. We're tough. We can handle it. That poor child beside you—she's utterly defenseless."

"We've got to help her, Em. At least we can help Corrie."

"I don't know how, luv. We'll be doing good to save our own skins."

"We can't let her be shipped to South America."

"We'll think of something, luv."

I tightened my arm around the trembling girl and stroked the short black curls that covered her head like a crisp cap. I remembered Cassie, the lovely Negro slave I had helped escape to freedom along with her husband Adam. I had no way of knowing what had ultimately happened to them, but they hadn't been recaptured, and I liked to think they were safely up north, living a good life with the child Cassie had been carrying when they fled the plantation. I had no idea how I was going to do it, but I was going to help this girl, too. As the boat drew nearer the ship, I resolved to protect her.

"Stop crying, Corrie," I said quietly. "Sit up. Wipe your eyes."

Corrie obeyed, making a valiant effort to stem her tears. The sun was a brilliant white ball now, climbing the pale blue sky and casting dazzling reflections on the surging blue-gray water. One of the boats ahead of us had already reached the ship. The women were climbing up a rope ladder and being pulled onto the deck by brawny pirates. Em nudged my side, pointing. To our left, perhaps a hundred and fifty yards away, two large gray fins were visible on the surface of the water, circling slowly.

"Sharks," she said. "I told you these waters are full of 'em."

"They must be enormous, judging from the size of those fins."

"I'm paralyzed, luv. I'll never be able to climb that ladder. One little slip and—splash. Jesus! Look at 'em! They're coming closer."

Em was quite pale, her greenish-brown eyes wide with fear. She closed them and moved her lips in a silent prayer.

The last woman in the boat ahead was hauled over the railing and onto the deck, the boat itself raised on ropes and lifted over, disappearing from sight. The pirate rowing our boat loosened his hold on the oars and let the boat drift. It clattered against the side of the ship with a mighty bang that jolted all of us.

"Jesus Christ!" Em roared. "Take it easy, you bastard! Do you want to dump us all in the water!"

"Up the ladder, wench!" he ordered.

"You must be joking, luv. If you think I'm going to shimmy up that flimsy hunk of rope, you're out of your mind."

The pirate smiled. He caught hold of her arm, jerked her to her feet and heaved her up in the air, tossing her toward the side of the ship. Em climbed up the ladder with remarkable agility, her skirts fluttering wildly up over her legs, ragged, ruffled petticoats soaring. As she reached the top, muscular arms reached out, caught hold of her, dragging her over the railing. I whispered encouraging words to Corrie, who had started trembling again. The pirate pulled Bessie to her feet and ordered her to climb. She merely stared at him. He slapped her across the face and shoved her toward the ladder, and she climbed slowly, heavily.

The other two women went up next, and then the pirate nodded to Corrie. She hesitated, terrified, and I squeezed her hand. Her frail body trembling visibly, she caught hold of the ropes and began to climb, pausing midway and clinging as the ship swayed. I caught my breath, afraid she was going to let go of the ropes. The pirates leaning over the railing yelled loudly, ordering her to keep climbing. She shook her head, her eyes closed tightly.

"Go on, Corrie!" I called. "You can make it. I'm right behind you."

The girl sobbed and moved up a few more rungs. Hands reached down, and she was pulled the rest of the way up. I caught hold of one of the rungs and put my foot in another, pulling myself up. The rope was coarse and scratched my palms. The ladder swung outward, swung back, slapping against the side, almost causing me to lose my grip. No wonder Corrie had been so frightened, I thought, moving up another rung. The wind blew heavy, copper-red waves across my cheeks and tore at my skirts. Out of the corner of my eye I could see the sharks circling, their bodies visible from this angle, long, sleek, moving in a lethargic ballet just beneath the surface. That didn't help at all. I clung to the ropes and willed myself to move up another rung, another, finally reaching the top. Two pirates caught hold of my wrists and heaved me over the railing, almost pulling my arms out of their sockets.

"Over there with the rest of 'em!" one of them barked.

The other women were clustered together near a stack of barrels containing gunpowder. Nadine was primping again, straightening her skirts, shoving pale blonde curls away from her sharp, thin face. Bessie stood to one side, staring at the water, and Em had her arm around Corrie's waist. Corrie's lovely brown eyes filled with relief when she saw me approach.

"I see you made it," Em said. "I wouldn't care to go through *that* again, I can tell you for sure."

"I kept thinking about the sharks."

"So did I. Here come the rest of the women. We'll be pulling up anchor as soon as they're all aboard. Michael told me. He's below deck now with the captain. Red Nick'll be coming up to inspect us in a little while."

"You think you know everything, don't you?" Nadine snapped. "Just because you're screwing that young pirate you think you've got inside information. You little whore! *I* could have had him if I'd wanted him."

"I didn't notice him paying much attention to you, luv. He was probably afraid you'd give him a dose of clap."

"The captain's going to set me ashore as soon as he finds out who I am. He's going to set me ashore with one of the men who'll take me back to New Orleans and collect the reward. Daddy'll give him a huge reward."

"I wouldn't count on it, luv."

One by one, the other women joined us. Overhead, the strong canvas sails cracked, snapping in the wind, causing the ship to rock slowly from side to side, the deck tilting. Ropes hung down from the masts like a tangle of heavy vines, and a pirate without shirt stood in the crow's nest, peering across the horizon, on the lookout for other ships. *The Sea Lyon* was enormous, heavily armed with twenty cannon, ten on either side. It was an elegant vessel, gleaming with brass and polished mahogany and showing few signs of combat. I couldn't help but compare it to the squalid prison ship on which I had crossed the Atlantic. It was like comparing a palace to a hovel, I thought, noticing the elegantly carved banisters leading down to the officers' quarters.

"It's something, isn't it?" Em said. "It was one of the finest ships in the Spanish fleet before Red Nick took it. One of the fastest, too. I don't know how many knots an hour —I think Michael said knots, I suppose that means miles. I'm not too good at nautical terms."

"We all know what you *are* good at," Nadine remarked.

"You know, luv, I could really grow to dislike you if I tried hard enough. I wish he *would* put you ashore—on a desert island. They're bound to be some around here somewhere."

Nadine made a face and continued to fuss with her hair. The shore seemed very far away, our campsite barely visible across the water. Quince and his men had already started back through the swamps. The men on *The Sea Lyon* were just as fierce and sullen-looking as the others had been, but they seemed much cleaner, their clothes less ragged and soiled. Draper marched over to us and stood with hands on hips, the sleeves of his green shirt whipping in the wind.

"What's wrong with the nigger?" he snapped.

"She's all right," Em said. "She's just upset."

"Red Nick don't like snivelin'. He don't like lip, either. Any of you sluts open your mouths when he's inspectin' you, he's likely to knock you down. Keep that in mind!"

"Hush up, luv," Em told Corrie. "Lord, I've never seen such tears. Here, wipe them away. That's better. Marietta and I are going to take care of you, luv, but you've gotta hold up your end."

"I—I'se just so scared. I won't cry no more, Miz Em. I promise."

"Line up, sluts!" Draper ordered. "Here comes the captain!"

Tremayne came up the stairs from the officers' quarters, young, muscular, looking terribly stern now. He was followed by a very tall, very lean man who appeared to be in his mid-thirties. Nicholas Lyon wore a pair of black leather knee

144

boots polished to a high sheen, the heels clicking as he moved across the deck. His black breeches were snug, hugging his calves and thighs, while his maroon shirt fit loosely, bagging slightly over the waistband. It was made of pure silk, heavy and shiny, open at the throat, the full bell sleeves gathered at the wrists. The maroon was a rich, dark shade, the color of wine. He wore no cutlass, carried neither knife nor pistol, and his face was expressionless, yet he nevertheless seemed far more formidable than any of his men. He exuded an aura of savage ruthlessness that made my blood run cold.

"Here they are," Tremayne said. "Seventeen of 'em."

A tiny frown of displeasure creased Red Nick's brow. He hadn't bothered to look at us yet.

"So few?" he inquired.

"Quince and his boys aren't findin' it as easy as it used to be, and their agents aren't supplyin' as many wenches as they used to. These ain't too bad, and there's one in particular, a redhead—"

"I'll make my own judgment, Tremayne."

His voice was perfectly level, but it had a harsh, metallic quality that reminded one of steel. He sauntered over to inspect us, maroon silk fluttering at waistband and wrists. He moved with the assurance and lazy grace of a panther, lithe and arrogant, and one sensed a tightly coiled strength in that lean body. As he moved slowly down the line, examining each of us without the slightest sign of interest, I studied his face. It was not handsome, no, much too lean and taut for that, but there was something undeniably fascinating about those sharp, cruel features.

His lips were thin, his nose a trifle long, flaring at the nostrils, and the skin was stretched tightly across his broad, sharp cheekbones. His eyes were light blue, piercing eyes, eyes that knew no mercy, his heavy lids half-shrouding them. Dark, copper-brown brows arched sharply above, satanic brows that flared at the corners. His skin was deeply tanned, making his thin lips seem a paler pink, and his hair was a dark reddish-brown, the color of tarnished copper. A heavy V-shaped wave slanted across his forehead, the point an inch or so above his right eyebrow.

He paused briefly in front of each of us, those piercing

eyes moving up and down, taking in everything, betraying nothing. His thin lips lifted at one corner in a faint curl of disapproval as he examined Bessie, and then he continued his inspection, examining Corrie, examining Em, finally pausing in front of me. I stood perfectly still, gazing straight ahead with a composure I was far from feeling. My heart was pounding. I knew instinctively that it would be a grave error to try and stir his interest in any of the usual ways. Nicholas Lyon was not the kind of man who would respond to an inviting smile or melting looks.

I was filthy, my hair in tangled disarray, my face probably streaked with dirt. My gown was soiled and torn. Could he see beyond the dirt, the dishevelment? Perhaps he would find me too regal and aloof. He might prefer a different type altogether. Was it my imagination, or did he hesitate just a moment before moving on down the line? Did those eyes linger a few seconds as he examined my face, my body? Was there a slight flicker of interest in their icy blue depths? I couldn't be certain. I didn't dare hope. He moved on and finished his inspection with Nadine, who stood at the end of the line, and as he turned she reached out to pluck his arm.

"Just a minute, Captain," she said, "there's something you need to know. There's been a mistake, you see. I'm not like these others. I—my name is Nadine Dujardin. My father is Raoul Dujardin, I'm sure you've heard of him. He's a *very* important man, very wealthy, too, and he'll pay an enormous reward for my safe return. I'm sure your men didn't *mean* to make such an error, and I know Daddy'll understand—he won't make any trouble. You can just put me ashore with one of the men and he can take me back to New Orleans and Daddy'll give him the money."

"Sweet Jesus," Em whispered.

Nicholas Lyon stood very still, his eyes moving down to rest on the hand that restrained him. Nadine smiled and batted her lashes, playing the coquette now, all playful and flirtatious.

"You're obviously an intelligent man," she continued, "obviously a gentleman, too, not like the rest of this riffraff. I know you'll be reasonable about this. Just pick out a man and send me back and all will be forgiven, I promise."

He raised his eyes to look at her face a moment, taking in

the simpering smile, the playful eyes, and then he pulled his arm free and stepped back. Nadine continued to smile, even as he curled his fist and drew it back. He hit her across the jaw with a shattering impact that sent her flying backward at least ten feet before she fell crashing to the deck, totally unconscious even before her head banged on the hard wood. Several of the women screamed, and Em went rushing over to fall to her knees and gather the girl in her arms.

"Goddamn you!" she yelled. "She's a bloody fool, sure, but you didn't have to kill her! She's not breathing! Yes, she is—just barely! Nadine, can you hear me? Can you open your eyes? She's out cold, and I think you've broken her bloody jaw!"

It was an act of incredible courage. Em detested Nadine and everything she stood for, but her natural compassion was far stronger than any personal dislike. She had flown to the girl's side without even thinking of her own welfare, and she glared at the pirate now with eyes literally afire with anger. A sudden hush fell over the ship. Red Nick's men were stunned by Em's foolhardy action, even more stunned by her words. Tremayne had turned quite pale. He stared at her with his mouth wide open in amazement. Nadine stirred in Em's arms and began to moan. Em held her close, stroking her hair.

"You'll be all right," she said. "Can you move your jaw? Thank God. I thought it was broken. You poor little fool!"

She helped the girl to her feet and led her slowly back over to the group of women. Nadine was crying silently, tears streaming down her cheeks in wet, sparkling rivulets. Red Nick hadn't moved. His expression hadn't altered. I could feel the tension crackling in the air. Draper was the first to respond. He charged over and seized Em roughly by the arm.

"Ten lashes?" he inquired. "Twenty?"

"Twenty should do," Red Nick said dryly. "Tie her to the mast. Perhaps the others will profit by watching her punishment."

"Hold on a minute," Tremayne protested. "Captain, look, the women—uh—they've been under considerable strain. This one—" He pushed Draper away and took hold of Em himself, "I have an interest in her. I don't want her cut up. I'll punish her myself."

Red Nick elevated one satanic brow, surprised by his

second-in-command's intervention. Michael Tremayne ran his tongue over his lower lip, working up more courage.

"I'll take her down to my cabin, keep her there. I'll give her a beating she won't soon forget." He seized Em's hair and jerked her head back, looking into her eyes with a fierce, menacing expression. "I'll see she learns to behave herself."

"She needs a lashin'!" Draper growled.

"You shut up, Draper!"

Red Nick hesitated a moment, calmly observing the two men who were clearly on the verge of physical combat. Draper was scowling, gray eyes glittering with hostility. Tremayne had hooked his left arm around Em's neck, holding her protectively. His right hand rested on the hilt of his knife, and his expression left no doubt that he was ready to use it if Draper persisted. The rest of the men waited eagerly, hoping to witness a good rousing fight before they resumed their duties.

"You want this woman, Tremayne?" Red Nick asked.

Tremayne nodded, drawing Em closer. Red Nick frowned, plainly displeased but willing to reward his man for services rendered.

"Very well," he said. "We'll postpone the lashing for the time being. I expect you to discipline her properly, Tremayne. I intend to hold you personally responsible for her conduct."

It was at this point that I heard a low, crooning noise and turned to see Bessie shaking her head. She shook her head and crooned and then, abruptly, so abruptly that it took everyone by surprise, she went rushing toward the railing. A pirate leaped in front of her, trying to grab her. She shoved him aside with superhuman strength, knocking him off his feet. Men shouted, rushing toward her, but Bessie jumped up onto the railing before any of them could reach her. She stood poised there for a moment like a tightrope walker, plump and ungainly, dark hair flying, blue skirts whipping, and then she dove into the water.

Several of the women screamed. Men rushed to the railing. I started to rush over myself, but Tremayne relinquished his hold on Em and seized my arm, restraining me. He shook his head, his dark eyes telling me that there was no hope of saving her. Corrie began to sob. I watched in horror as Bessie came bobbing up to the surface, thrashing her arms furiously, trying to swim. Em seized my hand as Bessie went under again and the two sharks we had seen earlier glided slowly toward her, their long gray-white bodies clearly visible just beneath the sun-drenched surface. Bessie came up again, hair plastered across her face, skirts wet and tangled.

The sharks circled her leisurely, one of them gliding over to investigate, nudging her almost playfully, circling again as the other shark swirled over and casually bit off a leg. The water turned scarlet. Bessie's scream was a shrill, ear-splitting cry of anguish that ended in a horrible gurgling as she was pulled under. The sharks grew frenzied, feasting greedily, and the water churned furiously, bright, bright red. It was all over in a very few moments. The enormous creatures disappeared. The crimson stain spread and turned pink, fading, and then the water was blue again and sparkling with sunlight. Bessie might never have existed. Three of the women had fainted.

"Hoist the anchor, men," Nicholas Lyon said dryly. "We've tarried too long as it is."

The deck became a beehive of activity as the men hurried about their duties, pulling up the anchor, tightening ropes, climbing the rigging to adjust the sails. The sails flapped, catching the wind. The ship rocked, beginning to move. Red Nick strolled over to where we were standing. Draper and one of the other men were pulling the unconscious women to their feet, reviving them with sharp slaps. Tremayne, remembering his promise, grabbed Em's hair again and made a fist, holding it in front of her face with a menacing gleam in his dark eyes that was extremely convincing.

"Think you can handle her, Tremayne?" the captain asked.

"I can handle her, all right. She's gonna be black and blue before the day's over."

"Amuse yourself," Red Nick said.

Tremayne released Em's hair, seized her wrist, and dragged her toward the stairs leading down to the officers' quarters. Em stumbled along beside him quite willingly, eagerly, in fact. The captain watched them for a moment and then turned to look at me. I didn't lower my eyes. I met his stare calmly, neither defiant nor intimidated.

"Draper, get these women below," Red Nick ordered, his eyes never leaving my own. "Not this one," he added.

Draper barked orders and four men came to help him, herding the women together and shoving them roughly toward a dark, narrow opening at the other end of the ship. Corrie glanced back at me with despairing eyes as one of the men dragged her away. Nicholas Lyon and I stood facing each other as men rushed about, yelling to one another in coarse voices, as the great sails snapped in the wind and the ship moved over the waves with remarkable speed. I was perfectly immobile, much calmer than I had any right to be. He folded his arms across his chest, heavy maroon silk flowing, fluttering softly. His piercing blue eyes slowly undressed me and then dared me to betray some kind of reaction.

"In two days time, *The Sea Lyon* will rendezvous with another ship," he informed me. "The women will be transferred to that ship and sent on to our agents in Brazil. *The Sea Lyon* will return to my island."

I made no reply. I continued to meet his gaze with cool composure.

"Your little friend, the one Tremayne has taken a fancy to, will remain on board. She's his property now. I gave her to him."

"That was quite generous of you. I'm sure he appreciates it."

"What do you call yourself?"

"My name is Marietta Danver."

"You speak in a refined voice. Are you an aristocrat?"

"I was educated as one. I was shipped to America as an indentured servant over five years ago."

"What was your crime?"

"I was accused of stealing an emerald necklace."

"From an aristocrat?"

"I was a governess in the London home of Lord Robert Mallory. When I refused to become his mistress, he placed his wife's necklace in my valise, summoned the Bow Street runners, and claimed the jewels had been stolen."

"You were innocent, of course."

"Of course," I said.

"You're a very clever woman, I can sense that, and I'm glad to hear you're a thief instead of a fine lady. I hate the aristocracy. I hate everything they represent. Were you a blue blood, I would send you along with the other women without a moment's hesitation and without a single regret."

"And as I'm not an aristocrat?"

"I might decide to take you on to the island."

If he expected me to show relief, he was due a disappointment. I showed no emotion whatsoever, and that bothered him. His thin lips curled. His nostrils flared. I was taking a great risk, I knew, but I also knew that a grateful, submissive creature would have bored him, would have awakened his cruelest instincts. Nicholas Lyon had every intention of taking me down to his quarters and making love to me, and there was nothing I could do to prevent it, but if I played it just right, I could prevent him from sending me to South America with the other women. If I was to win, I had to arouse his interest as well as his lust, and instinct told me that a man like Lyon would find resistance and cool indifference far more intriguing than meek submission.

"I'd as soon go to Brazil with the others," I said.

That genuinely surprised him. "You'd prefer a brothel to my bed?"

"I'd prefer a brothel," I replied.

"You're unusually bold, Miss Danver. Unusually brave as well. You saw what happened to the skinny blonde."

"Do you think I'm afraid?" My voice was perfectly calm. "I've seen enough cruelty this past week to make me completely immune. Nothing you could do to me could possibly matter at this point."

"No?"

"I'll go with the others, Captain."

I turned and started walking quite coolly toward the other end of the ship. Nicholas Lyon took three long strides, grabbed my wrist and gave it an excruciatingly painful twist. Seizing my elbow with his other hand, he thrust my arm up between my shoulder blades, twisting even more, applying so much pressure I had to bite my lip to keep from screaming. Holding me in front of him, jerking my arm up another few inches, he forced me to walk toward the stairs, and when I struggled he gave my arm an upward yank that caused me to cry out in spite of myself. He forced me down the stairs and down a long narrow hallway with doors on either side, and I continued to struggle, knowing I must.

At the end of the hall an elegant mahogany door was slightly ajar. Nicholas Lyon kicked it all the way open and thrust me into a spacious, sumptuously appointed room. Letting go of my arm, he gave me a shove that sent me sprawling. I landed on my hands and knees on the plush gold carpet, hair falling in heavy waves across my cheeks. Sitting up on my knees, I brushed the hair back and turned to look at the man who stood in the doorway.

"In one of the adjoining rooms you'll find soap and water," he informed me. "Wash yourself. Scrub yourself thoroughly. In one of the chests you'll find a selection of gowns. Put one on. I'll be back after a while. I expect you to be waiting—and willing."

"And if I'm not?"

"I'll make you wish you'd never been born."

He turned and pulled the door shut behind him. I could hear his footsteps moving back down the hall. I stood up, rubbing my arm. It was so sore I could hardly move it, but the pain didn't matter at all. What mattered was that I had won the first round, even though he didn't realize it, and I was determined to win the second as well.

Eleven

Red Nick's quarters were elegant indeed, the walls of this main room paneled in dark mahogany that gleamed with a rich patina, exquisitely colored parchment maps hanging in ornate gold frames. There was an enormous desk, a dining table, several chairs, those at the dining table with high, carved backs and seats upholstered in plush yellow brocade. A gorgeous brown and bronze globe with gold lettering stood in one corner in a mahogany stand, and more maps, neatly rolled, stood in a mahogany rack beside it. Crystal pendants dangled from ornate wall sconces, and a chandelier hung over the dining table, pendants tinkling softly as the ship moved.

Brushing errant locks from my temple and rubbing my arm, I stepped into one of the adjoining rooms. It was much smaller, obviously his dressing room. His clothes hung in an enormous oak wardrobe, a collection of highly polished boots lined up neatly beneath. A pair of razor-sharp cutlasses hung crossed on the wall, the hilts silver and gold filigree, and there were pistols, too, at least seven of them arranged in an ornamental pattern. They were different shapes and sizes, all of them shining, all deadly.

I examined his clothes quite brazenly, the fine brocade frock coats, the heavy silk shirts, the narrow trousers. Nicholas Lyon lived well, and he had a taste for splendor. I ran my fingers over the smooth, leaf-brown satin dressing robe embroidered with darker brown *fleurs-de-lis*. The clothes told me quite a lot about him, as did the collection of weapons. Killing meant nothing to him, but cleanliness and fine things meant quite a lot. No wonder he wanted me to scrub myself thoroughly.

Behind a large Coromandel screen with coral, turquoise, and black patterns against a silver-gray background, I discovered a large porcelain tub filled with clean water that was still quite warm. Towels, soap, and sponges were piled on a table beside it. I took off my filthy clothes and slipped gratefully into the water, arching my back, sighing with pleasure as the water surrounded me, warm, soothing, wonderfully relaxing. The soap had an exotic, musky scent. I used a whole bar, scrubbing, rinsing, scrubbing again, reveling in the thick, foamy lather. I spent almost an hour in the tub, washing my hair three times, rinsing it, and when I stepped out I felt gloriously clean.

I dried myself with one of the large, soft towels, using another to rub my hair dry, and then I slipped into the leaf-brown dressing robe and walked into the third room, the gold carpet caressing my bare feet. The bedroom was larger than the dressing room, not nearly so large as the study, dominated by a huge mahogany fourposter with canopy and hanging of dark, embroidered gold brocade, the counterpane a deep, rich yellow satin. There was a dressing table with silver-backed brushes and combs, a hand mirror with silver frame. A full-length mirror hung on the wall, reflecting the sunlight that streamed in through the port holes.

Three large, ornately carved chests set against the wall, and I was just getting ready to examine their contents when the door leading into the study from the hallway opened. I turned, surprised to see Em tiptoeing across the room, eyes full of mischief.

"In here," I said.

Em jumped, slapping a hand over her heart. "Lord, luv, you scared the wits out of me!"

"What are you doing here? If he finds you—"

"He's not going to, luv. He and Michael are up on deck, doing whatever it is the captain and second-in-command do. I heard him bring you down here, and soon as I knew the coast was clear I popped over. My, these rooms are fancy, aren't they? Michael's room isn't nearly so grand."

"Did—did he beat you?"

"He gave me a spanking," Em said, smiling impishly, "but it was quite enjoyable, a tantalizing prelude to what came after. That was even *more* enjoyable. He's a brute, of course, a villain through and through, but I've had worse, luv, believe me. At least he's young and fairly nice lookin', strong as an ox, too, I might add."

"He seems to be quite taken with you."

"He is. Oh, he'd turn on me in a minute, break my jaw without giving it a second thought—these men are dangerous—but I can manage him. I've had a lot of experience. I see you've had a bath."

"There's a tub of water in the dressing room."

"If I had time I'd nip in there and have a splash myself, but I dare not stay too long. Michael really *would* beat me if I got caught in here, and the captain would undoubtedly give me fifty lashes. Scary, isn't he?"

"Very."

"He makes my blood run cold, I don't mind admittin' it. Are you going to be able to handle him?"

"I think so. It's not going to be easy."

"I don't envy you, luv. Tremayne's a cuddly baby bear

154

compared to Red Nick, and his men are a pack of puppies. That one, if he didn't like the way you looked when you got out of bed in the morning, he'd run you through and step over your body on his way to breakfast."

"You're quite right."

"Is he going to take you to the island?" she asked.

"He hasn't made up his mind yet."

"But you're going to make it up for him?"

I nodded. "I told him I preferred to go on to Brazil with the other women. He had to bring me down here by force."

"Clever," Em said, "very clever. A man like that, anything he can take without a fight he doesn't consider worth taking. He's going to have to rape you, and you're going to resist like mad."

"The first time."

"You're going to do just fine, luv. I knew you would. You want to be very careful, though."

"I intend to be."

Em adjusted one of the sleeves of her tattered pink dress, and the bright, perky quality vanished. Her eyes, usually so merry, were serious now and full of genuine concern. She might prattle and prance like a frivolous sprite, but Em was blessed with a strong native intelligence. Tough, shrewd, one of life's survivors, she faced me now with her hands on her hips, her frown making a tiny furrow on the bridge of her nose.

"We're in a very tricky spot, luv. It's going to take all the strength, all the courage we've got to pull through it. I keep thinking of that idiot Nadine, a victim of her own stupidity."

"That was a very brave thing you did, Em, rushing to her defense the way you did."

"I don't know what came over me, luv. I must have been out of my mind. That addle-pated little ninny deserved what she got, but all the same—" Em shook her head. "There's nothing we can do to help her now, just as there was nothing we could do to help Bessie. That—that sight is going to haunt me for the rest of my life."

"It's going to haunt me, too."

"We've got to put it out of our minds. We've got to concentrate on savin' our own skins—and Corrie's. We don't have much time. Michael told me the other women are going to be put on another ship in a couple of days. We have to work something out before then."

"I know."

"There's no hope of one of the men takin' a fancy to her, takin' her back to the island. I brought the subject up with Michael, said that little Negro girl is extremely pretty, said I was surprised one of the men hadn't appropriated her. He said Red Nick has an aversion to Negroes, won't have 'em on the island."

"I have a plan, Em. I think it may work. What you just told me isn't going to make it any easier."

Em started to speak but cut herself short as we heard footsteps coming down the hall that led to the study door. Her face went white. Seizing her hand, I pulled her over behind the bed and shoved her down. She crawled nimbly under it as the study door opened and Michael Tremayne strolled across the room. He took two maps from the rack beside the globe, unrolled them, and began to examine them with close scrutiny. After a moment he rolled one back up, stuck it back in the rack, and left the room with the other map under his arm. He hadn't even glanced toward the bedroom.

"It's all right now, Em," I said as he closed the door. "You can come on out."

Em scrambled from under the bed and stood up, visibly shaken, chestnut locks falling to her shoulders in wild disarray. She brushed her skirts and straightened the low-cut bodice that barely contained her breasts. Moving over to the doorway, she peered into the study and breathed a sigh of relief.

"It was Tremayne," I told her. "He came to fetch a map."

"Hope he didn't peek into his room to see how I was doin'," she said. "I thought my heart was going to leap right out of me. I'd better skip on over to his room before someone else pops in on us."

"Be careful, Em."

"You, too, luv."

She gave me a quick hug and then scurried across the plush gold carpet to the study door. Cocking her ear against it, she hesitated, listening a moment before easing it open and stepping into the hallway. I was shaken, too. Slipping over here as she had was a foolhardy thing to have done, a terrible risk, and I shuddered to think what would have happened had she been discovered. Em was a remarkably brave young woman, remarkably perceptive as well. Talking to her had strengthened my conviction that I was using the right approach with Red Nick.

Moving over to the three chests, I opened the first one, lifting the heavy lid with considerable effort. It was filled with gorgeous Irish linen napkins and tablecloths, with sumptuous blue silk draperies, and with bolts of cloth of silver, of pink and soft beige velvet. The second chest contained a collection of Sevres china, dozens and dozens of pieces, each exquisitely patterned with royal blue and coral pink designs and lavishly adorned with gold. King Louis himself might have dined off such china, I thought, closing the lid.

The third chest contained a small case covered with white leather worked with gold and, carefully wrapped in tissue, several gowns that had never been worn. I took them out one by one, marveling at their elaborate beauty, finally selecting a deep saffron yellow satin completely overlaid with golden lace. It had a petticoat of frail yellow tissue cloth with at least a dozen skirts in varying shades of yellow and gold. I set gown and petticoat aside, folded the others up and put them back into the chest, and then I opened the lovely white leather case.

Springs within the case caused several blue velvet trays to lift up as I raised the lid. The bottom tray held six delicate crystal bottles with fancy stoppers, each bottle nestling in its own nitch and filled with perfume. The next tray held a silver comb, a brush with silver handle and silver back patterned with gold flowers and leaves. The other trays held tiny sable-tipped brushes, a white silk box filled with beauty patches, and an array of jars and pots made of fine white porcelain traced with gold. I had never seen such an elaborate makeup case, had never seen such a variety of eye shadow and rouge and powder and lip rouge. The case had been designed in France, I knew, and I suspected that it had been created for a queen.

I took the case over to the dressing table without a moment's hesitation. Removing the brush and comb, I began to work on my hair, combing out the tangles, brushing and brushing until the rich, copper-red locks gleamed with red-gold highlights and fell in a lustrous cascade that framed my face with heavy, natural waves. I spent considerable time selecting the right shade of rouge, the right eye shadow, tinting my cheeks with a soft, pale pink, rubbing a suggestion of mauve-gray shadow over my lids. I selected a deeper pink lip rouge, using it sparingly, knowing that the secret of makeup was a subtle enhancement of natural coloring.

I opened one of the bottles of perfume. The scent was tantalizing, elusive, vaguely suggesting a field of poppies under a hot summer sun. I dabbed it behind my earlobes, between my breasts, touching wrists and the curves of my elbows lightly with the stopper, using just enough to give a teasing hint of fragrance. Replacing the stopper, putting the bottle back in its blue velvet nest, I reflected that this was the first time I had deliberately prepared myself for a rape. I intended to be in full control during every moment, but Nicholas Lyon must never suspect that. I would allow him to conquer and crush, allow him the brutal domination his nature required, but I would be the victor.

I replaced brush, comb, and pots, closing the makeup case and moving over to the bed. I untied the leaf brown sash and let the dressing robe fall to the floor in a shiny heap. I intended to leave it there. It would undoubtedly irritate him. I intended to irritate him. I intended to tease and taunt, working on him until he was seething with passionate fury, and then I intended to fight him with all my might, resorting to melodrama if need be. Nicholas Lyon was going to have a highly satisfying time. When it was over, when he had satiated the passionate fury I would arouse, he was not even going to consider sending me to Brazil, even though I might pretend to want him to do just that. I planned all this quite coldly, feeling not the slightest shame.

There was no room for shame. Survival was everything now. I had wanted to die, would gladly have killed myself after Derek was murdered, but that was behind me now. Since that night, I had endured horror far worse than any before, worse than the sordid degradation I had suffered at the hands of the Bow Street runners, worse than the terrifying brutalities inflicted on me when Helmut Schnieder finally went mad, and I could endure anything now. If I had to plot and scheme and play the harlot in order to survive, I would do so willingly. I was going to save myself—I was going to save Corrie, too—and one day Roger Hawke would pay for what he had done.

Completely naked, I slipped into the petticoat. The frail yellow tissue cloth was semi-transparent, the bodice extremely tight, extremely low, and the skirts lifted, floated, spreading out like fragile petals in glorious shades of yellow and gold. I put the gown on over it and stepped back over to the mirror, reaching around to fasten the tiny hooks in back. The rich yellow satin gleamed beneath the layer of glittering gold lace woven in elaborate floral patterns. The gown had been created for a smaller woman. It was much too tight at the waist and so low I hardly dared breathe. The narrow puffed sleeves fell completely off the shoulder, the thin petticoat straps beneath. The bodice was form-hugging, barely covering my nipples, and the full, full skirt swelled out over the underskirts like a great golden-yellow bell.

I stood in front of the mirror, barefoot, examining myself with cool objectivity. Everything was perfect, the hair, the face, the spectacular, provocative gown. I wondered idly about the woman for whom it had been intended. The contents of the three chests were obviously booty Lyon was taking back to the island, the gowns and makeup case gifts for the woman named Maria whom Em had mentioned. Maria gave herself airs, Em had told me, and Red Nick was growing tired of her, looking for a replacement.

Moving back into the study, I examined the parchment maps on the wall, gave the globe a twirl, restless now, nervous, too, although I tried to deny it. The chandelier over the dining table tinkled, barely audible, and I could feel the ship moving with a slight swaying motion that was hardly noticeable. I strolled back into the dressing room to examine the cutlasses and the collection of pistols. I took one of them down, testing its weight, checking it closely. Hanging it back in place, I frowned and returned to the other room. An hour passed slowly, so slowly, and then another, and my nerves were stretched to the breaking point. It was only with the greatest effort that I managed to hold onto even a semblance of composure.

It must have been at least another hour before the door opened and Lyon came in with Michael Tremayne. I was standing by one of the chairs, my hand resting on its back. Neither man paid the slightest attention to me. I might have been invisible. Tremayne unrolled a map and spread it out over the desk, pointing out an area with his forefinger. If his calculations were correct, he stated, the French vessel would be in those waters in three or four days, bound for Louisiana and carrying a very rich cargo. It wouldn't be out of their way to intercept it, he added, and although it would undoubtedly be heavily armed, they could take it easily enough.

"The usual ruse," he said. "It still works dandy, fools 'em every time."

"You're certain about your information?"

Tremayne nodded. "Got it first hand. I was dressed like a toff, wearin' frock coat and cravat, mixin' among 'em with a cigar in my mouth and passin' as a businessman. No one questioned my right to be there. I kept my mouth shut, of course, didn't want my voice to give me away. I just strolled about, lookin' grave and listenin'."

"You did well, Tremayne."

"Figured I might as well make myself useful while I was waitin' for Quince and his men to round up the wenches. Are we going to take it?"

"I see no reason why not," the captain replied. "It'll keep the men from getting too restless before we get back to the island."

They talked for a few minutes longer, and then Tremayne left. Nicholas Lyon rolled up the map and placed it in the rack. My nerves were screaming silently, and I was weak from hunger, yet somehow I was able to look at him with a cool, steady gaze when he finally decided to give me his attention. He studied me for a long time in silence, that heavy dark copper wave dipping down over his brow, his blue eyes gradually darkening. He must have been at least six-foot-three, I thought, and that excessively lean, hard frame made him seem taller still. His sharp, bony features and the upward slanting eyebrows brought to mind a sleek, diabolical fox.

"The gown suits you," he said.

"I assume it was stolen, along with the rest of the things."

"You examined the chests? They were in the possession of

a minor ambassador who, unhappily, chanced to be on a ship we took two weeks ago. I believe the chests were intended as gifts to a cousin of King Louis, a lady of renowned beauty.''

"What happened to the ambassador?"

"He walked the plank, screaming every step of the way. Draper finally had to give him a prod. The men were quite amused.''

"And you?"

"I find such things tiresome, believe a clean, quick kill much more efficient, but the men relish their fun. I feel compelled to oblige them.''

I looked at him with disgust and horror, deliberately allowing my composure to slip a little, and that pleased him. A faint smile flickered on his lips, and the blue eyes gleamed with sardonic amusement. He clearly intended to toy with me, savoring every moment, and I didn't intend to disappoint him. Visibly repressing a shudder, I regained my composure with what appeared to be great difficulty, drawing myself up and facing him with cool defiance.

"You're utterly heartless," I said.

"Quite true," he admitted.

"You can kill me, too."

"I could," he said, "quite easily. I could take that lovely throat in my hands and choke the life out of you in a matter of seconds, but I have different plans.''

"I prefer death!"

"I seriously doubt that," he replied.

The words seemed to catch in his throat. That harsh, metallic voice had a new, low pitch that was like a scratchy purr, strangely melodic and extremely sensuous. Hands resting on his thighs, dark maroon sleeves ballooning, the heavy silk bagging loosely where it was tucked into his waistband, he looked at me with heavy lids half-shrouding blue eyes that were filled now with anticipation. I could see the desire swelling between his legs, pressing against the snug black breeches. He moved slowly toward me. I stood my ground with chin held high, my shoulders trembling slightly for his benefit.

He wanted a victim. He wanted to break me, humiliate me, and it would be a mistake to make it too easy for him. I was cool, aloof, gazing at him with haughty blue eyes as he stopped in front of me, so close I could smell skin and sweat and silk.

"Afraid?" he inquired.

"I'm beyond fear. I don't care what happens to me. You don't seem to understand that. You can kill me. You can send me to Brazil. It doesn't matter in the least."

"No?"

"The—the man I loved was murdered before my eyes. I was raped repeatedly by one of the 'agents' who supplies your men with women—a man named Hart. I have no reason for living."

"You're going to live," he promised. "You're going to live in splendor."

"Not with you."

"You seem quite sure of that."

"I'll kill myself first."

"You're going to live with me. You're going to be my woman. What's more, you're going to love it. I'm going to make you love it."

I said nothing, but my eyes told him that would be impossible, that I found him thoroughly reprehensible and would prefer death to his embrace. It excited him. I could see the excitement in his eyes, carefully contained, held in check as he stood there with his hands on his thighs.

"You're no stranger to men," he said.

"I've known a number of men," I replied.

"Intimately," he added.

"That's quite true, but I've always been extremely selective—when I had a choice."

He smiled at that, a wry, sardonic smile that lifted those thin pink lips at one corner. His face was deeply tanned. His dark copper hair was thick and heavy, gleaming with red-brown highlights. His hands were tan, too. He placed them on my shoulders, and when I tried to pull away those strong, sinewy fingers dug into my flesh with bruising force. I winced. He pulled me to him and curled one arm around the back of my neck and lowered his head, lips parting as they neared my own. I beat against his chest with my fists. I kicked his shin with my bare foot. He kissed me savagely, relishing my struggles, crushing me to him with arms strong as steel. I threw my hands up and caught his hair and tried to pull his head back, and he kissed me with even more fury.

When he finally released me, I swung my hand back and slammed my palm across his face with all the strength I had. The slap made an explosion of sound, and my palm stung violently. Red Nick didn't blink. Not a muscle in his face moved. I backed slowly away from him, edging toward the dressing-room door. He watched with wry detachment as I stepped into the room and returned a moment later with the pistol in my hand. I leveled it at him, my eyes hard even though my hand was shaking.

"If—if you take one step toward me, I'll shoot."

"Will you?"

"I mean what I say. I'll put a bullet through your heart."

"I think not," he said.

He sauntered toward me. I pulled the trigger, tensing in anticipation of the blast. There was no blast, was, instead, the loud, metallic click I knew there would be, but my performance was superbly convincing nevertheless. I looked at the gun with puzzled, worried eyes, pulling the trigger again and again as he approached. I dropped the gun and shook my head, showing fear now for the first time.

He reached for me. I darted past him, rushing toward the door, and he lunged, catching me around the waist, whirling me around. I struggled with all my might, fighting viciously, sincerely, trying my best to hurt him. His mouth settled into a relentless line. His eyes were hard, dark with determination. He was fully aroused now, ready to plunder, the cat-and-mouse games over. I fought, and he fended off my blows with ease, catching my wrists as I tried to claw his face, shoving me back, back, finally shoving me against the wall and pinioning me to it with his body. I tried to kick. I tried to hit. He took my throat in one hand and squeezed steadily until I was weak and dizzy and unable to struggle more. Still holding me in that deadly grip, he reached down with his other hand and raised my skirts, lifting them up over my thighs, and then he undid his breeches.

He released my throat and took hold of my wrists and spread my arms wide, plunging into me with one savage thrust that caused me to gasp. I continued to struggle as he

163

pumped vigorously, his chest and shoulders pressing against me, his hands pinning my wrists against the wall. I squirmed, my face half-buried in the curve of his shoulder, my mouth open and pressed against the heavy maroon silk. His hands tightened on my wrists, pulling my arms wider. His body tensed, crushing me against the wall as that final thrust brought the shuddering release he craved. He gave a pained, grunting noise that was half-growl, half-moan, his body still tense, and then, after a moment, he sighed and withdrew, letting go of my wrists. His knees wobbled slightly as he stepped back and pulled up his breeches, tucking his shirt back in.

He stepped to the door and barked an order. I leaned against the wall a few moments and then stood up, brushing my skirts and adjusting my bodice. I caught hold of the back of a chair, steadying myself for a few more moments before going into the dressing room to wash. When I returned, a clean-cheeked youth in stocking cap and jersey was placing food on the table which had been set for two. Nicholas Lyon was leaning against the desk, arms folded across his chest, chin lowered, the heavy copper wave dipping over his brow. He ignored me as I passed into the bedroom to brush my hair and repair my makeup. I heard the youth leave a few minutes later. Red Nick stepped to the bedroom door, and I lifted my eyes to observe him in the mirror.

"You're quite cool," he remarked.

"Would you prefer tears and anguished cries?" I asked. "I've been raped before, and I find hysterics a waste of time and energy."

"Cool as can be," he said. "I admire that."

"You're much stronger than I, Captain Lyon. You can overpower me, and you can break me physically, but you can't break my spirit."

"I've no desire to," he replied.

I stood up, paying no attention to him now, smoothing an eyebrow and adding a final touch of lip rouge. When I turned around, he was still lounging in the doorway, watching me closely through narrowed eyes, a wry curl on his thin pink lips. I moved toward the doorway, and he stepped aside to let me pass, extremely intrigued by my proud, glacial manner. Had I been abject, submissive, humiliated, he would have been bored, and I had no intention of boring him. Seating myself at the table, I waited coolly for him to join me.

"You could have spared yourself that unpleasantness," he said, taking his seat.

"Indeed?"

"You could have made it easy on yourself."

"No doubt I could have."

He poured wine into a silver goblet. There was a roasted chicken, a slab of beef, bread, cheese, a bowl of fruit. He ate with relish, taking an occasional sip of wine, tearing the chicken apart with ease. I ate nothing whatsoever. Even though I longed to tear into the food with a relish equal to his, I felt it would be unseemly under the circumstances. I sat there with chin held high, perfectly poised. Lyon pushed his plate aside and poured more wine into his goblet.

"Not hungry?" he inquired.

"I've no desire to eat at your table."

"Or sleep in my bed, it seems."

I gazed at him with level blue eyes, not deigning to answer. The pirate smiled to himself, a wry, sarcastic smile that curled lightly on his lips. He took a swallow of wine and set the goblet down.

"I suppose you still prefer to go to Brazil with the others," he said.

"I don't imagine my preference matters to you in the least."

"Not in the least," he told me. "You're a very lucky young woman. I've decided to take you back to the island with me. You're going to be my woman. It's an honor you'll soon come to appreciate."

"I doubt that."

He cut off a hunk of cheese and ate it, studying me with idle speculation in those piercing blue eyes. He seemed to be asking himself what it would take to vanquish my aloof composure. He had taken my body, had plundered violently, but there had been no real challenge involved. It had been merely a matter of superior strength. The true challenge faced him now, and it was one he was determined to master. He finished the cheese and ate a piece of fruit, his eyes never straying.

"You'll live like a queen," he said.

"Do you really think that matters to me?"

"It will eventually come to matter a great deal. One soon grows accustomed to luxury, to fine clothes, to jewels."

"I've no interest in such things."

The wry smile flickered on his lips again. "You're a woman. You're interested."

"Do you really want to have a woman who hates you with all her heart and soul, a woman who will gladly drive a knife through your ribs the first chance she gets?"

"You won't feel that way for long."

"I'll never come to you willingly," I said.

"You will," he promised, "not only willingly but eagerly as well. Before this day's over you're going to be purring like a kitten."

I looked at him with that same level gaze, toying with the empty silver goblet beside my plate. Red Nick smiled.

"Think not?" he inquired. "We'll see."

He stood up, a dark gleam in his eyes as he thought of pleasures to come. He took my hand and pulled me to my feet. I didn't intend to fight him again. I didn't intend to show any emotion whatsoever, at least not for a while. He had already proved his superior strength. Now he intended to prove his prowess. He led me into the bedroom and undressed me, and when I stood naked before him he examined me as he might examine a piece of sculpture he was thinking of buying. He circled me slowly, examining me from every angle, and then he placed his hands over my breasts, his palms rubbing my nipples, his fingers gently squeezing the soft mounds of flesh. I showed no reaction whatsoever as he continued to fondle and squeeze, as he lifted me up in his arms and lowered me onto the rich yellow satin counterpane. He took off his clothes and stood with his hands resting on his thighs, tall and lean and firmly muscled, smooth skin evenly tanned.

"The first time was for me," he said. "This time will be for you, Marietta."

He sat beside me, leaned over me, kissed my throat, my breasts, drawing me slowly into his arms. He kissed and caressed and stroked, summoning responses I refused to give. He lowered me, mounted me, made love to me slowly and with a taunting precision that stirred purely physical sensations inside me, sensations I found it difficult to conceal. Conceal them I did, forcing myself to remain rigid beneath him. He doubled his efforts, holding back, delaying his pleasure, striving mightily to stir me. Finally, unable to hold back any longer, he allowed release, trembled, fell limp on top of me.

He made love to me again later on, his blue eyes angry and determined, and again I managed to withhold any sign of response. The sunlight streaming through the portholes had turned from yellow to a dark, wavering orange when he made love to me the last time, when I finally moaned and stirred and clung to him and shuddered with pleasure and gave him the responses his ego demanded, my soft cries and passionate caresses assuring him he was a lover beyond compare. He had won, and he savored his triumph as I held him to me and ran my hands over his back and shoulders, rubbing the smooth skin, sighing, submissive at last. Neither of us spoke. There was no need for words. After a while he got up and slipped on the leaf brown dressing robe and gave me a triumphant look.

I stretched and gathered the sheets over my bosom and sat up, meeting his eyes with a new composure, conquered but no longer a victim, proud but no longer defiant, accepting his victory calmly and with a cool, worldly attitude that pleased him immensely. Nicholas Lyon didn't want a slave. He wanted a sophisticated and intelligent mistress. He looked at me a moment longer, an arrogant, self-satisfied smile on his lips, and then he gathered up his boots and clothes and went into the dressing room. I saw him pass through the study a short while later, fully dressed, his hair damp, an even darker shade of copper because of the wetness.

He left, going back up on deck to attend to duties, and I returned to the dressing room and bathed thoroughly, scrubbing away the perspiration and smells of sex. I dried myself and perfumed my body again before sliding between the cool silken sheets. Waiting for him in the darkness, lulled by the slight swaying motion of the ship, I felt a sense of triumph that matched his own. He was thoroughly amoral, a dangerous animal who knew no mercy, who killed without the slightest qualm, but I had bested him at every turn. I had planned everything that happened and had been in complete control the whole time, even though he believed the whip hand was his.

It must have been well after eleven when he returned. He lighted candles in the study and sat down at his desk. I could see him through the open door. He worked for some time, his eyes grim, a frown making a deep furrow above the bridge of his nose as he studied charts and made notations on a sheet of paper. After half an hour or so, he put away the charts and stood up and blew out the candles, striding into the bedroom. He undressed in the darkness and climbed into bed, pulling me to him roughly as though I were a pillow, not wanting to make love again just yet, wanting merely to savor his new possession. I sighed and placed my hand on the back of his neck, snuggling up against him as though not fully awake. Thin rays of moonlight wavered through the portholes, making pale silver patterns on the floor, intensifying the velvety black shadows that danced on the walls. Nicholas Lyon clutched me tightly and slept, never once suspecting that I had him exactly where I wanted him.

Twelve

The water was a deep indigo blue, faintly touched with purple on the horizon, the sky a pale pearl-gray lightly tinted with blue. Overhead the great sails swelled majestically, propelling us smoothly over the waves. Draper stood at the wheel, legs apart, hands steady as he steered, and Michael Tremayne moved about like an arrogant young bull, making an inspection and snapping terse orders. There was an air of expectation as the great cannons were cleaned and readied for firing, as the fierce, efficient crew moved briskly about their duties.

"They're expecting the French ship," Em told me. "If Michael's calculations are correct, we should spot it sometime this afternoon. They plan to take it."

"They'se goin' to sink it?" Corrie asked.

Em nodded grimly. "It's not going to be a pretty sight, luv."

Corrie's lovely dark eyes grew wide with apprehension, and her shoulders trembled just a little, but she didn't sob. She made a visible effort to be brave. She stood beside me in the pale orange-tan cotton dress which she had washed and mended, frail, docile, still fearful that something would happen to her even though I had assured her that she was safe now, that the captain had agreed to let her stay with me and none of the men would hurt her. She had a dark, tiny room down near the galley where, by candlelight, she was altering the sumptuous gowns that had been intended for King Louis' cousin. Corrie was a wonderfully skillful seamstress, and the one time I had let her do my hair she had performed miracles with brush and comb.

The Sea Lyon had made a rendezvous with the other ship yesterday afternoon, and the rest of the women were now on their way to Brazil. Poor Nadine had protested vehemently, sobbing and shrieking, but her fate was sealed. I tried not to think of that frightening scene, tried not to feel selfish relief that Corrie, Em, and I had been spared that particular fate. I knew full well that what lay in store for us might prove to be equally as bad, perhaps even worse. I squeezed Corrie's hand and suggested she go down to her room and try to rest. The girl nodded meekly.

"There may be some trouble, Corrie. There may be an awful lot of noise. You stay in your room. Don't be afraid."

"I'll try not to be, Miz Marietta."

The girl crossed the deck and disappeared down one of the hatches. Em and I continued to stand on the poop deck, out of the way and completely ignored by the men. Em was wearing a gown Tremayne had found for her, a deep violet taffeta lavishly trimmed with black lace ruffles, and I was wearing sapphire-blue brocade. Em looked quite fetching as she twirled the black lace parasol Tremayne had given her.

"I love this gown," she remarked. "I'd grown terribly weary of the pink, luv, and it was in shambles. Michael dug this out of a trunk—it fits nicely. He *insisted* I wear it, told me not to give him any lip when I said it was much too grand.''

"That's strange," I remarked. "Red Nick insisted I dress elaborately, too. Corrie washed and mended the gown I wore through the swamps, and I intended to wear it. He pulled this one out of the chest, ordered me to put it on."

"Michael told me not to forget the parasol. He said the parasol was very important—and it wasn't because he was worried about my complexion. They plan to use us in some way."

"I have the same feeling."

"I asked Michael about it. He scowled at me and told me to do what he said if I didn't want a beatin'. He's marvelous in bed, and he's really quite taken with me, but he can be terribly surly and rough. He's got a vicious temper. I have to mind myself around him and be careful not to rouse it."

Em twirled her parasol and watched Tremayne stride about the deck in his high brown boots, snug brown breeches, and black and tan striped jersey. His sun-streaked brown hair framed his face in ragged locks, and the tight jersey emphasized his powerful build.

"I suppose I could have done worse," Em remarked. "I could have ended up with Draper. He had his eye on me, luv. Still has."

"We've been very lucky, Em."

"Luck had very little to do with it," she observed. "I can think of a number of places I'd rather be than on this ship."

"You could be on *The Crimson Hawk*."

"Don't I know it, luv. Poor Nadine. She's not going to last very long, I fear. None of them are. Thank God you were able to save Corrie."

"It wasn't easy," I replied. "The first time I brought the subject up he flatly refused. He said he didn't want a nigger underfoot. He said he had servants on the island."

"What did you do?"

"I told him that Corrie was a wizard with needle and thread and that she could perform miracles with my hair. I told him that if I was going to be his mistress I wanted to look the best I could and Corrie could help. He still refused."

"And?"

170

"I pouted. I was very cool, very remote. He finally relented. He told me to keep her out of his way and said the first time she got uppity he would get rid of her. Corrie's terrified of him, of course. I've given her very careful instructions on how to conduct herself when he's around."

"Rotten bastard," Em said.

"At least she's safe, Em. Temporarily."

"And that's something," she agreed. "We're going to get out of this, luv. They've got pistols and knives and swords, but we've got our own weapons. Thank God we know how to use them."

"It's not easy, Em."

"I know. Michael's quite fond of me already, although he'd go to the stake before he'd admit it, but I keep reminding myself he's a bloodthirsty pirate. I know he could turn on me at any minute."

"I have the same feeling about Red Nick."

"Is everything under control?" she asked.

"He's quite satisfied. I intend to keep him that way."

Nicholas Lyon came up on deck at that moment, looking unusually resplendent in glossy brown leather boots, brown satin breeches, and a gorgeous bronze satin frock coat trimmed with gold braid, cascades of gold lace at the wrists. He wore a dashing broad-brimmed hat of brown felt, bronze and white plumes sweeping down over one side. He spoke to Tremayne for a moment. Tremayne nodded and went below, and Lyon examined the cannons, giving terse instructions to those who were to man them, and then he joined Em and I on the poop deck.

"You both look quite elegant," he remarked.

"Thank you," I said.

"I see Tremayne found a gown for you," he said, addressing Em. "We keep a supply on hand for just such occasions as these."

"What kind of occasion would that be?" Em asked.

"We're going to welcome compatriots of ours."

"I didn't know pirates had compatriots," she retorted.

Red Nick gave her a cold, thoughtful look that would have sent shivers up the spine of a less courageous lass. Em faced him without fear, saucy and defiant, and after a moment a wry smile twisted on his lips.

"It seems Tremayne hasn't performed his duties," he observed.

"He's performed 'em, all right. My backside's black and blue. Want a peek, Captain?"

Red Nick ignored her. "When we spot the ship," he said, "when they are close enough to see you, I want you both to wave. Where's the little nigger? She might add a touch of authenticity."

"She's in her room," I said. "I—I don't want her up here."

He elevated one slanted brow, his blue eyes hard as stone.

"She'd be terrified. She'd give the show away," I added, thinking quickly.

"She might at that," he agreed. "I suppose two lovely ladies, their courtiers and a dozen French soldiers will have to do."

"Just what I've always wanted to be," Em said, "bait."

"I see I shall have to speak to Tremayne," Lyon observed dryly.

Em started to make another saucy reply, but I gave her a warning look. She restrained herself, and Red Nick moved on to inspect twelve men who had just come from below, all twelve dressed in French naval uniforms. He gave them a careful scrutiny, ordering one to remove a gold hoop from his earlobe, ordering another to tie his hair back.

"I don't think I'm going to like this," Em remarked. "I might as well confess it, luv, I hate bloodshed. It makes me terribly edgy. I've a feeling we're going to see a lot of it."

"Do you think we could signal them somehow?"

"Warn them, you mean? Not a chance, luv."

Em gave the black lace parasol an extra twirl. "Maybe *they'll* win," she said. "Maybe we'll be rescued right away. That would be ripping. I've always had a weakness for Frenchmen."

"Em, you must learn to curb your tongue with the captain. Tremayne might tolerate your sauce, he might even find it appealing, but Nicholas Lyon is—he has no sense of humor."

"You're telling me," she replied. "I know I'm going to have to watch myself, luv, but sometimes I just don't think. This tongue of mine has gotten me into *so* much trouble."

"It's gonna get you into a whole lot more," Tremayne informed her.

Neither of us had heard him approach. He had changed into an outfit almost as resplendent as the captain's, black boots, blue satin breeches, and a matching frock coat trimmed in silver. His wide black hat was adorned with long, sweeping black and white plumes.

"Don't *you* look fancy," Em said.

"The captain spoke to me just now, said you'd been lippy, said I was ta give you a good beatin' when we get below. I mean to, too."

"I can hardly wait, luv, You do it so well."

He scowled, and Em sighed wearily and reached up to adjust the slant of his hat, setting it at a more rakish angle. When she was satisfied with the tilt, she patted his cheek and ran her thumb over his full lower lip.

"You actually look *handsome* in that getup," she told him. "You keep wearin' it, and I might even let you sleep with me."

"I ain't jestin', Emmeline. You're gonna get it."

"So are you," she promised.

Tremayne scowled again, obviously infatuated, a sullen bulldog bewitched in spite of himself by a playful kitten. He glared at her menacingly, hoping to intimidate her.

"He give you your instructions?" he growled.

"Yes, luv. We're supposed to stand here and look lovely and smile and wave and lure the Frenchmen to their doom."

"One false move," he said, "just one, and you'll feed the sharks. I mean it, Emmeline. This is serious business, and you're part of it now."

"Some girls have all the luck."

"I'm gonna keep my eye on you," he warned.

"Don't worry, Handsome. We'll play our roles to perfection."

He stalked away, the long black and white plumes billowing. There was a loud cry from the pirate perched high up in the crow's nest. Tremayne snatched a telescope from one of the men, put it to his eye and tensely studied the horizon. Far, far away, where the blue waters turned purple before merging with the pearl-gray sky, a tiny black speck was visible to the

173

naked eye. Tremayne put the telescope down and began to bark orders in a gruff, excited voice.

The skull and crossbones was lowered, a large, vivid French flag raised to the top of the highest mast where it fluttered in glory. The crew scurried about making last-minute preparations, priming the cannons, piling balls in place, readying the long tapers for lighting, checking knives, pistols and cutlasses. The black speck on the horizon gradually took shape, a tiny toy boat now, bobbing on the water like a cork in the distance, growing larger as *The Sea Lyon* drew nearer, skimming lightly over the waves toward its victim.

"All right, men!" Tremayne shouted.

Grappling hooks and planks were brought out, placed within easy reach. The ropes dangling from the masts were checked. Those pirates not in French uniform crouched out of sight, four huddling around each cannon on the leeward side, the others hiding behind boxes and barrels and hatches. One uniformed man took over the wheel from Draper. Another manned the tiller. The other ten idled about the deck in strategic spots, highly visible. Tremayne and Red Nick joined us on the poop deck. The French vessel loomed larger now, and I could see the sailors moving about on deck, brawny lads in tight white breeches and blue and white striped jerseys. A man in a handsome uniform with shiny epaulettes was holding a telescope to his eye, observing us closely.

"Heavily armed," Tremayne observed. "Heavily manned, too. Guess that's to be expected, considerin' what they're carryin'."

"I'd say they outnumber us two to one," Red Nick replied.

"Ain't no problem, Captain."

"I shouldn't think so."

I tried to control the nervous tremors inside as I watched the French ship loom larger still. Red Nick looked at me with indifferent blue eyes.

"You don't like this, do you?" he inquired.

"They—they're all doomed," I said.

"Quite so," he agreed.

"They haven't a chance."

"Not a chance. Smile," he said.

"I can't."

"Smile!" he ordered. "Wave!"

The breach between the two ships narrowed. The French vessel was large and solid, built to withstand just such an attack as the one Lyon planned. I could see the men on deck clearly now. They seemed terribly young, their faces bright and merry, and all of them were doomed. All of them were going to die, were going to be horribly butchered. I could feel myself trembling. The man with the telescope wore a suspicious expression. He gave an order and men raced to man the cannon, ready to fire if need be. I couldn't stand it. I had to go below. I started to turn. Nicholas Lyon took hold of my wrist and gave it a twist that sent needles of pain all the way up to my shoulder.

"Smile," he repeated.

I forced a smile on my lips. I raised my free hand and waved. Michael Tremayne was standing very close to Em, his arm behind her, a pistol jammed between her shoulder blades. Em's eyes were damp, but she was smiling, too. *The Sea Lyon* sailed nearer its prey, the sails ballooning majestically in the wind, the French flag fluttering high overhead. The pirates in uniform began to shout and wave now, greeting their supposed compatriots with great zest. Nicholas Lyon released my wrist and removed his plumed hat and executed an elegant bow to the captain across the water.

"Bonjour!" he shouted.

The captain returned the greeting, still suspicious.

"We're a passenger ship," Red Nick called, in perfect French. "A storm blew us slightly off course three days ago. We're relieved to see you. We're short on water. Have you any spare barrels?"

"We can give you three or four," the captain shouted.

"A million thanks!"

Suspicions gone now, the captain spoke to his men. They moved away from the cannons. Several of them began to smile and wave. The ships drew closer, moving slowly toward each other. Tremayne was grinning like a little boy who had just been given an armload of brightly wrapped presents. A grin played on Red Nick's lips, too, but his blue eyes were lethal. He waited until the other ship was no more than fifty yards away, then raised his arm and lowered it in a sharp, abrupt signal. The cannons boomed. Em screamed.

The Sea Lyon rocked so violently that I was almost thrown off my feet.

Four large, gaping holes appeared in the hull of the French vessel, and two of the masts came tumbling down like felled timber, the sails ripping, the masts crashing onto the deck, one of them landing on the captain, knocking him down and crushing him horribly. The pirates swarmed over the deck, yelling lustily, tossing the grappling hooks across the water, pulling the French ship alongside *The Sea Lyon*. Red Nick threw his hat aside, peeled off his bronze satin coat, and seized the cutlass Tremayne held ready. The two of them leaped eagerly into the fray as planks were placed across the railings of the two ships and the pirates raced across them, others scrambling up the rigging and grabbing hold of ropes to swing through the air and land on the other deck with barbaric cries.

The huge iron balls tearing into the hull and felling the masts had taken the French sailors by complete surprise, and the ship had pitched so violently that many of them had been thrown sprawling onto the deck, arms and legs akimbo. Red Nick and his men fell upon them with vicious energy, cutting and slashing and firing their pistols, yelling like demons from the depths of hell. It took the Frenchmen several moments to recover from the shock. During those brief moments, their ranks were depleted, the deck already running with bright red blood.

"Jesus!" Em cried. "Oh, sweet Jesus!"

Her green-brown eyes were filled with anger and horror, and with tears as well. She dropped her parasol and clung to me, and neither of us could look away. We were paralyzed, held captive by the multiple scenes of carnage taking place before our eyes, a noisy, swirling, constantly shifting kaleidoscope of bloodshed. I saw a blond French youth get to his feet and seize his pistol, saw Draper drive a sword through him before he could fire. The youth's eyes grew wider and wider, his lips moving in a silent prayer as blood spurted and he sank to his knees.

Another sailor with wavy brown hair struggled furiously as two laughing pirates seized him and lifted him in the air and hurled him over the railing, his body falling to the waves below, followed by another, another, yet another. Directly across from where Em and I stood four French sailors were fighting with Draper and two other men, fighting with super-human strength and determination as the three pirates closed in, cutlasses flashing. One of the sailors managed to fire his pistol, and the pirate beside Draper grabbed his stomach and crashed to the deck. Draper knocked the pistol out of the sailor's hand and, too close to thrust with his blade, gave the lad a fierce shove that sent him crashing against the railing with such force that the wood splintered and he went spinning into the water. Draper and the remaining pirate cut down the other three sailors, heaved them overboard, and rushed to find more victims.

It was horrible, horrible, so horrible I could hardly believe it was happening. It was something out of hell, demons yelling, blood gushing, flames leaping as one of the sails caught fire, and I watched with stunned disbelief, my senses numb with shock. The burning mast and sail crackled, toppled, falling into the water, a sheet of flame covering everything like a vivid orange banner for a moment before disappearing into the waves. I desperately wanted to hide my eyes, to go below, to shut off the horror, but I was rooted to the spot, compelled to watch, seeing everything through a haze of disbelief. Em's face was white. Her shoulders were trembling. I wrapped my arms around her, and she buried her head in my shoulder, sobbing quietly, the strong, courageous girl momentarily reduced to a frightened child.

Tremayne was having the time of his life, leaping around with great agility, wielding his knife with deadly precision, his sky-blue satin outfit splattered with blood. Somehow or other he had managed to keep his hat on, and the plumes waved wildly. He grabbed a sailor by the hair, yanked his head back, sliced his throat, and then shoved him aside to grab another man and drive his knife deep into the man's chest. He was laughing, his dark eyes alight with boyish glee as he stabbed and slashed, enjoying the slaughter as another man might enjoy a rousing physical sport. Heaving yet another victim aside, he leaped nimbly over a fallen mast to grab another sailor from behind, shoving his knife into the sailor's back and twisting it viciously, his lips spreading in a wide, delighted grin as the lad screamed in agony and shuddered and died.

Red Nick fought coolly, calmly, his face expressionless as he used his cutlass with dazzling skill. While most of his men jabbed and slashed and jumped about in a frenzy of bloodlust, Lyon fenced like an aristocrat, each thrust and parry sharp and clean, arm and cutlass moving as one in graceful, deadly swirls, the sleeves of his fine white lawn shirt billowing, ruffles aflutter. Three sailors converged upon him, backing him against a wall, two of them slashing with swords as the other leveled his pistol, preparing to fire. Lyon moved with lightning speed, ducking, twirling, his free arm swinging out to loop around the throat of one of the men with swords. Holding the man in front of him in a deadly stranglehold, using him as a shield, he continued to thrust and parry, driving his blade through the heart of the man with the pistol, extracting it quickly, fencing coolly with the other sailor. He knocked the sword out of his hand and killed him neatly, and when he unwound his arm from his shield's throat, the man fell limply to the deck, strangled to death.

The deck was littered with bodies now, blood flowing in bright scarlet ribbons. Only a few sailors remained. Half the pirates had gone below to seek out more victims. They didn't intend to leave anyone alive. I watched as several pirates came merrily back up on deck, dragging along three unfortunate passengers, two older men in satin and lace and powdered wigs and a plump middle-aged woman in wine-colored velvet. The woman was struggling and shrieking. The two men were dazed. Laughing, yelling with savage glee, the pirates hauled the two men over to the railing and tossed them into the waves that, by now, were alive with sharks.

The woman broke free. She ran shrieking around the deck, stumbling over the bodies, waving her arms in the air. The pirates pursued her, delighted by the game, making no real effort to catch her at first. The woman fell down and spied a pistol and grabbed it and tried to fire, but they were upon her before she could pull the trigger. Taking hold of her by the wrists and ankles, they carried her over to the railing and swung her back and forth, swinging her over the railing, swinging her back, laughing, yelling, finally giving a final swing and releasing their holds. She went sailing through the air and disappeared into the water with a gigantic splash.

It was over. Everyone who had been on the ship was dead,

and the ship itself was beginning to list dangerously. Pirates were coming up from below with chests and trunks, bringing them across the planks to deposit them on *The Sea Lyon.* Tremayne was wiping the blade of his knife and looking disappointed that there was no one else to kill. Red Nick was calmly issuing orders, his eyes as cold as blue ice, the heavy copper wave slanting damply across his brow.

Em straightened up and looked at me with eyes that were suddenly much older. Her features were taut, her mouth a tight line.

"Are you all right, Em?" I asked.

"I'm all right, luv. I'll never be the same again, but—I'm all right. I thought I'd seen a lot of terrible things in my life, but I—I've never seen anything like this."

"Thank God Corrie was below."

"I wish I'd been," Em said. "Oh, luv, I wish I'd been."

"We'd better go down now."

Em nodded, and we moved down the stairs and down the narrow hallway to the door of Tremayne's room. I was still in a state of shock. There was something hard and tight inside me, a grim, terrible resolution that had evolved without my even being aware of it. I knew what I was going to do. I had to do it. There was no alternative. Em looked at me, calm now, composed, fierce determination in her eyes.

"I wish I were on my way to Brazil," I said.

"No you don't, luv."

"I can't go through with this, Em. I just don't care anymore."

"I feel the same way, Marietta, but we've got to be sensible." Her voice was very firm. "We—we're going to have to forget what happened today. We're going to have to put it out of our minds and concentrate on surviving."

"I don't care about surviving, not any longer."

"You don't know what you're saying, luv. They're going to pay for what they did. I swear it. We're going to get away from them somehow, but before we do, they're going to pay. I don't know just how we'll go about it, but we're going to make them pay."

Her voice seemed to come from a great distance. I hardly heard her words. She took hold of my hands and held them tightly.

"We've got to be strong, Marietta."

"I'm tired of being strong," I said in a flat voice.

"You need a drink, luv. He has lots of fine brandy in that cabinet of his. Pour yourself a drink and you'll feel better. We'll be on the island in a day or two, and things will be easier."

She let go of my hands, her eyes full of concern. I nodded and left her at the door and went into the captain's quarters. I moved as though in a daze, not really conscious of what I was doing. I went into his dressing room and examined the pistols on the wall and finally took one down. I opened a drawer of the small bureau beside the wardrobe and, moving aside the piles of silk scarves and fine handkerchiefs, took out the box of bullets I had discovered some time earlier. I loaded the pistol and put the box back, closed the bureau drawer and went into the study to wait for him. I sat down and held the pistol at my side. It was hidden by the folds of my sapphire skirt.

I was perfectly calm, perfectly composed, and I felt no emotion whatsoever. I felt, instead, a curious detachment. I seemed to be entirely removed from the scene. I saw the woman with the copper-red hair who sat in a chair wearing a rich sapphire gown, a pistol at her side, and she had no connection with the woman who observed, removed, untouched, incapable of feeling. Time passed, perhaps half an hour, perhaps more, and when he finally opened the door and stepped into the room I was still in that strange, numb state which I vaguely realized was a state of complete shock.

He closed the door and looked at me and realized at once that something was wrong. He paused, examining me with expressionless blue eyes, his face inscrutable. He had killed at least half a dozen men, and he was totally unscathed, might just have returned from a leisurely promenade around the deck. His thick copper hair was dry now, the point of that heavy, slanting wave resting half an inch above his right eyebrow.

"You watched," he said.

"I watched."

"You should have come below."

"I should have, yes."

"Your voice sounds peculiar."

"Does it?"

"I'm sorry you witnessed it, Marietta, but perhaps it's just as well. You know now how we operate. Perhaps it will clear your mind of any foolish notions about the life you're going to lead."

"I'm not going to lead any kind of life with you."

"No?"

"I'm going to kill you," I said.

He showed not the least surprise or alarm when I raised the pistol. If anything, there was a hint of amusement in his eyes, and the faintest suggestion of a smile played on his lips.

"It seems we've gone through this before," he remarked.

"The pistol is loaded," I said.

He elevated his eyebrow. The blue eyes were definitely amused.

"I'm a crack shot," I told him.

Nicholas Lyon shook his head and the smile played full on his lips and he took a step toward me. I stood up and leveled the pistol at him, surprised at its weight, the strain on my wrist. My hand shook slightly, and he took another step. I pulled the trigger and the explosion was deafening in the confines of the room. The force of the blast caused me to reel backward and drop the pistol. The smoke cleared, and Nicholas Lyon stood there idly examining the red stain on the side of his arm.

"A crack shot, did you say?"

I was too stunned to reply. He shook his head again and, confirming the fact that the bullet had merely grazed the side of his arm, looked at me with mocking disappointment. He was actually pleased by what I had done. In some perverse way it made him admire me all the more. He reached into the waistband of his breeches and pulled something out, something long and flexible and glittering with a thousand fires.

"Melodramatics over? Yes? I picked up something for you, my dear, thought you might like it."

He tossed the strand of silvery-blue fire, and I caught it instinctively, not even thinking. The necklace was heavy, dozens of diamonds and flashing blue sapphires dripping between my fingers, alive with fire, dazzlingly alive, glittering with vibrant beauty. I knew that the necklace must have belonged to the woman in wine-colored velvet. I wanted to hurl it at him. I wanted to retrieve the pistol and shoot him through the heart, as I had intended, but I did neither. I examined the gems and then looked up at him with icy composure.

"Still want to kill me?" he asked.

"It can wait."

"You delight me, Marietta."

He stepped over to me, took the necklace, and moved behind me to place it around my neck. The jewels rested heavily against my collarbone, dripping down to the swell of my breasts. He rested his right hand on my shoulder and curled his right arm around my waist, drawing me back against him. I could smell blood and gunpowder and flesh.

"Such spirit," he said.

He raised his hand and lifted the hair from my temple and lowered his head to kiss the side of my neck. He pulled me even closer, his arm curling tightly, squeezing the breath out of me.

"You play such amusing games," he murmured.

"It wasn't a game."

"I must remember to keep dangerous toys locked up. Next time you might miss. Instead of grazing my arm you might put a bullet through me."

He turned me around and looked into my eyes, his own gleaming darkly. He actually thought I had staged the scene for his amusement. I was amazed, and I felt a new sense of power. He opened his mouth and ran the tip of his tongue over his lower lip and then fastened his mouth hungrily over mine. I relaxed, pliant in his arms, yielding to his strength and hardness. He believed that he was in control, but he was quite mistaken. As his kiss grew more demanding, I thought about what Em had said. We were going to get away somehow, but before we did, they were going to pay.

Nicholas Lyon was going to pay dearly.

Thirteen

The island was long and relatively narrow, separated from the mainland by perhaps a quarter of a mile. In the distance, it was brown and green and a light sandy yellow, the curving seaside harbor filled with ships. Above the waterfront, the land rose sharply, dotted with a ramshackle collection of huts and buildings. There were gray stone embattlements on the rim of the bluffs that rose above the beaches, and in the sparkling midmorning sunlight I could see the stout black noses of at least fifty cannon pointing out to sea.

"That's New Spain behind the island," Em informed me. "Texas, actually, I think they call it, but Spanish territory, a vast wilderness with just a few villages and a couple of medium-sized towns and a lot of Spanish missions. It goes on for*ever*, Michael told me, and it's filled with savage Indians, dozens of tribes."

"That's encouraging," I said dryly.

"You haven't heard the worst part yet, luv. The other side of the island is fortified, too, because of the tribe along the coast. Cannibals," she added.

"Cannibals?"

"That's what Michael told me. They don't just *eat* their victims, they eat them *alive!*"

I found that hard to believe, but Em assured me it was true. *The Sea Lyon* glided smoothly toward the distant harbor, and the island loomed larger, color and detail sharpening. The deck was aswarm with activity, both Draper and Tremayne snapping orders. Red Nick sauntered up from below and came to join us on the poop deck. He was splendidly dressed in midnight-blue satin breeches and a matching frock coat lavishly embroidered in silver, lace cascading at his throat and wrists. His wide black hat slanted at a rakish angle, three long white and blue plumes curling down. His black boots shone with a high gloss. His finest sword hung at his side.

"How do you like my stronghold?" he inquired.

"It's quite impressive," I said.

"Small but sturdy," he observed. "When I left the Caribbean to stake out my own territory, free from competition, I found the island ideal. The fortifications were already here, a number of buildings as well. Another chap had decided to take over the Gulf Coast as his private domain. We had a nice set-to. He changed his mind—while feeding the sharks. Most of his men joined me, and those who didn't joined their leader."

"You simply took over?"

"I took over," he said. "Imported builders and craftsmen to spruce up the town and build my house—you can't see it from here, it's above the town, beyond that line of trees."

"I suppose Maria is waiting for you," I remarked.

"I would imagine she is."

"She's not going to be happy when you arrive with me in tow."

Lyon didn't reply, but a wry smile twisted at one corner of his mouth. I could see that he was looking forward to the confrontation. Surprising his mistress with the arrival of her replacement would undoubtedly appeal to his perverse humor. Em and I exchanged glances, and then she tactfully withdrew to go below. Tremayne stopped her, spoke to her gruffly, and she nodded wearily, moving down the stairs. Nicholas Lyon watched the island as we drew nearer the harbor. A huge crowd had gathered below the town. They were cheering and waving their hats.

"How many men do you have on the island?" I asked.

"Three hundred and fifty men, seven ships. They're all in harbor now, as you can see. I'll be sending four of them out in a few days, each manned by a full crew with a trusted lieutenant in charge."

"You're very well organized."

"That's the reason for my success."

"You'll hang one day," I said.

"You think so?"

"It's inevitable."

"Not necessarily," he replied. "Perhaps I'll 'reform.' Perhaps I'll join the forces of law and order, like Henry Morgan. The British made an agreement with him, you know. They authorized him to go right on plundering, as long as he did it for them. He was knighted. They made him lieutenant governor of Jamaica as well."

"That was almost a hundred years ago."

"Ah, you know about Sir Henry?"

"I've read about him in history books."

"Perhaps I'll be in the history books, too. Sir Henry may have lived a hundred years ago, but man's venality hasn't changed an iota, my dear. As a matter of fact, I've already received an offer from the British myself. They wanted me to join forces with them to help subjugate the rebels."

"And you refused?"

He nodded, the long plumes billowing. "I admire the rebels. I admire any man or any group who defies authority. Were I to take sides at all, I'd be on the side of the rebels, but I'm much too independent, and my work is much too profitable. I'll wait a while before I become respectable. I have all the power now. The island is impregnable. I'm the terror of the gulf."

"And proud of it," I said.

"Naturally."

"You enjoy killing."

"On the contrary, I find it a bore—but necessary."

"I see."

"You're an enigma to me, my dear. Sometimes I think you're very satisfied with yourself and with your new position. Most women with your background would be. Sometimes I'm not so sure."

"No?"

"I know you enjoy making love with me. You're a marvelously passionate creature. Once I broke you down, you proved that—repeatedly."

"Against my will," I said dryly.

"You enjoy it, my dear."

"I'm human, and you're unusually skillful."

He smiled, pleased. I looked at him coldly.

"I state that as a fact, not as a compliment. I respond to the skill, not to the man. I happen to loathe you."

"I find that intriguing."

"I imagine you do."

"You're a challenge, Marietta, a most interesting challenge. I never know what to expect. I broke down your reserve in bed, and I'm going to break down your mental reserve as well. I'm going to turn that loathing into love."

"I'll never love you."

"You will, my dear," he promised.

I smiled to myself. Nicholas Lyon was utterly intrigued, just as I meant him to be. He had mastered my body, and now he wanted to master my emotions, too. He had conquered me, yes, but that conquest wasn't yet total, and as long as I held back he was in my power, not I in his. His ego required slavish devotion and adoration, and he was determined to have it. I would never love Nicholas Lyon, but he was already beginning to fall in love with me. I sensed that, and it suited my purposes ideally.

We were in the harbor now. I could hear the men on shore cheering. Nicholas Lyon lifted his hat and nodded to them, and they cheered all the louder. He was a king here, absolute monarch of the island, and he wielded his power mercilessly, I knew. No one dared defy or disobey him. The price was much too high. Public floggings and executions were common on the island, according to Em, and Red Nick's men lived under a stringent set of rules. They could kill and rape and plunder at sea, but thievery on the island was punished by death. There were canteens on the island where they could drink and brawl to their hearts' content, but serious fighting meant flogging, and fighting with weapons meant execution. Nicholas Lyon kept them under tight control, ruling his domain with an iron hand.

Close up, the island was much larger than it had seemed from the distance. The harbor was almost directly in the center, with the streets and buildings rising above it. On either side of the town, if that it could be called, the land was uninhabited, lush tropical woods stretching out. The streets, I saw, were cobbled. There were huts and shacks leaning precariously against one another in a disorderly jumble, with a number of sturdier buildings of whitewashed stone, the roofs a dark red-orange tile. There were stores, a smithy, at least half a dozen rowdy canteens where rum and other liquors were provided for a price. I noticed a number of women in the crowd awaiting us, disheveled, slatternly creatures as bizarrely dressed as the men.

"I'd better go below," I said. "I told Corrie to meet me in your quarters when we landed."

"You're fond of the little nigger, aren't you?"

"She's a sweet child. I thank you for giving her to me."

"Just keep her out of my way," he warned.

Corrie was in the bedroom, carefully folding the gowns and placing them in a valise. She had skillfully altered each one of them, including the one I was wearing, a dark golden yellow taffeta striped with silver. She looked up as I entered, alarmed, alarm turning to relief when she saw me. Nicholas Lyon made no secret of his dislike for her, scowling whenever he saw her, and Corrie was terrified in his presence, eyes lowered, shoulders hunched forward as though expecting a lash across them at any moment. I smiled at her and helped her finish packing the gowns, placing the necklace and makeup kit on top.

"Is we supposed to pack his things, too?" she asked.

"One of his men will do that later, Corrie."

"I'se glad, Miz Marietta."

"I *am* glad," I corrected.

"That's right," she said. "I remember. I'se goin'—I *am* goin' to learn to talk proper. All them lessons you done be givin' me, I listened real good, and I ain't goin' to talk nigger talk no more. I forget sometimes is all."

"You're doing beautifully, Corrie."

Shy, meek, docile, the girl not only had a sweet nature, she had a strong native intelligence as well and, until now, no opportunity to develop it. During the past few days I had been giving her lessons in grammar, correcting her speech, teaching her the alphabet. Corrie was a marvelous seamstress and could indeed perform miracles with brush and comb, but I intended to teach her to read and write and speak correctly, preparing her for that day when she would really be free. She looked up at me now with dark, lovely eyes, the soft black nimbus of hair framing her light brown, delicately featured face.

"Is—are they goin' to hurt us, Miz Marietta?"

"Everything's going to be all right, Corrie. The worst part is over now. We'll be getting off the ship in a few minutes, and you'll have a room in the big house and—no one will hurt you."

"I try not to be scared, but that Cook, he said I'd better watch my step. He said if I got uppity the captain would have my hide, said he'd turn me over to his men and they'd tear me apart."

"He was just trying to frighten you."

"The captain looks like he'd like to have my hide. He glares at me with them scary blue eyes and tightens his mouth up and—and I get all trembly inside. He don't like niggers, I can tell."

"You're—don't use that word, Corrie."

"But I *is* a nigger, Miz Marietta."

"You're a beautiful and intelligent young woman, and one day you'll be able to hold your head up with pride, not because of the color of your skin but because of what you *are*."

"You is so good, Miz Marietta," Corrie said.

I moved over to the mirror and looked at my reflection, touched by what she had said, saddened, too. The yellow and silver striped taffeta gown had puffed sleeves that fell off the shoulder, and even after Corrie's alterations the bodice was provocatively low and snug at the waist. I gazed at the reflection, but I didn't see the woman with copper-red locks and worldly blue eyes. I saw, instead, a very young girl who had been as pure of heart as the Negro child who stood beside the bed, fastening the valise.

"No, Corrie," I said, "I'm not good. Perhaps I was once, a long time ago, but—things happened."

Corrie stepped over to me and placed her hand over mine, and when she spoke, her voice was grave and as lovely as dark honey.

"But them things weren't your fault," she said. "It ain't right for you to blame yourself. Them men took my cherry, but that didn't make *me* bad, they's the bad ones. You let the captain poke his tool in you 'cause you have to, not 'cause you want to. You has a fine heart, Miz Marietta, and you is kind and them is the things what makes a person good."

"I wish I could believe that," I said dryly.

"Believe what?" Em asked, stepping into the room.

"Nothing," I replied.

"Jesus, can you believe we're finally going to get off this ship? I hope I can walk! Do you feel that? We've stopped moving. How am I going to survive without the floor tilting under my feet and the ceiling swaying overhead? Well, luvs," Em said, "we've made it to the island. The first hurdle is behind us, the next one coming up."

"You looks lovely, Miz Em," Corrie said.

Em had changed into a pale, creamy tan satin gown embroidered all over with tiny brown silk flowers and tiny emerald silk leaves. Her glossy chestnut waves were piled on top of her head, several long locks spilling down in back, and she was wearing a gorgeous pair of emerald earrings. Hazel eyes saucy, cheekbones lightly dusted with golden brown freckles, a rueful smile on her small pink mouth, she did indeed look lovely.

"Michael told me to fix myself up," she explained. "He wants to impress his chums on shore with his fancy new whore. He gave me the gown and gave me the earrings and told me if I behaved myself I'd get a necklace to match. You think I'm not going to be an angel? At least until I get the necklace," she added. "If I seem to be chattering like a magpie, it's because I'm terrified. Did you see that *mob* on shore?"

"I saw them," I said.

"Getting off this island isn't going to be as easy as I thought it was going to be, but we're going to do it, luvs. The three of us are going to escape as soon as possible, cannibals or no."

Corrie's dark eyes grew wide. "Cannibals?" she said.

"Nothing for you to worry about at the moment, luv," Em assured her. "I'd as soon face a tribe of cannibals as face that mob out there, but I suppose we'd better go on up on deck."

Em took hold of my hand and took hold of Corrie's and squeezed both tightly. She smiled a bright, rueful smile but wasn't quite able to hide the apprehension in her eyes. She was brave and feisty and determined to keep up a cheery front, but I could see that she was as dispirited as I.

"We *are* going to make it, Em," I said.

"Of course we are," she retorted, squeezing our hands again. "A bunch of pirates are no match for *us*."

She let go of our hands and Corrie picked up the valise and we joined the men on deck. Tremayne appropriated Em immediately, seizing her roughly by the arm and leading her away. He was foppishly attired in brown satin breeches and matching frock coat faced with gold braid, his wide brimmed brown hat festooned with curling gold and white plumes. He led Em down the gangplank, greeting his cronies with gusto and showing off his new acquisition with a boisterous, swaggering pride. Em wore a patient, resigned expression as lewd shouts and noisy catcalls filled the air. One of the slatternly women broke free from the crowd and spat, barely missing the hem of Em's gown. A pirate clipped the woman on the jaw, knocking her down, and as she climbed to her knees Em gave her a dignified look and extended a stiff middle finger. The crowd roared with raucous laughter.

Tremayne grinned and slung his arm around Em's shoulders, and they moved on up the street. Draper came over to where Corrie and I were standing. His gray eyes were fierce. The nostrils of his sharp, beaklike nose flared, and there was a sullen curl on his lips. He was wearing the clothes he had been wearing the first time I saw him, black boots, black breeches, the loose-fitting silky green shirt with full sleeves. His coal black hair was held back with a green bandana, and the gold hoop dangled from his earlobe, gleaming in the brilliant sunlight.

"Your little friend is much too sure of herself," he growled, watching Em and Tremayne with flashing animosity. "She may have a nice pair of teats, but she'd better watch her step."

"Tremayne will take care of her," I replied.

"Yeah, he's pretty cocky, too, gettin' much too big for his breeches. He dudn't watch it, I'm gonna take the wench away from him. I'd like to get my hands on those teats."

I gazed at him with repulsion. Draper's eyes continued to flash, the fingers of his left hand beating a tattoo on the hilt of his cutlass. An erection strained against the cloth of his breeches as he watched Em and thought of what he would like to do.

Red Nick strolled over to join us. He had been watching the scene, too, and there was a glint of wry amusement in his eyes. The amusement faded as he looked at Corrie. His thin lips curled down at the corners. Corrie cringed, her shoulders trembling. He glared at her with strong aversion for half a moment, then dismissed her from his mind and turned to me.

"Draper will accompany us to the house," he said.

"What a charming surprise."

"Are you ready?"

"I suppose," I said.

My voice was cool, my manner cooler. Nicholas Lyon smiled a twisted half-smile and extended the crook of his arm. I placed my hand in the curve, and we moved toward the gangplank. Corrie remained where she was, nervously clutching the valise, not knowing what to do. Draper gave her a savage prod, and the two of them fell in behind us. The wooden plank creaked a little beneath our weight as we descended. The crowd on the dock cheered robustly, those men with hats waving them in the air as their leader stepped into their midst.

It was a huge, horrifying mob at least a hundred strong. The men had surly, savage faces, many of them with scars or broken noses or eye patches. They wore jack boots and bandanas and many, like Draper, sported golden hoops in one earlobe. All carried knives and cutlasses and pistols, even though there would seem to be no reason to here on the island. There were at least twenty women in the crowd, plump, soiled creatures with coarse faces and long, tattered hair. I repressed a shudder as the shouting, smelly crowd surrounded us, reeking of rum and sweat and filth. This was human nature at its foulest and most depraved, a nightmare mass from the depths of hell. They screamed lustily, waving hats and arms and bottles.

Nicholas Lyon raised his arm, his features stern. Silence fell immediately. His eyes were expressionless as they swept over the mob, and I saw fierce, brawny men stiffen with fear, as though they expected him to find some fault and mete out severe punishment. Tall, harsh, handsome in a cruel, chilling way, he did indeed have them under tight control, subduing an unruly pack of cutthroats without a word. He exuded an aura of utterly ruthless power, and had he ordered them to, all of them would have fallen to their knees to pay obeisance. He held them in suspense a few moments longer, eyes like blue ice, his lips curling with a faint smile of satisfaction as he savored his power, and then he gave the smile full play.

"It's been a highly successful trip, men," he announced. "We've returned with a hold full of booty. There will be free rum in the canteens tonight to celebrate our return."

Cheers rose in a deafening roar. Hats were thrown in the air. Red Nick acknowledged the cheers with a curt nod and, when the cheering died down, took me firmly by the elbow and led me toward the cobbled street that rose immediately above the docks. I held my chin high, looking neither to the left nor the right, but I could see the men eyeing me with curiosity nonetheless. The women looked at me with active hostility they strove to conceal. Taunting Tremayne's new whore was one thing. Offending the captain's woman was quite another. As we walked past stores and shacks and large canteens with flaking white walls and red-orange tiled roofs, I reflected that the women would gladly have torn me limb from limb merely because I was young and attractive and wearing an elegant gown. Red Nick's patronage was all that protected me.

"Frightened?" he inquired.

"Not at all," I lied.

"They envy you, you know, the women."

"I imagine they do."

"They were young and beautiful once, when they arrived on the island. Rum and rough usage have taken a sad toll. I'm going to have to import some new women before long."

"What will happen to these?"

"They'll cook and scrub floors and make themselves useful in other ways," he said. "You needn't worry about them. As my woman, you're perfectly safe, and so is Tremayne's little whore. None of the townspeople are allowed up on the hilltop, unless invited."

The cobbled street curved to the right, past an ever thicker congestion of sheds and shacks, chickens and goats in the yards beyond. Ahead, a smooth road curved gradually upward, lined on either side by tall palm trees, their heavy, green-brown fronds rattling in the breeze. I could see a huge square structure beyond the trees, walls gleaming white in the sunlight, enclosing several buildings with multilevel red-orange tile roofs. I realized that it was an enormous stockade with a walkway on the inside and notches along the top with cannon pointing out. The only access was a huge pair of solid oak doors studded with brass. They stood open now, and I glimpsed green lawns and fountains and houses within.

"The island is impregnable," he explained, "but the stockade is a final precaution. Once the doors are closed, a handful of men could hold off an entire army."

"How many houses are there inside?"

"Seven," he said, "plus a small barracks. The main house is quite large, quite luxurious, as you will see, and the six cottages are comfortable. They're occupied by my lieutenants. Twenty of my best men live in the barracks."

We passed through the enormous doors. There was a spacious courtyard with palm trees and fountains and lush green lawns. The barracks was immediately to the right of the great doors, and the six small white cottages faced each other across the courtyard, three on either side. The main house was directly ahead, large and lovely with white walls and black wrought-iron grills over the windows and roofs that rose and slanted at different levels. Brilliantly colored flowers grew in beds on both sides of the main portico, wide white steps leading up to the recessed front door.

Everything was clean and peaceful and calm. The nightmare noise and fury of the town below might never have existed. Em and Tremayne were standing in front of one of the cottages. Em waved. Twenty men with muskets stood at attention outside the barracks, all tall, lean, powerfully built, dressed in attire similar to the other pirates' but much more neatly, boots polished, breeches clean, colored shirts full-sleeved, silky. Lyon stopped, turned to them, saluted sharply and told them to be at ease. The men lowered their muskets and moved lazily back into the barracks. Red Nick led me past the fountains and colorful flower beds and up the wide front steps. Draper and Corrie were following behind.

We stepped into a long, wide hallway with archways on either side opening into spacious, airy rooms filled with sunlight. At the end of the hallway a curving staircase rose to the second floor. Moving through one of the archways, we stepped into an enormous salon graciously appointed with the finest French furniture, deep blue brocade drapes hanging at the window, pale blue and rose Aubusson rugs on the golden brown parquet floor. With its graceful lines, delicate colors and carefully balanced elegance, the room would have delighted the most demanding Parisian aristocrat.

Red Nick turned to Draper. "Take the nigger to the servants' quarters," he ordered. "See that she gets a room, then report back to me."

Draper nodded, took Corrie by the arm and led her away. She cast a frightened glance at me over her shoulder as they left. Lyon removed his hat, tossed it onto one of the chairs. He looked at the elegantly molded white marble fireplace, the gleaming silver candlesticks, the two crystal chandeliers that hung from the ceiling with cascades of sparkling pendants. The wide skirt of his frock coat rustled as he strolled across the room to remove a glass and crystal decanter from the gilded white liquor cabinet.

"Wine?" he inquired.

"I think not."

"What do you think of the place?"

"It's beautiful," I said.

"I appreciate beautiful things. Beautiful furniture, beautiful objects, beautiful women."

"And don't care how you acquire them."

"I vowed I'd have all this one day. When I was young and hungry and cold, I vowed I'd have wealth and power. I was an orphan, you see, stealing food and pennies when I was no more than five years old. I was lucky. A gentleman whose watch I pinched took pity on me, took me into his home. He and his wife raised me as their son, gave me a fine education, the best tutors."

"And?"

"They died when I was sixteen years old, the fever, both of them within a week of each other. Their nephew arrived in Edinburgh to take over. He threw me out onto the street, literally. I climbed back in through a window and took a poker and cracked his skull open."

He stook a sip of wine, his eyes expressionless as he continued.

"I fled. The authorities caught me. I was scheduled to hang. I managed to escape. I overpowered a guard and wrested the pistol out of his hand, shot him, shot another guard who tried to rush me. I hid out in the slums for over a month before I finally managed to get out of the city and take to the sea, a fugitive from justice. There was no turning back."

"So you became a pirate."

"It seemed the logical thing to do."

He finished his wine as footsteps sounded on the stairway.

"Neek-oh-las!" an excited voice cried. "Neek-oh-las! Ess that you?"

The footseps clattered noisily down the hallway, and then Maria burst into the room, absolutely stunning in a dark pink brocade gown that made a striking contrast to her dark, creamy tan skin. Her hair was a luscious blue-black, spilling over her shoulders in rich profusion, and her eyes were a lively brown, flashing, full of expression. Her mouth was wide and red and undeniably sensual, a mouth designed for passion. Not nearly as tall as I, she had an extremely curvaceous body, the clinging pink brocade bodice accentuating smooth shoulders and full breasts and slender waist. Lovely though she was, there was a suggestion of greed in the petulant curve of the mouth, an acquisitive gleam in those dark, flashing eyes.

Halfway across the room, she paused and took a deep breath and placed her hands on her hips. I was standing by a table to the left of the archway, and Maria hadn't seen me yet. Her eyes were fastened greedily on Nicholas Lyon, a pouting, provocative smile shaping on her lips.

"You bring me a present?" she asked.

"I've brought you a surprise."

He watched her with a stony face that showed no emotion whatsoever, mouth held in a straight line, one slanted brow slightly arched and almost touching the heavy copper wave. Maria hesitated, puzzled, obviously expecting him to pull out a glittering bauble.

"Where is it?" she demanded.

Lyon nodded in my direction. Maria turned, curious. When she saw me her lips parted in surprise. She stared, her eyes full of dismay, alarm, anger. I couldn't help but feel sorry for her, even when the lovely features hardened into a vicious mask. I stood there with a cool, detached expression, refusing to display my feelings. I pitied her. I hated him for what he was doing to her. Maria knew immediately, of course. No words were needed. She stared at me for several long moments, clenching and unclenching her hands, and then she gave a furious cry and whirled around and flew at Lyon with nails extended, planning to rake them across his face.

He caught her wrists, restraining her, cool, sadistic amusement in his eyes as he bent her wrists back. Maria began to scream and kick, struggling furiously, her blue-black locks flying, tumbling over her cheeks, her eyes flashing with Latin rage. She bit his hand and broke his hold on one wrist and threw her hand back and brought it across his face in a stinging slap, at the same time delivering a particularly vicious kick to his shin. He hurled her away from him with such force that she fell to the floor in a sobbing heap.

"You can't do this to Maria!" she screamed. "You can't do it!"

Draper strolled into the room, showing no reaction whatsoever to the scene in progress. Maria climbed to her feet and stood there for a moment with angry tears spilling down her cheeks, and then she looked at me and screamed a curse and leaped toward me. Draper reached out and deftly caught her, slinging his arm around her waist. She reared and bucked like a wild animal. He grabbed her hair and jerked her head back, pulling her off her feet, holding her up in front of him. She continued to kick, her pink brocade skirts swirling wildly. Draper chuckled, tightening his arm around her waist, tugging at her hair with savage force, arching her head back across his shoulder.

"You want her?" Lyon inquired.

Draper hesitated, debating the wisdom of taking over the captain's woman, clearly deciding it might be unwise, might lead to future resentment. He shook his head, scowling.

Lyon arched an eyebrow, surprised. "No?"

"These Spanish wenches, they ain't my type."

"Let me go!" Maria shrieked.

"I see," Lyon replied.

"Whatja want me to do with her?"

"Take her over to the barracks," the captain said. "She can keep the men amused until the next ship leaves for South America."

"No! No! You can't do this to Maria!"

"You have your orders," Lyon said.

Draper dragged the screaming woman out of the room. Her cries echoed in the hall, ending abruptly. Apparently, he had clamped a hand over her mouth. There was the sound of a door opening, closing, then blessed silence. Red Nick poured more wine and sipped it slowly, completely unruffled. I was horrified, and it took superhuman effort to maintain my poise. The man was totally amoral, totally unfeeling, and I knew full well that the same thing could happen to me if I began to bore him.

"I'll take that wine now," I said.

He looked up, gazed at me for a moment with cool blue eyes, and then filled another glass. I moved across the room to take it from him.

"What will happen to her?" I asked.

"The men will enjoy her for a few days. One of the ships sails for South America next week to pick up provisions and make a few coastal raids. She'll be sold to one of the houses."

"You can do that to a woman who has lived with you?"

"Without a qualm," he replied. "Don't waste your pity on her, my dear. Maria was a greedy, grasping little whore. She reveled in her position, gave herself airs, treating everyone with disdain. I found it amusing for a while, and then it began to weary me."

"You'd do the same thing to me," I said.

"Undoubtedly—if you wearied me."

"I'll keep that in mind."

"Do, my dear."

He finished his wine and set the glass down on the cabinet, then took the glass from my hand and placed it beside the other. He rested his hands on my shoulders and looked down into my eyes. I gazed up at him, cool, composed, not the least bit intimidated. He smiled a wry smile, pleased with my composure, my icy reserve, determined to break it down with his sexual prowess. His lean, harshly attractive face tightened with desire, that familiar gleam shining in his eyes. As his fingers squeezed my bare shoulders, as he drew me toward him, I vowed that Nicholas Lyon was going to be sorry he ever met me. One day he would be sorry indeed, I vowed, but in the meantime he would be anything but bored.

Fourteen

The sand was gray and strewn with pebbles and tiny pink-orange shells and scraps of yellow-brown seaweed. The waves washed over it with a soft, slushing sound, leaving a residue of frothy white foam. The water was a light grayish-green and constantly moving, sloshing, sending the waves swooping over the sand. I walked slowly along the beach, relishing the solitude, thankful to be away from the oppressive confines of the great white stockade. It seemed incredible that we had been on the island over two months, kept in an elegant prison, Em and I serving our men, desperately trying to formulate some plan for escaping.

We were not allowed to go down to the town, which was just as well. Neither of us had any desire to mingle with the ruffians there. We had been kept inside the stockade, allowed to wander as we pleased within the walls, and it was only during the past week that we had been permitted to explore the beaches and woods. Red Nick, Draper, and Tremayne had taken *The Sea Lyon* to a rendezvous at sea, where booty from another ship would be transferred to *The Sea Lyon*, and Em had charmed the captain of the guards into allowing us to take short walks outside. It hadn't been easy.

A blond giant with suspicious brown eyes, a crooked nose

and wide pink mouth with lower lip thrust out belligerently, he had adamantly refused at first, telling her he was responsible for our safety during Red Nick's absence. Em employed considerable persuasion one night in the shrubberies that grew in the garden behind Tremayne's cottage, and the next day we were permitted to take a walk in the forest with an "escort" of two men, the blond giant, whose name was Cleeve, and a black-haired brute named Grimmet. They accompanied us the following day as well, bored with our questions about trees and flowers, longing to be back at the barracks to drink rum and gamble with their cronies.

Seeing that our strolls were innocent and knowing full well there was no way we could get off the island, Cleeve had relaxed his vigilance and allowed us to go out without an escort the third day. Em continued to use her genial persuasion each night in the shrubberies—she didn't dare allow him to enter the cottage for fear someone would see, meeting him well after midnight under the cover of darkness—and now we were permitted to come and go at will providing we avoided the town and returned in under two hours. Cleeve was taking a great risk, of course, but Red Nick hadn't strictly forbidden us to go outside the walls, and I had assured Cleeve I would take full responsibility when the captain returned.

Even this limited freedom was welcome. It was good to be away from the large, elegant house with its spacious rooms and sumptuous furnishings, to be able to stroll without the sight of walls surrounding me. It was good to feel the sun on my cheeks and hear the sound of the waves and the crisp rattle of the palm fronds in the breeze. To my left, the beach merged into a gently sloping land that climbed to the bluff above where the gray stone fortifications stood, chipped and weathered by sun and sea wind. I could see a cannon pointing toward the mainland. The fortifications weren't manned now, for there had been no trouble with the Indians in years.

Cannibals they might be, but they stayed on the mainland and never ventured to the island. Once, four years ago, they had foolishly launched an attack, hundreds of them swarming over the beaches. Their bows and arrows had proved almost useless against cannon and pistol and cutlass, and they had quickly retreated, leaving the beaches littered with dead and dying tribesmen. They had apparently learned their lesson, for there had been no more serious trouble. The pirates frequently went to the mainland on various missions, but always in force, always heavily armed, and although there had been skirmishes with the Indians, they had been minor.

I paused now, staring across at the mainland. Trees grew thickly beyond the beach, the space between them heavy with underbrush. It looked dark and forbidding, green and brown and black, shadowy thickets and leafy tunnels leading into the mysterious interior where savage Indians painted their bodies with black and white and smeared themselves with alligator grease to ward off mosquitoes and carried long bows six feet tall. It was hard to believe that beyond the coast there were verdant green hills and sweeping plains and villages where Spanish padres in long brown cossacks welcomed visitors into the dim coolness of great adobe missions. Red Nick had told me a great deal about New Spain, or Texas as the settlers called it.

I bent down to pick up one of the tiny seashells, a gorgeous, delicately wrought thing, a pale pinkish-orange as smooth as pearl, speckled with brown. The Indian women, I knew, made necklaces of these shells. I slipped it into the pocket of my yellow cotton dress to take back to Corrie. She was too frightened to join Em and I on our strolls, convinced she would be slaughtered the moment she stepped outside the stockade. Her lessons were coming along beautifully. She spoke now with barely a trace of her former accent and rarely made a grammatical error. She could already read a few words and could write her name with aplomb. The lessons were satisfying to both of us and helped to pass the time.

Would we ever escape? I felt a terrible frustration as I continued along the beach, passing under a cluster of palms, moving across a wide expanse littered with driftwood. The frustration had grown steadily over the weeks. Escape seemed impossible. Em and I had discussed every possibility. It might be possible for the two of us to swim across to the mainland, but then we would be at the mercy of the Indians who could very easily be watching me at this very minute. Em was much more optimistic than I. She constantly assured me we would find a way, and I tried to believe her.

Life was not hard for either of us. As Red Nick's woman, I lived in luxury, surrounded by beautiful things, and he treated me with a strangely sarcastic gallantry, playing a subtle cat-and-mouse game all the while, toying with me, trying his best to break down the icy reserve I maintained except on those occasions when we were in bed together. Wooing me with gifts, convinced I was captivated by his sexual prowess, he patiently waited for the day when I would make the first overtures of passion. I remained a challenge to him, for Nicholas Lyon wasn't content merely to have my body. He wanted me to become an abject, adoring slave, which, I knew, would cause him to despise me immediately. Although he didn't realize it, I had the upper hand, and he was already in love with me.

Love? No, it wasn't love. Nicholas Lyon was incapable of love, but he was enthralled, captivated himself, a captivation I did my best to maintain. I kept him off balance, playing a cat-and-mouse game myself, carefully, very carefully, denying him the emotional response he craved, responding in bed with a passionate fury that was magnificently gratifying to his ego. He left me alone most of the day, tending to his duties in town, holding conferences with his lieutenants, and planning new ventures. This left me time for lessons with Corrie and time to array myself in provocative splendor for his return each evening. I had an elaborate, breathtakingly lovely wardrobe and, already, a fabulous collection of jewelry. We dined off the finest plate, drank wine from exquisite crystal goblets, and the food was remarkable, would have satisfied the most demanding gourmet. No, life was not hard, but every minute of every hour I was aware of being a prisoner, no matter how grand the prison.

Em lived in great comfort, too, though considerably less splendor. Tremayne pampered her outrageously, spoiled her deplorably, lavishing her with gifts. Her gowns were not as elaborate as those I wore, her jewelry not as fine, but she was wildly elated each time he presented her with a bauble and showed her appreciation with such zest that he strove to give her even more. He was madly infatuated with her, so much so that it frequently worked against her. Insanely jealous, he flew into a rage at the least provocation and had beaten her brutally several times. Em said she didn't mind the beatings, claiming she had suffered far worse in days gone by and adding that a diamond and ruby bracelet was considerable compensation for a sore backside. I shuddered to think what would happen if Tremayne found out about her midnight trysts with Cleeve.

The waves rocked, grayish-green, sparkling with sunlight, swooshing over the sand. I moved slowly along the beach, the breeze lifting my yellow skirt and causing the petticoats beneath to flutter. Three months ago, I had been living with the man I loved, anticipating marriage and looking forward to the future, convinced I could make it bright with happiness, and now I was on an island off the coast of a wild and savage wilderness, living with a man who personified evil. Derek . . . Derek. . . . No, I mustn't think of him now. I mustn't allow myself the pain and anguish that would possess me, overwhelm me completely. I couldn't be weak. I couldn't give in to those tremulous emotions that were locked away inside along with the tears.

I must be hard, strong, cold. I must be shrewd and crafty and cling to that steely core of resolution. I didn't want to. I wanted to let down my defenses, give in to emotion and weep. I wanted to be feminine and frail and lean on someone stronger, but there was no one, no one but myself, and I had rarely had the opportunity to draw strength from others. During the past years I had had to rely on my wits, my stamina, using my beauty and sexual allure as weapons in a war I hadn't waged, a war I was fighting still. I wanted to give up, to give in, to surrender and forget about self-preservation.

I couldn't do that. I had promised myself that Derek's death would be revenged, and it was a promise I meant to keep. There were others involved now, Em and Corrie, both of them depending on me in their different ways. I took a deep breath and banished the weakness. I *was* strong, and I *could* be cold and crafty, whether I wanted to be or not. I wasn't going to give in. I was going to go right on fighting that war, faced now with my most formidable opponent, and, furthermore, I was going to win. The steely determination returned.

Turning my back to the water, I crossed the sand and started up the slope that was only partially covered with grass, sand and dark black earth visible between the heavy green strands that reached down from the bluff like elongated fingers. The sun was very warm, a pale yellow ball in a sky the color of polished steel, gray-white, glaring. When I reached the top, I could see the grassy knoll and, beyond, the forest, not nearly as dense as that on the mainland, treetops tall, spreading, a patchwork of green in varying shades. To my right there was another gray stone fortification, half-covered with a curious climbing plant with dark, tiny leaves and pale purple and white flowers that hung down like delicate pendants. Although the stone was crumbly and covered with a fine gray dust, the cannon gleamed in the sunlight, clean and free of rust, the pyramid of balls beside it like huge shiny black marbles. Red Nick insisted that all the cannon be kept in prime condition.

I glanced toward the stockade, the topmost walls just barely visible beyond the trees, at least three quarters of a mile away. It wouldn't be visible at all were it not situated on the highest point of the island. Surrounded by forest to the east, west, and north, the town sloping down to the harbor on the south side, it dominated the island, a huge white fortress with gardens and trees and houses and barracks within walls that were two feet thick. Once, during a hurricane three years ago, the entire population of the island had taken refuge in the stockade. Much of the town had been destroyed, shacks and lean-tos blown away, and several ships had been damaged, but those enormous walls had withstood the savage gales and torrential rains. Red Nick had known exactly what he was doing when he had it built.

A flock of sea gulls flew screeching over the tops of the palm trees below, winging over the water like scraps of gray-white paper in the breeze and making a terrible racket before they disappeared. I leaned against the fortification, gazing at the knoll without really seeing it. The delicate purple and white flowers smelled sweet, their fragrance mingling with the smells of damp earth and old stone and salt. The sunlight warmed my cheeks and stroked my bare arms. The breeze toyed with my hair, blowing fine copper-red skeins over my eyes. I lifted a hand to brush them away, still fighting a desire to think of Derek, forcing the thought of him out of my mind.

Suddenly, for no apparent reason, I saw a pair of merry, mocking eyes as blue as indigo, a slightly crooked nose, a full pink mouth curling audaciously in a grin that was strangely endearing. Jeremy Bond strode in my memory with a bouncy, jaunty stride, a rich brown wave flopping over his brow, outlandishly dapper in his elegant attire. I remembered that overwhelming charm and that carefree, ruthless air. He had come into my life so quickly and with such remarkable vitality. Although I had seen him only three times, during a span of no more than twelve hours, the memory of him was as vivid as it would have been had I known him for years.

Disturbed over my relationship with Derek, foolishly insecure because he hadn't yet married me, I had reacted to Jeremy Bond with a confusing array of emotions. I had seen him immediately for the rogue he was, irresponsible and irreverent, a jaunty scoundrel who lived with verve and abandon, thumbing his nose at convention, breaking laws and breaking hearts with equal aplomb, yet I had sensed strength and compassion, and a deep understanding as well. He seemed to have looked directly into my heart, sensing my insecurity, sensing my need, knowing me as no man had. I had been infuriated by him, and I had been intrigued, too. I couldn't deny that.

I recalled that evening in the courtyard with moonlight washing over the tiles and the fountain making soft, splattering music as shadows spread. He said that he loved me. He begged me to love him. I could hear that low, melodious voice beseeching me, and I could feel the touch of his hands and the strength in those fingers that gently caressed my shoulders and throat. When his lips brushed mine sweet sensations had blossomed inside of me. Emotionally vulnerable because of what I took to be Derek's rejection, disturbed and bewildered, I had responded in spite of myself with a tormenting ache that, even in memory, was shattering to my senses.

I had wanted to sleep with him. I admitted that now. I had wanted him as desperately as he wanted me, and that desire had seemed a treacherous disloyalty at the time. I loved Derek, yet there in the moonlit courtyard I had longed to give myself to Jeremy Bond. He was a skillful seducer, wooing with silken charm, playing on my weakness, speaking words of love he must have spoken dozens of times to dozens of women. He had vowed he would return and take me away from Derek. Even after I had summoned all my strength and rejected his pleas, he had stared at me with a grim, serious face, assuring me that he had been speaking the truth, that he loved me and meant to have me.

Now, as I leaned back against the gray stone fortification and toyed with one of the pale purple blossoms, I wondered what had happened when he returned to New Orleans. I wondered if he had made an effort to see me again. Had he gone to the apartment? Had he tried to locate me? Had he discovered that Derek had booked passage on *The Blue Elephant* and assumed we had sailed? Had he felt disappointment, regret, loss? I doubted it. I doubted if he had given me another thought after I refused to give in to his wooing and sent him away. He probably didn't even remember my name, yet after three months I remembered him vividly and remembered feeling intensely, marvelously alive each moment he was beside me.

Jeremy Bond had been the first person to mention Red Nick's name to me. I remembered his telling me about Red Nick as we were strolling through the market, just before he thrust the wad of money into the hands of the sad-eyed Negro woman who had been looking for edible scraps among the rubbish around the stalls. Bond had shown considerable knowledge about Nicholas Lyon, for he had once led a campaign against the pirates, Red Nick's men, who preyed on the smugglers in the swamps. And now I was on the island Bond had first told me about, a captive of the man he had found so very interesting. Fate played some cruel tricks, I thought, remembering that conversation as we had walked through the market, Bond in dark formal attire and billowing cloak, I in the rustling crimson gown Derek had found so objectionable.

I forced the memories of Jeremy Bond out of my mind. He was a stranger I had encountered on the streets of New Orleans, a jaunty rogue I had seen through at once. Fate had thrown us together briefly, under unusual circumstances, and I would never see him again. I turned away from the gray stone wall and started across the grassy knoll, and as I did so I saw a bright flash of blue among the trees. Em cleared the trees and hurried toward me, her blue skirt flapping in the breeze.

"I've been looking all over for you!" she cried.

She caught up with me and placed a hand over her heart, breathing rapidly, chestnut locks spilling over her shoulders in a bouncy tangle.

"I left early," I told her. "I wanted some fresh air."

Em sighed heavily. "I slept late. I *needed* to after last night. Cleeve is insatiable, luv, and he has the strength of a stallion."

"You really are taking quite a chance, Em."

"I know, luv, but I have my reasons. He's a surly, silent brute, true, but I figured I could get him to talk, figured he might say something that would be worthwhile. Well, last night he *did*. Let's walk this way."

She took hold of my arm and turned me around, and we started walking toward the west end of the island, away from the stockade. I was puzzled, but before I could question her she continued in an excited voice.

"Cleeve told me a very interesting story, luv. He said the pirates used to row over to the mainland and hide in the bushes and wait for an Indian woman to come along. They'd jump out and pounce on her and bring her back to the island for some fun on the beach. They did it several times—that's why the Indians attacked that time, the pirates were abducting their women and raping them."

"I knew that, Em."

"After the attack, Red Nick forbade his men to row over to the mainland and molest the Indian women, but that didn't stop them. Cleeve and some of the others continued to sneak over now and again. Not more than six months ago a group of them rowed over one night and caught one of the women and brought her back to the island. They gagged her so that she couldn't make any noise, then raped her and killed her."

"Was Cleeve with them?" I asked.

Em shook her head. "Lucky for him he wasn't," she said. "They buried her body and hid the boat and returned to town. A couple of days later her body was discovered—they buried her on the beach and the waves washed the sand away. Red Nick was furious!"

Em paused, trying to control her excitement. We had left the grassy knoll now and were walking through the woods, sunlight sifting through the limbs overhead to make bright patterns on the shadowy ground. Tall ferns and plants with large, heart-shaped dark green leaves grew under the trees, and there were clusters of dark purple and red flowers as well. Thick strands of ivy covered many of the trees, heavy, vinelike strands dangling down from the limbs.

"He discovered the names of the culprits," Em continued, "and he had all five of them flogged, a hundred lashes each. One of the men died. Red Nick made his point, and now none of the men would dare venture over to the mainland with mischief in mind."

"I fail to see why you find the story so exciting, Em."

"Think, luv," she replied.

"What could it possibly have to do with us?"

"Think," she repeated.

I hesitated, frowning, and then it dawned on me. "The boat," I said.

"Exactly! They kept it hidden, luv, and chances are it's still there! I questioned Cleeve thoroughly, had to be real careful about it, had to pretend I wasn't really interested, merely making idle conversation. I kept stroking his back and wiggling under him and sighing blissfully—I should have gone on the stage, luv. Tiny rocks were bruising my backside and leaves were tickling my feet and legs and Cleeve must weigh a ton, all solid muscle."

"Are you sure he didn't suspect anything?"

"I told you I was careful. I asked him about the trips to the mainland, told him it was very brave and daring, said he must have been scared. He said no, he wasn't scared at all, not an Indian alive scared him. I said I didn't mean he might be scared of the Indians, I meant he must have been scared Red Nick would find out, might find the boat and figure out what they were doing."

"And?"

"He said there wasn't much chance of that, said there were huge rocks on the west end of the island, all covered over with ivy, with a network of small caves behind them. They hid the boat in one of the caves, he told me. I said oh, that was clever, and he said yeah, the cave kept it dry and it was near the water and they could pull it out easy and row across, and I said we're wasting time with all this talk, luv, let's have some more action. He started plowing away again, kept at it half the night. I could hardly *walk* when I got up this morning."

"Do you think he'll remember the conversation?" I asked.

"He's not going to remember anything we *said*, luv. He's not overly bright to begin with, and he's convinced the only reason I keep meeting him is because I can't resist his gorgeous body. I must say," she added thoughtfully, "he certainly knows what to *do* with it."

"You're dreadful, Em," I teased.

"A girl learns to appreciate certain skills," she replied, very matter-of-fact. "If she's going to have to use her body to barter with, she might as well get a little fun out of it. I got the information I wanted, luv, that's the important thing. The rest was a kind of bonus!"

She smiled, cheerfully amoral, engagingly frank. Em was the bravest girl I had ever known, bright, bold, indomitable, and I admired her without reservation. If her attitude toward things of the flesh was casual and considerably less than saintly, she had a sunny disposition and an innate goodness of heart that would have been exemplary to the most pious of souls. She walked beside me now with a light step, keeping an eye out for snakes, convinced the island was infested with them.

"I really don't see what good a small boat would do us," I said. "Once we rowed across to the mainland, we'd be in an even worse situation. The Indians—"

"Who says we have to row to the mainland?" she interrupted.

"We certainly can't row out to sea."

"But we *can* row along the coast, luv, avoiding the mainland until we are many, many miles away, well past Indian territory, *then* we can land and take our chances."

"It's an extremely daring plan, Em."

"It happens to be the only one we have at the moment."

"That's quite true," I said.

"We can steal provisions—food, water, guns—and carry them to the boat on the sly until we have enough for our journey. Then we can slip out of the stockade at night, and by the time they discover we're gone we can be several miles up the coast."

"They'd be certain to come after us."

"They'll assume we've crossed over to the mainland—I'll

drop hints that I don't *believe* in the Indians and ask Michael carefully obvious questions about that settlement thirty miles inland Red Nick's men sometimes trek to. Is that a *snake!*''

"It's only a branch, Em," I said.

"Gave me quite a turn! Anyway, when we're gone he'll remember my questions, and they'll send a party to the mainland and spend a couple of days looking for us and, more than likely, assume we've been eaten up by cannibals. We can make it, luv."

It was, of course, a wild and utterly foolhardy plan, but Em's enthusiasm was infectious, and I began to think it just might work. There were big questions. How were we going to get the provisions, and, once we got them, how were we going to get them to the boat? We couldn't just walk through the gates carrying containers of water and bags of oranges and boxes of dried beef, nor could we saunter past Cleeve and his men with guns and ammunition. Em seemed to read my mind.

"We'll find a way to get food and water and things," she said, "and we'll find a way to get them to the boat. I've already got a couple of ideas, luv."

"I suppose it could work."

"It *will*," she assured me.

"First we've got to find the boat, if, indeed, there is one."

"There *is*, luv. I just know it!"

Her hazel eyes were full of determination as we continued to move through the thick forest, avoiding the dangling strands of ivy, stepping over logs and rocks. After a while the trees seemed to thin out, far more sunlight streaming through the limbs, and the ground was much rockier. Em caught her skirt on a branch, muttered a curse, pulled it free. A bird cawed loudly, causing her to jump.

"I'm really not a woodsy person," she admitted.

"Nor am I."

"At least you've had experience, luv, all those weeks you spent trekking down the Natchez Trace with that chap Jeff you told me about. How are you at rowing a boat?"

"I don't know. I've never done it."

"Neither have I, but I'm sure it's easy enough once you get the knack. I imagine we can muster through."

The trees ended up ahead. We could see sky and water

through the trunks. Moving under the last limbs, we found ourselves on a high bluff, enormous, ivy-covered rocks tumbling down in a sprawling cascade to the beach below. The ivy was a dark, waxy green, clinging in leafy clusters to the dark gray rocks mottled with rust and umber streaks. Some of the rocks were as large as houses, some much smaller, precariously piled together as though dumped by a capricious giant. The wind was quite strong at this end of the island, causing the ivy to rattle noisily, causing our skirts to whip about our legs.

"The caves would be down below," Em said. "Guess we'll have to get down there somehow."

"It shouldn't be difficult," I observed.

"Not for a mountain goat!"

I smiled and, leaving her standing there with a dubious expression on her face, stepped onto the nearest rock, caught hold of a thick strand of ivy and carefully lowered myself onto the rock jutting out beneath it. The wind seemed to blow even harder, tearing at my hair, tossing it across my face as I sought another foothold. My foot slipped. I clung to the ivy, hoping it wouldn't be torn from its roots. Em screamed. I hesitated a moment and then, still holding the ivy with one hand, reached down to remove my shoes, first the left and then the right. I tossed them down to the beach and continued my descent with much greater ease, lowering myself into a crevice, edging around a great, ivy-hung hump, stepping down onto a broad, rocky ledge that glittered with mica in the sunlight.

As I continued to climb down, I remembered that other descent, much more hazardous than this, when I had climbed down the cliff behind the inn in Natchez, attempting to escape from Jeff Rawlins. That seemed such a long time ago, another lifetime. I blotted the memory out of my mind and concentrated on finding another foothold, halfway down now. The rocks were much larger here, easier to move over, although the drop from rock to rock was much steeper, sometimes as much as ten or fifteen feet. It would have been difficult indeed if I hadn't been able to hold onto the thick strands of ivy, using them as though they were ropes. It was with considerable relief that I lowered myself down the last rock and stepped onto the sand.

Em dropped down beside me a few moments later, looking shaken but extremely pleased with herself.

"I'll tell you one thing right now, luv, we're going to find *another* way to get back up!"

"It wasn't so bad."

"Wasn't so bad my ass! Where are my shoes? Oh, there they are over there. I was afraid I might have hurled them into the water. You scooted down nimbly as could be, luv, like you've been climbing down rocks all your life. I don't mind tellin' you I was scared spitless."

"Now all we have to do is find the cave," I said.

"Cleeve said it was behind the ivy, and said you couldn't see it. Let me just get my shoes on, and we'll find it in no time."

After we had retrieved our shoes and put them back on, we began to part the strands of ivy, looking for crevices. We found one cave almost immediately, but it was filled with cobwebs and much too small, hardly more than a hollow, certainly not large enough for a boat. The second cave was wide and low, so low we had to crawl. We crawled for perhaps thirty feet, Em grumbling all the while, before we reached solid rock and could go no farther. I had to smile at Em's expression as we crawled back out into the sunlight and stood up. Her spirit of adventure had been sorely tested. She brushed her skirt and wiped a cobweb from her cheek, a stubborn frown creasing her brow.

"I'm not giving up!" she vowed. "It's got to be here somewhere."

It was, but it took us another half hour to find it. The ivy hung down in thick, green-black strands like a waterfall, parting easily. A large tunnel led into the side of the bluff, sloping upward. I draped the ivy back so that light would stream in, but even so it was extremely dim inside, the walls damp and clammy, the sand under our feet deep and slippery, difficult to walk on. Large cobwebs waved from the ceiling. Em eyed them apprehensively. The tunnel veered to the right, widened even more, and we stepped into a large cave. The boat sat in the sand against one of the rocky walls, a coil of heavy rope beside it, the rope they had undoubtedly used to pull the boat out to the water. A pair of sturdy oars rested against the hull.

Em and I were silent, staring at it for several long moments. The sight of it should have been reassuring, but it wasn't. The reality was somehow disturbing. It was all very well to chatter about a bold escape by rowboat, but now that we actually had the means to do so, it became deadly serious. I felt a curious apprehension, and I could tell that Em did, too. Her expression was grave, her manner unusually subdued.

"We've got to do it, Marietta," she said.

"I know."

"It's going to take guts."

"We have no alternative, Em."

"I thought I'd feel much more elated. I don't feel elated at all. I feel—nervous, jittery, don't know why."

Em sighed and stepped over to the boat. I followed her, and we examined it thoroughly in the dim light. It was ten feet long and five feet wide, built of hard wood that showed no signs of decay. The sides were high, and there were two wooden slats to sit on, one between the two brass rings that the oars fit into, one farther back. There was plenty of room for the three of us and the provisions we would need. Em kicked the hull.

"It's solid," she declared.

I picked up one of the oars, and although it was by no means light, it wasn't nearly as heavy as I had expected it to be. Setting it back down, I uncoiled the rope and tied the end to the hook in front of the boat, and when I pulled on the rope the boat slid easily over the sand. I let go of the rope and brushed a wave from my cheek.

"I think we can manage it easily enough," I said.

"Of course we can."

"We'd better get back now, Em. Cleeve will be suspicious if we're gone much longer."

Em nodded, and we left the cave, draping the ivy carefully back over the entrance. We were both silent, lost in thought. I agreed with Em that climbing back up the rocks would be far too hazardous, and we walked quietly along the beach, looking for another way up. After a quarter of a mile or so, the rocks gave way to a steep slope, and we discovered a narrow path that twisted up to the top, the path the pirates must have used. A few minutes later we were walking through the forest again, rays of sunlight slanting through the limbs overhead to make dancing patterns on the ground, strands of ivy hanging down in thick loops.

Cleeve and two other men were standing in front of the great oak doors as we neared the stockade. From the distance I could see that their expressions were extremely grim, and I knew immediately that they had been on the verge of coming to look for us. That disturbed me, but Em waved merrily and told me there was nothing to fear.

"I'll take care of Cleeve," she assured me. "I'll make up some story to explain why we were gone so long, and if he's still suspicious I'll sneak him into the shrubberies for a midmorning tumble. *That* should do it."

"You mustn't take any unnecessary risks, Em."

"Both of us are going to be taking some pretty big risks during the next few days, luv. We've got to figure out a way to steal food and guns and ammunition and smuggle them out. It's going to be risky as hell."

Em flashed a teasing smile as we neared the men. "Meet me in the garden this afternoon," she said under her breath. "We've got an awful lot of planning to do."

Fifteen

The house was very quiet, so quiet I could hear birds chirping in the gardens out back. Burke, Lyon's chief servant, had gone down to the town to join his cronies in one of the canteens, and the other servants were either out or taking an afternoon siesta. It was a perfect opportunity, everything clear, but I was still nervous as I left the small sitting room on the second floor and started down the hall to the staircase. It was very warm, and all the windows were open. The house was full of sunlight, rooms bright and airy, but there was a sinister atmosphere nevertheless.

I had the feeling that unseen eyes were watching every move I made, and although I told myself that was preposterous, the feeling remained. Nervous and apprehensive, I moved down the curving staircase and across the wide hallway. My footsteps seemed to ring much too loudly on the gleaming golden brown parquet. I paused, listening. The birds chirped. Draperies rustled quietly as a warm breeze blew in through the open windows. No one was about. I hesitated a moment longer and then moved slowly and cautiously down the narrow back hall leading to the kitchen and servants' quarters, expecting Burke to step out and confront me at any moment.

Burke was tall and thin with a pockmarked face, thin, mean lips, and eyes so dark brown they seemed black. His pewter-gray hair was clipped very short, covering his skull like a tight cap, and I had never seen him in anything but the old black suit that fit his scarecrow-thin body like a second skin. Burke ran the house with the harsh efficiency of a tyrant, cruelly bullying the other servants, sullen youths who had been pressed into service as footmen, a fat harridan from the town who wore a black dress, drank endless glasses of rum, and held the title of housekeeper. The cook was from France, a superb chef who had murdered a family in Paris with his butcher knife. Fleeing the authorities, he had eventually ended up in Red Nick's service and spent most of his time brooding over his pots and pans in the kitchen and, between curses, creating elegant and superbly delicious meals.

Burke hated me. His thin lips compressed into a hard, tight line whenever I happened to encounter him, his dark eyes glowing with animosity, glowing like coals. Fiercely loyal to Red Nick, he resented my presence, resented the hold he felt I had over his master. I knew that he had made life hell for the unfortunate Maria, spying on her, reporting on her movements to Lyon and frequently stirring up trouble. He tried to make life hell for me, too, but I refused to be baited, treating him with cool hauteur when it was necessary for me to speak to him and ignoring him the rest of the time. Corrie lived in terror of Burke, and I had to admit that I was terrified, too, now that I was engaged in highly dangerous activity. If Burke had the least suspicion of what was going on, all would be lost.

The doors to the servants' dining hall were open. I paused, listening once more, then quickly moved past them and past the kitchen, opening the small door that led to the storage room and wine cellar below. I closed the door behind me and moved down the wide stone steps. The air was cool and clammy, smelling of damp and cork and onions. It was very dim, but I didn't dare light the torches that stood in iron rings along the wall. There was just enough light to see by, and I knew my way around quite well. I had been down here several times during the past week, each time on the sly, usually late at night with a candle that I could snuff out immediately if someone opened the door above the stairs. Passing the great wooden barrels of rum and the tall racks containing dusty bottles of the finest wine, I stepped into the enormous storeroom where food was kept, bins of flour, sugar, and tea, containers of salt and spices, fruit and nuts and beans and corn.

I had smuggled out apples and oranges and a large cotton sack full of hard parched corn, and I had also returned to my room with three fairly large empty tin containers which, now filled with water, sat in the boat with lids firmly in place. Em and I had worked out an ingenious way to get things out of the stockade. Behind the garden a narrow flight of white stone steps led up to the walkway that ran around the top of the high walls. Slipping up the steps at night, long after everyone was asleep and Cleeve had returned to the barracks, we lowered the bags of food and the containers to the ground on the other side of the wall with ropes and, the next morning, after we had sauntered out the great oak doors for our morning walks, fetched them and carried them to the boat, keeping behind trees and shrubberies to avoid possible detection.

We had fruit and parched corn and an enormous bag of nuts which were quite nutritious, but we needed some kind of meat as well. We might be on the boat for days, Em pointed out, rowing constantly, and we were going to need all the strength we could get. Finding a nonperishable meat had presented a problem. Strolling casually into the kitchen this morning, I had complimented Pierre on last night's meal, delicate pieces of beef cooked in a thick, creamy white wine sauce and baked in a pastry shell. Idly, I had asked him where he had gotten the meat. The fish and fowl, I knew, came from town, but no cattle were raised on the island. Scowling moodily at the intrusion, he had continued to polish a copper pot and muttered something about a supply of beef in the storage room. Surely it would spoil, I remarked, and he sullenly informed me that the beef was dried in hard chunks. Soaked in water or, preferably, wine, and cooked thoroughly, it was quite as savory as fresh. Having acquired the information I was seeking, I complimented him again, smiled politely, and went on up to the sitting room to give Corrie her lessons.

And now, in the dim, shadowy storage room with its damp walls and the floor strewn with sawdust, I searched for the dried beef, which I had not spied on any of my other trips down here. I prowled among the shelves, pushing aside boxes and canisters, looking behind bins, wondering where it could possibly be. The smell of clove and cinnamon and pepper was heady, blending with the smell of sawdust and damp stone. Strings of onions hung from the ceiling, and a huge barrel brimmed over with coffee beans. There was another barrel beside it, the lid tightly sealed. I pried at the lid, finally loosening it, and when I removed it I saw the chunks of beef, each individually wrapped in thin white oilcloth. I took a chunk out and examined it, smiling as I realized this was exactly what we needed.

As I was contemplating how to get it upstairs without being detected, there was a sound from above. I froze. The door creaked as someone cautiously opened it, quietly closed it. Stealthy footsteps sounded on the stairs. My heart seemed to leap into my throat, and then it seemed to stop beating altogether. I looked around frantically for some place to hide, darting quickly behind an enormous bin and huddling down as the footsteps moved past the racks of wine and entered the storage room. It was Burke. It had to be. He hadn't gone down to the canteen after all. He had stayed behind to spy on me, hoping to catch me out in something, and he had seen me come down here and everything was lost, everything. I closed my eyes, praying he wouldn't look behind the bin.

"Miz Marietta?"

Relief flooded over me. I stood up abruptly, so abruptly that Corrie gave a loud gasp, frightened half out of her wits. She was clutching two large pieces of cloth, and she was trembling visibly.

"Corrie! Thank God it's you. You—you scared the life out of me!"

"You done scared *me*, too," she said in a trembly voice. "I thought you was some kind of ghost, jumping up like that. I don't like this place at all. It's spooky, Miz Marietta."

"Why are you here?"

"I seen you—I *saw* you going down the hall. I was in my room and heard a noise and looked out and saw you sneaking through the door. I knew you was coming to look for the beef that French cook told you about, and I figured you might need some help so I made sure no one was about and sneaked down, too."

"What's that you have in your hands?"

"Well, after our lessons this morning I figured it might not be too easy to get them chunks of beef back up without no one seeing, so I thought on it for a while and decided what we needed was some big pockets. I took these aprons and made great big pockets on 'em and, see, we can put the beef in the pockets, tie the aprons on under our skirts, and march right past anyone pretty as you please without 'em being any the wiser."

"Corrie, you're a wonder!"

"You and Miss Em has been taking all the chances," she informed me, "and I've been feeling guilty about it. I figured it was time I helped some, too."

She smiled shyly, and I gave her a tight hug.

"I'd just as soon get out of this spooky place soon as we can," she said, glancing apprehensively around the room. "Let's just fill up these pockets and tie the aprons on quick as we can."

I nodded in agreement, and in less than five minutes we had the pockets of the aprons bulging with chunks of beef, the aprons tied on under our skirts and completely concealed. I frowned, staring at the half-empty barrel.

"If Pierre comes down to fetch more beef during the next day or so, he'll be certain to notice a lot of it is missing," I said. "He'll start asking questions."

Corrie tilted her head to one side, thinking hard, and then she smiled and tipped the barrel over, emptying all the remaining beef onto the floor, setting the barrel back up. As I watched, she began to fill the bottom of it with apples from one of the bins. Wondering why I hadn't thought of so simple a solution, I helped her, and when we had enough apples in the bottom, we put the beef on top of it. When we had finished, the barrel seemed to be as full of beef as it had been before.

"Where we going to hide all this meat we got?" she asked.

"We'll take it up to my bedroom and put it under the bed until tonight," I said, "and then Em and I will drop it over the wall after everyone else has gone to sleep."

We moved back through the wine cellar, walking rather awkwardly because of the heavily laden aprons tied about our waists under our skirts. Corrie's pale lime green cotton skirt looked much fuller than it had been when she came down, but not too obviously so. The chunks of beef slapped against my legs as I went up the steps. I was exhausted, but I felt a great sense of triumph as we opened the door and stepped back into the hall. We had all the food we needed now, water as well. All we lacked were guns and ammunition, and Em was busily figuring out a way to acquire them.

I closed the door behind me and turned to Corrie with a smile. The smile died on my lips when I saw her face. Her lips were parted. Her eyes were wide with terror. I heard footsteps and turned to see Burke moving purposefully down the hall toward us.

"Relax, Corrie!" I whispered urgently. "Don't let him see you're afraid. Don't let him suspect we have anything to hide!"

"May I ask what you're doing?" Burke growled.

"You may," I replied coldly, "but I'm not certain you'll receive an answer. I don't care for your tone, Burke."

"What were you doing down there!"

I gazed at him with haughty disdain, the mistress of the house confronting an impudent servant. Burke stood his ground, tall and sinister in his old black suit, his pock-marked face tight with suspicion. The black-brown eyes glowered at me with fierce animosity, and I was so nervous I thought my knees might give way, but somehow I managed to maintain my hauteur.

"I went down to inspect the wines," I said in a voice like ice. "Nicholas will be returning any day now, and I want to have something special for his return. I intend to confer with Pierre about the meal, too. You object?"

"You have no business down there!"

"I happen to be mistress of the house, Burke. I'll thank you to keep that in mind."

Burke glared at me, longing to vent his hostility in a spew of venomous insults, but he didn't quite dare, not at this point. Instead, he turned to Corrie, his mouth tightening into a thin, vicious line. Pewter-gray hair covering his skull in short-clipped locks, heavy, dark brows lowered menacingly, he took a step toward her.

"What are you doing here, nigger!"

Corrie moved back, utterly terrified and unable to conceal it. "I—I'se with Miz Marietta—" she stammered.

"What are you hiding? You're hiding something, I can tell. You steal something while you were down there?"

"How dare you!" I cried.

Burke paid no attention to me. "Come here, nigger! Several bottles of wine have disappeared lately. You got a bottle under your skirt? You been sneaking down there and stealing it, haven't you!"

Corrie backed against the wall, shaking her head back and forth, tears of terror welling in her eyes. Burke snarled and started to seize her arm, and it was then that I slammed my palm across his face, slapping him so hard that his head snapped back. He was stunned, as, indeed, I was myself. I had acted instinctively, without thinking, and as his pock-marked cheek burned bright pink I drew myself up and gazed at him with cool sapphire eyes.

"Don't you *ever* make such an accusation again, Burke," I said. "Corrie is *my* servant, not under your supervision at all. If the wine is missing, I suggest you question the housekeeper. More than likely she ran out of rum."

"You're going to be sorry for that," he promised. His voice was a guttural rasp.

"I beg your pardon?"

"You're worse than the last one. She put on airs, too,

thought she was better 'n anyone else, thought she had him wrapped around her little finger, yeah, but she got hers. You'll get yours, too."

"Would you care to repeat those words when Red Nick returns?"

Burke made no reply. He had gone too far, he knew that, but he longed to go farther still. Had he dared, he would have torn into me with both fists, beating me to a pulp with the greatest satisfaction. For a moment, as he stood there rubbing his cheek, I thought he might actually do so, and I braced myself for the assault, determined to fight like a tigress. He hesitated, dark eyes glittering. Then he muttered a curse and turned and went back down the hall. I breathed a sigh of relief.

"Come along, Corrie," I said.

She was still frightened, too frightened to speak. She shook her head again and brushed the tears from her cheeks, making a valiant effort to pull herself together. I took her hand and squeezed it, and after a moment or so she managed a feeble smile. I was still shaken myself by the close call. My palm stung. Burke had been hostile to me from the beginning, but now he had become an extremely dangerous enemy. We were going to have to be even more careful.

"Are you all right now?" I asked.

Corrie nodded. "I—I wasn't going to let him look under my skirt, Miz Marietta. I was going to kick him hard."

"He didn't find out anything, Corrie. That's all that matters."

"He's going to have his eye on us."

"I know. We'll worry about that later. Now we'd better get up to the bedroom and hide this beef. It's terribly heavy."

We went upstairs and removed the aprons and I pushed them under the bed and sat down wearily. I was still weary that afternoon when I met Em on the lawn in front of Tremayne's cottage. Cleeve and several of the men were milling around in front of the barracks, idly watching us as we strolled past the flower beds and fountains. Em had washed her hair during the morning. It tumbled about her shoulders in lustrous chestnut waves that gleamed in the sunlight with rich highlights. She was wearing a poppy-red silk frock with full skirt, puffed sleeves that fell off the shoulders, and a bodice cut provocatively low. Her hazel eyes were grave as I told her about the beef and our encounter with Burke.

"Jesus, luv," she said, "you must have been petrified."

"I was. Poor Corrie almost fainted."

"Is he suspicious?"

"He's suspicious by nature," I told her. "I don't think he suspects what we've been up to, but he's going to be watching me very closely, Em. I've no doubt he's behind one of the windows, watching right now."

"No need to panic, luv. In a couple of days we should be long gone."

"A couple of days? But—"

"You've managed beautifully about the food, and with that dried beef added to what we already have we should be able to make it fine. We've got the water, too—lugging those containers down the slope and into the cave was the hardest thing we've done. I'd no idea water was so *heavy*."

"The guns, Em."

"I'm getting to that. You said you'd take care of the food, and I said I'd take care of the guns, and I've been working on it. Michael doesn't keep any weapons in the cottage and you said you couldn't find any in the big house either, so I got to thinking and asked myself what would happen if there was an attack or something."

Em paused. I waited patiently. She smiled.

"The barracks, luv. There's an armory in the barracks, right off the sleeping quarters. I got Cleeve to show it to me this morning while you were filling up barrels with apples and smuggling beef past Burke. I said I'd dearly love to see his quarters. He asked why, and I said I was interested in *anything* having to do with him. He was quite flattered."

"He showed you the barracks?"

"Every inch of it. The men were delighted, made all sorts of rowdy comments as I passed through—most of 'em know Cleeve's meeting me every night, the idiot had to brag about it. Men! They're his mates, though, and none of them have any great love for Tremayne so there's no danger there."

"I *wish* you would get to the point, Em."

"The armory is right off the sleeping quarters, like I told you, and it's *crammed* with muskets and pistols and powder horns and boxes of bullets, swords and things, too. Here's the best part, luv—there's a side door that opens onto the yard. The steps leading up to the walkway in front are right outside, you see, so if there's an attack or something a chap could pop down the stairs and pop into the armory for more ammunition or what have you without having to go through the sleeping quarters. Clever.''

"I assume the door is locked.''

Em smiled again, an impish light in her eyes. "Not any longer, luv. While Cleeve was laboriously explaining how you load a musket I sauntered over and unlocked it.''

"I see. You're going to slip into the armory tonight.''

"We're going to slip in, luv.''

"With all those men sleeping only a few yards away? It's far too dangerous, Em.''

"They're not going to be sleeping,'' she informed me. "They're going to be watching a fight.''

"How are you going to arrange that?'' I asked dryly.

"Easy,'' Em said.

She explained everything to me in great detail. I was exceedingly apprehensive, not at all convinced her plan would work, but, nevertheless, I strolled back out into the courtyard that evening. The sky was a dark blue-black sprinkled with frosty stars, and there was far too much moonlight, the lawns frosted with silver and spread with shadows. I kept to the shadows, moving slowly toward the big tree that stood beside the last cottage on the right. Light spilled out of the windows of the barracks. There was hearty laughter and the sounds of scuffling. Stationing myself under the tree, I waited, and soon I saw Em ambling along in the moonlight. She paused beside one of the fountains. A few minutes later a man joined her.

Not much taller than she was, with a stocky, muscular build and extremely broad shoulders, he strode purposefully over to the fountain and stood in front of her with his legs spread, his fists planted on his thighs, his stance that of a rough pugilist spoiling for a fight. I recognized him immediately, Grimmet, the black-haired brute who, with Cleeve, had accompanied us on our walks those first two days.

"Fancy meeting *you* here,'' Em said coyly.

"Whadda ya mean? Ain't no coincidence, is it?''

I could hear their voices clearly, and although I couldn't see their faces, I could visualize Em's flirtatious smile and Grimmet's sullen, determined expression. Em had chosen her man well. Grimmet was a hot-tempered, belligerent lout who was a natural born bully.

"You gimme a message," he said, "swishing around in that red dress you're wearin', makin' eyes at me. Made a point a tellin' me you'd be takin' a stroll and 'ud like some company."

"Did I?"

"Ya know ya did. I got your message, yeah. Guess Cleeve ain't enough for you."

"Whatever do you mean?"

"You know what I mean, wench. I can use me some, ain't had any since that slut Maria was shipped off to South America. She kept all a us happy, that one. Regular spitfire."

"I think you've made a mistake," Em said. Her voice was crisp.

"Whadda ya mean?"

"I *may* have smiled at you, and I may have mentioned that I planned to take a stroll this evening, but I certainly didn't intend to imply that I wanted *your* company. I like *men*, not surly, overgrown boys."

"You sayin' I can't handle it?"

"I'm saying you'd better not *try.*"

Her words incensed him. Grimmet snorted and seized her arm. Em tried to pull away. He slung his free arm around the back of her shoulders, jerked her to him, and slammed his mouth over hers. Em struggled furiously, banging her fists against his back, kicking at his shins, fighting so vigorously that Grimmet lost his balance and fell to his knees, taking her down with him, his mouth still locked over hers. A moment later Em was on the ground, on her back, Grimmet astride her. She seized his hair and tugged at it and, once her lips were free, let out a deafening scream that could easily be heard all the way down to the harbor.

Men came pouring out of the barracks in a mad rush. Stunned, Grimmet tried to get to his feet, but Em held him fast, struggling beneath him in a frenzy of thrashing legs and flying skirts.

"Rape!" she cried. "Rape!"

The men were upon them in a matter of seconds, Cleeve in the lead, grabbing the unlucky Grimmet by the shoulders and pulling him off Em with ease as she relinquished her hold. Sobbing, marvelously hysterical, she climbed to her feet, covering her face with her hands as Cleeve threw a mighty punch that sent Grimmet sprawling. The men yelled and cheered, urging them on as the fight began in earnest, Cleeve and Grimmet filled with murderous intent, hitting and grappling and rolling on the lawn in a tangled fury.

Em backed away, completely ignored, and once she was clear of the circle of jubilant, rowdy men who lustily encouraged Cleeve and Grimmet to kill each other, she dashed nimbly across the lawn to where I stood concealed under the shadows of the tree.

"How was I?" she whispered merrily.

"Magnificent."

"Come on, luv, we haven't a second to lose."

Keeping to the shadows, we hurried to the side door of the barracks. Em opened the door, and we darted into the armory. It was very dark, only a few rays of moonlight streaming through the windows, but Em knew where everything was and exactly what she wanted. She seized three powder horns and slung them around her neck and grabbed a musket and thrust it into my hands. Scooping up two pistols, she led the way back outside, and we dashed to a clump of shrubbery she had picked out earlier and deposited our loot under it. The fight was still raging, the men yelling louder than before, laughing and scuffling among themselves as Cleeve and Grimmet continued to pound each other.

"Quick, luv, we've got to make another trip!"

We raced back to the armory, and Em pointed out the wooden box of ammunition. We heaved it up together, for it was far too heavy for either of us to carry alone. We hurried back to the shrubbery and shoved it under the thick, leafy branches, both of us out of breath. I stayed there, heart pounding, while Em returned to the armory to grab two bags of buckshot for the musket and lock the door. She joined me in less than two minutes, and together we hurried to where the men were fighting, Em sobbing beautifully.

I wrapped my arms around her and tried to comfort her, telling her it would be all right, telling her it was over now. It hadn't taken us a full ten minutes to carry out our mission. Cleeve and Grimmet were standing, staggering, both of them bloodied and bruised, exhausted. Em cried out, begging them to stop. Grimmet threw a punch and missed and fell to his knees. The men yelled gleefully as Cleeve aimed a kick and smashed the toe of his boot into Grimmet's temple. Grimmet sprawled backward, out cold. The fight was over.

Burke stepped foward to peer at the unconscious man and turned to Cleeve with accusing eyes. I hadn't seen him before. How long had he been watching? Had he come running out when Em first screamed? He demanded to know how the fight had begun and reminded everyone that fighting was forbidden and that both men would surely be flogged. They all hooted at him, and one man told him that if he knew what was good for him he'd keep his bleedin' mouth shut or else have his tongue ripped out. They howled at that, pounding each other on the back. Burke was livid, but he knew better than to stand up to this lot.

"Lucky for you Red Nick isn't here," he grumbled to Cleeve.

"Shove off, mate!" Cleeve snarled. "If word of this gets out, you're gonna be sorry. I'll personally see ya are."

Burke muttered something under his breath and turned away to go back to the house. Seeing me standing with my arms around the sobbing Em, he paused a moment and glared at me as though I were solely responsible for what had happened. I ignored him, repressing a shudder as he moved on angrily. Deciding it was time to stop sobbing, Em straightened up and wiped the false tears from her eyes and let out a gasp when she got a good look at Grimmet.

"Oh my!" she exclaimed. "You men had better take him back to the barracks and tend to his wounds. What a dreadful, dreadful experience—I don't know what came *over* him. Unbridled lust, I suspect. Just couldn't help himself. You come with me, Cleeve. I'll patch *you* up myself."

She led away the unprotesting Cleeve, and the men picked Grimmet up and hauled him back to the barracks. After all the noise and excitement, it was very quiet, very calm. I strolled slowly across the silver-brushed lawn strewn with elongated velvety black shadows. Leaves rustled. A bird cried out. From the barracks came a single, husky laugh. I could hardly believe that Em's plan had worked so well, and, now that it was over, I was horrified at our boldness. While we were actually carrying it out, there had been no time for nerves, we had been much too busy, but now I was so weak I could hardly climb the wide stone steps and open the front door. If we had been caught . . . but we hadn't been. We had carried it off with marvelous aplomb.

I paused for a moment in front of the long mirror that hung in the huge foyer. Candles burned in silver brackets on either side of it, creating a softly diffused light that was highly flattering. Rich copper-red locks spilled down to my shoulders in tumbling disarray, and my cheeks were slightly flushed. Faint, delicate blue-gray shadows stained my lids, while my eyes were a deep, deep sapphire, weary, sad. My shoulders were smooth and creamy white, bare, the sleeves of my dark blue gown crumpled, the low-cut bodice lightly soiled from our exertion. I gazed at the reflection for several moments, remembering another Marietta, wondering if I would ever see her gazing back at me again.

I went up the stairs to the large, elegant master bedroom to wait. Red Nick always made love to me on that grand, ornately carved white bed with its mauve and silver hangings, its mauve satin counterpane embroidered with tiny *fleurs-de-lis* in rich purple silk. After he had satisfied himself and, yes, satisfied me, too, at least physically, he always returned to his own, smaller bedroom down the hall. I stared at the bed, thinking of his lean, tan, superbly conditioned body and his savage expertise. How was it possible to hate someone so much, to actively long for his death, yet still respond to his strength and that curious combination of brutality and tender calculation?

I hoped I would never see him again. It was too much to hope that his ship would sink, but perhaps we could make our escape before he and Tremayne and the others returned. Had they been here this past week, it would have been impossible for us to have accomplished what we had. Their absence had been providential indeed, and their return now would be disastrous, increasing the danger many times over. Putting out the lights, sitting down in one of the plush, ivory satin chairs to wait, I prayed we would be safely on our way before *The Sea Lyon* came sailing into harbor.

The darkness was soon alleviated by pale, hazy moonlight that fell across the balcony and streamed in through the open French windows. The house was still, the silence broken only by the ticking of the clock and the gentle rustle of the drapes billowing inward in the faint evening breeze. They were mauve satin like the counterpane, embroidered with identical purple silk *fleurs-de-lis*, billowing with a soft swoosh, falling back, billowing again as the breeze caught them once more. Moonlight silvered the parquet floor and rich Aubusson carpets, and I could smell the gardens and, more faintly, the salty tang of the water half a mile away. An hour passed, another, and it was almost two in the morning before the pebble finally plopped lightly against a window pane. I moved quietly out onto the balcony and, leaning over the railing, peered down into the darkness. I could just see Em standing in the shadows of a tall shrub.

Hurrying back into the bedroom, I pulled the aprons out from under the bed and dragged them back to the balcony. I dropped them over, one at a time, and they landed with dull thuds that seemed frightfully loud. I crept down the hallway and started down the staircase, peering nervously around me in the darkness. I paused halfway down, certain I saw someone standing against the wall in the foyer, a distinct form slightly more solid than the dark shadows surrounding it. My skin chilled. I actually seemed to be encased in ice. I stood there for a long time, frozen, terrified, my eyes never leaving that dark bulk, darker than the shadows. There was no movement, no sound. I realized at last that my imagination was playing tricks on me, and I continued on down the stairs, moving very, very slowly, damning myself for wearing taffeta when I knew it rustled much louder than other materials.

Reaching the bottom of the staircase, I paused again, peering once more at the mass of shadows against the wall. The darker bulk I thought I had seen was no longer there, had vanished completely. I had indeed imagined it, just as I now imagined a pair of eyes staring at me, hostile eyes staring so intensely it seemed I could actually feel them boring into me. That was absurd. Of course it was absurd. There was no one standing against the wall, and no one was staring. I hurried down the narrow passageway that led to the back door, and a moment later I stepped into the gardens. My skin was still icy when I joined Em. A bird warbled sleepily. The sound made me jump.

"I'm sorry," I said. "Nerves."

"I'm a bit jumpy myself, luv. Who wouldn't be?"

"I thought I saw someone in the foyer as I came down the stairs. I thought someone was staring at me. It was—very unnerving."

"You're certain no one was there?"

"It—it was so dark. I'm pretty sure I imagined it."

"Let's hope so, luv. I don't trust that fellow Burke. The way he looked at you tonight—it gave me the shivers."

"Did you have any trouble with Cleeve?" I asked.

"Oh, he's out cold. I sent him straight back to the barracks as soon as I got through washing his wounds and dabbing on a bit of ointment. He wasn't up to any *more* activity this evening."

"It's so late, Em. Why did you wait so long to come?"

"I crept over shortly after midnight, luv, thought we'd get an early start, but there was a light burning in the servants' quarters—Burke, probably—and I didn't dare signal you until the light went out. I didn't want you traipsing through the house while someone was still up. However, I *did* make good use of the time. You'll be pleased to know I've already brought the guns and things to the foot of the steps."

"You carried that box of bullets by *yourself?*"

"*Shoved* the bloody thing, luv, every inch of the way. It wasn't jolly, I assure you."

"You should have waited and let me help."

"I didn't know how long that light was going to keep burning, and time was getting short. We'd better get right to work, Marietta. It's going to take us quite a while to get all these things dumped over the wall."

We picked up the aprons and, crossing the gardens, carried them to the foot of the narrow white stone steps that rose to the walkway that ran all around the top of the walls, with cannon stationed at strategic points. I fetched the rope and basket we had hidden under a shrub and, filling it with powder horns and pistols, we climbed the steps and moved along the wide walkway until we reached the point near one of the cannons. Tying the rope to the handle of the basket, we lowered the basket over the wall, dumping its contents behind a clump of underbrush growing near the wall, then pulled the empty basket back up.

Although tall trees grew in the gardens, their spreading limbs rising higher than the walls and concealing our progress along the walkway from anyone who might otherwise have been able to observe us from the windows of the house, I was nevertheless thankful that the moon had gone behind a heavy bank of clouds. It took us three more trips to get the rest of the things, and we had an extremely difficult time with the box of bullets, carefully hauling it up the perilously narrow steps. There was no railing, and one slip could have sent us crashing down to the ground below. The box completely filled the basket, and once we had lowered it, we found it impossible to tilt over and dump. After several attempts, we finally just let the end of the rope drop over the side of the wall.

"I'm afraid we're going to have an even jollier time getting it down to the boat," Em observed.

"It shouldn't be too difficult," I said. "We'll simply pull it in the basket. Thank goodness that's the last of the lot."

The clouds began to drift, silver spilling over their edges, and finally the moon appeared again, illuminating the scene with pale light. Exhausted, we stood there on the walkway for several minutes, peering across the woods to the water, pewter gray in the moonlight and gleaming with silvery reflections. The mainland beyond was a solid mass of darkness, dense, forbidding. In the stillness we could hear the waves sloshing over the sand half a mile away, the sound like whispers in the night. I shivered.

"Frightened?" Em asked.

"A little. I never thought we'd get this far."

"Neither did I, truth to tell, but we've done magnificently, luv. We've been quite resourceful. We'll get everything down to the boat tomorrow—that's going to be quite a chore—and then—" she paused. "Then we'll be ready to make good our escape."

She turned and sighed, and, without speaking, we left the walkway and moved down the steps and crossed the garden, leaves rustling, the ground a patchwork of silver and black. Em walked to the back door with me, and we stood there for several moments, silent, awed by the enormity of what we had undertaken. I finally spoke.

"Do you really think we can make it, Em?"

"Resourceful girls like us? Of course we can."

There was a hollow ring to her words, and I knew that she was as apprehensive as I was. I reached for her hand and squeezed it, and we were silent for a few more moments, comforting each other, trying to quell the fear that suddenly possessed us both.

"Look at it this way, luv, the hardest part's behind us."

"I suppose so."

"We've got a boat, food, water, weapons—what could go wrong? We're going to do beautifully."

"I hope so."

"You *can* handle a gun?"

"I shot an Indian once. On the Natchez Trace. He was in a tree, ready to leap on Jeff with a tomahawk."

"Maybe—maybe we won't run into any Indians."

"Maybe not."

Em sighed again and let go of my hand. "I'd better get back, luv. It'll be dawn soon, and I don't want anyone to see me sneaking back into the cottage. We'll take our walk in the woods early tomorrow afternoon."

"And leave tomorrow night," I said.

"Tomorrow night it is, luv," Em replied. "The sooner we get off this bloody island the happier I'll be!"

Sixteen

Everything was in place, evenly distributed at either end of the boat, and we stared at it for a moment there in the dimness of the cave: guns, ammunition, enough food and water to last us for three or four weeks if we portioned them carefully. Satisfied with our accomplishment and extremely tired after two hours of work hauling everything down to the cave, we turned and moved down the wide damp tunnel and stepped into the dazzling late afternoon sunlight. Both of us were grimy, our dresses stained with perspiration, our hair all atangle, and I brushed a long cobweb from Em's cheek.

"Cleeve's going to be very suspicious," I remarked.

"Don't worry about Cleeve, luv. You've got a smudge of dirt on your left cheek."

I wiped it away and gazed at the waves washing gently over the fine gray sand littered with delicate pinkish-orange shells. Across the water the mainland was brown and green, festooned with long black shadows, and I wondered if the Indians were watching us. In my imagination every tree trunk concealed a tall, naked savage painted black and white, smeared with alligator grease and carrying slings of arrows and bows six feet long. Was it true that they actually ate men alive, slicing strips of flesh off a victim lashed to a stake and screaming in agony?

"Don't think about it," Em said, guessing my thoughts.

"I shouldn't, I know, but I can't help it. All those stories—"

"They're probably miles away, luv, holding a big powwow in another area. Indians migrate, you know. They're always packing up their tepees and moving to a cozier spot."

"That's quite true."

"Look at it this way, after what we've seen, after the pirates, a band of cannibals would seem downright friendly. We'd better get back to the stockade, luv, don't want the boys getting edgy. Have you told Corrie we're leaving tonight?" she asked as we started toward the slope.

"I told her this morning while she was brushing my hair. She's very nervous about it, but she's going to hold up fine."

"I'm sure she will," Em said. "The three of us are going to do marvelously well. We'll be back in New Orleans before you know it."

"Do you really think so, Em?"

"Of course we will, and we'll go to the authorities and tell them all we know about the island—its location, the number of men, the position of the cannons, the stockade, where the armory is. With that information they won't be so leary about invading. They'll wipe the place right off the map, luv. Red Nick and crew will be sorry they ever tangled with us."

"What are your plans, Em?"

"You mean when we get back? I've got plenty of plans, luv. I'm going to sell all that jewelry Michael's given me and have a whole lot of money and then I'm going to go respectable. I'm going to learn to speak proper and act proper, and then I'm going to charm the breeches off some unsuspecting man who'll jump at the chance to marry me."

"Sounds frightfully dull," I teased.

"He may be unsuspecting, luv, but he'll be big and strong and handsome and anything but dull. A military man, perhaps, I've always had a weakness for soldiers. Sailors, too, for that matter."

"You're incorrigible, Em."

"I know. It's a deplorable weakness."

She smiled pertly, and we climbed up the steep, rocky path cut in the side of the slope, pausing for a few moments when we reached the top. The woods were before us, green leaves dappled with sunlight, red and purple flowers growing in the shadows. Below, the rocks tumbled to the beach, waves leaving wet tracks and strands of yellow-brown seaweed on the sand.

"What about you, luv?" Em asked. "What do you plan to do?"

"I'm going to England," I said as we started through the trees.

"Still determined to get even with that man who had your lover killed?"

I nodded, grim. "Roger Hawke is going to pay for what he did. I wanted to die when Derek was killed, Em. There was no reason to go on living, not until I saw Roger Hawke. I vowed I'd have revenge."

"I wish you could forget it, Marietta."

"I'll never be able to forget it. I'll never be able to rest until I see him in his grave."

"I don't mean to be contrary, but—well, that doesn't sound like a very noble purpose, luv. Revenge may be sweet, like someone said, but it eats you up inside. I know. I longed to take revenge on my stepfather and his darling sons, longed to go back to Baton Rouge and give 'em what they deserved, and I finally realized I wasn't hurting anyone but myself. Men like that always get their comeuppance, luv. Your Roger will eventually get his, too, without any help from you.''

I pushed a tangle of vines out of the way, knowing full well that what she said was true. There was nothing noble about my desire for revenge, but it had given me a reason to go on living, and I wasn't ready to relinquish it yet. Em plucked one of the lush red flowers and toyed with it as we moved on through the woods, sunlight dappling through the leaves, the air laden with pungent odors of lichen and bark and damp soil.

"Seems to me you'd be better off building a new life," Em continued, studying the silky red petals. "You're still young and beautiful, Marietta, and you could have any man you wanted."

"I'll never want another man, Em. After Derek, I could never love anyone else."

"I don't believe that, luv, not for a minute. You loved him, yes, and that love will always remain in your heart, along with the grief, but there'll be another man, and you'll love him just as much as you loved Derek."

The hem of my skirt caught on a branch of underbrush and I pulled it free, not bothering to reply to Em's statement. She couldn't know, of course. Intelligent though she was, and as experienced in matters of the flesh, she had never known the kind of love I had shared with Derek. That kind of love happened but once in a lifetime, and anything after would be merely a pale imitation. I could never settle for that.

"What about the charmer you met in the market?" Em asked.

"Jeremy Bond?"

"There was something in your voice when you told me about him, luv. Something in your eyes, too."

"He—he's a thorough rogue."

"You made that quite clear."

"Utterly irresponsible."

"Dashing and handsome and dangerously appealing. You told me all that, and your eyes and voice told me a lot more, luv. He touched something inside of you that had never been touched before. You responded to him as you'd never responded to another man.''

"I admitted that I wanted to sleep with him, Em."

"I'm not talking about sex, luv. You said you felt he knew you, felt he understood you—despite the fact that he was clearly a jaunty scoundrel. A man like that—" Em paused.

"A man like that would wreak havoc on any woman foolish enough to become involved with him," I said crisply.

"But any woman would be willing to take that risk."

"I wish I'd never told you about him," I said, cross now. "I met him under unusual circumstances and, yes, he made a very strong impression on me, but I'll never see him again. Even if I did, I'd turn around and run as fast as possible in the opposite direction."

Em smiled a knowing smile I found utterly infuriating. I wanted to slap her, and I immediately felt guilty about it. Em had the best intentions in the world. I had no idea what she had been trying to prove, but she had merely succeeded in irritating me. I adored her and I could never have endured all this without her, but Em the expert on love needed a good shaking. The thought that I could love a man like Jeremy Bond was laughable.

"You'll love again," Em assured me.

"Think what you like! I really don't care to discuss it."

"Sorry, luv."

"I'm the one who's sorry. I shouldn't have snapped at you like that."

"We're both tense," she said as we stepped into the clearing in front of the stockade. "Tired, too. I've never worked so hard in my life—" Em paused, frowning. "What's that noise? It sounds like they're having a riot down at the harbor."

Though muted by distance, the lusty, excited yells were clearly audible. As we listened, Cleeve came out of the stockade and strolled toward us. There was a dark bruise on his right cheekbone and his lower lip was split and swollen at one corner. Stopping a few feet away from us, he placed his fists on his thighs, the full sleeves of his silky tan shirt ballooning, the tail tucked loosely into the waistband of his dark brown breeches. Blond hair spilling about his head in

234

tattered locks, brown eyes dark and brooding, he looked formidable indeed, the broken nose adding a particularly sinister touch.

"What's all the shouting about?" Em inquired.

Cleve grimaced. "*The Sea Lyon*'s been spotted through the telescope. It'll be in the harbor before sun sets. Your man Tremayne's coming back."

"Shit," Em said. "Pardon my French, luv."

"You ain't eager to see 'im?" Cleeve asked.

"You've no *idea* how uneager I am."

Cleeve looked pleased. "Guess you've got kinda used ta our meetin's in the bushes," he said.

"Guess I have, luv."

"So what're we gonna do about it?"

"I'm sure we'll think of something," Em told him, but her mind wasn't on arranging future trysts. She was extremely distracted, her cheeks pale as she looked at the road that led down through town to the harbor.

"I ain't ready to give you up," Cleeve growled.

"And I'm not ready to give *you* up, either, luv, but right now Marietta and I have to go in and clean up. Don't fret, gorgeous. I'll get back to you real soon."

She smiled and touched his bruised cheekbone and then led the way into the stockade. We paused in the gardens in front of Tremayne's cottage, Em thinking hard, her brow creased, hazel eyes still distracted. Several pirates were sitting out in front of the barracks, polishing weapons, preparing for the inspection Red Nick was sure to hold. Grimmet was in even worse shape than Cleeve, I noticed. He glared across the lawn at Em with pure venom.

"Why did they have to come back today," Em grumbled. "This spoils everything."

"We can't allow it to, Em. We can't change our plans now."

"We'll have to, luv."

I shook my head. "If we put it off we might never go through with it. We're leaving tonight."

"What about Michael? What about Red Nick?"

"I'll take care of Red Nick," I replied, "and I assume you'll be able to take care of Tremayne."

"What do you plan to do, crack a bottle over his head?"

"If it came to that, I would. I don't think it'll be necessary. I intend to don my finest gown and greet him calmly and see that he has a splendid dinner with the choicest wine."

"And then?"

"Then we'll make love and he'll go back to his room and go to sleep and I'll gather up my jewelry and meet Corrie downstairs and we'll slip out of the house. We'll meet you at the stockade entrance at—say one-thirty."

"Those doors are solid oak, luv. They're kept firmly locked at night."

"I've yet to see a lock I couldn't pick."

"It'll be easy enough for *you* to slip out once Red Nick's left the bedroom, but Tremayne sleeps beside me all night long. I suppose I could try to get him drunk, he does love his rum."

"If that doesn't work, crack a bottle over *his* head."

"I may have to."

"One-thirty, Em."

"I'll be there," she promised.

She went on into the cottage, and I crossed the courtyard and moved up the wide front steps. Burke was standing in the foyer, tall and thin and sinister in his old black suit. He was obviously lurking about to see when I came back, and his black-brown eyes stared at me with suspicion as I entered. I was acutely aware of my stained dress and tumbled hair, and I had the uncanny feeling that he knew exactly what Em and I had been doing. There was a hollow sensation in the pit of my stomach as I looked at that thin, pockmarked face, but I managed to speak in a voice that would have suited the most imperious duchess.

"I assume you're aware *The Sea Lyon* will be docking soon," I said. "Tell Cook I want him to prepare his finest meal and serve the very best wine. We'll dine at eight."

"Guess you won't be traipsing off for hours every day now," he said in his raspy voice.

"That's no concern of yours, Burke."

"You and that other wench—you get mighty sweaty and soiled, just strolling in the woods. What causes you to work up such a sweat, I ask myself. What causes you to get your skirt all streaked with dirt? I've been thinking about that a lot."

"You have your orders, Burke! See that they're carried out."

I moved past him with superb hauteur, and it was only after I reached the upstairs sitting room that I allowed myself to react to his words. Had Burke been standing in the foyer last night? Had he seen me slip out of the house? Had he followed Em and me this afternoon, staying out of sight and watching us as we hauled the beef and guns and ammunition down to the boat? I had several moments of terrible panic, and then I steeled myself and firmly banished it. I couldn't permit myself to panic or to entertain disturbing thoughts. It was going to take all the strength I had to get through this evening without giving myself away, and I didn't intend to let Burke unnerve me.

I summoned two of the surly young footmen and had them bring water for the ornate brass and porcelain tub in the spacious, sun-filled dressing room adjoining the bedroom. I took a long bath, using the exquisite French soap that felt like satin and made a creamy, luxurious lather. I washed my hair thoroughly and rinsed it with a special rinse Corrie made with lemon juice and vinegar. When I finally got out of the tub, dried off, and toweled my hair dry, it gleamed like burnished copper with rich golden-red highlights. Slipping on a thin white silk robe festooned with rows of lacy ruffles, I tied the sash around my waist as Corrie came in to arrange my hair and help me dress.

Her delicate features were drawn, the pale coffee-colored skin taut across her cheekbones. In her light blue cotton dress, she looked small and frail and helpless, soft black hair covering her head like a puffy cloud. I knew she was nervous and apprehensive, but she made a decided effort to conceal it, her luminous brown eyes full of determination as she gathered up brush and comb and put the curling irons on to heat.

"Your hair's still kinda damp, Miz Marietta. You sit down there in front of the mirror and I'll just rub it a bit more with a fresh towel. I see you done used that rinse I made up for you. I can always tell. Your hair's like beautiful copper fire, and it has body, too. Fine to work with."

Gently, skillfully, she rubbed my hair until it was completely dry, and then she began to brush it with brisk strokes until it fell about my shoulders in heavy, silken waves that gleamed even more richly. She began to gather up the waves and stack them on top of my head in smooth, glossy swirls, as intent as a master sculptor working with liquid copper, using thin, pale gold hairpins that, once in place, were completely invisible. Her hands were steady, her full pink mouth set in a firm line. Corrie wasn't going to panic either.

"They'se—they are coming back tonight," she said. "I heard them footmen talking about it."

"That's right, Corrie."

"Is—is—are we still going to sneak out?"

"We're going to meet Em at the front entrance at one-thirty tonight. I expect you to be waiting for me in the foyer shortly after one."

"I'll be there, Miz Marietta, quiet—quiet as a mouse."

Her voice trembled, and she frowned, irritated at herself for betraying her apprehension. Fastening the last pin in place, she took up the hot curling irons and began to work with the full waves she had left hanging in back, shaping them into long, perfect ringlets.

"We're going to make it, Corrie," I said quietly. "Everything's going to work out fine."

"What about Red Nick? He—he'll come after us."

"He'll think we've gone over to the mainland. Em intends to ask Tremayne a lot of questions about the Indians tonight and make inquiries about the settlement the pirates sometimes visit. When he discovers we've gone, he'll immediately assume we've headed for the settlement, and he'll tell Red Nick."

"Miz Em is mighty clever. We—we're really going to get away. I can feel it in my bones."

"In a few weeks you'll be completely free, Corrie. You'll have money, too. I'm going to sell all my jewelry. You can come to England with me, if you like. You could open a shop there."

"What kinda shop would I wanna open, Miz Marietta?"

"I don't know. You're so marvelous with hair. There are hundreds of ladies in London who would pay dearly to have you arrange their hair. They'd also pay to buy your special rinse and that cream you made up to give extra texture to my hair. You could sell the cream and the rinse, and you could hire girls and train them to work with hair like you do."

Corrie's lovely eyes widened. "A shop just for hair?" she said. "I never heard of such a shop, Miz Marietta."

"Neither have I," I admitted, "but there's no reason why yours couldn't be the first. I think it's a marvelous idea."

Corrie put the curling irons aside and toyed with the ringlets for a few moments, making sure they had the proper shape and bounce. Satisfied, she stepped back, admiring her handiwork. My hair had never looked more beautiful, a sumptuous crown of perfectly sculpted waves with several long ringlets dangling between my shoulder blades. Corrie was indeed an artist, and although I had come up with the idea for the shop on the spur of the moment, primarily to give her something else to think about and ease her apprehension, I was convinced she could make an enormous success of such a shop.

"What gown are you going to wear tonight, Miz Marietta?"

"The bronze satin, I think."

"You mean the peacock gown, the one with all them colored ruffles showing through like peacock tails?"

I nodded. It was the most spectacular gown in the wardrobe, and although Corrie had altered it to fit me perfectly, I had never worn it. She took it out of the wardrobe, along with the petticoat that went with it, carrying them into the bedroom and spreading them carefully over the bed while I opened the elaborate white leather makeup case and began to apply pale pink lip rouge. I rubbed the sides of my cheeks with a light gray-pink salve that, smoothed on properly, looked perfectly natural and emphasized my high cheekbones, and then I applied a pale mauve shadow to my lids. When I had finished, I gazed at myself in the mirror, cool and critical, looking for flaws.

The face with its gleaming crown of copper-red waves was beautiful and composed, sapphire blue eyes calm and level, cheekbones high and aristocratic, pink mouth generously curved. It was the face of a worldly, sophisticated woman, determined and self-assured, but the woman within was anything but confident. She was a mass of trembling nerves, fighting desperately to hold herself together and draw from inner resources of strength that had been sadly depleted of late. I wondered if I would be able to go through with it. How much longer would I have to be strong and hard and resilient?

I felt weary, so weary, and I knew that if it weren't for Em and Corrie I would already have given up.

Not really, I told myself, leaving the dressing table and stepping into the bedroom. I was merely low, feeling the tension. I had been born a fighter, and I would go right on fighting. Not for me the life of ease and pampered luxury so many women knew. I had had to battle merely to survive, and by this time it was second nature to me. Removing the robe, I took the frail bronze gauze petticoat from Corrie and slipped it on. The bodice was almost non-existent, cut so low, the cloth so thin, and half-dozen gauzy bronze skirts spread out from the waist like gossamer, lifting and floating as I moved.

I sat down on the edge of the bed to put on the elegant high-heeled slippers covered in bronze satin. They fit perfectly, as did the other shoes in the wardrobe, a fact I considered quite fortunate. Corrie helped me into the exquisite bronze satin gown, fastening the tiny, invisible hooks in back while I adjusted the narrow, off-the-shoulder sleeves and extremely low bodice which clung like a second skin. Corrie fastened the last hook and stepped back to help smooth down the skirt which spread out in scalloped panels that parted halfway down to reveal an underskirt made up of rows and rows of ruffles in green, blue, yellow gold and turquoise, the colors of a peacock's tail. The gown was a magnificent creation, designed, no doubt, for some Parisian courtesan.

"I never seen anything so lovely," Corrie said. "That bronze cloth shimmers, and when you move them—those ruffles underneath flutter just like peacock feathers."

I smiled and moved over to the full-length mirror. The bodice and scalloped overskirt were cut in clean, simple lines, unadorned, the multicolored ruffles beneath the scallops providing a striking contrast, the colors all the more vivid against the bronze. Jeremy Bond would have approved of the gown, I thought, and I frowned, wondering why he came to mind, wishing I were able to forget those merry, mocking blue eyes and that wide grin that was so devilishly attractive. Why must they continue to haunt me? I recalled the conversation Em and I had had this afternoon. Why had it irritated me so? Had my voice and eyes indeed conveyed something when I had first told her about him?

The clatter of musketry and sound of voices coming from

the courtyard drove all thought of Jeremy Bond out of my mind. I glanced at the clock. It was seven thirty. Red Nick and his entourage had entered the stockade, and he would be coming inside soon.

"I better get back downstairs," Corrie said. "I'll be waiting in the foyer for you tonight, Miz Marietta. I'll be standing in the darkness, still as can be."

She hesitated a moment, standing across the room, and then she hurried over to me and flung her arms around me. I held her close, hugging her tightly, and for several moments we clung together, this frightened child and I, both longing to burst into tears. When I finally released her, she stepped back and looked up at me with moist, shining eyes and a brave smile that was utterly heartbreaking. She was so young, so lovely, totally dependent on me. I wasn't going to let her down. I brushed a tear from her cheek and returned her smile with one I hoped was reassuring.

"You're going to have that shop, Corrie," I promised.

"I believe you, Miz Marietta."

"We've both got to be very brave this evening."

"We will be," she replied. "I'm not going to be scared. I'm going to be just as brave as you and Miz Em is."

She left the bedroom with a flutter of blue cotton skirts, and a few minutes later I heard the front door opening downstairs and footsteps in the foyer. I remembered the way Maria had flown down the stairs, calling his name and demanding to know what he'd brought her. I waited almost ten minutes before leaving the bedroom. I slowly descended the curving staircase, cool, regal, showing no emotion whatsoever. Nicholas Lyon was still in the foyer, talking with Burke. Both men looked up and, after a word from Lyon, Burke scowled and left, going down the side hall toward the servants' quarters.

Red Nick stood in the foyer, tall and lean, watching me with those piercing blue eyes that seemed a darker blue, dark with male appreciation as he watched me moving on down the stairs. His high black books were polished to a high sheen, his dark maroon broadcloth breeches cut narrow, closely fitting. His maroon frock coat fit closely, too, emphasizing his broad shoulders and slender waist, the full skirt flaring slightly at the hips. A white lace jabot spilled from his throat, and lace spilled beneath the cuffs of the coat as well. He carried a broad maroon hat adorned with sweeping black plumes. His dark copper hair was burnished by the candle-light, a gleaming red-brown, the heavy wave slanting over his right eyebrow. The blue eyes glowed darkly, yes, but the lean, harshly handsome face was immobile, thin lips curling faintly at one corner.

"Good evening," I said, pausing at the foot of the stairs.

"Hardly an effusive greeting," he observed dryly.

"You want dramatics?"

"I'd like to see a gleam of pleasure—or even anticipation. I've been away two weeks."

"Two weeks and three days," I corrected.

"So you did miss me?"

"Perhaps."

"You're a deliciously infuriating creature, Marietta. I don't know whether to thrash you or take you in my arms."

"The choice is yours."

The lips curled a bit more in the suggestion of a smile. The blue eyes were sardonic. He moved toward me, stopping a few feet away from where I stood, folding his arms across his chest. The lace at his wrists dripped down like delicate white foam.

"Maybe I *should* thrash you," he remarked. "Maybe then you'd learn to appreciate your position."

"As your prisoner?"

"As my woman. You look quite spectacularly lovely. You've never worn that gown before. You put it on in honor of my return?"

"Perhaps."

"Infuriating," he said, placing his hat on a table.

"You can always replace me."

Nicholas Lyon shook his head slowly, his eyes holding mine. "I fear you're irreplaceable, my dear. You've bewitched me."

"Indeed?"

"All the time I was gone I kept thinking of you. That disturbs me. I don't like for any woman to have that kind of hold on me. No woman has—before. What shall I do about it?"

"I've no idea."

He stepped closer, unfolding his arms, resting his hands on my shoulders. I could smell the clean, pleasant musk of his body, the virile smell of flesh. His fingers squeezed my shoulders, his grip growing tighter as he pulled me to him and parted his lips, the tip of his tongue flicking out as he tilted his head and lowered his mouth over mine. I was rigid and unresponsive, making him work, stirring him to force the needed response from me. After a few moments I yielded, curling my arms around his back, rubbing my palms over the maroon broadcloth and feeling the muscles beneath. Satisfied, he released me, eyes sardonic again, blue and faintly mocking.

"One day you'll respond quite eagerly, my dear."

"Will I?"

"One day you'll want me as much as I want you."

"Perhaps," I said for a third time.

Nicholas smiled a twisted smile and, taking my arm, led me into the spacious sitting room. He sat down in one of the chairs, spreading his long legs out, tilting his head down toward his chest and lifting his eyes to watch me as I went over to the liquor cabinet to pour him a brandy. He wanted me. He wanted me badly. I smiled at the knowledge. Despite his cool, mocking demeanor, he was filled with a sexual tension so intense it was almost tangible, crackling in the air. Other men would have ground their teeth, would have gripped the arms of the chair so tightly the fabric would tear, but Nicholas Lyon restrained himself, waiting, maintaining that icy detachment as the tension grew inside.

I carried the brandy over to the chair and handed it to him, and as his fingers curled around the glass I reached down quite casually and brushed the heavy copper wave from his brow. It splayed back down as soon as I moved my hand. He caught hold of my wrist, looking up at me, sipping his brandy. When I attempted to pull free, he gave my wrist a savage tug, twisting it as he brought me down to my knees in front of him. He took another sip of brandy and ran his tongue over his lower lip, heavy lids half-shrouding eyes dark with desire.

"Sit," he ordered.

"If that's what you wish."

He spread his knees apart, and I sat on the floor between

them, resting my back against the chair, shoulders against his thighs. I folded my legs under me, my skirt spreading out, indeed resembling a fan of peacock feathers against the bronze. He lifted the dangling ringlets and curled the fingers of his left hand around the back of my neck, massaging it as he continued to drink his brandy. It was extremely erotic, and I felt my nipples hardening, straining against the restraint of gauze and satin. I arched my back as his fingers pressed the side of my neck, his thumb digging against the top of my spine.

"I assume your mission was successful," I said.

"Quite successful."

"How many men did you kill?"

"It wasn't necessary to kill anyone. We merely rendezvoused with another ship, *The Green Parrot,* and transferred their booty onto *The Sea Lyon.* It was a bloodless expedition."

"For that you had to leave me for over two weeks?"

"I learned a long time ago that, when it comes to booty, I need to supervise things personally. So you did miss me?"

"Only at night," I said coolly.

He finished his brandy and set the empty glass on the floor. He stood up and pulled me to my feet, holding me loosely against him, eyes gleaming, mouth twisting with a sardonic curl. He seemed to vibrate with animal sexuality, so strong it was like a separate force enveloping him, yet he held back, controlling it, storing it up so that release would be even more potent. I tilted my chin back, looking up at that lean, harsh face. I detested him and made no effort to conceal it, yet as I gazed into those half-shrouded eyes I felt a physical response quickening inside.

"You're not interested in what I brought you?" he inquired.

"Not particularly."

"Maria would have begged and wheedled."

"I'm not Maria."

He took hold of my wrist and, reaching into the pocket of his frock coat, pulled out a heavy bracelet of square cut emeralds, each at least forty carats, burning with shimmering blue-green fires and completely surrounded by diamonds. He fastened the bracelet around my wrist and waited for some reaction. I gazed at it without feeling, and he grimaced and reached back into his pocket to pull out a matching necklace with even larger stones set in diamonds, emerald pendants dangling from the band of square cut emeralds. He turned me around roughly and fastened the necklace around my throat, drawing it tight.

"I should strangle you with it," he said icily.

"Emeralds aren't my stones," I said. "The green doesn't go with my eyes."

"You'll wear them tonight, wench, and later on—later on you'll show a little gratitude."

"And if I don't?"

"I'll keep on making love to you until you do."

"In that case, I shall make it a point to show no gratitude," I said in a faintly lilting voice.

Nicholas Lyon wrapped his arms around me, standing behind me, holding me in a hug so tight I felt my ribs might crack. He rested his head on my shoulder, breathing deeply, still holding back, scarcely able to restrain himself. His lips brushed the side of my neck, moving up to touch my earlobe. His arms tightened even more, hurting me.

"Dinner—dinner should be ready," I said, barely able to breathe. "I ordered Cook to make all your favorite dishes and serve the best wine. After that long voyage you must be hungry."

"I am," he replied. "Not for food."

"If you intend to do what you said, you'll need your strength. I suggest we—adjourn to the dining room."

"You're right," he said, releasing me. "Anticipation makes it even better. I've been anticipating for over two weeks—another hour or so shouldn't matter."

The meal was superb indeed, served on the finest Sevres china, two different wines accompanying the lobster tails cooked in butter and duck roasted with a sweet orange glaze. Nicholas had succeeded in temporarily stemming his sexuality, and as we dined his manner was once more cool and detached. He ate with leisurely appreciation, savoring each dish, but I merely toyed with the food on my plate, thinking of our escape plans, trying not to show my apprehension. The emeralds and diamonds glittered in the candlelight, heavy on my wrist and throat. I wondered whom they had belonged to, how many lives had been lost over them before they came into my possession.

"Burke tells me you've been leaving the stockade every day," Lyon said as fruit and cheese were brought in.

"Em and I have been—taking walks in the woods and along the beach."

"Who permitted it? Cleeve?"

"I take full responsibility. I told him you wouldn't mind. You didn't forbid it, Nicholas."

He sliced an apple deftly. "He said you arrived back at the stockade with tangled hair and a soiled dress. He said he thought you were up to something." He put the knife aside and looked at me with piercing blue eyes, the heavy copper wave completely hiding his right eyebrow.

"What could I be up to?"

"What indeed?"

"We walked on the beach and gathered shells. We gathered wild flowers, too. The stockade is—so confined. With you gone I grew restless, Nicholas. Em did, too."

"I see."

"Do you realize I've never been down to town?" I asked, hoping to change the subject.

"I'll have to take you to one of the canteens. You might find it amusing. Burke also said he found you prowling in the wine cellar."

"I wanted to check out the wines so that I could tell Cook which ones to serve tonight. Burke hates me—I don't know why. He'd love nothing better than to stir up trouble."

"That's quite true. Burke is extremely devoted to me— perhaps too devoted. He feels your presence is an intrusion on his domain. He felt the same way about Maria. I'm going to have to do something about him one of these days."

"Do we have to talk about him?" I asked, deliberately petulant. "If you've finished eating there are—better things to do."

"I quite agree," he said. "You go on up to the bedroom. I'll join you in a few minutes."

My heart was pounding as I went up the stairs. What exactly had Burke told him? I had the feeling much, much more had been said, that Nicholas was deliberately holding back information, that his questions had been very carefully worded in order to elicit a reaction from me. I had been uneasy, had betrayed that uneasiness by speaking too quickly, answering too glibly. Moving across the bedroom, I took hold of one of the bedposts, clinging to it for a moment with eyes closed, tiny waves of panic stirring inside, threatening to build and wash over me with demolishing force.

No, no, I mustn't let it happen. There was too much at stake. I had to be cool and calm. I had to be calculating and strong. If Nicholas Lyon was suspicious, I had to drive that suspicion out of his mind, using the only weapons at my disposal, my beauty, my body. I let go of the bedpost and, pushing aside the mauve and silver hangings, I turned back the mauve satin counterpane with its tiny purple silk *fleurs-de-lis*. I smoothed the cool white silk sheets and fluffed the pillows, preparing the battleground. That thick, potent sexuality stirring inside him was going to find glorious release, and when it was over, when he was finally satiated, any suspicion Burke might have aroused would be lulled.

I went into the dressing room and removed the emerald and diamond necklace, the bracelet as well, holding them for a moment in the palm of my hand and studying the flashing, shimmering fires. Emeralds might not go with my sapphire blue eyes, but these stones would bring a small fortune in the marketplace, as would the other jewelry he had given me. When all of it was sold, I would be a fabulously wealthy woman. I opened the elaborate jewelry box and added the newest pieces to the collection, dropping them carelessly on top of the pearls and the rubies, the diamond hair clips and the diamond and sapphire necklace he had given to me aboard ship.

As I stared at the collection, I remembered the spectacularly lovely diamond necklace Jeff Rawlins had given me, a gift he could ill afford and one I had been forced to sell after his death. Memories came flooding back, and I was dismayed to find my lashes damp with tears. I brushed them away and closed the jewelry box with a firm snap. Tears were a luxury I couldn't afford. Memories were a hazard I couldn't risk, not now. Standing in front of the mirror, I lifted my arms behind me and began to work with the tiny hooks in back of the bodice, unfastening them. When the bodice finally fell free, I struggled out of the gown and hung it up carefully in the wardrobe, removing the petticoat and shoes, putting them away, too.

I applied dabs of perfume behind my ears, between my breasts, in the curve of my arms, choosing a particularly subtle scent that brought to mind wild sunflowers baking in a hot sun, rich, erotic, provocative. Then I slipped into a nightgown as fine and frail as cobweb, a pale, hazy gold the color of morning sunlight, delicately embroidered with a scattering of miniscule bronze flowers. The thin straps were almost invisible, and the clinging, low-cut bodice provided the scantiest covering, flesh visible beneath, my breasts swelling full, nipples straining against the fragile cloth. The skirt fell in a full, pale gold swirl that only half-concealed my hips and legs.

It was a tantalizing garment, designed for seduction, and although I usually slept in the nude, it suited my purposes ideally tonight, adding an extra bit of provocation I knew he would appreciate. I put out all the lights in the dressing room and, moving back into the bedroom, put out most of the lights in there as well, leaving only a few candles burning, enough to create a pale golden haze, softly diffused. I opened the doors that led out onto the balcony, and a gentle evening breeze caused the draperies to stir with a quiet, silken rustle. Out in the gardens a bird warbled throatily in the night, a plaintive sound.

One hand resting on the door frame, the drapes billowing beside me, I looked out across the white marble railing, watching the treetops swaying faintly in the moonlight. The sky beyond was a deep blue-black, lightly brushed with silver and sprinkled with thousands of tiny, glittering stars. Several minutes passed, perhaps ten, perhaps less, and I was suddenly aware of his presence in the room. I hadn't heard him enter, but I could feel him there, feel his eyes on me as I continued to gaze at the night sky.

When I finally turned, Nicholas Lyon smiled a sardonic smile that curled lazily on his thin lips. He was wearing a loose-fitting garment of heavy bronze brocade that resembled a monk's robe. Unbelted, it fell all the way to his feet, the sleeves very full, the plush brocade embroidered with leafy patterns in an even darker bronze silk. His thick copper hair gleamed red-brown in the dim candlelight, and his eyes were so dark a blue they might almost have been black. He stood with legs spread wide, arms folded across his chest, looking at me with chin tilted down, dark eyes raised, the smile flickering. He exuded an aura of sexuality, thick, languid, smouldering, I gazed at him coolly, unmoved, and my indifference taunted him, as I intended.

"Waiting?" he inquired.

"I'm ready, Nicholas."

He lifted an eyebrow. "You sound less than enthusiastic."

"I'll perform my duty without complaint."

"Duty? Is that what it is?"

"I'm your captive. I have no choice."

The words goaded him, and they tittilated him as well. A man like Nicholas Lyon needed to feel power, needed to conquer repeatedly, and I had known from the first that meek submission would bore him. He strode toward me now in long, purposeful steps, the long robe swaying, and when he placed his hands on my shoulders the long sleeves slipped back, exposing his forearms. His fingers gripped tightly, digging into my flesh. I winced. He smiled.

"I've spoiled you," he said.

"Have you?"

"I've been too good to you, too kind, too lenient. I'm beginning to think I should have taken a stronger hand."

"You're hurting me," I said.

"I'm going to break you."

"You have my body, Nicholas. That should be enough. You'll never have my love."

"You're going to love me," he said.

I shook my head, and his blue eyes grew hard and determined. The challenge was there again, and he was prepared to meet it, to conquer, to taste anew that victory.

"I'm going to force you to love me."

His crisp, metallic voice was as determined as his eyes, and his fingers slid down to my breasts, curling around them, digging into the soft mounds of flesh that seemed to respond of their own accord, swelling under the pressure, nipples tightening. His mouth was a tight, angry line, the anger purely sexual, part of the excitement I had deliberately aroused in him. He squeezed my breasts until I gasped, and

249

then he slung one arm around the back of my neck and parted his lips and slammed them over mine, wrapping his other arm around my waist. He kissed me with a splendid fury that only increased as I refused to yield. Turning me in his arms until I was tilted backward, he thrust his tongue into my mouth, and I had to cling to him for support, my arms around his broad shoulders.

I could feel his fury mounting, mounting, and when it reached its peak, I made a moaning noise in my throat and melted against him, submitting reluctantly. He raised his head and looked down into my eyes, his own dark and gleaming with satisfaction. I gazed up at that harsh, handsome face, the face of a ruthless villain, mouth thin, nose sharp, cheeks lean, brows slanting over eyes dark, dark blue with desire yet still disdainful and mocking. I longed to dig my claws into his cheeks, longed to hit and kick and hurt. He sensed that. It pleased him. He would conquer now, turn my cool defiance into submission, prove his strength and prowess.

"One day you'll beg for this," he promised.

"I detest you," I said, knowing it was what he wanted to hear.

"You lie."

"I detest you with all my heart and soul."

"You enjoy these games as much as I do."

"Think what you will."

"I think you're magnificent," he growled.

He released me and stepped back, the need inside him growing, singing in his blood. The sardonic smile flickered on his lips as he looked at me, the creature who would fulfill that need, who would enable him to prove himself and relish his power. He took hold of my wrist and pulled me across the room to the foot of the bed. Then, catching his thumbs in the straps of my nightgown, he gave a jerk and tore them. He took hold of the top of the bodice, ripping it apart, and I stood very still as he continued to tear the delicate garment until it was a heap of gauzy shreds on the floor and I was completely naked. I gazed at him with a cool, passionless gaze, and again his sardonic smile flickered. Lifting me up into his arms, he dumped me roughly onto the bed. I gasped, shifting position on the silken sheets, copper-red waves spilling about my shoulders.

He stood at the foot of the bed, looking down at me, deliberately prolonging his pleasure, savoring the anticipation. Several moments passed before he pulled the robe over his head and tossed it aside. It fell to the floor like a shiny, dismembered bronze shadow. Nude, he padded across the room to put out the rest of the candles, tall and lithe, moving with panther grace, lean muscles rippling beneath the smooth tanned skin. The golden haze vanished, darkness quickly broken by the shafts of moonlight that streamed through the windows.

He moved back over to the bed and stood there for a few more moments, erect, ready, and then, abruptly, he heaved himself on top of me and pinioned my wrists to the mattress and sank his teeth into my shoulder. He took me with brutal abandon, thrusting deep in swift, savage strokes, plundering, conquering, but the victory was all mine. He had forgotten all about Burke, had forgotten everything but the moment, the madness. I allowed myself to respond at last, submitting to his fury, giving in, raking my nails across his back and praying all the while things would go well tonight and this fierce plunder would be his last.

Seventeen

I didn't dare light a lamp, and my nerves were wildly on edge as I dressed in the darkness, the rays of moonlight providing only the dimmest illumination. It was terribly late, well after two in the morning. Corrie had been waiting downstairs in the darkness for over an hour, and I knew her nerves must be in shambles, too. My delay had been unavoidable. After that first fierce session, Nicholas had made love to me again, lazily this time, languorously, deliberately prolonging each sensation until I had been ready to scream. As I slipped the dark blue cotton frock over the ruffled white petticoat, I remembered his husky, amused chuckle as I struggled tensely beneath him, praying he would hurry.

Completely dressed now, I paused, listening. The house was still. I could hear leaves rustling in the garden and, from the distance, the sound of waves. I moved quickly out of the bedroom and into the hall. The jewelry slapped against my thigh, all of it fastened in a small cloth bag securely tied around my waist beneath the underskirts. The hall was very dark, pitch dark, but I moved confidently through the layers of blackness, reaching out to catch hold of the banister, hurrying down the stairs. Every nerve in my body seemed taut, ready to snap, and stark terror loomed, threatening to overwhelm me, but I staunchly held it at bay.

At the foot of the stairs I paused again, peering into the darkness. I couldn't see Corrie. Had she given up and gone back to her room? The poor child must have been paralyzed with fear. I moved slowly down the wide foyer, studying the shadows.

"Corrie?" I whispered. "Corrie, are you here?"

I heard a small, barely audible whimper, and then Corrie materialized out of the shadows and hurried toward me. I caught her in my arms and hugged her. She was trembling.

"It's all right," I whispered. "I'm terribly late, but it couldn't be helped. You must have been terrified."

"I was, Miz Marietta. I was so scared—scared that Burke was gonna find me. He's been watchin' me. He suspects something, I know he does. I—I have a knife. I slipped into the kitchen and stole it."

She held it up. I could barely see the blade in the darkness.

"I—I was gonna stab him," she said. "If he came prowlin' and found me I was gonna stab him."

"You're a very brave girl, Corrie."

"I'm not. I'm—I'm still so scared my knees are shakin'."

"We'd better hurry," I said. "Em will be waiting. She'll be wondering what happened."

"Are we gonna make it, Miz Marietta?"

"Of course we are," I told her, sounding far more confident than I felt. "Come along now."

We moved on down the foyer, passing the large archways leading into nests of darkness. I had the feeling that we were being watched by several pairs of eyes, but I knew it was merely my nerves. Reaching the front door, I unlocked it and opened it quietly, cautiously, giving Corrie a little shove. She moved outside, and I followed her, pulling the door shut behind me and feeling a tremendous relief as we hurried down the steps. The house had been like a great, oppressive weight bearing down on me, and I felt much better now that we were free of those heavy walls and ceilings.

"We must be quick," I cautioned, "but we must be very quiet, too. There may be a guard posted. Follow me. Keep to the shadows."

Clouds had passed over the moon. The sky was the color of ashes, and the lawns were sable dark, cottages and barracks barely visible. We hurried toward the main gates, skirts fluttering in the breeze. As we reached the gates, the clouds parted. Silvery moonlight flooded the stockade. Em stepped out of the shadows of a shrub, seized our wrists, and quickly pulled us back into the concealment the large shrub provided.

"Jesus!" she whispered frantically. "I thought something terrible had happened! I've been waiting out here for hours!"

"Nick—Nicholas was in an extremely amorous mood."

"He *would* be, wouldn't he? So was Michael, but I got him so full of rum he passed out before he could lay a hand on me. He was sprawled out on top of the bed, fully dressed and snoring like an ox when I left."

"What if he wakes up?" Corrie asked.

"He's not going to wake up for a long time, luv," Em promised. "By that time we'll be well on our way. There's a guard," she told me, "he's been paradin' around all night, passed right by me a couple of times, so close I could've reached out and touched him. I was so bored waiting for you two I almost tapped him on the shoulder and asked him to chat with me."

"Where is he now?"

"On the other side of the barracks, maybe up on the walkway. If he keeps true to form, he'll be back over here by

253

the gates in a few more minutes. Are you *sure* you can manage that lock, Marietta?''

I nodded, removing a hairpin. The gates were gilded with bright silver moonlight. I didn't dare approach the lock until the clouds passed back over the moon. I frowned, impatient. Em sighed heavily, clearly disgusted. Corrie peered around the stockade, looking for the guard. Each minute seemed to drag on for an eternity.

''We can't wait much longer,'' Em said. ''Too much time has elapsed already. If we intend to make it, we'll have to be completely away from the island before dawn. *Damn* this moonlight!''

A thin veil of clouds drifted across the moon. Some of the silvery illumination vanished, though not nearly enough to suit me. Bracing myself, I moved over to the gates and examined the enormous lock in the hazy silver-gray light. It looked formidable indeed, much more formidable than anything I had ever attempted before, but I refused to be discouraged. Remembering those days on the prison ship when, to relieve the tedium and squalor, Angie had taught me how to pick almost any lock, I deftly inserted the tip of the hairpin into the lock and began to jiggle it, concentrating on touch and sound, eyes closed as I felt the tip of the pin scratching, exploring.

''Do hurry, luv,'' Em protested. ''The guard will be back any time now. I'm getting *very* jumpy.''

''Hush,'' I scolded.

The tip of the pin touched, caught on metal, and I began to pry gently, my eyes still closed. The pin slipped, scratched, twisted out of my hand, dropping to the ground. I cursed and knelt down to find it just as the thin clouds drifted away from the moon and brilliant silver rays spilled down with the brightness of afternoon sunshine. I spotted the pin, retrieved it, and inserted it back into the lock. I could hear heavy footsteps in the distance, moving slowly, moving closer. Em was gripping Corrie's hand with bone-crushing force, a tense expression on her face.

''Come on, damn you,'' I whispered, giving the pin a vicious jab. There was an extremely loud click. ''There!'' I said.

I gave the lock a turn. It clicked again, much louder, and

then, to my horror, it tore loose and crashed to the ground with a deafening clatter. Em gasped and grabbed my wrist and pulled me into the shadows as the heavy footsteps came running. Unlocked now, the heavy gates began to gradually ease open, swinging outward.

"What we gonna *do!*" Corrie exclaimed.

"I'll divert," Em said quickly. "You—find a rock or something, luv. Do what you have to do."

I nodded, understanding immediately, and Em stepped out of the shadows and stood in front of the gates with her hands on her hips and a disconcerted smile on her lips as the guard came rushing up, a long, deadly looking pistol aimed at her heart.

"What th' 'ell are you doin'!" he yelled.

"Not so *loud,* luv," she protested. "You'll wake the dead."

"It's you, is it—Tremayne's woman. Whatja doin' out 'ere at this time a night? Them gates—they're open!"

"No need to get yourself riled up, luv," she said reasonably. "I couldn't sleep and I—I thought I'd take a little stroll. It's a glorious night, isn't it? Don't you love the moonlight?"

"You—you was tryin' to sneak outta th' stockade!"

Em sighed heavily, shaking her head. "I was leaning against the gates, enjoying the moonlight, and the lock—it just fell *off.* It must have been terribly rusty. Shocking. I should think Red Nick would keep things in better repair."

"You're lyin'!" he bellowed.

"*Do* lower your voice, luv, and while you're at it you might lower that pistol, too. A big strong brute like you doesn't really need a gun in order to subdue a—a poor defenseless female like me."

There was a playful lilt in her voice, and her ploy was beginning to work. The guard scowled menacingly, his brows forming a straight, dark line, but he was a shade less belligerent. Em smiled coyly, adjusting one of the sleeves of her dark yellow cotton frock. For some reason, the exceedingly low-cut bodice slipped even lower. The guard lowered his pistol, taking a step nearer. Corrie was so terrified I thought she might faint. I gave her hand a squeeze and, putting a finger to my lips, cautioned her to keep silent.

"I'm takin' you back to Tremayne!" the guard said gruffly. "I've a feelin' he ain't gonna like this."

"He probably won't," Em admitted. "We—don't you think we might talk this over, luv? You seem a very reasonable chap—besides being so big and strong and attractive."

"None a your tricks! I saw what 'appened to Grimmet. Cleeve near killed 'im. Grimmet said it wuz all your fault, said you led 'im on. Me, I ain't gonna be made a fool uv."

"Of course not," Em replied. "You're much too sensible—and much too attractive."

She smiled again, using her wiles with outrageous aplomb, and the guard was definitely intrigued and more than a little bewildered, obviously torn between duty and desire. Should he take her back to Tremayne, or should he take advantage of the invitation she was so blatantly making? Em brushed a thick chestnut wave from her cheek and arched her back ever so slightly, causing the low-cut bodice to slip even lower.

"You're a man who does his duty," she said, "I can see that, luv, and it's your duty to take me back to Tremayne, but—we don't have to be in such a *hurry*, do we? It's such a lovely night."

"What're you gettin' at?"

"I might as well confess it, luv—I've had my eye on you for some time. I have this terrible weakness for shoulders, and yours are so *broad*. I noticed right away, the first time I saw you."

He was helpless now, utterly. Em tilted her chin down and peered up at him with melting hazel eyes and then, stepping forward, rested her hand lightly on his cheek. I spotted a rock on the ground a few feet away. It was large enough to do the job. Cautioning Corrie to silence once more, I crept forward, knelt down, and picked up the rock, grasping it firmly in my hand.

"You want it, don't ja?" the guard growled.

"Luv, how did you ever *guess?*"

He jammed his pistol into his waistband and made a noise in his throat and reached for her. Em wrapped her arms around his shoulders and turned him a bit so that I would have an easier target. I moved very quickly, leaping forward, bringing the rock up, bringing it down sharply on his crown. He didn't make a sound. He slumped immediately, sagging in

Em's arms. She staggered under his weight, almost toppling over backward.

"We'll have to drag him outside the gates," she said, "can't leave him here in plain sight. Give me a *hand*, luv, he weighs a ton."

I dropped the rock and took hold of the guard, and together we dragged him out the gates and propped him against the wall on the other side, half under a large shrub. He was like an enormous rag doll, limp and lolling. Em removed the pistol from his waistband.

"He's not dead, is he?" I asked.

"Not quite," she replied. "He'll be out for several hours, though, and when he comes to he's going to have a wretched headache. You wield a wicked rock, luv."

"I believe in being thorough."

"We make a marvelous team, don't we?"

"Is—is everything all right?" Corrie asked, joining us.

"Everything's fine, luv. Let's just push these gates shut and prop a log or something against them to keep them shut. We can't leave them sagging open like this—someone might notice."

We closed the gates, and Corrie held them shut while Em and I looked for a log or large rock. Finding none, we looked at each other and then looked at the guard. I sighed. Em shrugged her shoulders. We lugged him over and propped him against the gates.

"We'd better be on our way now, luvs. We've lost enough time as it is."

"Is—is there snakes and things in them woods?"

"Those woods," I said.

"Not a single snake," Em lied. "Come on, let's scoot."

I took Corrie's hand, and Em led the way. We hurried into the woods, moving at a killing pace. Em and I had come this way so often we knew every root, every rock, every hanging vine, and we were able to skirt every obstacle by instinct. The woods were very dark, only a few rays of moonlight seeping through the tangled limbs overhead. The air was damp and clammy, heavy with fetid odors. Branches seemed to reach out to scratch our arms and tear at our skirts. The hanging vines were a constant threat. After a while, panting, we were forced to slow down. The woods seemed to close in around us, dense, damp, a dark green-black lightly sprinkled with pale silver that only intensified the heavy shadows. Insects hummed. Scurrying, scratching noises abounded.

"How much farther is it?" Corrie asked. Her voice was laden with apprehension.

"Just a short way," I replied.

"What—what was that noise?"

"Probably a rabbit," Em said. "Keep moving. Ouch! Thorns. Watch out for that branch."

"I wonder what time it is," I said.

"Much too late. I—I'm a little worried, luv. We *must* be away from the island before dawn—well away—if they're to assume we've merely crossed over to the mainland."

"It's my fault, Em. I shouldn't have let him take me the second time. I should have pretended to—to have a headache or something, but I didn't want him to be suspicious. Burke had been talking to him—I've no idea what he said, but I had the feeling Nicholas was observing me very carefully."

"It couldn't be helped, luv. The path gets tricky here," she added, leading the way around a mass of tangled roots. "I wish there was a bit more light. Did you bring your jewelry?"

"Every single piece."

"Me, too, plus a few things Michael had—a solid gold watch, a set of silver hairbrushes, some diamond studs. I've got so much loot strapped around my waist I can hardly walk. Jesus! What was that!"

"It was just a bird calling out, Em."

"Sounded like a *wildcat* to me."

"Is—is there wildcats?" Corrie asked shakily.

"Of course not. Em's just being fanciful. Look, you can see the moonlight up ahead. We're almost there."

"We gotta climb down that cliff?"

"There's a path," I told her. "Em and I know the way. Everything's going to be fine, Corrie."

"I wish I was as brave as you, Miz Marietta."

I didn't feel at all brave at the moment. I was, in fact, so terrified I could hardly breathe. I wondered how long I would last. How long would it be before the terror completely overwhelmed me and I became a jibbering mass, incapable of taking another step? This whole scheme seemed wildly improbable, utterly foolhardy. We must have been out of our minds to think we could actually make it, I thought, shoving a hanging vine out of the way. Nicholas and his men would find us, and then . . . I couldn't allow myself to think of what might happen.

"Keep up, Corrie," I said sternly.

"I'm right behind you, Miz Marietta."

In the faint light I could see that she was still clutching the knife, and Em held the guard's pistol in her hand, casually swinging it back and forth. I saw that it was cocked and, horrified, took it from her.

"You'd better leave the guns to me."

"I was just getting the feel of it," she protested.

"You were just getting ready to blow your foot off."

"Really?"

"This is madness, Em."

"I know, luv, but we have no choice."

The trees were thinning now, the moonlight much brighter, and a few minutes later we cleared the woods entirely and moved rapidly across the rock-strewn open space above the cliff, making our way toward the narrow path that looked far more treacherous than it had in daylight. The enormous, jagged black rocks were frosted with silver, the waves below a deep pewter gray, churning furiously in the wind and sweeping over the sand with unexpected violence. I paused at the top of the path that scaled the side of the cliff.

"I'll lead the way down, Corrie," I said. "You follow closely behind me, and Em will bring up the rear. Watch your step and don't—look down. It's very narrow, but there's no danger. We'll be down on the beach in a matter of minutes."

Corrie nodded, and I hesitated just a moment and then started down, keeping close to the rocky wall, trying to ignore the open air and the sheer drop to the rocks below. The wind was fierce, much fiercer than it had seemed earlier. The waves pounded, pounded, making a furious noise. Cautiously, step by step, I made my way down the steep incline that, in places, was no wider than two feet. Hair blew across my cheeks, across my eyes. My legs were shaky, my knees so trembly I felt they might buckle beneath me. My terror grew, and I closed my eyes for a moment, trying to summon the strength to continue. I stepped on a small rock. It rolled under my foot. I lost my balance, swinging out into space.

"Miz Marietta!"

Corrie seized my arm, jerked me back. I slammed against the rock wall with stunning force, flattening myself against it with arms spread wide. Dark clouds seemed to whirl in my head, widening, darkening, picking up speed with a dizzying force. I started to sag. Corrie took hold of my arms. I straightened up, taking several deep breaths.

"Jesus, luv," Em said. Her face was white. "Are—are you all right?"

"I—think so. I stepped on a rock. It—rolled. Just—give me a minute to pull myself together."

The dark clouds ebbed. The dizziness vanished. Corrie was holding one of my hands, stroking it gently. I sighed and smiled shakily and pulled my hand free, and then I continued on down, moving around projecting boulders and keeping my eye out for loose stones on the path ahead. It gradually grew wider, the slope less steep. The wind howled, mist from the waves stinging my cheeks. It was with great relief that I stepped onto the sandy beach, stumbling a little. I turned to assist Corrie. She gave me a brave smile.

"We made it," she said.

"Barely!" Em exclaimed. "My heart almost stopped beating there for a moment, luv—you gave me such a fright! I'm still shaking."

"So am I," I said dryly.

We started trudging down the beach toward the cave. The sand was damp and slippery beneath our feet, making progress difficult, and the great waves continued to slosh over the sand, sweeping forward in foamy billows. The sky was a much lighter gray now, the color of pale ashes, the stars barely visible. The wind blew even harder, whistling against the rocky face of the cliff.

"This wind bothers me, Marietta."

"I know. Perhaps it'll die down."

"I certainly hope so. I—I'm horribly worried, luv. Don't let this jaunty, carefree manner fool you. I've never been so frightened in my life. If we *don't* make it, and they catch us—"

"You mustn't think about it, Em."

"Don't mind me, luv. I intend to be frightfully cheerful once we're in the boat and away from the island."

It seemed to take us forever to reach the mouth of the cave. I parted the hanging strands of ivy and fastened them back over a rock. Moonlight streamed in behind me as I stepped inside. The walls were damp and clammy, coated with liquid silver, it seemed. Em and Corrie followed as I moved down the tunnel, the sand dry here, even more slippery. I could hardly believe that we had made it this far. The apprehension I had felt earlier began to evaporate, replaced by steely determination. We were going to do it. We were going to get away. We were actually going to make it.

The boat was a shadowy outline in the darkness, the shape barely visible. I caught hold of the rope I had affixed to the front earlier and began to pull with all my might.

"Here," Em said, "let me help."

The boat slipped easily over the dry sand, heavy though it was with food, water, and guns. It took only a few moments for us to pull it to the mouth of the cave.

"The wind seems to have died down some," I said.

"A little," Em replied. "It still seems terribly fierce."

I went back into the cave to fetch the oars, placing them inside the boat when I returned. The three of us stood there for a moment, looking out across the beach to the churning pewter-gray water and the dark, sinister mainland beyond. In my imagination I could see naked savages crouching behind the trees, watching us, their long bows drawn, arrows ready to fly. Pushing the vision out of my mind, I took hold of the rope again and, with Em and Corrie helping, pulled the boat across the wet sand toward the waves.

"That's far enough," Nicholas Lyon said.

I whirled around. He stood there on the beach with Burke and three other men, his head lowered, his hands resting lightly on his thighs. His red-brown hair blew in the wind, whipping across his forehead, and in the moonlight his face was utterly without expression. Burke was leering. The other men looked extremely worried. Corrie gave a whimper. Em stood very still, holding the end of the rope in her hands.

"See!" Burke cried. "I told ja! I told ja I knew something was up. I had my eye on her. I knew she was planning something, the way she was slipping around. I kept my eyes open, just like I always do."

"I'm disappointed in you, Marietta," Nicholas said quietly.

"What are you going to do?" I asked. My voice was surprisingly calm.

"You're gonna be lashed!" Burke exclaimed. "You're gonna get fifty, at least. Maybe more. All three a you are gonna catch it now, and it's gonna be a pleasure to watch."

"Shut up," Red Nick ordered.

"You oughta kill her!" Burke continued. "She's a trollop, just like the other one. You oughta get rid of her! Let me do it. Let me do it for you! A bitch like that doesn't deserve to live."

Nicholas Lyon turned to him and glanced at him for perhaps a fraction of a second. Then he reached into his waistband and pulled out his pistol. He leveled it point-blank at Burke's forehead and pulled the trigger. The explosion was deafening, echoing against the face of the cliff. The impact knocked Burke off his feet, a spurting red hole blossoming just above the bridge of his nose as he crashed to the wet sand. Corrie screamed. Em gathered her into her arms, holding her fast.

Nicholas Lyon calmly blew on the barrel of the pistol and then thrust it back into his waistband. His harsh, handsome face was still without expression as he looked at me.

"Burke was right," he said. "You'll have to be punished."

"It was my idea," I told him. "It was all my idea. They—Em and Corrie didn't want to go along with it. I forced them to. I don't care what you do to me, but they're not to blame, neither of them."

He made no reply. He hadn't so much as glanced at the bleeding corpse on the sand. Burke might never have existed. The three other men were even more apprehensive, uncertain about what might happen next. The wind died down all at once, raging fiercely one moment, still the next. A faint pink hue began to stain the pale gray sky.

"I suggest we go back to the stockade," Nicholas said. "Men, you escort the other ladies back. I'll see to Miss Danver."

"No!" Corrie cried.

One of the men tore her out of Em's arms. Corrie struggled

valiantly. He frowned, doubled up his fist and slammed it against her jaw, catching her around the waist as she sagged forward, totally unconscious. He slung her across his shoulder and carried her down the beach as though she were a sack of potatoes. Em walked off with the other two without protest, one on either side of her. I faced Nicholas Lyon with cool composure that matched his own. Waves lapped at the prow of the boat, lapped at the grotesque corpse on the sand.

"Are you going to kill me, too?" I asked.

"I should," he replied.

His voice was calm, matter-of-fact. He had just murdered a man in cold blood, and he felt absolutely nothing. He had pulled the pistol and fired without giving it a thought, had not even bothered to look at the body. He was a monster, but I had known that from the beginning. I gazed at him now without fear, without feeling and with no hope whatsoever. I had matched wits with him, had thought myself crafty and clever indeed, and all the while he had been wise to my maneuvers. He had undoubtedly been amused by my feminine wiles, a sardonic smile playing on his lips as he let me continue making a fool of myself.

"I don't care what you do to me," I repeated, "but Em and Corrie are innocent. Neither of them wanted to help me. I made them do it."

"We'll discuss it later," he said. "Come along, Marietta."

He began to stroll casually down the beach toward the pathway cut into the side of the cliff. I followed meekly, stumbling on the damp sand. Nicholas Lyon never once looked back, but when he reached the foot of the path he turned, waiting for me to catch up. He took my hand, assisting me gallantly, letting me move up first so that he could keep an eye on me and take hold of me if I lost my footing. I climbed up the steep incline, not caring whether I slipped or not. When I was halfway up I paused, looking down. I could jump now. I could end it all. It would be over in a matter of seconds. Red Nick waited patiently, knowing what was on my mind, unperturbed.

I couldn't do it, of course. I truly didn't care what happened to me, but I couldn't desert Corrie and Em. Em might be able to fend for herself, but Corrie was utterly defenseless and I still might be able to save her somehow. I continued on up the path, feeling his presence behind me. The sky was more pink than gray now, taking on a faint golden-orange hue on the horizon. I reached the top, exhausted, depleted, swaying slightly. Nicholas took hold of my arm, steadying me, his manner strangely compassionate. I looked up at his face. It might have been sculpted in granite.

"I'm all right now," I said.

He let go of my arm and moved across the clearing toward the trees, lithe and graceful as a panther. Although he maintained complete silence, that curious gallantry prevailed as we moved through the woods. He took my hand now and then, leading me around a tangle of shrubbery, helping me over a fallen log. He held vines back out of the way as I passed, treating me in a manner that might almost reflect a tender, protective concern.

The sun had come over the rim of the horizon as we cleared the woods, and a dark golden-orange light streamed down in slanting rays as we passed through the gates and crossed the stockade. Several of the men were loitering out in front of the barracks, watching us, and I saw Em going inside the cottage door, Tremayne holding her arm in a firm grip. I had no idea what Nicholas was going to do to me. I didn't really care. I didn't seem to be able to feel anything at all as we moved up the steps and into the foyer.

"You're filthy," he said in a flat, toneless voice. "Go to your room and bathe and change. I'll be in the drawing room."

I went upstairs and removed my clothes and unfastened the cloth bag holding the jewelry and dropped it into the jewelry box. I took a long bath and brushed my hair until it gleamed and put on a frock of sky-blue brocade embroidered with tiny royal blue flowers. I adjusted the off-the-shoulder puffed sleeves and ran my hands over the snug waist and spread the full skirt out over the layered petticoats. I gazed at myself in the mirror with sapphire blue eyes that seemed utterly lifeless. My hair fell in a rich tumble of copper-red waves, spilling to my shoulders in thick profusion, but I didn't bother to pin it back.

I felt numb as I went downstairs. Nicholas was waiting in the drawing room, drinking a cup of coffee. He didn't look up as I entered. He continued to drink his coffee, lost in thought, it seemed, his blue eyes reflective. He had changed into a pair of snug dark brown breeches and a pale, creamy tan shirt open at the throat, the full bell sleeves gathered at the wrists. His dark brown boots were glossy. His tarnished copper hair was unbrushed, falling across his forehead in feathery locks. He finished his coffee, set the cup down and turned to look at me, his eyes still thoughtful.

"What am I going to do with you?" he asked gently.

"I don't know. I don't care."

"It seems those endearments you murmured last night were less than sincere. All the while you were planning to run away."

"I don't deny it."

"That distresses me, my dear," he continued. "I had hoped we had reached a new phase in our relationship. I had hoped you were actually beginning to enjoy my company."

His voice was low, gentle, almost crooning. He looked at me as he might have looked at a beloved child. The voice, the manner were far more chilling than anger would have been. The cold, harsh Nicholas was familiar. This tender, concerned lover was frightening indeed. I gazed at him with my chin held high, my eyes perfectly level. He sighed and shook his head, a regretful smile on his lips.

"Burke told me you were planning something. He wasn't sure just what, but he knew something was afoot. I chose not to believe him. I made love to you, and then I made love to you again, and you clasped me to you and rubbed your palms over my back and whispered sweet words. Apparently you meant none of them."

"I hate you, Nicholas. I always have."

"I went back to my room and slept, and half an hour later Burke awakened me and said that you and the little nigger were gone. I summoned the men, and we found the guard outside the gates, quite unconscious. You must have hit him very hard."

"I wanted to get away from the island. I wanted to get away from you."

"I was upset, naturally, but most of all I was concerned for your safety. I was afraid you might actually get off the island and fall into the hands of the Indians. It was then, my dear, that I realized I had fallen quite hopelessly in love with you."

"You're incapable of love," I said.

"I thought so myself," he admitted. "I'm not particularly pleased. Loving you makes me vulnerable, renders me incapable of meting out the punishment you deserve. Had Maria done what you've done, I'd have put a bullet through her heart and taken great satisfaction in doing so."

He sauntered slowly across the room toward me. I felt a tightening inside my stomach, but I held my ground, refusing to show fear, refusing to show any emotion whatsoever. Nicholas paused in front of me and studied my face with a tight smile on his lips. He shook his head again, regretful.

"I wish you hadn't done it," he said.

"I'll do it again, the next chance I get."

He slapped me across the face, so suddenly, so savagely that I almost fell down. He slapped me again, again, slamming his palm across my right cheek, my left, until both were burning with blistering pain. My head seemed to ring as blow followed blow, but I refused to cry out, even as he hit me yet again, so viciously that my legs crumpled and I fell to my knees. My cheeks seemed to be covered with liquid fire. Nicholas Lyon seized my hair and jerked my head back and slapped me once more, putting all his power behind it. I toppled backward, sprawling at his feet on the carpet.

He stood over me with his hands resting on his thighs, his chest heaving as he breathed heavily, blue eyes hooded, peering down at me without expression. I seemed to be whirling in a void, cheeks aflame, black curtains drawing over my eyes. I gasped and closed my eyes, and some of the dizziness left. I struggled to keep from crying, determined not to give him that satisfaction. I shifted my position and caught hold of his calf in order to pull myself up. He turned and walked away, and with the support removed so abruptly I fell face down, barely able to break the fall with my palms.

I reeled on the brink of unconsciousness again. The floor seemed to tilt and spin. After several moments I managed to crawl over and catch hold of the side of a chair and pulled myself up. I stood, clutching the chair for support, still not sure I wasn't going to pass out. Nicholas was standing at one of the windows, peering out at the lawns.

"Are you all right?" he asked. He didn't turn around.

"I—I'll live," I said.

He continued to stare out at the lawns, his back rigid, pale creamy tan silk draped across his broad shoulders. A ray of sunlight streamed through the window, touching his hair, turning it into a dark, fiery copper. I held onto the chair, my cheeks turning numb now, the burning gradually abating. I adjusted the bodice of my gown, tugging at the sky-blue brocade, straightening it across my bosom.

"I didn't want to do that," he said.

I made no reply. Nicholas turned away from the window and moved over to the liquor cabinet without looking at me. He poured himself a brandy, expressionless. He drank it slowly, staring straight ahead without seeing. My head was clear now. I let go of the chair and brushed my skirt and then rubbed my fingertips lightly over my right cheek, wincing as I did so.

"You got off lightly, Marietta. I should have beaten you until you passed out."

"Why didn't you?"

"I happen to love you," he said coldly.

"You have a—a curious way of showing it."

Nicholas set his glass down and looked at me for the first time with eyes a dangerous, chilling blue. I could sense the violence and hostility bristling just beneath the surface, ready to flare up again at the least provocation. I brushed hair from my cheek and, somehow or other, managed to summon a vestige of dignity, returning his glare with poise. He frowned, a deep furrow digging into the flesh above the bridge of his nose. I felt something wet and salty on my lashes and was amazed to discover tears streaming down my cheeks, and I let them flow, not bothering to brush them away, crying silently, unable to help it. His frown deepened.

"I don't suppose you regret it," he remarked.

"Not—not at all," I replied.

"The men will expect some kind of retribution—in public, in the square down in town. If I had any sense, I'd have you strung up and lashed in front of the whole island."

I reached up to brush away the tears, but I couldn't stop the stream. I didn't want to cry. I didn't want to give him the satisfaction. Those chilling blue eyes examined me closely, without emotion. His thin lips were pressed into a tight line.

"I don't imagine Tremayne will want his little whore's

back torn to shreds either. He'll administer his own punishment in private. It looks as though the little nigger will have to stand in for you both."

An icy knife seemed to pierce my heart. "What—what do you mean?"

"She'll be taken down to the square this afternoon. She'll be tied to the whipping post with her arms over her head. Her dress will be ripped away from her back, and my man will administer fifty lashes."

"No," I whispered.

"It will probably kill her," he observed. "That should satisfy the men."

"You can't—you can't do it, Nicholas. You can't."

"You'll watch, of course. So will Tremayne's woman."

"Nicholas—"

"After that, I imagine you'll think twice before attempting anything like this again."

"Please," I begged. "Nicholas—please don't do it. She—she's just a child. None—none of this was her fault. Please. Please don't do it. I'll do anything—anything you like. I'll promise anything."

"I have no choice, Marietta."

His voice was as cold and emotionless as his eyes. I was completely encased in ice now, and my heart seemed to leap. I couldn't let it happen. I couldn't. I had to do something, anything, to prevent it. He stood with legs spread wide, arms folded across his chest, immobile, unfeeling, the deep furrow above the bridge of his nose.

"You said you loved me," I pleaded.

"It has to be done."

"If—if you love me, you—you won't do this. You'll grant me this one thing. I'll never try to escape again. I promise. I'll be dutiful and submissive. I'll devote myself to—pleasing you in every way I can."

He didn't seem to hear. Not a facial muscle moved. I sobbed and turned away and started toward the door, filled with an anguish that was almost unendurable. He took several long strides and grabbed my wrist and jerked it brutally, whirling me around so that I was facing him again. He looked down into my eyes for a long time, irritated, indecisive, frowning fiercely.

"Please," I whispered.

"I'm a goddamn fool," he said harshly.

"No. No. You—you have compassion."

"It's not compassion, Marietta. It's weakness. The worst kind of weakness."

"No."

He hesitated another moment and then let go of my wrist. He walked back over to the liquor cabinet to pour yet another brandy, and several moments went by. My heart seemed to be in my throat. The suspense was shattering. I didn't think I could bear much more. He took another sip of brandy and looked at me with hooded eyes.

"Very well, Marietta," he said dryly. "I'll let your little nigger go, but I intend to hold you to your word. If you break it, I'll kill her myself. I swear it."

Relief swept over me, and I was suddenly so weary I could hardly stand. I moved over to him and took his left hand in both of mine.

"You won't be sorry," I whispered. "I'll keep my word."

Nicholas Lyon pulled his hand free, his thin lips spreading into a tight, disdainful line.

"You'd better," he told me.

Eighteen

Nicholas held my arm firmly as we moved past the outlying shacks and down the steeply inclining street toward the harbor. The sunset was bright with orange and gold and red, the sky ablaze with vividly colored streamers that began to fade and smear even as they appeared. Goats peered around corners at us with suspicious, belligerent faces, and chickens clacked, scurrying out of the way with much flapping of wings. I stumbled on the cobbles. His grip tightened, warningly, it seemed. I detested the town, detested coming down here to the canteens. Of late, sensing this, he had insisted we come down several nights a week. He seemed to derive some perverse satisfaction from seeing me ill at ease.

"Don't walk so bloody fast!" Em snapped, walking ahead of us with Tremayne on one side, Draper on the other.

"Shut up, wench!" Tremayne growled.

He gave her a shove. Em tripped on the cobbles. Draper caught her arm, steadying her. She cast a mutinous glance at Tremayne but held her tongue. Her lot had not been an easy one since our escape attempt two months ago. Tremayne had administered a beating that had left her immobile for almost a week, and, ever since, had been surly and brutal, cuffing her at the least provocation, treating her like chattel. He had begun to drink heavily, too, rarely sober after the sun went down. Em endured all with a grim, stoical attitude. Draper was beginning to seem more and more attractive to her.

Deep violet shadows were beginning to shroud the town as we passed the storehouses. The banners had almost faded. The sky was taking on a somber purple hue. Far ahead, through the crooked line of buildings, I could see the ships, masts towering like a skeletal forest. Raucous music and coarse laughter filled the air as we neared the canteens. I tensed, bracing myself for the ordeal. Nicholas smiled a twisted smile, wry amusement in his eyes. He knew I hated the noise and the filth and the horrible smells, the drunkenness and brawling good humor. He liked to sit and watch my reactions, savoring my discomfort. I never protested, never complained.

I had promised to be dutiful and submissive, and I had kept my word. I had promised to devote myself to pleasing him, and I had done so, causing our relationship to take on a curiously perverse tone that, I knew, gave him a great deal of satisfaction. I was no longer cool and defiant. I no longer held back. I served his meals myself. I poured his brandy. I lighted his cigars, and, when he took me into his arms, I melted against him at once and parted my lips and let him use me as he wished. He had found it amusing at first, but gradually his amusement had turned to disdain. He took to taunting me in subtle ways. He goaded me. His love-making was frequently extremely brutal, as though he were trying to force me to break down and rebel. We were playing new games now, and Nicholas definitely had the whip hand, his threat concerning Corrie keeping me in line even when he pushed me the hardest.

He claimed to love me. Perhaps he did, in his way, but his idea of love was strangely twisted, strongly allied with its reverse side. Love meant weakness to Nicholas Lyon. He hated this weakness in himself and, because I was the one who caused it, he felt compelled to make me suffer for it. He didn't beat me as Tremayne beat Em. No, his way was much more wily. He subjected me to constant humiliation, my pride broken, he thought, my spirit thoroughly subjugated. When he didn't ignore me completely, he scrutinized me carefully with that twisted smile curling on his lips, as a cat might scrutinize a mouse he contemplated pouncing upon. I played the new role to perfection, but I was beginning to feel the strain. He knew that. It pleased him. He was quite satisfied . . . and not yet bored.

A shrill scream split the air as a hefty woman with tattered, greasy blonde hair came tearing out of one of the canteens, her violet skirts flying. Two pirates rushed out in hot pursuit. One of them made a flying leap, catching her legs with his arms and bringing her down with a mighty thud on the cobblestones. She screamed again, fighting vigorously as he climbed atop her, and then both of them began to laugh lustily. The other pirate stood by on wobbling knees, guzzling rum from a bottle as he watched the jolly copulation.

"Charming," Em snapped as we passed.

"You think you're better'n she is?" Tremayne growled.

"A damn sight better!"

"Yeah, you think you're somethin' special, don't ja? Always givin' yourself airs. You're a whore, *my* whore, and don't you forget it!"

"Lay off, Tremayne," Draper warned.

"You keep your mouth shut, Draper! It ain't none of your affair. I know you been pantin' after her. Been pantin' after her from the first, haven't ya? You just find your own whore!"

"It would seem the bloom has worn off the rose,"

Nicholas observed dryly. "Tremayne's besotted, practically useless to me these past two months. That's what a woman can do to a man."

"Not to you, surely."

"Of course not," he said. "I have far too much good sense. I'm disappointed in Tremayne. He was the paradigmatic pirate, ruthless, amoral, a physical brute who knew no fear. His infatuation for your little friend changed all that, turning him into a surly rum-pot."

Nicholas' superior education frequently showed in his speech. He was a brilliant man, by far the most brilliant I had ever known. If all his drive and immense intellect had been channeled in another direction, he could have been a great statesman or anything he desired to be. Unfortunately, he had chosen to become a pirate, and he was the most feared, the most notorious pirate of the day.

"Here we are!" Tremayne cried, shoving Em through the door of the largest canteen. Draper followed, and Nicholas Lyon took my hand and led me inside with exaggerated courtesy, his blue eyes full of mockery. The smells assaulted my nostrils immediately, sweat and ale and vomit and dirt blending horribly together with the odors of stale grease and red peppers. I tried not to wince, moving through the crowd with my chin held high.

The tables were all full. Tremayne marched over to the largest table and, seizing a drunken pirate by the arm, jerked him out of his chair and shoved him to the floor. One of his mates leaped to his feet, ready to protest. Tremayne gave him a stunning blow across the jaw with his right fist, a blow so hard two of the man's teeth went flying, blood spurting in crimson threads. The rest of the men at the table deserted immediately, almost knocking over their chairs in their haste to avoid similar treatment.

Em and I exchanged glances. Her cheeks were pale, but her hazel eyes were dangerously bright, glittering with anger. Her small pink mouth was pursed. I prayed she would be able to control herself. Tremayne had grown progressively worse, and I was afraid he might actually kill her if she crossed him. Chestnut waves piled on top of her head and spilling between her shoulder blades in a cascade of curls, diamonds and amethysts sparkling at her ears and around her throat, she wore a rich purple brocade gown. The low-cut bodice was embroidered with tiny silver flowers, and silver flowers were scattered over the full skirt. She took a seat and began to toy with the diamond and amethyst bracelet on her wrist.

I sat down across from her, spreading out my bronze skirt, leaf-brown petticoats rustling beneath. Nicholas insisted we dress to the hilt for these occasions, knowing our finery would further irritate the sluttish women who consorted in the canteens. My copper-red waves were caught up with heavy strands of diamonds and pearls, and a pearl choker was around my throat, diamond pendants dangling from it in great, glittering drops. The jewels, the lavish gown made me feel even more ill at ease, which was exactly what Nicholas had intended. He took the chair next to mine and crossed long, muscular legs clad in skintight maroon satin, the matching maroon frock coat embroidered with black silk *fleurs-de-lis*. His black leather knee boots were polished to a high sheen, his tarnished copper hair gleaming with rich highlights, the heavy V-shaped wave slanting across his forehead.

"Rum!" Tremayne shouted, pounding the table.

"I'd like some whiskey," Em said.

"It's pure rotgut," Draper told her.

"So much the better," she replied. "The sooner I lose consciousness the better."

"You'll have rum and like it!" Tremayne ordered.

"My master speaks. Rum it is."

"Some white wine?" Nicholas inquired, addressing me.

"I suppose."

"White wine," he told the woman who slouched over to our table. "Bring the best. I mean the best. Rum, too, several bottles."

"And you might just wipe the glasses, luv," Em added.

"As soon as you wipe your ass," the slut retorted.

"Heaven," Em said. "Oh, she's heaven."

The woman scowled and slouched away, her filthy blue skirts swaying as she wagged her large buttocks. The noise blasted all around us, bottles breaking, gruff voices yelling, harsh laughter rumbling. The floor was slippery with spilled ale. The dirty white walls were blotched with yellow stains and draped with strands of onions and gourds and bright red-orange peppers. Candles smoked in the large, wheel-shaped fixtures hanging from the beamed ceiling. The woman returned with wine, rum and a tray of bread, cheese and hard sausage. Em gave her a dazzling smile and extended a stiff middle finger.

Nicholas examined the wine label carefully, nodded, and uncorked the bottle. He poured a few swallows into his glass and sipped it, his blue eyes full of concentration as he savored the taste. He nodded again. The woman frowned wearily and slapped the bottles of rum down in front of Tremayne. Nicholas poured wine into my glass, and I lifted it to my lips. The wine was cool and tangy, quite delicious. I drank the rest of it immediately. Smiling, he poured me another glassful.

"It's deceptively potent," he advised me. "I wouldn't drink too much of it, my dear, It goes straight to your head."

"Maybe I'd better try some," Em remarked.

"Shut up!" Tremayne bellowed.

"He's all charm tonight, I must say. Can't help it, the luv. It comes naturally."

I drank the second glass of wine and poured a third. Nicholas was amused, blue eyes dancing, wry smile curling at the corners of his mouth. I hated him. How long was I going to be able to endure that mockery without striking back at him? Corrie. I must think of Corrie. He had meant his threat. He would kill her. He would enjoy doing it. The wine was supposed to go to my head, but it only made everything sharper, clearer, the noise louder, the smells more offensive, colors brighter.

I looked at the man sitting beside me with cool appraisal. The face was indeed handsome, but harsh, so harsh. The nose was too long, the lips too thin, the skin stretched tightly across the sharp cheekbones. The hair was thick and rich, beautiful hair, so beautiful I wanted to touch it, and the piercing blue eyes would be beautiful, too, were they softened with compassion. A patina of cruelty overlaid every feature. If his childhood had not been warped, if bitterness had not etched those harsh lines, Nicholas Lyon would have been an incredibly attractive man.

"You seem unusually pensive tonight," he remarked.

"It's the wine," I said.

"You were looking at me with—unusual concentration."

"Was I?"

"Almost wistfully, my dear. Not, alas, with desire. You're unusually desirable tonight. The gown is lovely. The pearls and diamonds set off the color of your hair. I'm glad I gave them to you."

"You've given me so many lovely things."

"I wish you could give me something in return."

"What?" I asked.

"Your love."

"I wish so, too, Nicholas. I really do. I'm trying."

He lifted the corners of his lips and touched my cheek, then looked up as a roar of delight filled the vast room. "Pepita!" someone yelled. "Pepita!" The crowd parted as a woman with bare feet sauntered foward, two men with guitars behind her. Tall, with a narrow waist and extremely full breasts, she had dark tan skin and unusually long black hair that fell in a mass of glossy, tangled waves. Her black eyes gleamed greedily. Her full red mouth was curled in a surly pout. Her low-cut red blouse barely contained her breasts. Her white skirt was very full and slightly ragged, covered with bands of black and purple embroidery, a purple sash wound around her waist.

"Pepita!" the crowd roared. "Pepita! Dance for us!"

The woman ignored her admirers and padded across the room to our table, a provocative smile on her lips. She was at least thirty. Her face was heavily made up. She was attractive in a coarse, primitive way, exuding a raw sexual allure men of a certain kind found wildly exciting. I couldn't despise her. She had undoubtedly been brought to the island a captive, as Em and I had, and she had made a place for herself. Pepita was a survivor. I admired her for that, even as I recoiled from the cheap perfume she had splashed on her body.

"Dance for us, Pepita!" the men yelled.

Pepita placed her hands on her hips, tossed her hair back and looked directly into Nicholas' eyes.

"I dance for Red Neek," she announced throatily.

"Clear a space!" a man shouted. "Clear a space for Pepita!"

Eyes hungrily devouring Red Nick, Pepita smiled and lifted her arms in the air, whirling slowly as the two men who had accompanied her began to strum their guitars. The crowd moved back, clearing a space for her, and she moved onto the floor with provocative undulations, swaying, swirling, slowly, moving with a feline grace. Nicholas watched with amused blue eyes, sipping his wine as the woman arched her back, her breasts thrust out, her long hair almost sweeping the floor. She rocked back and forth, lifting first one bare foot, then the other, red lips parted.

The music was extremely sensual, Spanish music, evoking intense heat, passion, hot sunlight, sweat. Pepita undulated, swaying her torso, smiling, moving gradually back over to our table. She lifted her skirts, shook them, placed her hand on Nicholas' jaw, and then, turning, arched her back again until she was half-resting on the table. I moved my wine glass out of the way, my face expressionless as she writhed with her back on the table, her legs slowly lifting until her skirts fell back, exposing her thighs. Nicholas ran his hand along her leg, still amused.

Pepita clapped her hands and leaped to her feet and, as the music picked up tempo, began to whirl like a dervish, faster, faster, hands clapping loudly as the strumming became a passionate fury. The music stopped abruptly. She fell to her knees, spread them, arched back until her head touched the floor. There was thunderous applause and a shower of gold coins. Pepita jumped up, scooping the coins off the floor. Tying them in a handkerchief, which she tossed to one of the guitarists, she sauntered back to our table, tossing her long black hair. She smelled of sweat and garlic. Forcing herself between my chair and his, she smiled, stroking Nicholas' lean cheek.

"You like, Red Neck?"

Nicholas nodded, smiling his twisting smile.

"You buy Pepita a drink?"

"Certainly," he said.

"Here," I said, "why don't you take my chair."

I stood up and moved around the table, angry now. I wasn't angry with Pepita. She was only looking after her own interests, and I couldn't blame her. I was angry with him because I saw the game he was playing and felt it was beneath him. Pepita slid into my chair, glistening with a moist coat of perspiration. Her breasts were almost completely exposed, red silk clinging to her nipples. Her black hair was damp. Nicholas poured her a glass of rum, and I reached over to retrieve my glass and the bottle of wine, sitting down in the chair beside Em. Tremayne, on her other side, had a glazed look in his eyes. I poured another glass of wine.

"Easy, luv," Em warned.

"I need it," I snapped.

"You're reacting just as he intended you to react," she said under her breath, looking across the table at Nicholas and the dancer. "Don't give him the satisfaction."

"I don't know how much more of this I can take, Em."

"You can take a hell of a lot more, luv. So can I. We have no choice."

"What are you two mutterin' about?" Tremayne snarled.

"We were talking about you," she replied sweetly, "discussing your social graces and overwhelming charm."

"More rum!" he barked. "We're outta rum!"

Draper passed another bottle over to him. The gold hoop in his ear glittered in the candlelight. His fierce gray eyes had a crafty look, as though he were planning some devilment, and, beneath the beaklike nose, his thin mouth stretched into a tight smile. Tremayne seized the bottle. He smashed the top of it across the edge of the table, splashing rum into his glass and splattering it over his soiled pale blue satin breeches. His pale blue frock coat was soiled, too, the silver lace tattered.

"You reel-ly like Pepita's dance, Red Neek?" the woman asked coyly.

"I found it most interesting."

"I dance in private sometime. I give private performance sometime."

"I'll bet she does," Em observed.

"Sometime zee men—zhey want to have me dance for zhem alone, in private. Zhey pay much gold. You want Pepita to dance just for you?"

"Perhaps."

"I like to. For you, free."

"Jesus, she'd never make it on Rampart Street."

"Is honor for Pepita to dance for Red Neek in private. Zhere is room upstairs."

"Convenient," Em said.

"Hush," I told her.

"Ve go upstairs?"

277

"Later, perhaps," Nicholas said.

"Pepita has wanted to meet Red Neek for long time. She come to island as woman of one of his men. She pines for music. He sends for her two brothers. Zhey come to play music for Pepita. Jason, he die. Run through by a bad man on board a ship. Pepita all alone."

"My heart is breaking," Em remarked.

"Other men, zhey all want her, but Pepita dances instead. She dances for zhem all, and zhey give her gold. Zhey all love her, but Pepita sees Red Neek one day, and she long to dance only for him."

"Subtlety," Em said, "I've always admired it."

Nicholas was enjoying himself immensely. He was deliberately trying to provoke me, toying with this poor, pathetic trollop who had no idea she was being used. Confident of her allure, convinced he found her irresistible, she threw back her head and laughed huskily. The damp red silk blouse slipped half an inch lower. I could smell the sweat, the garlic, the dreadful perfume across the table. Nicholas' nostrils quivered. He lifted a scented handkerchief to his nose, ever so tactfully. Pepita began to gnaw a piece of sausage.

"We're outta rum again!" Tremayne roared. He whirled his torso around, glaring at Em. "Go get me some, woman!"

His dark brown eyes were full of menace. Sun-streaked brown hair tumbled over his brow. An ugly snarl curled on his lips. Em looked at him for a moment, debating whether or not to make a smart retort, and then she sighed and started to get up. She didn't move fast enough to suit Tremayne. He gave her a vicious shove that sent her reeling backward. She fell to the floor, brocade flying, the chair crashing down with her. I screamed, jumping to my feet, and Draper and Tremayne stood, too, Draper's eyes glittering.

"Bitch!" Tremayne cried.

"That's enough, Tremayne," Draper warned.

"I'm gonna kick your guts out, bitch!"

Draper caught his shoulder and whirled him around. I reached down, taking Em's hand, helping her up. Her cheeks were bleached of all color, chalk white, but she wasn't really hurt. The corners of her mouth quivered. I held her to me, looking over her shoulder at the two men who stood glaring at each other like two bulls ready to charge. The enormous room was silent, all eyes on our table.

Tremayne was sober now, stone sober, seething with cold fury.

"You afraid I might damage her?" he growled. "Afraid I might mess her up for you, is that it?"

"Could be."

"She been slippin' out to meet you in the bushes, too?"

"Not yet," Draper replied.

"You sonuvabitch! We're gonna settle this! We're gonna settle this right now!"

His hand flew beneath the skirt of his frock coat and came back out clutching a knife. Em shuddered. I held her tightly. Nicholas hadn't bothered to get up. He remained in his chair, calmly sipping his wine. Pepita held onto his arm, visibly excited by the prospect of bloodshed. Draper looked at his captain, knowing knife-fighting was forbidden, waiting for some signal. Nicholas set his glass down and lifted the handkerchief to his nostrils again.

Everyone watched him with eager anticipation. If Red Nick gave the word, the two men would fight to the death with knives, and it would be great entertainment, a rare and unexpected treat. Em freed herself from my arms and adjusted one of the sleeves of her elaborate purple brocade gown, composed now, awaiting his decision with stony calm. Draper stood with eyes narrowed, loose and lean, not at all impatient. Tremayne gripped the knife tightly, so tightly his knuckles were white. His chest was heaving. Nicholas pulled his arm from Pepita's hold and looked up at Draper, finally nodding.

"You may as well settle it," he said.

The crowd of burly pirates greeted his words with lusty cheers, the women among them cheering even louder. A dozen men surged over, taking hold of Draper and Tremayne and hauling them to the center of the floor. Draper pulled out his knife. An enormous red-haired brute with a broken nose seized Tremayne's left hand, seized Draper's, and tied their wrists tightly together with a soiled white handkerchief. The two combatants stood facing each other, holding their knives in their right hands, their left arms crossed in front of them, wrists bound so securely their hands must already be growing numb. The pirates moved back, clearing a space for them. Silence fell.

"It'll be all right," I told Em.

"I'm not worried at all," she said in a flat voice. "Draper's sure to win."

"Do you want him to?"

"He's no prize, luv, but after these past weeks anyone would be better than Tremayne."

In the center of the floor the two men circled each other warily, drawing back, tugging at their bound wrists, moving in a macabre ballet. Overhead, the candles flickered, spilling down a smoky yellow light that threw their shadows over the floor, elongating them. The shadows moved as they did, dancing, distorted black patterns shifting and changing over the filthy, slippery surface. Tremayne was tense, taut, his powerful muscles bulging as he pulled back with teeth bared. Draper remained loose, relaxed, almost nonchalant.

Tremayne made a growling noise and jerked his left arm violently, pulling Draper toward him, his knife flashing, glittering in the candlelight. Draper ducked, turned, made a sudden twist, throwing Tremayne off balance. The knife sliced through Draper's billowing sleeve. Green silk shredded, but there was no blood. Tremayne plunged the knife again, and Draper dropped to one knee deftly, swinging his own knife up. The blades scraped together with a horrible scratching noise that gave me chills. Em's face was perfectly immobile as she watched. She seemed totally unmoved, as though it had nothing whatsoever to do with her, but I knew it was because she wouldn't allow herself to give way to emotion.

The crowd of pirates cheered, waving bottles in the air, lustily yelling encouragement as the two men tugged and turned and slashed, Tremayne's knife nicking Draper's wrist, Draper's knife slicing a thin wet red line across Tremayne's jaw. Both men were covered with sweat now. Draper's green silk shirt clung damply to his back. Tremayne's sun-streaked brown hair was wet, splayed across his brow in dark locks. The floor was sticky with spilled rum that had dried to form a gummy coating. The soles of their boots slipped now and then, causing one or the other to lose balance. Tremayne, I knew, was a master with the knife, lunging, slashing, lunging again with renewed fury, and Draper didn't seem to be a match for him at first, seemed to be spending all his energy fending off those lethal blows.

Tremayne grew more and more energetic, brown eyes blazing as he waved the knife, plunging it toward Draper's heart, and Draper caught the blade with the edge of his own, deflecting it just in time. I was amazed at Draper's lack of spirit. He moved quickly, loosely, almost lazily, as though it were a wearying game he found faintly boring. I realized then what he was doing. He was deliberately conserving his strength, letting Tremayne work himself into a frenzy, wear himself out. The crowd roared obscenely, placing bets now, shoving each other, having an uproarious time.

Pepita had leaped up onto her chair, skirts swaying wildly as she jumped and yelled. Nicholas continued to sip his wine. He watched the combat with frosty blue eyes, clearly indifferent to the outcome. There was a deafening roar as more blood was drawn. Pepita jumped off the chair and grabbed another piece of sausage and began to gnaw it greedily, her eyes alight with excitement. Draper was on his knees, Tremayne hulking over him, panting heavily as he slashed and slashed, always hitting Draper's blade, the clicking, clashing noise ringing loudly. Nicholas looked up at me, a faint smile playing on his lips as he observed my pale cheeks and worried eyes.

Tremayne was exhausted now, lunging blearily, stumbling, his coordination gone. He growled, plunging the knife once more. Draper smiled and reared back, pulling his left arm forward with all his might. Tremayne seemed to fly through the air, describing a flailing arc before he crashed to the floor with a shuddering thud. Draper twisted, turned, swung himself over, and then he was on top of the fallen man's legs and, calmly, he drove his knife into Tremayne's heart. There were excited yells as blood spurted and Tremayne's body reared and bucked violently, once, twice, once more, then fell limp. Draper wiped his blade on the skirt of Tremayne's frock coat, sliced through the handkerchief that bound their wrists together and then stood up.

He ignored the cheers, the clatter of coins, the smashing of glass, pushed aside those pirates who rushed over to pound him on the back in congratulation. He came back over to our table, one sleeve shredded, his right wrist sporting a thin red cut. Pepita threw herself into his arms. He shoved her out of the way and looked down at Red Nick, awaiting his judgment. Nicholas sighed, gently pushing his wine glass to one side.

"I suppose you want the woman," he said.

Draper nodded. He glanced at Em with lascivious gray eyes, then turned his attention back to Red Nick.

"She's yours," Nicholas said. "Everything he had is yours now, including his cottage and his position. You're my chief aide now, Draper. I trust you won't let the woman turn you into a drunken incompetent."

"I'll keep her under control."

"See that you do. Take her back to the stockade now."

Pepita plopped herself down beside Nicholas again, taking hold of his arm and winding her own about it.

"Ve go upstairs now? Pepita dance for you?"

Nicholas ignored her. He looked at me with expressionless eyes. "Go back to the stockade with them," he ordered. "I'll join you later."

I didn't answer. I followed Em and Draper out of the canteen, averting my eyes as we passed the still bleeding corpse. The moon had come up, washing the town with pale silver light that gilded the crooked rooftops and intensified the darkness filling the twisting alleyways. The night air was cool, wonderfully refreshing after the stench of the canteen. We began to walk up the cobblestoned street. A dog barked at us. Lighted windows made misty gold squares in the black walls. After we had gone some way, Em paused, tore a piece of cloth from her petticoat, and, taking hold of Draper's wrist, tied the cut securely, knotting the cloth tightly.

"There," she said. "That's better."

"You're gonna take good çare a me, ain't ja?"

"You can count on it, luv. I'm going to make you deliriously happy."

"I had my eye on you from th' first, ever since I seen you standin' there on the beach with your teats bulgin' outta that pink dress."

"I know," she said wearily.

"We're gonna have us a grand time."

"Sure we are, luv."

We walked the rest of the way in silence. Draper was far more exhausted than he had appeared to be at first. He moved up the steep street with considerable effort, his arms swinging limply at his sides. Our skirts made a crisp rustling noise as Em and I walked beside him. Moonlight spilled over her face and bare shoulders in a soft haze. Her shoulders seemed to droop. She wore a resigned expression, and there was a hopeless look in her eyes I had never seen there before. I reached over to take her hand. She turned and gave me a tiny, reassuring smile, but the hopeless look remained.

We passed the shacks, the goats, the chickens. Someone was roasting meat over an open fire in front of one of the shacks. A woman laughed in the darkness. We moved up the winding road toward the stockade. It stood in sharp relief against the black night sky, the great white walls washed with silver, the cannon projecting from the slits at the top like grotesque black snouts. As we entered the gates I felt a hollow feeling inside. The horrible din, the smells, the violence had left me empty, depleted, incapable of feeling anything but this weariness that permeated my whole body. We passed the barracks and moved toward one of the fountains. Draper looked as though he were ready to drop. We paused again, and Em touched his cheek.

"Look, luv," she said, "why don't you go to your quarters and—and rest up a while. You can join me at the cottage later on. I'd like to freshen up a bit, and you're going to need a *lot* of strength tonight."

"That ain't a bad idea," Draper replied, trying to sound fierce.

"Take a nap, luv," she advised. "Don't sleep *too* long, though. I don't want to get lonesome."

Draper shuffled away into the darkness, disappearing in the shadows. Em and I stood by the fountain. The cool night breeze stroked our cheeks.

"Are you going to be all right?" I asked.

"I'm going to be fine, luv. After Tremayne, Draper will be a snap. I can handle him easily enough."

"It all seems so futile," I said.

Em didn't reply. There was no need to. She looked up at the starless sky for a moment, and then she sighed, straightening her shoulders. Leaves rattled quietly in the breeze. We could hear the guard pacing back and forth, his boots crunching heavily on the rocky ground. We stood there for several more moments, silent. Then Em sighed and passed a hand across her forehead and lifted the hem of her brocade gown and started across the night-damp lawn toward the cottage she had shared with Tremayne, the cottage she would now share with Draper. I moved wearily toward the big house where I would await the pleasure of Nicholas Lyon.

Was it really any better than a house in Caracas or Rio? I was beginning to wonder. We had escaped that, but had survival been worth it? My spirits were low indeed as I moved down the corridor and started up the stairs to the bedroom. A bleak depression had settled over me, as bleak, as grim as any I had ever experienced. It was not caused merely by the violence I had witnessed tonight, the bloody death that had been so gleefully enjoyed by those who watched it. It was a cumulative thing that had been building for weeks and had finally enveloped me like an impenetrable black cloud.

Soft lights were burning in the bedroom as I entered. They glowed with a hazy golden mist that washed over the luxury of elegant white wood and Aubusson carpet and mauve and silver hangings. I stepped over to the dressing table and opened the elaborate jewelry box heaped high with gleaming, flashing treasure. I removed the pearl choker with its diamond pendants and dropped it on top of the heap, the pearls glowing, the diamonds shimmering with liquid fires. I began to undo the strands of diamond and pearl that held my hair back, adding the exquisite ropes to the collection and closing the box.

I had luxury, yes, sumptuous gowns and incredible jewels and a magnificent room, but the jewels, the gowns meant nothing, and the room was a prison. The man who held me prisoner was superbly adept at love-making, was able to summon physical sensations that swelled and exploded inside until I was drowning in an ocean of ecstasy, but these same sensations filled me with self-loathing, seemed a betrayal of myself. He was a cold, inhuman monster who employed a subtle torture that, in many ways, was far worse than physical blows would have been. He didn't bruise my body, no, but he had bruised my spirit until it was ready to expire.

I picked up the hairbrush and began to run it through the rich copper-red waves, gazing at my reflection as I did so. The skin seemed to stretch tightly across those high cheekbones. The mouth seemed to droop. The sapphire blue eyes were filled with the same hopelessness I had seen in Em's. I had given up hope. Yes, that was it. After all this time, I had finally given up hope, and life had no meaning. The last spark had been extinguished, and only ashes remained. Ashes. Cold gray ashes.

"Miz Marietta?"

I turned, startled. Corrie stood in the doorway with her sewing kit, an elaborate blue and silver gown draped over her arm. Her soft black hair covered her head like a puffy cloud, and her lovely brown eyes were filled with concern as she looked at me. She was so small, so frail, so defenseless, yet there was a strength in her I had constantly underestimated.

"I heard you come in," she said. "I—I knew Red Nick wasn't with you, and I thought you might like some company. I wanted to finish alterin' this gown he brought back—there's just a little stitchin' left to do on the bodice—and the light in my room ain't—isn't strong enough. Mind if I sit over there in that chair and finish it?"

"Of course not, Corrie."

She moved over to the chair and set her sewing box down on the table beside it. She took out scissors and thimble, needle and thread and spread the gown across her legs, silver and blue folds spilling over the carpet. I continued to brush my hair, in no mood to talk. The long, frightfully sharp scissors flashed as she deftly snipped at threads. Putting the scissors aside, she threaded her needle and began to resew the bodice, making tiny gathers in the cloth. Her head was bent. Her eyes were lowered in concentration. Pale gold light streamed over her shoulder as she worked.

"You'se—you are low," she said quietly.

"Yes, Corrie, I'm low."

"You mustn't be, Miz Marietta. Things are going to work out."

I put the hairbrush down and, tossing my head, shook the waves away from my temples. "I wish I could believe that," I said.

"It's been hard," she continued, "but we're still alive."

"Yes, we're still alive," I replied. My voice was flat.

"Lotsa good has happened," Corrie's voice was low, soothing. "I can read now, at least if it isn't too complicated with a lotta big words. I can spell my name and write lotsa other words, too."

"You've done very well, Corrie."

"When we get back, I—I'll be ready to take my place in the world, just like you told me."

I was too dispirited to reply. Corrie made another delicate stitch, the thimble shining on her finger. She shook the bodice and held it up to examine it, then frowned slightly and continued to stitch. She still had faith. She still had hope. Em and I might have given up, but this lovely child still believed we would leave the island and safely return to the civilized world. I didn't want to discourage her, and I knew that in my present mood anything I might say would be bleak. Straightening the sleeves of my bronze satin gown, I turned, the skirt belling.

"I think I'll take a walk in the gardens," I said, trying to sound casual. "You go ahead and finish your work, Corrie."

She looked up apprehensively. "Will it be all right?" she asked. "If he came back and found me here—"

"Nicholas won't be back for some time," I assured her. "I imagine he'll be occupied for most of the night."

I left the bedroom and went slowly down the stairs, running my hand along the polished banister. My skirts made a soft, silken music as I walked down the narrow back hall and stepped outside. The flower beds were ragged in the moonlight, the large shrubs casting long shadows over the pathway leading toward the enormous trees that grew in back, near the wall. I shivered a little in the night air. It seemed much cooler than it had earlier. I really should go back in and fetch a wrap, I thought, folding my arms around my waist.

I strolled past the shrubs and moved under the trees, the limbs spreading out overhead, creaking faintly in the breeze. It was very dark here, very few rays of moonlight penetrating the canopy of leafy boughs. Shadows shifted and moved at my feet, great nests of shadows shrouding the wall. I paused beside one of the trunks, and as I did so I heard a heavy thud that sounded like something dropping. I turned toward the sound, but I could see nothing. I put it out of my mind, leaning against the trunk, shivering.

I stood there for a long while, listening to the night noises, the rustle of leaves, the creaking of boughs, the sleepy twitter of a bird, and I had the feeling someone was watching me. It was foolish, of course. I paid no attention to it. I stared into the darkness, wondering how much longer I could endure. How much longer would it be before I broke completely, just as he wanted me to? I had endured and endured, it seemed. Somehow, in the past, I had always found strength to go on when one treachery followed another, when hope gave way to despair and joy turned into anguish and grief, but the reserves of strength had all run dry now, and I no longer had the will to fight.

The air turned cooler still. I was shivering badly, my arms and shoulders freezing. I turned to go back inside, and it was then that I saw the man standing a few yards away, looking at me. I clasped a hand to my heart, so startled I almost fainted. A scream welled in my throat. He leaped forward, grabbed me, and whirled me around. A strong hand clamped over my mouth, jerking my head back until it was tilted against a wide shoulder.

"Easy, lass," a familiar voice crooned. "I've come a long way to get you out of this mess, and I don't want you mucking things up by screaming your silly head off."

Nineteen

He held his hand clamped firmly over my mouth while shock and dismay and a wild surge of conflicting emotions swept over me. After a moment, very cautiously, he removed his hand and took hold of my shoulders and turned me around so that I faced him. He gripped my upper arms, supporting me, and I would surely have crumpled to the ground if those strong hands hadn't held me. In the hazy darkness I could barely see his face, merry eyes, a slightly twisted nose, the wide, full mouth grinning saucily as though this were a delightful prank.

"Are you goint to faint?" he asked.

"I'm not sure," I whispered.

"Go ahead. I'll hold you. I'm terrific with swooning females."

"I'm not going to faint."

"Pity," he said.

"How—"

"You've got dozens and dozens of questions," he interrupted. "It's only natural. I'll answer 'em all eventually, when we've time, but for now all you need to know is I'm here, and ten of my best men are at this moment loading every ship in the harbor with explosives, plantin' explosives in the warehouses, too. In half an hour we're going to have a terrific fireworks display."

"Jeremy—it—it's really you."

"It's me, lass, in the flesh."

"I feel like I'm dreaming. It can't be true—"

288

"It's true," he assured me, his voice tender now, oh so tender. "You're not dreaming, Marietta."

I started to cry, and he folded me to him and held me close, gently stroking my head, murmuring soft words that were mere music, making no sense, making my heart turn over. I wrapped my arms around his broad shoulders and held onto him with all my might, afraid he would dematerialize and I would wake up and discover it had all been an illusion. He was wearing a buckskin jacket. I could feel the strong, soft leather under my fingers, could feel the fringe swaying as he rocked me slightly, his right arm a band of steel holding me, drawing me closer as his left hand continued to smooth my hair. I felt his warmth, his strength, that tall, muscular body supple and relaxed. I cried for several moments, my face buried in the curve of his shoulders, and after a while I finally looked up and he smiled and brushed my tears away.

"I—I'm sorry," I said. "I didn't mean to give way like that."

"It was my pleasure, lass. Weak, defenseless females are my specialty."

"I'm not weak."

"I know. You're strong, one of the strongest, bravest women in all the world."

"Don't patronize me."

"Wouldn't dream of it, lass. Are you all right now? Are you going to fold up and sink to the ground?"

"Just let me hold on a little longer."

He nodded, and I clung to him and closed my eyes and let the conflicting emotions swirl, reveling in the luxury of his strength, those protective arms enfolding me. The boughs creaked quietly. The leaves rustled. Jeremy Bond smelled of leather and sweat and dirt, and it was the sweetest smell on earth, a pungent, virile musk that filled me with euphoria. I tightened my arms over his shoulders, and he chuckled and squeezed me so hard I was sure I would snap in two.

"You came," I murmured.

"Did you ever doubt I would?"

"You—how did you—"

"I returned to New Orleans to discover you'd already left for England on *The Blue Elephant*," he said quietly. "My heart was broken, of course, and I vowed I'd go to England after you and tear you out of Hawke's arms and take you away with me, but things kept coming up. There was a job I had to finish, then another one. Three weeks ago I ran into your friend Will Hart in a rather sordid establishment in New Orleans. I lugged him out into an alley. He had some interesting things to tell me."

"He—"

"I know, lass. He told me everything. He was in considerable pain as he did so, I might add. I'm afraid I broke his arm before I finally got the whole story out of him—tore it right out of its socket, I fear, just like you might tear a drumstick off a roast chicken."

I shuddered. The muscles of his right arm grew tauter, drawing me closer to him.

"I finished him off, of course, took a great deal of pleasure in crushing his windpipe with my forearm. I dumped him behind a pile of garbage, and then I gathered up the best men I could find. One of 'em owns a small ship, no bigger than a tug, really. It's anchored three miles down the coast, in a secret cove. We rowed the rest of the way to the island. The boats are waiting down on the beach for our return to the ship."

I straightened up, letting go of his shoulders. He released me and moved back a step or two. I was composed now, even though my heart still seemed to leap, even though it all still seemed like a dream. I took several deep breaths, and when I spoke my voice was surprisingly level.

"How did you know I would be on the island? How did you know I wouldn't be in some squalid crib in Caracas?"

"I knew Red Nick wouldn't let a beauty like you get away, lass. I knew he'd appropriate you for himself. Are you steady now? Able to function without falling to pieces?"

"I'm all right," I replied.

"Sure?"

"I'm sure."

"Good. We don't have a lot of time. I've got to plant explosives in the armory—you're going to have to show me where it is—and then we've got to hightail it down to the beach. My men'll meet us there, and we'll be on our way."

I could feel the cool night air on my bare shoulders and arms, but I was no longer shivering. I paid no attention to the cold. Only a few moments ago I had been as low as I had ever been in my life, had given up all hope, weak, finally defeated, and now I felt strength and resolution charging through me like new sap. I was renewed, revitalized, filled with a fierce determination and eager for action.

"There's a guard," I said, "and the armory's attached to the barracks. There's a side door, but it's locked."

"I'll take care of the guard."

"And the lock?"

"I'll pry it off."

"And make such a racket every man in the barracks will be down on you, no doubt. I'll unlock it for you."

"How're you going to do that?" he asked.

"Wait and see. I'll have to go back inside the house, and I'll have to stop by one of the cottages."

"I'm not letting you out of my sight, lass."

"I'll do it while you're setting up your explosives," I continued, ignoring his remark. "You needn't worry about Red Nick. He's down at one of the canteens. There are two other women who're going with us. A girl, Corrie, and Em, a friend of mine."

"I guess we can manage two more," he said amiably.

"And I'll have to change. I can't go tearing through the night in bronze satin."

"You'll have to be quick about it, lass."

"And there're my jewels."

"Jewels?"

"I'm not leaving the island without them," I said firmly.

"Ah," he said, chuckling, "you *are* feeling better. The old spirit's returning. Sure Red Nick's not going to pop in on you while you're changing your gown and restyling your hair?"

"There's no one in the house besides the servants."

"All right then, but first the armory. Just let me fetch the explosives. I hid 'em behind a tree. We'll meet back here. There's a rope hanging over the side of the wall. I climbed up it, swung into a tree, dropped to the ground. When I saw you strolling about, I couldn't believe my luck."

"Get your explosives," I told him. My voice was impatient.

Jeremy Bond chuckled again and hurried into the shadows, returning a moment later with a bulky package wrapped in oilskin. I led him through the gardens and around the side of the house, keeping in the shadows as much as possible. As we cleared the side of the house, the moon came from behind a bank of clouds, silvering the lawns. I took Jeremy Bond's hand and led him quickly across a patch of bright silver to the protective darkness beneath a tree. We paused for a moment, then dashed toward another tree, the fringe on his buckskin jacket flying. I saw the guard pacing near the gates. The windows of the barracks were open, pools of yellow light spilling out.

"How many men in there?" he asked.

"Twenty or so," I replied.

"Christ!"

"They're gambling and drinking rum. If you're quiet about it, they won't hear you. The guard's out of sight now. Come on."

We passed Em's cottage and soon were hidden by the shrubberies growing near the armory, the same shrubberies under which Em and I had hidden the guns and ammunition we had stolen. As I led him cautiously toward the side door, I could hear rough voices and hearty laughter as the men in the barracks played cards and consumed their rum. Jeremy Bond shook his head in despair when he saw the lock on the door. I shoved him out of the way and removed a hairpin.

"Where'd you learn to do that?" he whispered as I set to work.

"On a prison ship. I'm quite expert at it. Damn! This one's difficult. I don't know if the pin is going to reach—there, I can feel it giving. Just another minute—"

"You're amazing, lass."

"Shut up, you're breaking my concentration."

"Lippy, too. I come all this way to rescue you from a fate worse than death, and you tell me to shut up. You and I are going to fight a lot during years to come, lass."

"There!" I opened the door.

"Amazing," he repeated.

"Do whatever you plan to do with your explosives, Mr. Bond. Em and Corrie and I will meet you in back of the house in fifteen minutes. And—and please be careful. I wouldn't want anything to happen to you."

"You *do* care. I knew it."

"I just want to get off this bloody island," I said dryly.

Jeremy Bond smiled and flung an arm around the back of my neck and kissed me quite suddenly, quite thoroughly. He was outrageous, utterly outrageous, jaunty and devil-may-care in the face of grave danger, refusing to be serious even when his life was at stake, taking the time to kiss me when every minute counted, kissing me with robust energy.

"There'll be more later," he promised, releasing me. "*You* be careful, Marietta. I'd like to get out of this without getting myself bruised up. Hate to fight. Prefer to sneak around in the dark."

He patted my cheek and stepped nimbly into the dark armory. I moved back behind the shrubberies, listening for the guard. When I heard him pacing heavily on the other side of the stockade, I hurried back to Em's cottage, keeping to the shadows. The front door was unlocked, a light burning in the sitting room. I stepped into the foyer. My heart was beating rapidly. I was out of breath. I paused for a moment, pulling myself together, then moved into the small sitting room.

Em was standing in front of the mantle, still wearing the elaborate purple brocade gown embroidered with silver flowers. There was a glass of brandy in her hand, and in her eyes there was a lost look, a look of total dejection, total defeat. She had taken off the diamonds and amethysts. They were scattered carelessly over the top of a small table in front of the pale blue sofa, shimmering in the candlelight.

"Get your things together," I said briskly.

"Lord, luv, what's the matter?"

"We're leaving."

A wry smile curled on her lips. "It must be the wine, luv. You drank an awful lot of it. Your cheeks are flushed bright pink. Your eyes—your eyes are like frozen blue fire."

"We're leaving the island, Em. We're leaving tonight."

"Red Nick wouldn't like that, I'm afraid. Neither would Draper. I'm expecting him any moment now. I really don't think it's a wise idea, your being here at this particular time."

"Em! Didn't you hear me? We're leaving. We don't have much time. Jeremy Bond and his men have come for us. He's planting explosives in the armory at this very moment, and they've put explosives in all the ships and warehouses. Everything's going to blow in a matter of minutes."

"My God!"

"I was strolling in the gardens. He dropped out of a tree and seized me and—I really don't have time to explain. We have maybe twelve minutes. I told him we'd meet him in back of the gardens."

"You—you're not drunk?"

"It's *true*, Em."

"Jesus," she said. She swallowed the rest of the brandy, set the glass down and hurriedly began to scoop up the jewelry. "I'll be there, luv. I've just got to get the rest of my jewelry and—and a few other things. Do I have time to change? Twelve minutes. I can do it. Corrie? What about—"

"I'm going to get her right now. Ten minutes, Em. Make it ten minutes. Meet us in the gardens behind the house in ten minutes, no later."

She nodded, curls spilling over her cheeks. She grabbed a tiny snuff box of solid gold set with pink and blue enamel, hesitated before a pair of silver candlesticks and then rushed out of the room. I hurried back outside and ran toward the house, bronze skirts billowing, whipping in the breeze. I was out of breath again as I entered the house, so excited I could hardly think. Calm, I told myself. You must be calm. You mustn't alarm Corrie. We've got a full ten minutes. There's so much to do. Ten minutes. Plenty of time if you don't allow yourself to panic. I moved up the stairs and stepped into the bedroom. Corrie was still sewing.

"Miz Marietta! You startled me. You look upset."

"Put down your sewing, Corrie. I want you to listen to me very carefully. We're leaving the island tonight. Some men have come to take us away. Don't ask me any questions. I want you to go down to your room and get your other dress and your cloak and then come back up here."

Corrie put her sewing aside and stood up, perfectly calm, as though she had been expecting this. Leaving scissors, sewing box, and thimble on the table, leaving the blue and silver gown on the floor, she moved quickly and silently out of the room. I took a deep breath and closed my eyes for a moment and then stepped over to the wardrobe, pushing aside gowns and reaching behind rows of shoes to retrieve the white cotton bag I had hidden there. Corrie had made it for me. It had straps like an apron, and I had worn it tied around my waist, filled with jewelry, when we had attempted our escape.

Forcing myself to remain calm, I took down a fine white cotton petticoat, skirts awhirl with ruffles, and then took down the simplest and sturdiest gown I had, thin tan linen with narrow brown and rust stripes. I carried the garments over to the dressing table and draped them over the stool and opened the jewelry box, dumping its contents into the bag. I set it aside and undressed, dropping bronze gown and leaf-brown petticoats to the floor, kicking them aside as I strapped the bag around my waist, letting its weight rest against the side of my left thigh. My hands trembled slightly as I tightened the knot, securing it firmly.

I put on the white cotton petticoat, smoothed the snug bodice down, and then put on the gown. It had short, narrow sleeves and a low, scooped neckline that revealed the swell of my breasts. The waist was tight, the skirt extremely full. It wasn't the ideal garment, no, but it was better than satin or velvet. I fastened the tiny hooks in back and ran my hands along my sides, adjusting the fit.

As I moved back over to the wardrobe to take down the tan linen cloak lined with rust-colored silk that went with the gown, I thought about Jeremy Bond and the extreme danger he was in as he moved about in the dark armory, placing those explosives he carried wrapped up in oilskin. What if he stumbled in the dark and knocked over a rack of guns? The clatter would alert the men in the barracks immediately, and they'd be upon him in a matter of seconds. What if he fumbled with the explosives and failed to set them up properly and they went off?

I forced the thoughts out of my mind and fastened the cloak around my shoulders. For all his jaunty, irreverent manner, Jeremy Bond was extremely capable, a professional mercenary who was apparently one of the best. He wasn't going to knock over a rack of guns. He wasn't going to blow himself up by accident. He would do his job quickly and efficiently and hurry back to the gardens to help us over the wall and down to the beach where the boats were waiting. So much had happened, so quickly. I still found it hard to believe that he was actually here, that escape was at hand.

Corrie should be returning any minute now. I glanced around the room, trying to organize my thoughts. I had the jewelry. I had changed. I had put on my cloak. There was still three or four minutes. What else did I need? Clothes. Perhaps I should grab a couple of other dresses. An extra pair of shoes as well. I could make a bundle of them. I took down a long blue cloak and spread it out on the floor, then returned to select the gowns, all so very sumptuous, cloth of gold, silver lace, deep garnet velvet, fine for the kept woman of a pirate chief but totally unsuitable for my present purposes. I finally selected a heavy blue silk and a golden yellow brocade. They were much too elegant, but they would have to do. I folded them up and put them on the cloak.

Shoes. I scanned the rows of them lined up on the bottom of the wardrobe. They were all so fancy. Satin slippers. High heels. Shoes with gem-encrusted buckles. My mind seemed to whirl. I could feel panic building. I snatched up a pair of dark blue leather slippers and tossed them on top of the gowns, then grabbed hairbrush and comb and added them to the pile. I kneeled down and began to bundle the things up, folding the heavy blue cloak over gowns and shoes, hairbrush, and comb. It was a shame I couldn't take the makeup case, I reflected, but it would make the bundle far too bulky.

Using the long blue ribbons meant to fasten the cloak under the chin, I tied the bundle up and placed it on the dressing stool, glancing anxiously at the clock. Eight minutes had passed since I first entered the room. I had moved fast indeed and, once again, was slightly out of breath. My nerves were beginning to jangle. Where was Corrie? What was keeping her? She should have returned by this time. Hearing footsteps in the hallway, I gave a sigh of relief and began to adjust the folds of the tan cloak over my shoulders, looking into the mirror as I did so.

"We must hurry," I said as I heard her enter.

"Indeed?" Nicholas Lyon inquired.

I whirled around. I could feel the color leaving my cheeks. He stood in the doorway, one hand resting on the door frame, the other thrust casually into the pocket of his maroon satin breeches. The maroon frock coat embroidered with black silk *fleurs-de-lis* hung open, revealing the fine white lawn shirt beneath. Frothy white lace ruffles cascaded from his throat and from beneath the cuffs of his coat. Those piercing blue eyes took in my change of clothes, the bundle on the dressing stool, the opened wardrobe doors. He slowly arched one brow, chin lowered, the heavy red-brown wave slanting over his forehead.

"It seems you were expecting someone else," he observed.

My throat was tight, constricted. I tried to speak. I couldn't. I felt a terrible sinking sensation in the pit of my stomach, and my pulse seemed to leap wildly just once and then vanish completely. My eyes must have reflected my alarm, for his thin lips slowly curled in a mocking smile. I wondered if my heart was going to fail me, if I was going to pitch forward to the floor.

"Going somewhere?" he asked.

I managed to nod, desperately trying to fight back the alarm.

"In a fit of pique, no doubt. My little flirtation with Pepita must have upset you."

"I—I thought you'd be gone—much longer."

"Obviously. Did you actually think I'd sleep with that coarse little harlot? I gave her some more rum, let her chatter on for a while, and then dumped a few gold coins down the front of her blouse."

He removed his hand from the door frame and folded his arms across his chest, his chin still tilted. He was enjoying himself immensely, enjoying my panic, my fear. I swallowed and passed a hand across my forehead, praying for strength.

"What's all this about?" he asked, jerking his head to one side to indicate the confusion of clothes on the floor, the bundle, the open doors of the wardrobe.

"I—I'm leaving, Nicholas."

"Are you?"

"You can't stop me."

"No?"

"Men have arrived. They came to—to rescue me."

"Do you expect me to believe that?"

"I don't care what you believe."

My voice was stronger now, a hard edge underlining

each word. The initial shock had worn off, and I could feel determination building inside me. I wasn't going to be intimidated. I wasn't going to let him interfere. I stared at him with defiant eyes, no longer afraid.

"You're being very foolish, my dear," he said gently.

"I'm leaving. I'm taking Corrie with me."

"Very foolish," he repeated, shaking his head. "I'm going to have to punish you, you know."

"I'm not afraid of you, Nicholas."

It was true. Fear had vanished entirely. I felt a steely hardness inside, strength such as I had rarely felt before. I stood very still, every muscle in my body taut, ready to spring, ready to strike. Nicholas unfolded his arms and tilted his head to one side, studying me with a reflective look in his eyes, a sad half-smile on his lips.

"This time I won't hesitate," he told me. "This time I won't allow personal feeling to interfere with duty. I told you I'd kill the little nigger, and I intend to do so. You'll watch."

"Corrie's already gone," I lied. "She left the house ten minutes ago."

"You're lying, Marietta."

"She's already with the men. They're going to blow up all your ships, the warehouses as well. He—the man who came after me—is setting a charge of explosives in the armory at this very moment."

"You do have a vivid imagination," he remarked. "No ship could possibly have approached this island without being observed."

"They anchored the ship in a secret cove down the coast and rowed to the island after dark."

A slight frown creased his brow as he considered this information, wondering if it could possibly be true. After a moment he rejected it as being altogether too improbable. I prayed Corrie wouldn't come in, prayed she would hear him and have the sense to go out to the gardens.

"I've been very lax with you, Marietta," he said. "Much too lax. I let my feelings for you get in the way."

"You have no feelings."

"I realize now I should have taken a firmer hand at the very beginning."

He sighed and took a step toward me, the skirt of his

embroidered maroon frock coat swaying, ruffles fluttering at chest and wrists. His dark copper hair was burnished by the candlelight, gleaming with rich red highlights. He smiled, his lips lifting at one corner.

"Don't come any closer," I warned.

"I don't know where your little nigger is, but rest assured I'll attend to her. Right now I shall attend to you—quite severely, I fear. I'm going to teach you a much needed lesson."

My hand flew behind me, groping on the dressing table. My fingers closed over the ivory handle of a hand mirror. I pulled it up and hurled it at him. He ducked as it sailed past his shoulder and continued moving toward me, slowly, smiling in anticipation. I rushed forward, trying to dart past him. His hand shot out, seizing my left wrist, wrenching it savagely.

"Let go of me!"

"Struggle all you like," he told me. "That'll only make it more interesting."

I pressed my lips into a tight line and kicked his shin with all the force I could muster. He winced in pain, bending forward, and as he did so I raked my nails across his cheek, digging deeply into the flesh, drawing blood. He let go of my wrist and stepped back and brought his right fist crashing against my jaw. Blazing pain shot throughout my body. I reeled backward, lost my balance, fell to my knees, stunned. Nicholas rubbed his bleeding cheek.

"You're going to be sorry for that," he promised. His voice was harsh now, metallic, filled with menace. "You're going to be sorry indeed."

He started toward me again and then stopped in his tracks as a thundering explosion sounded in the harbor, only faintly muted by distance. There was another and yet another. Nicholas Lyon wore a look of dismay, realization dawning on him as a fourth blast exploded with rumbling force. I touched my jaw, moving it gently to ascertain that it wasn't broken. As another explosion thundered he looked at me with blue eyes blazing, his cheeks ashen.

"It's true!" I cried. "Everything I said was true."

"You're responsible for this!"

"I'm glad. I'm glad! They're blowing up the whole island! The armory is going to go any minute now."

"You bitch!"

He leaped forward, and his hands flew out, seizing my throat, strong, sinewy fingers closing around it, thumbs pressing brutally into the soft flesh just beneath my windpipe. I gasped, grabbing his wrists, trying to break his grip, and he shook me viciously, squeezing even harder. Bright lights seemed to flash before my eyes, whirling rapidly, and I lowered my lids. The lights continued to whirl and my breath was gone and my lungs seemed about to burst as those thumbs crushed flesh and muscle. I grabbed his wrists again and opened my eyes and saw his face looming over me, his teeth bared, his eyes flashing blue fire. I tried desperately to pull those wrists apart, but my strength was going and I was beginning to sag. I knew I was going to die.

My head was filled with a shrill ringing noise, but I heard his yell nevertheless. He released my throat abruptly, staggering. I fell back onto the carpet in a limp heap, barely conscious. Through a shimmering haze I saw him above me, his legs wobbling and his torso swaying back and forth as his arms flew behind his back, reaching for something. He made a strange gurgling noise in his throat, beginning to topple, and I rolled out of the way as he fell crashing to the floor with a heavy thud, his arms thrown out. He lay there beside me without moving, and through the haze I saw Corrie standing a few feet away with the scissors held tightly in one hand, the shiny blades dripping with blood.

I coughed, trying to sit up. I was much too weak to make it. Everything went black. When I opened my eyes again, Corrie was on her knees beside me, trying to pull me up. I moaned and coughed and blinked my eyes. Her own were large and dark and filled with alarm as she helped me into a sitting position. My jaw still throbbed with pain and my throat was so sore I could hardly swallow, but I was fully conscious now . . . and alive. Corrie held me against her. Her arms were surprisingly strong.

"I thought you was dead," she said.

"I think—I'm all—right," I croaked hoarsely.

"I came up the stairs, and I heard him in here, heard him threatening you. I was afraid to come in. I stayed in the hall, leaning against the wall, and I was so scared, Miz Marietta."

"You should—have—gone on to—the gardens."

"Then he hit you and them explosions went off. I peeked through the doorway and saw him choking you and I—I didn't even think. I just came running in and grabbed the scissors and stabbed him."

"Help me—up—Corrie," I whispered.

"Is—are you hurt bad?"

She helped me to my feet. The floor seemed to tilt and sway beneath me, but the sensation soon passed. The dizziness vanished. My head cleared. I coughed again, wincing at the pain. Corrie still had hold of my arm, her brow furrowed with concern.

"I'll be fine," I said carefully. It hurt to talk, and I winced again, forcing myself to continue. "We must hurry. The gardens. Get the bundle on the—dressing—stool."

Corrie nodded and snatched up the bundle, and we left the room. As she paused to pick up the dress and cloak she had left in the hall, I looked back through the doorway at the man sprawled out on the carpet with arms thrown out and head turned to one side, copper hair gleaming richly. Red Nick was dead. The bloody scissors lay on the carpet nearby where Corrie had dropped them. Nicholas Lyon had loved me in his own, curiously twisted way, and that love had brought about his downfall. I looked at the body, feeling no remorse, feeling no horror, feeling nothing but relief. Corrie took my hand and I turned away. We started toward the stairs.

I held on to the banister, still weak, trying to move as quickly as possible. Corrie moved ahead of me, my bundle and her own dress and cloak under her arm. We were perhaps halfway down when the armory went. The explosion caused the walls of the house to shake. The banister trembled under my hand. One of the huge chandeliers in the foyer crashed to the floor, shattering. The entire lower floor glowed a bright, dazzling orange. Corrie paused for only a moment, then straightened her shoulders and continued down the stairs as the glowing light grew brighter, flickering wildly, as the first explosion was followed by a dozen smaller ones like a fireworks display gone mad. At the foot of the stairs she turned and took my hand, and we hurried down the narrow hallway to the back door.

It flew open before we reached it. Em and Jeremy Bond tore into the house with frantic expressions and stopped short when they saw us. Em took one look at me and gasped and gathered me into her arms, holding me tightly, and Jeremy Bond frowned and herded all three of us out the door and into the gardens. The noise was still deafening. We could hear loud, hysterical voices over the crackle of flames and the minor explosions as kegs of powder blew and boxes of ammunition caught fire and split open with the noise of a thousand firecrackers going off at once. The whole sky seemed to be a bright, blazing red-orange, and the gardens were as light as day as the flickering, flaming glow spread. Great clouds of smoke spilled over the house, filling the air.

"My God!" Em cried. "What happened to you! Your jaw! Your throat! We were waiting out here in the dark, and I was getting worried and then—"

"Later!" Jeremy Bond barked. "We'll talk later. Right now we've got to get our tails out of here before that crew comes looking for us."

"She's been hurt!"

"She's walking, isn't she? Shut up and follow orders!"

"Oh, he's charming, luv," she said spitefully. "You really can pick them, I'll say that for you."

She turned to pick up a large bundle from beneath one of the shrubs, and as she did so a tall, powerfully built man with straight golden-brown hair and stern brown eyes came rushing around the side of the house, his leather jerkin flapping open, a pistol in his hand. Corrie stiffened. Em clutched her bundle and gave a shrill scream. Jeremy Bond looked relieved, motioning for the man to join us.

"Damn!" the man yelled. "When you do it, Jeremy-boy, you do it *big!*"

"What are you doing here, Randolph? I thought I ordered everyone to meet on the beach."

"I know you did, lad, but I finished settin' up the explosives in the warehouse and figured you might be needin' a little help up here. I started up the road toward the stockade, got halfway up when the damn thing blew. The front of the place flew apart, stones hurtlin' in every direction. Flames shot up in the air, lickin' the sky."

"Who's *he?*" Em demanded.

Jeremy ignored her. "Since you're here, Randolph, you

can give me some help with the women. We have to get them over the wall and down to the beach.''

''Happy to,'' Randolph retorted. ''We'd best hurry it up, lad. The courtyard is swarmin' with pirates. No one paid any attention to me as I passed—too much confusion, guess they thought I was one of 'em—but some of 'em are bound to come back here any minute now.''

Jeremy Bond nodded tersely and scooped me up into his arms and started moving toward the trees. I clung to him, my arms wrapped around his shoulders. Randolph slung an arm around Em's waist and took Corrie by the wrist and hurried them after us. Em protested vehemently, struggling to break loose and informing him in no uncertain terms that she could walk unaided. Randolph merely grinned, tightening his hold and dragging her along. I closed my eyes, beginning to feel dizzy again, growing weaker by the second. I rested my head against the side of Jeremy Bond's neck and breathed in his musky odor, feeling I was in the middle of a nightmare that would never end. He carried me up the stairs and along the walkway and then set me down gently beside one of the cannons. Randolph brought Em and Corrie up, holding both of them firmly as the sky glared orange and great billows of smoke filled the air.

''You can let go of me now!'' Em snapped. ''I'm not a baby!''

''You're a saucy wench, aren't you?''

''I don't like being manhandled by a great brute like you!''

''My name's Randolph, Dick Randolph. You can call me Randy.''

''I'll bet you *are*,'' she retorted.

''Get 'em down,'' Jeremy ordered.

''Come on, Saucy,'' Randolph said cheerfully. ''You're first.''

Before Em could protest he bent down and wrapped his arms around her legs and slung her across his shoulders as though she were a sack of corn meal. Em let out a shriek and clutched her bundle. It rattled noisily as Randolph took hold of the rope tied around the base of the cannon and leaped over the side of the wall. Em continued to shriek as he scrambled down and deposited her on the ground. Jeremy held me in his arms. I felt faint, so weak I could hardly keep my eyes open. Randolph scrambled back up the wall and spoke very gently to Corrie. She nodded meekly and wrapped her dress and cloak over my bundle, holding them firmly as he picked her up and carried her over the wall.

"I—I'm so sleepy," I said. "I can't make it, Jeremy. You'll have to go without me. I—just—can't—make it."

"You're going to be fine, lass."

I closed my eyes, reeling, and I felt him sling me over his shoulder as Randolph had slung Em, but it seemed to be happening to someone else. I seemed to sway in midair as he moved slowly, carefully down the wall, one arm wrapped tightly around my legs, holding onto the rope with his free hand. He must be terribly strong, I thought, and then I seemed to be swallowed up by darkness, sinking into a blessed oblivion.

I opened my eyes later and saw trees and rocks and was vaguely aware that we were moving downhill toward the beach. I was nestled in his arms. He carried me lightly, easily, as though I weighed nothing at all. I sighed, closing my eyes again, swimming in darkness. Then I stirred and saw that we were on the beach. Several other men had joined us, and they all seemed to be talking at once. Three boats rocked on the sloshing waves. Em and Corrie were already sitting in one, Em having a spirited conversation with Randolph who stood waist-high in the water, steadying the boat. Moonlight shimmered, and in the distance the red glow spread over the top of the island. Jeremy Bond looked down at me, a worried frown creasing his brow.

"I'm perfectly all right," I told him. "I'm just sleepy."

"Of course you are, lass. Of course."

"Don't humor me. I'm not a child."

"We'll just get you in the boat, lass. You'll be fine."

He carried me through the water and set me down beside Em. She gathered me to her, stroking my hair.

"Delayed shock," Jeremy told her. "She'll rally in a little while."

I heard them talking about me, and then I heard the slap of oars in the water. The boat rocked pleasantly, and I rested my head against Em's shoulder. Later, much later, I sat up and brushed the hair out of my eyes, acutely aware of the cold.

My head was perfectly clear. Em sat beside me, her arm around me, and Corrie huddled on the other side, stroking my hand. Randolph was sitting at one end of the boat, Jeremy at the other, both rowing in strong, steady unison. An icy wind blew across the water, chilling me to the bone.

"How are you feeling?" Em asked.

"Not too marvelous," I replied. "I'll survive."

"Corrie told me what happened, luv."

"It's over now," I said. "It's all behind us."

Silvery strands of reflected moonlight danced on the dark water, and there was a heavy haze in the air. I could see another long rowboat up ahead of us, and, turning, I saw another behind. Far, far in the distance I could see glowing orange light as fires burned on the island. We must have come at least halfway, I thought, turning back around and gathering the folds of the cloak around my shoulders.

"They blew up every single ship in the harbor," Em told me, "all the warehouses as well. The whole island's aflame now. It looks like Red Nick's men are out of business—those that survived. Did you get your jewelry, luv?"

I nodded. "It's in a bag, strapped around my waist."

"Mine, too," she said, "and I've got some other things in my bundle. Randolph gave me a lot of trouble about the bundle, said it was too bulky and heavy. I told him to take a flying leap. He's something, that one, stubborn as a mule—and strong as an ox. I think I'm in love."

"You talkin' about me?" Randolph barked.

"Never you mind, luv," she called gaily.

The haze grew thicker, billowing across the boat in foggy clouds. The wind blew vigorously. Spumes of icy spray splattered us as the men continued to row. The boat rocked precariously, bouncing on the waves. I looked over my shoulder, but I could no longer see the island, nor could I see the boat that had been behind us. I huddled between Em and Corrie, shivering as needles of spray stung my cheeks and wet my cloak. We had survived the island and its horrors. We were on our way back to civilization at last. As the wind grew stronger and large, angry waves slashed the side of the boat, I prayed we would make it.

BOOK THREE:
The Rogue

Twenty

The wind stopped abruptly, so abruptly that it was startling. One minute the waves were hitting the sides of the boat, spraying us thoroughly, and the next the boat was rocking gently from side to side and the water was still. I was vastly relieved, but there was a worried look on Jeremy Bond's face. Through the fine cloud of haze I could see a deep furrow above the bridge of his nose. His mouth was set in a tight line. He looked over my head at Randolph.

"I don't like this," he said.

"I don't like it either, Jeremy-boy. Not a bit."

"What's wrong?" I asked. "The wind's stopped blowing."

"That's just it, lass," Randolph said.

"Jesus, you two are scaring me," Em exclaimed. "I don't like the tone you're using. Are we going to *sink?*"

"How far to the cove?" Jeremy asked.

"A mile, maybe, maybe a mile and a half."

"I think we'd better head for shore, Randolph."

"Aye, it might be a good idea."

"Will you two please tell us what's going *on!*" Em snapped.

"Maybe nothin'," Randolph retorted, "nothin' for you to get all stirred up about. You just sit there and keep that saucy tongue still for a few minutes while we row to shore."

"We'll probably be eaten by cannibals!"

"Hush, Em," I warned.

Jeremy Bond straightened his shoulders, took a firm grip on the oars and dipped them into the water. Randolph did the same, and the boat turned in the water, pointing toward the shore which was barely visible, a dark line in the darkness which, I realized, was gradually lightening. The haze swirled and lifted, thinning out. There was no sound whatsoever except the splash of oars dipping into water. Everything was still, frighteningly still. It was almost as though the earth were holding its breath, I thought, apprehensive now as the men rowed with grim determination.

"I'm getting a queasy feeling," Em observed. "I'll feel much better when we're on dry land."

"So will I."

Corrie looked up at us, silent, stoic, refusing to show the alarm I knew she must be feeling. Only a few minutes ago I had been shivering as icy wind assailed us, and now I felt warm. The sudden change in temperature was as disturbing as the abrupt stillness. The haze lifted, evaporating quickly, and a curious opal light began to seep through the semi-darkness. I realized that it was almost dawn. Layers of darkness melted away, revealing a sky the color of slate, deep, deep gray stained with the strange opal light that should have been pink and gold.

The oars struck bottom. Jeremy Bond climbed out of the boat, took hold of it, and began to pull us toward the beach. Randolph joined him, and a few moments later the bottom of the boat scraped on sand. Em grabbed her bundle and held it tightly as Randolph clamped his hands about her waist and heaved her out of the boat, setting her on the beach. She brushed her skirts and gave him a hateful look. He grinned, then turned to help Corrie out. Jeremy Bond reached for my hand, clasping it firmly. I climbed out and stood beside Corrie and Em. Jeremy picked up the remaining bundle.

"We'd better drag the boat over there behind those trees," he said, "and then we'd best hunt for shelter."

"Bound to be a cave or gully or somethin'," Randolph replied, taking hold of one side of the boat.

They dragged the boat toward the trees. The haze had vanished entirely. The dark opal light continued to spread over the dark gray sky. The water was dark gray, too, faintly tinged with green, perfectly still it seemed, barely lapping the shore. Not a breeze stirred, the air pressing down with almost physical force, so sultry I could feel sweat beginning to dampen my dress between my shoulder blades. I removed my cloak and took the bundle from Corrie, tying the cloak around it.

"It's going to storm," she said. "It's going to storm bad."

"How can you tell, luv?" Em asked.

"I seen it like this once before, when I was with Miz Henrietta. We was on the plantation near the coast and the air stopped breathing and everything grew still like it is now. The sky turned dark, like now, and there was that funny purple light. Mister Dale, he was the foreman, he got us all down into the storm cellar quick."

Em sat down on a piece of driftwood, spreading her pale blue cotton skirt out, revealing the ruffled petticoats beneath. "Just what we need," she said wryly, "a bloody storm."

"It was a hurricane, Miz Em. It done—did ever so much damage, uprooted trees and picked houses up and blew 'em away. There was a tidal wave, too, and land was flooded, shacks and chicken coops under water."

"I'm feeling cheerier and cheerier, luv. Keep talking."

The men returned. Their faces were grim indeed. Jeremy Bond stepped over to the edge of the water and slanted a palm across his forehead, peering up and down the shoreline, looking for another rowboat.

"No sign of 'em," he told Randolph. "I'm worried, Randolph. Those waves were pretty choppy, and there're a lot of rocks in these waters. The fog was so thick you couldn't see a foot in front of you."

"Them boys aren't stupid, lad. When the goin' got rough, they headed for shore, probably a lot sooner 'n we did. They'll turn up."

"I hope so. I feel responsible for those men."

"I know, lad, but right now we gotta worry about our own skins, and judgin' from the light I don't reckon we have a helluva lot of time to dally."

"You're right, of course."

Those blue eyes, usually so merry, were dark with concern as he turned to us. He was wearing tall brown boots and a pair of tan corduroy breeches that had faded to a light pinkish-orange. Beneath the fringed brown buckskin jacket he wore a thin white cotton shirt opened at the throat. An orange-red bandana was knotted around his neck, ends flapping over his lapel, and a leather holster hung from his belt, the butt of his pistol pushing the tail of his jacket up at one side. He bore very little resemblance to the foppishly attired dandy I had known in New Orleans.

"Are we going to have a hurricane?" Em asked.

"We're likely to have a bit of wind, a spot of rain," Randolph told her, "but don't you worry your pretty little head about it. We'll find us some place snug and cozy, and you and I can get to know each other better."

"That won't be any treat for me, luv, I can assure you. I've rarely seen an uglier lout in all my born days."

"You're joshin' me, gal. I'm as good lookin' as they come. Why, the women fall all over me, can't fight 'em off."

Em got up from the piece of driftwood and picked up her bundle. "There's no accounting for taste," she snapped.

Dick Randolph grinned. With his square jaw and broad, flat cheekbones he was far from good-looking, but there was a merry curl to his mouth and his dark brown eyes were merry, too. Thick golden-brown hair flopped over his forehead in unruly waves, and there was a tiny crescent-shaped scar at the corner of his mouth, pale pink against his tan complexion. Tall, lean, powerfully built with massive shoulders, he exuded brute strength and casual self-confidence. I suspected that his easygoing amiability could be quite misleading to any enemy he might encounter.

"Come along, gal," he said, slinging an arm around her shoulders. "We'll lead the way."

Em sighed and put on a martyred expression that fooled no one, Randolph least of all. He gave her a tight squeeze and led her toward the trees. Corrie picked up the bundle tied up in cloaks and followed them. I turned, looking at Jeremy Bond with a tight feeling inside. I knew he was terribly upset about the other men, and I felt it was all my fault. If it hadn't been for me, they would all be safely in New Orleans at this very moment. Although neither Jeremy nor Randolph had voiced it, I was sure both of them considered it likely that one or both the boats had either crashed on the rocks or capsized in the heavy fog and tumultuous waves.

Jeremy seemed to read my thoughts. He stepped across the sand toward me and took my hand.

"It's going to be all right, lass," he said quietly. "The

men are probably heading for shelter at this very minute, probably rowed to shore as soon as the fog grew thick."

"How many men were there?"

"Ten—no, nine, Cates was killed on the island. They're all right. We'll meet 'em at the cove as soon as this storm blows over. That's a nasty bruise you've got there on your jaw. How does it feel?"

"It doesn't hurt much. It's a little sore."

"And your throat?"

"I'm fine, Jeremy."

"I should never have let you go back to the house."

"I insisted. Remember? I was quite stubborn about it."

"You were stubborn, all right. Lippy, too, if I recall."

He smiled. It was a beautiful smile that made something melt inside of me. I looked up at his handsome face, the slightly twisted nose saving it from being too handsome, too perfect. I wanted to place my finger over that deep cleft in his chin, wanted to run my fingertips over those broad, smooth cheekbones. His rich, unruly brown hair was thick and silky, spilling over his brow, his eyes so very blue, so vivid and lively, filled now with feeling I had so rarely seen in the eyes of any man.

"I—I never thanked you," I said.

"Matter of fact, you didn't."

"Thank you, Jeremy. I had just about given up hope."

"You should have known I'd come. You should have known I'd eventually find out what happened and come for you."

"I never thought I'd see you again. After that night in the gardens I didn't think you'd give me another thought."

"I meant everything I said that night, Marietta."

I didn't reply. I didn't want to discuss it, not yet, perhaps not ever. I was grateful to Jeremy Bond, more grateful than words could ever express, but I had no intention of deluding myself that the gratitude I felt could ever develop into anything else. He was charming, yes, looking at me now with tender blue eyes and a softly curving mouth, virile in his buckskin jacket and faded corduroy breeches, the red-orange bandana tied around his neck, but I wasn't going to succumb to that charm, that potent male allure. I intended to keep my guard up at all times, for my own protection.

Once again, he seemed to read my thoughts. His smile widened, and he shook his head, eyes atwinkle.

"You intend to fight it, I see."

"I don't know what you're talking about," I said stiffly.

"Ah, lass, you're exasperating, the most exasperating female I've ever encountered, but fortunately I'm a patient man. With a lass like you a man *has* to be patient—or else resort to rape."

"I'll sleep with you, Jeremy, if that's what you want."

My voice was cold and deliberate, my manner aloof. He didn't like that at all. His mouth tightened, and there was a glint of anger in his eyes. For a moment I thought he was going to strike me.

"You will, lass," he said sternly, "but of your own accord, because you want it as much as I. I shan't take advantage of you—of your gratitude, nor shall I press you. I'm going to make you see what's in your own heart, and when you do, you'll come to me without hesitation."

"That day will never come, Jeremy."

He looked at me for a long moment, and I met his look with a level gaze, my chin held high. I had long since pulled my hand from his, and I reached up to brush a heavy copper-red wave from my temple. He clearly wanted to say something more, but he instead sighed heavily, turning to glance up at the sky.

"I shan't argue with you, Marietta. We haven't the time right now. It's going to start blowing like hell in just a few minutes, and we've got to find shelter."

He took hold of my elbow and led me toward the trees, holding me loosely but firmly, guiding me around a clump of driftwood. His moment of anger had passed, and our conversation might never have occurred. He was completely relaxed, moving in that long, bouncy stride that I had some difficulty keeping up with. The beach was soon behind us and we were moving quickly through the trees. The ground was wet and spongy, giving beneath our feet. This was marshland, cypress and willows in profusion, the whole area, as I was to discover, riddled with small lakes and narrow, greenish-brown rivers that snaked sluggishly along, twisting in every direction.

We soon caught up with Corrie and Em and Randolph.

Randolph had Em's bundle slung over his shoulder, one arm curled around her waist. The bundle still rattled noisily. I wondered what all she had managed to snatch up in those frantic ten minutes before she hurried to the gardens. Corrie trudged along calmly behind them, still wearing a stoical expression. I relieved her of my bundle and gave her a reassuring smile. She smiled back, but her heart wasn't in it. She was so exhausted she could hardly walk, no doubt still reliving the nightmare of that final hour on the island.

We waded through a river not more than twelve feet wide, the water no higher than midcalf, willows lining it thickly on either side, and, beyond it, the land began to slope upward somewhat. We passed a large clearing with long wooden poles driven into the ground in circular clusters, pulled together at the top to form oval frameworks. Sheets of mothy animal skin hung over part of one of them, and I realized they had been huts. In the center of each framework there was a deep hole surrounded by rocks and filled with charred wood. The clearing was littered with dried gourds and strangely shaped vessels and pots covered with a rocky white substance Jeremy identified as asphaltum, but by far the most striking sight was the enormous pile of shells. It must have been at least ten feet in circumference and seven feet high at its highest point.

"Jesus!" Em exclaimed, holding close to Randolph. "What—what is this place?"

"Karankawa village," he replied, "or at least it was until a short while ago."

"Karankawa! Aren't they the cannibals!"

"Don't get yourself all riled up, gal. They're gone. The Karankawas are a migratory tribe, rarely stay in one spot more 'n a few weeks at a time. They move about from place to place, stay as long as the food is plentiful, and when it begins to give out they pick up and move again."

"What are those shells?" she asked.

"Oyster shells, from the looks of 'em. There must have been a big bed of 'em nearby."

"I thought they ate *people*."

"They eat whatever's at hand," he said teasingly, "fish, roots, berries, the occasional deer, the occasional white man."

"That's not funny!"

Randolph chuckled, and we moved on, passing through a heavy grove of cedar trees. The ground seemed firmer here. The sky overhead was almost completely opal colored now, dense, opaque, hardly a patch of gray showing, and it was so sultry that all of us were sweating freely. Jeremy was beginning to look worried again, his mouth tight, his eyes grim. Em let out a wild shriek as something dropped out of a tree and slithered across the pathway. Randolph held her close, chuckling again. She kicked him viciously in the shin, whereupon he let out a yell that startled birds and sent them flapping out of trees in a great cloud. Em smiled, extremely pleased with herself.

"Here, minx!" he said angrily, slinging the bundle at her. "Carry your own bloody loot. It weighs a ton!"

"I love a gentleman," she remarked, heaving the bundle over her shoulder with considerable effort.

"I'll carry it, Miz Em," Corrie said.

"No you won't, luv. It *does* weigh a ton. Those bloody candlesticks. I should have left them, but they're solid silver. Six pairs."

Up ahead, through the trees, we could see a hillside covered with trees and great gray rocks. Halfway up there was a large, gaping hole, the entrance to a small cave. Jeremy urged us to move faster, and we stumbled on, Em bent almost double under the weight of her bundle. After a short while Randolph grimaced, shook his head, and took it away from her, slinging it back across his broad, muscular shoulder. She gave him a lovely smile.

I stepped on a rock and lost my balance. Jeremy Bond seized my arm, steadying me, and as he did so there was a rumbling noise in the distance, like no thunder I had ever heard before. It sounded as though a gigantic iron roller was rumbling over the earth, flattening everything in its pathway. The ground seemed to shift under our feet as the rumbling continued, growing louder. The wind began to blow, singing through the treetops, mildly at first, the breeze a pleasant relief after the oppressive heat. I felt light drops of moisture as a cool scattering of raindrops sprinkled over us. In a matter of seconds the wind was blowing fiercely, howling, howling like a banshee, and the rain pelted us in swirling sheets.

"The cave!" Jeremy shouted. "We've got to make the cave!"

We were running now, the wind at our backs, pushing us forward like an invisible giant bent on smashing us to the ground, the rain swirling, blinding us as we rushed toward the hillside. Corrie slipped, but she didn't fall. She flew forward, feet off the ground, arms flailing at her sides, her skirts billowing up over her legs. Em screamed as Corrie crashed to the ground. Jeremy rushed forward, picked the girl up and said something to Randolph. Randolph nodded and scooped Em up into his arms and started running. Jeremy set Corrie back down and came toward me, his buckskin jacket flapping wildly as he struggled against the wind.

"What are you going to do!" I yelled as he seized my arm.

"You'll have to trust me, lass!"

He quickly untied the bandana from around his neck and tied one end of it around my right wrist. The rain pelted us with the force of bullets, and we could hardly stand. Corrie, crouched on the ground, seemed to skid as the wind slammed against her. Jeremy tightened the knot around my wrist and then pulled me over to the trunk of a tree.

"No!" I cried.

"Trust me! I'll be back for you!"

He forced both my arms around the trunk of the tree and tied the other end of the bandana around my left wrist and left me trussed up there, hugging the rough trunk of the tree. The wind tore at my skirts and hair as I turned my head to watch him scoop Corrie up and carry her off after Em and Randolph. The wind howled with the sound of a thousand demons, and limbs began to break off and fly through the air. They were gone now and I was alone, tied to the tree that shook and trembled and seemed intent on uprooting itself. A limb from another tree came hurtling toward me, crashing against the trunk only a few inches above my head.

The world had gone mad. The elements raged. The air was full of flying debris and rain, rain that crashed down in solid sheets of gray, great waves of wetness that slammed against me and turned the ground into mud. The noise was horrendous, the howling wind, the crashing rain, the shrieking of wood splintering. A thunderbolt darted from the sky, splitting the air with silver fury. It slammed into a tree only a few yards away from me. There was a great cloud of smoke and a burst of searing flames, and the tree split in two, splintering apart with a tearing, shrieking noise that was like a demented wail.

Lightning struck again, and again, and a limb overhead split and flew into the air. I saw flames explode over my head, flaring quickly, doused immediately by the rain. I clung to the tree, my eyes closed now, my cheek resting against the rough bark. I could feel the trunk swaying, swaying, straining against the wind, and I knew that in just a matter of minutes it was going to snap in two and I would be torn apart as well. I was drenched from head to toe, and still the great waves slashed against me, pounding my body. The wind continued to scream, shriller and shriller, and the rumbling grew louder as the giant roller drew nearer, crushing everything.

I prayed they had made it to the cave. I was going to die, I knew that, but perhaps the others had made it to safety in time. A tremendous gust hit the tree and the tree swayed, roots tearing from the ground, and I was picked up and thrown into the air and would have been blown away had my wrists not been tied. I slammed back against the trunk with an impact that knocked the breath out of me, and there was a painful slap against my thigh as the heavy bag of jewelry hit against flesh with bruising force. I held on, eyes closed still, waiting for the inevitable.

Great roots had been pulled out of the ground. The tree was at an angle now, and I was no longer standing. I was swaying, held only by that tightly knotted bandana. Sheets of rain slammed against me, and water rose, swirling above my ankles, above my calves. If I wasn't torn free and blown away, flying to a shattering, splintering death as I crashed against tree trunks and rocks, I would surely drown, tied here, helpless as the water rose, whirling higher by the second, coating my skirt and legs with mud. Another limb tore free above my head, sailing away, and bolts of lightning flashed all around like jagged silver serpents striking with venomous force.

I was going to die. I faced the fact with curious objectivity, beyond terror as I swayed from the trunk that tilted at a forty-five-degree angle. More roots pulled free and the tilt grew lower and I dropped down into the raging water that was waist-high, rushing in torrents that would have carried me off were I not tied. Minutes passed, hours, it seemed, and reality faded and I was in the middle of a howling, shrieking, pounding nightmare that would never end. My mind seemed to quicken and spin, and images flashed with dizzying speed and vivid color.

I saw an auction block and two men, one tall and stern with hard features and gray eyes and black hair, the other lean, lounging against a tree, his blond hair all atumble. They were bidding for me, both of them. Then I saw a wagon and a run-down plantation house and Derek Hawke was delirious from snakebite and I was smoothing his brow. I looked into his eyes and they turned from gray to dark brown, and Jeff Rawlins was teasing me as we organized a ball in the gambling hall in New Orleans. I shook my head to clear it, and I saw oak trees and mist and saw the pistols and heard the shot and Jeff fell to the ground and I hurried toward him and he looked at me with the harsh brutal face of Helmut Schnieder and I was in the mansion at Natchez, Roseclay, and it was burning and he was laughing, pulling on my wrists, pulling them apart.

"Let go of me!" I screamed. "Let go!"

"Easy, lass! I've got to untie you!"

I opened my eyes and saw his face only a few inches away from mine as he struggled to untie the bandana. His brown hair plastered over his skull in thick, wet locks and splayed across his forehead, and his mouth was set in a determined line and his blue eyes were determined, too. I shook my head, trying to tell him it was useless, unable to speak as my legs kicked in the rushing water, skirts weighing me down, pulling me. He caught hold of my arm and held it tightly as my other arm swung free, the bandana still tied around my wrist. The suction of the water pulled me away from him, but he held on, somehow he held on. It seemed my arm was going to be pulled out of its socket as he drew me toward him, gathering me in his arms.

He was standing. Legs spread wide, he was standing in the raging waters that rushed violently, swirling with debris, threatening to carry us both away. He looked into my eyes, and his own were calm, deliberately calm, reassuring me and warning me not to panic. He held me tightly, so tightly I felt certain my ribs would crack. Over the shrieking wind and pounding rain I heard him tell me to wrap my arms around his shoulders and hold on fast. He was yelling directly into my ear, yet I could hardly hear him over the nightmare din, and I didn't try to answer. I merely obeyed.

He swung me around and ducked and for a brief instant both of us were under water as he moved beneath the trunk of the tree I had been tied to only moments before. He pulled me up and I coughed, water spilling from both of us as he half-walked, half-swam away from the tree. There was a great, groaning noise as the trunk tilted more and roots tore free. The trunk fell into the water with a great splash and immediately swirled away, banging against the sides of other trees, limbs splintering, shattering. Had Jeremy Bond not arrived when he had I would have been crushed to death, every bone in my body broken.

Jeremy wrapped one arm around me, reached with the other and caught hold of a tree trunk and pulled with all his might. I held on to him, knowing it was futile, knowing we would never make the cave. He let go of the tree trunk and took another step, his foot slipping, then holding, his legs trembling as he took yet another step and then another. The water was up to his thighs and any moment now his legs would give way and both of us would go cascading to our deaths. A bolt of lightning struck. Half a tree crashed into the water directly in front of us. Jeremy caught hold of it, swung it around and let go. It swirled away.

He could have saved himself, and he had come back for me. Now both of us would die. He claimed to love me. He must. He must love me. He had risked his life and the lives of all his men in order to rescue me from the island, and now he was risking his life again and we would die together. I had wanted to die before. Before, after Derek was murdered, I had longed for death, but now, as those strong arms held me pinioned tightly against that muscular chest, as the wind shrieked and the rain slashed and treetops swayed and broke and limbs flew into the air, I wanted desperately to live, if only to thank this man for all he had done. I clung to him, my face buried in his neck, and I could feel every muscle in his body straining as he continued to move through the torrential waters.

It was no longer waist-high. It was up to his knees now. How far had we come? How much more could he endure? His knees were growing weak from the effort. I could feel them give slightly as he struggled upward. Yes, upward, he was climbing now, moving up that first gentle slope of the hillside. I lifted my head and through the raging gray sheets of rain it seemed I could see someone moving toward us. Jeremy called out and took another step. I felt him sway violently as his right leg slipped, and he fell face forward, his arms flying out instinctively to break the fall.

I spun underwater, thrashing, and I could feel the tug of the water carrying me away. I went plummeting downward in the water, and then I screamed in pain as the roots of my hair threatened to tear out of my scalp. Jeremy Bond pulled, dragging me back toward him by my hair, and I threw my arms out and reached back to seize that hand that was tearing my hair out. He took hold of my wrist and pulled me forward, on his knees in the water. For a moment we wrestled together as I struck out in blind panic. He finally slung an arm around my throat, caught both my wrists in his free hand, and lifted me, dragging me out of the water, half-strangling me as he did so.

Enormous hands reached out, clasping his arm, clasping mine, heaving, and I was vaguely aware of Dick Randolph swinging me over his shoulder. Rain pelted my back. The wind slammed at me with incredible force. The shrieking howl never ceased, the din so loud I thought my eardrums would burst from the agony of it. Randolph climbed, carrying me, Jeremy Bond behind us, and then we were moving through the mouth of the cave. As Randolph set me on my feet, holding my arms so that I wouldn't fall, I caught a quick glimpse of purple-gray rock walls and a blazing fire and a curious heap of mossy rugs and broken pots. I looked up into Randolph's eyes and started to say thank you, and then my head started spinning and I collapsed in his arms.

"My God!" Em cried.

"She's all right, gal. Just faint."

"Bring her over here by the fire! She's half-drowned!"

I was aware of strong arms moving me, lowering me onto grassy softness. I was aware of the dancing yellow-orange flames and the smoke and the heat and it was lovely, so lovely, for I was shivering and my teeth were chattering. I saw Em leaning over me with concerned hazel eyes, Corrie behind her, and I tried to sit up because I had to ask about Jeremy. Did he make it? Was he behind us? Em pushed me back onto the softness and then wrapped me up in something equally as soft. I shook my head because I couldn't sleep, I had to know about Jeremy. I tried to speak again, and then I saw him standing beside the fire, peeling off the buckskin jacket.

I could hear the wind screaming and the rain lashing, but the sound was muted, not nearly as loud as the crackle of flames, lovely flames that danced merrily and cast flickering black shadows on the purple-gray walls and warmed me. I sighed, drawing the grassy softness closer about me, and I wondered what it was, wondered about the broken pots I had seen. I closed my eyes, sinking slowly into soft, luxurious darkness. When I opened them again I saw his face leaning over me, polished by firelight, eyes tender, brown hair dry, falling forward over his brow. I heard the wind and rain and heard him say something, and then darkness claimed me again as his hand touched my cheek and gently stroked it. I had rarely known such bliss.

Twenty-One

I struggled into a sitting position, dry, warm, surprisingly refreshed. The soft, sweet-smelling rug of dried, woven moss fell away from my shoulders as I stretched, looking around the cave. The fire had gone out, only a pile of cold, charred wood remaining, and rays of sunlight streamed through the opening. Corrie and the men were gone. Em smiled and came toward me with one of the curiously shaped white vessels.

"Here, luv," she said, "drink this, it's water, and try not to let the fact that cannibals drank out of it bother you."

I took the vessel by its slender white neck and drank greedily, giving no thought whatsoever to other lips that might have touched the rim. The water was wonderfully cool and satisfying. Em watched me drink as a mother hen might watch an ailing chick. I finished the rest of the water and handed her the vessel. She set it down gingerly.

"How are you feeling?" she inquired.

"I'm sore all over. My jaw aches. My throat feels raw. The roots of my hair sting and, yes, my wrists hurt, too, but I feel wonderful, lucky to be alive."

"You slept for hours, luv. It's midafternoon now, and the storm passed over a long time ago."

"Where are the men?"

"Hunting for food," she replied. "Corrie went with them. It seems she knows quite a lot about roots and berries and things. They've been gone over an hour—should be back soon. I don't know about you, but I'm starving."

"I could use a bite," I admitted.

"Randolph thinks he's going to find game and kill it with a bow and arrow. As soon as the storm was over he went out and came back with a long willow branch and a bunch of sticks he'd cut. He peeled the bark off the sticks and notched them and sharpened the ends to points, making arrows, then took a piece of thin wire out of his pocket and fastened it to the willow branch and made a dandy bow."

"Why go to all that trouble? Why not just use his gun?"

"That's what I wanted to know, luv, thought it was silly as hell when he claims to be such a terrific shot. Know what he told me? He told me that if there still *were* any Karankawas lurking about the neighborhood he didn't want to alert 'em of our presence with gunfire."

"He thinks there might still be some around?"

Em nodded. "They're migratory, he says, but it seems that when they migrate they don't migrate *far*. They move all through the area in long canoes they make by hollowing out logs. They could be ten miles away or they could be half a mile away, and here's the lovely part, luv, there isn't just one big tribe of 'em. There're *bands* of them all over the place."

She shivered, folding her arms around her waist. I stretched again, not at all alarmed. The moss rugs made a soft, crackling sound. At least four of them were beneath me, making an unusually comfortable mattress.

"Some of them were in this cave," Em continued. "They left the rugs and the pots. While you were sleeping Randolph told me all about them, told me a lot more than I cared to hear. He was trying to scare me, of course, and I'll have to admit he *did*. They eat their victims *alive*, luv. They tie them to a stake and dance around them with knives and then nip over and cut off a piece of flesh and—"

"Please, Em," I protested.

"And they cut their victim's entrails out and *roast* them right in front of him. He had me cringing, all right. I was white as a sheet, actually trembling, and he put his arms around me and chuckled and told me not to worry, said he'd protect me, the bastard."

"He was probably making most of it up, Em."

"No he wasn't, luv. He just confirmed the stories I heard on the island. After he'd finished scaring me he told me about their culture and habits and things. He seems to know all about them. The men are very tall and wear only breech-cloths and paint themselves up, usually in black and white. Each pattern they use on their bodies has a special meaning, a kind of message to the others. They tattoo themselves, too, like the Seminoles in Florida. I never heard of the Seminoles, but apparently the Karankawas have a lot in common with them, only the Seminoles don't eat human flesh.''

She was determined to regale me with information, and I stood up, stretching once again. I was sore all over, it was true, but it seemed I could feel the life force quickening in my veins. I ignored the aches and pains, brushing bits of dried mud off my skirt.

"The women are quite attractive, he says," Em continued. "They are tall, too, and wear skirts of dried moss, like those rugs, and strings of shells and green glass beads. The Karankawas are extremely promiscuous, Randolph says, and they have very close family tries. Some explorer named Cabeza de Vaca wrote about 'em in a book—Randolph read it, didn't know he could read. This de Vaca fellow was shipwrecked off the coast in the early fifteen hundreds and wandered around the southwest for a couple of years, gathering information for his book, I suppose.''

Em warmed up to her subject, quite clearly fascinated, and I let her talk, paying very little attention. I continued to brush dried mud off my dress, my mind on Jeremy Bond.

"Anyway, luv, *he* found them quite friendly, de Vaca did. He called them Capoques and Hans instead of Karankawas, but Randolph says they're the same Indians. They move around the lagoons and bays in their hollowed-out log canoes and catch fish in cane weirs and eat the root of an underwater plant when they can't find anything else. This part's going to bowl you over, luv—de Vaca recorded that the women nurse their young until the children are twelve years old! He was quite amazed.''

"I shouldn't wonder," I said, smiling.

Em sighed and shook her head and, momentarily forgetting the Karankawas, examined me with close scrutiny.

"You really had us worried, luv. I thought surely you were going to be killed.''

"So did I.''

"When I saw Jeremy Bond intended to tie you to a tree and

leave you out there I screamed and kicked something awful, but Randolph wouldn't put me down. He finally had to hit me, knocked me clean unconscious. I woke up in the cave just as Bond brought Corrie in. She was wailing, too."

"There was nothing else he could do, Em. He was thinking of all of us. He saved my life."

"Cocky chap. Can't say that I take to him, although I'll have to admit he's terribly good-looking. Brave, too."

"Extremely brave," I said quietly.

"He squawked like the devil when I made him climb the tree, though. Said no dress on earth was worth climbing that high for. I put my hands on my hips and looked him straight in the eyes and told him if he didn't get his ass up there I'd kick it so hard he wouldn't sit on it for a week."

"What are you talking about?"

"Your bundle, luv. You dropped it—don't imagine you remember in all the excitement. It flew away and caught in the branches of one of the trees, and I saw it as soon as we stepped out of the cave. Your cocky gentleman shimmied up after it, grumbling all the way. Corrie and I dried everything over the fire. Your dresses and shoes weren't wet, just the cloaks. Corrie's things were only a little damp."

"Were the brush and comb still there?"

Em nodded. "I've already used them, imagine you'd like to, too. I'll get them."

She handed me the brush and comb a moment later, and I combed the tangles out of my hair and then brushed until it fell to my shoulders in thick, smooth waves. This simple act made me feel much, much better somehow, and as I gave brush and comb back to Em I contemplated taking off my filthy dress and putting on one of the others. Reason told me it would be extremely foolish. We still had to trek to the boat they had left anchored in the secret cove, and a fresh dress would soon be as dirty as this one. I decided to wait until we reached the boat to change. I brushed the rest of the dried mud off my dress and then straightened the bodice, stepping over to the mouth of the cave to peer out at the storm-wracked terrain.

The damage wasn't nearly as extensive as I would have imagined it to be. Limbs were torn off trees, true, and trees were split and broken, but the majority of them were undamaged, spreading leafy green limbs toward the radiant silvery-yellow sunshine. The torrents of water were gone, of course, and the ground was already dry. Overhead the sky stretched blue-white and cloudless, polished with sunlight, and from this elevation I could see a network of swollen rivers and lagoons, half-concealed by willows and the sturdy gray cypress. It was hard to believe that only a few hours ago all this had been obliterated by torrential rains and raging winds that crushed and destroyed.

"Incredible, isn't it?" Em said, coming to stand beside me. "It's all so peaceful and calm now. Pretty, too, if you like scenery. Never could get too excited about it myself."

"It's wonderful to be free, isn't it?"

"If you don't mind cannibals lurking behind every tree. Me, I'll be much happier once we're in New Orleans."

"At least we're off the island, Em."

"And have two strapping men to protect us. I feel terribly secure with that Randolph around. He gives me a cozy, cuddly feeling inside—I want to snuggle up and purr, and at the same time I want to scratch."

I gave her a wry look, arching one eyebrow.

"Oh no, luv," she protested, "this time it's *serious*."

I merely smiled and shook my head, savoring the brilliant sunlight that stroked my cheeks and bare arms and shoulders. It was very warm, although the heat lacked the sultry, oppressive quality it had had earlier. I felt a marvelous energy surging through me, and there was a light, lovely, tremulous sensation I hardly recognized—it had been so long since I felt it. I realized that I was happy. For the first time in months and months I felt relaxed and radiant, smiling naturally, easily, at peace with myself and the world. I didn't care to examine the reasons.

"Here they come," Em said. "Lord, he's got two huge birds in his hand! Holding them by their feet."

"Wild turkeys," I told her.

"Just look at that satisfied look on his face. Mighty pleased with himself."

Randolph saw us standing in front of the cave and lifted the turkeys over his head, waving them triumphantly. Em made a disgusted noise. Randolph came on up the hill, Jeremy and Corrie behind him. Corrie was carrying a basket of woven willow that must have been in the cave along with the other things. It was filled with plump, purple-black berries. Jeremy took her elbow, guiding her past a large boulder. He climbed the rest of the way with that long, easy stride, loose and bouncy. The fringe on his jacket swayed, and I noticed that the red-orange bandana was back around his neck, none the worse for wear.

"Success!" Randolph cried. "Look at 'em! Aren't they lovely?"

"Get those bloody things away from me!" Em snapped.

"Got 'em both with my bow and arrow, and you thought I was going to come back empty-handed, didn't you?"

"I was hoping you wouldn't come back at all," she said dryly.

"Joshin' again. Bet you pined for me the whole time. Corrie here found a blackberry bush, filled the basket with 'em, and Jeremy-boy spent the whole time sittin' with a fishin' pole. Nary a nibble."

"Don't rub it in," Jeremy grumbled. "They just weren't biting. Never could abide fishing. Bores the bejesus out of me."

"You just don't have the knack, lad. It's an art."

"Glad to see you up and about," Jeremy told me.

"I feel wonderful."

"Can't say the same about myself. Skinned my knees climbing that bloody tree to fetch your bundle. Hurt my hands, too."

"Poor baby," Em said.

"You shut up!"

"Isn't he adorable? I love a man with a sunny disposition. What do you intend to do with those birds, Randolph?"

"I intend to cut their heads off, and then you're going to pluck out all the feathers and we're going to make a spit and roast 'em."

"*I*'m not going to pluck them," she retorted, recoiling with horror. "I'm not going to *touch* them! Gives me the shivers just to think of it."

Randolph grinned and took out his knife, and Em scurried back into the cave so she wouldn't have to witness the decapitations. I sat down on a rock, took one of the turkeys, and deftly began to pluck the feathers. Corrie took the berries inside, and Randolph followed her in order to tease Em some more. Jeremy stood with his hands on his hips, head cocked to one side as he watched me pull the feathers out.

"You do that quite well," he remarked.

"I've had lots of experience."

"Oh?"

"I've plucked many a chicken in my time, usually dipped them in boiling water first. It makes the feathers come out more easily. Here, this one's done. Hand me the other."

"It seems you have talents I never suspected," he said, handing me the other turkey. "You mean you can actually cook?"

"I'm a superb cook," I retorted.

"I don't believe it!"

I plucked out a handful of feathers and dropped them on the ground, not bothering to look up at him. "I make a peach pie that melts in your mouth," I informed him, "and you haven't lived until you've tasted my pot roast. I use special herbs to give it just the right flavor."

"You jest, lass. No woman who looks like you could possibly find her way around a kitchen. Next you'll be telling me you polish boots."

"I've polished my share."

"Wanna polish mine?"

"Here. This one's done, too. If you'll hand me your knife, I'll cut them open and remove the entrails."

"I don't think I want to watch."

"You're as bad as Em," I told him.

I took the knife from him and took the turkeys and moved down the hill a little way to perform the task. After I had finished, I wiped my hands off in the grass and returned to the cave with the turkeys ready to be roasted. Em gave a horrified look as I handed them to Randolph, who had already set up a crude spit over the remains of the fire, driving two Y-shaped sticks into the ground on either side. He skewered the turkeys on a third stick and placed it on top of the other two.

"There!" he proclaimed. "Now all we need is a fire, and in a little while we'll be eating like kings. Any more wood over there in the corner? Fetch it for me, saucy, and stay away from those blackberries! You'll spoil your appetite."

"Bossy brute, aren't you?"

There was some water left in one of the vessels. I rinsed my hands off and then asked Corrie if she would like to take a walk while the turkeys were cooking. She shook her head and smiled and told me she'd had quite enough exercise for one afternoon. I squeezed her shoulder and strolled out of the cave, moving leisurely down the hillside. A moment later I heard Jeremy Bond clumping down after me. I didn't turn around, ignoring him even after he caught up and strode along beside me. The light, lovely feeling seemed to dance in my blood, and I felt gloriously alive.

"Don't mind me," he said, "I just thought I'd keep you company."

"You needn't have bothered."

"Wouldn't want you to stumble into a band of Karankawas, lass. The area is swarming with them. Randolph and I found two hollowed-out canoes down by the river, half-hidden under some shrubs. The men who left 'em there might be coming back for 'em."

"You're trying to scare me, Mr. Bond."

"Reckon I am," he admitted. "You're supposed to shiver and throw yourself into my arms so I can be strong and protective."

"I don't scare easily."

"I can see that, lass. You called me Mr. Bond again. Reckon you did it just to irritate me. You're in an unusually skittish mood, I must say. Frisky as a colt."

"I feel very good. In spite of the way you manhandled me in the storm. You almost pulled my hair out."

"Had to grab something, lass."

"Thank you, Jeremy," I said quietly. "I seem to be saying that an awful lot."

"I'm not complainin'."

"You saved my life. Again."

"You know, in China they have a belief that when you save a person's life you're responsible for that person from then on, responsible for his health and happiness and general well-being."

"We're not Chinese, Mr. Bond, and you're certainly not responsible for me in any way."

"Oh, but I am," he replied.

330

I turned to glance at him. He grinned, bouncing along beside me with his arms swinging, buckskin fringe bouncing, the bandana flapping at his neck. I felt the full force of that overwhelming charm that was so virile, so playful and boyish, and I wanted to smile. I didn't, of course. I knew better than to give him any kind of encouragement, even though I might have enjoyed it. I continued walking, turning left as we reached the bottom of the hill and moving under the trees. Jeremy was silent, shortening his stride to match my own, and we were soon surrounded by willow trees, long, dangling strands of jade-green leaves brushing our arms.

When we reached the mossy banks of a small, twisting river, I moved under one of the willows and leaned against the trunk, completely surrounded by dangling strands. Jeremy Bond parted them and joined me. Sunlight gilded the tiny green leaves, turning them a light, golden green. He smiled again, and I pretended to ignore him, acutely aware of his nearness, his smell, the masculine allure that was only enhanced by the rough clothes. I listened to the river that moved sluggishly, almost silently, and watched the long strands shimmer with sunlight as they swayed ever so slightly.

I arched my back, rubbing it against the slender trunk, and my bosom rose, straining against the low-cut neckline. It wasn't a deliberate provocation, but I saw the look in his eyes and saw how it affected him and immediately straightened up, folding my arms across my waist. Jeremy parted his lips, his blue eyes very intense, and the air around us seemed to crackle with sexual tension, something I certainly hadn't planned. Or had I? I frowned, confused by the emotions inside. I didn't want him. I was wary of him. I knew him for what he was, and I certainly didn't intend to become involved with him, yet I was grateful, so very grateful for all he had done and when I was with him I seemed to be so marvelously alive.

"Where did you learn to cook?" he inquired.

"I was an indentured servant, surely you know that. I was a cook-housekeeper."

· "On Hawke's plantation?"

I nodded, feeling a sharp twinge of pain, immediately banishing it. Jeremy seemed to be aware of it, and I could see that he was sorry he had asked. I had never known a man so sensitive to my moods, a man who seemed to know what I was thinking, what I was feeling.

"I really can cook," I told him, making it light.

"I'll bet you can."

"One day I'll bake a pie for you."

"Is that a promise?"

"It's the least I can do."

"Peach?"

"If you like."

He leaned forward, placing his right palm on the trunk a few inches above my head, his chest almost touching me, his face inches from my own. I tilted my chin back, looking up at him, and I saw the soft roll of flesh beneath his jaw, creasing into a small double chin as he lowered his head with lips parted. He was going to kiss me, and I wanted him to, I suddenly wanted it very much. I placed my palms on his chest and, as his mouth covered mine, slipped them under the buckskin jacket and around his ribcage, letting them rest on his back. I could feel the muscles beneath the thin cotton shirt, could feel the warmth of his skin. I rubbed his back, yielding to the tenderness of his kiss.

He kissed me for a very long time, lazily, savoring my lips, and I moved my hands over the smooth muscles of his shoulders and allowed myself to drift along a river of pleasure, floating without effort, the sweetness filling me as he made a moaning noise in his throat and drew me to him, lazy still, not at all hurried, kissing me without urgency because it was natural and right and both of us wanted it. I drifted, eyes closed, feeling sleepy and sweet, all my defenses gone, melted away. Jeremy lifted his head and looked into my eyes and kissed me once more, very lightly.

"I love you, Marietta."

His voice was low, slightly husky, and his eyes told me the same thing. I felt a terrible confusion and indecision. I wanted him. I couldn't begin to deny that. Every fiber of my being seemed to be drawn to him, to demand completion. The sweetness filled me and I yearned to submerge myself in his strength and warmth, to drift again on that lazy river of pleasure, but I knew it was wrong. It was not the man, it was my own hunger, my own need, and sexuality had little to do with it. For months I had known nothing but harsh brutality. I craved tender words, tender caresses, gentility, longed to relinquish my steely control and lean on someone else, draw from strength not my own.

My palms were still resting on his shoulders, beneath the jacket, and I wanted desperately to draw him closer and cling to him, wanted desperately to gather him to me and have his lips on mine again and lose myself in the sweetness. Confused, indecisive, I looked up into his eyes, and he understood everything and waited for me to make up my mind. He wasn't going to press me. He wasn't going to do anything I didn't want him to do. I wanted it with all my heart and soul but knew it would be a mistake to give in to the yearning so urgent and demanding. I unwound my arms from him and leaned away, my shoulders pressing against the willow tree.

"It wouldn't be fair," I whispered.

"Fair?"

"To you. I don't love you. I never could. I'm grateful and I find you—appealing, but—"

"I understand, Marietta."

"I—I've been through a great deal. I'm extremely vulnerable—"

"I shan't take advantage of that."

He stepped back and thrust his hands in the pockets of the pinkish-orange corduroy trousers that had once been tan. A gentle smile played on his mouth, and he was not at all angry, not at all perturbed. His rich, unruly brown hair tumbled over his brow. His blue eyes were tender, looking at me as they might look at a beloved child. The pale jade-green leaves shimmered in the sunlight, dangling all around us in long, swaying strands. I looked at him, grateful for his understanding, and gradually the sleepy languor and the yearning ebbed and common sense returned. I sighed and straightened up. I had resisted temptation, and the temptation had been very strong indeed. The victory gave me no sense of satisfaction. I felt, instead, something that was very like disappointment.

"Thank you, Jeremy," I said. "Any other man would have pressed on."

"I'm very patient. I told you that. I'll wait until you're ready, until you see what's in your own heart."

"Shall we return to the cave?"

"Yes, I imagine the turkeys are roasted by now. I'm starving."

"So am I."

He grinned, relaxed, and took my hand and parted the strands of willow and led me away from the river, his manner extremely easygoing. He continued to hold my hand, squeezing it now and then, and I didn't try to pull it free. Both of us were silent as we climbed up the hillside, but there was no strain whatsoever. I could smell the roast meat as we neared the cave. I realized I was weak from hunger, so hungry I couldn't possibly wait any longer to eat something.

"There you are!" Em exclaimed. "I was beginning to worry, luv."

"Is it ready?"

"Cooked to perfection," Randolph informed me, "and Corrie has already cut it into neat pieces and fetched some leaves for us to spread it on. Want a drumstick?"

"Anything," I said.

He chuckled and handed me a large green leaf with a piece of turkey on it. I ate greedily, sitting on the ground with my back against the purple-gray rock wall. I had two more pieces after that and drank half a vessel of water and ate several handfuls of blackberries as well. It was the finest meal I had ever had.

When the last piece of turkey had been devoured, when the blackberries were all gone and the water vessels empty, we sat for a few moments, replete and satisfied. Em gnawed a bone, finally, reluctantly, tossing it aside. Randolph climbed lazily to his feet and stepped over to the mouth of the cave, spreading his arms out and resting his palms on either side of the opening. The sunlight touched his straight golden-brown hair which was, I realized, actually very dark blond, golden-blond so dark it seemed almost brown.

"Guess we'd better mosey on to the cove," he remarked.

"I couldn't move an inch," Em said.

"Reckon we could make it before nightfall," he continued, ignoring her remark. "We'll have to press hard, though."

"I want a nap," Em protested.

"You can nap on the ship, gal. Up, up everyone! Let's get stirring."

I could have used a nap myself, but I climbed wearily to

my feet, reaching down to give Corrie a hand. Jeremy Bond picked up both bundles. Em's rattled noisily. He gave her a nasty look as he slung it over his shoulder with mine. She smiled sweetly and told him that solid silver candlesticks would fetch over thirty pounds each in New Orleans. This bit of information failed to humor him one bit. He gave her another look and moved out of the cave, Randolph ahead of him. In a matter of minutes we had left cave and hillside behind and were wading across the shallow, sluggish river Jeremy and I had seen earlier. Em kept a sharp eye out for cannibals and eyed the river dubiously as we waded through it.

"There're alligators," she informed me. "The Karankawas smear themselves with alligator grease to ward off mosquitoes and other stinging insects, so it stands to reason these waters are swarming with 'em."

"I'll watch for them," I said.

The land was very marshy on the other side of the river, cypress and willow trees growing thickly along with other trees, much smaller, that Corrie identified as wild plums, pointing to the purple-red fruit hanging from the branches. We crossed several more rivers, one of them waist-deep, and circled around a number of small lakes. Exotic-looking birds rose in the air, fluttering enormous wings that caught the sunlight. The sunlight wasn't as bright as it had been. The sky was beginning to lose its color, blue giving way to the gray-white that preceded sunset. Jeremy and Randolph forged on ahead, Corrie a few steps behind them. Em took my hand, motioning for me to move a bit slower. We lagged behind the others so that we could talk in private.

"What happened back there?" she asked.

"When?"

"When you and your handsome Mr. Bond took your walk."

"Nothing happened, Em."

Em looked crestfallen. "Nothing at all?"

"Well, he did kiss me," I admitted.

"And?"

"And we turned around and came back to the cave."

Em stepped over a tangle of cypress roots and looked suspiciously at a log half-hidden by long grass. The going was much rougher now, trees closer together, roots tangled, the ground spongier, water all around. We waded a small river, only to cross another a few moments later, the water calf-high. The banks were very muddy, and I saw something that did indeed look like an alligator. Em, fortunately, didn't see it.

"He's in love with you, you know," she continued. "He sat beside you for the longest time when you were asleep— after he brought you in from the storm. He held your hand and looked at you and, luv, his eyes were so full of feeling I could have cried. I've never seen such tenderness and concern."

I pushed a branch out of the way. A bird swooped up, startling me.

"He came all this way, risking his life to rescue you from the island," Em continued, "and then he risked his life again during the storm. He *must* love you."

"I'm very grateful for all he's done. I've told him so."

"But you don't love him?"

"Not in the least," I replied.

"I suppose it's just as well, luv. He's a heartbreaker, that one. I can tell. Too jaunty, too charming, and *much* too good-looking. A woman could go to pieces over a man like that."

"I don't intend to go to pieces over any man," I said. My voice was extremely firm. "I've come too far. I've been through too much. I'm not going to be hurt again."

"He could do that. He could break your heart, luv."

"It's not going to happen," I assured her.

"Me, I'll take a straightforward, uncomplicated brute like Randolph. He tried to take liberties this afternoon in the cave. You and Jeremy Bond had gone for your walk and Corrie went out to gather leaves and the two of us were left alone. He *did* take liberties, actually."

"What did you do?"

"I told him he had exactly fifteen minutes to stop that nonsense."

She looked at me with mischievous eyes. I smiled, and a moment later we both burst into laughter. The men turned around to see what was the matter. We had lagged very far behind. Randolph yelled for us to catch up immediately, and we joined them, both of us unreasonably lighthearted. Jeremy insisted I walk beside him. Corrie had picked an armful of wild flowers, sprays of exotic blossoms that looked like tiny mauve orchids speckled with bronze and red. She handed me a spray. I toyed with it as we moved on.

"How much farther do we have to go?" I asked.

" 'Bout a half a mile, I'd say," Jeremy replied. "What were you two laughing about?"

"None of your business," Em said over her shoulder.

"Wonder you didn't get gobbled up by alligators, lagging behind like that," Randolph told her. "We passed a whole swarm of 'em."

"Oh, you're just trying to scare me."

"We did, Miz Em," Corrie said. "I saw them. They were sleeping on the bank of that river."

"Jesus!"

Em held onto Randolph's arm, staying as close to him as possible. I exchanged smiles with Corrie. She seemed to have undergone a transformation since we'd left the island. Her timidity had vanished, and she was proving to be both hearty and resourceful. I remembered the promises I had made to her on the island. I intended to keep every one of them. She trudged along, wading through the water, climbing over roots, examining everything with interest.

The land grew swampier, even more difficult to traverse, one river twisting into another, thick groves of trees giving way to stagnant lakes that reflected the fading rays of sunlight. Moss hung from the cypress trees in long ghostly strands. I could see why the Karankawas used canoes. It was almost impossible to get through this area on foot. None of us complained, however. We forged ahead resolutely, and half an hour later we reached the cove.

The ship wasn't large. It had a rusty-brown hull and only three sails and certainly no more than two large cabins below deck. The hull was crushed at one end, sinking into the water. The masts were broken, the sails a tangle of wet canvas, floating on top of the water. We stood on the bank, looking at the destruction the storm had wrought. None of us spoke. There was no need for words. We were stranded in the wilderness.

337

Twenty-Two

The sails floated heavily, tangled on the broken masts that banged together in the water like logs as the waves rocked gently. The front of the ship rose as the end sank, inch by inch, those decks above water slanting precariously. In half an hour or less the entire ship would be under water. I tried not to think of what it meant. I tried to banish the terrible sinking feeling and the fear. Em's cheeks were pale, her hazel eyes grim. Corrie stood beside her, still holding the sprays of wild flowers. Jeremy and Randolph looked at the ship with eyes that were hard and strangely calm.

"There's still time to salvage a few things," Jeremy said.

"It's too risky, lad."

"The galley, the armory are up front, not underwater yet. We could save a few guns, ammunition, a few cooking utensils. We'll need 'em. I'm swimming out there, Randy."

"I'll go with you."

"No, one of us has to stay with the women. Besides, you've never been able to swim worth a damn."

"You'll need help, lad. Even if you're able to salvage things you won't be able to get 'em back here by your-self."

Jeremy had already peeled off his buckskin jacket. He sat down on the bank now, removing his boots. "I'll manage," he retorted.

He removed his holster and gun, brushed the hair from his forehead and then waded into the water. When it was up to his waist, he leaped forward and started swimming toward the ship in strong, steady strokes. The cove wasn't very large, the ship no more than three or four hundred yards from shore. He reached it in a matter of minutes, catching hold of the railing that was half-submerged, pulling himself up onto the slanting deck. It seemed to vanish beneath him, sinking behind him. The ship rocked, tilting as he climbed the deck on his hands and knees, moving uphill, disappearing down an open hatch. He was going to be killed. The ship was going to sink and he was going to be trapped inside, and I would never see him again.

Em took my hand, squeezing it so tightly I felt my fingers were going to be crushed. Randolph continued to stare at the ship, unable to conceal his worry now. Corrie took a deep breath, laid the flowers on the ground, and stepped out of her shoes.

"What do you think you're doing?" Randolph said harshly.

"I'm going to help him," Corrie replied. "You said he'd need help."

"No you're not, gal! I'm not about to let you go out—"

Before he could finish the sentence Corrie had whipped off her dress. She dove into the water, swimming awkwardly toward the ship in her white petticoat. I was horrified, so horrified I could only stare as she thrashed her legs and flailed her arms, sinking under the water, appearing a moment later with hair plastered over her skull like a shiny black cap.

"She's not going to make it!" Em exclaimed. "She's going to drown!"

Randolph clenched his fists, knuckles white, desperately wanting to go after the girl, knowing that if anything happened to him Em and I would be alone. He was torn with indecision, his face etched with misery as he watched Corrie splutter and flail, going under again. My heart seemed to fail. I felt faint. Em was crushing my hand in hers, and I didn't even notice. Corrie's head appeared again, and she lunged forward like a seal, kicking her legs, swinging her arms in windmill fashion, swimming erratically toward the ship.

She reached the railing, caught hold of it and pulled herself up, crawling onto the deck. She rested there a moment, obviously catching her breath, and then she turned and waved to us and crawled up the deck to the open hatch. The ship was sinking faster now. At least two yards of deck had disappeared under water since Jeremy had climbed aboard. I could hear the creaking, groaning, sucking noise as the water claimed its victim, pulling it under, and as the front of the ship rose higher in the air I could see the barnacles clinging to the bottom like gray-green rocks. How long before the whole ship would slide under? Five minutes? Ten?

"Corrie," I whispered.

"She wanted to help, luv. She feels she owes us so much and feels she hasn't held up her end. This is—this was her way of showing us she can do her share. She's a very brave girl."

"They're going to die, Em."

"Maybe not, luv. They'll get out in time."

I was numb, held there in the grip of horror as I watched the waves slap and suck, pulling another foot of the ship under, another, the water only a few yards from the open hatch now. I was filled with dread such as I had never felt before, thinking of that frail, lovely girl who had shown such heroism, thinking of the man who loved me, who genuinely loved me, whom I had denied. There was a great gulping noise, and the top of the ship rocked violently from side to side and seemed to leap out of the water, sucked back by the water, slipping under at an alarming rate now.

"Look!" Em cried.

A huge black bundle seemed to fly out of the hatch, sailing over the railing and landing in the water with a great splash, bobbing on the surface only a couple of feet from the tangle of sails. The three of us on the shore waited, watching the hatch, expecting to see Corrie and Jeremy emerge at any second. I held my breath, praying silently, but the ship continued to sink and no one appeared. Hope ebbed, my dread even greater now. Em had let go of my hand and was standing at the very edge of the water. Tears were spilling down her cheeks, but my own eyes were dry.

A full minute passed, another, another, and there was nothing I could do but wait and watch and pray. The water was not more than two feet from the open hatch now. In a matter of minutes it would pour in and flood the cabins below, and they would be trapped. Em looked as though she was going to dive into the water and swim after them herself.

Randolf took hold of her arm and pulled her away from the water's edge and curled an arm around her waist. She rested her head against his shoulder, tears streaming.

It happened then. There was another great gulping noise and a loud creaking and the ship rocked and water poured through the open hatch. In a matter of seconds the whole thing submerged, great bubbles churning on the surface. I stared at the sails and the bobbing black bundle and the spot where, half a minute ago, the prow had jutted out of the water. They were gone. Jeremy and Corrie were gone. I couldn't cry. I couldn't scream. I could only stare at the churning bubbles.

Something bobbed to the surface. A second bundle, wrapped in black oilcloth. It bobbed and bounced, rocking on the surface, and then Corrie's head appeared beside it and her frail coffee-colored arms wrapped around it. Em cried out, and the sound seemed to come from a great distance. Jeremy Bond surfaced, head and torso plunging up through the water. He shook his head to get the hair out of his eyes and then swam over to the bundle and wrapped his arm around Corrie's shoulders. They stayed there for a few moments, treading water as the bubbles continued to break like huge wet balls all around them.

I felt no relief. I was beyond relief. It seemed I had died myself and come back to life, and I was too numb to feel anything. I saw Corrie winding her arms around Jeremy's shoulders, half-lying on his back as he pushed away from the bundle and started swimming toward shore with the same strong, steady strokes he had used earlier. Corrie clung to him, and he swam as though she weren't there at all, his arms slicing effortlessly through the water. When he was able to touch bottom with his feet he paused and pulled her around in front of him and gave her a mighty hug. Both of them were laughing. They had almost died, and they were laughing like noisy children.

I took my bundle and untied the cloak strings and pulled the cloak free, hardly aware of what I was doing. Jeremy brought Corrie to shore, and Randolph took her hand and pulled her out of the water. Em took the cloak from me, wrapping Corrie up in it. Corrie was smiling, beaming, pleased with herself. I wanted to shake her. I wanted to slap her. I pulled her into my arms and hugged her so tightly she gasped, squirming.

"I'm all right, Miz Marietta," she protested. "I'm fine."

"Damn you, Corrie. Damn you!"

"We got lotsa good things. Mr. Jeremy put 'em on wooden planks so's they wouldn't sink and then wrapped 'em up in big black sheets and tied 'em up with rope."

"Why! Why did you *do* it?"

"I wanted to help. 'Sides, I swim like a fish."

I couldn't say anything more. I cried. I cried at last, and Corrie was comforting me, smiling gently as she stroked my hair with her wet hand. Jeremy had swam back out toward the soggy canvas sails and broken masts, fetching one of the bundles, swimming back with it. Randolph waded out into the water and took hold of the bundle and Jeremy turned around, splashing like a porpoise, deliberately showing off. I was angry, so angry I was trembling, and I was so relieved I wanted to laugh just as they had laughed, joyously, like a child. I cried instead, and Corrie sighed as though I were being very unreasonable.

Jeremy Bond returned to shore with the second bundle, climbed out of the water and shook himself like a great puppy, water flying in every direction. The pinkish-orange corduroy breeches were sodden, clinging wetly to his legs and thighs, and the white cotton shirt was like a second skin, his tanned flesh visible beneath the wet cloth. The orange-red bandana hung wet and limp around his neck. He shoved wet tendrils of hair from his brow and looked at us and grinned. I wanted to slap *his* face.

"We made it," he said.

"Sure did," Corrie added.

She pulled away from me and began to dry herself off with the cloak, grinning just like he was.

"Little lass saved my life," Jeremy said.

"Sure did," Corrie said.

"Damn you *both!*" I cried.

"What's the matter with her?" Jeremy asked.

"Nerves, I guess," Corrie replied.

"What happened?" Randolph asked.

"I climbed in and went down the passage toward the

342

armory, slipping, sliding, banging my head on the wall. The ship was rocking something terrible, but the water hadn't reached the armory or the galley, thank God. I half-stepped, half-fell into the armory and tore down one of the wooden shelves and set it on the floor and began to pile things on it, three rifles, several powder horns, a couple of bags of shot. I tore down another shelf and put it on top and wrapped it all up in oilskin, hoping the wood'd keep it afloat.''

"Sure enough it did,'' Corrie said.

"Then I started to get another shelf down, and the ship pitched forward and I crashed against the wall and caught my foot in that big rack, you know which one I'm talkin' about, Randy, the big rack where we kept the muskets. Anyway, I tried to pull my foot free, but it was stuck, stuck bad, and the ship rocked some more and I knew I was a goner. I knew I'd never get my foot loose in time. Hell of a way to die, I thought, stuck in a rack like a rabbit in a trap. Real ironic, after all the danger I've faced in my lifetime.''

"For Christ's sake, get *on* with it!'' Em snapped.

"You'll be pleased to know I didn't panic. Didn't panic at all. Resigned myself to the inevitable, and then this little lass here come stumbling in like an apparition, wringing wet, and she saw my problem at once. Didn't say a word, didn't want to waste the time. She just grabbed a rifle and held it by the barrel and banged the butt against the rack, broke it to pieces, the rack, that is. I was mighty grateful, I can tell you.''

"I've a feeling you will,'' Em said dryly.

"I gave her a quick hug, but I didn't say anything either, didn't want to waste time askin' questions and expressin' thanks. I picked up the bundle and the damned thing musta weighed a ton. The ship was rockin' from side to side, and I knew we only had a few minutes. I could feel it sinkin'. I started out of the armory and without bein' told Corrie here took hold of my belt in back of me, and I struggled back up the passageway, Corrie holdin' on for dear life.''

"You fell down,'' she prompted. "Don't forget that part.''

"Yeah, I fell down, dropped the bundle, started slipping, and here's the scary part—I could see the water at the other end of the passageway! Could see it risin', drawin' nearer. I scrambled back up and helped Corrie up and reached the hatch and heaved the bundle through it. Heard it splash.

Corrie had already stepped into the galley. She was pulling down things, a big bag of coffee, a bag of sugar, a tin coffeepot, a big fryin' pan. I knew we oughta get out immediately, but I figured I might as well give her a hand. I tore down a couple of wooden shelves and—''

''Do you have to tell us everything!'' I cried.

''I forgot the oilskin. It was back in the armory. I dashed back for it and brought it back and bundled everything up, tied it securely with a piece of rope and started toward the hatch again, Corrie right behind me. We had almost reached it when there was a great, scary lurch and water started pourin' in and the ship started sinkin' with us still aboard. We were underwater in less time than it takes to tell. I grabbed Corrie and put her hands between the bundle and the ropes and gave her a great shove through the hatch. I saw her shooting up, her legs disappearin', and then I started swimmin' myself and broke surface a minute later.''

''Christ! You could write a book about it,'' Em said acidly.

''Might do that one day.''

''I hope the sugar and coffee and stuff didn't get wet,'' Corrie remarked. ''It doesn't matter about the skillet, of course.''

''Everything should be dry as can be. I wrapped the oilskin around it several times, tied it securely. Damn! I've got water in my ear.''

He banged the side of his head with the flat of his hand and then shook his head and sighed with relief. His clothes were already beginning to dry, for even though the sky was stained with pink and gold smears it was still quite warm. I was in control of myself now, tears dry, anger repressed, my manner cool and composed as I watched him plop down on the ground to pull on his boots. Corrie had retrieved her dress and was pulling it on while Randolph untied the bundles. Em looked as put out as I still felt.

''What do we do now?'' she asked.

''We make camp for the night. Here on the shore will do. You and Marietta might gather some firewood. I'll catch some fish. We'll fry 'em.''

''Our hero probably frightened them all away.''

''I'll make some coffee,'' Corrie said, straightening her

dress. "I got some tin cups, too. Only three, but we can share."

"Dandy," Em said.

"Fetch that firewood, gal!"

"If I weren't a lady I'd tell you to take a flying leap at the moon."

"It ain't out yet," Randolph retorted.

Em gave an exasperated snort, and she and I left the others on the shore and moved into the surrounding woods. Em had momentarily forgotten about Karankawas and alligators and such and marched ahead quite intrepidly. Both of us had been shaken by what had happened, reacting in different ways. Her hands still shook a little as she picked up a small log and a handful of long sticks. The ground was much drier here, slightly sandy, and the cypress and willows had given way to tall palms and exotic, feathery-limbed trees I couldn't identify. We could hear waves washing over the shores beyond the cove and the sound of hearty voices as Jeremy and Randolph examined the things he had salvaged.

"I was scared to death, luv," Em said.

"So was I, Em."

"It was bad enough when Jeremy climbed aboard that horrible wreck, but when Corrie leaped into the water I thought I was going to have heart failure. I don't ever want to go through another twenty minutes like that."

"Neither do I."

"It looks like we're going to have to walk home."

I nodded, adding another small log to the armload I was already holding. Em clutched hers to her bosom, and we started back, walking slowly, palm fronds rattling overhead.

"I know it sounds foolish, but I feel frightfully optimistic, luv. After all we've been through, walking to New Orleans should be a snap. At least we have two strong men to look after us, although I've got a sneaky feeling we're going to spend most of the time looking after *them*. Babies, both of them. A couple of overgrown boys."

"I don't imagine we'll have to walk *all* the way, Em. We'll reach a settlement long before New Orleans and buy horses or something."

"And guess who'll pay," she retorted. "Neither one of

them have a penny in their pockets. We're going to have to sell a piece of jewelry or some of my candlesticks."

"Got the wood, I see," Randolph said as we rejoined them. "Pile it up over there in that circle of rocks I set up. We'll build a fire a bit later. Right now I'm going to mosey on down a way and catch us some fish. I'm hungry as a bear."

Em dropped her wood in the circle of rocks. "After all that turkey?" she inquired.

"That was hours ago."

"I'll go with you, Mister Randy," Corrie said. "I know all about fishing. I used to catch lotsa catfish when we were at the plantation. There was a river, and I went there lots when Miz Henrietta didn't need me."

"I'll let you bait my hooks."

"You got hooks?"

"I got wire. I'll make us some dandy hooks."

"What are we going to use for bait?"

"Reckon we can find some worms."

"Grasshoppers would be better."

"Jesus! Will you two *go*? On second thought, I'd better go with you to see you both don't fall in. I've never been fishing before. I'm sure I'll be fascinated."

"Come on, then, if you're comin', but you'll have to keep quiet. Don't want to scare the fish."

Em gave him one of her looks. He chuckled, and the three of them moved down the bank as though on their way to a party. Jeremy Bond was on his knees, sorting out powder horns and bags of shot. His clothes were completely dry now, but his hair was still damp, beginning to feather at the ends. He hadn't put his jacket back on. The thin white cotton shirt clung to his back and shoulders as he worked. After a while he stood up and brushed the dirt from the knees of his breeches and gave me a satisfied nod.

"Everything's dry, you'll be pleased to know. Even the coffee and sugar and corn meal. Corrie promised to pan-fry some corn bread as soon as we could find some turkey eggs. Shouldn't be too difficult."

"You both gave us quite a scare."

"Were you worried about me?"

"I wasn't worried about *you*. I was worried about Corrie."

"She's quite a lass. She really did save my life. What do you mean, you weren't worried about me?"

"Maybe I was a little."

"A lot," he told me. "Wouldn't want your future husband drownin' on you."

"You never give up, do you?"

"Never," he admitted, grinning.

I gazed up at the sky. It was dark gray now, the pink and orange smears beginning to fade. The fading colors were reflected in the water, which was beginning to take on a dark, inky hue. Insects hummed and leaves rustled quietly and birds called in the treetops. I folded my arms across my waist and strolled over to the water's edge. After all the tumultuous emotions I felt curiously serene as I watched the colors blurring on the water, dissolving into the inky black. I felt Jeremy's presence behind me, although I hadn't heard his approach. Neither of us spoke, and after a moment he placed his hands on my shoulders and began to gently massage them. It was soothing, so very soothing, and I didn't attempt to pull away.

"Are we going to make it, Jeremy?" I asked quietly.

"Of course we are."

His voice, behind me, was low, melodious, confident. Those strong hands continued to massage my shoulders, his fingers kneading my flesh, gently, yet with considerable force, easing taut muscles. I arched my back, trying to remember my resolve to be wary of him, to resist that charm, but it was so nice to relax and leave worry behind and lean upon his strength. I could feel the weakness steal over me, wonderful weakness I had so rarely been able to indulge in. Dangerous weakness, I told myself, but the warning was so faint I paid it no mind.

"I can't believe we're actually going to be back in New Orleans."

"We will be," he assured me. "There's a settlement—oh, seventy miles or so from here. We'll have to travel over fifty miles of marshland, but after that it'll be much easier."

"We'll buy horses," I said.

"And all the supplies we need. You're a wealthy woman."

"You'd let me pay for everything."

"I have no scruples about taking money from a woman. Besides, I consider it part of your dowry."

He chuckled softly and curled one arm around my waist, drawing me against him. Dangerous, the faint voice whispered inside, pull away, be cool and distant, don't let this happen. He curled his other arm around my throat and bent his head forward to rest his cheek against mine. It was warm, smooth as the smoothest leather.

"The Indians," I said.

"A few Karankawas aren't going to bother Randy 'n me. We've been in much tighter spots than this. We've got plenty of guns and ammunition, and both of us are crack shots."

"So am I."

"Really?"

I nodded, and he tightened his arm around my waist and massaged my throat with his forearm, his cheek still touching mine. Danger, sweet danger, and I longed to ignore it and give in to the sweet euphoria that was stealing through me. It would be a mistake, such a mistake. I needed tenderness and words murmured quietly and gentle hands softly caressing me but the price would be so high. I wouldn't be hurt again. I wouldn't allow myself to be hurt, and every instinct told me that if I gave in to these feelings the results would be disastrous.

He turned his head slightly and kissed my temple, and I closed my eyes and took hold of his arms and pulled myself free, reluctantly, abandoning the warmth and blessed sense of security. He didn't object. He stepped back and looked at me and shook his head, patient, willing to wait. I began to stroll slowly along the bank, and he fell into step beside me. All the color was gone now, the water black, the sky a dark, dark gray tinged with purple. The first stars were beginning to appear.

"I'm sorry, Jeremy," I said.

"Don't be, lass. I'm content to wait."

"You'll wait in vain."

"I think not."

"I have something I must do."

"Tell me," he said.

And I told him about Roger Hawke and the vow I had made and told him how that vow had given me the will to live. He listened quietly, asking no questions, making no comments, and as I spoke my words seemed hollow, the motivation behind them all wrong. One couldn't live for revenge, not if one wanted to really live, yet even so I knew I must destroy Roger Hawke.

"I wanted him dead at first," I continued. "I wanted to kill him, as he killed Derek, but now—" I hesitated. "I will indeed be a wealthy woman when I sell my jewels. I'll find another way to destroy him."

"Oh?"

"I intend to own Hawkehouse. I intend to spend the rest of my life there. It's where I belong."

"You loved him that much?"

I didn't reply, and Jeremy didn't press me. He was silent, lost in thought, his hands thrust into the pockets of his breeches. It was growing darker by the minute, the sky a deep purple that merged into black, the stars growing brighter in contrast. We walked, listening to the night noises, and that splendid closeness was gone and we might have been strangers. For all his jaunty aplomb, his cockiness and irreverent, irresponsible facade, he was a deeply sensitive man, far more sensitive than I had suspected. I had disappointed him, and I sensed that I had hurt him as well.

"We'd better go back," he said. "I'll get the fire started."

He turned and strolled away, the bounciness missing from his long stride. I stood there by the inky water for several minutes, alone, feeling the loneliness, feeling, for those few minutes, as alone as I had ever been in my life, and I couldn't understand why. It was growing cooler, surprisingly cool after the earlier warmth. In the distance I saw a flicker of orange, and soon a fire was blazing and I could see him standing nearby, arms folded over his chest as he watched the flames.

I heard laughter. Corrie and Em and Randolph were returning. I saw them approaching, mere silhouettes in the darkness. Em and Corrie were both chattering. I stood there for another moment, crestfallen, alone, apart, and then I deliberately banished the mood and hurried to meet them. Em was startled and told me I'd given her quite a turn. She'd thought I was an

349

Indian, and Randolph laughed. Corrie told me that she'd heard a gobbling noise and figured if a wild turkey was around there must be eggs.

"And I found *two*, Miz Marietta!" She pulled one from each pocket of her skirt, holding them up. "Aren't they lovely? We're going to have fried cornbread tonight. I promised Mister Jeremy."

"Fish, too," Randolph said. "Look at these, seven of the finest fish you ever saw."

"You're never going to believe this, luv, but *I* caught one of them," Em informed me.

"The littlest one," Randolph said. "I started to throw it back."

"You're lying! Mine's the biggest of the lot."

They continued to squabble amiably, even after we had joined Jeremy by the fire. The fire burned down to a heap of glowing red-orange coals as Randolph cleaned the fish and prepared them. They were soon sizzling in the iron skillet Corrie had taken from the galley, and coffee was boiling in the coffeepot, the smell heavenly. When the fish were done, Corrie fried cornbread in their grease. The others ate heartily, and I forced myself to swallow a few bites. I had no appetite whatsoever.

"Reckon we'd better turn in now," Randolph said after everyone had finished and Corrie and Em had rinsed out skillet and coffeepot in the water. "Tomorrow is going to be a rough day."

"I'm sure I won't be able to sleep a wink," Em declared.

"I can hardly hold my eyes open," Corrie admitted.

"You want me to take the first watch, Jeremy-boy?" Randolph asked.

"I'll take it. You get some sleep. I'll wake you up in a couple of hours."

I took my cloak and, using the bundle for a pillow, settled under one of the trees. Em and Corrie settled themselves nearby, and Randolph sat down, leaned against a tree trunk and folded his arms across his chest. He was soon fast asleep. Em tossed and turned for a while, grumbling about the hard ground and speculating about the possibility of snakes, but she, too, was soon asleep, as was Corrie. Half an hour later I was still wide awake, surreptitiously watching Jeremy Bond as he paced idly around the camp, pausing frequently to gaze at the water or look up at the sky.

He had put the fringed buckskin jacket back on, for it was chilly now, and he carried a rifle. Although his manner was extremely relaxed, I knew he was very alert, cocking his head at every noise. We hadn't spoken since he had left me on the bank to go start the fire. Em, Corrie, and Randolph had kept up a merry chatter throughout the meal, but Jeremy had been silent, not obviously so. I had been the only one to notice. He had been at ease, had eaten with relish and had smiled at Em's more outrageous remarks, but he hadn't said a word to anyone, nor had he looked at me.

He disapproved of my plans for revenge. He thought them unworthy of me and thought less of me for entertaining such plans. I didn't expect him even to begin to understand. I didn't expect anyone to understand. I didn't care what he thought. Why should I care? What could it possibly matter? He thought I was a fool for wanting to own Hawkehouse and spend the rest of my life there, but what could a man like Jeremy Bond know about my reasons for wanting to do so? Hawkehouse would have been my home had Derek lived. . . . Derek. . . . I didn't want to think of him just yet. The pain was still too fresh, too strong inside.

I had made it quite clear that I wanted no part of Jeremy Bond. Hadn't I? I could never love a man like that. I could never love any man again, not after what I had known with Derek. One day, Jeremy had said, I would see what was in my own heart, and then I would go to him. I knew what was in my heart already. Of course I did. I was fond of him, yes, that was the right word, one couldn't help but be fond of him, and I was grateful, but love? The mere idea was totally absurd. I might be physically drawn to him, but that was something entirely different . . . of course it was.

A twig snapped. Shrubbery rustled. Jeremy Bond whirled around, rifle at the ready. I sat up, terrified. A small, furry creature scampered across the ground, snatched a piece of leftover cornbread and scrambled back into the underbrush. Jeremy grinned and lowered his rifle. Seeing that I was awake, he told me in a very quiet voice that it was merely a raccoon and ordered me to go back to sleep. I rested my head back on the bundle and pulled the cloak around me again, but I didn't sleep. I couldn't sleep.

Perhaps half an hour passed, half an hour during which I listened to the hum of insects and the rustle of leaves and the gentle slapping of water. Then I was aware of him standing over me, and I lay very still, my eyes closed, my breathing carefully controlled. He knelt down beside me and adjusted the folds of the cloak about my shoulders and then brushed a strand of hair from my temple, his touch light as air. He stroked my cheek with the same light touch and ran his thumb over the curve of my lower lip. I made a sleepy noise and turned over on my side. He moved quickly away and resumed his lazy pacing.

It seemed I could still feel that light, tender touch on my cheek and my lip. My eyelids were growing heavy now, and the slapping of water against the bank was a soothing sound, finally lulling me to sleep, but I felt his fingertips on my skin even as I slept and it was a lovely feeling, and I wasn't asleep at all, I was still awake. He was leaning over me again and smiling, and I lifted my arms and drew him to me and the beautiful weakness spread through me and I clung to him, sad, so sad that it was only a dream.

Twenty-Three

It was already extremely warm, even though the sun had been up less than an hour. Em and I had wandered away from the camp to perform our ablutions beside a small stream nearby. Unlike most of the other streams we had seen, this one was clear and sparkling in the morning sunlight, the sandy gray banks littered with tiny pinkish-white shells. After Em had convinced herself there were no alligators about, we had removed our clothes and washed ourselves as thoroughly as possible with no soap. Now, dressed again but still barefoot, we shared the brush and comb I had brought along.

"Corrie never ceases to amaze me," Em remarked, pulling the comb through her long chestnut waves. "She was up at the crack of dawn, chipper as could be. Before I'd even rubbed the sleep out of my eyes she'd already nipped off to wash herself and fetch fresh water."

"She's a different person," I agreed.

"Lord knows she's been through enough to change anyone. Some people break under adversity. Others show their true mettle. Corrie's got mettle enough for half a dozen girls."

"I imagine she'll have coffee ready by the time we get back."

"A four-course breakfast wouldn't surprise me either. Trade you the comb for the brush, luv."

I handed her the brush and took the comb.

"Jesus, I'm sore all over from sleeping on the ground. I feel like my bones have been pulverized. I must say, though, *you* were sleeping soundly enough. It took me forever to wake you up."

"I was awake most of the night."

"I shouldn't wonder with all the snakes and things about. I'm surprised I was able to sleep a wink."

We put on our shoes, refreshed. My thin tan linen dress with its narrow brown and rust stripes was much the worse for wear, torn at the bodice, several rips in the very full skirt that belled out over my petticoats. Em's pale blue was in no better shape.

"Did you bring any gowns?" I asked idly. "Or were you too busy snatching up candlesticks and enamel and gold boxes?"

"Grabbed a couple of things," she admitted, "a rich red brocade and that white silk embroidered all over with deeper white flowers, you remember the one I'm talking about."

"Vaguely."

"I never wore it. It looks too much like a wedding gown. I imagine I'll be married in it."

I arched an eyebrow. Em grinned.

"A girl has to look out for herself, luv. Randolph told me yesterday he reckoned he'd have to marry me when we got back to civilization just to keep me in line. I may take him up on it. I adore brave men."

"What if he changes his mind?"

"He's not that brave, luv."

We both laughed and started back toward the camp, Em chattering blithely about her future plans.

"I look at it this way, luv, once I sell all my jewelry and things I'll be a rich woman and all the men'll be after me and I won't know if it's me or my money they're after. Randolph, now, he's smitten already and hasn't an inkling how rich I'm going to be. Besides, I think it's high time I turned respectable. All this adventure gets wearying after a while."

"Are we going the right way?" I asked.

"Of course, the camp's beyond those trees. I can hear the men moving about. Randolph's no prize, of course," she continued, "but he's big and strong and honest and sweet in his way and, truth to tell, luv, I'm terribly fond of him already."

"Em, we're going the wrong way. I distinctly remember that thick clump of cypress trees. There were several cardinals perched on the branches, remember? You said you'd never seen such red feathers."

"You're right, luv. But those footsteps—"

We paused. The footsteps were drawing nearer, moving stealthily through the underbrush. The color drained from Em's cheeks. She clutched my hand in hers. We were completely surrounded by trees, and the camp was at least a quarter of a mile in the opposite direction. The footsteps stopped. A heavy silence fell over the woods, broken after a moment by the shrill cawing of a bird. I could sense others nearby, sense them straining to listen just as we were. All the horrible stories I had heard about the Karankawas came back to me, and I knew Em was remembering them, too.

"What—what are we going to do?" she whispered.

"I don't know."

"I think I'm going to faint, luv."

"Run. We must run—"

"I couldn't move. I'm paralyzed. Oh, Jesus!"

The footsteps sounded again, approaching cautiously. A sense of unreality possessed me. We were standing in the center of a clump of trees, and Em was holding my hand in a crushing grip. The morning sunshine streamed down in pale silver-yellow rays. The shrubbery ten yards away began to tremble, branches parting slowly, and in a moment a savage, tattooed Indian was going to step out, and none of it was real. I was unable to move, unable to speak, completely numb with terror.

The shrubbery parted. A man stepped out, letting the branches fall back behind him.

"I'll be damned," he said. "White women."

He was of medium height with burly shoulders and a broad, genial face and brick red hair. He wore muddy brown boots and brown cord breeches and a brown and gray striped jersey torn in several places. He carried a long pistol, and there was another in his belt, along with a knife. Three other men came out from behind the shrubbery, one of them a muscular blond youth who couldn't be more than twenty years old. All four of them stared at us in amazement, and Em and I were amazed, too, and flooded with relief. Em quickly recovered and placed her hands on her hips.

"What's the matter?" she snapped. "Haven't any of you seen women before?"

"Not in the middle of the bloody wilderness," the redhead told her. "We heard you. Thought you might be Indians. Crept up quietly, ready to fire."

"Not quietly enough," she retorted. "You scared us silly!"

"Sorry," he said amiably.

"I *hope* you're with Jeremy Bond," she said.

"How'd ja guess?"

"Logic, luv. There were two other rowboats, and, besides, I think I saw you on the beach. It was dark, of course, but a girl couldn't miss a hulk like you."

"Name's Marshall, Frank Marshall. This here's Chris Sampson—" he indicated the blond youth, "and Hurley and Roberts."

"Delighted to meet you, I'm sure. Just glad you're not wearing feathers."

Frank Marshall laughed. Young Chris Sampson looked

355

stern and apprehensive. Hurley was tall and lanky with straight black hair and shifty gray eyes beneath scowling brows. His face was pockmarked. Roberts was a husky brute with curly brown hair, wide pink lips and friendly blue eyes. All four men were dirty and bedraggled and heavily armed.

"We're awfully glad to see you," I said.

"Where are the others?" Marshall asked.

"Jeremy and Randolph are back at the camp."

"Not any longer," Randolph said, moving toward us. "You two gals seemed to be takin' an inordinate amount of time bathin' an' such, thought I'd come see if you were all right."

"Thought you might get a peek, too, didn't you?" Em said.

"Mighta had somethin' like that in mind. Hello Chris, Frank, relieved to see you. You, too, Hurley. Ain't too happy about seein' you, Bobby Roberts. Never could stand that plump choirboy's mug of yours."

Roberts grinned. He did indeed resemble a husky choirboy, I thought, a hulking, pugilistic choirboy full of mischief.

"Glad you boys made it," Randolph continued. "Me 'n Jeremy had just about given you up."

"Fog got mighty thick, couldn't see a thing. Waves were bangin' the boat. We figured it'd be smart to head for shore. Damned near got blown away in the storm, crouched in a gulley, prayin' somethin' fierce. Tree blew down and hit Bobby on the head. Didn't hurt him none. Thick skull."

"What about Wallace and the rest?"

Marshall shook his head. "We found the rowboat, Randy. It was washed up on shore, had big, gapin' holes in it. Hurley found Jack Green yesterday afternoon. He—uh—he wudn't a pretty sight, banged up bad on the rocks, bloody gashes all over his body. We buried him on the shore where we found him. Wallace and the other three musta washed out to sea."

There was a moment of silence, and then Randolph sighed, accepting the information with a lack of emotion that, on the surface, seemed callous.

"Boys knew the risks involved when they signed on," he said. "It can't be helped. Reckon we'd better get back to camp. We got a lot of trekkin' to do. Ship's sunk. We're returnin' on foot."

We started back toward camp, silent, the men forming a phalanx around Em and me. I felt a heavy sadness inside as I thought about the five men who had drowned. How many more lives would be lost before we reached New Orleans? I could see that Em shared my thoughts. Her hazel eyes were grave, her vivacious manner completely subdued. Jeremy Bond was waiting for us at the campsite, Corrie beside him. He questioned Marshall carefully and, like Randolph, showed no emotion whatsoever when he learned of the fate of the other five men.

"It'll be the six of us, then," he said, "and the three women. I imagine we can make it."

"Sure we can, Jeremy. Why, me 'n Bobby could hold off a whole tribe of Indians all by ourselves. Is that coffee I smell?"

"There's a whole pot," Corrie said. "I can make more when it's gone."

"You're a lass after my own heart. What's your name, gal?"

"Corrie."

"Mine's Marshall. You can call me Frankie."

Corrie smiled, warming to the burly, genial redhead immediately. She gave him a tin cup full of coffee and apologized for not having enough breakfast to go around.

"If I had some more turkey eggs I could make cornbread."

"Young Chris here's good at findin' eggs an' such. He'll help ya hunt for some, won't ja Chris?"

Chris Sampson nodded, very stern. At least six feet tall, with a powerful, muscular build, he had even, attractive features and grave brown eyes. He wore tan knee boots, snug tan breeches, and a loosely fitting yellow shirt of silky material. His yellow-blond hair was very thick, very wavy. Polite, formal, ever so stern, he took Corrie's arm and led her into the woods. She looked up at him shyly, intimidated by his formality and good looks.

"He seems terribly young to be on a mission like this," Em observed as the two of them disappeared.

"Nineteen years old," Marshall said. "As fine a lad as ever drew breath."

"Then what's he doing with you all?"

"Lad's an orphan," Randolph told her. "Both his parents

were carried off in the last fever epidemic. His father was one of Jeremy's best men. Chris is young, but I'm damn glad to have him with us. He could shoot the wings off a fly buzzin' fifty yards away, best damn shot I ever seen, and there ain't no one better at hand-to-hand combat. Lad's a killer."

"He seems so quiet and gentle," I said.

"Oh, he is," Randolph assured me, "disposition of a lamb, but when he has to fight he's a cold-blooded terror."

"We're going to need a big breakfast," Em said. "I suggest you go catch some more fish."

"That's a good idea. Come on, Bobby, you an' me'll catch a big batch of 'em. You can wait for your coffee."

Roberts groaned, eyeing the coffeepot longingly. Randolph threw an affectionate arm around his shoulders and led him away. Hurley stepped over to help Jeremy separate the supplies into six easily portable bundles, and Em and I went to gather more firewood. Corrie and young Chris returned a quarter of an hour later. Corrie was beaming, walking very carefully with her skirt held up in front of her. It was full of eggs. Chris seemed much more relaxed, a faint smile on his lips as he guided her along. He stuck close by her as she cooked breakfast, his manner extremely solicitous.

"Corrie's found herself a friend," Em remarked as we washed the utensils after breakfast. "Young Chris is positively smitten."

"He has every reason to be," I replied, dipping a tin cup into the water. "She's a lovely girl."

Em shifted her position. We were on our knees, at the water's edge. "I feel much better with the other men around. Safety in numbers. Jesus, this skillet's impossible to clean!"

"Hand it to me. Here, take these cups back to Jeremy so he can pack them."

"Is everything all right there, luv?" she inquired. "You haven't spoken to him since we returned from fishing last night. Jeremy hasn't spoken to you either."

"You noticed."

"I *always* notice, luv."

"Everything's all right, Em," I said dryly. "I told him what I planned to do with the rest of my life. He didn't care for my plans."

"You told him about Roger Hawke?"

I nodded, scrubbing the skillet furiously. Em shook her head and stood up, the cups clattering in her hand.

"It's none of my business, luv, but you're making a big mistake. The past is the past, over and done with. You could have a wonderful future with a man like Jeremy Bond."

"I know what I want, Em."

"Do you, luv?" she asked. "I wonder."

She took the cups over to Jeremy, and, a few minutes later, I handed him the skillet. He packed it away without a word, and we began our trek, moving inland. Jeremy led the way, Hurley and Marshall behind him, Roberts and Randolph bringing up the rear. Chris Sampson walked beside Corrie, directly ahead of Em and I, and the two of them talked quietly, Chris pointing out a bird, a plant, a flower, telling her about them. She looked up at his stern, handsome profile with dark eyes that were rendered even lovelier by the soft, feminine glow I had never seen there before. She worshipped him already.

Chris slipped his arm around her shoulder, leading her around a tangled clump of cypress roots. The loose, silky yellow shirt clung damply to his broad shoulders. Corrie stumbled. He held her tightly for a moment and reluctantly let go when the way was clear and there was no excuse to hold her. She walked very close beside him, seeming even smaller, frailer because of his height, his powerful build. Her step was light, lilting, almost kittenish, and she constantly touched his arm, as though to reassure herself. Chris looked down at her now and then, that faint smile on his wide, full lips.

I frowned, worried. Corrie was little more than a child, with a fragile beauty and tender heart that would appeal to any youth, but that beauty could become a curse, that heart could be broken so easily by someone like Chris Sampson. He was a fine lad, yes, I could see that, and he was fond of Corrie, but nothing but grief could come of such an affiliation. He might fall in love with her, and he might love her deeply and sincerely, but ultimately he would turn to his own kind. She would lead a doomed, hothouse existence in some opulent, perfumed room in the Quarter, seeking release in other arms, in alcohol. It was a sad history repeated over and over again when forbidden lines were crossed.

"I shouldn't worry, luv," Em said.

"About what?"

"About Corrie." Her voice was low so that they wouldn't overhear. "His mother was black. Randolph told me about it. She was a mulatto, actually, a very beautiful free woman of color. His father was the son of a white planter, a rugged, rowdy fellow who disgraced himself in his early teens and turned his back on respectable society. He moved in with his mistress and became a smuggler, eventually became a mercenary, one of Jeremy's best men. He taught young Chris everything he knew, took him along on several missions."

"Then—"

"Chris could pass, of course, but he's very proud of his heritage, and he has only disdain for those who deny their blood. When his parents died a year and a half ago, he moved in with his black grandmother. She ran a boardinghouse in New Orleans, a free woman with skin the color of ebony and features pure African. He was devoted to her. She passed away, too, only three months ago. Chris was at loose ends and very grateful to Jeremy and Randolph for taking him on and bringing him along on this mission. He and Corrie could be very good for each other, Luv."

"Perhaps you're right," I said, still doubtful. "I just don't want to see her hurt."

We moved on in silence, stumbling over roots, ducking under limbs, the way becoming more and more difficult to traverse. The trees grew thicker, crowding in on either side, heavy with tangled vines and strands of purple-red wild flowers, dripping with moisture. The air was damp, steamy, the ground spongy underfoot, frequently muddy. The twisting rivers were everywhere, shallow, sluggish, clouds of insects buzzing over the greenish-brown surface. Brownish-green logs littered the banks, covered with mud, and it was only when I saw them stir that I realized they were Em's dreaded alligators. One yawned, making a low hissing sound, revealing rows of razor-sharp teeth. I thought Em would faint.

"They won't hurt you none," Randolph called.

"That's what *you* say, luv. Jesus!"

We waded across the river, climbed the muddy bank and made our way beneath the tangled branches of the cypress trees, the men parting low-hanging vines and great clusters of grayish-tan moss. We moved very, very slowly, of necessity, and after a while each step seemed an agony. The heat was intense, pressing down like a tangible force, and the air was heavy, laden with pungent odors of mud and slime and decay. My limbs ached dreadfully. My feet seemed to sink into the muddy ground, and it took great effort to pull them out, take another step. All of us were perspiring, but no one complained. We trudged on and on, finally stopping at the edge of a great brown lake.

"We're going to hafta cross it," Randolph said. "It'd take hours to go around it."

"You're right," Jeremy agreed.

"How deep is it?" Em asked.

"Plenty deep, from the looks of it," Hurley remarked. "It's too big for us to try to swim across, Jeremy."

Jeremy nodded, grim. I leaned against a tree trunk, thoroughly exhausted and ravenously hungry. From the position of the sun I judged it to be well past two in the afternoon. Em sank down on the ground, heedless of the mud. Corrie seemed to be wilting, leaning limply against Chris who stood very straight with an arm curled around her shoulder. Bobby Roberts looked at the great expanse of water and shook his head. Frank Marshall grimaced.

"Looks like we're going to hafta build rafts," he said. "Won't take too long. I gotta hatchet. Hurley does, too. We can use them vines to tie the logs together."

"No one's getting *me* on a raft," Em informed him. "That lake's bound to be crawling with alligators."

"There's one right behind you!" Randolph cried.

Em screamed and leaped to her feet, and the men all laughed. She gave Randolph a look that should have turned him to stone. He merely grinned. Bobby Roberts began to pass around the canteens, which he had been carrying, and after they had drunk the men began to chop down small trees and cut vines. Corrie strolled away, exploring, returning a short while later with some perfectly vile-looking yellow-orange roots which, she assured us, were quite edible. Em made another face, accepting one grudgingly.

"It tastes like a sweet potato," she exclaimed, "only softer, sweeter, too."

"I told you, Miz Em. You ought to trust me."

Corrie went away to fetch more roots, and Em went with

her. They washed them in the water and then passed them around to the men who, by then, had cut down enough small trees to make two rafts. Hurley and Marshall were cutting branches off and trimming them all down to uniform size, while Roberts and Randolph lashed them tightly together with the thin, sturdy vines. Chris and Corrie were talking quietly, Chris eating one of the roots, and Em was pestering Randolph, warning him that she bloody well wasn't going to get on one of those flimsy things no matter how tightly they were tied together.

I finished eating the pulpy, surprisingly delicious root and stood at the water's edge, looking across. The flat brown surface of the water had a curious purple hue, and the trees across the way were gray and black, casting deep purple shadows over the bank. The sky was gray-white, ablaze with sunlight, and the air seemed strangely opaque, shimmering with heat. Several logs floated near the bank, half-submerged in the water. One turned violently, lashing a long, scaly tail, and I shuddered, realizing that Em had been right. The lake *was* crawling with alligators.

"You're not frightened, are you?" Jeremy asked.

His voice startled me. I turned to find him standing just behind me, his buckskin jacket abandoned on the ground, the thin white shirt clinging damply to his chest, the red-orange bandana limp around his neck. There was a streak of dirt on his jaw, and his rich brown hair was wet with perspiration, falling in wet tendrils across his brow. I noticed faint gray-mauve smudges beneath his eyes, etched there by exhaustion, and they made his eyes seem ever bluer, incredibly blue. He smiled a weary smile.

"We'll make it across easily enough," he told me. "I've built any number of rafts in my day."

"I'm not worried, Jeremy," I said.

My voice was cool, much cooler than I had intended, and my manner was remote, aloof. I hadn't intended that either. He gazed at me with those weary blue eyes, too tired to make a jaunty reply. This was the first time he had spoken to me all day, and I realized he had been trying to relieve the tension that had been building between us. I frowned and reached up to rub the streak of dirt from his jaw, massaging it vigorously with my fingertips. After I had finished, I smoothed the damp tendrils from his brow, silent, my face expressionless.

The others worked and chattered several yards behind us, but they might not have been there at all. The two of us might have been alone there at the edge of the still brown lake with soft clouds of insects swarming low over the surface. Our eyes met, held, and I refused to look away, refused to bend. He wasn't going to make me melt, oh no. I stood my ground, stiff and unyielding. He didn't approve of me. It didn't matter in the least. I owed him no explanations. I gazed at him with cool, indifferent eyes, and Jeremy finally scowled and jammed his hands into the pockets of his breeches.

"I ought to slap you," he said.

"Would it make you feel better?"

"Much better. I'd like to shake you until your teeth chatter, but I don't imagine it would do any good."

"It probably wouldn't," I snapped.

"You're a stubborn wench."

"I happen to know my own mind."

"Your mind, perhaps, but not your heart."

"I don't care to discuss it, Jeremy."

"We're going to," he said. "Not now, perhaps. When I get you alone. I intend to talk some sense into you—if I have to use my fists."

"You can't bully me."

"No?"

"No," I retorted.

I realized how foolish and childish this exchange had become, and it irritated me no end. I turned my back on him, folding my arms around my waist and staring resolutely across the lake. After a moment I heard him turn and stride angrily back toward the others. He could be as angry as he liked. It didn't matter a jot to me. I really had treated him shabbily, though. He had tried to make amends, to ease the tension, and I had been poker stiff. I was grateful to him, yes, he had rescued me, had saved my life, but I wasn't about to succumb to that virile allure, that magnetic charm.

I had a fortune in jewels hanging in a bag against my thigh. Half the money they brought would be his. Jeremy Bond would be properly paid for his services. He could keep the money or divide it among his men or hurl it into the wind, I didn't care. I would be under no further obligation to him. I intended to go to England and do what I had to do, and Jeremy Bond could go hang. I told myself that repeatedly, but it was little consolation. I watched the heat waves shimmer in the air and heard the alligators splash and saw a flock of large, long-necked blue-gray birds settle on the bank across the lake.

"We're ready, Miz Marietta," Corrie said, taking my hand. "The rafts look safe enough to me, not a single crack between the logs. Chris cut some poles to use."

Roberts and Hurley dragged the rafts to the edge of the water, all our bundles already on them. The alligators glided nearer, curious. Em was holding onto Randolph's arm so tightly he winced. Her face was white. I hesitated only a moment, then, still holding Corrie's hand, stepped onto the middle of one of the rafts and sat down, pushing one of the bundles aside. Corrie sat down beside me, showing not the least sign of fear. Em clung to Randolph's arm, and then, taking a deep breath, joined us, watching the alligators with wide, frightened eyes. Randolph climbed aboard, and Chris Sampson gave the raft a shove. It floated onto the water. He grabbed a long pole, vaulted onto the raft and began to pole easily, smoothly, without apparent effort.

The raft rocked, bobbing lightly on the muddy brown water spread with purple shadows. The alligators followed us, four of them, gliding lazily, snouts and eyes barely visible above the surface, long, heavy bodies swaying back and forth, making few ripples. Chris paid no attention to them, digging the pole into the mud, heaving, pushing, the muscles of his arms and shoulders bunching under the silky yellow shirt, his legs planted wide apart. Jeremy and the others were on the second raft, several yards behind us.

Em's eyes were closed now. Her lips were moving. Randolph chuckled.

"What's the matter, gal?" he teased.

"Shut up, you bastard! Can't you see I'm praying?"

One of the alligators snaked closer, much too close, its wide jaws opening, water pouring over its snout. Chris grimaced and jerked the pole up and jabbed the creature viciously. The alligator thrashed in the water, bleeding, and the other three were suddenly upon him and there was a whirling, splashing, spewing confusion, horrible, horrible, tails lashing in the air, jaws snapping, biting. I looked away, shuddering, and Chris continued to pole. We were more than halfway across now. My skirt was wet. Water was seeping through the logs.

"Don't worry," Randolph said. "It'll hold."

The alligators were far behind us. That horrible splashing, whirling mass of scaly brown-green bodies was gone, and three placid, lazy creatures glided leisurely back toward the shore. Jeremy's raft was closer, Hurley poling skillfully, his pockmarked face intent as he dug in, pushed, dug in, pushed. Jeremy had put his jacket back on, despite the heat, and he held his rifle loosely, the butt resting on his knee. Bobby Roberts and Marshall were chattering as blithely, completely unconcerned.

I was vastly relieved when we reached the shore. Randolph scooped Em up and set her on the bank. She shook her skirts out and sighed, picking her way through the mud and onto dry ground. Randolph took my hand and helped me off the raft and then assisted Corrie. Chris pulled the raft out of the water as Jeremy's raft nudged the muddy bank. I joined Em, and we watched as the men gathered up the bundles, slapping at the swarms of buzzing insects that filled the air.

The lake behind us, we continued our trek, moving through the tangle of trees, the thick underbrush, water all around, sluggish, brown, twisting in a muddy network. Tree trunks were green with moss. Willow dripped listlessly. Gray cypress roots reached out like giant, deformed fingers trying to trip us up, and wild flowers made vivid splashes of red and purple. Exotic birds called out shrilly, snakes slithered, and the hum of insects was constant. An hour passed, two, and we waded across a river, then another, waist-high, and moved through a narrow tunnel of trees and came to another smaller lake and circled around it, the sun beating down with punishing intensity.

"Jesus," Em moaned, "I don't think I can move another step."

"I know," I said. "I feel the same way. We'll stop soon."

"I'm going to have nightmares about those alligators, luv. I just know I am. Storms, shipwrecks, snakes, alligators. What next? Don't answer that, luv," she added hastily.

"We'll make it, Em," I told her.

"Sure we will," she replied, "but I'd kinda like to make it all in one *piece*."

"Stop grumbling," Randolph called. "Keep walking."

"He doesn't know it yet," she confided, "but the romance is definitely over."

We kept walking.

Twenty-Four

The pond was small and crystal clear and completely surrounded by willow trees that trailed long jade-green strands in the water. The water was cool, wonderfully cool, and Corrie and I luxuriated in it, filling our hands with it and pouring it over our shoulders, splashing leisurely. It was bliss, pure bliss, and both of us were reluctant to leave, even though we knew the men would soon be ready to press on. Em had already bathed, dressed, and departed to go squabble with Randolph. The men had bathed earlier, leaping in with relish as soon as Chris discovered the pond near the spot we had stopped for our midafternoon break.

Corrie, ever ingenious when it came to plants and such, discovered some soft green moss and had shown Em and I how to use it as soap, rubbing it in the water until it dissolved into a rich, thick lather. We had bathed thoroughly, had washed our hair as well, and Corrie, ever practical, had washed our dresses with the foamy lather and spread them over the willows to dry, along with our petticoats. It was marvelous to feel clean again after three long days of trekking through the wilderness. Each day had been more grueling than the last, and it seemed an eternity since we had been sheltered in the cave.

"Your hair's all shiny," Corrie remarked, slithering in the water like a sleek, lovely brown seal. "It's the color of fire, not red, not gold, not copper, a combination of all three."

"It feels deliciously clean."

"It's going to smell good, too. That moss has a lovely scent."

"This is so nice," I said, splashing dazzling sprays over my shoulders. "I suppose Chris filled all the canteens?"

"He filled them before the men jumped in. We won't even have to boil this water before we drink it."

"I'm eager to taste those mushrooms you two gathered this morning."

"I'm going to make a stew," she told me. "With the mushrooms and those roots I dug up and the meat Mister Randolph had left over. It'll be tasty, I promise you."

"I don't know what we'd do without you, Corrie. You've been ever so helpful. You and Chris."

"He's really a nice gentleman, isn't he, Miz Marietta?"

"He's a very nice boy."

"He's had a—a lot of sadness in his life. He doesn't talk much, and he frowns a lot, but I think he's grand. He treats me like I was somebody special. He treats me like a lady. And, Miz Marietta, he ain't—hasn't even tried to kiss me, even though I wouldn't have minded a bit."

"He respects you, Corrie."

She sighed, treading water, a pensive look in her lovely brown eyes. Her black hair was wet and shiny, clinging to her skull like a tight satin cap. A glow seemed to suffuse her as she thought about the stalwart blond youth who had captured her heart. She was painfully, poignantly beautiful as the water glistened on her clean, coffee-colored skin, her small breasts and delicate pinkish-brown nipples.

"No one's ever respected me before," she said quietly. "I guess I love him, Miz Marietta."

"I think that's wonderful, Corrie."

"I never thought I'd fall in love. I never figured I had the right to love anyone, particularly anyone like Mister Chris.

When he looks at me I feel all trembly and sweet inside, like my blood was singing a lullaby. I guess that sounds silly."

"It sounds beautiful."

"Have you ever felt that way, Miz Marietta?"

"I have, Corrie. Once."

"That man you was going to marry? The one who was killed? He made you feel that way?"

I nodded, dipping my hair into the water again, wringing it out until it seemed to squeak. Sunlight sparkled on the surface in brilliant silver-yellow sunbursts. Our dresses and petticoats, spread out over the willows, were already dry, fluttering slightly in the breeze. The bag that held my jewelry rested on the bank near a mossy gray rock, my shoes beside it. Corrie floated on her back, treading water with her feet and palms, gliding easily, gracefully. After a while she darted under the surface and swam back to where I stood in waist-high water.

"I think Mister Chris might love me, too," she said.

"I'm sure he does. He couldn't help but love you."

"I told him about the shop, Miz Marietta, the one you said I was going to have in London. I told him I was going to fix fine ladies' hair and put it up in fancy hairdos and sell them my special cream and rinse in real pretty bottles and jars with gold stoppers. He said he wondered if such a shop would be a success, and I told him sure it would, you said so."

"You'll be a sensation, Corrie."

"They—they won't mind that I'm colored?"

"Your color will be an asset, Corrie. They'll find you very exotic, different. We'll call the shop 'Mademoiselle Corrie's' and have it painted on the glass in fancy gold letters. They'll be mad for you."

"I could sell perfume, too," she said. "I make lovely perfume, Miz Marietta, just give me some flower petals and spirit and water and a low flame to cook 'em over. It smells much nicer than that perfume Miz Henrietta used to get from France. She said so herself. I told Chris about the perfume—he asked me to not call him 'Mister' Chris, but I keep forgetting—and he said he thought it was a clever idea."

"Do you think he might come to London with you?"

Corrie grinned, nodding. "He said someone would have to keep the books and look after the business details while I was making the perfume and doing up the ladies' hair. He said I was sweet, but he didn't reckon I was very efficient. He said I needed someone tough and hard-headed to keep the business going on an even keel. He likes the sound of London, Miz Marietta. Since his granny died, New Orleans isn't a happy place for him, it's never been a happy place for folks like him who ain't—aren't neither black nor white. Maybe London will be different, he says.''

''I'm sure it will be,'' I told her.

''I'm so happy, Miz Marietta. I never thought I could be so happy. Only thing I wish, I wish Mister—I wish Chris wasn't so stern and stiff. I wish he'd break down and kiss me 'fore I get all impatient and kiss *him*.''

She laughed and paddled to shore, climbing out and standing in the sunlight between the dangling strands of willow, small and naked and glistening wetly. She shook herself and squeezed water from her hair and began to dress, pulling on her petticoat, her pale-colored dress.

''You'd better hurry, Miz Marietta,'' she called. ''Mister Jeremy will be rarin' to move on, and he'll grumble something terrible if you don't come soon. He's been real snappy and fretful lately. I guess you've noticed.''

''I've noticed, Corrie.''

''Reckon I know *why*,'' she teased. ''You really ought to be nicer to him,'' she added. ''He's ever so brave, ever so nice. I can't help but be sorry for him, mopin' all the time 'cause you won't talk to him.''

She fluffed her skirts out and smiled again and disappeared through the curtain of jade-green willow strands. I deliberately lingered in the water, knowing that what she said was true, knowing that Jeremy would be furious with me if I held everyone up. Well, he could just be furious. It would be good for him. I swam leisurely across the pond, reveling in the cool, sparkling water that seemed to caress my skin. The men had taken their time in the water earlier on, splashing and yelling like a pack of banshees. We had heard them hooting and carrying on, and Em had confided that it took all the will power she had to keep from sneaking through the willows to take a peek.

The past three days had been grueling indeed as we penetrated deeper into the wilderness, making precious little progress it seemed, spending most of our time wading through rivers and crossing lakes. The trees were gnarled and thick, hung with vines and moss, bizarre trees like none I had ever seen, and there were eerie ferns like giant, lacy green fans and purple-green plants with tentacles and curious flowers. It was a primeval land very few white men had seen, a handful of Spanish explorers in breastplate and helmets, perhaps. The air was damp, steamy, oppressive, shimmering with heat, the land alive with the hum of insects, the rattle of fronds, the cries of strange birds. Neither swamp nor dry land, it was full of game, at least, and shellfish were plentiful.

Ponds like this were rare indeed, most of the water sluggish and brown with muddy banks littered with shells, alligators frequently dozing in the deep shade provided by overhanging branches. I swam slowly in the clear, deliciously cool water, knowing full well it might be days before I would have another opportunity. If Jeremy was angry, he could just be angry. He had been driving us without mercy, pushing so hard that even the amiable Bobby Roberts had complained. We couldn't lag, Jeremy insisted, we must push on if we intended to get out of this wilderness and reach the settlement.

I was seeing a new side to him. The jaunty, raffish charm had been supplanted by a grim, ruthless determination. He was hard on us, yes, hardest of all on himself. Though the men might grumble, they clearly admired him and respected his judgment, and I had to admit he was a superb leader. The man who set his mouth in a tight line and forged ahead with blue eyes stern, rifle at the ready was totally unlike the cocky, elegantly attired dandy of New Orleans. There was strength I had never suspected, sturdy character that had been hidden by the merry, irreverent manner and lighthearted patter.

We spoke but rarely, and then we were extremely polite. My manner toward him was slightly condescending, his toward me extremely strained, as though it took great effort to be civil. Even though his voice was oh so polite he looked as though he wanted to strangle me. I kept away from him as much as possible, and it was just as well, for there were times when I wanted to kick his shins and claw his cheeks and hold him close, very close, and lean on him and dissolve with tenderness and end this terrible tension once and for all. I was not in love with him, of course not, the mere idea was absurd, but he aroused a whole plethora of bewildering emotions inside me.

I kept remembering the night I had been unable to sleep and he had been on guard and the raccoon had stolen a piece of corn bread. I remembered the way he had leaned over me and, thinking me asleep, had touched my cheek and run his thumb over my lower lip, lightly, gently, the touch so tender. I glided through the water, remembering, and I found it hard to reconcile that Jeremy with the stern, ruthless leader or the devil-may-care fop who chattered foolishly and with such overwhelming charm. Did I really know him? Did I really want to?

Sighing, I stood up in the water, near the bank, lifting my arms to push long, wet tendrils from my face, and as I did so I was aware of someone watching me. The sensation was undeniable, almost physical. I could feel alien eyes observing me closely, but when I turned I could see no one, could see nothing but the dangling, pale jade-green willow strands. I frowned, wondering if I had imagined the sensation, but no, it was still there. Someone was looking at me. Alarm began to grow as I felt those eyes burning, boring into me. There could be no mistake about it.

The willow strands swayed, ever so lightly, and in the blue-gray shadows beyond them I finally saw the woman. She stood very still, tall, brown, wearing only a short skirt made of dried moss, a few strands of shells around her neck. Her face was broad, her eyes as black as coal, and a large, purple-blue tattoo completely covered one cheek. Her long black hair was coarse, falling to her shoulders in a tangled mass. I stared at her, terrified, and for one horrible moment our eyes met. Then the willow swayed again, and she was gone, disappearing swiftly, silently into the shadows.

My heart seemed to have stopped beating. I seemed to be paralyzed, standing there naked in the water, waiting for some unknown horror to descend. An eternity seemed to pass, though it could only have been a few seconds. I leaped toward the bank, climbed out of the water, and snatched up my shoes and the jewelry bag. I tore my dress and petticoat from the willows and held them in front of me and ran through the swaying jade-green curtains, clearing the willows, running wildly toward camp.

He caught me. He held me. I stammered, trying to speak. I couldn't. I shook my head, and he scowled, his eyes stern and blue, frozen blue fire, his lean, tan face etched with anger. Don't be angry, please don't be angry, I begged silently. He realized then that my panic was genuine and he was not the cause, and he held me very tightly, his arms around my naked back. I shuddered, my cheek against his buckskin jacket, and he said something I couldn't understand. I sobbed.

"Get hold of yourself!" he said sternly. "What is it? What's wrong?"

"She—she was—watching me!"

"What are you talking about?"

"A woman. An Indian woman. She was wearing a moss skirt and shell beads and—and, Jeremy, there was a horrible tattoo on her cheek. She stared at me, and then she just disappeared."

"When?"

"Just moments ago."

He let go of me and stepped back. I was suddenly aware of my nakedness, my wet hair. His cheeks were slightly pale. His eyes were deeply troubled, his full mouth held in a tight, straight line.

"Get dressed," he ordered. "Quickly."

I hesitated for a moment, and then I turned my back and dropped my shoes and stepped into them. I tied the bag around my waist and slipped on the white cotton petticoat and smoothed it down at the sides. I pulled the dress over it and reached around, fumbling to fasten it, panic beginning to sweep over me again. Jeremy marched over, shoved my hands away, and fastened the dress, rough, irritable, finishing just as Randolph and Hurley came up, both of them carrying rifles.

"Thought something might have happened," Randolph said casually. "You were gone a mite too long."

"Everything's all right at the moment," Jeremy retorted, "but we've got to get the hell out of here—as quickly as possible."

"Karankawas?"

"Marietta saw an Indian woman by the pond. The woman

372

was alone, probably came to fetch water. That means there's a whole band nearby.''

"Christ Almighty!"

Jeremy seized my arm and jerked savagely, almost pulling me off balance, and we began to run toward camp, Randolph and Hurley right behind us. When we reached the others, Jeremy let go of my arm, shoved me toward Em and barked a few terse orders. Guns were grabbed. Bundles were snatched up. In a matter of seconds we were moving rapidly away, half-running, and we kept up that pace for almost an hour. I thought my lungs would burst. I thought I would surely keel over with exhaustion. I kept moving, every muscle of my body straining, on fire.

Jeremy, up ahead, raised his arm, signaling us to stop, and I leaned against a tree trunk, panting. Em, for once, was silent, as exhausted as I was, sinking onto the ground at my feet. Corrie stood beside Chris. He held his arm around her. Hurley, Roberts, and Randolph held their guns and turned to watch the path we had just followed. Marshall, sweating profusely, joined Jeremy, and they talked quietly in low, worried voices. After a moment Randolph joined them.

"No sign of pursuit," he said grimly. "Perhaps the band was farther away than we reckoned."

"They know we're here, Randy. They may not have given immediate pursuit, but they know we're here. No way of knowing how many there are. Could be half a dozen. Could be a hundred."

"Coupla dozen at least," Marshall said. "Bands ain't usually any smaller than that, usually a lot bigger."

We had come at least a mile, perhaps a mile and a half, and the danger was real, all around us. The very air seemed to vibrate with it. I finally caught my breath and wiped perspiration from my forehead and looked back at the twisting, vine-draped trees behind us, expecting to see a band of naked savages come racing toward us at any moment. Em sighed, some of the color returning to her cheeks. She brushed flecks of dry leaf from her blue skirt and looked up at me with worried hazel eyes. Both of us were remembering the stories we had heard about the Karankawas.

"Thing to do is stay calm," Randolph was saying. "We

got a head start on 'em. We need to press on, find a good place to camp for the night where we can build a barricade."

"You're right," Jeremy agreed.

"One of us ought to go on ahead, scout the area, find the right spot."

Jeremy nodded, straightening up, clutching his rifle with steady hands, a determined set to his jaw. His face might have been carved from granite, hard and grim, his eyes so dark a blue they seemed almost blue-black. Weak late-afternoon sunlight streamed through the treetops in dusty yellow shafts like wavering, ghostly fingers reaching down to gather us up. Jeremy gazed at one of them, frowning. His wavy brown hair was damp with sweat. The red-orange bandana was wet, his fringed buckskin jacket soiled with dirt.

"I'll go," he said.

Randolph shook his head. "No, lad, the others need you here. Besides, I'm better at findin' campsites, always was. I'll go on, scout around some, pick out a place."

"I'd rather go myself, Randy."

"Hate to admit this, lad, but—hell, I might as well confess it. You're a much better shot than I am. If anything were to happen, you'd be able to do much better shootin', be much better protection for the women. I'm goin' now, ain't gonna argue about it."

"We'll rest for a few minutes, Randy, then move on. As soon as you find a likely spot, circle back."

Randolph took a canteen from Hurley, crammed an extra pistol in his waistband and hurried on, soon disappearing in the trees. There was a long silence followed by the cry of some wild creature in the distance. Em sighed and stood up and, taking the canteens from Hurley, began to distribute them. All of us drank sparingly, knowing instinctively that the water might have to last for some time. Hurley collected the canteens and slung them back over his shoulder. Bobby Roberts, sitting with his back propped against a tree, pulled out his knife and began to whittle idly at a stick.

"Ten minutes," Jeremy told us. "No longer."

He walked several paces back the way we had come and stood guard, his rifle cocked, his back to us. Corrie, calm and efficient, began to gather berries from a bush nearby, putting them into a large white cotton bag she took from her pocket.

Chris examined his rifle carefully and then checked his pistol, while Frank Marshall watched the treetops with a deceptively casual air, studying the shadowy branches, his finger on the trigger of his pistol. Em, too nervous to rest, went over to help Corrie gather berries.

I hesitated a few moments and then brushed my hair back and went over to stand beside Jeremy. He glanced at me and then resumed his watch, his profile stern. Ahead was the shadowy green tunnel through which we had come, the trees thick on either side, leafy, low-hanging limbs making a canopy above. Very little sunlight penetrated the gloom. Birds twittered. The sounds seemed to echo, coming from every side. A bluejay swooped down, grabbed a twig in its beak and flew back into the trees. A twig snapped. Jeremy stiffened, alert, aiming his rifle in the direction of the sound. When nothing happened, he relaxed a little, ignoring me.

"I want you to give me a pistol," I said calmly.

"I don't think that's a good idea."

"I'm a very good shot, Jeremy."

"Are you indeed?" he inquired.

"I can handle a pistol as well as any man."

He hesitated, then pulled the extra pistol from his waistband and handed it to me. It was long and heavy with a smooth, polished butt and a sleek barrel. I tested its weight in my hand, finding the right balance, aiming it at a branch with my finger curled lightly around the trigger. He watched with an impassive face.

"If they come, Marietta," he said, "if they overpower us, I want you to use it on yourself."

"Jeremy—"

"I don't imagine it'll happen," he continued quickly. "They may attack, probably will, but once they taste the bite of our bullets they'll undoubtedly fall back. We've got plenty of guns, plenty of ammunition."

"Jeremy—" I repeated.

He looked at me, and words failed me. There was so much I wanted to say, so very much, and I realized, quite calmly, that I might never have another opportunity. I wanted to ask his forgiveness. I wanted to express my gratitude. I wanted to express all the other things inside, and I couldn't say anything at all, I could only look at that stern, worried face with a terrible ache in my heart. Before this day was over one or both of us might be dead, and the words wouldn't come.

I lowered my eyes, gazing at the pistol, and Jeremy took a deep breath, knowing, understanding. He placed his hand on my arm, and I looked up into those blue, blue eyes. The tension between us evaporated, and we were closer at that moment than we had ever been before. Words weren't necessary. I should have known that. This man seemed to know my every mood, my every thought, seemed to sense every emotion inside me, understanding instinctively, understanding more than I understood myself.

"You'd better go back and get off your feet," he said quietly. "We'll be moving on in a few minutes."

"I'm frightened, Jeremy."

"Of course you are. I'm scared out of my wits."

"If it weren't for me, you—you wouldn't be here."

"That's quite true," he admitted.

"I feel so guilty."

"That's foolishness."

"Those men who were lost—"

"They signed on to do a job, Marietta, fully aware of the risks they'd be taking. If it hadn't been this mission, it would have been another, equally as dangerous."

"There is so much I want to say—"

"You will," he promised. "One day."

I studied his lean, handsome face, the full mouth, the twisted nose, the broad, flat cheekbones with skin so taut across them. His rich brown hair was damp with perspiration, wisps of it sticking to his brow and temples. I lifted my hand and smoothed it back and then ran my fingertip along the deep cleft in his chin. His blue eyes were grave. A deep frown creased his brow.

"Go join the others, Marietta," he ordered.

His voice was harsh, and I understood the reason. This was neither the time nor the place for the feelings that had begun to surface. He was thinking of the welfare of all of us. I nodded and turned, feeling much better as I sat down under a tree. We were in grave danger, but the strain between Jeremy and I was gone, that terrible tension removed. If we got out of this, I vowed, I would make it up to him. I looked at the pistol again, calm, refusing to give in to the panic that could so easily sweep over me.

Em came to sink down beside me, sighing heavily.

"We picked a whole bag full of berries," she informed me. "We might be grateful for them later on. Jesus, luv, are you as scared as I am? I feel like I'm going to start shrieking any minute now."

"You won't, though."

"I don't imagine I will. I'll be admirably brave."

"We have to be, Em."

"I know. The men have enough on their minds without worrying about panicky females. I'm worried sick about Randolph. I wish he hadn't gone off like that by himself. I know it was necessary, but—"

"He'll be all right. Randolph can take care of himself."

"Jesus, here comes Jeremy. We're going to start moving again. The Karankawas aren't going to get us, luv. We're all going to keel over from exhaustion!"

Jeremy set a killing pace, driving us mercilessly, and tree trunks and huge, lacy ferns seemed to fly past as we half-ran, skirting around roots, ducking to avoid low-hanging branches, wading across shallow rivers. My lungs began to burn again, the muscles of my legs aching furiously, but I kept on, kept up, Em beside me with a stoical expression. I gripped the pistol firmly, and the feel of it in my hand gave me a feeling of security.

We reached another river, much wider, much deeper than the others had been, too deep to wade across. Jeremy stopped, and we clustered around him, Bobby Roberts standing in back, watching for pursuit. Hurley volunteered to go across first and discovered that the water was only shoulder high at its deepest point. He returned and scooped Em up, his pockmarked face expressionless as he hoisted her up onto his shoulders. She clutched his hair, terrified as he started across again, almost dropping her at one point.

Chris carried Corrie across, and, handing my pistol to Marshall, I dove in and swam across. Hurley took my hand, pulling me out of the water. Jeremy and Marshall and Roberts came after me, holding their rifles high. I wiped damp tendrils from my face and took the pistol from Marshall. We

377

stood there for a few moments, catching our breaths, watching the opposite bank. The trees looked thick and ominous. The sun was going down, deep red-orange smears staining the horizon, dusk falling. Jeremy and the other men checked their guns. Em fanned herself. It was so warm that my dress and hair began to dry immediately.

There was a noise behind us. The men whirled around. Jeremy shoved me behind him. Em and Corrie were already crouching behind tree trunks, Chris in front of them. Randolph stepped around a huge shrub and strolled casually toward us, sweating profusely. He glanced at the guns leveled at his chest and grinned.

"No need for 'em yet, lads," he said. "It's just ole Randy."

"Did you find a spot?" Jeremy asked.

"Sure did, 'bout a half a mile from here. There's a wide river and on the other side there's a kinda sandy clearin' juttin' out into the water, littered with dead trees. I figured we could use the trees to make a barricade—they're all fallen down, roots stickin' up in the sand."

"Good," Jeremy said, relieved.

"We'll have the river in front of us, thick woods behind, with a barricade of dead trees makin' a kinda fort. It ain't ideal, but I reckon we could hold 'em off easily enough."

"Half a mile, you say?"

"'Bout that, maybe a little more. We oughta make it by dark."

"Let's get moving," Jeremy said. "You women get up here behind Randy and me. Chris, you and Marshall stay close behind them. Hurley and Bobby will bring up the rear."

"I didn't see any signs of 'em up ahead," Randolph said. "If they're anywhere, they'll be behind us. Anything happen while I was scoutin'?"

Jeremy shook his head, and we continued on our way, moving at a slower pace than before. The sky was taking on a light purple hue now, gradually darkening, and the air was thick with a pale violet-blue haze. Tree limbs cast long black shadows over the ground, nests of shadows thickening all around us. Hurley and Roberts lagged behind a little, turning constantly to keep an eye out on our rear. Randolph looked around at Em and grinned. She made a face at him, much too

378

tired to summon up a smart remark. Corrie stumbled, clutching the bag of berries. I took her arm, steadying her. She smiled up at me, the corners of her mouth quivering slightly.

She was determined to be brave, to be bright, to hide the terror I knew she must be feeling, just as I did. I smiled back at her and gave her arm a squeeze. We waded across a shallow river and wound through a thick grove of cypress trees and on into a denser, thicker woods with towering trees, trunks huge, limbs spreading in a leafy tangle overhead. Exotic plants grew around them, plants with gigantic purple-green leaves shaped like elephants' ears, spiky plants like spears. Wild ivy climbed over every surface.

Twenty minutes passed, perhaps more. It was much darker now, colors beginning to fade, brown and yellow and a dozen shades of green melting into a dark grayish-black tinged with purple. The shadows were deep blue-black, swallowing up everything. With visibility gone, we were forced to move at an even slower pace. This worried Jeremy. He turned around to look back, and in the dim light I could see the tense lines in his face. The wilderness was dense, threatening, seemed to close in on us.

"How much farther?" he asked brusquely.

"We're almost there. The river's just up ahead. We'll be safe and snug behind them dead trees in less'n ten minutes."

"I don't like this, Randy. It's too quiet."

I noticed the silence then for the first time. Except for the sounds of our progress, the woods were still, frightfully still. No leaves rustled. No birds sang. The hum of insects had ceased. I was puzzled, growing more apprehensive by the moment. I turned to glance over my shoulder. Chris and Marshall were close behind us, Hurley several paces behind them. Bobby Roberts was lagging so far behind I could barely see him in the gloom of shadows. Holding his rifle firmly, glancing from left to right, he seemed unusually on edge, as though he sensed something.

Em sighed and started to say something to me. At that moment a bird called out. It was a coarse, cawing sound, coming from our right. The sound seemed to go through me like a spear, causing me to start. There was another caw, from our left, then another and another until the sounds seemed to come from all around. Jeremy and Randolph exchanged looks up ahead. Behind us, Chris said something to Marshall, his voice so low I wasn't able to make out the words.

I turned around, and I knew then, knew even before I heard the shrill, demonic yells and saw two fierce, naked giants with tattooed bodies drop from the trees and pounce on Bobby Roberts. Hurley cried out and began to fire, running toward Roberts. Roberts dropped his rifle, struggling valiantly, but they were too strong, too savage. All three of them disappeared into the shadows and the cawing stopped, the silence far more frightening than the noise had been.

Jeremy grabbed my arm, whirled me around, jerked his head at Em and Corrie.

"Run!" he said tersely. "I want all three of you to run like hell! Get to the river. Get across it. Get behind those dead trees and stay down. Run. Now! And whatever you do, don't look back!"

Twenty-Five

We obeyed immediately, tearing ahead toward the river as the demonic yells filled the woods and gunfire exploded. Em was slightly ahead of Corrie and me, her blue skirt flying, white petticoats billowing, her long chestnut waves all atumble. We were in the middle of a shrieking, deafening nightmare, all the demons of hell loose, leaping, yelling, pursuing us. We ran, flying past trees and underbrush, the sounds not so loud now, not so deafening, the river still not in sight. I tripped, and Corrie seized my arm and kept me from falling. Em was far ahead of us.

I saw the tree limb shaking. I saw the naked brown legs among the leaves directly in front of Em. With horror I saw the savage leap from the tree and grab her, pulling her away. She fought like a wildcat, kicking and scratching at the naked brown giant with tattooed chest and face, long black hair falling to his shoulders. She raked her nails across his cheek and drove her knee into his groin. He let go of her, fell back and pulled a knife, plunging it toward her.

A bright red fountain gushed from his forehead, and he was thrown against a tree trunk with arms and legs akimbo and crashed to the ground in a heap. The pistol in my hand smoked and my arm ached from the jerk and I wasn't even aware I had fired. Em looked at me, her cheeks ashen, but we didn't hesitate. We continued to run, seeing the river now, moving even faster, splashing through the water, moving toward the sandy land that jutted out on the other side. The river was wide, deep, too, the water soon up to our thighs, our shoulders. We swam, reaching land, climbing over the fallen gray trees.

The yells, the gunfire were in the distance now, muffled by the woods, and it was eerily peaceful here, quiet, not yet night, the sky purple, the air thick with violet-blue haze. A bird warbled nearby. The water gurgled as it moved, sloshing against the banks. All three of us were panting. None of us spoke. Em was trembling. Corrie took her in her arms and held her very tightly, and I closed my eyes, resting my forehead against the rough gray bark. The bird continued to warble. Crickets chirped in the woods behind us, making a raspy music that blended with the soft slosh of the water.

Several moments passed, and I finally opened my eyes and sat up, summoning all my strength, looking around. The sandy piece of land jutted out into the river, perhaps fifty yards wide, and there was water on three sides, woods along the shoreline. There were at least twelve dead trees, half-rotted, bark peeling, heavy limbs broken off and littering the sand. We could build a barricade quite easily. We could hold them off. If . . . if the men joined us, we could hold them off. If the men didn't come . . . I refused to think about it. I wouldn't allow myself to entertain that possibility.

"Are you all right?" I asked Em.

She nodded, removing Corrie's arms from around her. "I kneed that bastard good, and then—then he pulled the knife. He was going to stab me, I saw the look in his eyes. It was—it was horrible. If you hadn't fired when you did, luv, I'd have been a goner."

"I don't even remember firing. I just—suddenly he was flying through the air and the blood was spurting and—God!"

"I wonder how many there are?"

"It seemed like hundreds."

"It's true what they say about the alligator grease. The smell! I almost keeled over when I got the first whiff. He must have been six-foot-five, maybe taller, and that horrible tattoo on his face!"

"Someone's coming," Corrie said.

We stared across the river and saw Chris and Hurley. They splashed into the water, starting across. There was still gunfire in the distance. Marshall appeared, looking over his shoulder, and then he started across, too, holding his rifle high. The gunfire ceased. There were no more yells. Chris and Hurley joined us behind the fallen trees, and a moment later Marshall scrambled over. They began to remove the bundles strapped on their backs. Em's tumbled to the ground, clattering. The string broke and the top burst open. A silver candlestick rolled out. She picked it up, holding it by the end as though it were a bludgeon. I stared at the line of trees on the opposite shore, waiting, holding my breath, praying the others would appear.

"Set the guns out over here, on this piece of oilskin," Marshall ordered. "Powder. Ammunition. We got plenty. Make sure all the guns are loaded. You women know how to load a pistol, load a rifle?"

"I do," I said, still watching the shore.

"I can learn, luv," Em told him. "You just do it once. Let me watch."

"I'll show you," Chris said. "You, too, Corrie. You're both going to need to know how. Hand me that powder horn, Frank."

They still hadn't appeared, and it was so quiet, so still, the water flowing, the crickets chirping, quiet rattling, clicking noises behind me as rifles were handled. Chris began to speak to Em and Corrie, explaining steps in a low voice, and I tuned it all out, resting my elbows on the log, staring, straining to see as the haze grew thicker and the shadows increased, spreading thick, velvety darkness. I didn't dare ask the other men what had happened. If they told me, if I knew, hope would be gone, and I had to cling to 'hope, I had to believe they were still alive.

"There," Chris said. "It's simple as can be."

"Hand me that one, luv. Let me load it."

"Here. You load this one, Corrie."

"We'd better start building a barricade," Marshall told Hurley. "There're plenty of dead trees. Randy picked a good spot. We'll have us a small fort in no time."

What if they were dead? What if I never saw Jeremy again? I hadn't told him all the things I wanted to say. I hadn't let him know how I felt. I hadn't expressed the feelings inside. I wished fervently that I had given way to them. I had been so stiff, so thorny, so defensive. I had been afraid. I realized that now. I had been afraid to examine those feelings too closely, afraid I might have to acknowledge them. I wished now that I had melted into his arms, given way, had succumbed to that dangerous charm, that virile strength. I wished I had let him make love to me, how I wished it now, how I longed to be in his arms at this moment.

"You did fine," Chris said quietly.

"Nothing to it," Em replied. "It's ready to fire?"

"Ready," he told her.

"This one is, too," Corrie said.

"Now I'll show you how to load a pistol. It's a little different. Pay close attention."

The rough bark cutting into the flesh of my forearms, the bodice of my dress clinging wetly to my skin, I peered at the line of trees, willing them to appear, and I saw a man step onto the bank, tall, stalwart, rifle in hand. It was Randolph. He looked behind him and then started across the river, wading slowly, constantly glancing over his shoulder. I stood up and climbed over the log, heedless of the protests behind me. Marshall shouted for me to get down, get down, and Em called out, and Chris, and I paid no mind. I waited. Randolph swam easily across the rest of the way and climbed out.

"Where is he?" I asked. My voice was barely audible.

"He's all right, gal. He's coming."

"Where is he?" I repeated.

"They fell back. Soon as they tasted our bullets, they fell back, and he wanted to look around a bit before he joins us."

"Randolph—"

"He's all *right*, gal. Here, get back behind this log. Damn foolish of you, standin' in plain sight, easy target. They fell back, but they're still out there, probably watchin' us right now."

"And Jeremy is—"

Randolph made a face, impatient, half-shoving me over the log, climbing over himself, pulling me down beside him. He was lying. I knew it. He was lying because time was of the essence, they were going to attack any moment now, and he was afraid I would grow hysterical if I knew Jeremy was dead. He was being kind. He wanted to give me a few more hours of hope. I could feel the hysteria building inside me. I couldn't take it. I couldn't. Randolph took hold of my shoulders, gripping me so tightly I winced.

"Jeremy can take care of himself. Ain't a better man alive for creepin' through the woods. He'll be here in just a few minutes."

"He's alive?"

"He's alive, gal," he assured me.

I sat quietly, still not believing him, and he got up and began to help Marshall and Hurley build the barricade all around us. They dragged the fallen trees through the sand, piling them up, constructing rough walls while Chris and Em and Corrie loaded all the guns and lined them up on the oilskin, setting out the ammunition, the powder horns, preparing. I was numb, unable to feel anything it seemed, unaware of the gritty sand, the rough log I rested against, the mosquitoes humming in the air. Em came to sit beside me. She took my hand. I looked up at her and shook my head.

"It's going to be all right," she told me. "Randolph says they aren't likely to attack now. They don't like to fight in the dark. They'll wait until dawn, and we'll be ready for them then. Corrie and I are going to gather up some of these broken limbs and make a fire. She's going to make stew with that meat Randolph has in his pack and the mushrooms she gathered. You'll feel better after you eat, after you've had some coffee."

I nodded, forcing myself to respond. I brushed a wave from my cheek and told her I would help. Like a zombie, I got up and helped gather limbs and placed them over the hole

Chris had dug and lined with rocks. Hurley and Randolph and Marshall finished building the barricade, piling the dead trees in a circular wall four feet high all around us. Corrie made coffee and put the stew on, and everything was peaceful, calm. It was totally dark, now, the sky a deep purple-black frosted with stars. Em handed me a cup of coffee. The fire cast flickering yellow-orange patterns over the sand. Chris and Randolph patrolled, moving around the hastily improvised walls with their rifles. The water lapped against the banks. Behind us, the woods were full of night noises.

I sipped the coffee without tasting it. An hour must have passed since we had first climbed over the logs, dripping wet, exhausted, terrified. It seemed much longer. It seemed an eternity. I was functioning quite well. I finished the coffee and handed the cup to Corrie. She filled it again, and I carried it to Hurley. There weren't enough cups for all of us. We had to share. I told him the stew would be ready shortly. No one guessed that I was numb. I was admirably calm, composed. No one guessed.

The moon came out, silvering the water, accentuating the blackness of the woods. I moved back to the wall that faced the opposite bank, leaned my elbows on it and stared across at the blackness beyond the rippling silver water. I was convinced now that he was dead, that I would never see him again, and I tried to resign myself. I tried to be brave and rational about it, but I wanted to scream. Jeremy was gone, and I knew I couldn't endure the loss. Not this time.

"The stew's done, luv," Em said, coming to stand beside me.

"I'm not hungry, Em. Let the others eat first."

"He's going to come back, Marietta. He stayed behind to look for Bobby. The Karankawas fell back almost immediately, the men shot at least a dozen. Randolph figures there're about fifty of them."

"Bobby—"

"They took him. They dragged him away. Jeremy thought maybe he could follow the trail and—and help. He promised Randolph he wouldn't take any unnecessary risks. It was something he had to do."

I didn't reply, and Em fell silent, standing close beside me with her hand on my arm, trying to comfort me. She understood what I was feeling and knew the reasons why. There was no need for words. We could hear the men talking quietly behind us. Corrie's voice was low and melodious as she served the stew. The river rippled, silver shimmering on the black water, under the purple-black sky. The fire made a soft crackling noise, and tree limbs groaned as they stirred in the faint night breeze.

Randolph came over to join us, peering across the river at the dense black trees.

"They ain't gonna attack tonight," he told us. "You gals might as well get some rest. Might as well sleep."

"I don't think I could," Em said.

"You're gonna need all your strength tomorrow. It ain't gonna be pleasant. They'll come shrieking across the river soon as the sun comes up. We'll hold 'em off, but it may be hours 'fore they give up. They may be at it all day."

"Go ahead, cheer us up."

"Oh, we'll be all right," he said, not at all perturbed. "We got plenty of water, enough food, ample ammunition, and every man here's a crack shot. I been in a lot worse spots. The Karankawas'll come and they'll lose a lot of men and when they've had enough, they'll give it up."

He paused, listening intently, gripping his rifle tightly. From across the river came the faint sound of scuffling. There was a moment of silence, and then there was another loud caw, a hideous sound all the more terrifying now that I knew it wasn't a bird. A second caw answered, coming from nearer the river. The other men joined us, alert, ready to fire. A shot rang out in the woods beyond the water, the explosion reverberating loudly, drowning out the shrill yell that sounded simultaneously. Silence followed.

"There he is," Chris said.

I could barely see the dark form silhouetted against the darkness of the shore. I sensed rather than saw. He stepped to the water's edge and turned to look back at the woods. I was frightened, terribly frightened, because he was alive after all and in grave danger. He backed into the water, watching the trees. Silver splintered about his calves as he moved through the water, away from the bank, his back toward us.. He was clearly visible now, moving in the brilliant moonlight, a perfect target. I held my breath. My heart was pounding. He turned toward us, moving quickly, soon up to his waist in water. I saw the two Indians merge from the darkness, padding silently to the edge of the water.

Jeremy turned, fired. One of the Indians fell forward, his knees hitting the sand, his torso landing in the water with a mighty splash. The other savage let out a bloodcurdling shriek and plunged forward into the water, swinging his knife in the air. There was no time for Jeremy to reload his rifle. He turned and hurled it through the air, and even before it landed in front of the barricade he had whirled back around to meet the assault.

Em seized Randolph's shoulder.

"Shoot!" she cried. "Why don't you shoot!"

"Too dark, too far," Randolph said calmly.

The Indian yelled and leaped upon Jeremy. Jeremy grabbed his wrist and kept the blade fom plunging into his heart, and they both fell into the water and began to thrash and whirl and flail in a life-and-death struggle. Dazzling geysers of silver water shot up all around them. They rolled and tumbled, going under, surfacing, fighting, and it was impossible to tell who was on top, who was trapped in a death lock. The water splashed wildly, shimmering, shooting up in brilliant fountains. Then they went under again, and the water was still.

Five seconds passed, ten, and there was no movement. Fifteen, twenty, and I felt an invisible hand clutching my heart, squeezing, squeezing, and then, after a full half-minute, a man stood up in the water and a limp, broken figure popped onto the surface, floating face down. We were silent, watching. Jeremy shoved the corpse away from him. It began to float downstream as he turned and began to swim toward us. He climbed onto the sandbank and picked up his rifle.

"Glad you could make it," Randolph said amiably.

He reached out and took Jeremy's rifle. Jeremy climbed over the barricade, dripping wet, hair plastered over his head, across his brow. He pushed it back, his eyes inscrutable in the firelight.

"Bobby?" Marshall asked.

Jeremy shook his head. "No sign of him. I picked up their

trail and followed it over a half a mile, lost it when they crossed a river. I kept hoping I'd stumble across his body. No such luck. They took him away. Alive.''

He spoke in a cool, matter-of-fact voice. We all knew what it meant. I thought of the plump, amiable Roberts with his curly hair and choirboy's face, and I prayed fervently that he was already dead. Em looked faint, leaning back against the barricade with ashen cheeks. Chris wrapped his arm around Corrie's shoulders, holding her tightly. The men were calm, betraying not the slightest emotion. Jeremy unfastened the pack on his back and let it drop. He peeled off his buckskin jacket and tossed it near the fire.

I went over and took an empty tin cup and filled it with coffee, handing it to him. He took it from me, seemingly unaware of what he was doing. I placed my hand on his arm.

''Come sit by the fire,'' I said quietly.

He let me lead him across the sand. He sat down and sipped the coffee, and the others left us alone. I stood over him, watching him. The firelight bathed his face. His wet shirt clung to his back and shoulders. His hair began to dry slowly, feathering at the ends. When he had finished the coffee, I fetched stew, and he drank it slowly and set the cup down. I reached down to smooth the hair back from his forehead. The fire was beginning to burn down, crackling quietly, charred wood popping as tiny flames licked it.

''More stew?'' I asked.

''Don't hover over me,'' he snapped.

''I—I'm sorry.''

He looked up and grimaced, his mouth turned down, and then he shook his head again and stood up. His clothes were dry now, his wavy brown hair still slightly damp. His face, in the firelight, was lined with exhaustion, almost gaunt. His twisted nose looked thinner, his eyes much larger and filled with emotions he sternly repressed.

''Forgive me, Marietta. I shouldn't have snapped.''

''You've been through a great deal. You should rest, Jeremy.''

He moved away from the dying fire and stepped over to the barricade. Em and Randolph were talking quietly. Hurley and Marshall were standing guard at either side, watching the moonlit water for any sign of movement, while Chris stood facing the trees directly behind us, Corrie beside him. The crickets no longer chirped. It was a lovely night, black and purple and silver, serene and so peaceful with the sound of the water and the rustle of leaves in the evening breeze. The horror was out there in the night, waiting, waiting.

"I thought you were dead," I said. "When you didn't come back I was certain you'd been killed."

"I'm not an easy man to kill," he said lightly.

He turned to look at me, his face polished by moonlight now, all smooth planes, shadows beneath his cheekbones, his mouth wide and full and soft. The cleft in his chin seemed deeper. Standing so close to him, I felt his strength and his warmth, and I was filled with tender emotions that seemed to blossom inside. I was sad, too, and I found it difficult to hold back the tears. Jeremy touched my cheek.

"I was so worried," I said.

"You care," he said.

"Of course I care."

He curled his fingers lightly around my throat, and I tilted my chin, looking up into those eyes that seemed to caress me. He leaned his body forward and lowered his head and brushed my lips with his own. I wrapped my arms around him, holding him close. He didn't respond. He stood very still, looking over my shoulder at the river, and after a moment he stroked my hair.

"You'd better get some sleep," he said.

"All the while I kept thinking of—all the things I wanted you to know, all the things I was unable to say. I want to say them now, Jeremy. If anything happens, I want you to know how I—"

He placed his hand over my lips, looking down at me with sober eyes.

"I want you to say them," he told me, "but not now, not like this, when you're distraught, overwhelmed by emotion. When you say them, I want to know they come from the heart. You're very tired now. You've been through a terrible ordeal."

"And you think I—you think it's just because—because I'm distraught?"

He didn't answer. I stepped back, feeling the separation, feeling alone and cold, wanting so to lean on his strength, to feel his warmth and the security of those arms enfolding me. He looked at me, knowing what I felt, and he made no move to draw me to him. Deep, deep inside me I knew he was right, knew I was a prey to emotions brought on by circumstance, and I admired him for refusing to take advantage, yet the disappointment was real, the feeling of rejection acute.

"Get some sleep, Marietta."

I turned away from him, knowing I wouldn't be able to sleep. I unwrapped the cloak from my bundle and spread it on the sand beside one of the rough gray logs. I retrieved my pistol, loaded it and then stretched out on the cloak, gazing up at the stars that glittered dimly against the night sky. Corrie soon stretched out beside me, and Em joined us, the silver candlestick at her side. Hurley and Randolph and Marshall stretched out on the sand, too, on the other side of the fire, a mere heap of glowing coals now, while Jeremy and Chris took the first watch.

I wasn't at all frightened. I was too exhausted to be afraid, so exhausted I was numb. What was it like for every bone and muscle in my body not to ache? I couldn't remember. I closed my eyes, listening to the flow of water and the quiet rustle of leaves and the hum of insects. A frog croaked nearby. There was a soft plop, a tiny splash. Em made a low moaning noise in her sleep and turned over, flinging an arm out. Chris and Jeremy moved slowly around the perimeter of the barricade, their footsteps crunching lightly on the sand. Tomorrow the Karankawas would come and there would be more horror, and I was much too exhausted to worry, exhausted through and through, so exhausted sleep was out of the question. The sand was surprisingly soft beneath the cloak, yielding slightly under my weight, shifting as I moved.

Another frog croaked and an owl hooted. It really was an owl, not an Indian. The woods were full of Indians. One of them dropped from a tree and I shot him as Em broke away, the whole scene replaying itself, growing darker as I watched, darker, merging into blackness, melting away. I slept deeply, heavily, and then I sat up with a start. Em grabbed my hand. She was listening to something. Screams. I could hear them plainly, coming from the trees across the river.

"What is it?" I whispered.

"They're at it, luv. They just started."

There was another piercing scream, a shrill, anguished cry that seemed to be torn from a body and hurled into the night with shattering force, rising to a high pitch that vibrated and hung in the air. Everyone was awake inside the barricade. The men had their guns. The sky had lightened to a pale violet, and the stars were barely visible. Even though the sky was lighter, the shadows seemed darker than ever, spreading across the ground like opaque black veils. Em gripped my hand tightly as another scream split the air. I realized it was Roberts. I realized what they were doing to him.

"Oh God," I said. "Oh God. God."

"They want us to hear, luv. They want us to know. They brought him back so they could—so they could torture us as well, so we could hear the screams and—and know what was happening."

I stood up and moved over to stand beside the men. None of them spoke. Across the river, through the trees, I could see a flickering orange glow. It was indistinct and shapeless, shifting and spreading, fading, flaring up again, dimly illuminating a tiny section of the vast darkness. I judged it to be perhaps a quarter of a mile from the river, not too close but close enough for us to see, close enough for us to hear. There was another anguished scream, and I knew I couldn't stand it. I knew I would go mad with anguish myself.

"They plan to take their time," Marshall said. "They plan to keep it up until dawn."

"We've got to do something!" I cried.

"Nothin' we can do," Hurley said grimly.

Corrie was crying quietly. Em took her into her arms and led her away from the barricade and set her down, kneeling beside her, holding her. In the moonlight I could see Jeremy's face, as hard as granite, expressionless. He handed his rifle to Chris, pulled the pistol from his waistband and started to climb over the barricade. Randolph grabbed his arm, restraining him.

"No you don't, lad. I ain't gonna let you do it."

"Let go of my arm, Randolph." His voice was hard, flinty.

"I ain't lettin' you do it. Bobby's *my* friend, lad. He's like a brother to me, always has been. I'm goin'."

"The responsibility is mine. If you don't let go of my arm I'll break your bloody jaw."

391

That flinty voice was without emotion. He meant what he said. There could be no mistake about that. Randolph sighed, shook his head sadly and released his hold. Jeremy nodded curtly. Randolph's mighty fist flew through the air with the weight and force of a sledgehammer, making a terrible thud as it slammed into Jeremy's cheekbone. Jeremy crumpled, out cold. Hurley caught him before he could fall to the ground, holding him under the arms, carefully lowering the limp body and stretching it out.

"Sorry I had to do that," Randolph remarked, extremely casual. "He always was a stubborn bastard. Take care of things, boys. I should be back 'fore too long."

He turned to look at Em, giving her a smile that was heartbreakingly shy and sheepish, almost self-deprecating. She kneeled there with her arms around Corrie and looked at him with solemn eyes, unable to smile back, unable to make a bright, careless remark. Randolph saluted her, seized a pistol, holding it high, and climbed over the logs. He moved silently into the water and seemed to merge with it, barely visible. I was watching carefully, but I didn't see him leave the water and slip into the woods on the other side.

The orange glow flickered in the distance, and there was another prolonged scream that rose and rose, growing shriller and shriller and finally splintering into silence. It began again seconds later, even more horrifying, breaking into racking sobs. I turned away, folding my arms tightly around my waist and trying not to be sick. Jeremy began to moan. He sat up and rubbed his cheekbone and then climbed to his feet.

"He's gone," Chris said. "He had to do it, Jeremy."

"I know, Chris. He and Bobby were—very close."

"He'll make it, Randy will. He'll do the job and get back safely. Here, take some of this."

He handed Jeremy a canteen. Jeremy drank and then handed it back. There was a bad scrape on his cheekbone where the fist had slammed against it. Chris dampened a handkerchief and dabbed at the scrape. Jeremy winced, scowling. The screams had ceased for the moment. Roberts must have passed out from the pain. They would revive him. They intended to keep him alive as long as possible. We waited, silent, and the sky grew lighter. The shadows began to melt from black into a light gray-black.

Em came over to where I was standing. She was in control of herself, but her cheeks were stark white, her hazel eyes dark with worry.

"He's so goddamned brave," she said.

"He'll be all right, Em."

"The sonofabitch has to be a hero."

"That's the kind of man he is. That's one of the reasons you love him."

"I do, you know. Who'd have thought a great big hulk like that would ever make me feel this way. When I think of all the men I've known—" She sighed and shook her head. "Jesus, just my luck to fall in love with a lug like that, without a penny to his name."

Corrie had piled twigs and small limbs over the coals and was filling the coffeepot with water. Chris lighted the fire. The shadows were fading quickly now. The sky was a pale, pale violet gradually turning into light gray. The stars were gone. Pale tendrils of mist rose from the water, dissolving immediately. Minutes passed. The coffee began to boil.

Another agonized scream broke the silence. It rose in the air and seemed to hang there with nerve-shattering clarity, followed by a second scream that was even more unnerving, more animal than human, the scream of a being in terrible, excruciating pain. A shot rang out, sharp and clear. The scream ended abruptly. There was a moment of stunned silence, and then the woods on the other side were filled with angry, barbaric shouts.

Em was holding my hand. I winced, certain she was going to crush my fingers, but I made no attempt to pull away. We both stared across the water at the dark line of trees. There was no movement, no sign of anyone. We waited, all of us, and it was not until he was halfway across the river that we saw Randolph. He swam the rest of the way with ease and climbed out of the water. His face was expressionless as he joined us behind the barricade.

"It's done," he said. "I got him between the eyes. The demons had already—" He cut himself short, unable to continue.

Em wrapped her arms around him. He hardly noticed.

"The sky's turnin' pink," Marshall said. "We'd better get ready. They'll be headin' over here any minute now."

Twenty-Six

The waiting was the worst part. Every minute seemed to stretch out intolerably, and still they didn't come. The mist evaporated, and the sky was a pale pinkish-orange that slowly bleached to white. Shapes and colors materialized, the gray trees turning grayish-brown, leaves turning green, thin sunlight growing stronger. The pink and orange faded completely. Dawn brightened into a clear, sunny morning, and already the heat was intense. We waited, staring across the river, and all was silent, all was still. Not a leaf trembled. The Karankawas might have been swallowed up by the night.

The men stood with rifles aimed. The river flowed along the banks with a quiet gurgling sound. A bluejay sailed across it, scolding noisily. Em, Corrie, and I organized the powder horns and ammunition and lined the extra guns up on the oilskin, ready to pass them out, ready to reload. The sun rose higher, streaming bright yellow light over the bleached white sky. I wanted to believe they were gone. I wanted to believe they had satisfied their lust with Roberts and had turned back, but I knew that they were waiting, too. For what? It was morning now. Why didn't they come?

Another half-hour passed. Corrie insisted the men drink coffee and eat some of the meat Randolph had dried earlier. I thought I was going to scream. I couldn't endure the suspense much longer. My nerves seemed to stretch tighter, tighter, ready to snap. I helped Corrie serve the coffee and meat, refusing to give in to the tension, presenting a calm demeanor that belied the jangling inside. I drank a cup of coffee myself when the men had finished and then picked up my pistol, checking it carefully.

"I don't know how much more of this I'm going to be able to take," Em said, speaking low so the men wouldn't hear. "I'm about to jump out of my skin, luv."

"So am I, Em, but we can't let them down."

Em brushed sand from her pale blue skirt and nodded. We would both hold on and do our best to keep a brave front, if only for the sake of the men who needed our support. We both had stoical expressions and, on the surface, seemed totally unperturbed, as, indeed, did all the men. Randolph seemed almost nonchalant as he stood at the barricade with his rifle resting on the top log, his lids drooping lazily over impassive brown eyes. A thick golden brown wave fell across his brow. He reached up idly to push it back, yawning as he did so.

"Reckon they intend to take their time," he remarked. "Guess they ain't in no hurry to get themselves slaughtered."

"They're thinkin' it over," Hurley said. "Maybe they'll decide it ain't worth it."

"Wish they would," Randolph replied. "Don't imagine they will, though. They gotta at least make a show of standin' up to us. Can't go skulkin' back to camp without a coupla wounded. Their squaws'd think they'd lost some of their manhood. Manhood's real big with 'em, I hear. They gotta prove it constantly."

"Probably gets tedious as hell," Marshall observed.

"Dangerous, too," Hurley added.

They chatted casually as the sun beat down, growing even hotter as the morning wore on. All of us were perspiring freely. The banks were deep with shade from the trees, looking cool and inviting, but there was no shade here on the sandy half-acre that jutted out into the river. Swarms of tiny insects swooped over the surface of the river, making a soft buzzing noise, and birds called out in the woods, twittering merrily. Corrie stepped over to place her hand on Chris' arm. He looked down at her with a gentle, reassuring smile, and Corrie smiled back, silently conveying her confidence in him. I found it incredibly poignant. They were so young, so innocent, and, together, represented all that love should be.

"They're beautiful together, aren't they?" Em said quietly.

I nodded as Chris touched Corrie's cheek and leaned down to say something to her in a low, loving voice. They were so perfectly matched, I thought, Chris tall and stalwart, blond and stern and protective, Corrie dark and frail, lovely and trusting. They were beautiful indeed, like two halves of a whole, united at last.

"Corrie's very fortunate," I said. "She's known hardship and horror, far too much of it, but Chris will make her forget all that. He'll take care of her and make her happy. Happiness—"

I paused, letting the word trail into silence, pleased for Corrie and Chris yet inexplicably sad at the same time. Em sensed what I was feeling, and she understood instinctively.

"You'll find it, too, luv," she promised. "Both of us will, and it'll be all the finer because of what we've been through."

"Do you really believe that, Em?"

"I have to believe it. Neither of us will ever know that innocent, trusting kind of love—I don't think I was ever innocent—but we'll have our day, luv."

"Maybe you're right," I said doubtfully.

"I intend to make it happen for me. Last night when Randolph left I realized what I felt for him, and I vowed that if he got back I was going to hold on to him, hold on fast. He's no prize, of course, but then neither am I. I'm going to hold on to him and make him the happiest man alive. The sonofabitch has no *idea* how happy he's going to be."

Em glared at him almost defiantly, and, as though feeling the force of her glare, Randolph turned and grinned at her. She gave him a look of mock exasperation and shoved a long chestnut wave from her temple.

"He doesn't know it yet," she confided, "but he's going to settle down, and so am I. It's high time—God knows I've done everything *else*. I've got a sneaky feeling I'm going to like it."

She sighed and fell silent, thoughtful now, and after a few moments passed, she looked up and gazed across the river with a deep frown.

"I wish this were *over*," she said. "I wish those bloody savages would attack and be done with it."

Another half-hour passed, the sun intensely hot, the woods silent, insects skimming over the water in humming swarms.

All of us grew more and more restless. I fetched canteens and carried them around to all the men, serving Jeremy last. He drank sparingly and fastened the lid back on, handing me the canteen. His thin white shirt was damp with sweat. His brow was moist, wisps of hair sticking to it, and his cheekbone was discolored, a deep bluish-mauve. I sensed the tension in that tall, lean frame, even though he seemed to be completely relaxed.

"Will they ever come?" I asked.

"They'll come," he assured me.

"Why—why are they waiting?"

"I'm not sure, but I suspect they're waiting for reinforcements."

His suspicion proved to be right, for not more than ten minutes later four long canoes were sighted upriver, gliding smoothly over the greenish-brown water and keeping close to the far bank. A warrior stood at either end of each canoe, guiding it with long, straight poles, four other warriors sitting in between. Chris and Randolph, Hurley and Marshall gripped their rifles, ready to shoot, but Jeremy shook his head curtly and told them to hold their fire. The canoes glided past silently, and not one of the Indians glanced in our direction. We might have been invisible. The canoes were made from tree trunks with the bark still on them, trimmed flat and hollowed out, the ends blunted. Coarse but serviceable, they seemed to move of their own volition, the warriors dipping their poles into the water only infrequently.

As they passed, I stared in horrified fascination. The Karankawas were extremely tall, if one were to judge from those who stood immobile with the poles. They were well over six feet and powerfully built, their dark, copper-brown skin glistening in the sunlight. Coarse black hair fell to their shoulders in loose, shaggy locks, and their faces were broad and flat, features indiscernible, for each face was completely covered with black and white paint in a wide variety of hideous designs. Quivers of arrows were slung across their backs, and each warrior not poling held a long, sturdy bow. Even though they were on the other side of the river, only a few feet from the bank, I could smell the odor of rancid alligator grease.

The canoes moved downstream, disappearing around a

bend, and I shuddered. Never had I seen such terrifying creatures, and as I remembered the accounts of their savagery, as I remembered the flickering orange glow in the night and those shrill, agonized screams, it was hard to believe they were actually human. They seemed more like creatures from the depths of hell, fierce, barbaric demons who personified the darkest evil. A new terror possessed me, and I didn't realize I was trembling until Jeremy placed his hand on my shoulder.

"Don't fall apart now, lass," he said gently. "We're going to need you to load the guns."

"I—I'm not going to fall apart. I just—they're so frightening—"

"They're merely men," he told me, "smeared with paint and armed with primitive weapons. We'll hold them off."

His fingers gripped my shoulder tightly, and as those blue eyes looked into mine I seemed to feel the strength in him entering me, strengthening me. The terror evaporated. I nodded, and he let go of my shoulder and touched me lightly on the cheek and turned back to face the river. Em was shaken, too, and her fingers trembled slightly as she lined the extra guns up again, keeping herself busy, trying not to think of what was about to happen. Tension seemed to crackle in the air as we waited those last few moments. When the first yell split the silence, we were almost relieved.

The Indian rushed out of the woods, yelling, waving his bow, splashing in the water, his face painted black with white circles around his eyes. He turned toward the woods and raised his bow over his head. At least twenty more Indians came tearing out from the trees, hooting and howling, leaping into the water and charging across. Jeremy raised his rifle, fired. The first Indian let out a yowl and flew up into the air, vivid scarlet streams spurting from his chest. He fell into the water with a giant splash, and another Indian leaped over the body and charged on, his body flung sideways as Randolph's bullet ripped into his chest.

I grabbed a rifle and thrust it at Jeremy, took the first and began to reload it, trying to ignore the noise, the yowls, the steady explosions that seemed to burst my eardrums. Don't think about it, don't think about it, just load the gun. Just load the gun. I took the powder horn and the rod and the barrel was so hot it scorched my fingers, but I didn't even notice. I rammed the rod down and finished the job and thrust the rifle at Chris and began to load another, Em and Corrie working beside me, calm and efficient, much calmer than I was. Powder, rod, bullet, calm, keep calm, do it properly. There. I handed the rifle to Hurley and took up another, spilled powder and started to panic and refused to let it take hold of me.

I loaded another rifle, another, another, paying no mind to the splashing and howling, the steady firing. The barricade was surrounded now, they were on all sides, and all five men were firing, firing, tossing their rifles down and grabbing fresh ones. The air was thick with smoke, the smell of powder overwhelming. It couldn't go on much longer. It couldn't. I refused to believe it could continue much longer. I worked steadily, emotionally numb now, picking up a rifle, loading it, handing it to one of the men, grabbing another and loading it, my fingers burning, my eyes smarting from the smoke.

Chris tossed his rifle down, and I got up and hurried over to him with the one I had just loaded. There was a twanging, zinging noise and an arrow flew past my head. Chris grabbed the rifle and shoved me down, and the air seemed to be full of arrows that plunged into the sand and sprouted on the logs as though by magic. One ripped through my skirt, pinning it to the sand. I pulled the cloth free and crawled back to the rifles and loaded another, another, no longer thinking, working mechanically as the smoke grew thicker and the screeching grew louder, much nearer now, shrill, demonic, punctuated by the explosions of rifles that never stopped.

I rammed the rod home and shoved the rifle to Jeremy and grabbed up another and loaded it and saw the Indian leap over the barricade and land in the sand a few yards away. He screamed and raised his knife and started to hurl himself on Chris' back. I aimed the rifle and fired. The butt rammed into my shoulder with a painful thud, and the barrel spat a bright orange-red streak that ripped into the Indian's head. His head flew apart, and there was a grotesque bloody smear where his face had been. I paid it no mind. I had grabbed another rifle before he even hit the sand and loaded it quickly, calmly, and I tossed it to Hurley and saw two more savages leaping over the barricade.

Randolph seized one of them, and they were rolling on the sand, thrashing and flailing. There was no time to watch, no time to worry. I loaded a rifle, and Marshall grabbed it and fired. The second Indian fell to his knees with a terrible screech and blood spewed and he flopped face forward. Three more Indians leaped over the barricade, and I realized vaguely that they were going to overpower us, we were going to be killed. Jeremy fired, and an Indian fell. Hurley was on the ground, a howling, screeching savage on top of him. Randolph wrested the knife from the brave he was fighting and plunged it into the Indian's chest. Then he leaped up, and grabbed the hair of the Indian on top of Hurley, yanked his head back and slit his throat.

Chris fired, and a brave crashed against the barricade, clutching his chest, blood spurting through his fingers. Before Chris could grab another rifle an Indian leaped on him. Chris seized his wrist and slung an arm around the back of his neck and dipped forward abruptly, sending the Indian flying over his shoulders. Chris seized a rifle, fired again. Jeremy scooped up two pistols and shot a brave who leaped over the logs, shot another who rushed him. The chaos was unbelievable, a mad frenzy of carnage, bullets flying, savages howling, blood splattering over the sand. Em and Corrie and I loaded the guns, quickly, quickly, never quick enough, it seemed, our eyes smarting from the smoke.

I tossed a rifle to Hurley and loaded a pistol and Marshall seized it and ran to the other side of the barricade. I picked up a rifle, and a Karankawa leaped over the logs and landed only a few feet away from me, yowling with savage glee. He was tall and brown and muscular and his face was painted black with streaks of white in a jagged lightning pattern. His long, coarse hair was tangled, and his black eyes held mine for an instant, burning with lust as he let out another hideous yowl. I raised the rifle and pulled the trigger. There was no streak of orange, no puff of smoke, no crushing thud against my shoulder. The rifle wasn't loaded. The brave cackled and leaped forward to grab me. I saw his eyes burning and saw the flash of silver and heard the deafening crunch as Em slammed her candlestick against his skull with all her might. His skull split open. Em dropped the candlestick and covered her face with her hands. I grabbed her wrist and pulled her down as arrows flew.

We loaded guns. The men were all back at the barricade now, firing rapidly. No more Indians leaped over the logs. Time passed, and the howling grew distant, and then, miraculously, it ceased altogether. The smoke lifted, and it was over. For a while it was over. Marshall and Hurley were heaving the corpses over the logs, into the water, and the river carried them away like bobbing logs. Blood dried on the sand, a dark red-brown, and arrows dotted the logs like porcupine quills. I stood up, my muscles sore, my bones aching. The sun was high, the sky a cloudless blue. Across the river the woods were still, tree trunks brown, leaves dark green in the sunlight, the bank deep with blue-gray shade. There was no sign of the Karankawas.

"Is everyone all right?" I asked.

"I got a lump on my head the size of a egg," Hurley said.

"I feel like hell," Marshall added.

"Me, I feel terrific," Randolph said, "rarin' to go again. Ain't had so much fun since I don't know when."

"Jesus," Em moaned.

I wiped sweat from my brow. "No one's hurt?"

"Can't hurt men mean as us," Randolph informed me. "It ain't possible."

"Will they be back?"

"Not soon," Jeremy replied. "They'll regroup and count their losses and have a big powwow about it. Probably won't hit us again till late afternoon, if then."

"They're not going to let us go," I said in a flat voice.

Jeremy shook his head. "We've killed too many of their men. They can't go back to camp now without captives or—souvenirs."

"You mean scalps?" Em asked.

"The Karankawas have never heard of scalping. That's a European refinement that hasn't spread to these parts yet."

"European? What do you mean?"

"Before the white men came, the native American Indian didn't scalp. He merely decapitated his enemy. During the colonial conflicts, when the French and English were battling it out up north, our distinguished British officers placed a premium on the—uh—heads of the French, and the Indians brought them in by the basketful."

"Jesus! I'm sorry I asked."

"As you can imagine, it got rather cumbersome, all those baskets piling up, and then someone had the bright idea of just accepting the hair. It was much tidier. Scalping caught on fast. The French placed a premium on English scalps, too, and later on, in various parts of the country, a bounty was placed on Indian hair. White men are much better at scalping than the Indians, better knives, I suppose."

"So if the Karankawas don't take us alive, they won't take our hair," Randolph said cheerily. "They'll just whack our heads off and wag 'em back to show all their pals."

"You go to hell, Dick Randolph!"

Randolph grinned and began to rub the butt of his rifle.

"They'll hit us again," Jeremy said calmly, "and we'll hold them off and deplete their ranks even more. There were maybe fifteen in the woods yesterday, twenty-four more came down in canoes. That's forty, more or less, and we picked off at least twenty of them."

"Hardly enough left to shake a stick at," Marshall observed.

"They'll hit us this afternoon, and when they fail to overpower us they'll either give it up or send for more reinforcements."

"Dandy," Em said.

"If they're not going to hit us again till late afternoon, I suggest you men get some rest," I said. "You're going to need all your strength."

"That's a good idea," Randolph agreed. "The rest of you chaps sit down a spell. I'll keep watch. If I see 'em comin', I'll holler."

I picked up the canteens by their straps and began to distribute them to the men. Randolph lounged against the barricade, idly watching the woods, and the others sat leaning against the logs in a patch of shade, sweaty, exhausted, faces drawn. Corrie and Em began to gather wood for a fire, and after the men had all had water I put the canteens aside and began to hunt through the packs for food. All my senses seemed to have been deadened by the carnage, the horror, and I moved as though in a trance.

"Corrie's putting coffee on," Em said, kneeling down beside me. "I could use something a hell of a lot stronger, I don't mind telling you. Do we have any food left?"

"There's some dried beef, some mushrooms, the bag of berries Corrie picked yesterday. It'll have to do."

"You're so *calm*, luv."

"I'm not calm at all. I'm just—numb."

"I'm still shaking all over. I've never killed anyone before. When I hit that Indian with the candlestick I just—I just meant to *stun* him. Jesus, his head cracked open like a melon—"

She shuddered and reached for the bag of berries.

"There was blood all over the candlestick," she said in a shaky voice. "I felt like hurling it into the river."

"Did you?" I inquired.

Em got to her feet and brushed sand from her skirt. "Of course not," she replied. "I wiped it off and stuck it back in my bundle. A girl has to be sensible about these things, luv."

She began to pass around the berries, encouraging the men to eat heartily, and I handed out the beef and mushrooms. The sun had passed behind the woods now, and the trees spread long shadows over the sand. Although it was still intensely hot, we were no longer in the blazing sunlight. The smoke had long since lifted, but the acrid smell of gunpowder still hung in the air along with other smells too horrible to contemplate. The river flowed with a soft, lapping sound. Leaves rustled in the trees behind us. The birds had begun to twitter again.

Jeremy relieved Randolph after a while, and I joined him at the barricade. The others were very quiet. Chris and Corrie were sitting together, her head resting against his shoulder, his arm curled loosely around her. Hurley lazily cleaned rifles, and Marshall was stretched out in the shade, sound asleep. Em was going through her bundle, examining her treasures in an effort to keep her mind off what was to happen. I began to tug at one of the arrows sticking in the log in front of me.

"Be careful," Jeremy warned. "They're poisoned."

My hand flew back as though it had been stung. Jeremy broke the arrow off and tossed it into the river.

"They dip the arrowheads in venom," he explained. "A Karankawa arrow will kill, even if it doesn't hit a vital area. Takes the poison no more than ten or fifteen minutes to do its work."

"How horrible."

"They're not a particularly engaging tribe," he admitted.

I gazed across the river. The trees were still, serene. The bank was deep with blue-black shade. Sunlight sparkled on the river, paler now, a dull silver. I wondered if they were watching us, planning their next attack.

"Are we going to get out of this?" I asked quietly.

"Of course we are. The worst part's over."

"What if they send for more reinforcements?"

"Don't anticipate, Marietta. Try to put it out of your mind. It'll all be over soon."

He spoke in a quiet, matter-of-fact voice that was extremely reassuring. I believed him. I had complete confidence in him, and I wondered how I could ever have thought him carefree and irresponsible. The handsome, jaunty, fashionably attired rogue of New Orleans seemed a figment of my imagination, and it was hard to believe that this strong, resourceful leader was the same person. I had misjudged him dreadfully, had been completely misled by the dazzling and glamorous facade he had assumed in the city. Facade? No, that Jeremy was real, too, merely another part of an extremely complex man who was tough, tender, gallant, grave, full of contradictions.

He noticed my hands and took one of them in his, examining it with a frown creasing his brow. My palms and the insides of my fingers were badly scorched, the skin stiff and dry and lightly discolored.

"Do they hurt?" he asked.

I shook my head. "I hardly noticed. They'll heal."

He folded his fingers over mine. "You women did a wonderful job," he told me. "We couldn't have made it without you, you know. You were very brave. Most women would have gone to pieces."

"I doubt that. We're not the weak, clinging creatures you seem to think we are, Jeremy."

"I'm finding that out."

"You've obviously known the wrong women," I said.

He grinned, thinking, no doubt, of the lovely, pampered, perfumed creatures he had known so well, and in such quantity. I felt a slight twinge of jealousy as I thought of that parade of beautiful women who had spoiled him so thoroughly ever since he was in his early teens. He looked at me, the grin still playing on his mouth, and I was acutely aware of my tattered, filthy dress, my tangled hair and dirty face. He seemed, again, to read my mind, and the grin softened into a smile.

"I remember a gorgeous creature in a sumptuous red brocade gown," he told me, "her skin like pale satin, her hair glistening like dark red gold, and you know what?"

"What?"

"She didn't look half as lovely as you look right now."

"Filthy? Bedraggled?"

"Brave. Courageous. Unafraid."

"I suppose you thought I was merely another pampered courtesan," I said, looking away from him.

"I thought you had the saddest eyes I'd ever seen, lass," he replied. "I thought I'd never seen a creature so completely vulnerable, so intent on hiding it."

I gazed at the river, thinking of his words, moved by them and amazed, too, for Jeremy Bond understood things about me no other man had ever even suspected. He knew the woman behind the mask, the Marietta who kept those secret, innermost feelings carefully concealed and faced the world with a defiant show of strength and thorny pride. Several moments passed in silence, and then he placed his hand on my shoulder.

"Get some rest, Marietta," he said.

"I don't think I could."

"Rest," he ordered. "We're going to need you later on."

I left him and sat down in the shade and listened to the hum of the mosquitoes and the lapping of the water, aching all over and utterly depleted. I refused to think of the horror that had engulfed us such a short while ago, and I refused to contemplate the repetition that would surely occur before the afternoon was over. I thought, instead, of the remarkable man to whom I owed so much and wondered what I was going to do about him when this was over, when we reached civilization again.

I pulled my bundle over and rested my head against it, closing my eyes, trying to rest. A fine coat of perspiration covered my skin. It was so dreadfully hot, even here in the shade, and they were out there, waiting. Randolph and Jeremy made light of it and presented an optimistic front, pretending the worst was over, but they were worried nevertheless, deeply worried. If more reinforcements came, if more and more canoes glided down the river, filled with those savage warriors with their bows and arrows and clubs. . . . I shut the horror out of my mind. With great difficulty, I forced myself to think of nothing but the gentle lapping music of the water, the soft, splashing melody that was so soothing, so relaxing. Peaceful.

Corrie shook my shoulders, and I sat up, startled. She smiled a reassuring smile. I rubbed my eyes, and then I heard the shrill, cawing noises coming from across the river and saw that the men were all in position around the barricade, waiting with rifles cocked.

"How long have they been—making that noise?" I asked.

"They just started a little while ago," Corrie said calmly. "You've been sleeping for almost four hours, Miz Marietta. Mister Jeremy said let you sleep, you needed it, not to wake you up till we needed you."

I stood up and looked across at the opposite bank. The hideous, birdlike cries grew louder, nightmare sounds that seemed to split the air. Late-afternoon sunlight bathed the bank, mud and mossy rocks gleaming, vines dangling from the trees in thick loops. The Karankawas were not yet in sight, working themselves up to a frenzy behind the trees, cawing, yelling. Corrie saw the expression on my face and took my hand, giving it a tight squeeze.

"It's not going to be nearly as bad this time, Miz Marietta. There aren't nearly as many of them. Chris says they'll probably fall back real soon. They won't even get across the river."

Her voice was calm and gentle, betraying not the least sign of fear. She squeezed my hand again, small, fragile, lovely, so much stronger than I was, so confident in her newfound love and the happiness it brought her. She let go of my hand and

406

told me that she and Em had already loaded all of the extra guns and had everything set up.

"Don't be afraid," she said.

"I'm not afraid, Corrie."

"It's going to be over soon. Chris promised. We're going to get out of this and then everything is going to be beautiful."

She believed that. She was still young enough, still innocent enough to believe everything would be beautiful. I had believed that once, so long ago, but life had taught me that such belief was fantasy, wishful thinking. Perhaps it would be different with Corrie. Perhaps everything really would be beautiful. She was in love with Chris and Chris was in love with her and he was a fine young man, honest, stalwart, strong, tender, too, not afraid to express his tenderness.

"We'd better get ready," I said quietly. "They'll be coming any minute now."

Corrie smiled again and nodded. As she did, the Indians came tearing out of the woods, yelling and dancing on the bank and waving their bows in the air. It happened quickly, so quickly, in one terrible instant that seemed, strangely, to take forever. The Indians started across the river, and the men began to fire, and the arrows flew before Corrie and I could step over to where Em was kneeling beside the neat row of rifles lined up on the oilskin. I saw the brave leap into the water, splashing it vigorously with his feet, saw him draw an arrow from his quiver and position it in his bow, all in that instant as the rifles exploded and puffs of smoke rose and the shrill screams grew even more frenzied.

The brave let loose the arrow and it spiraled through the air, the feathered end fluttering. I saw it coming. I heard the zinging whistle it made and heard the splatting thud as it jammed into Corrie's shoulder. Her eyes grew wide with amazement, and she frowned, bewildered. I grabbed her hand and pulled her down to the sand and gathered her into my arms, stunned, unable to believe what had happened. The arrow protruded from her shoulder, long and sleek, still quivering slightly as she moved in my arms, straightening up, that bewildered look on her face. Deafening explosions sounded all around us, so loud we could no longer hear the yells. Arrows thunked into the logs.

"It didn't hurt, Miz Marietta," Corrie said. "It dun't hurt at all. I can't—I can't feel anything but a—a stinging, a funny stinging feeling in my shoulder."

"It—it's got to come out, Corrie."

"I'll be all right. I'll just rest here. Miz Em needs you to help reload the rifles."

"Marshall's helping her. See? He's kneeling beside her, helping her. Sit still, Corrie. Please, please just sit still."

"It's going to be all right," she said.

"Of course it is."

"It's just my shoul—shoulder."

Chris dropped down beside us. His face was taut, cheekbones chalky. Corrie smiled at him, her small pink lips curving sweetly, her dark eyes glowing as she looked into his. His blond hair was damp with perspiration. There was a powdery black smear on his cheek. His brown eyes gave nothing away.

"I'm going to have to pull it out," he said.

"Sure. I'se not—I'm not scared."

"Hold her arms," Chris ordered.

I held her, and Chris pressed his lips tightly together, grasped the arrow, and jerked quickly, savagely. Corrie gasped, her whole body twitching violently, but she didn't cry out. She didn't scream. The corner of her mouth was bloody where she had bitten it. Chris staunched the stream of blood that flowed from her shoulder with his handkerchief and told me to hold it there. He handed me a canteen and looked into my eyes, and I nodded, knowing as he did, knowing we must keep it from Corrie.

"I've got to get back to the barricade," he told her.

" 'Course you do. You're the best shot there is. Mister Jeremy said so. I'm going to be all right. It don't hurt, Chris. Honest it don't."

He leaned forward and kissed her lightly, lovingly, on the mouth, and then he turned quickly away before she could see the tears in his eyes. He grabbed his rifle and hurried back to his post and fired. I held the handkerchief against the wound and rocked Corrie gently in my arms as the smoke grew thicker and the explosions thundered. Marshall had left his post and was helping Em reload the rifles. Corrie began to tremble ever so slightly, looking up at me with a new bewilderment. I held her close, forcing back my own tears, and Corrie frowned again.

"I—I feel funny, Miz Marietta. It's stinging all through me. It itches—it itches in my blood."

"Try to relax, darling," I said. My voice was tight. I wasn't going to break down. I wasn't. "Here. Drink some water."

"I'se not thirsty. It's gettin' cold, isn't it?"

I nodded, afraid to speak again. I managed to smile down at her, and Corrie sighed, the delicate frown still creasing her brow. Her eyes were puzzled as she felt the sensations spreading through her. I prayed it would be quick. I prayed she wouldn't suffer too much. Chaos raged around us, rifles spitting their deadly fire with deafening blasts, yellow-gray smoke swirling in the air in thick puffs. Em and Marshall worked furiously, grabbing the rifles, reloading them, tossing them to the men, and the men darted from side to side of the barricade, grim, determined, yelling to each other. It all seemed to be happening elsewhere, on a different plane, and nothing was real but the terrible anguish tearing me apart and the lovely, gentle child who was dying in my arms.

"I'se gettin' sleepy," she murmured.

"Go to sleep, darling. Just close your eyes and—sleep."

"It itches, Miz Marietta. It's gettin' so cold."

I held her tightly, folding her against me, and she sighed again and nestled her head on my shoulder, her soft, cloudy black hair brushing my neck. I felt her trembling. Her body jerked in a series of spasms, and then she raised her head to look up at me with velvety brown eyes that were worried now. Her pink lips quivered as she tried to speak. She jerked again, and then her body seemed to melt against mine as she relaxed.

"I'se so tired," she said. "I—I'se scared, too, Miz Marietta. I can't help it. It—it itches so bad—in my blood, and it's so—so cold."

"Try to sleep, darling."

"It's going to be all right?"

"It's going to be all right," I assured her. "You're going to have your own shop in London. Mademoiselle Corrie's. It's going to be so grand, so elegant."

"Gold letters on the glass?"

"Big gold letters. All the fine ladies will come."

"And—and I'll do their hair and—and sell them my creams and perfume. Chris will be there, too."

"Chris will be there."

"He'll take care of things. I'm going to sell the perfume in pretty glass bottles with—with gold stoppers. Oh—" She stiffened again, her eyes wide. "Somethin'—somethin' stabbed me, Miz Marietta."

"Relax, darling. Close your eyes."

She obeyed, resting her head on my shoulder as I stroked her hair. The men weren't firing as often now. Arrows no longer thunked against the logs. Em looked at us, tears spilling down her ashen cheeks as she reloaded another rifle. She knew about the poison, too. She thrust the rifle to Hurley, sobbing as she grabbed up another. Corrie stirred in my arms, sighing once again.

"I can see it, Miz Marietta," she murmured. "I can see the gold letters on the shop window. My own shop. And Chris. Chris is there, smiling at me. He has such a pretty smile. He loves me."

"He loves you dearly. I—I love you, too, Corrie."

"I know you does."

Her eyes were still closed. Her voice was so faint I could hardly hear her. The men were firing infrequently now, almost idly. I could hear savage yells as the Indians retreated across the river. Corrie moaned and snuggled close, nestling against me like a kitten. I could no longer hold back my tears. I stroked her hair, blind with salty liquid, blinking.

"It's beautiful, Miz Marietta. I can—can see it so clear."

"Sleep, darling. Go to sleep."

"I've got you and—and I've got Chris. I'se so—so—" She looked up and smiled that lovely, gentle smile. "So happy," she whispered.

The firing stopped. The smoke began to lift. Corrie was limp and still against me, and Chris was standing over us, his handsome young face etched with grief. He gazed at the body in my arms with all that pain in his eyes. After a moment he turned away, unable to look any longer without breaking down completely. He moved over to the barricade and stared at the river without seeing it. Jeremy came over. Our eyes met. He was at a loss, wanting to comfort me and knowing it was impossible.

"They've retreated," he said quietly.

"Will they be back?"

"Not until morning. We'll be gone by then. As soon as it's dark Hurley and I are going to slip down there and steal a couple of their canoes. She—she's gone?"

I nodded.

"Luv," Em cried. "Oh, luv—"

"She's gone, Em. Corrie's dead. Why—why couldn't it have been me?" My voice broke. "Oh dear God, why couldn't it have been me?"

Twenty-Seven

Soap and warm water were a luxury I couldn't seem to get enough of, and Juanita patiently indulged my eccentricity, shaking her head in dismay when I asked for yet another tub of water. Plump, amiable, her warm brown eyes full of pretended exasperation, she lugged the pails of water up the stairs of the inn without complaint. She filled the small tin tub and set out a large fluffy towel and a thick bar of the verbena-scented soap she made herself every Saturday after she finished the laundry. Juanita's father owned the large, rambling inn which dominated one side of the square, its dusty abobe walls a dark golden tan, and the girl worked from dawn to dusk, chattering merrily and displaying an absorbing interest in the guests.

"Zeehs ess zhe last pail," she exclaimed, dumping the water into the tub with much splashing. Steam rose in misty clouds. "You'd better let eet cool a while before you climb in, Mees Danver. It'd scald you now!"

"Thank you, Juanita."

"You are going out?"

"Yes. I thought I'd take a short walk."

"Ess good!" she declared, nodding her head emphatically. "Ess *not* good you staying here in your room all zhis time, nev-air going out, brooding, taking all your meals on zhe trays I bring up. You've hardly left zhis room since you got here a week ago."

"I know, Juanita."

"Zhe oth-air one, zhis Mees Em, she ess rarely *in* her room. She and zhat Mees-stair Randolph gallivant all over zhe place, visiting zhe ranchos outside of town, taking long rides over zhe countryside. I know a secret."

"Oh?"

"This morning, zhey visit zhe padre."

I removed my dress and spread it over the bed. "Indeed?" I said.

"I see zhem go into zhe mission togeth-air," the girl replied. "Mees Em, she looks real dreamy. Mees-stair Randolph, he looks nervous as can be. When zhey come out, zhe padre is with zhem, and Mees-stair Randolph says something to him and zhe padre nods."

Juanita smiled. She was wearing a white cotton blouse and a bright pink cotton skirt embroidered with red and blue and yellow flowers. Earrings made from golden coins dangled from her ears, and a long black braid was draped over one shoulder. Pleasantly overweight, not more than seventeen years old, she was a bustling, vivacious, gossipy creature abounding in good humor. During this past week my comfort and well-being had been her major concern, and it worried her that I spent so much time in my room, that I didn't eat every bite of the enormous meals she brought up on trays.

"I think zhey have *plans,*" she observed. "Mees Em, zhat red silk gown she has, she *gave* it to me."

"That was very sweet of her."

"I'll have to let it *out*, quite a lot, but when Manuel sees me in it, he's going to give me another pair of earrings. Mees Em, she tells me she won't be needing zhe dress any longer.

412

'My red silk days are over, luv,' she tells me, and she begins to brush zhat lovely white gown she has, *such* a look in her eyes as she examines it.''

Another smile played on her small, cherry-red mouth, and her brown eyes twinkled merrily. She stuck her finger in the tub of water, made a face and informed me that it was still too hot.

"All zhese baths, and in the middle of zhe afternoon, too. Crazy. I think maybe she wears zhe white dress real soon. Mees-stair Randolph won't let her out of his sight, and when another man looks at her—*all* zhe men look at her, zhere aren't zhat many white women in zhese parts, and most of zhem middle-aged and married—when another man looks at her, Mees-stair Randolph growls and looks real menacing. Mees Em grins.''

"They're very much in love, Juanita.''

"I know. It's wonder-ful to be in love. I've been several times, Mees Danver. I may be plump and may talk too much, everyone says I talk too much, but I have—what you say in English? Person—personality. Yes, zhat's it. Zhe men all want to cuddle with me. Manuel, too. He gives me earrings and tries to get me to meet him in zhe garden out back when everyone is asleep. I tell him I'm a good girl.''

"That's very wise,'' I said.

"I tell him as soon as zhe padre joins us together he can cuddle me all he wants. Manuel's very handsome. His father owns a big rancho, many horses, but he spends most of his time here at the inn, mooning over me. It's great fun. My girl friend Chita says I've got him bewitched.''

Juanita sighed, thinking of her Manuel with a thoughtful look in her eyes. She tested the water again and then stepped over to the heavy wardrobe to examine the contents. The heavy blue silk and the golden yellow brocade I had brought from the island hung in solitary splendor beside the petticoats that went with them. Juanita had taken charge of them, too, brushing them, pressing them, mending a tear on one of the hems. For the past week I had been wearing two cotton frocks Juanita had provided, the one I had just removed and a pale tan sprigged with tiny rust-brown and orange flowers. Freshly laundered, it was spread over a chair now with a clean white cotton petticoat.

"And you, Mees Danver?" she asked. "Are you in love?"

I shook my head, suddenly uncomfortable under her close scrutiny.

"Mees-stair Jeremy, he ees always asking me about you. Are you feeling better? Are you going to come down to zhe taproom for dinner? Are you eating all zhe food I bring you? Do you need anyzhing? He looks worried all zhe time when he asks about you, and at night he paces his room, back and forth."

"He's concerned, Juanita. I—something happened that—that upset me very much. I've needed time to get over it."

Juanita nodded, brown eyes sad now, her mouth drooping. "Mees Em, she told me about zhe Indians and zhat sweet little nigra girl who got killed. She said you loved her very much, and it broke your heart to leave her buried there beside zhe river."

"I don't want to talk about it, Juanita."

"I understand," the girl said quietly. "But—staying in zhis room all zhe time, it doesn't help, Mees Danver. You need to see people and get fresh air and try to go on. I'm glad you decide to take a walk. Ess beautiful day today, but hot. Ess siesta time for everyone but zhe gringos."

She tested the water again and then sprinkled a bottle of fragrant-smelling bath salts into it. I removed the cotton petticoat and, naked, slipped into the water. It was wonderfully warm. As I reached for the bar of soap, Juanita took the clothes I had removed and draped them across her arm.

"I launder zhese for you, bring zhem back in zhe morning all clean and crisp. I bring a tray up zhis evening?"

"I think not, Juanita. I think I'll eat with the others tonight."

The girl beamed, nodding happily. "Ess good!" she declared. "Mis-stair Jeremy will be most glad. He keeps busy, selling zhat bracelet you gave him and buying supplies and a wagon and horses, but he mopes, too. He wants to hold you in his arms and comfort you."

"Thank you, Juanita," I said in what I hoped was a tone of dismissal. "If I need anything else, I'll pull the cord and ring for you."

Juanita grinned and bustled out of the room, pink skirt

rustling, earrings tinkling brightly. I sighed as she closed the door and sank deeper into the water, savoring its warmth and the silky softness the bath salts created. I closed my eyes for a moment, arching my back, relaxing. Then I began to lather myself thoroughly, squeezing the sponge, making floating heaps of suds. It had been two and a half weeks since Corrie's death, since that dreadful night when we buried her and then slipped away in the canoes Jeremy and Hurley had stolen from the Karankawas. It seemed a lifetime ago. That night and the week and a half of travel that followed was like a half-remembered nightmare. I seemed to have been in a trance, so crushed with grief I could barely function. Em had watched over me like a mother hen, her concern for me helping her bear her own grief.

I remembered few details of that journey, and once we reached this small Spanish town I had been ill and so exhausted I had wanted to sleep forever. Juanita had watched over me, and Em had come to my room every day, trying her best to cheer me up. I had seen Jeremy only twice, when I had given him the bracelet to sell and when he had returned with the money, a surprisingly large amount of money. I had turned it all over to him and told him to purchase anything we needed. Then I had slipped back into my lethargy. I had remained here in this cool, comfortable room with its gigantic brass bed and bright rag rugs and whitewashed walls, nourishing my grief, reluctant to let it go, completely uninterested in anything going on around me.

It was over now. This morning, when I awakened, I had realized that the time had come to let go, to make peace with myself. Corrie was gone, and no amount of grief could bring her back. The world was still revolving, and I could no longer hide from it. I had to go on. I had to face reality. Staying closed up in this room solved nothing. The grief was still there inside of me, it would always be there, but I had come to terms with it at last. I was ready to go on now, difficult as it might be. I was physically rested for the first time in weeks and, surprisingly, eager to be up and out. When Em had come by the room shortly before noon, I had promised to meet her in the square, and I found myself looking forward to it.

I bathed and washed my hair and then, getting out of the

tub, dried myself thoroughly and slipped into the freshly laundered white petticoat. It was very snug at the waist, and the bodice barely covered my breasts, but Juanita had done the best she could. The clothes, I knew, had belonged to her mother who, bored with the town and weary of working all day at the inn, had run off with a handsome gringo, leaving the girl in care of her father. Juanita was quite philosophical about it. She had been eight years old at the time, yet she had kept her mother's things in perfect condition. I was extremely grateful for the garments, ill-fitting though they might be.

I toweled my hair dry and then sat down in front of the window to let the bright afternoon sunlight finish the job, gazing out at the square. The cottonwood trees spread pale blue-gray shadows over the grass, and sunlight bathed golden-tan adobe walls and the few frame buildings. The enormous, majestic mission dominated everything, much older than any of the other structures. It had once squatted alone against the sky, a sanctuary in the wilderness, and the town had gradually grown up around it. The thick adobe had weathered to a dark reddish-brown, and although the ornate molding had begun to crumble, the three exquisite stained-glass windows over the portico retained their full glory, circular in shape, spilling colored patterns over the wide steps.

The town was very small, surely no more than two hundred inhabitants, most of them Spanish. The Mexican government constantly encouraged white settlers, luring them with lavish spreads of land and promises of wealth, but few of the settlers lived in the town itself. A handful of hardy pioneers had established farms and ranches in the area, and more had come after the Indian threat had diminished. The Karankawas never left the coastal marshes, and after several fierce skirmishes with the determined settlers, the Comanches had moved farther west, where fewer rifles spit fire and picked off their warriors. More and more white people were coming to Texas, and already they were grumbling about the restrictions the government forced upon them. Mexico wanted settlers, yes, wanted them to clear the land and develop it and establish new settlements, but it wanted to keep very tight control.

My hair dry, I moved over to the dressing table and sat down in front of the mirror in its ornately carved wooden frame. I brushed the long copper-red waves until they gleamed with rich, fiery highlights, and then, putting down the brush, I examined my face in the glass. My skin seemed drawn, slight hollows under my cheekbones, and there were faint mauve shadows about my eyelids, making my eyes seem a deeper, darker blue. There was sadness in them still, and the corners of my mouth had a subtle, sad droop. Would I ever be able to smile again? I left the dressing table and put on the pale tan dress sprigged with tiny rust brown and orange flowers. It, too, was snug at the waist, and the square-cut neckline was lower than I would have liked, but the full skirt belled out over the petticoat, rustling crisply as I stepped into my shoes.

I hesitated just a moment and then left the room, moving quietly down the narrow, shadowy stairway and across the large lobby crowded with heavy, ornately carved Spanish furniture. Brightly colored rugs hung on the whitewashed walls, and there were plants in profusion, dark green and dusty. The enormous taproom was a shadowy cavern to my right, shuttered and empty at this time of day. The town seemed deserted as I stepped outside, windows shuttered, not a person in sight. Strolling across the narrow dirt street to the square, I sat down on one of the benches beneath the cottonwood trees.

The sky was vast, a pale, endless blue mottled with soft white clouds that met and bunched together, changing shapes, floating on. It was very warm, true, but not nearly as warm as it had been nearer the coast. Here the heat was dry, with none of the muggy humidity, not at all oppressive. I spread my skirts out and watched a squirrel darting among the branches of a tree, scurrying nimbly as a bluejay swooped, fussing at him. Leaves rustled quietly overhead, shadow and sunlight dancing at my feet in shifting patterns. After my week of seclusion it was lovely to smell the grass and earth, to savor the fresh air and to watch the clouds skimming slowly across the sky.

I wondered where Jeremy was. At one of the ranches, perhaps, arranging to buy horses and a wagon for our return to New Orleans. The journey would not be arduous, but we would need many supplies. Jeremy had sold the bracelet to one of the Spanish landowners, and the money it had fetched would more than pay for all we needed. His manner had been grave, polite, deferential when he had come to my room, and although he had limited our talk to matters of business, I had felt that there was much more he wanted to say. He had managed to purchase new clothes for himself, had been dressed like a Spanish *vaquero*, wonderfully handsome in the slim tobacco-brown pants with a band of tiny silver studs and blue embroidery running up the sides and the short, form-fitting tobacco-brown jacket adorned with bands of similar design. His white shirt had been open at the throat, and a vivid blue scarf had been knotted carelessly around his neck. I wondered if he had purchased a sombrero, too.

Jeremy. What was I going to do about him? I owed him so much. I owed him my life. He was in love with me, there could be no doubt of that, and I was extremely fond of him. Did I love him? There had been moments when I was certain of it, other times when the very idea seemed absurd. I was physically attracted to him, no woman could be immune to that potent magnetism, and during these past weeks I had come to admire him for his strength, his resolution, his stern, uncompromising will and his remarkable bravery, character-istics so out of keeping with the jaunty, devil-may-care charmer I had met in New Orleans. I was attracted to him, yes, and I admired him, but . . . love?

As I sat there under the cottonwood trees in the silent, sleepy town in the middle of a vast, alien land, I realized that I was afraid. I was afraid to let myself love him. I was afraid to make any kind of commitment. I had loved Derek with all my heart and soul, and that love had almost destroyed me. There had been so much grief, so much anguish, and I couldn't go through that again. Deep inside I knew that if I allowed myself I could love Jeremy Bond as wildly, as unreasonably, with every fiber of my being, and I was not going to put myself in that position again. There were too many dangers, too many risks involved, and I would be vulnerable, exposed, at the mercy of emotion. No, better by far to bury any feeling I might have for him and face the future alone, relying on no one, depending on nothing but my own strength.

The sound of hoofbeats brought me out of my reverie. I looked up, startled to see Em riding down the street on an enormous red-brown horse whose shiny coat gleamed in the sunlight. She tugged on the reins, brought the horse to a halt in front of the inn and dismounted nimbly. Tying the reins to a hitching post, she stroked the horse's cheek, said something to it in a low, gentle voice, and, giving it a final pat, hurried across the street to join me. Her chestnut hair was in a long, thick braid that flopped from shoulder to shoulder as she ran, and she had acquired a light, lovely tan. The extremely low neckline of her white cotton peasant blouse was embroidered with pink and turquoise flowers, the small puffed sleeves pulled off the shoulder. The vivid turquoise skirt that billowed over her petticoats was embroidered at hem and waistband with pink and silver flowers. She wore a pair of thin brown leather sandals that left her feet almost bare.

"Here you are, luv!" she exclaimed. "I was afraid you wouldn't come, and I forgot the time and had to *race* to get back to town."

"Em, where on earth did you get that horse?"

"Rusty? He's *mine*, luv!"

"When did you learn to ride?"

"This week. Randolph taught me. Nothing to it. I was scared spitless the first time, of course, absolutely terrified, but I soon got over it. I've been riding all over the countryside, and I *love* it."

"It seems a lot has happened this week."

"You've no idea," she said, smiling. "Like my outfit?"

"It's quite different."

"Gabriella gave it to me. She's just my size. I think it's ever so fetching, and I thought my hair would look nice pulled back like this, braided. Randolph says I already look like a senorita."

"Who is Gabriella?"

"A lovely girl, luv. She speaks perfect English. So does her father. The two of them are going back to Mexico City, then on to Madrid. They own a gorgeous rancho ten miles outside of town, hundreds and hundreds of acres. They raise horses, stables like you've never seen, and there's a great, sprawling house with thick white adobe walls and red tile roofs and patios and fountains and gardens and everything."

"I see."

"I *own* the place, luv."

I gazed at her in amazement. Em caught her breath, so full of news she could barely contain herself.

"Maybe I've lost my mind, luv, but I'm gloriously, deliriously happy! Señor Lopez has been trying to unload the rancho for two years, ever since his wife died. He wants to take Gabriella back to Madrid where she'll have an opportunity to meet fine Spanish gentlemen and get herself a suitable husband. I fell in love with the rancho the minute I saw it, all those green, green pastures and cottonwood trees, that wide, sparkling river."

"You bought it," I said.

"I didn't have any money, of course, but I had all the loot I brought back from the island. The candlesticks, the gold and enamel boxes, the jewelry, all of it together worth a bloody fortune. Señor Lopez' eyes lit up when he saw it. We made a trade then and there. He got the loot, I got the rancho. All the servants are going to stay on, besides Gabriella's personal maid, and I'm afraid I'm going to have trouble with that cook."

"You're going to raise horses?"

"Randolph is, luv. I'm going to sit in the parlor and run the house and fan myself and be the best bloody wife a man ever had. We're going to be married next week. At the rancho. We've already talked to the padre."

"I think it's wonderful, Em."

Em plopped down beside me on the bench and fanned out her turquoise skirt, admiring the lavishly embroidered hem. The long, thick braid had fallen over her left shoulder, and her lightly tanned cheeks were flushed a soft pink. She was silent a moment, lost in thought, and then she looked at me with hazel eyes that were grave now, full of worldly wisdom.

"I couldn't go back to New Orleans, Marietta. It has too many memories and none of them good. I was—the life I led there—" She hesitated, frowning. "I vowed to make a new start, luv, and I have. I'm damned lucky to have a man like Dick Randolph at my side. He's ready to settle down, too, and he passes no judgment on me, on my past."

"You're going to be very happy."

"Damned right I am. Randolph made male noises about not letting a woman set him up, he couldn't let me buy the rancho, he had his pride, that sort of nonsense. I told him if he didn't shut up he was going to get a boot up his ass."

"What did he do?"

"He grinned," she said. "He's staying out at the rancho now, in one of the bunkhouses, getting the lay of things. Chris and Hurley and Marshall are with him. They're going to stay with us, luv. They're going to work at the rancho and share in the profits."

"How is Chris, Em?"

"He's bearing up nicely. He doesn't talk much. He goes off by himself a lot, wandering along the river or riding over the range, spends a lot of time in the stables. He's wonderful with the horses, luv. He didn't want to go back to New Orleans."

"I can understand that."

"He's young, luv. He'll get over it eventually."

"Being with friends will help."

"Hurley and Marshall said they didn't have anything better to do, and Randolph's delighted. They'll be a great help, and I'll feel much better having three more crack shots around, too. There's still an occasional Indian scare, you know, small bands of Comanches roaming about, looking for horses to steal. We'll be well protected at the rancho, all those handsome *vaqueros*. They're going to stay on, of course, and work for Randolph."

"When are Gabriella and her father leaving?" I asked.

"Right after the wedding. The rancho will be completely furnished, by the way. Señor Lopez is leaving all the furniture, that was part of the deal. He has a magnificent wine cellar, too."

Em fell silent, a thoughtful look in her hazel eyes. She toyed with the heavy chestnut braid that fell across her shoulder and gazed across the square. I could tell that something was bothering her. After a moment she sighed and suggested we stroll around the square and take a closer look at the mission. We crossed the grass, walked under the cottonwood trees on the other side and began to move down the street opposite the inn. The town was so quiet it might have been deserted. It would come alive in an hour or so, would be noisy and festive when the canteens opened up and the *vaqueros* and ranch hands swarmed in for liquor and merriment.

"I'm happy for you, Em," I said quietly. "Randolph is a very lucky man."

"I'm lucky, too, luv. Men like him don't grow on trees, I can tell you for sure. I should know."

"That's bothering you, isn't it? The other men."

"It doesn't bother Randolph," she replied. "At least he says it doesn't. He's fully aware he's not getting a blushing virgin. He knows about my past—most of it. He loves me, luv, and I guess I love him. I've never felt this way before. So much has happened—" She paused. "Jesus, maybe I *have* lost my mind."

"Nonsense."

"Emmeline Jones, a respectable wife. Can you picture it? I've always been on my own. I've always been on the move. I've never depended on anyone. When I think of settling down in one place with one man, it makes me nervous as hell."

"You mustn't feel that way."

"Do you think I can pull it off, luv?"

"I think you'll pull it off beautifully. You've never had an opportunity to be respectable before, Em."

"Maybe I'll take to it," she replied. "One thing about it, in this country no one gives a hang about your past. All the people I've met have been friendly as can be. I think they *like* me."

"They're all going to love you," I assured her.

"We'll see," she said.

We stopped in front of the mission and gazed up at the stained-glass windows in their ornate, crumbling molding. Sunlight reflected in the lovely, multicolored panes, and color spilled over the steps in wavering patterns. The deep recess beyond the portico was full of shadows. I could barely see the huge, carved doors, closed now against the midafternoon heat. In the tower that rose above the roof a great bell hung silent, tarnished a moldly copper-green with age. I saw bird nests under the eaves.

"You'll stay for the wedding, of course," Em said.

"Of course."

"There's going to be a fiesta. Señor Lopez has arranged everything. All the *vaqueros* and their lady friends will be there to celebrate, most of the settlers, too. There'll be lights and music and food and liquor and—Jesus, luv, I'm so nervous!"

"You'll get over that."

"What if he backs out?"

"He won't."

"What if *I* do?"

I gave her an exasperated look, and she sighed heavily. Then she grinned and took my hand, and we started back toward the inn. The clouds had all disappeared from the sky, leaving it a pure, pale blue that was almost white. Soft violet-gray shadows were beginning to spread over the adobe walls. Juanita's father was out front, opening the heavy wooden shutters. He smiled at us. Em stroked her horse's neck and began to untie the reins from the hitching post.

"Are you going back to the rancho?" I asked.

"Randolph and I are having dinner with the Lopezes. Afterward Randolph will go back to the bunkhouse, and Señor Lopez will bring me back here in one of the carriages. Everything *very* proper until the wedding. I wish you would come, luv. Gabriella and her father are eager to meet you. I could have a carriage sent back for you when I return."

"I'd better not, Em."

Em looked at me closely, concerned.

"You're not going to have Juanita bring up another tray?"

"No. I'll dine in the taproom."

"And tomorrow you're coming out to the rancho with me, whether you want to or not. I've been worried about you, luv. All of us have."

"I just had to be alone for a while, Em. I'm all right now. I'm ready to get on with the business of living, no matter how trying it might be. When I get to New Orleans and sell the jewelry, I'll be an extremely wealthy woman. That should be some consolation."

"Luv—"

"I'm sorry, Em. I—I didn't mean to sound so grim."

"Things are going to work out for you, too, luv. I know they will. Jeremy loves you. I've never seen a man so much in

423

love. He's been worried sick this past week, hanging about like a puppy dog, asking about you, wanting to see you, afraid to intrude."

I didn't reply. The wooden shutters clanged as Juanita's father unfastened them and slammed them back. Em's horse whinnied, arching its neck, its silky red-brown mane waving. The town was beginning to come alive. Siesta time was over. Em's eyes were still full of concern, and I forced myself to smile, not wanting to dampen her own joy with my low spirits. The smile didn't deceive her at all. She frowned, clutching the reins as Rusty whinnied again.

"You love him, too, Marietta."

"Perhaps. I don't really know."

"You love him," she repeated. "The past is over, luv, it's over and done with. You've been hurt, and you're afraid. I understand that, but you can't let the past destroy the future. You're young and beautiful and you have a whole lifetime ahead of you."

"I can't make any decisions, Em. Not now. Not yet."

Em hesitated. She clearly wanted to say more but was reluctant to do so. I reached for her hand and gave it a reassuring squeeze.

"I just need a few more days," I said lightly. "You go back to the rancho and have a grand time. I'll see you tomorrow morning."

"You'll let me show you the rancho?"

"Every inch of it," I promised.

She smiled, relieved, and gave me a quick hug before slipping her sandaled foot into the stirrup and swinging herself into the saddle. She did this with astonishing ease, long braid flapping against her shoulder blades, her turquoise skirt billowing up over her petticoat. She tugged the reins gently, digging her knees into his flanks as Rusty reared and turned, eager to be gone. He galloped down the street, and Em turned in the saddle to wave merrily. I waved back and watched until she disappeared, amazed at her equestrian prowess.

I was very, very pleased for her. The feisty, scrappy little street sparrow who had known such hardship, such adversity, was finally going to have her day of triumph, and I knew that she and Randolph would be very happy, perfectly matched and far more in love than either would admit. They were going to make a new start in a new country. They would grow with it, and their future would be bright, exciting, full of challenge. As I visualized it, my own seemed even bleaker in contrast. A pensive sadness filled me as I turned to go back inside the inn.

Why was I so afraid? Why did I feel so lost, so disoriented? What was I going to do about Jeremy?

Twenty-Eight

Through the open windows of the spacious bedroom assigned to me I could hear the romantic twang of guitars and the merry babble of voices as the guests assembled on the patio. There must be at least a hundred people, I thought, but the lovely, tiled patio shaded by cottonwoods and surrounded by gardens could easily accommodate them. Señor Lopez and his daughter would depart tonight to stay at the inn, beginning their long journey tomorrow, and as a parting gesture to the couple who would be taking over the rancho they had spared no expense. Em's wedding and the fiesta following it would be the most elaborate social affair yet seen in these parts.

Colored lanterns hung from the branches of the cottonwood trees. Tonight they would spray red and blue and golden shadows over the dancers who whirled to the tunes played by guitars and fiddles. Servants bustled about the tables set up on the lawn beyond the gardens, laden already with food and liquor, and in a gigantic pit two steers were cooking over smouldering coals. Señor Lopez had even exhumed fireworks that had been brought all the way from Mexico City some time ago and stored in the basement for just such an occasion.

There was an air of excitement and anticipation that seemed to have infected everyone at the rancho for the past week as arrangements were made and invitations sent out.

I glanced at the clock. Less than half an hour remained before Em and I were due downstairs. Señor Lopez would escort her out to the patio and to the flower-bedecked altar where Randolph would be waiting with the padre. I would march behind them carrying a lavish, dripping bouquet of camellias, white roses, and lacy white fern. I stepped over to the mirror for a final examination, the skirt of my deep blue silk gown making soft, silken music as it rustled over the ivory lace underskirts. It was wonderful to feel fine silk caressing my skin again, to be wearing subtle, exquisite perfume and makeup, these last courtesy of Gabriella, whose bedroom this had been.

Glistening red-gold waves were sculpted on top of my head, rich with copper highlights, a mass of long ringlets dangling down my back. My lids were softly etched with pale mauve-blue shadow, my cheeks brushed with the faintest touch of pink that made the hollows less pronounced. I had applied a touch of lip rouge as well, the deep pink emphasizing their natural color. I looked at the reflection with cool objectivity. The tired, haggard look was gone, yes, but the eyes were still sad, the mouth still drooping faintly at the corners. The radiant glow that love alone supplies had been missing for some time, and the woman in the glass seemed older, wearied by life.

Tomorrow morning, after breakfast, Jeremy and I would leave on the first lap of our journey back to New Orleans. He had purchased horses and a sturdy wagon, and it was waiting in the carriage yard, already loaded with food and supplies. I had seen very little of him this past week. Four days ago he had come to stay at the rancho with Randolph and the other men, while Em and I remained at the inn. We had dined together once in the taproom before he left, his manner polite and deferential, my own subdued. The conversation had been desultory, the evening leaving me even more indecisive than before. There was so much unsaid, and that left unexpressed seemed to widen the gulf between us. I didn't look forward to our long journey alone together.

There was a knock at the door. I turned as Gabriella

entered, a vision of youthful loveliness in pale pink tulle. Not yet eighteen, the girl had a creamy tan complexion, warm, gentle brown eyes and gleaming blue-black hair worn now in long ringlets that framed her face. A smile curved on her soft pink lips. Shy, virginal, sheltered by her doting father and her stern, sharp-eyed duenna, she exuded an aura of touching, childlike innocence.

"How lovely you look," she said in her low, musical voice. "Your gown must have come from Paris."

"It did," I admitted.

"I suppose I shall have Paris gowns, too, once we reach Madrid. I look forward to it, but it's sad to be leaving all my friends here. Papa wants to find me a wealthy, aristocratic husband."

"I'm sure the gentlemen of Madrid will be mad for you, Gabriella."

The girl shrugged, clearly finding the idea highly improbable. Her pink tulle skirt belled out, awash with pink tulle ruffles that seemed to float as she moved across the room. Her handsome, silver-haired father had great expectations for her, and I felt certain they would be fulfilled. Gabriella was going to have the noble Spanish grandees in a stir.

"It's so lovely of you and your father to have gone to so much trouble and expense for my friends," I said.

"Papa wanted to do it, and it is for us as well. We will be saying goodbye to our friends. It is almost time to go down, Miss Danver, and Miss Em—" She hesitated, a delicate frown creasing her brow. "I think you had better go to her."

I was vaguely alarmed. "Is everything all right?"

"She won't move," Gabriella said. "She sits in her chair and stares into space and refuses to speak. I brought her a lovely white lace veil, as fine as cobweb, a gift for her to wear. She refused to look at it."

"I imagine it's merely nerves, Gabriella."

Gabriella sighed, unable to comprehend such conduct. "I will be downstairs in the salon with my papa," she said. "If you need anything, please ask one of the servants."

She left, and it was my turn to sigh. Em had grown more and more nervous as her wedding day approached, bouts of wild, non-stop chatter alternating with bouts of moody silence. She had flatly refused to come to the rancho this morning, and it had taken me half an hour of frantic persuasion to get her to budge. It was going to take even more to get her downstairs, it seemed. I picked up a flat white leather box from the dressing table, left the room and went down the hall to the master bedroom.

Em sat in a chair upholstered in blue velvet. She didn't look up as I entered. She was wearing the gorgeous white silk gown she had brought from the island. It was embroidered all over with flowers in a deeper white silk, and the full puffed sleeves left her shoulders bare. Her chestnut hair was pulled sleekly from her face and worn in a tight bun in back, a semi-circle of creamy white magnolias fastened to the side of her head. Her mouth was set in a stubborn line, her expression that of a recalcitrant child.

I set the box down and sighed once more.

"It's no use trying to reason with me," she said flatly. "I'm not going through with it, and that's that."

I didn't argue with her but, instead, stepped over to the bed to admire the lace veil Gabriella had mentioned. It was indeed as fine as cobweb, delicate flower patterns spun together in translucent patterns.

"I've got a plan, luv," Em said.

"Oh?"

"Your wagon's all loaded, right? The two of us will slip down the back way and hitch up the horses and make a quick getaway. We'll drive back to the inn, and Jeremy can join us there tomorrow."

"We're really not dressed for it," I observed.

"We'll be on our way back to New Orleans, and all this will be behind us and I can *breathe* again."

"What about Randolph?"

"He gets to keep the rancho."

"I suppose we *could* drive back to the inn in these clothes," I said casually. "I rather looked forward to showing off this gown, but it doesn't really matter. What do you want me to tell Señor Lopez?"

"Tell him—I don't know—tell him I just couldn't—" Em cut herself short, exasperated. "You're not being very *helpful*, luv."

"And you're not being very sensible."

"I can't help it. I'm scared to death!"

"That's perfectly natural."

Em stood up and stomped over to the full-length mirror. She plucked irritably at the full puffed sleeves, her hazel eyes flashing a bright green-brown. Her mouth curled wryly.

"The whole custom's barbaric!" she snapped. "Tying yourself to one man, standing in front of a priest and mouthing silly words. Wearing *white!* Jesus, talk about hypocrisy. The red silk would be far more appropriate. I should never have given it away."

"Are you about finished?" I inquired.

"Jesus, luv, I feel so—"

"I know how you feel," I said gently. "You'll get over it. Try to calm down. We haven't got much time."

Em seemed to droop. "I'm such a coward," she said lamely.

I picked up the veil and moved over to the mirror, standing behind her and meeting her eyes in the glass. She was on the verge of tears now. Carefully, tenderly, I placed the veil over her head and draped it about her shoulders. Em didn't protest. She stood very still, gazing into the mirror with eyes welling. The tears glistened on her lashes.

"You're beautiful," I said. "Breathtakingly beautiful."

"Every bride's beautiful," she retorted, brushing at the tears. "You ever see one who looked frumpy?"

"You're going to be very happy, Em."

She frowned and reached up to adjust the veil. "I'll go through with it," she said, "but if that sonofabitch thinks he is going to *own* me he's sadly mistaken. He gets smart with me once, just *once,* and I take the first wagon back to New Orleans. Do you *really* think I look nice?"

"I really do."

Em sighed and turned away from the mirror. "You'll have to forgive me, luv. I'm not my usual scintillating self today."

I studied her with a critical eye. "The gown's lovely," I remarked, "and the veil is just right, but—" I paused, tilting my head, "something is lacking."

"Lacking?"

"All that white—you need a touch of color."

"You think I could persuade Juanita to give me the dress back?"

429

I ignored her, concentrating, thinking, and then I snapped my fingers. "I have just the thing!" I declared.

I stepped over to the table where I had placed the box when I entered the room. I opened it and took out the shimmering diamond and emerald necklace it contained, the necklace Nicholas had given me when he returned to the island. The emeralds flashed, alive with dancing green fire, and the diamonds surrounding each square-cut emerald seemed to leap with dazzling light.

"This should do it," I said.

"*Jesus*, luv!"

"Put it on, Em."

"I couldn't. Why—why it's worth more than all the loot I brought back put together. It's worth a bloody fortune!"

"It's my wedding gift to you. I have nothing else to give you, and there are plenty more jewels left in my pouch. Here, put it on, darling. I want you to have it."

"I'm going to start crying again. I just know it."

"Don't you dare," I said sternly.

Em put the necklace around her neck and fastened it, and her eyes sparkled almost as brightly as the emeralds. Her full, belling skirt swayed and rustled as she came across the room to hug me tightly, so tightly I gasped, and then we both almost burst into tears. Em stepped back, sighed, and adjusted the veil which had gone askew.

"I guess we might as well go on down now, luv. I'd rather face a firing squad, I don't mind telling you, but I brought this all on myself. I should have told the big oaf to get lost, and I still might do it if he gets too uppity. Take my hand, luv. Hold on tight. I don't want to go tumbling down the stairs head first. Is there time for a quick drink?"

"I'm afraid not, Em."

"Hell, I could use a nice healthy slug of whiskey. Well, here goes, luv. I still think I've taken leave of my senses."

Despite her words she was as cool as could be as we moved down the broad, winding spiral staircase with its carved mahogany banister, and as we stepped into the grand salon to join Señor Lopez and Gabriella, she was the picture of serene composure, a demure smile on her lips. The nervous histrionics might never have occurred. Gabriella handed us our bouquets, Em's identical to mine but twice as large. She held it as a madonna might hold a child, but I had the feeling she longed to chuck it across the room and make a mad dash. Gabriella kissed her cheek and hurried outside in a flurry of pink tulle.

Señor Lopez beamed. Tall, distinguished, with silver-gray hair and a profile that looked as though it belonged on an ancient coin, he wore a black brocade suit with short, Spanish jacket and an emerald-green satin cummerbund. He took Em's hand and lifted it to his lips.

"I've got a terrific idea," she said. "Why don't we forget all this nonsense and run off together? I never could resist a man with silver hair. Why couldn't I have met you *first*, luv?"

Señor Lopez smiled, flattered. The guitars began to twang, and Em gave me a look of panic and rested her arm on Señor Lopez'. They moved slowly out the wide French doors onto the patio. I moved in step behind them as the crowd parted, creating an aisle toward the flower-bedecked altar where Randolph stood, the padre in front of him, Jeremy beside him. The crowd smiled and whispered, full of admiration for the radiant, gorgeously attired bride and the handsome older man who held her arm in his. As we drew nearer the altar I observed that Randolph was as nervous as Em had been, shifting uneasily from foot to foot and looking as though *he* wanted to make a mad dash.

Señor Lopez deposited Em beside the groom and stepped back into the crowd. I took my place at her side. Randolph looked inordinately handsome in his dark charcoal Spanish *vaquero* suit and maroon cummerbund. His golden brown hair was brushed sleekly, gleaming in the late afternoon sunlight, and his eyes were full of panic. Jeremy stood at his side, his blue eyes expressionless, a rich brown wave spilling over his brow. The guitars continued to twang in a low, romantic melody throughout the ceremony, which the padre conducted in Latin. Em and Randolph were both confused. The padre had to whisper his instructions over again in English.

Jeremy handed Randolph the ancient, polished gold band Señor Lopez had provided. Randolph grabbed Em's hand and jammed the ring onto her wedding finger. Em winced and gave him a furious look. The padre completed the ceremony, blessed both of them and told Randolph he could kiss the bride. Randolph seized her in a rough bear hug and slammed his mouth over hers with such nervous force that her head snapped back and she almost lost her veil. The crowd cheered as he bent her at the waist and swung her around. Em pounded on his back and broke free, eyes flashing angrily as she straightened up and adjusted her veil.

"That's all you're getting right now," she hissed, "so just keep your distance. You almost broke my bloody finger when you jammed the ring on it!"

Randolph grinned. "I meant it to stay."

"I didn't understand a word he said. Are you *sure* we're married?"

"We're married, Mrs. Randolph."

"Jesus," Em groaned. "I'm going to rue this day. I just know it!"

Randolph kissed her again, and Em melted against him. The guests roared their approval. Señor Lopez beamed. Marshall and Hurley tossed their hats into the air. Em turned to smile at the guests, her eyes shining, and then she threw her bridal bouquet. Gabriella seemed startled when it landed in her arms. There was another loud cheer. The guitars twanged loudly. Champagne corks popped with the sound of firecrackers. The bride and groom were swept up into the crowd and besieged with noisy congratulations. Festive mayhem prevailed. I put my bouquet down on the altar. Someone handed me a glass of champagne.

The crowd shifted, moving constantly, a bright kaleidoscope of color, everyone babbling merrily, drinking. I caught glimpses of Em and Randolph, Em radiant with cheeks a bright pink and eyes sparkling, Randolph already a bit tipsy as he downed glass after glass of champagne. Marshall pounded him on the back, and Randolph stumbled, grinning foolishly. I finished my champagne, smiling and responding to people who spoke to me but feeling strangely apart. The twanging guitars, the popping corks, the boisterous voices merely intensified this feeling.

I saw Juanita across the patio, plump and jolly in the red silk gown Em had given her. A new pair of earrings dangled from her ears, and she was talking to a tall, good-looking Spanish youth who seemed thoroughly smitten as she chattered and smiled and toyed with her black lace fan. He leaned forward and whispered into her ear. Juanita rapped him sharply on the shoulder with her fan, giggling as she did so. I accepted another glass of champagne from a servant and drank it much too quickly. Jeremy seemed to have disappeared. I hadn't spoken to him all day. I wondered if he was deliberately avoiding me. It didn't matter. Not at all.

I drank the champagne and smiled and talked, and the melancholy feeling grew stronger. I felt trapped amidst all this festivity and desperately longed to escape. Em and Randolph had already left the patio. People were beginning to move through the gardens toward the tables set up on the lawn. Chris came over to me, grave and handsome in a pale tan *vaquero* outfit he had borrowed from one of the men. The sides of the narrow breeches were stitched with brown patterns, as was the short, form-fitting jacket. The shirt beneath was yellow silk, the identical shade of his neatly brushed hair.

"Enjoying yourself?" he inquired.

"I'm trying, Chris."

"Me, too," he replied. "It's not easy."

"I understand you're staying here with Em and Randolph."

Chris nodded, eyes lowered. "I like it here," he said quietly. "There's a lot of room to wander around in, lots of work to keep a man occupied, keep his mind off—things."

I touched his arm lightly. "You're going to do fine, Chris."

"I'll never forget her, Miss Danver. I loved her, and she loved me. I'll always remember."

"She would want you to remember, Chris, and she would want you to be happy. You must try to be happy for her sake."

Chris didn't reply. He was very young, I thought, and although he would always remember Corrie, he would, in time, get over his grief and meet a young woman who would appreciate his special qualities. The light was beginning to fade. The patio was almost deserted. I saw Jeremy strolling through the gardens with a very attractive Spanish señorita in a violet silk gown. There was a magnolia in her hair, and she looked up at him with dark, admiring eyes. He seemed to be enjoying himself immensely.

"Everyone's eating," Chris said. "Shall we join them?"

"I think not, Chris. I'm afraid all this excitement has given me a headache. I think I'll just—be alone for a while."

"Can I bring you a plate?" he asked. "Perhaps something cool to drink?"

I shook my head. "You go ahead, Chris," I said. "Perhaps I'll join you later."

Chris nodded gravely and started toward the lawn. I stood on the patio for a moment, listening to the merry noise coming through the trees. Servants began to clean up the litter and light the colored lanterns as the light faded even more, and others dismantled the altar and carried the flowers away. I left the patio, strolling under the cottonwood trees in the opposite direction, strolling aimlessly away from the house, the music, the oppressive festivity. The land was rolling and green, cottonwoods and pecan trees casting long shadows as the sun went down. I could hear the river ahead. A horse whinnied, galloping across a pasture.

The sky was a pale turquoise blue, gradually fading to gray and streaked with spectacular tangerine- and apricot-colored banners that blazed and melted into golden mist while, above, banks of clouds burned a fiery red-orange. I stood very still, watching the incredibly gorgeous sunset, the most beautiful I had ever seen. Flaming orange and red and gold blazed with majestic splendor as though the sky itself was on fire. The color faded by degrees to a bright rose pink that darkened to maroon, finally bleaching to a pale, pale pink that grew dimmer and dimmer until there was just a faint blush against the gray. That, too, faded as I continued to stroll.

By the time I reached the river everything was gray and black, long velvety shadows lengthening. The moon rose slowly, thin and pale, providing very little light, and the stars were dim, tiny pinpoints of silver that glimmered faintly, barely visible. I could hear music in the distance, the sound soft and muted, a lively Spanish tune not nearly as loud as the rushing swoosh of water. I should go back. I knew that. For Em's sake I should return to the fiesta and dance under the swaying lanterns and pretend an elation I didn't feel. The melancholy I had felt earlier swelled inside.

A deep yearning accompanied it, a curious yearning I couldn't fully define. I felt alone, and lost, and the future loomed ahead a bleak expanse of days with nothing to alleviate the bleakness. I had no one to turn to and nothing to look forward to, and the desire for revenge that had enabled me to go on after Derek's death had deserted me entirely. It had never been an admirable desire, had been, in reality, a foolish pipe dream. Roger Hawke would have his comeuppance, but I would have nothing to do with it. My plan to bury myself at Hawkehouse and devote the rest of my life to Derek's memory was foolish, too. I was alive, alive with every fiber of my being and full of emotions that struggled for release, yet they remained locked up inside, tightly contained for much too long a time. The need, the yearning that plagued me like a physical ache was actually quite easily defined, but I was too proud and too stubborn to acknowledge the truth.

"Thinking of me?" he inquired.

I whirled around, slamming my palm against my heart. Jeremy Bond grinned in the pale moonlight.

"Did I startle you?" he asked.

"I almost had heart failure!"

"Sorry. Guess I didn't make much noise. Learned to move real quiet when I was stalking Indians and such."

"I'm hardly an Indian!"

"I *said* I'm sorry."

"Is that what you were doing—stalking me?"

"I missed you," he said. "One of the servants said he saw you wandering off in this direction. Thought I'd come look for you."

"I'm surprised you could tear yourself away," I said acidly.

"Oh, you must have seen Dolores, the girl in the violet gown. Her father has one of the biggest ranchos in the territory, richer than Croesus, I understand. Chap's shopping for a son-in-law."

"What a marvelous opportunity for you."

"Dolores is a beautiful girl," he admitted, "but she doesn't speak a word of English. My Spanish is rotten."

"I don't imagine you'd have too much trouble communicating."

The grin still curled on his lips, and his eyes were full of teasing mockery. I longed to slap him silly. He was so insufferably handsome in the moonlight in the tobacco-brown *vaquero* outfit with its silver studs and dark blue embroidery. The breeches were very narrow, the short jacket form-fitting, accentuating broad shoulders and slender waist. The blue silk bandana was knotted around his neck.

"I left the fiesta because I wanted to be alone," I said, emphasizing the last word.

"Can't have you wandering about like this," he replied. "Much too dangerous."

"I suppose you're going to tell me there are Indians."

"None that I know of, but there are rattlesnakes. Coyotes, too."

"Coyotes?"

"Vicious animals. Travel in packs."

"Only in wintertime," I said, "when they're looking for food. And rattlesnakes are more prevalent farther west, where it's hotter and drier."

"Where'd you hear that?"

"Em told me. She checked before she bought the rancho."

"Okay, so I merely wanted to be with you. Is that a crime?"

I was at a loss for an answer. Jeremy moved closer, his broad cheekbones polished with moonlight, shadows beneath them. His lips were parted, and his eyes were very dark. He smelled of soap and leather and a woody scent I recognized as pine. Behind him, far, far in the distance, I could see the swaying splotches of color from the lanterns hung around the patio. Music drifted across the night, lilting now, very faint. The dancing had begun.

"Shouldn't you be dancing with Dolores?" I inquired.

"Probably should be," he said. "Poor girl will pine. I'd rather be with you."

"I—I'm not in the mood for company."

"That's too bad."

"Jeremy—"

"Look, lass, you wanna fight, we'll fight, but I intend to stick close by your side. I've missed you."

"Indeed?"

"A lot," he said.

A lovely, tremulous feeling shimmered to life inside of me, welling up and making me almost giddy. I sternly repressed it, irritated with myself and irritated with him. Jeremy smiled and took my arm, and we turned away from the river. I went along willingly enough, but I held my chin high nevertheless. Instead of heading back toward the rancho, we moved across a gently rolling pasture, a line of trees in the distance. I frowned, fully intending to protest, but for some reason the words remained unspoken.

It was completely dark now, and the stars that had been silver pinpoints before were blazing, thousands of stars blinking radiantly against the dark black sky. I had never seen such stars, flashing, sparkling, glimmering bright and so close it seemed I could reach up and touch them. There was a warm, gentle breeze. My skirts billowed lightly. The bandana around Jeremy's neck flapped against the lapel of his jacket.

"The stars are gorgeous," I said. "They're so big."

"Yeah, they're something. I like to sleep under them."

"Oh?"

"Fixed me up a place, a heap of straw, some blankets. I'll show you."

"I really don't think—"

I paused, slowing my step, and his hand tightened on my arm. I tried to pull free. He gave my arm a jerk. I stumbled. We had reached the trees now, and he led me through them, limbs groaning overhead, leaves rustling, blotting out the stars. I was angry, irritated, afraid, and that glorious, giddy feeling was stronger than ever. I felt as though I had drunk a whole bottle of the finest champagne. We entered a small clearing, completely surrounded by trees, and the stars flashed and gleamed overhead again.

Jeremy released my arm. In the light of the stars his face was grim and determined, the mouth set in a firm line, his eyes dark under lowered brows. I knew the time had come, knew it would be useless to protest, and I didn't really want to. I wanted him to pull me into his arms. I wanted him to hold me tightly, so tightly I would forget my doubts, my fears, forget everything but feeling. I was tired of thinking, tired of fighting, tired of being strong. I wanted to love him—I already loved him—but I was still afraid of the commitment. I couldn't bear to be hurt again.

"You planned this?" I said.

"I've been planning it for a long time."

"I—"

"You want it, too, Marietta."

"I—I'm afraid."

"Of me?"

I didn't answer. I folded my arms at my waist, clutching tightly, afraid of the emotions that threatened to overwhelm me, desperately trying to remain aloof, above feeling, to use my head and avoid disaster. Behind him, in the middle of the clearing, I saw the small pile of hay covered with blankets. He had planned this very carefully, knowing full well the rancho was too crowded to allow us privacy. Starlight filled the clearing with a fine silvery haze. The makeshift bed looked soft, inviting. I was so weak I could barely stand. My knees, at any moment, were going to give way.

"Love me," he crooned. "Love me, Marietta."

"I can't," I said. My voice was surprisingly cool, my manner composed. "I can't—I won't allow myself to—to love anyone. I've been hurt, Jeremy. I couldn't bear it if—"

He pulled me to him and placed a hand over my mouth, silencing me.

"Ah, lass, do you think I could ever hurt you? Do you think I could ever cause you pain?"

His voice was low and melodious and soothing, beautiful. He removed his hand from my lips and curled his fingers lightly around my chin, tilting my head back. I looked up into those dark, determined eyes, fighting the weakness that had become a sweet, seductive ache in my blood, in my bones. He curled his left arm around my waist, drawing me nearer, and his warmth and strength seemed to envelop me. His lips parted in a thoughtful half-smile.

"There've been times, true, when I've longed to shake you," he continued, each word a husky caress. "I've never known a lass so stubborn, so proud, so willful. You're infuriating, exasperating, and I love you—ah, lass, I love you to the point of distraction."

"Don't," I whispered. "We need to—to talk."

He shook his head. "I'm tired of talking. I'm tired of being patient. I want you. I intend to have you—now."

There was a stern note in his voice, and his face was suddenly hard. Leaves rustled. He tilted his head to one side and lowered his mouth until his lips brushed mine. Then his arms crushed me to him and I was lost, utterly lost. He kissed me as I had never been kissed before, with a passionate frenzy that mounted and mounted. I clung to his back, caught his hair with my fingers, and tugged, fighting still, but it was futile, futile, and I didn't really want him to stop.

I was whirling, drowning in sensations that were bright and new and blazing inside me. Never, never had it been like this, and I was afraid now that he might release me, that the cool, sensible Marietta would return and ruin the happiness that had been within my grasp for so long. This was meant to be, I told myself. This man, this moment, this magical glory that swept all reason aside. My lips parted. I melted against him, pliant, submissive, no longer my own person, his, completely his. He made a moaning noise in his throat, thrust his tongue into my mouth, and held me so tightly I gasped.

The kiss lasted for a blissful eternity that was all too short, and then he grasped my upper arms and lifted his head and looked into my eyes. I would have fallen had he not been holding me so firmly. He kissed my lids, my cheeks, my chin, my throat, tenderly now, murmuring soft words that were even sweeter than the tender touch of his lips. I was trembling, and my eyes were moist with tears. Jeremy led me over to the pile of hay covered with blankets. I stumbled, so weak I could barely walk. Arms curled around me, he kissed me again, passionate frenzy restrained but still there, deliberately, painfully held back.

"I've been waiting," he murmured.

"And—and I."

"Too long, it's been too long. I should have taken you that first night in New Orleans."

I turned, gazing up at the stars, and, behind me, he curled an arm around my throat and kissed my temple. With his free hand he began to undo the back of my gown. The bodice loosened, fell forward, the sleeves slipping down to my elbows. His arm was warm and strong, a tender bar across my throat, and with his lips brushing my earlobe he cupped his hand around my left breast, his fingers digging beneath the frail cloth of my petticoat to grasp and squeeze, his palm rubbing across the nipple that swelled and hardened, hurting. He caught my lobe between his teeth and nibbled gently, and I closed my eyes, whirling in a delirium that threatened to eclipse consciousness. I may actually have fainted for a moment, for when I opened my eyes he was in front of me, holding me up and slipping the sleeves from my arms.

I managed to stand while he fumbled with the blue silk, clumsily removing the gown. I stepped out of the circle of silk and, wearing only the frail petticoat, collapsed into his arms. He kissed me again, a long, lingering kiss, his lips firm, warm, his throat working as he moved his head from side to side with lips locked on mine. The sensations inside blazed, the sweet ache a torment now, each moment of delay exquisite torture. He moaned and drew back and parted his lips, flattening them against the edge of his teeth. He made a low growling noise, a splendid male animal, reason gone, driven away by the savage urge throbbing inside him.

He caught my shoulders and lowered me onto the blankets. The hay beneath them crackled, rustling crisply. The pallet was soft. I arched my back, every fiber of my being aching for fulfillment. He removed his jacket, tossed it aside, and unfastened his belt and began to fumble with the buttons in front of his trousers. I sighed, aching, writhing on the blankets and lifting my arms. Jeremy scowled, impatient, too impatient to finish undressing. He knelt down and raised the hem of my petticoat and lowered himself on me, entering me with a forceful thrust that made me cry out.

Pinioned beneath him, crushed by his weight, I spread my legs and wrapped my arms around his back, my fingers tearing at the silk of his shirt. Jeremy Bond filled me, pulsating inside me, moving, thrusting, strong as steel and soft as velvet, the torment unbearable, growing, growing, building as he thrust deeper and deeper and the dam of sensation weakened, crumbling, a flood of feeling ready to drown us both. He growled again, sinking his teeth into the soft flesh of my shoulder, his body tense, rigid atop mine as the moment of release drew nearer, nearer.

When he had scaled the highest peak, when he hung suspended over the abyss of ecstacy, he paused, deliberately, waiting for me. I shredded his silk shirt with my nails and moaned, moving beneath him, wrapping my legs around him, and that great dam of sensation began to give, began to topple. I opened my eyes and stared up at the stars flashing, glittering, dancing with silvery brilliance. He dove into me with one final thrust and broke the dam. Tumultuous waves of sensation swept over us, and it seemed all the stars in the sky exploded inside me. I cried out, clinging to him as wave after wave crashed, and Jeremy shuddered violently, finally growing limp as we washed to shore.

We made love again and yet again, and when, depleted, I lay in his arms, I knew a peace such as I had never known before. He slept, limp, heavy, breathing deeply, half atop me still, and I reveled in his weight and his warmth and the strong, virile scent of his flesh. I stroked his hair, so thick, so silky, and he made a grumpy, grunting noise and snuggled closer, pulling me nearer, throwing a leg over mine. I smiled, the ashes of aftermath still glowing beautifully inside me. I looked over his shoulder at the stars. They were beginning to fade now, slowly disappearing as a faint pink blush touched the sky.

Slowly, carefully, I pushed him off of me. He grunted again, rolling heavily to one side. The hay crackled beneath the blankets. I climbed to my feet and stretched, languorous, my limbs aching with a lovely ache. I adjusted my petticoat and retrieved my gown, slipping it on, fastening it in back. I straightened the bodice and smoothed the skirt down and ran my fingers through my hair. He sat up, blinking in the early morning light.

"We'd better get back to the rancho," I said.

"Yeah," he said. "I suppose so."

He brushed a heavy wave from his brow, rubbed his eyes and got to his feet, wobbling just a little. He did up his trousers and fastened his belt. I handed him his jacket. He put it on, wearing a sheepish grin, and then he pulled me to him and gave me a long, lazy kiss. I pulled away, smiling, and he shook his head and yawned. We started back toward the rancho, moving slowly through the trees and across the rolling pasture as the pink faded to a pale gold and a bird warbled sleepily.

"Happy?" he inquired.

"I've never been happier."

"It's gonna be this way from now on," he promised.

"Yes," I murmured.

"We belong together, Marietta."

"Yes."

"The future is ours."

I nodded, moving along beside him, my step light, youthful, all the weight of the past years lifted from my shoulders. I had made the commitment, and it was right. With Jeremy Bond I would begin a whole new life. I smiled, believing again in happy endings. I could see the rancho in the distance. I could hardly wait to tell Em of my newfound happiness.

"I guess you've put that nonsense about Roger Hawke out of your mind," he said.

"That—that belongs to the past, Jeremy."

"Just as well," he remarked. "Roger Hawke is dead."

I was startled. I stopped. Jeremy looked at me.

"He got his, Marietta. He was murdered. Two weeks after that night on the docks he was shot to death in an alley in New Orleans."

"Who did it?" I asked.

Jeremy hesitated, suddenly uncomfortable. He looked down at his boots, not wanting to answer.

"Who killed him, Jeremy?"

Jeremy lifted his head, frowning. His eyes held mine for a moment, and then he gazed at the rancho, still hesitant.

"His cousin shot him," he said.

"His cousin? But—"

"Derek Hawke murdered him."

The ground seemed to give way beneath me. I started to reel. He grabbed my shoulders, supporting me. I shook my head, refusing to believe what I had heard. Jeremy held my shoulders tightly, and it was several moments before the dizzy sensation receded. I felt cold, icy cold. His eyes were dark with concern when he saw the expression on my face.

"He wasn't killed, Marietta. He was wounded, badly wounded in the shoulder. A couple of sailors fished him out of the water. He was barely alive. They found a doctor. The doctor patched him up, kept him for over two weeks. Hawke was in a delirium most of the time. When he was finally able to be up and about, he set off in search of his cousin."

"He—he thought I was dead."

"I don't know what he thought. He found Roger Hawke. He killed him. He took the next boat to England. All this

442

happened before I returned to New Orleans. Hart told me about it before I crushed his windpipe.''

''You knew,'' I whispered. ''All along you knew—''

''Hawke left for England,'' he said sternly. ''He made no effort to find you. I'm the one who tracked you down. I'm the one who—''

''He thought I was dead! He wouldn't have gone if he—''

''He doesn't deserve you! You belong to me!''

I swung my arm back and brought my palm across his face with all the force I could muster. The slap exploded loudly. My palm throbbed. I felt certain I had broken my wrist.

''I'll never forgive you!'' I cried. ''Never!''

I turned and ran toward the rancho as fast as I could, my skirts billowing about my legs, my eyes blind with tears. I ran, stumbling, sobbing, leaving behind the shards of a beautiful dream that had been broken into a thousand jagged pieces.

BOOK FOUR
The Beloved

Twenty-Nine

The road was long and narrow and dusty, and the oak trees on either side spread heavy boughs overhead, creating a shadowy tunnel. Ghostly streamers of Spanish moss hung down like tattered gray veils, waving slightly in the breeze. Only a few rays of sunlight seeped through the thick canopy of boughs, wavering columns of pale yellow aswirl with motes of dust. The crude wooden wagon creaked noisily. The two stout gray horses plodded on patiently, unaware that we would soon reach our destination and the ordeal would be over.

I sat on the raised front seat beside Jeremy Bond, stiff, silent, aloof, as I had been ever since we had left the rancho almost three weeks ago. He was relaxed, nonchalant, clicking the reins every now and then and indifferent to my icy hauteur. At the beginning of our journey he had made a few feeble attempts to bring me round, to establish some kind of rapport, but they had been futile. I had made it quite clear that I tolerated his company only because it was absolutely necessary and that I wished to have nothing whatsoever to do with him. He finally accepted things with a weary resignation and made no more attempts at reconciliation.

The trip had been long, arduous, extremly uncomfortable, but I had refused to bend. There had been days on end when we had not seen another soul. We had slept out in the open, huddling under the blankets, close to each other physically but miles apart. I had done my share. I had helped gather firewood. I had cooked the meals, cleaned the utensils, packed and unpacked the wagon. When, after a rainstorm, the wagon had bogged down in the mud, I had helped get it unstuck, pushing with all my might at the back as Jeremy pulled on the reins. We had forded rivers, had trudged up hills, guiding the horses on foot, had shared all the hardships without my once giving way.

We spoke only when it was absolutely necessary. My voice was invariably icy and crisp with contempt. Jeremy pretended to ignore my tone, unperturbed, acting as though nothing had happened. On the rare occasions when we had been fortunate enough to find an inn along the road, we had dined together and shared a room, Jeremy lolling in a chair or on the floor while I slept in the bed. The intimacy we had shared under the stars the night of Em's wedding might never have happened. We might have been strangers, thrown together by circumstances and barely civil.

We had ferried across the Mississippi earlier this morning. We would be in New Orleans before nightfall. I would take a room and sell the jewels and, somehow, get a berth to England. Derek was alive. Derek was in England. He would be living at Hawkehouse, alone, lost, desolate, convinced the woman he loved was dead. I couldn't dwell on that or, I knew, I would go mad. I must be cool, patient. It would be weeks, perhaps months before we were reunited, and I would have to take it a day at a time.

The only man I had ever loved was alive. . . . I wanted to seize the reins and urge the horses forward at a mad gallop. I wanted to leap from the wagon and run. The thought of him alone there in that great house, grieving, could, if I let it, drive me into a frenzy. I kept tight control of my emotions. That was the only way I could endure the delays. Each day brought me nearer and nearer to that reunion, and I had to be satisfied with that. Sitting on the hard wooden seat beside a man I detested, I smoothed down the skirt of the pale tan dress sprigged with tiny rust-brown and orange flowers, the dress Juanita had given me. It was worn and dusty now, a jagged tear in the hem revealing the limp, ruffled petticoat beneath.

The wagon bumped over a deep hole in the road. It wobbled dangerously. I prayed we wouldn't lose another wheel. One had fallen off several days ago, and it had taken

Jeremy hours and hours to repair it and put it back on. We had lost a full day of travel. I couldn't endure another delay now, not when we were so close to our destination. I brushed a lank, dirty copper-red wave from my cheek and held on to the seat as we moved over yet another hole, careful not to fall against the man beside me. I sat as far away from him as possible and, chin held high, pretended he wasn't even there.

Derek was alive. Derek was the only man I had ever loved, truly loved. Any feelings I might have had for Jeremy Bond had been . . . an aberration, brought about by proximity and an unusual set of circumstances. I had seen him for what he was from the beginning, a charming rogue, a handsome, ruthless scoundrel, and I had staunchly resisted him. I had resisted him with all my might until . . . until my own sense of loss and my gratitude toward him had caused me temporarily to abandon judgment. I had given myself to him at last, only to learn of his treachery.

He had known all along. He had let me go on thinking Derek was dead. He had deceived me, all the while pressing his case, wooing me with his charm, his tenderness, his bravery, making a fool of me. He had saved my life, yes, on more than one occasion, and I was grateful to him for that. He would be well paid. When I sold the jewels I would give him half the money. Half? I would give him more. I would give him everything except what it would take to pay my fare to England. Money didn't matter. The only thing that mattered was getting to England, and I didn't want to be beholden to Jeremy Bond in any way. He had risked his life repeatedly to rescue me and bring me to safety, and he was going to be a very wealthy man.

A dangling strand of moss brushed my cheek. The wagon rocked from side to side, creaking, the tail end bumping. Up ahead, in the distance, I could see another wagon approaching us. It was similar to ours and piled high with furniture and household goods, mattress, chairs, boxes, a birdcage. Three small children rode in back, clinging to the furniture. A thin woman in a faded pink dress sat in front, holding the reins. The man who sat beside her was thin, too, almost emaciated, his gray coat hanging loosely. He leaned against her, his head resting wearily on her shoulder.

As the wagon drew nearer, the woman eyed us with great

suspicion, her mouth tight. She pulled the horses over to the far side of the road, as far away from us as possible. Jeremy lifted an arm in salute. The woman pretended not to see it, clutching the reins tightly and urging the horses on. Her green eyes glittered with something almost like fear. As the wagon passed ours, the children stared at us with sad, haunted eyes. The man up front never even raised his head. How strange, I thought. Strange, too, that this was the only vehicle we had seen since we had ferried across the river.

I frowned, puzzled. I had been so immersed in my thoughts that I hadn't noticed the lack of traffic. There should have been coaches, wagons, rigs, fine carriages. This road was ordinarily a busy thoroughfare, the main road between New Orleans and Natchez and all points in between. This close to New Orleans it should have been teeming, yet the wagon with its strange occupants was the only one we had passed. The children had seemed listless. The man had seemed ill. The woman driving had definitely been afraid of us, had acted as though she had expected us to stop her and bar the way.

I glanced at Jeremy. He was puzzled, too. A deep frown creased his brow. I longed to discuss my concern with him, but pride prevented me from saying anything. I stared straight ahead and continued to ignore his existence. There was undoubtedly a perfectly logical explanation for the lack of traffic, and the family on the wagon had probably been tenant farmers who had lost their place on one of the plantations. That would explain the pile of furniture and the woman's peculiar behavior. I put it out of my mind, shifting my position on the miserably hard wooden seat I had grown to loathe these past weeks.

I was getting hungry. Eager to catch the first ferry, we had foregone breakfast, and it must be almost noon now. There was food in back, cheese, bread, hard sausage, fruit, even a bottle of cheap red wine, all purchased at the inn we had stayed in two nights ago. I contemplated fetching an apple and eating it as we rode, but once again pride prevented it. When he was ready to stop for lunch, he would stop, and hell would freeze before I would suggest it. He was certainly as hungry as I was, more so probably, for he had an extremely hearty appetite.

Another half-hour passed before he finally pulled over to the side of the road. He climbed down, fetched two bags of oats and began to feed the horses. I got down without assistance, catching the hem of my skirt on a nailhead in the process and tearing it even more. Intent on the horses, Jeremy didn't even look up as he heard the cloth shredding. Irritated, stiff and sore from the long, uncomfortable ride, I took the food basket from the back of the wagon and stepped between the oaks, moving down the grassy slope beyond that led to the muddy bank of the river.

The great Mississippi moved sluggishly, terribly wide, the greenish-brown water slapping the banks. There was no traffic, no boats, no barges, no rafts. That was odd, too, but I was too hungry to give it much mind. The proprietress of the inn had, for a hefty price, packed the basket generously. The fried apricot pies were already gone, as were the hard-boiled eggs and the roast chicken. I removed the blue and white checked cloth from the top of the basket and spread it out on the grass, then took out food, wine, a knife, and two glasses.

I sat down and sliced bread, cheese, and sausage. Jeremy joined me a few minutes later. I poured wine into a glass and handed it to him without speaking. I placed cheese and sausage between two slices of bread, placed it on a napkin and handed him that, too. We ate in silence. The river flowed with a monotonous, sloshing sound. Birds twittered in the oak boughs. As I finished my wine, a swarm of butterflies fluttered nearby, their delicate wings a golden yellow in the sunlight. It was very peaceful and serene here by the river. If only it weren't spoiled by the presence of Jeremy Bond.

I glanced at him. He had finished eating, too. He was staring at me with solemn blue eyes, his expression stern. Afraid he was going to speak, I hastily put the things back into the basket and stood up. I folded the table cloth, put it on top of the food and then strolled down to the edge of the river, praying he would have the good judgment to leave me be. Several moments passed before I felt rather than heard him approaching. I didn't turn. I stiffened my back, clenching my hands at my sides.

"Don't you think this has gone on long enough?" he inquired.

I continued to stare across the river, intently studying the mossy logs that littered the opposite bank and pretending that Jeremy Bond did not exist. Wisps of hair blew about my temples. My skirt billowed in the breeze. I heard a heavy, exasperated sigh and waited for him to walk away. He didn't. He seized my shoulders and whirled me around to face him.

I was appalled. My eyes flashed with anger. I broke free and swung my hand back, fully intending to smash it across his mouth, but he caught my wrist in a powerful grip and twisted it so savagely that I gasped. His vivid blue eyes were unperturbed, his handsome face without expression. When I tried to pull away, he gave my wrist another twist. Needles of pain shot up my arm. I bit my lower lip, refusing to yield.

"I've had about all I'm gonna take," he said calmly.

"Go to hell!"

"I mean it, Marietta. This nonsense is—" He grimaced, searching for the right words. "I've put up with all I intend to. I've let you pout and sulk and act the icy aristocrat—I've indulged you, yeah, because I figured you needed a little time to get your thoughts together, but, by God, I'm not havin' any more of it."

"You're hurting me!"

"I'm fully aware of that."

He gave my wrist another savage twist. I kicked his shin. He released me and looked at me for a long, menacing moment before shoving me viciously into the river. I landed with a loud splash, immediately drenched, muddy waves engulfing me. Livid, spluttering, I tried to stand but couldn't get a footing in the slippery river bottom. I fell again, completely submerged, dress and petticoat turning into leaden coils that pulled me down. I thrashed and got my head out of the water and coughed, shoving sodden waves from my eyes.

Jeremy Bond stood calmly on the bank, watching me with those cool, expressionless eyes. The sonofabitch is going to let me drown! I thought, and I would drown willingly before I'd let him help me. I planted my feet as firmly as I could on the muddy bottom, managed to stand, and then took a step toward the bank, only to fall again. It was a full five minutes before I was finally able to crawl up on the bank. Dazed, drenched, panting, I rested for several moments before climbing to my feet.

Jeremy Bond hadn't moved. His face was still expressionless, but the faintest suggestion of a grin was beginning to curl on his lips. The fury I had felt earlier had vanished entirely. An icy calm possessed me as I straightened the wet, clinging bodice of my dress and began to wring out my skirts.

"You okay?" he asked.

I hesitated, thinking, and then I nodded weakly. "I'm fine," I said, closing my eyes. I reeled just a little, staggering. "I—I feel a bit faint."

I started to swoon, and he gallantly rushed over to grab me. I sidestepped nimbly and got behind him and slapped my palms against his shoulder blades and shoved with all my might. Jeremy Bond pitched face forward into the water with a startled yelp. I stood there for a moment, watching him thrash about, and then I sauntered slowly back up the slope, retrieved the food basket and took it back to the wagon. The horses were still lazily munching oats from the bags Jeremy had hung over their heads. A wavering ray of sunlight slanted across the road.

I dug into my bag and removed towel, brush, shoes, a plain white cotton petticoat and the pale violet-blue cotton dress Juanita had found for me before I left the inn. Leaving the wagon, I sauntered through the oaks until I located a large clump of shrubbery. I removed my wet clothes, draped them over the shrubs and, completely naked, began to towel myself dry. I was still calm and strangely serene. The intense hostility I had nourished these past weeks was gone, for some reason, and I felt nothing but indifference toward Jeremy Bond.

Half an hour passed before I returned to the wagon. My hair was dry, and I had brushed it until it fell in thick, gleaming waves. The pale violet-blue dress fit snugly at bosom and waist, the full skirt spreading out over the multilayered petticoat. I felt clean, refreshed, revived as I put the still damp clothes back into the wagon and dropped the mud-encrusted shoes beside them. Jeremy had removed the bags of oats from the horses' heads and was sitting up on the seat, the reins in his lap and a sullen look on his face.

He hadn't changed clothes. His shirt had dried but his breeches were still wet, clinging to his legs. His boots were muddy, and there was a streak of mud across his cheek. His hair was damp, too, a mass of dark brown tendrils plastered over his brow. I couldn't resist a smile. He curled his lip and looked at me with venomous blue eyes. I caught hold of the seat and pulled myself up beside him, affecting an airy indifference that caused him to gnash his teeth. I glanced at him, amused. He scowled.

"Don't you think we'd better press on?" I inquired.

"That was a nasty trick you pulled back there," he muttered.

"Sure was," I said.

"I wouldn't of thought it of you."

"You don't know me very well, Mr. Bond. I rather hoped you'd drown."

"I almost did!"

"Pity."

"Goddamnit, Marietta—"

"If you're too upset to drive, I'll gladly take the reins. I'd like to reach New Orleans before evening."

Jeremy Bond gave the reins a savage click. The horses began to plod forward. The wagon creaked. I sighed, feeling better than I had felt in a long time. Impatience and animosity were behind me, and I felt something that was almost akin to happiness. I wondered now why I had been so cold and silent and thorny. Jeremy Bond wasn't worth the effort. I'd soon see the last of him, and that was something to look forward to. I sighed again, swaying as the wagon rocked.

"Are you ready to talk?" he asked.

"We have nothing to talk about, Mr. Bond."

My voice was light, casual. He tightened his grip on the reins.

"You're the most unreasonable woman I've ever encountered!"

"That's your misfortune," I said airily.

"Anything I did, I did because I happen to love you."

"I don't care to discuss it."

"You love me, too, goddamnit."

I turned, looking at him with utter disdain. He was frowning deeply. His hair was beginning to dry now, fluffing into feathery wisps. His jaw was set, his mouth a straight, determined line.

"You're quite mistaken, Mr. Bond."

, "That night in the clearing—"

"That night was an aberration. It meant nothing whatsoever."

He lashed angrily at a strand of moss that brushed his cheek. "You're lying!"

"Think what you like. I don't intend to argue with you."

Jeremy did his best to control his emotions. He took a deep breath and held it for a moment. His hands clenched the reins so tightly that his knuckles were white. He breathed deeply, evenly, forcing the tension away, and after a short while he sighed, in control now. When he spoke, his voice was normal, his tone matter-of-fact.

"All right, Marietta, I knew Derek Hawke was alive. I admit that. I knew all along, and I guess maybe I should of told you, but I didn't. I kept it from you deliberately, but I had my reasons."

"I'm not at all interested in your reasons."

"He doesn't deserve you. He never did. He bought you, treated you like a slave, and when you displeased him, he sold you to Jeff Rawlins, fully believing you'd end up in a brothel in New Orleans."

"He was angry. He—"

"Later on, he took up with you again," he continued, still speaking in that calm, emotionless voice. "You belonged to another man, but he wanted you and he took you and then abandoned you after Jeff Rawlins died."

"He came back for me."

"And told you he intended to marry you—and didn't. He never intended to marry you. Derek Hawke marry the illegitimate daughter of an aristocrat and a barmaid? Unthinkable."

"You don't know anything about it. He—"

"He made you his mistress, and he planned to take you back to England as such, but he wasn't going to marry you, Marietta. Once he got you back to England he would have set you up in London. He would have delayed, procrastinated, made excuses until finally, one day, he would have explained to you all the reasons why marriage was out of the question."

I paid no attention to his words. He was desperate now, trying to cover his own guilt, and he understood nothing whatsoever about the situation. Derek loved me. He loved me. He had proved it over and over again, and had it not been for his cousin Roger we would have been married long since and living happily at Hawkehouse. Jeremy Bond wanted me for himself and would stop at nothing. He was deliberately trying to destroy my faith in Derek, I saw that, and it wasn't going to work.

"When he recovered from his wounds, Hawke assumed you were dead, and he had one thing and one thing only on his mind—revenge. He tracked down Roger Hawke. He shot him. He returned to England to take over his inheritance, and—"

"He thought I was dead. He almost died himself. He—"

"He made no effort to verify it. He made no effort to find you."

"I'm not going to listen to—"

"If he had loved you the way you claim, he would have moved heaven and earth until he found you. I *did*."

"I'm grateful for what you did," I said coldly.

"I don't want your gratitude!"

"And I intend to see that you are well paid for any inconvenience."

"God *damn!*" he exclaimed. "Why I didn't strangle you to death a long time ago I'll never know!"

He fell silent then, and that suited me perfectly. I smoothed down my skirt, stared at the dusty brown road and the ghostly gray strands of Spanish moss and the slanting rays of sunlight. We would be in New Orleans soon. I would pay him off, and it would all be over. I wasn't going to let him upset me again, not at this point. I would stoically endure his presence as long as it was necessary, and then I would start my journey to England and never give Jeremy Bond another single thought.

Half an hour passed, perhaps more, the horses plodding patiently, the wagon creaking, bouncing, the flat wooden bed shaking from side to side as the wheels bumped over potholes. The pungent smell of the river was ever present, mud and moss and water blending to form a strong, not unpleasant, odor. I was beginning to grow weary again, already, and it seemed I had spent half my life on this damnably uncomfortable wooden seat. How wonderful it was going to be to have a room in the city, a proper bed, a proper bath, a hot meal prepared by an excellent chef. Jeremy Bond sighed. He was weary, too.

"Would you like for me to take the reins?" I asked, prepared to be civil.

"No need for that," he snapped, and then he looked at me and frowned. "I'm sorry, didn't mean to bite your head off."

"That's quite all right," I said coldly.

"Look, I said I'm sorry. I have a lot of things on my mind. I've got the feeling something's wrong."

"What do you mean?"

"We're the only wagon on the road, have been for hours. We can't be more than a few miles from the city, and there's absolutely no traffic. No one's leaving New Orleans."

"That family a while back—"

"Something wrong there, too. The man looked ill. The woman looked scared to death. There might be a perfectly logical explanation, of course, but somehow I doubt it. We'll soon find out, at any rate."

His voice was grave. His expression was grave, too, and I felt a dreadful sinking sensation inside. Something *was* wrong. I had sensed it much earlier in the day. We had been away from civilization so long, had been completely out of touch with what was going on. Had the terrible conflict raging up north finally reached this part of the world? Was there fighting in New Orleans? Had the city been taken over by troops, a blockade set up? Try though I might to banish it, my apprehension grew, and when, a short while later, I saw the barricade ahead, I knew my worst fears had been realized.

It was a very crude barricade, flimsy wooden boxes and old sawhorses piled untidily across the road, three mothy-looking mattresses heaped on top. Two men paraded back and forth, ancient muskets resting on their shoulders. One of them was a shambling giant with tattered, dirty gold locks. His nose was broken, his brown eyes fierce, his demeanor extremely menacing. He must have been at least six-foot-seven. The other man was thin and bony, almost emaciated, his face pitted with pockmarks. His black hair was clipped close to his skull, and, as the wagon drew nearer, he glared at us with cold gray-blue eyes as hard and lifeless as marbles.

"They look like pirates," I whispered. "Surely they're not soldiers."

"They're not soldiers," Jeremy said tersely. "Keep calm, Marietta. Let me handle this."

"Halt!" the blond giant bellowed.

The man with the pockmarked face leveled his musket at us. Jeremy calmly tugged on the reins, bringing the horses to a full stop a few feet away from the barricade. I gripped the edge of the seat, curling my fingers tightly around the wood, trying to still my alarm. Jeremy seemed to be completely unperturbed, even when the bony man thrust his musket forward.

"You want to be careful with that," Jeremy remarked. "It might go off."

"Turn that wagon around, mister," the man ordered. "Ain't no one gettin' past us. Ain't no one enterin' New Orleans, ain't no one leavin' either."

"Would you mind telling me what this is all about?"

"Th' fevah," the giant growled. "Fevah's been ragin' over a week now an' folks're droppin' like flies. Hogan an' me, we got orders. We got orders to shoot anyone who tries to get past us."

"Yeah," Hogan agreed in a sepulchral voice. "Me an' Flint, we shoot first an' then ask questions. I told ja to turn that wagon around, mister, an' you better get movin', lessen ya wanna get your guts blown out."

Jeremy arched one brow. I couldn't tell if he were angry or amused. The blond, Flint, stepped over to the wagon, his mouth twisting in a sullen curl. Both men were obviously illiterate, dregs of humanity hired for a paltry sum to do a job no one else would take. Both were obviously vicious, too, and, invested with a small amount of authority, full of self-importance. Neither of them had bathed for several weeks, that was painfully evident, and their clothes were filthy. Flint's brown and yellow striped jersey looked ready to disintegrate, and his brown cord breeches were caked with dried mud, as were his boots.

"Ya better do as Hogan tells ya," he said. "Hogan, he gets impatient, gets real ugly."

Jeremy ignored this remark and turned to face me. "The fever," he said. "You know what that means?"

I nodded. Although I had never been through an epidemic during my years in New Orleans, I had heard chilling tales about the dreaded fever that turned the whole city into a charnel house, with thousands dying, particularly those in the congested slum areas. It struck without warning, picking its victims at random. Men in the bloom of health died in a matter of days, while others remained completely unscathed. I had heard of the white crosses painted across the doors of houses where there was illness, of wagons rattling through the city piled high with corpses to be deposited in trenches that served as community graves. I had heard of the looting and lawlessness that always prevailed during times of crisis, the criminal element taking full advantage.

"I know what it means," I said.

"We'll have to turn back. We can go to Natchez, stay there until the worst is over."

"No," I said.

"Marietta—"

"We'd lose weeks, and I don't intend to lose a single day. I feel quite sure these—these gentlemen are not incorruptible. The other wagon got past the barricade. It probably cost them every penny they had, but they got past. We have money."

"That's not the point—"

"Ain't no one gettin' past me an' Hogan," Flint snarled. "You two keep chattin', you're gonna find yourselves in trouble. Turn that wagon around!"

Jeremy glanced at the man with a complete lack of interest, as he might have glanced at a mildly worrisome insect. Flint scowled, mouth twisted beneath the broken nose, brown eyes filled with a savage gleam. Hogan, however, had lowered his musket. At the mention of money his whole demeanor had changed.

"Let's not be too hasty, Flint," he drawled. "These folks might have important reasons for gettin' into the city. We don't wanna be unreasonable about it. Might be an emergency or somethin'."

"Think they can bribe us!" Flint bellowed. "Think we're gonna let 'em get past us for a handful a pennies!"

" 'Magine they're thinkin' bigger 'n that. 'Magine they'd be willin' to pay a lot."

"We're turning back," Jeremy told me. "I don't mind taking the risk myself, but I'm not going to expose you to danger. We'll lose a few weeks, yes, but in the long run—"

"You go to Natchez if you want to," I said calmly. "I'm going on into the city."

"No you're not. I can't let you expose yourself to—"

"It's not your decision!" I snapped.

"Listen, goddamnit, you have no idea what it's like when there's an epidemic. It's too risky!"

"How much do you gentlemen want?" I inquired.

"Well, now," Hogan began, "a fine lady like you, you oughta be able to pay a nice sum iffen we wuz amind to let ya through."

"We're turning around, Marietta!"

"You go right ahead," I said airily. "I'll take my things out of the back and walk the rest of the way."

"Fifty pounds," Hogan said. "Yeah, fifty pounds. That oughta do it."

"Very well," I replied.

"Goddamn!" Jeremy thundered.

I started to climb down from the wagon. He seized my arm, holding it in a bruising grip. His jaw was thrust out. His vivid blue eyes were flashing. He glared at me, and I gazed at him with a cool serenity that infuriated him even more. Several moments passed before he released my arm. He took a deep breath and slowly expelled it.

"Okay," he said. "You win."

"You needn't accompany me, Mr. Bond. I'm perfectly capable of—"

"Shut up! Ten pounds," he told Hogan. "That's all you're getting."

"Ain't enough. The lady here's willing to pay—"

"Ten pounds. Take it or leave it."

Hogan and Flint exchanged looks and then looked back at Jeremy and saw the expression on his face, saw it would be futile to haggle. Ten pounds was a great deal of money to men like these, and as Jeremy clearly didn't want to go into the city to begin with, they decided to take what they could get while they had the chance. Jeremy took out the ten pounds, and Flint began to shove boxes and saw horses and mattresses aside. In a few minutes we were on our way again. Jeremy was remote, silent, still seething with anger he found difficult to contain. I had won. I was quite pleased with myself, yet as the wagon approached the city doubts began to creep in. I hoped I hadn't made a terrible error.

Thirty

Sunlight slanted through the louvered wooden shutters, making bright yellow stripes across the floor as I stepped into the shadowy pantry in back of the large, bottom-floor apartment I had been sharing with Jeremy Bond these past four days. As I had expected, the shelves were almost empty. He had bought food three mornings ago, but those scant provisions were gone now. I would have to go to the market, there was no getting out of it, and as I left the pantry I was almost relieved to have an excuse to get out of the apartment. I had grown to loathe it already.

I hadn't wanted to come here in the first place, but he hadn't given me any choice in the matter. I couldn't check into a room, not with an epidemic raging, the inns were all closed tight, taking no new guests, and so I had reluctantly agreed to come here. He had maintained the apartment for years. It had been in a shambles when we arrived, the furniture covered with sheets, dust everywhere, and I had been scandalized to find a pile of dirty dishes on the drainboard. He blithely explained that he had been in a bit of a hurry when he departed the city and had had far more urgent matters on his mind than a stack of dishes.

Everything was spotless now. I had scrubbed and cleaned and dusted and aired, not because I was fond of housework but simply because there was nothing else to do. He had sternly forbidden me to leave the house except to fetch water from the cistern in the backyard. He had been gone for hours every day, attending to "urgent" business about which he was extremly mysterious. He had sold the horses and wagon and, his own business attended to at last, had left this morning with all my jewelry, assuring me he had connections and would be able to get the best available price for each piece.

It was well after two o'clock in the afternoon now. I should never have let him have the jewelry, I thought, moving down the hall to the front parlor. I wouldn't be at all surprised if the rogue skipped town with them, leaving me flat broke. It was an unkind thought and, I admitted, grossly unfair. For all his faults, and they were legion, Jeremy Bond was honest, and in his way he had as much integrity as any man I had ever known. He'd be back, all right, and God only knew how much longer we'd be cooped up in this wretched apartment, windows and shutters tightly shut to keep out the air.

I couldn't stay inside any longer, not without losing my mind. The lack of food gave me a perfect excuse. I'd as soon risk the fever as risk insanity, I told myself. I was extremely familiar with this neighborhood. The market was only a short walk from here. With luck, I could go and get back with ample provisions before he returned. I hesitated nevertheless. Jeremy would be livid when he found out, and much as I longed to go I couldn't help feeling a twinge of apprehension. I would be taking a risk, yes, there was no doubt about it, but then he had been jaunting around the city every day and hadn't been affected in the least.

Squaring my shoulders, I moved resolutely into the bedroom. We needed food. I needed to get out of the apartment, if only for a little while. If he didn't like it, that was just too bad. I stepped over to the mirror and removed the apron I had been wearing and smoothed down the skirt of the violet-blue cotton dress. It was beginning to look the worst for wear, but I saw no reason to change just to go to the market. I brushed my hair back, peering at my reflection in the dim light. I looked a little pale and drawn, but that was to be expected. Who wouldn't be pale after being confined like this for so long?

I fetched my reticule, checked to see that I had enough money and then, as an afterthought, stepped over to the chest beside the bed and took out the small pistol he kept in the top drawer. After verifying that it was loaded, I dropped it into the reticule, pulled the drawstring tight and moved into the foyer, praying he wouldn't choose this moment to return and catch me in the act of leaving. I unlocked the door and stepped outside. The sunlight seemed blinding, and I paused, blinking my eyes. Four days inside with all the shutters closed had left me unprepared for the radiant light, and it took me a moment to adjust.

The courtyard was deserted. Most of the flowers were dead, and the shrubbery was beginning to wilt and turn brown. The sulphur fumes were responsible for that. Great iron vats of sulphur were kept burning night and day on almost every corner as a preventative measure against the fever, and I wondered if the noxious fumes really helped. As I moved across the courtyard and opened the ornate iron gate the smell seemed overpowering, growing stronger as I walked down the street toward the corner. A vat was burning there, great yellow-gray clouds of smoke filling the air. Ardently wishing I'd thought to bring along a scented handkerchief, I put my hand over my nose and mouth and hurried around the corner.

The smell seemed less potent as I continued toward the market, but perhaps I was merely getting used to it. I seemed to be the only pedestrian. It was just as well, I thought. The fewer people I encountered, the better. As I passed a row of houses, I couldn't help but notice the large white crosses slashed across three of the doors in white paint. Up ahead, a woman in brown, with a heavy brown veil, stepped out of a courtyard and started walking toward me. When she saw me she stopped, hesitated a moment and then scurried across the street so she wouldn't have to pass me. I could understand her precaution and was relieved myself.

It was really foolhardy of me to come out like this. I realized that now, but I stubbornly refused to turn back. I moved on resolutely, passing another burning vat, coughing. A wagon passed on the street, rumbling noisily over the cobblestones. The man driving it had a scarf tied around the lower half of his face. He glanced at me suspiciously and kept a firm grip on his whip, almost as though he expected me to leap at him. The whole city was obviously in a state of terror. Jeremy had told me about the looting, the fighting, the murders. Thank goodness I had brought the pistol. I wouldn't hesitate to use it if the need arose.

When I finally reached the market, I wasn't at all surprised to see that most of the stalls were shut tight, a gray, ghostly atmosphere supplanting the bustle and color and vitality that usually prevailed. The few people who were shopping cautiously avoided each other whenever possible. Most of the men had scarves covering their noses and mouths, as had the driver of the wagon, while the women kept heavily scented handkerchiefs over their nostrils. Several of them carried oranges poked full of cloves as well. The air was filled with a thick, billowing fog from the dozens of sulphur vats.

"You gonna buy, lady, or are you gonna stand there thinkin' about it?"

The proprietor of the stall I had stopped in front of was a big, burly man in blue shirt and black leather apron. His manner was gruff, suspicious, and with the scarf over his face he looked exactly like a bandit. There was a pistol on the shelf behind him, deliberately kept in plain sight. I purchased three plucked chickens, four pounds of beef, a roll of hard sausage, and when he told me how much it was going to cost I was appalled. He was indeed a bandit, charging five times what the meat would have cost under ordinary circumstances.

"But that's absurd!" I protested. "You can't charge—"

"I can charge anything I wanna charge, lady! I'm riskin' my life bein' here. Pay up or move on! I don't fancy bein' contaminated."

"It seems I have no choice," I said acidly.

"Ain't no one gotta choice. You wanna eat, you gotta pay."

I placed the money on the countertop. He took it gingerly and thrust it into his pocket.

"You gotta basket?"

"I forgot to bring one."

"I gotta basket here under the counter. It'll cost ya a pound."

"A pound!"

"You gonna buy food, you gotta have a basket to carry it in."

I slapped another pound note down, livid. He placed the

meat into the basket and shoved it toward me. I moved on angrily, my anger growing as I was forced to pay exorbitant prices for bread, cheese, fruit and vegetables. When I left the market I had only a few coins remaining, and the basket was so heavy I could barely carry it. I walked slowly, frequently stopping to shift the basket from one hand to the other, gripping the handle tightly and feeling as though my arm were being pulled from its socket.

"Marietta!"

I had only come a short way from the market when the woman called my name. I turned, startled to see an apparition in black hurrying toward me. Her black taffeta dress rustled crisply. The feathers on her black hat bobbed, and heavy black veils cascading from the brim completely covered her head and shoulders. She stopped a few feet away from me, catching her breath, and the scent of her perfume was so strong it almost knocked me down. She was literally drenched in it.

"My dear!" she cried. "I thought you were in England. No, no, don't get too close, stay where you are! No offense, dear, but we all have to take precautions."

"Lucille? Is—is that *you?*"

"I scarcely *know*, my dear! These past three weeks have been so horrible I'm not sure *who* I am. The girls have left me, every last one of them. Fled the city immediately, as *I* should have done, of course, if I'd had any sense. I was afraid to leave the shop, all this dreadful looting. It's boarded up, windows, doors, everything, and I've finally found a man to guard it for me. I'm leaving for the Devereaux plantation tonight."

"I didn't know anyone could leave the city. I thought—"

"It costs a *fortune*, my dear. These wretched, wretched men smuggle one out in boats in the dead of night, it's *extremely* dangerous. I just made the arrangements half an hour ago—that's the only reason I'm on the *street*, my dear, that insufferable lout wouldn't come to the shop."

Lucille pulled out a large white lace handkerchief and, moving back a few steps, cautiously lifted the heavy black veils, draping them over the brim of her hat. For the first time I could see the bright, shrewd, not unkind eyes, the heavily rouged cheeks, the thin, avaricious mouth painted a vivid red.

A few gray curls dangled across her brow, and the dangling garnet earrings I remembered so well still swayed at her ears. She raised the handkerchief to her nostrils and sniffed audibly. Overwhelming waves of Parisian scent filled the air, completely eclipsing the scent of sulphur.

"The Devereaux girls have been after me to come to the plantation ever since the first cases were reported—they want me to sew for them, of course, they're planning a ball and want new gowns, but I shall naturally be treated as an honored guest. *No* one should stay in this city a day longer than it's absolutely necessary to stay. I'm surprised to see *you* here, my dear. I was under the impression you were in England with your handsome Hawke."

"I—that didn't work out, Lucille. It's a long story.".

"You must tell me all about it. Later, when this is all over with and we can talk in safety. That *dress* you're wearing! Don't tell me where you got it, my dear, please spare me the sordid details. Cotton! And I made you such gorgeous things!"

Lucille shook her head, raising her eyes heavenward at the same time. The earrings swayed vigorously. One of the veils tumbled back down. She whipped it back up and took another sniff from the perfumed handkerchief. I had set the basket down beside me, and I rubbed my arms.

"You've been to the market, I see," she said. "I suppose one has to eat—I've been living on champagne and petits fours, had a *huge* supply in my rooms over the shop. You want to cook *everything* carefully, my dear, boil all the vegetables, don't dare eat anything raw. Lettuce! You bought lettuce! Don't risk it, no matter how long you rinse it, and, of course, you don't drink *water*."

"I've been boiling it first."

"Folly, my dear, sheer folly! As soon as it cools it's as bad as ever. Champagne's the thing. I still have two cases left—I wish there were some way I could get them to you. Ordinarily I'd send a boy over with them, but of course one daren't trust *anyone* now."

Lucille waved the handkerchief in front of her nose and looked up and down the street as though to verify that it was still safe to talk. She moved back another step and raised her voice.

"How long have you been here?" she asked.

"Four days."

"Four days! Then you have no idea what it's been like. My dear, over two thousand have died! More dying every day—men, women, children. No funerals, no decent burials. They've dug these grotesque pits outside the city. The dead are carried there in wagons, dumped into the pits, lime poured over them. Not just the dead, either!"

"What do you mean?"

"My dear, the authorities have hired the scum of the earth to do the dirty work—guard the roads, drive the wagons, collect the dead. Horrible ruffians from the waterfront. They're worse than the worst criminals! Crosses are painted on the doors where there's sickness—you've seen them. These men march into the houses to collect the dead and, my dear, sometimes a poor soul is still alive, and they just chuck him into the wagon with the corpses in order to save themselves another trip the next day!"

"How horrible!"

"It's true, I swear it. I've seen it with my own eyes. I was watching from my upstairs window when one of the wagons stopped across the street from the shop—I shan't describe it to you, I couldn't bear to!—and two terrible men got down and went into the house. They came out with poor Mr. Jacobson, he was wrapped in filthy sheets. His wife was shrieking and wailing, running after them. My dear, Mr. Jacobson was still alive!"

Lucille paused dramatically, her dark eyes wide with a curiously gleeful horror. "He would have died in a matter of hours, of course," she continued, "but that's beside the point. When they dumped him on top of the corpses, I saw him *move!* He tried to get up, but he hadn't the strength. I'll never forget it, my dear—it was horrible, *horrible.*"

"Surely the authorities—"

"The authorities don't want to be bothered! Most of them are safe and snug on plantations downriver. They've turned everything over to these hooligans and a few brave doctors who're working themselves to death. But let me finish my story! Mrs. Jacobson tried to pull her husband off the wagon, and one of the men knocked her down, knocked her unconscious. Then both of them went back into the house and came out a few minutes later with her Sevres vases and her silver candlesticks and jewelry box."

She paused again, lifting the handkerchief to her nostrils. "I happen to know her jewelry was all paste—the pearls may have been genuine, perhaps, but they were decidedly inferior."

"Can't something be *done?*" I asked.

Lucille shook her head. "Respectable citizens are arming themselves. You never know when those ruffians are going to break into your house under the pretense of doing their official 'duty.' There've been several shootings."

"I've heard about that," I said.

"Looting on a grand scale, rioting on the waterfront, and hundreds dying all the while. Thank *God* I'm finally getting out of the city, even if it *is* costing me a small fortune. I'd suggest you get out, too, my dear, as soon as possible."

"I hope you have a safe journey, Lucille."

"It's going to be dreadful. A tiny *rowboat.* Swamps! But at least I'll be getting out of this hellhole. You take care, my dear, and when this is all over come by the shop—we'll have a lovely gossip, and I'll see that you have something better to wear than that hideous cotton!"

"Take care yourself."

"I will. I must fly! I hope the shop is still *standing!*"

Lucille dropped the veils over her face and shoulders, waved the handkerchief at me and scurried away in a flurry of rustling black taffeta. I sighed and picked up the basket and continued on my way, deeply disturbed by what she had told me but not sure I believed all of it. Lucille was a magnificent seamstress and a very shrewd businesswoman, but she was also flighty and excitable and prone to exaggeration. She thrived on gossip and drama, and it was obvious that this fever epidemic was the greatest drama that had come her way in a long time. She had almost seemed to be enjoying herself in a perverse sort of way, I thought, although surely I had imagined it.

I turned another corner, my free hand over my mouth and nose as I passed the vat of sulphur. There was no need to panic, I told myself. The worst of the epidemic would soon be over, the fever would run its course, and things would return to normal. I would simply sit it out inside the apartment, and then I would take the first available ship to England. I might have to endure two or three more weeks of Jeremy Bond's company, true, but that was an ordeal I could face easily enough. He might grumble about having to sleep on the sofa in the parlor each night, may have hinted that the bed was plenty big enough for both of us, but at least he hadn't made an overt attempt to try and share it with me. He wouldn't dare!

Gripping the handle of the basket with my left hand, I walked alongside a crumbling gray brick wall festooned with strands of withered purple bougainvillaea. A fountain splashed mournfully in the courtyard beyond. As I passed the wrought-iron gates, I saw the white cross slashed across the door of the house. Someone was sobbing inside. The sound was muted by the thickness of the walls but clearly audible nevertheless. I shifted the basket to my right hand and moved on hurriedly, eager now to be safely back inside the apartment I had been so ready to leave earlier on.

I wasn't more than three streets from the apartment when I heard the wagon approaching. I turned, looking behind me, and then I stopped, a cold chill of horror turning my skin to ice. I could feel the color leaving my cheeks as the wagon with its grotesque cargo moved down the street. It was pulled by a bony brown horse that looked ready to drop in its traces, and two men sat on the high wooden seat in front, rough, surly-looking men in filthy clothes. Neither of them wore scarves over their faces. The driver was chewing a wad of tobacco. The man beside him was busily scratching his filthy straw-colored hair. Both were oblivious to the cargo.

The back of the wagon was heaped with corpses, bodies piled helter-skelter like so much cordwood, legs and arms akimbo, some dangling over the sides. There were women, children, old men, lifeless eyes wide open and staring at nothing. Some were in night clothes, some wrapped in sheets, a few completely naked, and as the wagon moved over the rough cobbles the bodies on top rolled and shifted about. I felt faint. My knees seemed to give way. I flattened myself against the wall, staring in stark horror, unable to look away as the wagon drew nearer and nearer. The driver spat out his tobacco and tightened his grip on the reins as the wheels bumped over a rough stretch.

One of the bodies jerked, slipping over the side, dangling there with arms hanging down, swaying, lifeless hands trailing over the cobbles. It was the body of a gray-haired old man, skeleton thin, prevented from falling completely off only by the weight of the body of a corpulent woman thrown over its legs. I saw the torso swaying from side to side, saw the fingers trailing, and I closed my eyes tightly, willing myself not to swoon. I kept my eyes closed until I could no longer hear the sound of hooves and creaking wheels, and when I finally opened them I felt dazed, disoriented.

I wasn't going to be sick. I wasn't going to faint. I was going to be perfectly calm. I gripped the handle of the basket and moved on resolutely, trying to shut the horror out of my mind, trying to forget, but the sight seemed to be burned in my mind in graphic detail. I shuddered, and it seemed to take me forever to get back to the apartment. I opened the gate and crossed the courtyard as though in a trance, dug the door key out of my reticule and unlocked the door with trembling hand, half-expecting to find Jeremy Bond waiting for me in the foyer with hands on thighs and eyes blazing with anger.

He hadn't returned. That, at least, was a relief. I sighed, pulling myself together with great effort. I took the basket into the pantry and put the food away. I would cook a large meal. I would keep busy. That would help. Yes, when he returned I would have a hot meal waiting for him, but first I had to bathe. I had to scrub myself thoroughly. I fetched water from the cistern in the backyard and heated it and poured it into the large white porcelain tub behind the screen in the bedroom. I poured perfume and bath powders into the water and took off my clothes and dropped them into the hamper.

I must have stayed in the tub for half an hour. I scrubbed and scrubbed, washing my hair as well, and then I soaked in the warm water, relaxing at last. When I finally climbed out and dried myself off I felt much better, although I still had a queasy feeling in the pit of my stomach. I put on a fresh white petticoat and the deep blue silk gown I had worn the night of Em's wedding. I toweled my hair again and brushed it until it was completely dry. The clock on the mantle chimed. It was five o'clock. I wondered why Jeremy hadn't returned. He should have been back much earlier.

I wasn't going to worry about it. I was going to keep busy. I pailed the water out of the tub and emptied it in the backyard, cleaned the tub out and started a fire in the large black iron stove in the small kitchen in back of the apartment. I washed vegetables and put them on to cook. I put a chicken in the oven to roast. I made fresh bread. The clock chimed again. I could hear it in the distance, a pleasant metallic sound. Six o'clock. It couldn't possibly be six! Where was he? Why hadn't he returned? I took the vegetables off the stove, put them in bowls, and buttered them. I sliced some bread and checked the chicken and decided to let it cook a few more minutes.

The sunlight was almost gone. I lighted all the lamps and set the table in the dining room, carefully arranging silverware and plates, folding the linen napkins, deliberately dawdling. Six-ten. Six-fifteen. I smelled the chicken and hurried back into the kitchen to take it out of the oven. The skin was a crisp golden brown, but it wasn't burned. I placed it on a platter and told myself that he would be coming in any minute now, I might as well take the food into the dining room.

I wasn't at all hungry myself. I was too worried to be hungry. Yes, I was worried, damn it, and when he came in I intended to give him a tongue lashing he wouldn't soon forget. How could he be so inconsiderate? How could he be so thoughtless, staying gone all this time, leaving me alone to worry myself sick? The bastard was probably at a bar somewhere, drinking with cronies and blithely ignoring the hour. It was absolutely infuriating! He might keep me shut up in this apartment like a prisoner and forbid me to go out, but it was perfectly all right for him to sally about all over the city oblivious to the danger all around him.

I set the food on the table and refolded the napkins. Wine. We would have wine with our meal. There were dozens of bottles in a heavy wire rack in the pantry. I chose a bottle and returned to the dining room with it and then stood there, holding it, unable to keep the alarm at bay a moment longer. My hands were trembling. The back of my throat ached.

There was a terrible hollow feeling inside. Something had happened to him. I knew it. I could feel it in my bones. I set the bottle down on the table and moved to the doorway and gripped the frame with my right hand, steadying myself as wave after wave of alarm swept over me.

Something awful had happened to him. He wasn't coming back. I would never see him again, and I had been so cold, so hateful, so remote, and he would never know that I hadn't meant any of it. I had been angry with him, it was true, dreadfully angry, with good reason, but I didn't hate him. How could I possibly hate him? How could I have treated him so badly after all he had done? I had no illusions about him. He was a thorough rogue, a scamp, a scoundrel, and I could never love a man like that, but. . . . Oh, sweet Jesus, I couldn't stand any more of this. I was beginning to tremble all over. My legs wouldn't hold me up much longer. I clung to the doorframe, silently praying that he would come through the door.

Several moments passed. I heard footsteps in the courtyard. I heard a key turning in the lock. He opened the front door and stepped into the foyer, a bulging black bag in his hand. He sighed and brushed a heavy brown wave from his brow. He looked weary. His face was pale. There were deep mauve shadows under his eyes. He was wearing blue breeches and frock coat and a darker blue waistcoat patterned with black silk leaves. The clothes seemed to hang limply on him. His black silk neckcloth was crumpled. He sighed again and looked up and saw me standing in the doorway and smiled a jaunty smile.

"Been waiting for me?" he inquired.

"Have you any idea what *time* it is!"

"Haven't the least notion, lass."

"It—it's almost seven o'clock! You should have been back hours ago!"

"Been busy," he said.

"I was almost out of my mind! I thought—*damn* you, Jeremy Bond! You saunter out of here like you're on your way to a picnic and leave me alone all day and—"

I cut myself short, unable to go on without spluttering. He shook his head, a smile playing on his lips, and I glared at him, desperately wishing I had something to throw. The heavy wave dipped over his brow again. His blue eyes were full of amusement. He was very pleased with himself, insufferably pleased with himself. I longed to slap him.

"I take it you've been worried about me," he said.

"I never gave you a thought," I said venomously. "I was worried about my jewelry."

I was lying. I had forgotten all about the jewels.

"Sold every last one of 'em," he told me. "Took quite a while. I had to call on quite a few of my—uh—contacts. None of 'em could afford to buy the whole lot, had to sell a few pieces at a time." He hoisted the bag and grinned. "I drove a hard bargain, lass. This bag's full of money, and you're a very rich woman."

"You look tired. Your forehead's moist."

"There're thousands and thousands of pounds, *thousands*. I wouldn't take anything but cash, counted every note. I probably should have put it in one of the banks, but I don't trust 'em, never have. I've got a safe in the bedroom, in back of the wardrobe, solid iron. Figured I'd put it there where I can keep an eye on it. Do you realize how wealthy you are? Do you realize—"

"Will you stop *babbling!*"

He looked hurt. "Sorry, lass," he said. "I kinda figured you might be interested."

"You're mad, stark raving mad. Carrying that much money around, deliberately *asking* someone to hit you over the head. Sometimes I think you haven't got a bit of sense!"

"I've got a pistol in my waistband, kept my coattail whipped back so everyone could see it."

"Your cheeks are pale."

"It's been a long day. I'm a little tired. I'll just take this into the bedroom and put it in the safe. What's that I smell? Have you been baking bread?"

"I cooked a big meal. Everything's cold now."

"No problem, lass. You can warm it up right quick."

"Go to hell!" I snapped.

Jeremy grinned and sauntered into the bedroom with the bag. I brushed a tear from my eye, incensed to find it there. I took the food back into the kitchen and put the vegetables back on top of the stove and put the chicken in the oven. I began to slice bread, hardly aware of what I was doing, so relieved I felt weak. I could hear him moving around in the bedroom, and it was a lovely sound, sweeter than the finest music to my ears.

When the food was warm, I took everything back into the dining room. It was dark outside now. The lamps filled the apartment with a pleasant golden glow. I opened the wine, poured it, took a sip. It was taking him a terribly long time in the bedroom. Perhaps he was counting the money. Half of it was his, I was going to insist on that. He could divide it among the families of the men who had been killed and Randolph and the others. He could do anything he wanted with it. I took another sip of wine and, carrying the glass, moved into the parlor, growing a bit impatient now.

"You might *hurry*," I called. "I refuse to warm it up a second time."

"Be right with you, lass."

His voice sounded peculiar, strained. He was tired. I was going to see that he went right to bed after dinner. I had been much too hard on him, I decided. I was going to keep my distance, and I certainly wasn't going to encourage familiarity, but there was no need for me to be quite so cool and distant. If we were going to be living in such close quarters for the next two or three weeks, it might as well be on amiable terms. I finished the wine, feeling relaxed for the first time.

"Jeremy, *do* come on. Forget the money. I'm hungry."

I heard him approaching. He moved hesitantly across the foyer and stepped through the doorway of the parlor and stood there just inside the door, looking at me. I set the glass down, instantly alarmed. His face was even paler, his skin like damp white wax. The shadows beneath his eyes were much darker, and he had a dazed, confused look, a furrow between his brows, his lips parted. I started toward him. He shook his head and held his arm out as though to push me back.

"No, no—don't come near me. I feel funny, dizzy. I—I think I'm sick."

"Jeremy!"

He shook his head again. He frowned, and then he crumpled to the floor in a dead faint.

Thirty-One

He was sleeping peacefully at last, at long last, and I was so weary I could hardly sit up, but I didn't dare relax. I took the cloth out of the bowl of water on the bedside table and wrung it out and bathed his brow and smoothed his hair back. His cheeks were flushed, his skin warm, but at least it wasn't burning as it had been off and on all during the night. He wasn't tossing and turning and thrashing about so violently I had to use force to keep him in bed. He wasn't shivering, his teeth rattling, his eyes wide open and glazed. He was sleeping. I wondered how long it would be before he had another seizure.

I bathed his cheeks. He moaned and murmured something in his sleep and rolled over on his side. The mattress sagged. The sheets were wringing wet from his perspiration. I'd have to change them. I'd have to get some food into him. Soup. I'd make soup. He had to eat something. I put the cloth back into the bowl of water and stood up straight and massaged the back of my neck. My bones felt as though they had been pulverized. My eyes were sore, lids heavy. I desperately needed sleep, just an hour or so. How long had it been since he had keeled over in the parlor? An eternity seemed to have gone by, but the thin, pale rays of sunlight seeping through the louvers informed me it was early morning. No more than twelve hours had passed.

Jeremy moaned again, shifted his position and then lay still. Several moments passed. Dare I leave him alone? I watched him, frowning, and I finally left the bedroom, moving quietly, wearily down the hallway to the kitchen. I built a fire in the stove and put a pot of coffee on to boil and tried to collect my thoughts. There was so much to do, so much to do, and I was so weary and sleepy and sore I could barely stand. I closed my eyes for just a moment and a hazy gray fog enveloped me and I stumbled, almost falling. I braced myself against the drainboard. I couldn't give in. I couldn't give way. I had to keep my eyes open. I had to keep busy.

The coffee began to boil. I poured a cup and drank it scalding hot. It helped just a little. I had a second cup, and then I washed vegetables and cut them up and put them on to boil and cut the beef into tiny cubes and put it in the pot and added salt. It would be at least an hour and a half before the soup was ready. I cut three oranges in half and squeezed the juice out into a glass and carried it back into the bedroom.

He was still sleeping. His face had lost the waxy pallor. His cheeks were a vivid pink, much too pink. I set the glass down on the bedside table, sat down on the edge of the bed and managed to lift his torso up, holding him in my arms. He groaned and opened his eyes and looked up at me with a confused expression.

"Wha—what—" he murmured.

Supporting him with one arm, I reached for the glass of orange juice.

"Drink this," I said gently.

He scowled and shook his head and closed his eyes, leaning heavily against me. I could barely hold him up. My backbone felt as though it would snap in two. I lifted the rim of the glass to his lips, forced them open and tilted the glass. He swallowed. He opened his eyes again and grimaced and tried to push me away.

"Doan—don't want—"

"Drink it."

He struggled. I held him firmly and, somehow, managed to force him to drink all the juice. I eased him back onto the pillows, and he seemed to relax. The vivid flush had faded somewhat, but his forehead was warm when I stroked it. He was perspiring again. He breathed deeply and moaned again and blinked, lifting his eyelids to look at me. He squinted, as though I were far away and he couldn't focus properly.

476

"Ma—Marietta?"

"I'm here, Jeremy."

"No—no—shouldn't be—"

"Don't try to talk."

"Fe—fever. Go. Lea—leave me. Dangerous—"

"Hush."

"Conta—tagious. You—danger—"

He murmured something I couldn't understand and then began to struggle with the sheets, pushing them down to his waist. I bathed his face again and bathed his torso with the damp, cool cloth. He relaxed, sleeping again. He was completely naked under the sheets. I had no idea how I had found the strength to drag him into the bedroom, undress him and get him into bed last night, but I had somehow. He had struggled, fighting me, delirious, finally collapsing on the bed in a dead heap. Boots, breeches, coat and waistcoat, shirt and neckcloth, somehow I had removed them and gotten him under the covers.

I dropped the cloth back into the bowl of water and carried the bowl into the kitchen. The soup was cooking nicely, simmering now, filling the room with a pleasant smell. I stirred it, tested the vegetables with a fork and added a few herbs. I fetched more water from the cistern in back and boiled it and set it aside to cool. I was still weary and sore, but the dreadful grogginess had vanished. The apartment was quiet, filled with dim, hazy sunlight. I longed to throw the shutters back and open the windows, but I didn't dare. I stirred the soup and, when the water was cool, took it to the bedroom.

Jeremy was awake. He looked at me with feverish blue eyes and tried to sit up. I shook my head and placed my hands on his shoulders and shoved him gently back onto the pillows. He frowned, wanting desperately to speak but too weak to do so. I smiled reassuringly and stroked his cheek.

"I'm going to bathe you again," I said, "and then I'm going to change the sheets. Just—just lie still. All right?"

His skin was clammy with dry sweat now. The flush was gone. He fell asleep again as I bathed him with the cool water and continued to sleep as I pulled the covers off him and edged the sheet out from under him, rolling his body first to the left, then to the right, finally pulling the sheet free. It was much more difficult to get a fresh sheet under him. He was limp, heavy, resisting me in his sleep, but I managed at last, tucked the hem of the sheet under the mattress and tenderly covered him with clean sheet and counterpane.

Gathering up the soiled bedclothes, I put them in the hamper and then sat down in the chair beside the bed, weary, watching him, trying to think. My eyelids were growing heavy again. If only I could close them for just a few minutes . . . I mustn't. I dared not. The soup would be ready in a little while. I had to feed him, and then I would have to leave him alone in the apartment while I went to fetch a doctor. Lucille had said a few brave doctors had remained in the city, doing what they could to help. I had to find one and persuade him to come here.

I frowned, contemplating the problem. How to find one? How to get him here? Hundreds of people were dying each day, thousands more were ill, raging with fever, in need of care, and the doctors who had stayed to combat the fever would be horribly overworked, going without sleep, making rounds all over New Orleans. The city was in chaos, and I didn't dare leave Jeremy alone for more than an hour, two at the most. How was I going to locate a doctor and get him back here in that time? I didn't know any doctors. I didn't know where to start looking for one. I couldn't just go out on the streets and search for a plaque in a window.

Plaque . . . window . . . I remembered the small, elegant bronze plaque in the window of a building near the pharmacy. I had passed it dozens of times when I was on my way to Lucille's shop. Yes, Dr. Jean Paul Duvall. I remembered him well. Although I had never had occasion to consult him, he had come to Rawlins' Place a number of times with his lovely quadroon mistress. He was tall, thin, extremely handsome, and the fashionable courtesans of the Quarter had flocked to him with imaginary ailments. He had treated them with impatient contempt, his manner brusque. I remembered one of the women complaining about him, deeply offended that he had turned her out of his office so that he could go nurse the poor.

"*He* calls it being dedicated," she had wailed, "*I* call it madness. A man like that; those dark brown eyes, those silver temples, visiting river-bottom trash in squalid hovels when all of us *pine* to keep him occupied."

I knew that if Dr. Duvall still had his practice he would undoubtedly be here in the city. It had been at least two and a half years since I had seen him. Would he remember me? My chances of finding him in his office were slim indeed, I realized that, but I could leave an urgent message. I might well be wasting my time, but I had to try.

Jeremy stirred in his sleep, restless again. He threw one arm out, slamming it back against the headboard, and then he sat up with a start, staring into space with wide, frightened eyes. The bedclothes fell down to his waist, exposing his damp torso. He mumbled angry, inaudible words, his cheeks flaming, and when I tried to ease him back down he shoved me viciously. I gripped his shoulders firmly, pushing him back onto the pillows, holding him there, and after a few moments the fight went out of him and he relaxed.

The color left his cheeks. His skin, pink and flushed before, took on a grayish pallor faintly tinged with yellow. Locks of damp brown hair clung to his forehead, plastered there with perspiration. I smoothed them back again, and he looked up at me, fully conscious now, fully aware of his surroundings. His lips were dry, beginning to chap.

"How—how long have I been—been here?" he asked weakly.

"Several hours. Since evening."

"It—it's the fever, lass."

I shook my head vehemently. "We don't know that yet. I'm going to get a doctor. We can't be sure until he examines you."

"I have it," he murmured. His voice was barely a whisper. "You—you must stay away."

"I'm going to nurse you."

"N—no. Too risky."

"Nonsense!"

"Can't let you—"

"I'm not going to fight with you, Jeremy," I said firmly. "You're much too weak. When you have your strength back, when you're up and about, we'll fight all you like."

"Stu—stubborn wench."

"If you're just now finding that out, you're even denser than I gave you credit for being."

"W—when—" he began feebly.

"Yes?"

"When I—get up—"

479

I waited. He struggled to get the words out, and, even in his illness, there was the suggestion of a smile on his dry, cracking lips. It was absolutely heartbreaking.

"When you get up?" I prompted.

"Go—going to beat—hell—out of you—"

"We'll just see about that, Mr. Bond. Right now you're going to stay in bed and do exactly what I say. I've made some soup. I'm going to go get it. You're going to eat it."

"Can—can't eat."

"Oh yes you can."

I gave him a very stern look and, maintaining my front, moved briskly out of the bedroom. As soon as I reached the hall I stopped, closing my eyes, biting my lower lip. Tears I couldn't control spilled over my lashes and streamed down my cheeks. Sobs welled up, and it was all I could do to hold them back. I couldn't give way. I couldn't. He mustn't hear. The emotions swelled, and I clenched my fists, willing them away, praying for strength. Several moments passed. I brushed the tears from my cheeks and squared my shoulders and moved down the hall with a resolute expression.

Later. Later, when it was all over with, when Jeremy was well again, I could give way. Now I had to be strong. I had to be firm, cool, collected. I took the soup off the stove, took down a bowl and filled it. He *was* going to get well. He was. I was going to see to it. I refused even to think about the possibility of his not recovering. If Dr. Duvall wouldn't come, I would get another doctor somehow and bring him here, at gunpoint if necessary. Jeremy was going to get well. I made myself that solemn promise, and I felt much better.

Putting soup, spoon, and napkin on a wooden tray, I carried it back to the bedroom. He was still awake, weak, so weak. There were dark smudges under his eyes, and that sickly pallor was even worse, as though the fever burning inside had left his skin an ashy gray faintly tinted with yellow. I gave him a no-nonsense look and set the tray down and helped him into a sitting position, propping the pillows behind him. He didn't resist, but I could see that it took a terrible effort for him to sit up.

I sat down beside him and, dipping my finger into the bowl of water, moistened his lips.

"The soup is rich and thick. I want you to eat it all."

He merely looked at me, too weak to say anything. His blue

eyes were beginning to take on a distant, foggy look. It was growing harder and harder for him to focus. I filled the spoon with soup and lifted it to his lips. Jeremy opened his mouth, swallowed, meek and obedient.

"There. Isn't it delicious?"

"Aw—awful—"

"How dare you! I may be a lot of things, Jeremy Bond, but a poor cook I'm not. This happens to be the best soup you've ever eaten. It's perfectly delicious."

He tried to make a face and couldn't quite manage it. I continued to feed him until, with half a bowl still left, he raised his hand and pushed the spoon away, sagging limply against the pillows. I set the spoon aside and eased him back down. His body was relatively cool, the burning fever temporarily gone. With any luck, he would be able to sleep for an hour or so after eating, and I could go to Dr. Duvall's office. He closed his eyes as I pulled the sheet and counterpane up over his shoulders.

I took the tray back to the kitchen, threw out the soup still in the bowl and put bowl and spoon in a pan of water. Almost a quart of soup remained in the pot. I emptied it into a jar, sealed the jar and, opening the door of the larder, placed it into the cool, tin-lined recess. It would keep for a while, not for long. I'd have to go to the market again tomorrow. I would also have to wash dishes and launder the sheets and. . . . There were dozens of things to do, and I was glad. As long as I kept busy I could continue to ignore the terrible fear suspended over me like an ominous cloud, ready to swallow me up if I so much as acknowledged its presence.

Returning quietly to the bedroom, I found a lead pencil and a piece of paper and composed a message for Dr. Duvall, identifying myself and stressing the urgency. Then I put the message into my reticule along with several twenty-pound notes. Jeremy moaned softly as I stepped over to the mirror, but he didn't wake up. The pale, haggard woman who gazed back at me in the glass seemed a total stranger.

The blue silk gown was crumpled, the puffed sleeves limp, the bodice clinging damply, moist with perspiration. The skirt was deplorably wrinkled, soiled with water spots. My hair hung in listless waves of dull, dark copper-red, and my face was drawn, skin taut across cheekbones. There was a dark, haunted look in my eyes, and my lids were etched with deep mauve-gray shadows. I looked ten years older, but that didn't matter in the least. Nothing mattered now but Jeremy. I pushed the heavy waves back from my cheeks and tossed them over my shoulders, too weary to brush them.

Turning away from the mirror, I took a handkerchief out and soaked it with cologne from the bottle on the dressing table. Jeremy woke up with a start, jerking his body into a sitting position and staring at me with alarmed eyes.

"Wh—what—"

I hurried over to him and took hold of his shoulders. He struggled, glaring at me. His cheeks were blazing again. His eyes were a fiery blue. When I tried to ease him onto the pillows he flung his arms out, knocking the back of his left hand across the side of my face. I maintained a firm grip on his shoulders and shoved him back. He went limp, moaning, his eyes foggy now.

"N—no. No, no—"

I bathed his face with the damp cloth and stroked his hair. Eyes closed, he took hold of my hand. His own was damp, clammy, his fingers curling limply around mine.

"Ma—Marietta?" he whispered.

"I'm here, Jeremy."

"Fe—fever. Danger. Don't—don't want you to—"

"Hush," I crooned. "Hush, darling."

"N—not him. Me."

"Shhhh. Don't try to talk."

"L—love you."

"Go to sleep."

"Real—really do. Must be—lieve me."

"I believe you."

"M—me. Not him—"

He dropped his hand onto the mattress and muttered something unintelligible and then sighed, asleep at last. I sat beside him for several moments before carefully easing myself off the bed. He might well wake up again while I was gone, but that was a risk I would have to take. Fetching my reticule from the dressing table, gathering up the handkerchief, I moved quickly and silently out of the bedroom.

When I stepped outside, the sulphur fumes seemed even worse than they had the day before, but I paid them no mind. Holding the handkerchief to my nostrils, I hurried through the courtyard and opened the gate. The sky was overcast today, a

482

mottled gray-white without a trace of blue, the atmosphere bleak as I walked down the street. Everything was brown and black and gray, orange flames leaping from the vats of burning sulphur and filling the air with haze. New Orleans was like a different city, ghostly, deserted, all color and vitality bled away.

My footsteps rang loudly on the pavement, reverberating against the dusty courtyard walls with an eerie, echoing sound. I turned a corner, shielding my face with the handkerchief as I passed a roaring vat. The heat of the flames seemed to singe my skin. The great puffs of smoke were smothering. I hurried on, moving resolutely through the labyrinth of narrow streets. A closed black carriage clattered past, moving at a dangerous speed. The driver cracked his whip, urging the horses on as though all the demons of hell were in hot pursuit.

Jeremy would be all right until I got back. I tried to convince myself of that, but I worried nevertheless. Suppose he had another of those dreadful chills like he had had during the night, shivering violently, his teeth chattering? I hadn't left any blankets on the bed, and even if I had he would be too weak to gather them around him. He had been freezing, freezing, his skin actually taking on a bluish hue, and it had been almost half an hour before the first chill left, followed immediately by a violent fever that seemed to burn him alive. I shouldn't have left him, even for a few minutes. I should turn back immediately. If he had another chill and I wasn't there to look after him . . . I forced the thought from my mind.

I had to get a doctor for him. That was my first priority. He would be all right. He would probably sleep the whole time I was gone. I quickened my step, forgetting the weariness that was like a leaden weight, filled with new determination. I was going to hold up. I could keep going as long as I needed to. Sleep, rest, they didn't matter. I could sleep later. I could rest when Jeremy was well. It was my fault that he was ill, all my fault. He had wanted to turn back at the barricade, had insisted on it, but I had adamantly refused, stubborn, inflexible, deaf to his reasoning. We had come into the city against his will, and now. . . . He was going to get well. I was going to see to it. Nothing was going to stop me. I passed another vat and started down yet another narrow street lined with silent houses behind dusty courtyard walls.

Two men turned a corner and started in my direction on the opposite side of the street. I stopped, watching them closely as they hooted with laughter and stumbled along, obviously drunk. One of them clutched the neck of a bottle of gin. The other carried an exquisite cloisonné vase. Both had brutal faces and shaggy hair, their clothes filthy. A heavy middle-aged woman in a bedraggled coral velvet gown came panting around the corner, tottering after them on high heels, as drunk as they were. Her plump, sweaty face was caked with powder, cheeks bright with rouge. Masses of brassy gold ringlets bounced from her incredible coiffure.

"Aw, come on!" she cried. "Lemme have it, lemme have it! Ain't no use to you, and it'd look grand in my parlor. Th' gents'd love it!"

"Go on, you old whore!" one of the men called over his shoulder. "Steal your own vase. We're sellin' this one!"

"Thieves! Ruffians! Gimme that vase!"

She caught up with them and tried to grab the vase. The man with the bottle gave her a vicious shove. As she reeled backward one of her heels snapped, and she lost her balance and fell, sprawling on the pavement in a heap of tangled velvet and thrashing limbs and bouncing ringlets. The men laughed all the louder, standing over her as she shrieked and spluttered. When she tried to get up, the man with the bottle poured the rest of the gin over her face. His companion roared with glee and turned around and saw me across the street. A lewd grin twisted on his lips. He set the vase down on the pavement and tugged at the other man's arm.

"Hey, Davey, lookee there! A bloomin' duchess! All by herself, too!"

"She shore is! Fancy that!"

"Reckon she might like some company, hunh, Davey?"

"A coupla 'andsome lads like us, she'd love it."

I stood my ground, fully prepared to pull the pistol out of my reticule if I needed to, but it wasn't necessary. While the men were staring at me and making rude comments, the woman scrambled to her feet, snatched the vase and took off with it. Hearing her clattering footsteps, they whirled around just in time to see her disappear around the corner, and, yelling with rage, they forgot all about me and stumbled after her. I continued on my way, not the least bit shaken but furiously regretting the loss of precious minutes.

Leaving the residential area, I passed a row of shops, all of them boarded up tightly, wooden planks nailed across windows and doors. The painted wooden signs hanging over the pavement swung listlessly, colored paint faded and chipping. A cat prowled mournfully on the steps of the pharmacy. Dr. Duvall's office was just down the street. I hurried on, passing an old Negro woman who was wearily dragging a worn pillowcase half full of some kind of rubbish. I was relieved to see the doctor's bronze plaque still in the window. At least he was still practicing. The door was locked, and as I knocked on it I noticed that the old woman had stopped and was staring at me with a peculiar expression on her face.

I continued to knock, but there was no answer. Dr. Duvall wasn't in. I hadn't really expected him to be. I took the note out of my reticule and was preparing to slip it under the door when a carriage turned the corner and pulled up in front of the steps. The driver was a husky lad with thick blond hair and amiable blue eyes. A black silk scarf covered the lower half of his face. He climbed down, patted the horse's rump affectionately and opened the carriage door.

Dr. Duvall climbed out, a worn black leather bag in his hand. He looked incredibly tired, his handsome face lined with fatigue. There was a distracted look in his gentle brown eyes. His silvered brown hair badly needed brushing, and he clearly hadn't changed clothes in days. His black frock coat was wrinkled and shiny, his maroon neckcloth crumpled. He sighed heavily, running a hand through his hair. He started to say something to the driver, and then he saw me standing in front of the door.

"Dr. Duvall, thank goodness you've come. I was just getting ready to leave a message."

His mouth tightened. His expression grew stern. "Are you out of your mind, woman?" he said gruffly. "Don't you know it's dangerous for you to be out here on the street?"

"You don't understand. I—it—"

"You don't even have anything over your face!"

"Dr. Duvall, don't you recognize me? I'm Marietta Danver. You used to come to Rawlins' Place."

He frowned. "Miss Danver? Of course, of course! I remem-

485

ber well. But, my dear, what are you doing standing out here on the street? It's absolute insanity."

"I didn't know who to turn to. I remembered you—I hoped you'd remember me. I didn't know if you were still practicing or—"

I cut myself short and closed my eyes for a moment, trying to pull myself together. Dr. Duvall moved up the steps and took hold of my arms. The gruff manner was gone now. He was all tender concern, his lovely brown eyes studying me carefully.

"I—it's not me," I said, "I just haven't had any sleep. It's a friend of mine. He's very ill."

"You've been nursing him?"

"Since last night. He fainted. He's been running a terrible fever. His skin is—it's ashy, and during the night he had awful chills."

Dr. Duvall nodded gravely. I didn't have to say anything else. He knew. His expression confirmed my worst fears.

"Can you come?" I asked. "Can you examine him? I know you're tired. I know you must have dozens of calls to make, but—"

Dr. Duvall silenced me with a look. "Of course I'll come, my dear," he said. "I just have to step into my office for a minute to put a few things in my bag. That's the only reason I came by the office—to fetch new supplies. I haven't been back here since yesterday afternoon."

"I'm so grateful. I can't begin to tell you how—"

"Angus will help you into the carriage, Miss Danver. You give him directions, and I'll be right with you. Try to relax, my dear. We'll do all that we can for your friend."

The youth with the amiable eyes took my hand and gently assisted me into the carriage as Dr. Duvall unlocked the door and stepped into his office. I told the young man how to get to the apartment and then settled back against the dusty cushions. The interior of the carriage smelled of camphor and ancient leather. Frayed brown velvet curtains hung at the windows. I was beginning to feel faint again, and I realized that it had been almost twenty-four hours since I had eaten anything.

Dr. Duvall climbed into the carriage, closed the door and settled wearily beside me with the bag on his knees. I didn't speak. He seemed relieved. As the carriage pulled away, I noticed that the old Negro woman was still standing in front of the boarded-up shop, watching as we passed. Dr. Duvall sighed again and once more ran his hand through his tousled brown and silver hair. He allowed himself to relax, taking full advantage of these few minutes of respite from his arduous duties. In repose, his handsome face seemed older, his skin like fine old parchment.

When the carriage stopped and the husky young driver opened the door and helped me out, I noticed that the sky was much darker, a deep slate gray, low and ominous. A strong breeze drove heavy clouds across its surface, and dry, dying leaves rattled in the courtyard. It was very warm, the breeze like hot breath on my skin as I opened the gates. Dr. Duvall told the driver he would be back out in a few minutes and followed me into the courtyard. His face was stern again, his manner brisk and official.

Jeremy woke up when we entered the bedroom. The sheets were tangled about his legs. His skin gleamed with sweat, and hair clung to his skull in wet tendrils. Frowning, he blinked his eyes, clearly unable to focus properly, and as Dr. Duvall moved over to the bed, he moaned, rolling his head from side to side on the pillow. Dr. Duvall set his bag on the floor and took Jeremy's pulse and then placed a palm over his brow. I stood near the doorway, clasping my hands and watching with anxious eyes. Dr. Duvall glanced up at me.

"Leave us for a while, Miss Danver. I'll call you when I'm finished with my examination."

I nodded numbly and went back to the kitchen and, in order to have something to do, put more wood in the stove, lighted a fire and put a pan of water on the flat iron surface. When it was warm enough, I took it off and began to wash the dishes, working mechanically, without thought. I rinsed the dishes in a second pan of water, dried them, put them away. The apartment grew darker as more clouds gathered in the sky. Leaving the kitchen, I stepped into the parlor and began to light lamps.

Dr. Duvall joined me there. I set down the lamp I was holding and looked at him. His face was utterly expressionless, revealing nothing, but I knew. I felt a strange calm come over me.

"Is he going to be all right?" I asked.

"I've given him some medicine. He'll rest easily for a while. I've left a bottle of medicine on the bedside table. I want you to give him a tablespoon full every four hours."

"Will it—"

I couldn't complete the question. Dr. Duvall maintained his cool, objective manner, and I understood. He couldn't afford to show compassion, couldn't afford to offer false hope. In order to accomplish his work, facing death as he did several times a day, he had to remain completely detached. I accepted that. Compassion, kind words wouldn't have helped at all.

"It's bad, isn't it?" I said.

"It's very bad, Miss Danver."

"The medicine—"

"It's laudanum. It will ease his pain, help him sleep."

"Then—"

"There's nothing more I can do for him. He's too far gone."

"So soon?"

"It happens that way sometimes."

"How long?" I asked.

"Another day. Possibly two. Three at the most."

"I see."

My voice was flat. Dr. Duvall looked at me, gripping the handle of his bag tightly, wanting to say more but knowing it would be useless. I thanked him and offered to pay him, but he refused to take any money. I led him into the foyer and opened the front door. He hesitated, letting his guard down at last. His brown eyes were full of tender compassion, and when he spoke his voice was low and gentle.

"You're taking a grave risk, nursing him like this. You realize that?"

"I'm not going to let him die, Dr. Duvall."

"I'll have to report the case. It's necessary."

"I understand."

"Take care of yourself," he said. "Eat. Get some sleep. Your friend will rest with the laudanum. I—" He paused, frowning. "I wish I could offer you some hope, but—"

"Thank you again, Dr. Duvall. I appreciate your coming."

I showed him out, closed the door and stood there in the foyer for several minutes, still possessed by that curious calm. I wasn't going to let go. I wasn't going to break down. I couldn't, not while Jeremy needed me. Dr. Duvall had given up on him, believed there was no hope, but . . . I wasn't going to accept that. I went back into the bedroom. Jeremy was sleeping peacefully. I sat down on the bed and took his hand, holding it with both my own, looking down at him with a tenderness I had never permitted myself to show before. He breathed deeply, his lips parted, cracked. His skin had a deep yellow tint beneath the gray pallor.

"You're going to get well," I said. "You're going to get well, my darling. I promise you. I promise."

I said the words for my own benefit. Jeremy never heard them.

Thirty-Two

They put the white cross on the door late that afternoon. The paint gleamed in the dying gray light, an obscene symbol that spelled the end of hope for those within. I knew full well what it meant, but I refused to let it unnerve me. I brought the sheets in, folded them, and, around seven, got Jeremy to drink another half-glass of orange juice. He slept fitfully during the night, and I slept in the chair beside his bed, waking twice to give him a tablespoon of laudanum. In the morning, stiff, sore, my back and neck aching dreadfully, I changed the sheets again, gave him more laudanum and then set off for the market.

It hadn't rained yet. The sky was full of ominous black clouds so heavy, so low it seemed one could almost reach up and touch them. The sultry breeze was stronger, blowing scraps of debris along the pavement and causing the fog of sulphuric smoke to lift and swirl and separate. I moved rapidly, the empty basket in one hand, the loaded pistol in the other, the reticule swinging from my wrist. I wanted anyone I encountered to see that I was armed, and my grim, determined expression left no doubt that I would shoot at the slightest provocation. A group of rowdy men had broken into one of the shops, tearing boards away, breaking glass, and they were looting it merrily as I passed on the opposite side of the street. Intent on their plunder, they paid no attention to me.

The market was even more deserted than it had been two days ago. I paid a small fortune for a dozen eggs. Oranges were so dear they might have been pure gold. I refused to pay that much for them. I argued vehemently with the woman behind the booth and finally, nervously, eyes on my pistol, she sold them to me for half what she had been asking. I bought beans, coffee, flour, a bunch of bananas, another chicken. An aging whore in a soiled green velvet gown and a wide-brimmed green velvet hat draped with masses of limp black and white plumes burst into hysterical sobs when she couldn't afford a roll of sausage. A violent fist fight broke out between a heavyset man in a blue broadcloth frock coat and the burly proprietor of the fish stall. Bins of eels were knocked over, the slippery black creatures writhing on the cobbles in tangled masses.

I made my last purchase and left the market with a heavily laden basket. My neck was still sore, and my spinal cord felt as though it had been twisted out of shape. When I arched my back, tiny bones popped, and I felt some relief. Walking rapidly, gripping the pistol firmly, I passed a wagon with a mattress in back, a pile of blankets scattered on top. Two men were leading a man in nightclothes toward the wagon. He was delirious, stumbling feebly as they wrenched his arms, forcing him forward. A third man carried a brass figurine and a pair of silver candlesticks, velvet draperies slung over his shoulder and trailing on the ground behind him.

Although they were sturdy, rough-looking specimens, the three men were relatively clean, their clothes relatively neat, and there was . . . yes, there was a military air about them, the short-clipped hair, the brisk movements and stern, confident expressions. Reaching the corner, I turned to watch, extremely curious. When they got to the wagon, the sick man began to struggle, shaking his head, trying to break free. Calmly, indifferently, one of the men gave his arm a savage wrench, twisting it up between his shoulder blades, and, clapping a hand over his mouth, forced the poor creature up onto the back of the wagon. The man fell onto the mattress, scrambled to his knees and tried to leap out. A savage fist across his jaw knocked him unconscious. The men pulled an olive green blanket over him and stood by the wagon, talking idly and examining the items brought out of the house.

I moved on, puzzled. Had the city authorities at last turned to the military for help in this time of crisis? It seemed a logical move, far more logical than hiring hooligans and riffraff, but, if so, then why had the men been loading the sick man onto the wagon? Gathering up corpses and taking them to communal graves was one thing, but this man had been very much alive, strong enough to walk, to struggle. I frowned, passing another burning vat, coughing as the breeze blew noisome puffs of smoke into my face. I couldn't help but be alarmed by what I had seen. The military, I knew, could be far more dangerous than the worst ruffians, particularly if given authority in civilian matters. The three men had treated the fever victim with a brutal indifference, and they had clearly stolen the figurine, the candlesticks, the velvet draperies.

It didn't affect me. It wasn't my concern. Terrible things were happening all over the city, and I couldn't afford to dwell on them. Nursing Jeremy back to health was my only concern and required all the time, thought, and energy I had. I couldn't worry about anything else. Forcing the incident out of my mind, I moved briskly down the street, and it was with a feeling of great relief that I finally stepped into the courtyard.

The crudely painted white cross seemed to leer at me as I closed the gate, almost as though it were an animate thing with a malevolent spirit, flattened there against the door and waiting to pounce. I closed the door behind me and sternly admonished myself for such bizarre fancies. Looking into the bedroom, I saw that Jeremy was still asleep. I dropped the pistol back into my reticule and placed the reticule on the dressing table, then carried the basket of food into the kitchen. As I put the food away, I arched my back again, vowing not to spend another night in the chair. I would make a pallet instead.

I made a pot of coffee, sliced bread and toasted it and sat down at the round wooden table. The coffee was rich, delicious, and, with butter spread over it, the toast was delicious, too. I was going to have to eat more, if only to keep my strength up. I couldn't take proper care of Jeremy if I was weak and stumbling from lack of nourishment and sleep. As I sat there in the silent kitchen, sipping my second cup of coffee, it seemed as though I'd been nursing him for weeks, yet a full forty-eight hours hadn't passed since he had crumpled onto the floor of the parlor and the nightmare had begun. It was going to get worse, I knew that, and I had to brace myself for it.

Finishing the coffee, I left the table, took the chicken out, washed it, cut it up and dropped it into a pot of water. I put more wood into the oven and put the chicken on to boil. When it was tender, I would debone it, cut the meat into small pieces and cook it in its broth with noodles and cabbage leaves to make a thick, nourishing soup. It was growing more and more difficult for Jeremy to swallow, and it was imperative that he eat as much as possible. When the chicken began to bubble in the pot, I moved the pot from the flame and put another pot of water on to boil. Ten minutes later I carried a bowl of warm water into the bedroom along with a fresh washcloth.

Jeremy was still sleeping. I hated to disturb him, but I needed to bathe him and then change the sheets, which were soaked through with sweat. He made moaning noises as I bathed him, although he didn't open his eyes. When I began to roll his body over in order to change the sheets, he muttered angrily in his sleep and began to shiver. Moving over to the wardrobe, I took down a rich dressing robe of heavy maroon brocade and struggled to get him into it. As I slipped his arms into the sleeves of the sumptuous garment, I wondered about the woman who had given it to him. Men never bought robes like this for themselves. I could visualize some woman picking it out, stroking the luxuriant, silky material, smiling to herself as she thought of how he would look in it. Folding the lapels across his chest, tying the sash loosely at his waist, I eased him back onto the pillows.

Many, many women must have loved him, I thought, smoothing a damp lock from his brow. They would have found his virility appealing, his ruthless air exciting, his charm irresisitible. Buxom barmaids, elegant countesses, blushing virgins, worldly courtesans—all must have longed to touch him as I was touching him now. How they must have vied for his attention, spoiling him deplorably, hoping to entrap him, each doomed to find him as enchanting as foxfire and just as elusive. How many hearts had he broken? How many women lay awake in lonely beds, the interminable hours of the night filled with memories of the handsome charmer who had loved so well and left so nimbly?

He had stopped shivering. His skin was slightly warm to the

touch, but it wasn't burning, and he seemed to be sleeping a deep, restful sleep. I attributed that to the laudanum. The opiate was extremely strong, and I was a bit concerned about giving him so much. Although it undoubtedly eased pain and induced sleep, it frequently had dangerous side effects if taken too often or in too great a quantity. Bizarre nightmares, hallucinations, violent behavior often resulted if the drug was used improperly. Giving his brow a final stroke, I stood up and rubbed the back of my neck. Dr. Duvall had given me specific instructions, and I felt sure he wouldn't have left the bottle if he thought there was any danger.

Jeremy stirred, opening his eyes. Moaning groggily, he tried to sit up, the maroon brocade rustling. I put my hands on his shoulders, gently easing him back down.

"It's all right," I said softly. "I'm here."

He frowned deeply, scrutinizing me with feverish blue eyes that seemed to look right through me.

"W—who—"

"It's Marietta, Jeremy."

"Ma—Marietta?"

He might never have heard the name before. Those feverish eyes continued to scrutinize me, suspicious, apprehensive. He scowled angrily, muttering something I didn't catch.

"H—hot," he said.

"I know, darling."

"Thirs—thirsty."

"I'll get you some orange juice."

When I returned from the kitchen with the glass, he drank greedily, although I could see that it was painful for him to swallow. As soon as I removed the glass from his lips he dropped his head back onto the pillows and closed his eyes. In a few moments he was sound asleep again, breathing heavily through parted lips. I stood beside the bed a while longer, watching him, then returned to the kitchen.

Taking the chicken off the stove, I removed the tender, juicy meat from the bones and cut it into small pieces, dropping them back into the rich broth with a cupful of small noodles and cabbage leaves I had carefully washed and shredded into thin strips. A wonderful aroma filled the kitchen as the soup began to simmer. I stirred it listlessly, adding a few herbs and a pinch of salt. I wondered how long it would take him to get well. After the fever was gone, after the danger was over, how long would it be before he was back on his feet and able to go about his business? Two weeks? Three? I couldn't leave New Orleans until he was fully recovered.

He *was* going to recover. I wouldn't even consider the alternative, despite Dr. Duvall's grim words. Jeremy was young and strong and red-blooded, bursting with vitality and energy. A simple fever wasn't going to down him, not if I had anything to do with it. I would see that he got plenty to eat. I would bathe him repeatedly with cool water when the fever raged, and when he was cold, when he began to shiver and his teeth began to chatter, I would keep him warm. As I stirred the soup, I felt total confidence, but my eyes grew moist nevertheless. It . . . it wasn't just whistling in the dark, I told myself. He *was* going to get well.

Setting the wooden spoon aside, I wiped my eyes and straightened my shoulders. I needed more sleep. I needed more food, too. After I fed Jeremy, I would eat a bowl of soup myself and make a pallet in the bedroom and try to nap for a little while. I was worn to the nub, tired through and through, so weary I could hardly stand and, as a result, my nerves were frayed, my emotions dangerously near the surface. I wanted to sit down and sob and sob and sob until all the anguish and anxiety were released, but I couldn't let go. If I did, I might not be able to stop.

There was a distant rumble. The walls seemed to shake. Gunfire? It took me a moment to realize it had been thunder. I opened the back door and looked out. Ponderous gray-black clouds roiled in the dark gray sky, hanging low, and it was so dark I could barely see the large round wooden cistern that stood beside the giant fig trees. As I watched, silvery flashes of lightning illuminated the sky like a dazzlingly brilliant web, but it still didn't rain. I closed the door and took the soup off the stove.

Jeremy made an angry face when I pulled him up into a sitting position and propped the pillows behind him. He grumbled, looking at me with vivid blue eyes that saw something else. The rich maroon robe slipped from his shoulders, sliding down his arms. I pulled it back up, adjusted it and retied the sash. Jeremy made another face, pushing me away.

"I've brought soup," I said gently.

"N—no—"

"You must eat."

"Going to let it hap—happen, not *going* to—"

"Jeremy—"

"Wrong—bad—"

"Here. Open your mouth."

He pressed his lips tight, glaring at me. His fists were clenched, and I realized that he was seeing some highly disturbing scene that was vividly alive inside his mind. I bathed his forehead and cheeks with a damp cloth. He muttered to himself, and then the snapping sapphire fire left his eyes and he had a confused, bewildered look. He squinted, trying to clear the fog, seeing me at last.

"Ma—Marietta? Is—is that—"

"It's me, Jeremy. I've come to feed you."

"F—food? Not—not hungry—"

"Open your mouth."

He grumbled unpleasantly, obeying at last. The muscles of his throat moved painfully as he swallowed, but I managed to feed him the entire bowl of soup nevertheless. I wiped his lips and gave him water and then carefully filled a tablespoon with the thick, syrupy brown medicine and gave it to him. He grimaced as I wrapped my arm around his shoulders and lowered him back down, moving the pillows and placing one under his head. He fell asleep almost immediately, his lips parting, his breathing heavy, labored. I studied his face, trying to convince myself that some of the pallor was gone, the yellow fading, but in my heart I knew there had been no change.

At the kitchen table, I ate a bowl of soup and a slice of buttered bread, wanting more coffee but deciding against it. As soon as I finished washing the dishes, I would pile some blankets on the floor in the bedroom and try to take a nap. After the soup and the laudanum, Jeremy should sleep for three or four hours, and I would wake up if he stirred. Putting water on to warm, stacking the dishes on the drainboard, I wondered if I could possibly drag the sofa from the parlor into the bedroom. It would be far more comfortable than a pallet on the floor. No, it was far too heavy, and the mere thought of exerting myself left me weak.

There was another loud clap of thunder as I washed the dishes. Splashes of silver light flickered through the louvers of the shutters, causing weird shadows to dance on the walls. When the storm finally broke, there was going to be a torrential downpour, but I knew it could go on this way for hours before a single drop fell. More thunder sounded, noisy, insistent, echoing in the front foyer. It was almost as though someone was pounding repeatedly on the door. It took me a moment to realize that someone *was* at the door, rapping so hard the wood was likely to splinter.

Drying my hands, frowning, I hurried down the hall, snapped the lock open and cautiously turned the door handle. I didn't open the door all the way, I didn't dare, and I silently cursed myself for not having the foresight to get the pistol.

The man who stood on the doorstep was tall and lean with a lean, tan face and steely gray eyes beneath highly arched, sooty black brows. His dark golden brown hair was clipped close to the skull, and his thin pink lips spread in a tight, disgruntled line. As I opened the door a few more inches and he got a good look at my face, the gray eyes lost their steely hardness and took on an all too familiar gleam. The lips lifted slowly at one corner into an appreciative grin.

"What do you want?" I asked. My voice was like stone.

"Well, now, ain't very neighborly, are we?"

I started to slam the door. He placed his palm against it, pushing hard. I stumbled back. He shoved the door all the way open, and I saw the two men behind him then, saw the wagon in front of the gate with at least seven people huddling miserably under the blankets. My heart seemed to stop beating. My blood turned icy cold. I recognized them now, all three of them.

"Who are you?" I demanded.

"Corporal Sanders, ma'am, and this here's Private O'Hara and Private Hopkins."

O'Hara, a husky redhead with sullen brown eyes, nodded curtly. Hopkins was short and stocky and stood in a pugilistic stance, legs spread wide, shoulders hunched, fists planted on his thighs. He seemed to bristle with hostility, black eyes glaring at me as though he longed to knock me down. All three men wore black boots, dark breeches, and silky shirts, O'Hara's and Hopkins' navy blue, Sanders' a deep yellow-beige.

"O'Hara and Hopkins, they're my helpers. I got orders to gather up all th' people in th' neighborhood who got th' fever.

City's transportin' 'em to a camp ten miles outta town. Got beds for 'em there, got people to look after 'em."

"You—you're with the army?"

"That's right. Second Regiment."

"You're not in uniform."

Sanders grinned. "It's pretty ugly work, ma'am. Didn't none of us want to get our uniforms all soiled. I got my orders. Hopkins and O'Hara are here to help. Where's th' fever victim?"

Don't panic, I told myself. Don't panic. Think. Think. Calm. Keep very, very calm. Don't let them see how frightened you are. Shoving a long copper wave from my cheek, assuming a haughty air, I stared at the tall, not unattractive man with the lean tan face and short golden-brown hair.

"There must be some mistake," I said coolly. "There's no one here with fever."

"No?" Sanders drawled.

"My—my husband has an extremely bad cold. The doctor came and examined him and said he was very weak and needed a great deal of rest and needed to drink a lot of liquids, but—it isn't the fever."

"How ya gonna explain this cross on the door?"

"It was painted there by error. Someone was confused. My husband has a bad cold."

Sanders' thin pink lips curled mockingly. "Don't see no wedding ring on your finger," he said. "Bet that man in there ain't gotta ring, either. I think you're lying to me."

"She's gotta nice body, ain't she?" O'Hara called.

"Yeah," Sanders agreed, gray eyes studying me. "Real nice."

"Wouldn't mind some of that, would you?"

"Wouldn't mind at all."

"Let's get on with it!" Hopkins barked. "We ain't got time for none of that."

"Hopkins ain't got no appreciation a th' finer things," O'Hara remarked. "He gets his fun by shovin' people around, beatin' 'em up. I don't see that we're in an all-fired hurry."

"No hurry at all," Sanders said.

His eyes held mine. The grin curled on his lips. The iciness inside me was numbing. I had to do something. What? What? I couldn't let them take him. I couldn't let them put him on that wagon. They were taking the ill away to die, of that I was certain. The conditions at the camp were undoubtedly primitive and squalid, they had to be. Without personal attention, without constant care, Jeremy wouldn't have a chance of surviving. They weren't going to take him. They weren't. What was I going to do? Think. Think.

"Let's get on with it!" Hopkins urged. "She gives you any trouble, let me handle her!"

His black eyes burned. His whole body was charged with brutal energy he could barely contain. Rocking on the balls of his feet, knees bending, he reminded me of a bulldog on a leash, and I knew he longed to attack. Sanders seemed to read my thoughts.

"We ain't gonna turn him loose," he said, "not lessen you try'n keep us from doin' our duty."

"I—I told you, there's no one here with fever. You're wasting your time."

Sanders shoved me back and stepped into the foyer. O'Hara and Hopkins crowded in behind him. I moved quickly into the parlor, praying they would follow and stay away from the bedroom. Sanders strolled in after me, still grinning. O'Hara followed him and began to examine the furnishings with a covetous eye. He fingered a silver box, stroked a pink silk cushion, moving about the room, taking stock. Hopkins hadn't come into the parlor. Where was he?

"Lotta nice things here," O'Hara observed. "Real fine things. Reckon that fancy clock'd fetch a nice sum. Them little figures on it're real gold. Looks like we got us some rich folks here."

"You can take anything you want," I said quickly. "I won't protest. Take anything you want."

"Right generous of you, ma'am," Sanders said.

"I—I'll make a bargain with you."

His eyes undressed me. He ran the tip of his tongue along his lower lip, savoring the situation, anticipating delight. I steeled myself.

"You gotta lot to bargain with," he drawled. "Ain't seen a body shapely as yours in a long time. Real tasty lookin'."

"She gonna let ya?" O'Hara asked.

"Reckon she is. Reckon she don't have much choice."

O'Hara chuckled and thrust the silver box into his pocket. I

498

looked at Sanders, calm now, prepared to give myself to him. If it meant saving Jeremy, I would give myself to all three of them. Sanders rubbed his chin with his thumb, his gray eyes full of amusement and kindling desire. He pulled me to him and thrust his hand into the bodice of my gown, grasping my breast and squeezing hard, his other arm curling around the back of my neck. I tried to conceal my disgust as he slowly lowered his head, lips parted.

"He's in here!" Hopkins thundered.

Sanders frowned, annoyed. "Go help him, O'Hara!" he ordered. "I got business with the lady. After you've taken him out to the wagon you 'n Hopkins can come back and gather up some loot."

"You bastard!" I cried.

I kicked him in the shin, breaking free. He caught my wrist and jerked me in front of him, slinging an arm around my throat, brutally pressing his forearm again my windpipe as I struggled to escape. O'Hara chuckled again and sauntered out of the room. Sanders loosened his hold a bit and bent his head down, his lips brushing my earlobe. I stopped struggling, standing very still, his forearm firm across my throat but no longer pressing.

"You 'n me, we're gonna have some fun," he taunted.

"We made a bargain," I said hoarsely.

"You made an offer, I didn't promise nothin'. Just relax. Me, I know how to make a gal feel good, real good. We're gonna move over there to that sofa, an' when we're done you're gonna beg me to do it all over again."

Forearm tightening across my windpipe, he forced me across the room and shoved me onto the sofa. I looked up at him, desperate now, desperately trying to think. The pistol. I had to get the pistol. It was in my reticule. Reticule. Money. I would offer him money. He stood over me, leering, delaying his pleasure. I sat up, the bodice of my soiled blue silk gown slipping low, almost exposing my nipples. He liked that. He opened his mouth, his tongue flicking out to lick his lip again.

"I have money," I said.

It worked. "Money?"

"A great deal of money," I replied. My voice was level now. "Before my friend fell ill, he went to the bank. We were planning to leave New Orleans. He took everything we had out of the bank."

Sanders forgot his throbbing member and pulled me to my feet.

"Show me!" he ordered, shoving me toward the door.

I led the way across the foyer and into the bedroom. Hopkins and O'Hara had pulled Jeremy out of bed, each holding one of his arms. He sagged between them, moaning, his eyes closed, the maroon robe hanging limply to his calves. I moved calmly over to the dressing table, picked up the reticule and turned around. Sanders waited near the doorway with a new kind of lust in his eyes. O'Hara and Hopkins gave him puzzled looks. I pulled the pistol out and leveled it at Sanders' heart. O'Hara gasped.

"Jesus! She's gotta pistol!"

I stared at Sanders with eyes as hard as marble. "Tell them to put him down," I said.

He heard the deadly deliberation in my voice. His cheeks turned pale, and he valiantly tried to hide his fear from his mates. I cocked the pistol, holding it steady, my eyes never leaving his own.

"Hey—hey now," he protested. "You don't wanna interfere with th' army, ma'am."

"Tell them to put him down."

"You ain't gonna let no woman intimidate you!" Hopkins snarled. "Knock her down and take that toy outta her hand."

"Looks like I—uh—looks like I'll have to," Sanders said nervously. "Why don't ja put th' pistol down, ma'am."

"Move a muscle," I said, "and I'll fire. I mean it. Tell them to put him down."

Sanders hesitated a moment, then gave the order.

"Gently," I warned.

Hopkins scowled savagely. O'Hara was visibly shaken. They lowered Jeremy onto the bed and straightened up, and then Hopkins roared and lunged at me. I whirled around and pulled the trigger and the explosion seemed to rock the room. The blast knocked Hopkins halfway across the room. He fell to the carpet, his shoulder shattered, bones splintered, blood gushing a bright crimson. In the confusion I whipped open the top drawer of the dressing table and pulled out the pistol Jeremy had been carrying. O'Hara stared at me in horror through the curling smoke.

"She's got *another* one!" he exclaimed.

"I happen to be a crack shot," I said. "I could easily have put the bullet between his eyes."

"I *believe* you, lady!"

"Sanders?"

"I—I ain't gonna argue with you."

Hopkins was moaning in anguish, on his knees, his face chalk white as he stared at the jagged, gushing hole in his shoulder with bits of bone protruding. His eyes rolled back. He pitched forward, arms flopping out in front of him, one of them slamming against O'Hara's leg. O'Hara shuddered, looking as though he might faint. Sanders stared at the pistol in my hand, his gray eyes wide and frightened.

"Pick him up," I ordered. "Get him out of here. If any of you come back, I'll shoot to kill. Do you understand?"

Sanders nodded briskly. "We made a mistake. This fellow ain't got th' fever, he's gotta bad cold. Right, O'Hara?"

"Right!"

"Help me get him up. Let's get th' hell outta here!"

They got the wounded man to his feet and, supporting him between them, led him out of the bedroom. I followed them into the foyer, holding the pistol in front of me. Sanders fumbled with the doorknob. Hopkins sagged, crying out in agony as his shoulder wrenched, then passed out again. Sanders pulled the door open, and they started to step outside.

"Just a minute!" I called.

"Jesus," O'Hara whispered. "What now?"

"The box," I said. "The silver box you took from the parlor. Give it to me."

O'Hara hastily complied. I took the box and jabbed the pistol forward, indicating the door. They stumbled outside, dragging Hopkins with them.

"This whole bloody town's gone to hell," O'Hara complained. "Folks just ain't *friendly* any more!"

I closed the door and locked it, then leaned against it and closed my eyes for a moment, beginning to tremble as delayed reaction set in. Taking several deep breaths, I stepped into the parlor and set the box down and looked out the window. The wagon with its pitiful human cargo was pulling away from the gate. I doubted seriously that any of the three men would return. Hopkins would be out of commission for a long time, and

Sanders and O'Hara, cocky and confident when terrorizing a helpless woman, had cringed fearfully when I pulled out the pistol. None of the brave, stalwart soldiers would want it to be bandied about that they had been bested by a lone woman.

Jeremy was sprawled sideways across the bed when I returned to the bedroom, and it took me a long time to get him back under the covers. He resisted me in his sleep, shoving me with surprising strength, muttering angrily and groaning all the while. When I drew the covers up over him, he thrashed about, pushing them back, and then he sat up abruptly, eyes wide, burning a fiery blue, lips drawn back. There was a deafening clap of thunder, a sudden gust of wind that caused the shutters to rattle. Lightning flashed, streaks of silver-blue filling the dimly lit room. Shadows danced on the wall. Rain began to pound on the roof. Jeremy glared at me with a murderous expression on his face, in the grip of a waking nightmare, and when I took him by the shoulders and tried to ease him down onto the pillows he roared and drew back his fist and slammed it across my jaw.

Violent silver-yellow-orange lights exploded in my head as a million red-hot needles of pain stabbed my jaw. I stumbled back, and my knees turned into rubber and folded under me. I was swallowed up by smothering folds of inky blackness.

Struggling, struggling, I fought through the layers of blackness, moaning as the pain returned, a dull ache now, no longer burning, and the rapping noise was a constant irritant, coming from a great distance. Black melted into gray, and I opened my eyes, blinking. Where was I? What had happened? It took me a minute to realize I was on the floor. What was I doing on the floor? I touched my jaw carefully as memory returned. Jeremy. He had grown violent, had struck me. Catching hold of the bedpost, I pulled myself to my feet. He was asleep, breathing heavily. The thunder and lightning had gone, and it wasn't raining any longer, although rain still dripped from the eaves. How long had I been unconscious? I clung to the bedpost for support, dizzy, my legs still weak.

As my head cleared, I was aware of the rapping noise once more. What was it? I frowned, and then I realized that someone was knocking at the door. I almost sobbed. No. No. I couldn't take any more. I couldn't face anything else, not today. Go away, I pleaded silently. Please go away. The rapping continued. Whoever was there had no intention of leaving. Oh God.

Oh God. I ran a hand across my forehead and stepped over to the dressing table and picked up the pistol. Staggering wearily into the foyer, I set my mouth in a tight, determined line, unlocked the door and threw it open.

The old Negro woman I had seen lingering near Dr. Duvall's office looked at the pistol with large, luminous black eyes that registered not the slightest alarm. Lifting them to look into my own eyes, she frowned, and I saw deep concern stirring. She was wearing a faded blue cotton dress patched in a dozen places, and there was a tattered purple shawl around her shoulders, held together in front by a brooch of blue and black enamel. Her thinning pewter-gray hair was pulled away from her face and fastened in a tight bun on the back of her neck. The ancient, wrinkled brown face had a curious and touching beauty all its own. Her clothes and hair were wet, and she was carrying a large bag that looked as though it had been made from a single piece of dirty, flowered carpet.

"I'se Mandy," she said. Her voice was low, scratchy. "I'se come here to help the young gen'leman get well."

I stared at her, much too startled to speak. The woman brushed raindrops from her withered brown cheeks. Behind her, raindrops dripped from tree limbs, and the bougainvillaea was like limp, drenched purple silk. Seeing the confusion in my eyes, she gave me a reassuring nod.

"I heard you talkin' to the doctor. I knowed who you were. I remembered, you see, yessum, and I knowed it must be that young gen'leman who wuz sick, the one who give me all that money."

My confusion grew. "Money? I don't—"

"You wuz wearin' a glorious red dress that night," she rasped, "an' he wuz dressed grand, too, handsome as a prince. Y'all wuz passin' through the market, and I wuz prowlin' around the stalls, tryin' to find something to eat an' he give me all that money and moved on 'fore I could even thank him."

I recalled the shadowy market place with only a few torches burning here and there, most of the stalls closed as we strolled through. I recalled the smell of nuts roasting, and I remembered the woman now. She had been picking through the scraps and rubbish on the ground, moving wearily, her back bent as she gathered up limp carrots and cabbage leaves. Jeremy had been incensed by by her plight, had angrily thrust several large bills into her hands and then ranted about the heartlessness of slave-holders who freed their slaves without providing them with any means of livelihood. That night seemed a lifetime ago.

"You remember?" she asked.

I nodded. I seemed to be in a daze. My vision was blurry.

"Mandy never forgot his kindness," she said in that ancient, scratchy voice. "Nobody ever give me so much money, it wuz over fifty pounds. I wuz able to set me up my own stall in the flea market an' sell the things I gather up from the alleys, things people throw away."

She was still standing on the doorstep, I motioned for her to come inside. I seemed to be standing a long way off, observing the scene with complete detachment, yet everything was blurred, hazy.

"I remembered," she said as I closed the door, "an' when I saw you on the street, I knowed it wuz you. When I heard what you said to the doctor, I knowed I had to help. I'd 'uv come sooner, but I didn't know where you lived, I couldn't hear you when you was givin' directions to that young fella what helps the doctor."

"How did you find us?" The voice seemed to belong to someone else.

"He told me where to come, that boy, Angus. I waited and waited, waited all night, hopin' they'd come back so I could ask him, but they didn't return till this mornin', and then I had to go get my things."

"Things?"

"Roots, herbs, powder. I brought lemons, too, an' a honey-comb that's drippin' with honey. Got everything I need here in the bag. Mandy knows all about the fever, knows what to do."

I shook my head. None of this was real. Mandy looked at me with those beautiful eyes, ancient eyes full of ancient wisdom. A frown creased her brow as she gently touched my jaw.

"We'll put somethin' on that," she said.

"He—he hit me. He didn't mean to."

" 'Course not. He wuz havin' a spell."

"Those men were here and tried to take him away, and I had to shoot one of them in the shoulder. When you knocked on the door, I thought—"

"Hush, child. Everything's going to be fine."

I shook my head again, unable to believe she was here, unable to believe any of this was happening. Mandy asked me to take her to Jeremy. I led her into the bedroom, moving as though in a trance, unable to focus. She stepped over to the bed and examined him, touching his skin, frowning deeply when she saw the yellow tint beneath his pallor. I was still holding the pistol. I set it down, watching as she leaned down to listen to his heartbeat. After a moment she straightened up, the frown digging a furrow between her brows. Her black eyes were extremely worried.

"I'se goin' to have to get started right away," she muttered.

"I appreciate your coming," I said, "but he's very sick. I—" My voice broke and the tears spilled over my lashes. "I—I don't think he's going to—"

I couldn't continue. The tears streamed down my cheeks in salty rivulets, and I didn't even try to stem the flow. Mandy came over to me and reached out a gnarled old hand and patted my shoulder.

"Don't you cry, child. Mandy's here. I'se goin' to take care of him, an' I'se goin' to take care of you, too. Stop that cryin', hear? Mandy's goin' to make everything all right."

Thirty-Three

He sat up in bed, cocky, confident, and altogether too smug, grinning at me as I entered the room. Cheeks freshly shaven, hair brushed to a sleek gloss, he wore an outrageously opulent brown brocade robe embroidered with lavish black silk leaves, and he smelled of soap and pine. Ignoring him, I walked over to the mirror and began to arrange my hair. In the glass I could see a crestfallen look appear on his face, quickly turning into one of petulance.

"So you bathed and shaved and brushed your own hair," I said dryly, not bothering to turn around. "You want a medal?"

"*I* think it's quite an accomplishment."

"Most men do it every day."

"You're so damned querulous!"

"You've been spoiled quite enough these past three weeks, Mr. Bond. It's high time you started taking care of yourself. I'm sick and tired of 'Marietta, do this,' 'Marietta, do that,' 'Mandy, bring me another glass of milk.' A person would think you were a bloody pasha."

"A person *might* show a little sympathy for a convalescent."

"Convalescent? You've been perfectly fit for several days. You just like being waited on."

"Wanna rub my back?"

"Indeed I don't!"

"You're very good at it."

I let that pass. He had taken terrible advantage of me, of Mandy, too, lolling about while we waited on him hand and foot. I had rubbed his back every day, had shaved him and brushed his hair, and Mandy delighted in cooking up special dishes to tempt his appetite. If he'd eaten one piece of sweet potato pie, he'd eaten two dozen, not to mention all the caramel custards and bowls of rice pudding. Despite it all, he still had a slightly gaunt look, hollows beneath his cheekbones. Another week of Mandy's cooking would take care of that, I mused.

"New dress?" he inquired.

I adjusted the sleeves of the pale violet and sky blue striped silk and nodded, putting the hair brush down. "Lucille finished it yesterday morning, did a rush job so I'd have something decent to wear. I'm going back today for more fittings."

"Preferred customer, I suppose."

"I'm paying her a fortune. She can afford to give me special treatment. I expect a whole new wardrobe to be ready by the end of the week."

Jeremy stretched his arms and settled back more comfortably on the pillows. Although he was still too thin, most of his color had returned, and he looked wonderfully handsome in the elaborate robe. Brilliant rays of silvery-yellow sunlight streamed through the opened windows, burnishing his hair. I longed to go smooth that heavy wave from his brow and feel its rich texture against

506

my fingers. Instead, I stuffed a few bills into my reticule and gave him a cool look.

"What's for lunch?" he asked.

"I believe Mandy's making pork chops and applesauce. I'm not having anything."

"Her applesauce is wonderful, much better than that horrible inky concoction she had me drinking. And those mustard plasters—" He made a face and pretended to shudder.

"That horrible inky concoction and those mustard plasters just happened to have saved your life."

He shook his head. "It was the charms that did it, those and all the feathers she burned. When's it going to be ready? Lunch, I mean."

"It will be ready soon enough. You couldn't be hungry, not after eating all those pancakes for breakfast."

"You made those, didn't you?"

"What if I did?"

"They were soggy," he accused.

"Go to hell, Jeremy Bond."

"Ah, lass, I love you. You cook and you rub backs and you're so gorgeous I could look at you all day long."

"I, on the other hand, can't wait to be rid of the sight of you."

"You don't mean that," he assured me.

"I haven't time to banter with you, Jeremy. Lucille is expecting me."

"I might just go out myself this afternoon," he said as I started toward the door.

I whirled around, giving him a look that should have reduced him to ashes. "You're not leaving this house!" I ordered.

"You're the one who says I'm perfectly fit. I've been doing exercises for the past week. Sit-ups. Push-ups. Secretly. Didn't want you and Mandy yelling at me."

"Damn you, Jeremy, I—"

"I'm getting fed up with this room, this bed. I feel perfectly well enough for a little outing. It'd do me good. Fresh air. Sunshine."

"Not a chance," I said. "Not for another week at least."

He scowled, a rebellious look in those vivid blue eyes. Mandy stepped into the room at that point, carrying a tray heavily laden with pork chops, applesauce, broccoli and flaky popovers.

507

She set the tray down on the bedside table and smiled at him, a tender, maternal smile that would have melted the heart of Attila the Hun. Jeremy smiled, too, basking in her loving attention. I sighed and shook my head.

"Watch him, Mandy," I warned. "He's getting feisty."

"Don't you worry none, Miz Marietta. I'se goin' to keep an eye on him. He's goin' to eat all this lunch, an' then he's goin' to take a nice nap. You run on an', get them dresses made."

I left, vastly irritated. He wouldn't dare go out, I told myself. He wouldn't dare defy me. He wasn't nearly strong enough to go jaunting about the city yet, and he knew it. He had merely wanted to rile me, something he delighted in doing. At any rate, Mandy would look after him. I smiled ruefully. Mandy would look after him, yes, but the rogue had already wrapped her around his little finger. She was completely under the spell of that infuriating charm. She treated him like a frisky, cuddly, thoroughly engaging puppy, her eyes lighting up whenever she was near him, a broad smile on her lips as she hurried to do his bidding. Mandy was, after all, female, and she would gladly face a firing squad for him.

I moved briskly down the street, still seething. Sunlight sparkled on the cobbles and the sky was a glorious, cloudless blue. Carriages and carts rumbled past. Brightly clad pedestrians crowded the pavements, men bustling about with an air of self-importance, women in silks chattering like merry magpies as they returned from shopping, servants carrying packages, Negro women with baskets of fruit balanced on their heads. The quarantine had been lifted over a week ago, the fever epidemic was over, and New Orleans wore a festive air, dreary gray shrouds replaced by gaudy, brilliant trappings that dazzled the eye. The air seemed to be charged with a new vitality now that the ordeal was behind us.

A wagon stood in front of Lucille's shop. Three husky men were busily carrying heavy bolts of cloth through the opened door, and a shabbily dressed boy with a bucket of soap and water was cleaning the windows. Shrill, agitated voices split the air. I entered the shop to find one of Lucille's assistants in tears and Lucille herself arguing vociferously with a plump, middle-aged woman in purple taffeta who clutched a bolt of ivory lace to her breast and shook her head adamantly, black ringlets dancing, bright pink spots blazing on her chubby cheeks.

"Out of the question!" Lucille shrieked. "I told you, I have a very important order to complete, an entire wardrobe. I can't *possibly* do your dress for another two weeks, and *then* I wouldn't dream of using that dreadful lace! I don't know *where* you got it, Madame Roland, but it's cheap, cheap, cheap, will fall apart in less than a year. I use my *own* material, you know that! Will you shut *up!*" she snapped at her sobbing assistant. "Take these men to the storeroom, show them where to put the cloth—"

"I'm one of your very best customers!" the plump woman yelled. "If you can't come to my aid in a time of need—"

"Need! You don't *need* an ivory lace dress. If you had any sense you'd wear nothing but *black!*"

"Well! I've never been so insulted in—"

"What *is* this!" Lucille cried, grabbing one of the men by the shoulder. "I said *plum* velvet. This is *puce!* You take it straight back to the warehouse and tell those idiots that if they can't deliver what I order they can find a *new* customer to rob! *Mon Dieu! C'est* too bloody *much!*"

She rolled her eyes heavenward and flapped her hands in the air. When the man started to argue with her she shooed him away and reached for smelling salts and then saw me standing just inside the doorway.

"My dear! I'm surrounded by idiots. You're early. This place is a madhouse! Marie wants the day off so she can meet her butcher boyfriend for an afternoon tryst, and Madame Roland wants a *lace* ball gown for next Tuesday, and these *men* have only brought half of what I ordered!"

"I'll never step foot in this shop again!" Madame Roland screamed.

"That's fine with *me*, Fatty! I've never liked dressing you in the first place. You make my finest creations look like something a *scrub* woman would wear! Out! Out! Go eat another pound of pralines!"

Cheeks flaming, Madame Roland marched out of the shop in a wild flurry of purple taffeta. One of the men handed Lucille a receipt to sign, and she studied it with narrow eyes, marked through four items, jotted notes beside the lines and then scribbled her name. The men left hurriedly. Marie came out of the back room, wiping her eyes. Outside, the boy leisurely swabbed the windows with soapy water.

"This hasn't been one of my better days," Lucille sighed,

putting on a martyred expression. "The shop was closed for so long, and now everyone wants everything at once. I only have two hands and *no* one I can depend on. Stop sniveling, Marie! You can meet him tonight, and he'll appreciate you all the more for waiting."

"He's not a butcher! He's a fine young man and his father just happens to sell meat and—"

"Where's Camille?" Lucille interrupted.

"She's in the fitting room, getting out Miss Danver's gown and pinning up the hem."

"Stop her at once! *I'll* do Miss Danver's hem. Camille *knows* this is a very special order! I never had problems like these when I was sewing for Pompadour," she confided. "Jeanne gave me my own apartment in Versailles to work in, such gilt, such crystal chandeliers! A *far* cry from what I had at the Devereaux plantation, I can assure you."

"Oh?" I said patiently.

"Can you believe it, my dear, they expected me to stay in the attic! A horrible, stuffy little room not fit for a scullery maid. They *begged* me to come, and I went through *hell* in that wretched rowboat, going through swamps you wouldn't believe, and I expected to be treated like a *guest*. I was stuck up there like a common *servant*, sewing by the light of a single candle till all hours of the morning. I had no choice, my dear, but when it was finally safe to leave I gave them *all* a piece of my mind!"

I shook my head in pretended sympathy. Lucille sighed wearily.

"*Everyone's* giving balls now that the fever's over. I've never had so many orders—the city's gone pleasure mad, and all the women expect *me* to dress them. I've given *you* top priority, my dear. It's been quite an ordeal, but I think everything will be ready on time. I've been working night and day, and, I must say, my dear, I think I've outdone myself."

I gave her an appreciative smile. Lucille might go on and on about giving me such preferential treatment, but, in fact, I was paying her three times what I would ordinarily have paid in order to have the new wardrobe prepared in such a short time. At those prices the engaging old fraud could afford to work night and day.

"Come on into the fitting room, my dear. You're going to be enchanted when you see the gown. We'll have some champagne, and I'll do up the hem and make a few adjustments—I'm still not satisfied with the bodice. You *must* tell me all about that devilishly handsome Jeremy Bond. I've never been as surprised as I was when I learned you were living with *him*.''

Groaning inwardly, I followed her into the fitting room and, stepping behind the screen, began to undress. I had been extremely guarded in what I had told Lucille, merely informing her that Derek and I had been separated, that I was sharing an apartment with Jeremy prior to leaving for England. She was an inveterate gossip, voraciously consuming any scrap of information about the private lives of her customers and embellishing lavishly in the retelling. I knew better than to give her any but the sketchiest details.

Lucille handed me the exquisite pale gold tulle petticoat, and I slipped it on, stepping from behind the screen just as the much put-upon Marie entered with a bottle of chilled champagne and two elegant crystal glasses. Camille, an unfortunately pudgy girl with large, rough hands, opened the bottle and poured the sparkling beverage, and then Lucille shooed them both out of the room. I took a sip and set the glass down.

''I don't know *what* I'm going to do with those girls,'' Lucille complained. ''Marie thinks of nothing but bedrooms, and Camille, alas, stumbles about like a dimwit. I suppose I'm lucky to have *anyone* working for me in this wretchedly backward city. Things just aren't the way they were in Paris.''

She picked up the shimmering golden-brown brocade gown embroidered all over with gold and brown flowers and helped me into it. When she had finished fastening it in back, I stepped up onto the round ivory footstool. The gown had narrow, off-the-shoulder sleeves, a low, clinging bodice and a very full skirt that belled out gorgeously. Lucille finished her champagne and, grabbing a packet of pins, got down on her knees to work with the hem.

''Any other customer would have insisted on rows of ruffles and fussy gold velvet bows, but you, my dear, have *unerring* taste. Simple, flowing lines, absolutely uncluttered. With cloth like this you don't need anything else. I'm not going to tell you what I *paid* for it, but you're getting it at a discount, my dear.''

''I'm extremely grateful.''

''Pompadour would have gone mad over this material, but then, of course, she couldn't wear brown, even as rich a golden brown as this. Such magnificent embroidery! Jeanne could only wear the palest colors, you know, mauve, pale blue, light mint green. Anything more dramatic would have washed her out completely, and with her complexion—''

Bending over, I reached for the glass of champagne I had set aside. I had the feeling I was going to need it. As Lucille continued to chatter about her most famous customer, I studied the gown in the full-length mirror on the wall across the room. It was indeed a sumptuous creation, the embroidered gold and dark brown silk flowers gleaming against the golden brown.

''—*such* a delicious man!'' Lucille was saying. ''Every woman in New Orleans was after him, and you end up sharing his apartment. I do hope he's quite recovered.''

''He's much better, Lucille.''

''So fortunate you were there to nurse him! It must have been a dreadful ordeal for you, my dear.''

''It wasn't pleasant,'' I said. ''If Mandy hadn't come along when she did, I couldn't have saved him.''

''Oh yes, that Negro woman. I believe you told me about her.''

''She made mustard plasters and made medicine from roots and herbs, forced him to drink it. It was perfectly vile-smelling.''

''I can imagine!''

''She also made medicine from lemons and honey and vinegar. It was touch and go for a while, but—it's over now.''

''Turn to the left a bit, my dear. And now?''

''Now I'm going to England to join Derek.''

''Ah, the magnetic, brooding Mr. Hawke. I never understood exactly what *happened*, my dear. The two of you were going to England to be married, and then you show up back in New Orleans with Jeremy Bond.''

''I told you, Lucille. We were separated.''

''I see. I see. A lovers' quarrel.''

''Something like that.''

''And the dashing Jeremy Bond provided comfort and solace.''

''I suppose you could say that.''

''A little to the right now,'' she directed, moving around on her knees. ''He knows you're still in love with Derek Hawke?''

''He's known from the first. I made no secret of it. Derek is the only man in the world I'll ever love that way. The bond between us is stronger than time, stronger than distance. I love him with all my heart and soul, and he loves me. The day of our reunion will be the happiest day of my life, and we'll never be separated again.''

Lucille finished pinning up the hem and got to her feet, moving back to examine her handiwork. I finished my champagne and set the glass down. She tilted her head to one side, eyes narrowed, thin lips tight, and then she told me to turn around slowly.

"Perfect!" she declared. "I'll sew it up at once. I want to let out a couple of tucks in the bodice—how does it fit under the arms?"

"It feels fine."

Lucille examined the bodice, frowned, nodded briskly and then moved back and poured herself another glass of champagne. I stepped behind the screen and removed the gown and petticoat. Lucille clapped for Camille and, when the girl appeared, told her to take the garments into the sewing room. I put on the violet and blue striped silk.

"Love," Lucille sighed. "It's glorious, and you've certainly had your share, my dear. *So* many adventures! Women commit suicide over men like Jeremy Bond."

"The world is full of idiots."

"And you blithely abandon him to cross the ocean for another man."

"I'm not abandoning him," I informed her, fastening up the dress. "He and I are merely—" I hesitated. "There's nothing between us, Lucille. He came to my aid when I needed help. He's being paid nicely."

Lucille's shrewd eyes gleamed knowingly. "There's nothing between you, yet you risk your life nursing him back to health."

"I had no choice. He needed me."

"And he doesn't need you now?" she asked as I stepped over to the mirror to adjust my sleeves.

"The only thing Jeremy Bond needs at the moment is a swift kick."

"Ah! Something *is* there. I knew it!"

"You're quite mistaken," I said haughtily, irritated by her persistence. "When shall I return for the next fittings?"

"All the other things should be ready for final fittings day after tomorrow, and, my dear, you know the black and white striped taffeta? I've found a pair of long red velvet gloves to go with it, and I'm making a hat as well, an enormous brim covered with black taffeta, lined with white, *dripping* with magnificent black and white plumes. One red velvet ribbon. My gift to you.''

She hugged me impulsively, and it was impossible to stay irritated with her. She was a shrewd, mercenary, gossipy old fraud who probably had never so much as set eyes on Madame de Pompadour, but beneath that brittle, avaricious exterior was a genuine heart. Pompadour or no, Lucille was a superb artist, and I was grateful for all she'd done for me over the years. I returned her hug, had another glass of champagne with her and left the shop.

Taking a shortcut through the market, I was pleased to see the thronging, bustling crowd, the vitality and color stronger than ever as housewives picked over mounds of bright red apples, vivid oranges, pale green pears and bargained over bins of shrimp and eels and silvery fish. Carts of flowers made splashes of vibrant color, and the smell of freshly baked bread and a hundred different spices perfumed the air. A strange, melancholy mood hung over me nevertheless, increasing as, leaving the market, I passed the building that once had housed Rawlins' Place, the glittering gambling house where so many changes had taken place in my life. Memories of Jeff stirred as I moved on, the old grief returning. The past seemed to haunt me now that I was about to leave this city I had grown to love.

I thought about Derek, something I hadn't allowed myself to do during the past weeks. I had firmly put all thought of him out of my mind, concentrating on Jeremy, on making him well again, but now that that had been accomplished, I felt the impatience and anguish that had plagued me ever since I had learned he was still alive. I saw again that beloved face with perfectly chiseled features, wide pink mouth set in a stern line, cheekbones broad and strong, gray eyes grim as he contemplated a life of bitter disappointments. He had at last claimed the inheritance that had been wrested from him, at last he was living at Hawkehouse, but his victory was a hollow one, I knew, and little consolation for the loss of the woman he loved. Soon, my darling, I promised him silently, soon we will be together again and joy will fill those eyes and happiness will be ours after all these years.

Opening the gate and crossing the courtyard. I banished the image from my mind, determined to concentrate on the present. That was the only way I could maintain my sanity. I would take each day at a time, and each day would bring me closer to that moment when his eyes met mine and his arms enfolded me and a flood of joy swept over us both. I opened the front door that still bore signs of the white cross, jagged marks where the paint had been scraped away. As I stepped into the foyer a wonderful smell wafted on the air. Mandy was baking another spice cake.

She was taking it out of the oven as I entered the kitchen. Setting it on the drainboard to cool, she sighed wearily and ran a hand across her wrinkled brow, her back to me. Unaware of my presence, she reached into the cabinet and took down a jar of plum preserves.

"Really, Mandy," I said. "Another cake? You're spoiling him dreadfully."

She turned around, startled.

"Miz—Miz Marietta. I didn't hear you come in. Did you get them pretty new dresses done?"

"They'll be finished in a few days. The cake looks delicious. You make all these things for Jeremy and *I'm* the one putting on weight."

"That ain't so, Miz Marietta. You'se much too skinny."

She seemed nervous for some reason, and I noticed a worried look in her eyes. I asked her if something was wrong, and she hesitated, wiping her hands on her apron and looking anxiously about the room as though searching for something else to do that would allow her to avoid answering my question.

"You—you'se goin' to be real upset. Miz Marietta."

"He's gone out, hasn't he?"

"I tried to stop him. 'You ain't strong enough yet, Mister Jeremy,' I told him. 'You ain't got no business gallivantin' around, get back in that bed.' He grinned at me an' said I was bein' silly, said not to fuss over him like he was a baby."

"Did he say where he was going?"

Mandy shook her head. "He just chucked me under the chin and sashayed out like he wudn't ever sick a day in his life. I been worried somethin' awful. Weak as that boy is, he's likely to pass out on the street."

"I hope he does," I said acidly.

"You don't mean that, Miz Marietta," she protested.

"If he insists on acting like an imbecile, he deserves anything that happens to him. I don't care to discuss it any more, Mandy. It's almost time to start dinner. I'll help you fry the chicken."

"You ain't doin' nothin' in this kitchen in that fancy silk dress," she informed me. "If you'se goin' to help me, you go change."

I obeyed, angrily removing the dress in the bedroom and putting on the sprigged tan cotton Mandy had skillfully mended and laundered. I assured myself that I didn't give a damn what happened to him. I certainly wasn't going to waste time worrying about him. He'd love that, the bastard. He'd love to think I was fretting and wringing my hands and imagining all sorts of disasters. He could go straight to hell and stay there. Tomorrow, first thing in the morning, I was going down to the booking office and buy passage on the very first ship leaving for England, and Jeremy Bond could rot in hell. I had put it off much too long as it was, fretting over him, rubbing his bloody back, waiting on him like a servant. I should have booked passage as soon as the quarantine was lifted.

My mood hadn't improved much when I returned to the kitchen. Mandy looked apprehensive as I cut the chicken into pieces, attacking it vigorously with the butcher knife. I dipped the pieces into flour and egg batter and dropped them into the pot of hot grease on the stove, taking great satisfaction as they began to pop and sizzle noisily. I washed broccoli and put it on to cook and then began to mix up batter for popovers. Mandy turned the chicken over with a long fork, watching me knead the dough.

"He'll be back, Miz Marietta," she said quietly.

"I couldn't care less," I retorted.

"You—Miz Marietta, you ain't really gonna go off to England and leave him, are you? You ain't gonna go off and marry that other man?"

"Of course I am."

"But—" She hesitated, frowning. "You loves Mister Jeremy."

"I detest him!"

"That ain't so. I know it ain't. I seen the way you nursed

him, the way you looked at him, all tender an' concerned, so worried he wudn't goin' to make it. Then, when he started gettin' better, I seen how pleased you were when he started teasin' you, how much you enjoyed it.''

''Nonsense!''

''This other man—I don't know nothin' about him, Miz Marietta, but I know you can't really love him, not feelin' the way you do about Mister Jeremy. You might *think* you do, but—''

''It's none of your concern, Mandy!'' I snapped.

I was immediately sorry, of course. Mandy meant well, and I shouldn't have snapped that way. My anger evaporated. I set the bowl of dough aside to rise and sighed, suddenly weary. Mandy turned the chicken over again and dropped pats of butter into the broccoli. I owed her so much, so very much. Freed by her master just before his death three years ago, she had been rummaging about the city ever since, struggling to survive, absolutely alone. She had no family, no friends. The money Jeremy had given her had enabled her to set up her stall in the flea market, but selling broken pots and discarded lamps and other odds and ends brought in barely enough to live on. That was all going to change. I intended to see to it. Before I left for England I was going to open an account for her in one of the banks in the Quarter that welcomed people of color, and Mandy would never have to worry about money again.

''I think that's dough's ready now,'' she said. ''I'll just get them popovers ready for the oven.''

''I'll set the table in the dining room. If he's well enough to gad about the city he's well enough to eat at the dinner table. I'm sorry I snapped at you, Mandy. I didn't mean it.''

'' 'Course you didn't. You wuz just upset.''

Jeremy came sauntering in twenty minutes later, looking infuriatingly chipper. His rich brown hair was windblown, tumbling over his brow. He was wearing dark blue breeches and frock coat, a maroon brocade waistcoat and a neckcloth of sky-blue silk. Although the coat hung rather loosely, he presented an undeniably dapper picture, and his new thinness made him seem even taller. If his mysterious outing had wearied him, he showed no signs of it. He seemed to be bursting with vitality.

"I'm famished!" he declared.

I ignored him. He seemed to find that amusing. I maintained a stony silence during dinner, and he chattered merrily with Mandy, complimenting her on the meal. When Mandy set a piece of spice cake in front of him and spread plum preserves over it, I gave an exasperated sigh, threw down my napkin and left the table. Going into the parlor, I lighted a lamp, took a book from the shelf and tried to read. Jeremy came in a short while later. I didn't bother to look up from my book.

"Fantastic meal," he observed. "You should've stayed for dessert. Mandy's spice cake was sheer heaven."

"I'm glad you enjoyed it," I said stiffly.

"You sound more like you wished I'd choked on it."

I made no comment. He grinned. I slammed the book shut and put it down. His grin widened.

"I'd better go help Mandy clear the table," I said, getting to my feet.

"She told me to tell you not to bother, said she'd clear the table and do the dishes and you were to rest your bones. Something the matter? You seem a mite put out."

I wasn't going to lose my temper again. I wasn't going to give him the satisfaction. I sat back down and calmly picked up the book and pretended to resume my reading. Jeremy stepped over to the mantle and propped one elbow on it, his frock coat hanging open.

"Guess you're mad 'cause I went out," he said.

"What you do doesn't concern me at all, Jeremy."

"No?"

"I'm not the least bit interested. I'm trying to read."

"Dull book. Couldn't get through it myself. Too much moralizing. Not enough action."

I turned a page. Although I paid not the least bit of attention to him, I was acutely aware of his presence. I could feel him watching me. It made me very uncomfortable, but he'd never know that. A full minute passed as I ran my eyes over the print without seeing a single word. He was growing impatient, I could tell. He was dying to reveal where he'd been. Hell would freeze over before I asked.

"Ship leaves in two weeks," he remarked casually.

The bastard had my attention now. I put the book back down and turned to face him.

"What ship?"

"The ship that's taking us to France. I went down to the booking office. You've never seen such a mob. Only a few ships leaving, most of 'em booked up months in advance. Had to bribe a few people, naturally, but I finally got us a cabin."

"*Us!*"

"We'll sail to France, then cross the Channel to England. I understand the cabin's quite comfortable. Couldn't get two separate cabins, had enough trouble getting one. We'll be sailing as Mr. and Mrs. Jeremy Bond, but that little bit of subterfuge shouldn't hurt anyone."

I was on my feet now, cheeks flaming.

"*We! Us!* What do you—"

"Did you really think I was going to let you go to England by yourself? A long voyage like that, you need someone big and strong to take care of you. I'm going with you, Marietta."

"Oh no you're not!"

Jeremy chuckled. "Wanna bet?" he asked.

Thirty-Four

The great white sails swelled in the breeze, carrying *Le Bon Coeur* over an endless expanse of water that rippled gently like watered gray silk, all blue long since faded. The sky was gray, too, a deepening pearl gray smeared with blurry gold and orange streaks in the wake of the sun that had already disappeared on the distant horizon where sea met sky. It was cool. I should have brought a cloak with me from the cabin. Resting my hands on the smooth mahogany railing, I stared at the emptiness, barely aware of movement as the huge prow cut smoothly through the water. Passengers leisurely strolled the deck, talking quietly, all of them elegantly clad. It took a great deal of money to sail on *Le Bon Coeur* and, with the revolution still raging in America, passage was even more expensive now.

I was in a pensive mood, a mood that had prevailed ever since our departure over two weeks ago. That had been a busy, bustling, frantic morning with hundreds of people crowding the dock, friends and family seeing passengers off with noisy festivity or even noisier sobs, men carrying heavy boxes and trunks up the gangplank, sailors swarming about the ship, bells clanging, incredible confusion on every side. I had been surprised when Lucille came to see me off, her shrewd old eyes full of genuine sadness, her thin face stiff as a mask as she tried to hold back her tears. She had hugged me so hard I thought my ribs would crack, and when I finally reached our cabin I discovered a case of champagne, an enormous basket of fruit and several brightly wrapped presents she had smuggled there earlier. I would miss the outrageous old fraud.

I would miss Mandy, too. She hadn't come to the dock. We had made our farewells at the apartment, which she would continue to occupy during Jeremy's absence. She had plenty of money now. I had taken her to the bank and opened an account for her, and she had protested that the amount was far, far too much, more than she would ever need. She was planning to start an herb garden in the backyard, in the shadow of the cistern and fig trees, and Camille was eager to help her. The clumsy, disorganized, great lump of a girl who caused Lucille so much distress had been elated when I asked her if she would like to share the apartment with Mandy and watch over her while Jeremy was gone. I wasn't sure who would be watching over whom, but the two had taken to each other immediately, an instant affection established between the ungainly French orphan and the withered old woman I had grown to love so much.

The sadness had haunted me ever since the ship set sail,

and it continued to haunt me now. I should be filled with a wild elation. I should be charged with excitement. I had finally left America behind me, and I was on my way to join the man I loved. After all these years, I was going back home to England, returning to my roots, but, curiously, it seemed I was leaving my roots in the great, sprawling, tumultuous country now forever lost to me. Loss. That's what I felt. The past seven years had not been easy. They had been filled with turmoil and tragedy, with conflict and disaster, but I had known great happiness as well and joy that sang in my blood like glorious music, and, somehow, without my being aware of it, I had become a part of that country in which I had spent those years. England, with its stately homes and sleepy villages and misty green fields, could never stir those feelings inside me that the country I was leaving did. I was English, but after all this time I no longer felt a part of the land of my birth.

As the orange and gold streaks faded against the dark gray sky, as sails billowed and cracked stiffly in the breeze, propelling the enormous ship over the gently rippling water, I thought of Em, longing to have her here beside me, longing to pour my heart out to her. My heart ached as I realized she was lost to me, too, that I would never see her again, nor Mandy, nor Lucille, nor any of the others whose lives had become a part of mine during those years in America. I thought of Adam and Cassie, whom I had helped escape from Shadow Oaks and sent north to freedom. Had they found happiness there? I thought of Helmut's sister, Meg, and her beloved James, young people free at last to love openly after Helmut's death in the blazing Roseclay. So many people. So many memories, not all of them painful.

I sighed, shivering a little as the cool breeze stroked my bare arms and shoulders. Seven years ago I had left England in chains, falsely accused of a crime I hadn't committed, terrified of a future of bondage but determined to survive, learning quickly in that squalid prison ship, learning from Angie, the blonde, angelic-looking guttersnipe who had become my closest friend and taught me to pick locks, learning from Jack, the brawny sailor who had made love to me in a secluded spot on deck and had brought me food so I wouldn't starve or succumb to scurvy like so many of the other prisoners. Auctioned off like a slave in Carolina. I had survived . . . and I had experienced a shattering love that racked my very soul and was still alive inside of me.

Derek. I would be with him soon. Derek was in England, and when he finally clasped me into his arms and held me tight, this perplexing melancholy would vanish forever. I belonged to him. My place was at his side. Once there, I would forget everything else and share with him a future that would be filled with a happiness few women were fortunate enough to know. All the anguish, all the conflict would be behind me at last.

I rubbed my arms to warm them, hesitating to return to the cabin. The sky was an even darker gray now, streaked with amethyst, and there were purple reflections on the water. Turning away from the railing, I saw Madame Janine Etienne strolling down the deck toward me. I stiffened, staring at her with a hostility that startled me. Madame Etienne smiled to herself, sensing the hostility, delighting in it. Thirty years old, undeniably beautiful with her sparkling green eyes flecked with brown, her glossy blue-black hair and cool, aristocratic features, she was returning to Paris to join a wealthy, middle-aged husband who had left New Orleans several months earlier on business, sending for her when he discovered it was going to keep him in France for the next two years.

Madame Etienne nodded to me as she drew nearer. I didn't return the nod. I observed that her rouged pink lips were a bit too full, her eyelids too heavy, and her nose was definitely too long. She was gorgeous nevertheless, her rich jet hair pulled back sleekly from her face and worn in an elaborate stack of waves in back, fastened with diamond clips. Her low-cut green velvet gown and the sweeping green velvet cloak edged with soft gray fur were chic indeed, as chic as anything Lucille ever created, and the diamonds that flashed in her hair, at her throat, and on her fingers were quite genuine. Janine Etienne had that special quality only certain French women seemed to attain, a combination of worldly allure and aggressive self-confidence. Her demeanor, her eyes proclaimed her a woman with numerous love affairs to her credit, and that was all very well, but I bitterly resented the fact that her latest was with a man who was traveling as my husband.

She stopped and smiled a coy, mocking smile. Her perfume was heavy, exotic, suggesting crushed flowers and bedrooms. I longed to grab the hussy by her hair and hurl her overboard.

"Good evening, Madame Bond," she said in that purring, heavily accented voice. "Where is that handsome husband of yours?"

"I've no idea," I retorted. "I assumed he was with you."

She lifted one of those perfectly arched eyebrows, pretending a surprise she was far from feeling. "La! *Avec moi?* Whyever would you think that?"

It came out *fie-evah vould jew zink zat*, charming, so French, so quaint. I might not hurl her overboard. I might just scratch her eyes out. The taunting smile continued to curl on her lips. The flecked green eyes sparkled with feline amusement.

"It's a habit he seems to have acquired of late," I said.

"La! *Such* a thoughtful man, so kind, so attentive to a poor woman traveling all alone. We play the cards. We sip the champagne. It helps to pass the time."

"I'll just bet it does."

She pulled the cloak closer about her shoulders, the soft, silvery gray fur framing the lower part of her face. Her chin was too sharp, I noted, her cheekbones a bit broad, much too heavily rouged. The overall effect was devastating, though, I had to admit that. She exuded a brazen sexual magnetism that made every man on board long to bed her. I wondered if Jeremy was the only one who had. Probably not. We had been sailing for over two weeks, and there were twenty-four hours in a day.

"You are upset?" she inquired.

"Not at all. Should I be?"

"Some wives, they would resent it. You, though, you are very wise. You understand men. Is very French of you."

I'll tell you one thing, sweetheart, I said silently, if I really wanted him you wouldn't have a prayer. You're doing me a favor. You just don't know it.

"Well," she said, "ta-ta, as you English say. Perhaps we

will see each other when we dine. Filet of sole tonight, I believe.''

Maybe you'll choke on a fish bone, I thought as she strolled on down the deck, wafting perfume in the air behind her. Several men turned to watch her progress, openly longing to sample her delectable wares. A shy, rather handsome blond man with a book in his hand trailed after her, trying to summon up enough courage to speak. Janine paused, gave him a provocative look over her shoulder and waited for him to catch up. The blond blushed, closed his book and stammered something I couldn't hear. The two of them moved on together, Janine showering him with admiring looks. Jeremy just might find her cabin a bit crowded tonight.

It really was quite amusing, I thought, going below, and it was foolish of me to let it bother me this way. Jeremy Bond and I were traveling together as husband and wife, yes, and we were sharing a rather luxurious cabin, but I slept in the bed alone and had, from the first, let him know that it was worth his life if he dared try to climb in with me. There was a chaise longue under one of the portholes, perfectly comfortable with soft, plump pink satin cushions. He had slept on it exactly four times, grumbling and complaining bitterly that it was much too short for him, which it was, and adding that if I had any style at all I'd give *him* the bed and take the chaise longue myself, unless we could work out some other arrangement. I coldly vetoed that ''other arrangement'' and refused to give up the bed. Jeremy had not spent another night in the cabin. I couldn't really blame him.

The movement of the ship was much more pronounced as I walked down the narrow but richly paneled passageway with doors on either side. I had to admit that we had been fortunate indeed to get passage on this ship with its elegant dining salon, its luxurious trappings and its courteous crew. *Le Bon Coeur* accommodated only fifty passengers, transporting a cargo of dry goods in its hold, but those fifty passengers were treated like royalty. I opened the door to our cabin and stepped inside. Jeremy wasn't in. He only came to the cabin to change clothes. It was just as well. The less we saw of each other the better.

It was seven o'clock. Jeremy and I dined at eight. As the plush dining room could only seat twenty people at a time, each passenger had been assigned a different hour for dining, six, seven and, by far the most desirable, eight. The captain dined then, as did the most fashionable passengers. I wondered how Janine had managed to get on the eight o'clock list. All those diamonds, perhaps. More likely a quick and satisfying tumble with the right ship's officer. Jeremy, of course, had bribed our way onto the list, putting the proper amount of money into the proper palm. Charming he might be. Fashionable he wasn't, nor was I, for that matter.

Although the gown I was wearing was perfectly suitable, I decided to change for dinner, particularly if I was going to have another encounter with the formidable Madame Etienne. Examining the gowns that hung in the wardrobe trunk standing open in the corner, I selected a deep red satin with narrow black stripes and laid it out on the bed along with the matching petticoat with its layers of floating red tulle underskirts. That should do it, I thought, removing the clothes I was wearing and hanging them back up. I would wear the long black velvet gloves as well, and perhaps a narrow black velvet ribbon at my throat. No, that would be too much, too obvious. The gloves would be enough.

Twenty minutes later, wearing only the red tulle petticoat, I was still at the dressing table, putting the finishing touches on my makeup, lips a bit redder than usual, cheeks subtly rouged, eyelids brushed with a suggestion of pale brown shadow. I had brushed my hair, arranged it on top of my head, and then decided to let it fall in natural waves. As I opened a bottle of perfume, Jeremy stepped into the cabin. He looked slightly rumpled, his frock coat wrinkled, his neckcloth loose.

"You might have knocked!" I snapped.

"Why the hell should I?" he snapped back. "This happens to be my cabin, too. You needn't go all modest on me. I've seen you in your petticoat before, you know."

"Go to hell!"

"Aren't we in a dandy mood."

"Aren't we just."

"You know, lass, you're turning into an awful shrew."

"And you, mister, are turning into a surly brute."

"Who's to blame for that?"

"Certainly not I," I said airily.

"Expecting me to sleep on that bloody chaise longue that's a good two feet too short. Acting like a terrified virgin."

"I've *never* acted like a terrified virgin. I refused to let you share the bed, yes, but—"

"Forget it!" he snarled, removing his coat.

"If you're going to undress, I'd prefer you do so behind the screen."

"You've seen me without my breeches before, too," he retorted, peeling off his shirt.

He sat down on the edge of the bed, pulled off his boots and then stood up and proceeded to remove his breeches. I dabbed perfume behind my ears and between my breasts, carefully ignoring him. He pulled on a robe, tied the sash, and then, just to aggravate me, lighted a perfectly foul-smelling cigar. I was not going to give him the satisfaction of complaining about it. I got up and slipped the gown over my head, pulling it down, putting my arms into the short puffed sleeves, adjusting the bodice.

"Planning a seduction?" he inquired.

"Hardly."

"All that perfume. All that makeup. A red dress. Have your eye on one of the officers?"

"I'm going to ignore that remark, Mr. Bond. Damn, I can't get it fastened properly—"

He stalked over, shoved my hands away and fastened up the tiny, invisible hooks in back with a nimble skill that proved he had had a considerable amount of practice. The job done, he marched over to his trunk and took out a new set of clothes, black broadcloth breeches and coat, fine white lawn shirt, a splendid sapphire-blue neckcloth. Cigar clenched in the corner of his mouth, he took off his robe and began to dress.

"I ran into the delectable Madame Étienne on deck," I remarked.

"Yeah?"

"She seemed lonely."

"Pity," he said, pulling on his breeches.

"I naturally assumed you'd be with her."

"You assumed wrong."

I took out the long black velvet gloves and began to put them on. Jeremy snapped his fingers, took out the deep pearl-gray brocade waistcoat he had forgotten and put it on over his shirt, smoothing it down with his palms. Picking up the neckcloth, he stepped over to the mirror and began to fasten it around his neck, carefully arranging the folds. He was a terrible dandy, I thought, but when he put his boots back on and slipped on the frock coat, I had to admit he looked dashing indeed. I couldn't blame Janine for snapping him up like a plate full of bonbons.

Jeremy crushed his cigar out in a small porcelain tray, tugged at the lapels of his coat and patted the sapphire neckcloth.

"How do I look?" he asked.

"You might just brush your hair."

"Guess I'd better at that. I know you're much too proud to ask, but just in case you're interested, I spent the day playing cards down in the hold with some of the more affluent male passengers. Won a bundle of money."

"How nice," I retorted. "You probably cheated."

"Didn't have to. The chaps on this boat don't know the first thing about cards. There," he said, putting down the brush. "Ready to go? I didn't eat any lunch, and I'm famished."

We left the cabin, and, clasping my elbow firmly, he led me down the passageway, walking with that brisk, bouncy stride. I almost had to trot to keep up. People nodded politely as we entered the dining salon and moved toward our table. Janine Etienne was sharing her table with the shy, handsome blond. He no longer had his book, I noticed, and he seemed a bit nervous and apprehensive about dining amid all these fashionable people at this unaccustomed hour. I pegged him at once as a six o'clock diner. Perhaps, though, he was merely apprehensive about being with the seductive Janine who devoured him with her eyes and clearly planned to have him for dessert. As we took our seats, I couldn't help but smile.

The great ship rocked a little, tilting slowly from side to side, though not enough to be disturbing or to prevent the waiters from serving the excellent meal with superb courtesy. Jeremy was silent, sullen now, toying with his food and making no effort to be sociable. Mouth tight, lips turned down at the corners, blue eyes lost in thought, hair neatly brushed for once, he was severely handsome, stern and formidable. Jeremy loved to squabble as much as I did—yes, I had to admit that our spats were curiously invigorating—but when he was in a mood like this, I knew better than to agitate him.

"Someone spotted a school of whales this afternoon," I remarked, spooning more cheese sauce over my asparagus.

"Yeah?"

"They were a long way off, I understand. Mrs. Tyler said they looked like gleaming black rocks floating in the water."

"Fascinating."

"I'd have loved to have seen them. I've never seen a whale."

"You haven't missed anything."

"This sole's delicious. It amazes me that one can dine in such luxury on board a ship."

Jeremy merely snorted, more sullen than ever. I was beginning to grow irritated.

"The weather's been marvelous," I observed. "We had that storm last week, it's true, but it wasn't a bad one, a bit of wind, some rain. The ship hardly tossed at all. The water's been smooth as glass today, and—"

"Is it absolutely necessary for you to keep on babbling like an empty-headed fool?"

That stung. I could feel spots of color burning on my cheeks.

"I was merely trying to be pleasant," I informed him. "That's a hell of a lot more than one could say for you."

"I don't happen to be in a pleasant mood."

"That's quite apparent. Perhaps it's the company. Perhaps you'd rather be chatting with Janine Etienne."

"Perhaps I would."

I started to get up. He reached across the table and seized my wrist in a tight clamp and told me in no uncertain terms to finish my meal. His voice was threatening. His eyes were full of smoldering blue fires. People were beginning to stare. I settled back down into my chair and, when he released it, rubbed my wrist.

"You hurt my wrist," I said.

"You're lucky I didn't break it."

"You bastard!"

528

He looked surprised. "You're really mad, aren't you?"

"You're bloody right I am!"

"Lower your voice. You're making a spectacle of yourself. People will think Mr. and Mrs. Jeremy Bond are having a marital spat."

"I don't give a damn what they think. I've had just about enough of this, Jeremy. I never wanted you to come on this trip in the first place. I tried to stop you. This charade is beginning to wear thin. And as for what people *think*—what the hell do you think they think when you spend every single night in the cabin of that simpering whore over there?"

"Touchy about Janine, aren't you?"

"I don't give a *damn* what you do!"

"Janine Etienne is an interesting woman. I've played cards with her a few times. I've had champagne with her. I'm a man. I have an ego. The woman I love treats me like a leper, and it's pleasant to spend time with a woman who finds me appealing."

"Don't flatter yourself! Anything in a pair of breeches is appealing to a woman like that."

"Be that as it may—"

"I've no intention of sitting here and discussing your sexual adventures. You can hump her twenty-four hours a day for all I care. I imagine she'd adore it."

"Probably would," he admitted.

I stabbed the sole with my fork and viciously decapitated the asparagus. Then I put knife and fork down and tried to control my anger and hold back the tears that threatened to splatter at any second. *Damn* him for making me feel this way. I took several deep breaths and, after a while, managed to lift my glass and take a sip of wine. After having toyed with his food earlier on, Jeremy now began to eat with apparent relish. The sonofabitch was pleased with himself for having upset me. He loved getting me riled, took a savage glee in seeing my cheeks burn, seeing my eyes flash. I fought back the anger and made a valiant effort to salvage my dignity.

Jeremy finished his sole. The waiter removed our plates and asked if we would care for dessert. Jeremy nodded. I maintained a stony silence. Janine Etienne left the dining salon with a flash of diamonds, a swirl of green velvet, the handsome blond trotting behind her like an obedient, lovesick schoolboy. Jeremy paid no attention to them. Our dessert came. He ate his slowly. I didn't touch mine.

"You more or less threw me out of our cabin," he said in a calm, reasonable voice. "I couldn't sleep on that bloody chaise longue. I had to find a place to spend my nights. An officer, Lieutenant Girdot, chap I played cards with, kindly volunteered to let me share his quarters—he has an extra bunk. I've been spending my nights there."

"Do you really expect me to believe that?" I asked dryly.

"Believe what you will, Marietta, but I assure you that the only woman on board this ship I care to sleep with is sitting across the table from me right now."

I met this comment with a brooding silence. My anger had vanished, and I no longer felt I might cry. The melancholy I had felt earlier on enveloped me again, deeper, more disturbing than ever. I felt utterly lost, utterly alone, and life itself seemed a hopeless, meaningless ritual. Not even the thought of Derek could lift the black depression that settled over me.

"Finished?" Jeremy inquired.

I nodded, and we left the dining salon. When he started to lead me back to the cabin, I shook my head and told him I wanted to stroll on deck for a while. He said he would keep me company, and I was too weary to object. All the fight had gone out of me. Jeremy said it would be cool and went to fetch a wrap for me. I moved up to the deck, folding my arms about my waist as the chill night air struck me. The night was deep blue and black and silver, only a few stars twinkling against the black, black sky, the moon obscured by clouds. I stepped over to the railing as the huge sails caught the wind overhead, belling out and snapping crisply. The water was much choppier than it had been earlier, and the ship moved ponderously, creaking and groaning as if protesting the strain. An occasional sailor scurried past, but there were no other passengers on deck.

"Rough night for a stroll," Jeremy said, coming up behind me.

"I don't mind. It suits my mood."

"That bad?" he inquired.

I nodded, and he placed a cloak over my shoulders. The heavy folds fell to my feet, covering me completely. Jeremy moved around in front of me and fastened the strings at my throat.

"Couldn't decide which one you'd want," he said, "so I just brought one of my own. It ought to keep you warm."

It was of heavy black broadcloth, lined with white satin, warm indeed and smelling of him. I adjusted the sweeping folds and began to stroll slowly down the deck. Jeremy sauntered along beside me, matching his stride to mine, hands thrust into the pockets of his breeches. The sails snapped. Wood groaned. A sailor called out to one of his mates. Waves sloshed against the hull with a monotonous, slapping sound.

"Low?" he asked.

"I have been ever since we left," I said quietly.

"I guess I'm responsible for that."

I shook my head. "It's not your fault. It's a lot of things. I should be happy, I know, but—" I let the sentence trail into silence, unable to explain what I was feeling.

"I understand, Marietta."

"Do you?"

"I know you, lass. I know you better than you know yourself. I understand, all right. I'm hoping you'll come to understand, too, before it's too late."

"You're speaking in riddles."

"Not at all," he replied. "It merely seems that way because you refuse to see what's in your own heart."

"You—you've said that before, several times. One day, you said, I would see what was in my own heart. I know what's in my heart, Jeremy. I know who I am, where I belong."

"Ah, lass, if only that were true."

He spoke softly, tenderly, and I looked up at him as we continued to walk slowly around the deck. His handsome face was sad, his eyes dark, reflective. He claimed to know me, but he didn't, not really, and I realized that I didn't really know him either. He was complex, a creature of many moods, constantly shifting. The charming, bantering, bickering Jeremy was merely a facade, and beneath that flippant surface were depths I had never fully appreciated. Once or twice I had sensed them, but I had never made an effort to genuinely know the man who dwelled there.

531

Clouds rolled slowly across the sky, spilling silver over their edges as they moved past the moon, and the moon appeared at last, round and full, pale silver-gold. The deck was washed with misty light. A million flecks of silver danced on the water like glittering spangles. Jeremy sighed, hunching his shoulders, thrusting his hands deeper into his pockets. He hadn't brought a cloak for himself, and it was growing cooler. He shouldn't be out here after such a serious illness, I thought, but I knew if I said anything to that effect it would irritate him.

We moved on in silence, each lost in our own thoughts, and after a while I stopped. We had completely traversed the deck, reaching the spot where I had been standing when he brought the cloak. The ship rocked, plowing on through the waves, the deck tilting slightly as we stood there without speaking. Jeremy stood at the railing, gazing out at the water, a stranger to me, it seemed, a man I didn't know at all. I wrapped the heavy cloak closer about me, the satin lining smooth and warm, caressing my skin.

"We'll be in France soon," I said.

"Yes, the days are passing quickly."

"Then England."

Jeremy turned to look at me. His face, sculpted in moonlight, was without expression now. He seemed remote, untouchable.

"That's right," he said. His voice was hard. "Soon we'll be in England, and you'll join your lover and live happily ever after."

"Jeremy, I—" I hesitated. "Why did you come? Why?"

"You know the answer to that, Marietta."

"You knew I—"

"Yes," he snapped, "I knew."

"Then—"

"I hoped there might still be a chance," he told me. "I hoped you might still come to your senses. I was wrong. I was a fool to hope. I shouldn't have come."

"I'm sorry. I wish—"

"It's not your fault, Marietta," he said tersely. "Each of us creates our own hell. We've no one to blame but ourselves."

He wanted to say more, I could see that, but he cut himself

short. I wanted to say more, too, wanted to say kind, wise words that would make it easier for us both, but the words wouldn't come. We stood there, silent, looking at each other in the moonlight as waves slapped against the hull and sails snapped in the wind, separated by silence and deep emotions tightly contained. After a moment Jeremy scowled and looked away. "Good night, Marietta," he said, and then, abruptly, he went below, leaving me alone with the loss, leaving me alone with my own pivate hell.

Thirty-Five

Carts and lorries and carriages of every description rumbled down the street at frightening speeds, horses neighing, wheels clattering over the cobbles, people darting through the traffic at the risk of life and limb. An urchin with flaxen hair and dirty face skipped nimbly in front of a carriage, dodged a cart and leaped in front of a lorry laden with great wooden casks of beer. The driver jerked violently on the reins. The horses reared. A cask of beer rolled off the lorry and crashed on the cobbles, wood splintering, beer gushing in foamy waves. Cheeks red with anger, the driver shouted fearsome curses and grabbed his whip. The urchin laughed, extended a stiff middle finger and danced merrily onto the pavement, swallowed up by the congestion of pedestrians. The traffic grew even more tangled and lethal as vehicles swerved to avoid the slats of wood.

The din was incredible. Hawkers cried their wares with shrill insistence, urging passersby to purchase sausage rolls, paper windmills, beads, copper pots and pans, tasty chestnuts freshly roasted. Horribly deformed beggars pleading for pennies were coldly ignored or harshly shoved aside by finely attired gentlemen who strode briskly along pavements as congested as the street itself. London was a city of great excitement and even greater contrasts, gorgeous, majestic buildings back-to-back with slums, quiet, lovely parks sheltering serenely amid densely overpopulated neighborhoods. It was a city of theaters and palaces and cathedrals, brothels and gin shops and flophouses where, for pennies, destitute vagrants could sleep in squalor four to a bed. Thieves and pimps rubbed elbows with clerks and advocates and the frenzied gentlemen of Fleet Street. Gaudily dressed prostitutes moved brazenly past aristocratic ladies in towering hats and rustling satin gowns.

It was invigorating, it was stimulating, it was a colorful, confusing panorama. Foul smells assailed the nostrils, amazing sights captured the eye, and the noise was incessant, splitting the air. It was all new to me, for as governess to Lord Robert Mallory's children I had been restricted to the elegant confines of Montagu Square, with an occasional, carefully planned afternoon with the children in the park nearby. I had never wandered down the streets, had never seen the gorgeous buildings, the gigantic piles of rubbish, the filth and splendor that gave London its unique flavor. But the proprietor of the White Hart had given me specific directions, and I felt sure I could find the coaching station easily enough.

As I moved down the street, besieged by beggars and accosted by hawkers who thrust various wares in front of me, I wished I had dressed a little less grandly. The taffeta gown with its broad black and white stripes and red velvet waist hugger was inappropriate, to say the least, as were the long red velvet gloves and the hat Lucille had especially created to go with the outfit, black and white plumes dripping over a broad black taffeta brim, an enormous red velvet bow holding them in place. Hat and gown were constantly imperiled as women dumped slops from second-story windows, and the lavish attire marked me as easy prey for the beggars and appallingly aggressive hawkers.

Jeremy had volunteered to see to the arrangements for me, but it was better this way. The streets of London were alarming, yes, but I wasn't in any danger. The beggars, the hawkers were merely an irritation, and, after all I'd been through, a relatively minor one at that. I could fend for myself, and I certainly didn't want Jeremy hiring the coach that would take me to Hawkehouse tomorrow.

He had been distantly polite ever since that night on board *Le Bon Coeur* when he had left me alone at the railing. The rest of the journey had been arduous indeed. The weather had grown steadily worse, culminating in a treacherous storm that had lasted for three full days. The ship had been damaged, and we had limped slowly on to France, arriving over a week late. The political situation between France and England being what it was, we had encountered a barrage of difficulties, and it had been necessary to make several hefty bribes before we could safely cross the channel. I had felt enormous relief when the towering white cliffs loomed out of the morning mist. Jeremy had hired a coach in Dover, and we rode in silence, polite strangers, arriving in London late in the afternoon and taking rooms at the White Hart Inn.

I hadn't joined him for breakfast this morning in the tap room, but he had come up to my rooms afterward, standing stiffly in front of the mantle in the sitting room and coldly volunteering to hire a coach to take me to Hawkehouse. Remote, restrained, he gazed at me with chilly eyes, waiting for my reply. Polite, as remote as he, I had informed him that I was perfectly capable of making my own arrangements, and, nodding curtly, he left. I knew that he had left the White Hart immediately afterward. Did he have friends in London, business to attend to? I wondered if I would see him again before I left tomorrow morning.

I hoped not. It would be much easier for both of us if . . . if he would just stay away until I was gone. I couldn't take any more of that distant manner, that polite, clipped voice, those blue eyes so frosty yet filled with pain. Being with him had become an ordeal, both of us strained, separated by an invisible wall of experiences recalled, words unspoken, emotions unexpressed. We had been through so much together these past months, and in many ways I had been closer to him than I had been to any man, but . . . it was over now. In a sense we had said our goodbyes that night on *Le Bon Coeur*.

Dodging a splattering downfall of slop as a woman emptied a bucket overhead, ignoring a beggar with twisted leg and horribly scarred face who shambled over with hand extended, I turned a corner and made my way down another street, looking for the great brick archway leading into the yard of the coaching station. I found it at last. Passengers were disembarking from a coach as I crossed the yard, and another coach was being loaded with bags. I entered the office. It was extremely crowded, the harried clerk barking orders to an underling, turning the pages of a ledger, trying his best to fend off passengers who besieged him on every side. One woman had lost her luggage. A fat man in a brown top hat demanded immediate transport to Brighton. People shouted and argued, pushing around the counter. Several drivers came in, one of them obviously tipsy, all of them barking instructions. I waited patiently, standing to one side, until finally all the others were gone. The clerk looked at me with belligerent eyes and asked me what I wanted.

"I'd like to hire a coach for tomorrow," I informed him.

"A 'ole coach? You wanna 'ire a 'ole coach all to yourself?"

"That's right."

"Might be one available, I'd 'ave to check. It'd cost you a pretty penny, though, I don't mind tellin' you."

"You *do* hire private coaches."

"When folks've got th' means, yeah, we do, providin' there's one available. You don't wanna pay that much, I can book you on a regular coach. You'd 'ave to share it with other passengers, but it wouldn't cost you a bloody fortune."

"I'm perfectly prepared to pay whatever it costs."

He eyed my black and white taffeta gown, the red velvet gloves, the elaborate hat, and his whole manner changed. A look of calculating greed glowed in his eyes as he studied me, clearly wondering just how much he could take me for. Putting on an official mien, he opened a ledger and asked me where I wanted to go in a 'ole bloody coach all by myself. I gave him the name of the village, and he ran his finger down a list on the page in front of him.

"Six 'ours it'd take you. You leave at eight o'clock in the morning, it'd get you there around two in th' afternoon. Six 'ours goin', six 'ours gettin' back to London, that's a 'ole day for coach an' driver. Cost you plenty." He ran his finger down another list and then consulted a schedule. "The driver'd probably want extra, drivin' all that way with just one passenger."

"I'll gladly pay the extra fee."

"In a 'urry to get there, ain't you?"

"Is a coach available?" I asked sharply.

"Let's see—mmmmmm, Ogilvy's free, but we don't want *im*—" He continued to study the schedule, his face growing more and more crestfallen. "Damn!" he finally exclaimed. "Ogilvy's th' only one! It 'ud 'afta be 'im, wouldn't it, an' all th' other chaps eager as I am to make a bit of— Maybe I can talk 'im into—" He scowled and pushed the schedule aside. "You wait right 'ere."

He stepped out into the yard. He planned to charge me an exorbitant fee, I could see that. The fact that I was female and expensively dressed made me an easy mark. It didn't matter. I merely wanted to be done with it. Hearing loud, angry voices outside, I stepped to the door. The clerk was arguing vehemently with a tall, muscular man wearing polished brown boots and dusty brown livery, a heavy black cape falling from his massive shoulders.

"I told you, Arbutt," the man thundered, "I ain't 'avin' any parta your crooked dealin's. I 'ave my pride. I 'ave my 'onesty."

"But she's rollin' in money. She's in a 'urry, too. We could charge 'er at least—"

The clerk turned and saw me standing in the doorway. All the air seemed to go out of him. He sighed and shook his head, returning wearily to the office with the driver behind him.

" 'Ere's Ogilvy 'imself," the clerk announced, "just in from Oxford. 'E's free tomorrow, all right, says 'e'll be glad to drive you."

Ogilvy nodded politely. In his late twenties, he had thick, unruly blond hair, rough-hewn, ruggedly attractive features and sky-blue eyes that were surprisingly gentle. He gave me a bashful smile, and I smiled back, liking him immediately.

"I'll be glad to take you, ma'am," he said in a gentle voice, "an' there won't be no extra charge, either."

The clerk snorted, plainly disgusted. Ogilvy gave him a fierce look. The two of them had obviously tangled before.

"I'd like to pay in advance," I said.

537

"Might be a good idea," Ogilvy agreed, eyeing the clerk.

The clerk told me what it would cost, and I gave him the money. He took it begrudgingly, put it away and made an entry in the ledger, all under the stern eye of the strapping driver.

"Goin' all that way, it'd be best if we left early," Ogilvy informed me. "Where shall I pick you up?"

"I'm staying at the White Hart Inn. Do you know where it is?"

Ogilvy nodded. "I'll be there shortly before eight in the mornin', 'elp you with your trunks an' things. Don't you worry none, ma'am. You're goin' to be in good 'ands."

"I have the feeling I will be," I replied. "Thank you, Ogilvy. I'll see you tomorrow."

The clerk snorted again as I left the office. I felt certain he and Ogilvy were going to start arguing again as soon as I was out of the way. As I crossed the busy yard and passed under the brick archway, I felt an enormous relief. It was done now. All the arrangements had been made, without Jeremy's help. Tomorrow, I thought, tomorrow I would be away from this noisy, alien city. Tomorrow I would be on my way to Hawkehouse. After all this time, I would finally be reunited with the man I loved.

The flood of joy I should have experienced at that thought failed to sweep over me. Curious. My heart should be dancing. There should be silent music inside, and I should feel a glorious, heady elation. Later. It would come later, when I was actually on my way. The constant strain of these past weeks with Jeremy had left me depleted, incapable of feeling anything but a bewildering combination of anxiety and aggravation and something strangely akin to guilt. Why had he insisted on accompanying me? Why had I ever allowed it? Why hadn't I told him to go straight to hell? I had, as a matter of fact, on more than one occasion, but it hadn't helped at all.

Ignoring the beggars, snubbing the hawkers, I made my way back to the White Hart and went up to my rooms. The door to Jeremy's bedroom stood open, and as I passed I could see Tibby, the tiny, energetic maid, making up his bed, humming as she did so. So he hadn't returned yet. It was almost four o'clock as I stepped into my sitting room.

Sunlight streamed in through the opened windows, making brilliant pools on the polished hardwood floor, reflecting in the glass of the framed hunting prints that hung on the walls. Removing my hat, setting it on a table, I moved over to one of the windows and peered out.

Tower Bridge reared up in the distance, silhouetted against an indigo sky, and the glorious dome of St. Paul's was visible far to my left. From this vantage point, London was a breathtaking panorama of majestic buildings, brown and rust, pale tan and gray marble, of wavering, leafy green trees and slanting, sooty rooftops and quaintly tilting chimneys. The festering slums were not visible, the filth and squalor concealed. Across the way, beyond Oxford Street, the park was a sanctuary of calm, trees clustered on green lawns, ponds sparkling a silvery blue in the sunlight, people strolling leisurely along the winding pathways.

Why did I feel so out of place? Why did I feel like a foreigner in an alien land? This was my homeland, the country of my birth, and yet . . . and yet something seemed to be pulling me, calling me, an inexplicable force originating from that vast, sprawling country across the sea. I thought of New Orleans and of the ruggedly beautiful countryside of Texas that had impressed me far more than I had realized at the time. I thought of Em and Randolph in their lovely hacienda, and I remembered the night sky so full of stars, dazzling, flashing, flickering stars so brilliant, so bright. I remembered the night all the stars in the sky seemed to explode inside me. . . . No, no, I wouldn't think of that. I mustn't. I must harden myself, banish that memory entirely.

Leaving the window, I moved briskly into the bedroom and began to repack my trunks and the small bags, laying out the clothes I would travel in tomorrow. I was merely killing time. I realized that. It was much too early to go down to the taproom for dinner, and I had nothing to read. I refolded the last chemise, closed the last bag. Footsteps rang out, moving down the hallway. Jeremy? I went into the sitting room and waited for the knock at my door, but the footsteps moved on down the hall. I told myself I was relieved. I tried to believe it. I didn't want to see him. We had nothing more to say to one another. Restless, growing more so by the minute, I put my hat back on and left the inn, heading for the park.

I had to harden myself against him. I realized that. I had to harden myself against the memories and those feelings that came upon me when I least expected them. I was fond of him, I couldn't deny that. He was infuriating and thoroughly exasperating, moody, mercurial, flippant one moment, grave the next, and one never knew what to expect, but. . . . Yes, I was fond of him, but I loved Derek. Pausing on the pavement as the traffic rumbled up and down Oxford Street, I frowned, damning Jeremy anew. There was no reason at all why I should feel guilty. I hadn't asked him to come along. I had protested vehemently and at length. He had insisted. . . . I had to put it out of my mind. Seeing a momentary break in the traffic, I hurried across the street, paused for a moment to catch my breath and then entered the park.

It was lovely indeed. The trees cast long shadows on the lawns, limbs leafy overhead, and as I moved deeper into the park the jangling noises of London grew muted, a background to the rustle of leaves, the pleasant warble of birds. Neatly dressed little boys played with toy sailboats at one of the ponds while their governesses sat on a bench nearby, gossiping quietly and clicking their knitting needles as they kept watch over their charges. Ladies in beautiful gowns walked arm in arm with men in top hats and elegant frock coats, nodding as they passed acquaintances. The air was fragrant with the scent of grass and rich soil, and flowers grew in colorful profusion, adding their own perfume. An atmosphere of serenity prevailed, something I badly needed.

I strolled slowly, pausing now and then to admire a bed of flowers, to lean against a tree trunk, to watch a little boy racing over a lawn with kite string in hand, the kite waving overhead like a gigantic red butterfly with wings outspread. People stared as I moved under the trees, past the fountains, the women critically examining my black and white striped taffeta gown with its red velvet waist hugger and matching gloves, the men displaying another kind of interest altogether. Lucille had done herself proud, I reflected, for the gown and the hat with its red velvet bow and sweeping black and white plumes were as fashionable as anything I had seen in London.

An hour and a half must have passed before I finally decided to start back. The shadows were beginning to lengthen, gradually changing from deep gray to violet-blue, and the sunlight sifting through the tree limbs was thinner, no longer so bright. It would soon be twilight, I thought, passing the pond where the little boys had been playing. I would have a light dinner in the taproom, and then I would go to bed. Perhaps I could sleep tonight. I hadn't been, not recently. Sleep had evaded me, and the nights had been long, full of restless tossing and turning, full of memories I managed to avoid during the day.

The cries and clattering noises grew more pronounced as I neared the Oxford Street entrance. A tall, rather hefty middle-aged man was just coming into the park, looking disgruntled and disoriented. He wore no hat, and his hair was badly powdered, a dull pewter-gray with black showing through. Although his clothes were well cut, they had a worn, rubbed look, just this side of shabby, the purple waistcoat soiled, the charcoal breeches and frock coat decidedly shiny. Puffing slightly as he moved up the pathway toward me, he had all the earmarks of a gentleman who had fallen on hard times, and as he drew nearer I suspected the reason why. He reeked of alcohol, tobacco, and sweat as well. I looked away, moving toward the entrance. The man mumbled something to himself and then looked up, noticing me for the first time.

He stopped. His flushed cheeks grew pale. He stared at me as though I were a ghost.

"Marietta?"

I was startled, rather alarmed as well. The man knew my name, yet I had never seen him before in my life. He was blocking my way now, standing there with an incredulous look in his eyes. I stared at him with a cool, haughty gaze, prepared to cry out if necessary. People were passing back and forth on Oxford Street only a few yards behind him. Although the man looked much too besotted to present any serious threat, I wished Jeremy were beside me.

"Is it really you?" he asked in a shaky voice. "Is it really Marietta, or am I seeing things?"

I looked at that fleshy, once handsome face, and recognition slowly came. It seemed altogether too incredible to believe that I should have accidentally encountered him on my first day in London, yet Lord Robert Mallory was actually standing there before me. It was one of those improbable coincidences that fate presents us far too frequently, and Lord

Robert seemed far more bewildered and upset than I. My initial alarm had evaporated, and I gazed at him with a surprising indifference. I had every reason in the world to hate him. This man had raped me and branded me a thief, hiding an emerald necklace in my bag and watching with a sardonic smile as the Bow Street runners took me away. He was directly responsible for all the misfortunes that followed, yet I could summon no emotion whatsoever. He shook his head, frowning, befuddled.

"It *is* you," he said. "I'm *not* imagining it."

"Please step aside, Lord Robert."

"I knew it. I knew it. Those eyes, that hair—there's never been hair like that, like copper fire. Marietta—Marietta—I've never forgotten you."

There was a whining note in his voice as he spoke these last words. I remembered the handsome, arrogant lord who had stalked through the rooms of the house on Montagu Square like some magnificent, predatory panther, and it was hard to associate that man with this stout, puffy-faced creature who reeked of port. He was still in his early forties, I calculated, yet he looked much older. The past seven years hadn't been kind to Lord Robert Mallory.

"Agatha left me," he said, as though reading my mind. "She took Robbie and Doreen and moved to the country. Agatha—she, she controls the money, Marietta. She always did."

"I seem to recall that."

"She sends me a pittance each month, expects me to live at Montagu Square on next to nothing. I can't even keep servants. They refuse to stay. There's no one. All my friends have deserted me."

He shook his head, as though unable to comprehend such a thing. There was a nervous twitch at the corner of his mouth.

"There were gambling debts," he continued, "a lot of them, and I couldn't pay my bill at the club and—" He hesitated, looking at me with bloodshot eyes full of entreaty. "It could have been so good for us, Marietta."

You poor fool, I thought. You poor, deluded fool.

"I often thought of you, wondered what happened. I—I didn't want to do it Marietta. I didn't want to plant those emeralds in your bag. It was Agatha. She made me. She said if I didn't go along with her she'd tighten the purse strings, stop paying my bills.''

''I see.''

''I felt bad about it,'' he whined. ''I wanted you so.''

The last time he had seen me I had been in chains, wearing rags, a felon convicted of theft and sentenced to fourteen years of indentured servitude. Besotted with liquor, afloat on a sea of self pity, he didn't seem to find it at all unusual that I was back in London, that I was dressed in splendor Lady Agatha could never have matched, nor had he shown the least bit of curiosity. Lord Robert had never been concerned with other people. They existed merely to serve him, to satisfy his various needs and appetites. He hadn't changed at all in that respect. He was still totally immersed in his own world, a world that had crumbled all around him, and he couldn't see beyond it.

''It isn't too late for us,'' he said.

My God. My God. Was he that far gone? Was he that great a fool?

''We could start over, Marietta. If only you'd forgive me, we—''

''Forgive you?'' I said. ''I should thank you, Lord Robert. Because of you I met the man I love. Because of you I'm an extremely wealthy woman.''

The words didn't seem to register. ''Come back with me,'' he pleaded. ''Come back to Montagu Square.''

''Goodbye, Lord Robert,'' I said.

''Goodbye? You don't mean—''

''I'm in rather a hurry.''

His dark eyes were full of pain, full of entreaty. ''You can't leave me. I have no one. I'm all alone. I have no money—''

He seemed on the verge of tears, eyes welling, the corners of his mouth beginning to quiver. I looked at this pathetic ruin of a man with stale powder on his hair, run-down garments on his bloated body, and I should have felt a sense of ironic justice. I should have felt great satisfaction at how the tables had turned, but I didn't. Reaching into my reticule, I pulled out all the money inside and thrust the folded bills into his hand. Then I walked briskly toward the entrance. He called my name, the word an anguished plea. I moved on

543

without looking back, leaving him with the private demons that would soon complete their destruction.

By the time I reached the White Hart I had already put the encounter out of my mind. Lord Robert Mallory belonged to the distant past, and I was concerned with the future now . . . and with the immediate present. Had Jeremy returned? Would he be in the taproom when I went down to dine? Tibby was in my bedroom when I entered, turning down the bedclothes and laying out a sheer, pale golden nightgown she had taken from one of the bags. She gave me a cocky, merry grin and told me she'd bring me a bedwarmer before I retired.

"Gets nippy, it does," she said. "Your feet'd be like ice without a 'ot brick wrapped up in flannel. I'll just slip it under th' covers in case you're still dinin'."

"Tibby, has the gentleman I arrived with come back yet?"

"You mean that 'andsome, saucy fellow with th' blue eyes? No, he 'asn't. I was in 'is room just a few minutes ago, makin' everything cozy. Know what 'e told me this mornin'? 'E told me I was so tiny 'e'd like to put me in 'is pocket and take me 'ome with 'im. Such cheek! Will you be wantin' anything else, miss?"

"I don't think so, Tibby. Thank you."

Grinning again, a charming creature not a full five feet tall, she bustled out, scurried through the sitting room and closed the door noisily behind her. I removed my hat and gloves, ran my fingers through my hair, and, a few minutes later, went down to the taproom to dine. It was cozy and pleasant with framed prints on the paneled walls, candles glowing, small bowls of flowers on all the tables. Heavenly aromas wafted in from the kitchen. There were few diners, for it was still a bit early, and I received special attention. I was quite hungry, but when my roast beef and Yorkshire pudding arrived I ate very little of it and turned down the raspberry treacle. My appetite had vanished. I kept looking toward the door, afraid he might wander in, dreading it.

I was just leaving the taproom when I saw him entering the lobby, moving in that long, bouncy stride. I stepped back in the doorway, praying he wouldn't see me. His rich brown hair was windblown, attractively tumbled, and his cheeks had a healthy flush as though he had been walking briskly. He was wearing pearl-gray breeches and coat, a dashing maroon

544

and white striped satin waistcoat, a sky-blue neckcloth. His coat flapped loosely, tail swinging as he strode to the stairwell and moved up, disappearing from sight. I waited several moments before following. His door was closed as I passed down the hall, and I heaved a sigh of relief as I reached my sitting room.

It was almost eight. Perhaps he had already dined. He knew London extremely well. Perhaps he had a favorite restaurant. He must have mány friends here. Female? Of course. Those glamorous older women, those depraved countesses. Why should I care? I didn't. Of course I didn't. No doubt he would come rapping at my door later on tonight to ask how my day had gone. I would be very cool, very polite. I sat down on the sofa, composing myself, waiting, and at ten o'clock I went into my bedroom and undressed, a quivering, tremulous feeling inside. Slipping into the filmy, pale golden nightgown, I folded my clothes carefully and put them away and then put out all the lights.

True to her word, Tibby had placed the hot brick under the covers at the foot of my bed. I stared at the dark ceiling that was gradually mottled with silver as moonlight streamed into the room. The windows were open. A bell tolled somewhere in the night. Sleep wouldn't come, and it must have been well after midnight when I finally got out of bed and stepped over to one of the windows, resting my folded arms on the sill and gazing out at the city. London was lovely under a black sky marbled with silver gray, clouds floating slowly. Below everything was black and gray and dark brown with tiny yellow-orange squares where lights glowed. Steeples and spires rose, bathed in moonlight, the dome of St. Paul's a soft, silvery blur, Tower Bridge an inky black sketch against the lighter sky.

The night air was cool, chilling my bare arms, and soft tendrils of hair blew against my cheeks as a cool breeze stirred. The curtains on either side of me billowed, lifting, falling, lifting again with a whispering sound. I searched the sky for stars, but none were visible. Would I ever see stars again like those gleaming in Texas? Such stars, such.... I forced the thought from my mind. In the morning I would begin the final journey. In less than twenty-four hours I would be in the arms of the man I loved. I had come so far, so far, and it was so close now. At last we would be together . . . but where were the stars?

Thirty-Six

Ogilvy nodded, smiled politely and swung the last trunk up onto his shoulder as though it weighed no more than a feather. He carried it out through the sitting room and clumped noisily and purposefully on down the hall. Dazzling silver-yellow sunlight streamed in through the bedroom windows. We were going to have a beautiful day for traveling, Ogilvy had assured me, and, indeed, the sky was a pale, cloudless blue-gray. It was not yet eight o'clock. I hadn't slept more than an hour or so during the night, and Tibby had brought me coffee and a buttered sweet roll shortly before seven, indignant when I refused a more substantial breakfast.

I had dressed with care, had paid my bill, had left a generous tip for Tibby. There was nothing more to detain me. Ogilvy would be strapping the bags on top of the coach now and, in a matter of minutes, would be ready to depart, yet I lingered still, reluctant to leave the room. He knew I planned to leave this morning. Surely he was awake. Surely he would at least say goodbye. Was he so bitter he couldn't bear to endure that final courtesy? It didn't matter, I told myself. I would have preferred us to part as friends, but if he wanted it this way, it was probably best.

Stepping over to the mirror, I made a final inspection of myself. My hair had been brushed to a coppery sheen and carefully arranged for the hat I had yet to put on. Deep mauve shadows tinted my lids, the result of so many sleepless nights, and a subtle application of rouge accentuated my high cheekbones and relieved some of the pallor. My lips were a deep, natural pink. Would Derek find me changed? Did I look older? Had the experiences of this past year left an irrevocable stamp? The eyes that stared back at me seemed a darker blue, sad, disillusioned, eyes that had seen far too much and would never again shine with that youthful sparkle of expectation.

The gown, at least, was perfect. The form-fitting, deep black velvet bodice had a low, square-cut neckline and long, tight sleeves, while the skirt that belled out over half a dozen bronze underskirts was of the finest satin with narrow stripes of black, bronze, mauve, royal blue, and turquoise. The black velvet hat with its high crown and broad, slanting brim had a huge spray of bronze, pale mauve, and royal blue feathers spilling down on the right side, held in place with a turquoise bow. I put it on, fastening it carefully, pleased with the tilt that exposed a stack of sculpted copper waves on the left, three long ringlets dangling down to rest on my left shoulder.

A bell somewhere nearby tolled eight times. I could delay no longer. Leaving the room, closing the sitting room door behind me, I moved down the hall. His door was closed. He was probably still asleep. I went on downstairs and through the lobby, stepped out onto the cobbled courtyard where the coach stood waiting. It was a modestly elegant vehicle of light golden brown, two sturdy bays stamping restlessly in harness, their coats gleaming a rich reddish-brown in the brilliant morning sunlight. Ogilvy had strapped the trunks and bags on top in a neat pyramid, a large, unfamiliar basket tied in front. He was wearing fresh brown livery, and the heavy black cape spilled down from his broad shoulders. He smiled, opening the door, and I saw the plush interior with seats covered in heavy fawn velvet.

"I gave everything a good goin' over this mornin'," he told me, "polished things up a bit. I took the liberty of bringin' a lunch basket, ma'am. There's no decent wayside inn 'tween 'ere and there, and I thought we might stop and eat by the road, give the 'orses a rest."

"That will be lovely, Ogilvy."

"See that little window up there, right behind the driver's seat? It opens up. You need anything, want to give me

547

instructions or anything, you just open it and speak up. I'll
'ear you.''

"Fine. I suppose we're ready to leave."

"Guess we are," he said.

He smiled and took my hand, ready to help me inside.
Jeremy strolled out of the inn and came toward us. Ogilvy
released my hand and, polite and deferential, moved to stroke
the horses' heads as Jeremy joined me. I looked at him,
silent, not knowing what to say, and he was silent, too,
gazing at me for a long moment with eyes that were no longer
remote, eyes filled with tender emotions that belied the pain.
The moment passed and still we did not speak, not in words.
I felt as though an invisible hand clutched my heart, squeezing tighter and tighter, and there was a lump in my throat.

"So you're off," he said quietly, at last.

I nodded, looking into his eyes. There were so many things
I wanted to say, but I knew I would never be able to say them
now. The hand squeezed my heart. I swallowed, forcing the
lump to dissolve. Somehow I managed to compose myself
and assume the polite, distant manner I knew would be my
only defense against the emotions welling inside me.

"I want to thank you, Jeremy," I said. "I want to thank
you for all you've done."

"No thanks required," he replied. "You finally convinced
me to take half the money, remember? I've been well paid for
services rendered."

There was another silence. It seemed to last forever.

"What are you going to do now, Jeremy?"

"In a week or so I'm leaving England. I'm going back to
America. There's a spread of land for sale in Texas, adjacent
to Randolph's. Randy showed it to me, encouraged me to buy
it, build a house, go into partnership with him. I told him I'd
think about it."

"You're going to settle down?"

"Figure it's high time," he said. "I can't think of a better
place to do it in. You remember the land. We were there."

"I don't think—"

"That night, Marietta. After the wedding."

The memory was a stabbing pain. I looked away from him,
desperately striving to retain my composure. The horses

stamped. Sunlight splattered the brown cobbles, bathed the front of the inn. Tibby had stepped outside, and Ogilvy had joined her near the door. They were flirting outrageously, Tibby twisting her apron in her hands and looking up at him with a cocky grin and a mischievous twinkle in her eye. Three geese ran across the courtyard, honking noisily, the proprietor's small son racing after them. In control again, I turned back to Jeremy.

"I'm glad you'll be in Texas," I said. "You'll be with friends."

"Randy, Chris, Em, too, for that matter. Look forward to seeing them again. A man needs friends around him."

"You're going to build a house?"

"A big house," he replied, and a quiet smile played on his lips. "I'm a rich man now. I can afford it."

"I hope you'll be happy, Jeremy."

"I haven't given up," he said.

"What do you mean?"

"I still hope you'll come to your senses."

"And—see what is in my own heart?"

"That's right. I haven't given up. I'll be here at the White Hart for a week. I'll be hoping. I'll be waiting, Marietta."

"Jeremy—"

He touched my cheek lightly, the smile soft on his lips, his blue eyes tender, gazing into mine as he stroked one of the long ringlets that dangled down to rest on my shoulder. The polite, remote stranger was gone, and the man who stood so near was a Jeremy I had seen only rarely. I seemed to melt inside. I bit my lip, looking away from him again.

"Goodbye, Jeremy," I said in a tight voice.

"I'll be waiting," he repeated.

I climbed into the carriage and settled back on the fawn velvet seat facing the front of the vehicle. Jeremy closed the door and moved back as Ogilvy told Tibby goodbye and came over to climb up onto the driver's seat. He said something to the horses and clicked the reins. The carriage began to move. Tibby waved from the doorway. Jeremy watched with hands thrust into his pockets, the heavy brown wave dipping over his forehead. I realized it was the last time I would ever see him, and there was another stabbing pain. I turned away from the window, unable to bear it, and soon we were out of the courtyard and moving down the street, in the thick of the morning trafffic.

London passed by the window, gorgeous marble facades, rows of shops, parks, slums, brown and gray, swarming with people, and I saw it all through a blur. I took several deep breaths, jostled about as the carriage clattered over a particularly rough stretch. The wheels made a lighter, whirring sound as we moved over a bridge. I could see the Thames below, the water a turgid blue-gray with several barges docked along the embankment like flat brown boxes, bobbing gently. We passed several large warehouses, more slums, and before too much longer the city was behind us and there were trees and rolling green fields with sheep grazing on the horizon.

I would forget him. As soon as I saw Derek again I would forget everything but the joy I had been waiting for for such a long time. I felt better now that we had left London. The worst part was over. It was only natural that I should feel this sadness, only natural that I should feel a part of me had been left behind. I had felt the same way when I had left Em in Texas, when I had left New Orleans and Mandy and Lucille. One by one the chapters of my life had been closing, becoming the past, and Jeremy belonged to the past now, too. The future was ahead, waiting for me at Hawkehouse, the future I had dreamed of and had come so close to realizing before it was brutally wrested from me on a dock in New Orleans. All that had happened since that night would cease to matter once we were in each other's arms.

Ogilvy slowed as we passed through a small village. I saw tan stone cottages with steep thatched roofs, kitchen gardens with cabbages and beans; a blacksmith's shop, a pub of buttery yellow brick, thatched like the cottages, a painted sign swinging over the door. A hefty blonde girl in blue dress and apron carried a pail of milk across a yard. Three old women in shawls gossiped listlessly as they drew water from the pump in the square. A man led a cow by a rope, taking it toward a pasture. Beyond the village there were fields of hops, the vines draped thickly over wooden trellises that bowed from the weight. The sunlight was even brighter now, streaming down in dazzling rays, and a few fleecy clouds had appeared, floating lazily across the sky.

I would learn to love this land. Eventually I would become a part of it, and I would forget that other land with its rolling plains, its rivers with cottonwood trees shading the muddy banks, its mockingbirds and the coyotes I had heard about but had never seen. That land was fresh and new and boisterous and demanded much from those who would dwell there. Jeremy would fit right in, I thought. He had the drive, the vitality, the strength to conquer that land. I could see him riding across a plain in his *vaquero* suit, the wind in his face, his hair whipping about his head. I wished him well. I wished him all the happiness in the world. I hoped he would find it, just as I had found mine.

The carriage rocked gently from side to side as we covered mile after mile, the horses moving at a leisurely trot, their hooves making a steady clop-clop on the hard-packed road. The wheels skimmed with a whirring sound, and harness jangled. I could see the back of Ogilvy's head through the little window behind the driver's seat. How long had it been since we left London? Two hours? Three? I leaned back against the padded velvet cushion, remembering a much younger woman who stood on an auction block in Carolina, remembering the tall, severely handsome stranger who coolly outbid the blond man in buckskins and took her away in a wagon to a run-down plantation house surrounded by cotton fields. That seemed so long ago. It might have happened to someone else.

I had loved him from the first, and I had tried so hard to please him, cooking his favorite foods, keeping the house shiny and clean and smelling of lemon and beeswax, polishing his boots, mending his clothes, loving him, wanting him so as I retired alone to my narrow bed each night. Embittered by a disastrous marriage, hating all women, he had denied the feelings I stirred in him until finally, unable to deny them any longer, he had taken me with brutal force, resenting me even as he acknowledged the love that burned fiercely inside him. He had never been comfortable with that love, for he believed it somehow diminished him and made him vulnerable. He had fought against it, had thrust me out of his life not once but twice, selling me to Jeff Rawlins and, much later, abandoning me after he had killed Jeff in a duel. But in the end he had come back, at last accepting the fact that he couldn't live without me.

Mile after mile after mile, wheels spinning, hooves clopping, through another village, past verdant green fields behind low, gray stone walls, low hills rising on the horizon, each moment that passed bringing me closer and closer to the man who still believed I was dead. Perhaps I should have sent a letter ahead of me, I thought, but no, no, this way was better. I wanted to be there to stem the shock, to see the joy in his eyes when he realized it was actually true. He would seize me. He would crush me to him. We would never, never be apart again, and I would make him happy . . . so happy. The green fields gradually vanished, merging into moors that stretched endlessly on either side of the road, grayish-brown grass taking on a pale lavender hue in the sunlight, stretches of peat like elongated black ponds.

The sun was directly overhead when Ogilvy slowed the horses and pulled over to the side of the road. Ogilvy climbed down from his perch and, a moment later, opened the door for me and helped me alight. My legs were a bit unsteady. Ogilvy smiled and clambered up to fetch the basket secured in front of the pyramid of luggage. The sunlight was warm. A faint breeze blew over the grassy moors, and there was a pungent, earthy smell. I could see part of an old Roman wall crumbling in the distance, the ancient gray stones streaked with rust and covered with patches of dark green moss.

"We'll just stop for a short spell," Ogilvy said, hauling down the basket. "Give the 'orses a bit of a rest."

"How much longer will it take?" I asked.

"Coupla 'ours, once we get goin' again. Plenty of food 'ere, ma'am, 'ard-boiled eggs, cheese, pork pies."

"I'm not very hungry, Ogilvy. You enjoy your lunch."

"Sure you won't join me?"

I nodded, giving him a polite smile. He shrugged and took the basket over to the low stone wall.

"Wish that Tibby were 'ere to share it. She's somethin', that one, tiny as a kitten an' just as playful. I plan to call on 'er as soon as I get back to London."

Ogilvy cracked an egg and peeled it, and I stretched my

legs, walking slowly along the road, enjoying the peaty smell of the moors and the strange, eerie beauty. There were more clouds in the sky now, floating slowly across the blue and casting purple-gray shadows that floated over the moors. Two more hours, I thought. The full realization of it seemed to hit me all at once, and for the first time I acknowledged the apprehension I had been feeling all day long. It had been building slowly, steadily mounting. What if he weren't there? What if he . . . . I forced the doubts from my mind, refusing to give shape to them, but a nervous tremor remained.

We were soon on our way again, Ogilvy stowing the basket away and helping me back into the carriage, the horses moving at a brisker clip now after their short break. The moors gave way after a while, replaced by hilly terrain dotted with trees, and then there were pastures, a patchwork of brown and tan and yellow and green. An hour passed, ten minutes, twenty, an hour and a half, and I tried to hold the bewildering confusion of emotions at bay, tried to hold on to some semblance of calm. We reached the village. Ogilvy pulled up in front of the large, sprawling inn. I opened the tiny window and told him someone inside would surely be able to give him directions to Hawkehouse. He climbed down and disappeared through the door.

I was tense now, so tense I could hardly sit still. Ogilvy came back out a couple of minutes later and climbed back onto the seat, turning to speak to me through the window.

"It's outside th' village, ma'am, three or four miles. We'll be there in no time."

I shut the window and sat back, fingernails digging into my palms as we began to move again. It seemed to take us forever to get out of the village, each minute an eternity. We passed more fields and a wooded area and then turned up a drive that went on and on and on until we finally passed through two thick brownstone portals surmounted by an ornamental black iron archway with a black hawk in the center, amid the curlicues. We were in parkland now, enormous oaks shading the grassy, rather unkempt lawns. A small herd of deer grazed serenely a short distance away, looking up with a singular lack of concern as the carriage passed. Ogilvy had slowed down. We seemed to be crawling.

The drive curved, parkland giving way to formal gardens,

equally unkempt, and I saw the house in the distance, a huge brown Elizabethan mansion with towers on either side, a fake battlement stretched between them, multilevel roofs rising behind, a rusty-green in the sunlight. Dozens of windows caught the afternoon sunlight, reflecting it, and wide, flat steps led down from the massive portico. It was ancient and ugly, but, to my eyes, the loveliest sight I had ever seen. Flowers grew in wild, multicolored profusion in front of the house, and there were terraced gardens on both sides, ancient fountains splashing, trellises laden with shabby vines partially covering the walkways.

I was in a daze as Ogilvy drove past the beds of flowers and pulled up before the steps. He climbed down, helped me out. I stared up at the aged brown structure, so much larger close up, steeped in history and tradition, undeniably intimidating. I hadn't the strength to move up the steps. I couldn't. Now that we had arrived I was paralyzed with terror. The windows seemed to stare down at me like accusing eyes, haughtily assessing me, demanding to know what right I had to be here. Sensing the state I was in, Ogilvy quietly asked if I would like him to fetch someone.

"No—no. You wait here, Ogilvy. I—we'll see about the luggage. I'm sure there'll be someone to help you with it."

"Very well, ma'am."

My legs were so weak they would hardly carry me up the steps. There was a large black iron knocker in the shape of a hawk's head in the center of the huge oak door, but before I could reach for it the door opened. A tall, skeletal servant in shabby, royal blue velvet livery and a powdered wig looked at me with watery, inquiring eyes. He was very old, well into his seventies, I judged. His skin was like wrinkled parchment. The wig was slightly askew.

"Yes?" he demanded.

"Lord Hawke," I said. "I've come to see Lord Hawke."

The servant held the door back and ushered me into an immense hall with faded Oriental rugs on the parquet floor. Heavy chests stood against the walls, and a suit of armor stood sentinel. A huge staircase of polished wood led up to the gallery above. The servant asked my name. I shook my head, much too nervous to speak. He hesitated, looking me up and down, taking in every detail of my person and attire, finally padding away. Minutes passed. I stood there in the hall, wondering if I were going to swoon. Then I heard footsteps and turning, saw Derek coming through a doorway.

He was tall and slender and handsome as a god with those perfectly chiseled features, that unruly, raven-black hair, those grim, gray eyes. He was wearing high, polished knee boots and snug black breeches and a shirt of fine white lawn opened at the throat, exquisite white lace spilling from the wrists of the full, gathered sleeves. He sauntered toward me with a questioning look in his eyes, not recognizing me at first. The tilt of my hat concealed part of my face. I turned slightly, facing him directly.

He stopped in his tracks, staring, and the color drained from his face. He shook his head, those dark gray eyes stunned, full of shock.

"My God," he said. "Oh my God."

He shook his head again, staring at me in stunned amazement, and I waited for him to rush to me and crush me into his arms and cry out with joy. He didn't. He continued to stare at me, trying to take it in, trying to master those emotions that must have been raging within. A long moment passed before he finally spoke again. He was in control now, but there was a tremor in his voice nevertheless.

"I—I thought you were dead."

"I know. I know, my darling. I thought you were dead, too. For months and months I thought you'd been murdered. I didn't want to go on living, and then I finally learned that you were alive, that you'd returned to England."

Why didn't he rush to me? Why didn't he fold me to him and hold me tightly and weep with joy? Why did he stand there so hesitantly, a perturbed look in his eyes? His mouth was a tight line. A deep, disturbed frown cut a furrow between his dark, arched brows. He wasn't pleased. Something was bothering him, and as I looked at him a strange, icy calm came over me. I knew. Even then I knew, and I felt no reaction whatsoever.

"I thought you were dead," he repeated. "I didn't think you could possibly survive. Roger told me. Before I killed him he told me you'd been sold to pirates and—"

"And you made no effort to find me," I said quietly.

"Marietta, you don't understand. You—Christ! Christ!" He slammed a fist into his palm.

"I came as soon as I could," I said.

"If only I'd known!" he exclaimed. "If only—"

She came slowly down the stairs. She was cool and blonde and elegant, every inch the patrician, unquestionably lovely. Her eyes were a clear light blue, her silvery-blonde hair pulled away from her face and worn in a loose bun at the nape of her neck. She wore a loose, flowing pink velvet dressing gown with long, full sleeves. The garment was gathered tight beneath her swollen breasts and fell in heavy, sumptuous folds to her feet, designed to conceal the fact that she was extremely pregnant and failing to do so. She paused at the foot of the stairs and looked at us with mild inquiry, waiting for him to introduce me.

His frown deepened. His mouth grew tighter. For a moment he was completely at a loss, and then he took a deep breath and plunged in.

"Angela, this is—this is a friend of mine. From America. Marietta Danver. Marietta, my wife."

"How do you do," she said pleasantly.

"Angela, Miss Danver and I have—business to conduct." She accepted the explanation with remarkable grace.

"I was just on my way to the music room. Perhaps you'll both join me there later on. You must ask Miss Danver to stay to tea, Derek."

She smiled at me, polite, unsuspecting, charming. She hadn't overheard us. I was certain of it. Those lovely eyes were completely without guile. She was the perfect wife for him, I thought, born to pour tea from a silver pot, born to be chatelaine of a great house like this one. He was extremely fortunate, I reflected. Lady Angela was ideal. Giving us another smile, she moved on down the hall, heavy pink velvet rustling softly. Derek watched until she was out of sight and then turned back to me.

"She's lovely," I said.

"Marietta, you must let me explain. I—"

"You owe me no explanations."

"I don't love her. I never did. I felt I had to marry, felt I had to sire an heir as soon as possible. Angela's pleasant.

556

She's very undemanding, very placid, utterly content. She—''

''I don't care to hear any more, Derek.''

''If only you knew how often I've—I went through hell, Marietta. When I lost you I went through hell. I didn't think it was possible to go on. I love you, damnit! I love you still. I've never stopped loving you. I can't let you go!''

''It seems you have no choice.''

''We can work something out.'' There was an edge of desperation in his voice. ''We can—I want you. I want you! There hasn't been a night since I first saw you standing on that auction block that I haven't wanted to—''

He came to me at last. He seized my upper arms, holding them tightly, and I looked into his eyes and saw the misery in them and knew that he did indeed love me. He loved me, yes, in his own selfish way, and he wanted me still. An apartment in London? Discreet visits several times a year? We could work something out, yes, and it would be enough for him.

''We have to talk,'' he said urgently. ''Not here. Not now. I—the inn. I will come to the inn tonight, as soon as I can get away. Take a room there, Marietta. Wait for me.''

I was silent for a moment, and finally I nodded. He released me, filled with relief. He sighed and brushed a hand across his brow. He took my hand and led me to the door and opened it, and we stepped outside. The coach stood in front of the house with the pyramid of luggage strapped on top. Ogilvy was stroking one of the horses, speaking to it in a gentle voice. Hearing the door close, he turned around and stood up straight, waiting for instructions.

''Go to the inn, Marietta,'' Derek told me. ''Have your man take your bags in, get you a room, then send him on his way. We'll use the inn until we can make other arrangements.''

I didn't say anything. He squeezed my hand so tightly I winced.

''I love you, Marietta,'' he said. ''I love you. I *need* you.''

''I know,'' I said quietly.

He led me down the wide, flat steps and opened the door of the coach. Ogilvy gave me a questioning look. I told him to take me back to the inn. He nodded and climbed up onto his seat. Derek looked into my eyes for a long moment, still holding my hand, and finally, rather curtly, handed me into the coach and closed the door. "Tonight," he said. He moved back to the steps and stood there with hands resting on his thighs, watching as we departed.

We drove slowly past the wild, unruly flower beds amok with vivid splashes of color, past the formal gardens so carefully laid out over two hundred years ago. The drive gradually curved, and I could see the house again, small from this distance, a child's dollhouse, brown and ugly. He was still standing on the steps, a tiny figure, details indiscernible, and his wife was beside him, a vague blur of pink and silver-blonde. I wondered idly what he was going to say to her. We turned into the parkland and the house was lost to sight, and as we drove past the unkempt lawns with the lovely oaks and the deer, grazing still, not bothering to look up, I waited for the shattering pain.

It didn't come. There was a feeling I couldn't quite identify, but it wasn't pain. It wasn't grief. All these years, I thought, all these years I have loved him with all my heart and soul, and now that love is gone and I don't even feel the loss. We passed through the portals again and started through the wooded area, and I gazed out the window, frowning as I tried to identify the elusive feeling inside. As the woodland vanished and the sun-splattered fields stretched out on either side under the pale blue sky, I realized it was relief. I felt relief, and slowly, slowly, a marvelous elation began to stir.

I had loved him, yes, and for years that love had been an obsession, even after I had realized its futility, even after I knew he could never return my love in kind. Doubts and apprehensions had begun to assail me in New Orleans, for I had known then that he never intended to marry me. I had denied the knowledge, clinging to my illusions, and even after I believed him dead I had clung to the ghost of that love . . . even after it had been supplanted by another love much stronger than anything I had ever felt before, a love so beautiful, so bright, so elating it had filled my heart and made music inside. I had stubbornly refused to acknowledge it. I had almost thrown it away. I had almost. . . . What a fool I had been. What a fool!

Tears of joy spilled over my lashes as I saw at last what

was in my heart and realized it wasn't too late. Thank God. Thank God it wasn't too late. He was waiting for me, for he had known. All along he had known. . . . The elation stirred, swelling, sweeping through me, filling me with a magical bliss so beautiful I could scarcely endure it. He loved me. He loved me. I loved him, too, with every fiber of my being, and I couldn't wait to tell him so, couldn't wait to throw myself into his arms and beg him to forgive me. As the carriage drove into the village and began to slow down I tapped furiously on the window behind Ogilvy's head and threw it open.

"Don't stop at the inn!" I cried urgently. "Drive on. Take us back to London, and—and, Ogilvy, please hurry! Please hurry!"